SIR PHILIP SIDNEY

# The Countess of Pembroke's Arcadia

EDITED WITH AN
INTRODUCTION AND NOTES BY
MAURICE EVANS

PENGUIN BOOKS

Penguin Books Ltd, Harmondsworth, Middlesex, England
Penguin Books, 625 Madison Avenue, New York, New York 10022, U.S.A.
Penguin Books Australia Ltd, Ringwood, Victoria, Australia
Penguin Books Canada Ltd, 2801 John Street, Markham, Ontario Canada L3R 1B4
Penguin Books (N.Z.) Ltd, 182–190 Wairau Road, Auckland 10, New Zealand

—

Published in Penguin English Library, 1977
Introduction and Notes Copyright © Maurice Evans, 1977

—

Made and printed in Great Britain by
Cox & Wyman Ltd, London Reading and Fakenham
Set in Linotype Juliana

FOR PATTY

*Et in Arcadia Ego*

# Contents

# Introduction

*The Countess of Pembroke's Arcadia* has been one of the most widely read and best-loved books in the whole of English literature. In the century after its original publication in 1593 it went through thirteen editions and inspired two sequels and countless imitations, as well as being translated into all the major European languages. Shakespeare took the Gloucester plot of *King Lear* from it, and *The Faerie Queene* draws on it in innumerable ways, especially in Book VI, 'Of Courtesy'. Tradition declares that Charles I quoted Pamela's prayer when he was on the scaffold, and Milton, though censuring it as a work of pagan morality, yet admitted that it was 'in that kind full of worth and wit'. As late as 1725 it was still popular enough to provoke a fourteenth edition and, in the same year, to be completely rewritten in modern English. For the rest of the eighteenth century, selections from the *Arcadia*, usually of the more sentimental parts, appeared at regular intervals, in response to the new cult of 'sensibility'; and these, in keeping the romance form alive, also helped to stimulate the interest in chivalry with which the term 'romantic' was initially associated, and which formed so important a dimension of the Romantic Revival. At the same time, the *Arcadia*, by its handling of character, motive and moral situation, contributed to the development of its successor in the narrative mode, the new novel. Its influence on the work of both Fielding and Richardson is unmistakable, though still largely unexplored: it is no accident that Richardson gave the name of Pamela to his first heroine. Pope had a copy; Joseph Wharton praised it as the archetypal romance; Scott and Lamb treasured it: only Hazlitt attacked it for reasons to be discussed shortly. Yet its days as a best-seller were over, and in the nineteenth century it was wholly superseded by the novel. The last complete edition appeared in 1907, and the total work in its traditional form has long been out of print. From being a best-seller, it has been completely taken over by the scholars and

9

become the centre of a thriving industry very far removed from its original intention.

The object of this edition is to make a great English classic available once more in the form in which it was read for three centuries. A book which pleased so many for so long can be no mere period piece; and besides affording perhaps the best insight we have into the tastes of the Elizabethan Age, the *Arcadia* is a great work in its own right, offering ample rewards to the modern reader who is willing to adjust to the demands made by its conventions. This introduction, therefore, will attempt to define the nature of these demands.

1

The work which has come down to us under the title of *The Countess of Pembroke's Arcadia* is a curious patchwork, assembled after Sidney's death and comprising parts of two different versions by Sidney himself, together with modifications introduced by his sister, the Countess of Pembroke, and additions by Sir William Alexander in the early seventeenth century. The precise dates of composition are uncertain; but it is probable that Sidney began his first version as early as 1577 and finished it while he was staying with his sister at her country house at Wilton in 1580. His letter to her, printed with the first published edition of the revised *Arcadia* in 1590, indicates the manner of composition – 'Your dear self can best witness the manner, being done in loose sheets of paper, most of it in your presence; the rest by sheets sent unto you as fast as they were done.' The *Old Arcadia*, though circulated in manuscript among friends, was never published until Feuillerat brought out his edition in 1912. It is a straightforward, relatively modern-sounding piece of fiction which tells its story in chronological order and uses traditional narrative techniques. It is divided into five books or acts, separated from each other by collections of pastoral eclogues which reflect the theme and mood of the narrative at the point where they are introduced, and at times carry on the action, forming little pastoral plays within the bigger dramatic structure. The characters break into song at every opportunity – there are over fifty songs in addition to those of the pastoral interludes – and this gives to the *Old Arcadia* at its most superficial level something of the quality of light opera.

The story concerns Basilius, king of Arcadia, who impiously wishing to know the future, consults the oracle and is punished in consequence with a very frightening reply in riddle form: his elder daughter shall be stolen away 'by princely mean, and yet not lost'; his younger shall embrace an unnatural love; he himself shall commit adultery with his own wife, and his sons-in-law shall be accused of his murder. Lastly, a foreign power shall sit in his throne: 'All this on thee this fatal year shall hit.' To escape these horrific prophecies, Basilius abandons his kingly responsibilities and goes into pastoral retreat, taking with him his wife, Gynecia, and his two daughters, Pamela and Philoclea, with no other attendants than an uncouth shepherd, Dametas, and his family, whose job it is to act as watchdogs over the princesses and keep all suitors away. This unkingly and unnatural behaviour itself precipitates the sequence of events through which the oracle is ultimately fulfilled. Two wandering princes, Musidorus and Pyrocles, happen to see the pictures of the princesses and fall in love, but are forced, by Basilius' measures, to disguise themselves as a shepherd and an Amazon respectively to gain access; and from this all manner of complications, both comic and serious, ensue. Basilius' irresponsibility leads to rebellions in his kingdom which in their turn force the princes to attempt elopement with the princesses; and when the four are captured, they find themselves arraigned for the apparent death of Basilius. The story ends with their trial and the fulfilment of the oracle to the letter although in a manner which no one had anticipated. Under cover of this romantic story, Sidney examines the responsibilities of kingship and the workings of providence; but his main preoccupation is with the uncontrollable nature of love. The two princes are noble heroes, yet Pyrocles succeeds in consummating his love for the virtuous Philoclea before marriage, and Musidorus is only prevented from raping Pamela by the unexpected arrival of bandits. Sidney takes a long, ironic look at love, challenging its claims to be outside the normal restraints of human law and yet, in the dénouement, demonstrating the limitations of even the highest human justice in the face of a mysterious and ultimately loving providence.

A few years later, between 1582 and 1584, after some tinkering with the text, Sidney began to rewrite what he called his 'toyfull book', and had redrafted the first two books and a part of the third before his death in 1586. He discarded little of the original material, although he redeployed it in new contexts, but he added so much that the new portions are in themselves longer than the whole of the earlier version. The additions consist of an account of all the heroic adventures which the two princes undertook before they reached Arcadia, and of the tragic love and rebellion of a further major character, Amphialus, in which both princes are subsequently involved. Sidney developed the heroic potential of his story, at the same time omitting most of the songs and attempting a more sophisticated narrative technique and a more elaborate rhetoric.

This revised portion of the *Arcadia* which ends abruptly in the middle of a fight and a sentence was published in 1590 under the supervision of Sidney's friend and biographer, Fulke Greville. It was superseded in 1593 when the Countess of Pembroke, whether to meet a public demand for a complete text or merely to assert her claim to her brother's material, brought out a folio consisting of the revised version together with the rest of the story as contained in the *Old Arcadia*. From our knowledge of the original version we can now see that she made certain emendations to the parts of the earlier work which she included. Besides bringing the names and references more or less into line with the revised version, she suppressed the more disreputable episodes: the scene where Pyrocles consummates his love with Philoclea was changed to one in which the two spend the night in virtuous chastity, and Musidorus' attempted rape of Pamela was quietly omitted. The intention was clearly to bring the behaviour of the princes into harmony with the more heroic roles which Sidney had assigned to them in the revised *Arcadia*; and modern scholarship inclines to the view that the Countess's bowdlerizations followed Sidney's own instructions or, at least, fulfilled his intentions.

The 1593 folio leaves a gap in the story between the end of the new version, where the princesses are still prisoners in Amphialus' castle, and the resumption of the old, where they are safely at home. To make this good, Sir William Alexander wrote a bridging passage (pp. 595–625), which appeared in the fifth edition of 1621 and in subsequent editions. This is the version traditionally known as *The Countess of Pembroke's Arcadia*, and it is not in any sense a single entity. John Florio, the Elizabethan translator who may have helped Greville with the 1590 quarto, railed at the Countess's attachment of the old ending to the new story on the grounds that 'this end we see of it, though at first above all, now is not answerable to the precedents'. This criticism is not wholly fair: the great trial itself which formed the original ending of the book is compatible with the revisions Sidney made, and though he would have added to it, there is no reason to suppose that he would have altered it except in detail. Nevertheless, to pass from one version to the other by way of Alexander's quite skilful tailoring feels like putting on a strait-jacket: the old plot with its amorous intrigues and misunderstandings cannot accommodate the new heroic relationships which have been forged, and the descent from the epic to the ironic is too abrupt. The 1593 version, which makes no attempt to suggest that the work forms a single whole, is perhaps more satisfactory for the literary purist.

It should be stressed, however, that apart from Florio who had an axe of his own to grind, no critic until modern times is on record as complaining about the lack of unity of the work. Having no knowledge of the unpublished original version, the intermediate generations of readers appear to have read the *Arcadia* without objection, and when Hazlitt castigated it in his *Age of Elizabeth* as 'one of the greatest monuments of the abuse of intellectual power upon record', it was upon different grounds.

Hazlitt's attack is relevant to us since it expresses in extreme form the main reasons why, in the nineteenth and twentieth centuries, the *Arcadia* has ceased to be a popular work and has been relegated to the world of scholarship. Hazlitt's main objection is to the style which he analyses with great perception but with a total lack of sympathy. Like Wordsworth, he mistrusts the traditional rhetoric which had dominated the conception of literary style since the Renaissance, and his onslaught on Sidney's rhetorical prose parallels that of Wordsworth on the rhetorical poetry of the eighteenth century: it is art, not nature: 'The quaint and pedantic style here objected to was not . . . the natural growth of untutored fancy, but an artificial excrescence transferred from logic and rhetoric to poetry.' We have moved a long way from the romantic assumptions about style since Hazlitt's day, yet Sidney's rhetoric is still probably the most formidable though not the only barrier in the way of our enjoyment. An Introduction to the *Arcadia* for the general reader, therefore, may best begin with this aspect of the work which will be found most immediately alien.

2

The sixteenth century in England, as in every other European country, was a period of intense pride in the vernacular language and of patriotic desire that it should show itself capable of rivalling the classical languages in eloquence. The Elizabethan liked his nature embellished by art, provided that the two worked in harmony with each other, and he felt none of the automatic distrust of artifice in itself which is a feature of romantic and modern taste. John Hoskins, for example, a contemporary of Sidney, whose *Directions for speech and style* was written round 1599, expresses the universal assumption of the Renaissance that the command of style and the mastery of rhetoric are the mark of the civilized man, the true evidence of human dignity. It is not surprising that he takes most of his illustrations of the beauties of style from the vast panoramic display of the *Arcadia*, and the examples which he singles out for especial praise are often those with which the modern reader has least sympathy. He admires Sidney's skill in periphrasis, for the 'charming variety' which it gives to the work: he likes it when Sidney replaces the common term 'thresher' by the phrase, 'one of Ceres' servants', and he prefers 'make his sword accursed by any widow' to the plain 'kill any married man':

For *having risen early*, he saith: *having striven with the sun's earliness*. Instead of *Mopsa wept ill favouredly, Mopsa disgraced weeping with her countenance*. Instead of saying *they that guarded Amphialus were killed themselves*, it is said: *seeking to save him they lost their fortresses which nature placed them in*.

Hoskins is typical of the period which produced and admired the style of the *Arcadia*, and a complete response to the work must

14

include the enjoyment of its rhetoric as well as of its more accessible qualities. In an age of rhetoricians, Sidney was the most varied and skilful, and the *Arcadia* is a gladiatorial display of oratory which outshines anything achieved in English before and perhaps since. No opportunity for a set oration is ever missed: both Pyrocles and Musidorus make set speeches to the rebels at different points of the story, and every discussion turns into a formal debate – between Pamela and Cecropia on atheism, between Pyrocles and Philoclea on suicide or Pyrocles and Musidorus on the after-life. It is in keeping with the nature of the book, as C. S. Lewis pointed out, that the climax should be one not of action but of debate in the forensic oratory of the trial at the end; and the range of models which Sidney produces at this point, from the purely emotive rhetoric of Philanax to the pithy, logical, dispassionate summary of Euarchus, is staggering in its virtuosity.

But set orations are only an especially formal use of the rhetoric which is fundamental to the style as a whole and which permeates the descriptions, the narrative and the ordinary level of dramatic exchange between characters. The nature of classical rhetoric is to take a normal human response and intensify its expression by means of repetition, or by converting it into an appropriate verbal pattern, or by defining it in a metaphor, so that the essential quality is forced upon the reader's attention with greater emphasis than would otherwise be the case. In this way the natural cry of grief is amplified into the formal exclamation; the process of self-questioning becomes a more rigid sequence of question and answer, and the normal exaggerations of feeling are blown up into hyperbole. A rhetorical style is the formal equivalent of a naturalistic one and bears the same sort of relationship to it as does ballet to straight acting. The *Arcadia* is an immense verbal ballet in this sense. Every impulse of sorrow finds expression in a patterned lament (p. 565):

Unhappy eyes, you have seen too much, that ever the light should be welcome to you. Unhappy ears, you shall never hear the music of music in her voice. Unhappy heart that hast lived to feel these pangs ... Philoclea is dead, and dead is with her all goodness, all sweetness, all excellency. Philoclea is dead, and yet life is not ashamed to continue upon the earth. Philoclea is dead ...

Each protest at the contrariness of things is heightened into rhetorical question and formal paradox (p. 456):

O dear though killing eyes, shall death head his dart with the gold of Cupid's arrow? Shall death take his aim from the rest of beauty? O beloved though hating Philoclea, how, if thou be'st merciful, hath cruelty stolen into thee? Or how, if thou be'st cruel, doth cruelty look more beautiful than mercy ever did?

In every battle, the natural opposition of the fighters is sharpened by verbal antithesis (p. 593):

There was strength against nimbleness; rage against resolution; fury against virtue; confidence against courage; pride against nobleness ... The Irish greyhound against the English mastiff; the swordfish against the whale; the rhinoceros against the elephant ...

In the longer dramatic sequences, the characters relate to each other like figures in a dance. The scene in which Musidorus first discovers Pyrocles disguised as an Amazon (pp. 132-9) is a good illustration, although it is too long to analyse in detail. In essence it depicts a brisk quarrel between the two in which they come as near to direct abuse of each other as their princely dignity will allow, until their normal feelings of love for each other reassert themselves and they embrace in tears. The progress of this quarrel from self-righteousness and evasion, to anger, to dismay and so to love again, is expressed by means of an elaborate verbal choreography which, beginning with long set addresses, develops into the opposition of formal stichomythia as feelings run higher, and subsides into a freer, more flowing rhetoric when the deeper emotions come into play. The leisurely formality of the treatment should not blind us to the precision with which Sidney delineates the range and development of the underlying emotions; and the passage, indeed, owes much of its humour as well as its peculiarly touching quality to the juxtaposition of highly formal rhetoric with all too human feelings. As the young men play their parts with the earnestness and ceremony of a duel, one is made conscious of the nature and tensions of civilization itself.

I have considered rhetoric so far only in relation to the noble characters, but even the low comedy figures at their raciest and most colloquial are presented through the same formal medium, though at a level appropriate to their less dignified roles. An example of this is the story which the sluttish shepherdess, Mopsa, insists on telling when the noble princesses are about to exchange tales (p. 311). Mopsa's tale is, ironically, that of Cupid and Psyche, although she is naturally ignorant of this fact and tells it as if it were an old wives' tale:

'In time past,' said she, 'there was a king, the mightiest man in all his country, that had by his wife the fairest daughter that ever did eat pap. Now this king did keep a great house, that everybody might come and take their meat freely. So one day, as his daughter was sitting in her window, playing upon a harp, as sweet as any rose ... there came in a knight into the court upon a goodly horse, one hair of gold and the other of silver; and so the knight, casting up his eyes to the window did fall into such love with her that he grew not worth the bread he eat; till many a sorry day going over his head, with Daily Diligence and Grisly Groans he won her affection, so that they agreed to run away together. And so in May, when all true hearts rejoice, they stale out of the castle without staying so much as for their breakfast ...'

The preoccupation with food is very natural to such a one as Mopsa, and Sidney makes it an aspect of her character; yet the sequence is not one of dramatic naturalism. Sidney has intensified the expression of Mopsa's illiteracy by heightening the native formlessness of her narrative – 'and ... and ... and so ... so ... and so ...' – and weaving into it more clichés and literary tags than would normally be there. It is rhetoric, but rhetoric for the lower classes – what Sidney elsewhere calls 'such a kind of rhetoric as weeded out all flowers of rhetoric' (pp. 95–6).

A love of formal language of this kind is natural to an age in which ceremony and splendid clothing played so large a part, and where the daily activities of the Court were a long and elaborate ritual. Sidney reflects the taste of his period when he makes his two heroes dress themselves in their most magnificent garments to go to their trial and, as they imagine, their execution. It is important to recognize, however, that Sidney's rhetoric is not merely pleasurable embroidery, but that it conditions in a fundamental way how we read the work. It is art open and unashamed, making no attempt to conceal itself, and this fact draws the reader's attention from what is being described to the method of description. Instead of involving us, it keeps us at a distance from the action, so that tragedy is turned into spectacle and admiration aroused in place of pity and fear. Early in the story Sidney describes a private combat within a battle 'which was so much inferior to the battle in noise and number as it was surpassing it in bravery of fighting and, as it were, delightful terribleness' (p. 98). The phrase 'delightful terribleness', derived, of course, from Aristotle's discussion of the tragic pleasure, defines very accurately the effect which Sidney seeks to achieve; and the self-conscious art is the means by which terribleness can give rise to delight. An extreme example of this is the account of Parthenia's bloody and tragic death at the hands of Amphialus (p. 528):

... in her cheeks the whiteness striving by little and little to get upon the rosiness of them; her neck, a neck indeed of alabaster, displaying the wound, which with most dainty blood laboured to drown his own beauties, so as here was a river of purest red, there an island of perfectest white, each giving lustre to the other ...

The playing with colours divorced from their physical causes, the geographical conceit which severs the connection between blood and human body, the suggestion of an alabaster statue, all combine to dehumanize the description and turn tragedy into something ornamental. The same technique is used in much religious verse of the early seventeenth century, where the intention is to display the wounds of Christ as objects for joyful contemplation. A similar effect is produced by different means at an even more serious moment of the story, when Philoclea is scourged by Cecropia (pp. 551–2):

The sun drew clouds up to hide his face from so pitiful a sight, and the very stone walls did yield drops of sweat for agony of such a mischief: each senseless thing had sense of pity; only they that had sense were senseless. Virtue rarely found her worldly weakness more than by the oppression of that day: and weeping Cupid told his weeping mother that he was sorry he was not deaf as well as blind ...

Here the very hyperboles which express the horror of the moment are the means by which the feeling is controlled: it is the sun and the stone wall which we think of as suffering rather than poor

Philoclea, and even the weeping is transferred to Cupid and made the source of a conceit. It is this systematic transmutation of life into artifice throughout the whole work which made it possible for a book so full of rebellion, suffering and bloodshed to become the favourite reading for generations of the ladies to whom Sidney addressed it. The reader can put it down or take it up again without being too deeply and painfully involved: he can look into it as into a picture gallery, dip into it and linger over the individual moment without worrying about what is to follow. The local pleasures of the journey are at least as important as those of reaching the end.

3

This is only to say that the *Arcadia* is a romance, not a novel. Although it anticipates many of the features which the modern reader is apt to think of as peculiar to the novel, it was in fact conceived in terms of a very different narrative tradition. Hoskins names the models on which he believed Sidney based his work: 'For the web, as it were, of his story, he followed three: Heliodorus in Greek, Sannazaro's *Arcadia* in Italian and *Diana* by Montemayor in Spanish.' Hoskins could have added at least two more major sources to this polyglot collection: the popular late medieval French romance, *Amadís de Gaula*, from which Sidney took much of his plot and chivalry, and a further Greek romance, namely *Clitophon and Leucippe*, from which, as from Heliodorus' *Aethiopica*, he borrowed the occasional episode. Modern scholars such as Wolff and Zandvoort have examined Sidney's sources very thoroughly, but a knowledge of this area is only relevant to us in so far as it helps to explain the conventions in terms of which Sidney was writing. The Italian *Arcadia* and the *Diana* were among the most influential works of Renaissance literature. Both were written in the pastoral mode; the former, a collection of verse eclogues given continuity by brief links in prose; the latter a sequence of pastoral love stories held together by a common theme and diversified with frequent songs. From these, Sidney took his Arcadian shepherd setting and the combination of prose narrative, eclogue and song which is especially characteristic of the *Old Ar-*

*cadia*. The Greek romances, written in the decadence of Greek literature in the early years of the Christian era and revived like so many other classical works by the sixteenth-century humanists, provided Sidney with his mixture of love and heroic adventure against a background of ancient Greece. The briefest comparison between Sidney's work and its sources, however, shows that although he shared with them a common idiom, his treatment is immeasurably more controlled and more serious; and for this reason there has been much discussion about the precise genre to which the *Arcadia* belongs. It has been called a pastoral romance, an Arcadian epic, a Greek romance, an heroic epic, an heroic romance; and this is not merely a matter of label, for each of these literary 'kinds' had its own body of theory and its own set of conventions.

The most likely supposition is that Sidney tried his hand at the fashionable Greek romance in the *Old Arcadia*, and was in process of converting it to the more serious and didactic mode of the heroic in his revision. In this he was plunging into the middle of one of the major literary controversies of the sixteenth century, that concerning the claims of the epic or the romance to be considered the highest form of the heroic. The debate centred on the use of single or multiple plots, whether the single great action of a single hero as in the *Iliad* or the *Aeneid* was preferable to the multiplicity of interwoven actions and characters as in Ariosto's *Orlando Furioso*, for example. It was the perennial debate between the ancients and the moderns, between the authority of Aristotle's newly discovered *Poetics* on the side of epic, and the patriotic appeal of the native tradition on that of romance. The Italian writer, Cinthio, whose important work *On Romances* (1554) influenced Sidney's *Apology for Poetry*, defended the romance on the grounds that 'this kind of poem, moreover, came from neither the Greeks nor the Latins; indeed it came laudibly from our own language'. He considered it the form appropriate to the genius of the Italian language, as the more prestigious epic to that of Latin and Greek, and he saw it as parallel, therefore, not inferior. As is so often the case with English writers, Sidney seems to have attempted a compromise between the rival claims. The structure of the revised *Arcadia*, for all its complexity, is more direct and logical, its plot more the projection of character in action than is usual in the romance: it has something of the probability and necessity which belongs to single-actioned tragedy and epic, as Aristotle defined them. On the other hand, the number and variety of its plots, and its capacity to include, in Cinthio's words, 'frequent love affairs, and besides the kings and the queens and other great personages, nymphs, shepherds, shepherdesses, pages, boys, servants, hermits, peasants and the other kinds of people', demonstrate its fundamental basis in romance. It is interesting that the only other comparable English work of the period, Spenser's *Faerie Queene*, comes down on the side of the heroic romance against the epic even more emphatically than the *Arcadia*, and both were perhaps inspired by the same patriotic motive. There was a long tradition of the romance in English, but none of the epic, and the two writers seem to have felt that it embodied in English the same greatness which had found an alternative form of expression in Latin and Greek.

Sidney had however other than merely patriotic reasons for choosing the romance. The tradition which he inherited was derived not only from the relatively flippant Greek romances but from the great Arthurian cycles of the Middle Ages with their strongly didactic emphasis. The range and flexibility of the form, the multiple plots which made it possible to explore a common theme from different angles, the loose narrative structure allowing story to be manipulated in the service of ideas, all combined to produce the ideal vehicle for the 'delightful teaching' which was his aim. We are fortunate in having Sidney's own account of what he understood the purpose of literature to be in his *Apology for Poetry*, written between 1581–3, at the time that he was beginning to revise the *Arcadia*. Although it contains no direct allusion to the *Arcadia* itself, the *Apology* makes some comments on Sidney's source-books which are relevant. He notices, for example, that there is literary precedent for mingling 'matters heroical and pastoral', and he comments on the fact that Sannazaro 'mingled prose and verse'. He finds *Amadís de Gaula* a fountain of moral teaching, and he claims that Heliodorus, like Xenophon, wrote 'an absolute heroical poem ... yet both these writ in prose' (p. 103). Sidney's assumption that there can be poetry in prose is in line with the common Renaissance conception of poetry, derived from Aristotle's 'Imitation'. 'Poesy therefore is an art of imitation, for so Aristotle termeth it in his word *mimesis*, that is to say, a representing, counterfeiting, or figuring forth – to speak metaphorically, a speaking picture – with this end, to teach and delight' (p. 101). Its essence consists in its particular power of fiction, 'verse being but an ornament and no cause to Poetry ...' (p. 103). It is a point Sidney emphasizes strongly and makes the very centre of his defence of poetry: '... it is not rhyming and versing that maketh a poet ... But it is that feigning notable images of virtues, vices, or what else, with that delightful teaching, which must be the right describing note to know a poet by ...' (p. 103). He admits that 'the senate of poets' have chosen 'that numbrous kind of writing which is called verse' as the 'fittest raiment' for their fictions, but only because the dignity of their subject demanded a more elaborate language than that of ordinary speech; and there are other ways of creating dignified language. His own elaborate and consistent rhetoric in the *Arcadia* is compatible with poetry, so carefully matched as it is to the situation, so elevated for the noble characters, so debased for the clowns but never, as we have seen, the language of plain speech. Ben Jonson among others in the period described the *Arcadia* as a poem; and Sidney's very systematic revision of the work suggests that he was bringing it into line with his own theory of poetry.

Sidney valued the active life more highly than the contemplative, and 'well-doing' more than 'well-knowing': as Greville described him, 'his end was not writing, even while he wrote'. Literature, he believed, had the very practical function of promoting virtuous action. His argument for the superiority of poetry to philosophy, for example, hinges on the difference between knowing and doing, between merely teaching the nature of virtue and moving men to practise it. He begins with the traditional assumption that everyone is born possessing the inner light of Right Reason, what Hooker called that 'light of Reason, wherewith God illuminateth everyone which cometh into the world, men being enabled to know truth from falsehood and good from evil'. Although the Fall has tended, in Hooker's words, 'to smother the light of natural understanding', yet some vestige of it still remains in all men, by virtue of which they instinctively love the highest when they recognize it; and Sidney believes that the poet, above all others, can help them to this recognition. Sidney shares the common Renaissance belief that the poet has retained a relatively unfallen vision, that his erected wit is less clouded by the infected will than in other men, so that he can see truly into the nature and purposes of God's creation. The poet has, in Sidney's Platonic description, 'the Idea and fore-conceit' of things and can through the liberty of fiction deliver them forth 'in such excellency as he hath imagined them'. In this way the poet holds up the perfect unfallen pattern of that which in nature appears only as a tarnished copy: he creates a world of things as they should be instead of as they are, of general and universal truths instead of local and particular variations, a world in which good appears absolutely good, 'each thing to be followed', and evil totally evil, containing 'nothing that is not to be shunned' (p. 110). This is achieved by means of the imagination, in its traditional sense, the image making and receiving faculty which operates through the highest of the human senses, the sight. With its aid the poet creates his 'speaking pictures' which reveal the divine law in 'sensible form': they speak through and to the imagination, waking up the slumbering truths within the soul of the reader and uncovering the innate forms of virtue as the sculptor uncovers the statue lying within the block of stone. Pope is referring to this process when he defines true wit as

> Something whose truth convinced at sight we find,
> That gives us back an image of our mind

and Dr Johnson is still thinking in the same terms though in a different metaphor when he describes those general truths which find an echo in every bosom. For Sidney, the philosopher, lacking this imaginative power, can only bestow 'a wordish description, which doth neither strike, pierce nor possess the sight of the soul'; his learned definitions 'lie dark before the imaginative and judging power' because 'not illuminated or figured forth by the speaking picture of poesy' (p. 107). The historian is equally ineffective because his images are 'captived to the truths of a foolish world' and unable, therefore, to evoke a reflection within the right reason. In contrast to both, the poet can embody his universal truths in images which penetrate at a subliminal level. He alone is able to move the unconverted, those who 'feel not the inward reason they stand upon' but who, through delight, 'so steal to see the form of goodness (which seen they cannot but love) ere themselves be aware, as if they took a medicine of cherries' (p. 114). By the knowledge which it creates, poetry is able 'to lift up the mind from the dungeon of the body to the enjoying his own divine essence' (p. 104).

The *Arcadia* is a poem in this sense: its aim is to awake the love of virtue by an infinity of 'speaking pictures', as Sidney's own contemporaries clearly recognized. Greville calls Sidney 'this excellent image-maker' and praises him for turning the barren precepts of philosophy into the 'pregnant images of life' – pregnant, in the sense that they breed virtuous actions, as Sidney himself envisaged the poet able 'to bestow a Cyrus upon the world to make many Cyruses' (p. 101). His purpose, says Greville, was 'to limn out such exact pictures of every posture of the mind'. Hoskins too praises the 'many notable and lively portraits' of human attitudes and situations with which the *Arcadia* is stocked, and the printer of the 1590 edition shows how it struck a contemporary, in the little abstracts which he gives at the beginning of each chapter: 'A verbal crafty coward *portrayed* in Clinias ... Brave courage *imaged* in Amphialus.'

It is here, of course, that the romance form lends itself so unreservedly to Sidney's purposes, with its picture gallery inviting the reader to look and to linger. What he sees will be the speaking pictures which Sidney describes in the *Apology*, archetypal images of virtue and vice which awake the imagination and inform the mind, which move men and 'make them know that goodness whereunto they are moved' (p. 103). A typical example is the description of Pamela at prayer, when the two princesses are being held and tortured by Cecropia (p. 464).

But this prayer sent to heaven from so heavenly a creature, with such a fervent grace as if devotion had borrowed her body to make of itself a most beautiful representation; with her eyes so lifted to the skyward that one would have thought they had begun to fly thitherward to take their place among their fellow stars; her naked hands raising up their whole length and, as it were, kissing one another, as if the right had been the picture of Zeal, and the left of Humbleness, which both united themselves to make their suits more acceptable ...

The description is explicitly a picture, 'a most beautiful representation' of devotion. As Pamela kneels there, her eyes gazing upwards to heaven, her hands raised yet folded in prayer, her attitude turns her into the emblem of piety itself, a figure which, like patience on a monument, evokes all the traditional attributes of the virtue she examplifies. At the same time the visual emblem is illuminated by the moral commentary which Sidney weaves into his description, defining the loving combination of zeal and humility towards heaven which are the constituent parts of prayer. Even the hard-hearted Cecropia is abashed and moved by the image which Pamela presents, though she cannot tell why. The hard-hearted reader is made both to see and to hear. A more self-conscious example is Sidney's description of Argalus and Parthenia as a pattern of perfect married love. The messenger arrives to find Argalus in his parlour reading aloud the stories of Hercules' labours, while Parthenia looks at him rather than at the book, asking him 'pretty' questions not because she wants an answer but for the pleasure of causing him to look at her (p. 501):

A happy couple: he joying in her, she joying in herself, but in herself, because she enjoyed him: both increasing their riches by giving to each other ... where desire never wanted satisfaction, nor satisfaction ever bred satiety; he ruling, because she would obey, or rather because she would obey, she therein ruling.

The picture of the couple has the same archetypal quality as Blake's little illustrations of nurses and children or children and old folks in his *Songs of Innocence*, which are in the common tradition of emblem; but again Sidney defines the implications of the scene in a way which turns the visual image into one which articulates. It is in line with Sidney's own theory, for example, that Argalus shall be reading of the exploits of Hercules whose heroic deeds, described in poetry, will move him to a like heroism. It is fitting, too, that Parthenia shall look up to her husband and learn of nobility through him: like Milton, the Elizabethans had a keen sense of the hierarchy of the sexes – 'He for God only, she for

God in him'. Sidney's description, however, involves in addition to that of hierarchy, a further image of the circle of love, where each gives and takes and grows the richer by giving. Behind the circular pattern of language in this little description lie the circular dance of the Graces and all the ramifications of circle imagery, both Christian and Platonic, by which the Renaissance symbolized the nature of love, human and divine. In this way the visual image is given a speaking voice to define its own felt significance.

These are both examples of positive images of virtue, but the process works in reverse, to depict evil in terms which present 'nothing that is not to be shunned'. Sidney's account of Amphialus' rebellion contains many illustrations of this, of which the following picture of the first great battle against Basilius' forces is typical (p. 469):

The clashing of armour, the crushing of staves, the jostling of bodies, the resounding of blows, was the first part of that ill-agreeing music which was beautified with the grisliness of wounds, the rising of dust, the hideous falls and groans of the dying. The very horses, angry in their masters' anger, with love and obedience brought forth the effects of hate and resistance, and with minds of servitude did as if they affected glory. Some lay dead under their dead masters, whom unknightly wounds had unjustly punished for a faithful duty. Some lay upon their lords by like accidents, and in death had the honour to be borne by them, whom in life they had borne ... The earth itself (wont to be a burial of men) was now, as it were, buried with men; so was the face thereof hidden with dead bodies ... In one place lay disinherited heads, dispossessed of their natural seignories ... There lay arms, whose fingers yet moved as if they would feel for him that made them feel; and legs, which contrary to common reason, by being discharged of their burden, were grown heavier.

This excerpt from a long and most elaborate description uses the same methods as many of the battle paintings of the sixteenth century. There is no attempt at realism: the painter compiles a series of images illustrating the various activities of a battlefied and then assembles them into what is less a picture than a hieroglyph of battle. In this way Sidney assembles all the basic properties – the arms, the assaults, the horses, the dead and mangled bodies, each described in isolation; but the verbal medium makes possible a moral dimension which a painting lacks. Music is one of the great Renaissance symbols of divine and human harmony, and the monstrous disharmony of Sidney's battle symphony serves, therefore, to set the episode in a metaphysical context by which it is condemned. As the description develops, the contradiction inherent in the conception of inharmonious music is amplified into a vision in which all natural order is perverted, all normal functions are reversed and all healthful impulses produce monstrous results. The horses, if in their proper place beneath their masters, are only so because foully slain, but more normally reverse the natural order by lying on top of those whom they should have borne. The earth is buried instead of burying, against nature the legs made heavier instead of lighter by the loss of their load. The metaphor of the disinherited heads, dispossessed of their natural seignories, implies a violation of both the human and the social hierarchy, and drew special commendations from Hoskins for this reason. The description adds up to a total image of rebellion as something hostile to the very law of nature, yet all embodied in the picture itself without overt commentary. There are significantly more of these 'speaking pictures' in the Revised than in the Old Arcadia, and they achieve their greatest elaboration and power in the third book. As Sidney's art matures and he grows increasingly away from the first versions in his latest work, he becomes more intent on turning his original romance into a heroic poem.*

4

The ceaseless moral pressure which the Arcadia exerts on the reader through its pictorial detail is only a part of the larger strategy of the book. If, as Sidney believes, the nature of poetry is to reveal the universal behind the particular, the law of God operating within the seeming chaos of the world, then the Arcadia is a poem both in detailed image and in underlying theme. The theme of Sidney's 'poem' is the subject of this section. The Arcadians are a

* For a fuller treatment of 'speaking pictures' see The Shape of Things Known. Sidney's Apology and its Philosophical Tradition. Forrest G. Robinson (Harvard, 1972).

pagan people of ancient Greece, lacking the Christian revelation but possessed, like More's Utopians, of right reason which, so long as it is not obscured by passion, provides an innate sense of right and wrong and is sufficient to comprehend the Law of Nature and deduce the existence of providence. The conflict between right reason and unregulated passion is fundamental in Sidney's work both at the personal and the political level. Right reason, sensing the existence of a universal order, judges all actions in relation to that order; whereas passion, lacking such knowledge, can see only the particular and immediate, and pursues its aims as in a moral and metaphysical vacuum. The issue is debated between Cecropia and the imprisoned Pamela in a sequence which forms the centre-piece of the whole *Arcadia* and defines its metaphysical assumptions. Cecropia can concieve of nothing beyond this life (p. 488):

Yesterday was but as today, and tomorrow will tread the same footsteps of his foregoers: so as it is manifest enough that all things follow but the course of their own nature, saving only man, who while by the pregnancy of his imagination he strives to things supernatural, meanwhile he loseth his own natural felicity.

She believes there can be no wisdom 'but in including both heaven and earth in oneself', and her moral attitude towards love and beauty, therefore, is one of frank hedonism, just as on the political level she wishes her son, Amphialus, to possess the crown at no matter what cost. Her late husband was indeed, she tells him, 'a man worthy to reign, thinking nothing enough for himself' (p. 445). In a world with no other dimension to consider, the only virtue lies in the fulfilment of desire. Pamela, in contrast, is the virtuous pagan, led by her reason to the belief in a first cause and divine order, all embracing, all powerful and eternal. In her view, therefore, love, beauty and power must be defined in terms of their function in the total scheme, and used responsibly, in conformity with the eternal laws.

The distinction forms the criterion for virtue throughout the whole action, both in public and private affairs. Pamela and Philoclea believing in absolute virtue accept its restraints and bear their trials with patience because they know them to be sent by an all-powerful providence. The princes, Musidorus and Pyrocles, exhibit the same rational virtue in all their chivalrous exploits, fighting always in defence of justice and order; but on reaching Arcadia, they are faced with a new kind of problem, that of love which is a passion not to be escaped and scarcely to be controlled. When he discovers that Pamela loves him, Musidorus becomes 'a child of passion' and, in Sidney's very significant metaphor, is not 'content to give desire a kingdom, but that it must be an unlimited monarchy'. He steals a kiss, and would steal more in the *Old Arcadia*; but he is punished for it as Pyrocles, too, is schooled for his unbridled desires. By the end, both have learned the true nature of rational love, which is to give rather than to take, to bear patiently rather than to rebel, to accept whatever comes as the will of God; both (in terms of Sidney's favourite *topos*) to do and suffer: so their heroism is made complete. Not all, however, are given the chance to educate themselves, and the book is full of violent loves and disorders, of characters swept along by un- thinking passion, like Andromana or Erona, or the even un- happier characters like Gynecia and Amphialus who have enough reason to know that they are wrong but not enough to govern their actions. These suffer the worst of both worlds.

Basilius shows that he lacks any real belief in a divine order by his attempt to escape the fulfilment of the oracle; and inevitably, therefore, both his private and his public actions are tainted by the same basic error. As a man he is prepared to sacrifice wife and children to embark upon an unvirtuous love-affair: as a ruler he treats his kingship as if it were a private possession for his own gratification instead of as the human counterpart of the divine law. In every issue he follows his desires as a lover in opposition to his responsibilities as a king, against the advice of Philanax to 'set down all private conceits in comparison of what for the public is profitable' (p. 549), and in direct contrast to Euarchus, for whom absolute Justice overrules even parental love. In consequence his kingdom sinks, logically, almost to the level of a democracy, which is for Sidney the ultimate form of social chaos, where each man is governed only by his own desires.

Amphialus follows the same pattern, driven by his uncon- trollable passion for Philoclea to violate the laws of God and of society, and encouraged to do so by the situation which Basilius has created. In abducting Philoclea he destroys the very harmony which is the essential nature of love, and in resorting to rebellion, he allows his own rebel passions to dictate the conduct of public affairs. Knowing that he is wrong, but unable to master the passion which drives him on, his answer is to veil his actions under an extravagant code of honour and old-time chivalry which, however noble it may appear, represents in fact the same confusion of private with public values as in the case of Basilius. He treats war as if it were an affair of private honour and conducts his campaigns as if they were tourneys, so that on more than one occasion he has to be reprimanded because 'he would rather affect the glory of a private fighter than of a wise general' (p. 495). His reason is so blinded by desire that he cannot recognize the chaos which he is creating, and sees it all as legitimate in terms of chivalry (p. 473):

And now the often-changing fortune began also to change the hue of battles. For at the first, though it were terrible, yet terror was decked so bravely with rich furniture, gilt swords, shining armours ... that the eye with delight had scarce leisure to be afraid: but now all universally defiled with dust, blood, broken armours, mangled bodies, took away the mask and set forth horror in his own horrible manner. But neither could danger be dreadful to Amphialus' undismayable courage, nor yet seem ugly to him whose truly-affected mind did still paint it over with the beauty of Philoclea ...

The complete emblem of this, and one of Sidney's most powerful speaking pictures, is the terrible fight between Amphialus and Argalus, who is only drawn into the affair because of 'the tyranny of honour'. The battle itself, in its elaborate chivalry and refusal ever to take unfair advantage, is more like a relationship between lovers than foes (p. 507):

A notable example of the wonderful effects of virtue, where the conqueror sought for friendship of the conquered, and the conquered would not pardon the conqueror: both indeed being of that mind to love each other for accepting, but not for giving mercy, and neither affected to over-live dishonour ...

Yet the end of this display is the bloody death of the most noble

Argalus and the subsequent sacrifice of Parthenia; and even here, Amphialus can only half recognize the truly evil course he has chosen. The fact that Philoclea sees him defeated by the Black Knight causes him more shame than all the suffering he has brought about.

Sidney is involved here in a very sensitive area of Renaissance thought, at a time when basic conceptions of social morality were in a state of flux, and the old attitudes to honour and chivalry, though by no means dead, were under fire from a new sense of public law and real-politik. It is an issue which Shakespeare debated in *Troilus and Cressida* or again in the opposition between Hotspur and Prince Hal or Antony and Octavius – Antony, it will be remembered, challenged Octavius to a duel. Like Shakespeare, Sidney is clear in his mind that wars cannot be managed in this way, and that there is no room in the modern hierarchical state for uncontrolled chivalry and private honour. Phalantus, who joined Basilius in his siege of Amphialus' castle, 'desired to keep his valour in knowledge by some private act, since the public policy restrained him', and so challenged Amphialus to a 'hateless' duel, making sure that his mistress should hear about it. There is no mistaking Sidney's disapproval of such an exhibition in the middle of serious matters; and yet it is equally obvious from his splendid descriptions of the armour and the devices, and the admiration which he reveals for the valour and generosity of the fighters, that there is a side of him which loved the old ideals and enjoyed the game of chivalry. His own private life illustrates the dichotomy within himself and his age. On one side he was a leader in the revival of court chivalry and a constant protagonist in the frequent joustings which were arranged for the Queen's entertainment. Unlike Malory, for example, in his many accounts of battles and tourneys, Sidney shows a first-hand, professional knowledge of the techniques of fighting with sword and lance, the proper manège of a horse, the finer details of armour and similar matters. And yet at the same time he is the modern politician calculating how best to out-manoeuvre Spain by timely intervention in the Low Countries.

This dichotomy is itself part of the even wider debate about the relationship between public and private morality which had been forced upon the conscience of sixteenth-century Europe by Machiavelli. His low estimate of the level of reason and morality among the populace led him, in *The Prince*, to formulate a double set of moral standards for private and public affairs. Since the common people are not amenable to reason they must for their own sakes be governed by whatever combination of deceit, tyranny and bribe will be most effective. The end is good government and for a prince the end justifies the means. Sidney, like any educated man of his century, was familiar with this revolutionary doctrine, and as a budding statesman only too aware of the problems of governing, he could see that Machiavelli had a point. Euarchus, for example, is a benevolent Machiavellian in his recognition and exploitation of the fact that the common people are 'naturally taken with exterior shows far more than the inward consideration of the material points'. In making his judgement on the two princes at the end of the story, therefore, he spends much thought on stage-managing the occasion, because 'in these pompous ceremonies he well knew a secret of government much to consist' (p. 807). The princes themselves act as though the end justifies the means in the ruthless and unsentimental way they manipulate Gynecia or Mopsa for their own purposes; and Sidney shows no pity for the victims, although he implies, I think, that the princes were at fault in ever getting themselves into a position where they had to descend to such shifts.

But however much he may have flirted with Machiavellianism in its detail, there can be no doubt that Sidney denied its fundamental assumptions. There is for him one absolute standard for good and evil, one divine order, one all-controlling providence, and there is no ambiguity in his moral attitude towards it. The laws of nature and of God are realities and will not suffer violation to go unpunished, whether men acknowledge their existence or not. The inescapable logic of events produces its inevitable results, and retribution follows atheism in the form of rebellion and tragedy descending on the heads of the guilty and of those innocently involved with them. At the trial of Gynecia and the princes in the final book, Euarchus metes out justice according to the strict letter of the law, and counters the princes' plea for mercy on the grounds that they acted through love with the harsh assertion that 'love may have no such privilege' (p. 837). Euarchus is the very embodiment of Law, the defender of the law of nature, with more than a hint of the symbolism of the Old Law in his actions. His justice reasserts the order which has been denied by so many of the actors throughout the book.

Yet even this is not the end. In the last page, there comes the surprising dénouement which absolves all present from the penalty of the law and allows the story to end in happy reunion and marriage. In the last resort providence shows itself more mysterious than right reason can fathom, more merciful than human justice can aspire to be. There are circumstances where 'reason cannot show itself more reasonable than to leave reasoning in things above reason' (p. 587). The divine purpose is fulfilled through the very means by which Basilius seeks to thwart it, and all he has done is to create for himself a painful and roundabout route to a destination which he would have arrived at in any case. At the beginning of Book Four, Pyrocles' well-laid plans to elope with Philoclea are brought to nothing by the actions of Dametas which follow inevitably from Musidorus' plan to elope with Pamela. At the same time, Musidorus himself is captured in the woods by the same rebels who fled there because Pyrocles had defeated them earlier in the story. Sidney comments on the dark logic of this in a passage which he developed in his revision (p. 715):

The almighty wisdom (evermore delighting to show the world that by unlikeliest means greatest matters may come to conclusion, that human reason may be the more humbled and more willingly give place to divine providence) as at the first it brought in Dametas to play a part in this royal pageant ... so ... for an end, made his folly the instrument of revealing that which far greater cunning had sought to conceal.

When Euarchus arrives in Arcadia on his way home to what he expects will be a happy reunion with his son and nephew, he finds instead that he has to judge and condemn them to death. 'In such a shadow or rather pit of darkness the wormish mankind lives, that neither they know how to foresee nor what to fear, and are but like tennis-balls tossed by the racket of the higher powers' (p. 817). Sidney's comment is Websterean in its suggestion of a harsh and unloving providence, and it is not until the closing pages, when the complex chain of cause and effect is worked out, that providence is shown to be not only omnipotent but benign. At this point the whole great pattern becomes apparent, and even the machinations and failures of Cecropia fall into place. The fact that her husband unexpectedly died just as he was about to depose Basilius, that her plan to destroy the princesses by her wild beasts miscarries almost as by miracle, and that when at last she has them in her power, she cannot murder them as she wishes because her son has fallen in love with Philoclea: the fact, too, that Anaxius is struck down with love at first sight for Pamela at the moment that he goes to kill her – all these unexpected contretemps demonstrate that providence has a special care for the princesses and is reserving them, in the words of the second oracle, 'for such as were better beloved of the gods' (p. 587).

The princes for whom they are reserved share in the same benevolent destiny. Sidney exploits the normal tolerance of extraordinary action and coincidence which the Romance form possesses to carry the heroes through a series of hair-breadth escapes which cumulatively amount almost to miracle. The actions 'beyond mortal power' (p. 269) which they repeatedly perform; the king of Pontus' dream which saves them from Plexirtus (p. 280); the accident by which Pyrocles recovers his sword after the shipwreck (p. 374), and the fact that he trips and so is saved from the suicide he intends (p. 564); the constant if unobtrusive reference to a guiding providence which leads Dametas, 'guided by a far greater constellation than his own', to discover Pyrocles and Philoclea in bed (p. 722), or brings the rebels, 'guided by everlasting justice' to prevent the flight of Musidorus and Pamela (p. 754) – all show a divine power at work to fulfil the oracle.

The mechanics by which this great plan is completed normally, however, spring from the nature of the characters themselves and are not overtly imposed upon them. The predestination which controls the story is of ends only, not of means: Providence foresees and forewills the conclusion but leaves men free to choose their own route there. As Basilius tiptoes out to his adulterous assignation, Sidney comments, 'Thus with a great deal of pain did Basilius go to her whom he fled, and with much cunning left the person for whom he employed all his cunning' (p. 678). There are, of course, good ways and evil ways, and most men choose the latter, but whichever is taken will be used by Providence to fulfil its own inscrutable purposes. The only human duty, therefore, is to follow virtue in the immediate act and to trust the outcome to providence. No end, however good, can justify a deliberate violation of virtue.

The most important theme of the *Arcadia* is the mysterious but benevolent working of providence, and the oracle itself is the central fact and symbol of this process. It is impious to consult the oracle on flippant grounds, but even more so to try and evade its prophecies, as not only Basilius but the neighbouring princes, who try to destroy Musidorus when they learn of the greatness foretold for him, discover to their cost (p. 257). Even the virtuous Philanax errs in ignoring the second oracle which bids him 'to give tribute but not oblation to human wisdom' (p. 587). His immoderate attack on the princes at their trial, springing out of a blind and sentimental veneration for his dead master Basilius, shows a failure to study the oracle with sufficient care; and this point would perhaps have been underlined if Sidney had completed his revision. But Philanax would certainly have been spared for his other virtues as, I think, would Amphialus. He is not actually dead, although beyond the help of normal medicine, when we see him being carried away by Queen Helen in Book Three. But we are told earlier of the most excellent physician at her court, who had already achieved the miraculous cure of Parthenia; and because Amphialus is a great and noble figure in spite of all his wrong headedness, and because the light of reason is never wholly dead in him, it seems likely that he would have been regenerated in a completed version.

The *Arcadia* embodies this reassuring assertion of order and purpose beneath apparent chaos in its own 'sensible' form. It offers us a picture of anarchy, in which princes become shepherds and shepherds have the authority of princes, in which Pyrocles fights as an Amazon and Parthenia as a knight: yet the whole disordered pattern of action is presented in terms of a complete and orderly literary hierarchy. The level of style throughout is controlled with an impeccable decorum, every character speaking a language appropriate to his standing, each description in terms nicely graded to its social level and moral seriousness. Amphialus' battles are treated in a higher style than those involving the common rebellious rout, as Pamela's narrative differs from Mopsa's tale; and when the disguised princes take part in the shepherd eclogues, their songs are in the fashionable 'highbrow' classical metres as opposed to the common ballad-metres of the lower orders. In this way, with enormous attention to detail, Sidney insists on the permanence of hierarchy even when all order and decorum seem to have been lost. The literary form itself carries as strong a symbolism as do the shapes of altars and Easter wings in which George Herbert composed some of his religious lyrics.

5

The symbolism of style throughout the book leads us back to the symbolic significance of its title, the *Arcadia*. From Theocritus onwards, Arcadia has been the setting for the pastoral idyll, an innocent world where the sun always shines and the shepherd inhabitants pass their time playing their pipes, competing in eclogues and wooing their mistresses. The pressures of society, the obligations of work, are not there and man and nature are in accord with each other. Even Shakespeare's Forest of Arden which is not immune from winter and rough weather at least is free of the complexities of normal living. No one ever mistook the Arcadian idyll for reality; it was always the embodiment of man's yearning for a simpler less artificial life than that imposed by civilization. For the Renaissance, a period extremely rich in the poetry of pastoral idyll, Arcadia was specifically a country of the mind through which the poets projected their vision of an innocent happiness where love and poetry are the only serious matters. This is Spenser's pastoral image in Book VI of *The Faerie Queene*, and because its values are contrary to those of real life, it can be set up in contrast to its opposite, the Court, and so used for satiric purposes.

Sidney shows himself to be very familiar with the Arcadian tradition. The shepherds who perform his eclogues make no pretence at reality, and from time to time we are reminded that Arcadia itself has a very literary genesis. Basilius' country bower is surrounded by 'such sort of trees as either excellency of fruit, stateliness of growth, continual greenness, or poetical fancies, have made at any time famous' (p. 175); and the countryside is dotted with figures out of the conventional pastoral: 'here a shepherd's boy piping as though he should never be old: there a young shepherdess knitting and withal singing...' (pp. 69–70). And because Arcadia is the accepted symbol for whatever the poets find lacking in the world, Sidney invests his ideal Arcadia with his own symbolism particularly relevant to the theme of his book. The first glimpses we have of it reveal it as a place of order and hierarchy, where the operation of the divine law is explicity manifested in the workings of nature (p. 69):

There were hills which garnished their proud heights with stately trees; humble valleys whose base estate seemed comforted with refreshing of silver rivers ... thickets, which, being lined with most pleasant shade, were witnessed so to by the cheerful deposition of many well-tuned birds; each pasture stored with sheep feeding with sober security ...

Everything is in its proper station gladly performing its proper task. Nor is this true only of nature; the works of man share in the same ideal order: Kalander's house combines beauty with the capacity to perform its proper function of hospitality: 'The lights, doors and stairs rather directed to the use of the guest than to the eye of the artificer; and yet as the one chiefly heeded, so the other not neglected ...' (p. 71). The servants are all 'serviceable in behaviour', and the garden, both fruitful and beautiful, in the middle of which is a statue of Venus with a babe at her breast – not however, Cupid, but the young heroic Aeneas. This initial symbolism is picked up from time to time throughout the book in the natural activities of the country, in the description of the hunting for example, or the hawking where the very birds of the air know their proper places and are punished if, like the heron, they seek to exceed them.

But this first image of an idyllic Arcadia is undercut even before it is established, and we are only introduced to it after an opening to the book which suggests that the real world is very far from sharing this ideal nature. In the first pages we see the two Arcadian shepherds, Claius and Strephon, lamenting that their lady Urania has left them; and it must be remembered that Urania was the common Renaissance symbol for spiritual love – the Venus Urania of neoplatonism whose departure from the world Spenser laments in Book V of *The Faerie Queene*. While the two are talking in praise of her goodness, their speech is interrupted by the sight of an apparently dead man being washed ashore and the bloody remains of a sea battle a little way out (p. 66):

... a sight full of piteous strangeness: a ship, or rather the carcase of the ship, or rather some few bones of the carcase hulling there, part broken, part burned, part drowned – death having used more than one dart to that destruction ... but that the chief violence was grown of human inhumanity: for their bodies were full of grisly wounds, and their blood had (as it were) filled the wrinkles of the sea's visage, which it seemed the sea would not wash away that it might witness it is not always his fault when we condemn his cruelty.

The description, one of Sidney's most elaborately constructed pictures, insists that death has entered the world with all our woe, and that man is no longer in accord with nature. The ideal Arcadia, therefore, is used throughout as a point of reference to remind the reader of what ought to be, and its values are kept alive in the pastoral eclogues, while Sidney turns the actual Arcadia of his story into a Greek state surrounded by other Greek states which it comes increasingly to resemble as its ruler continues to ignore the obligations of his position. Throughout the book we are conscious of the two Arcadias, the ideal one of poetic tradition and the real one of the story from which the pastoral peace has been driven by the neglect of human reason; yet by the end, when order has been re-established and the transgressors have either repented of their sins or been eliminated because of them, even then the Golden Age is not reborn. The Elizabethans were realists in the last resort, and like Spenser and Shakespeare who both used the Arcadian myth, Sidney saw it as an ideal to be striven for but never achieved in full. The Arcadian idyll owes both its poignancy and its appeal as myth to the fact that it can never be attained.

The double level of his treatment of Arcadia itself provides a key to Sidney's attitude towards heroism in his 'heroic poem'. The reader is constantly struck by the enormous gulf between the nobility of the princely heroes and, to an even greater degree, of the two princesses, and the ignoble behaviour of almost everybody else. Sidney's picture of democracy is a justly famous one (pp. 383-4): in a state where self-interest is the only motive, the anarchy of Hobbes's State of Nature will inevitably prevail. It has sometimes been assumed from this description that Sidney is the aristocrat sneering at the illiterate lower orders, but a glance at his treatment of the nobility suggests that he viewed them too with an equal cynicism. The accounts of Timautus' campaign for power against Philanax in Book Four (pp. 766-70), or Amphialus' methods of recruiting allies by appealing to self-interest (pp. 452) show the same selfish motives in operation at the upper as well as the lower levels of society; and the *Arcadia* is full of little 'asides' which reveal an acute consciousness of fallen human nature. The description of the lamentations of the Arcadians when they think that their king is dead: 'they yielded themselves over to all those forms of lamentation that doleful images do imprint in the honest but over-tender hearts, especially when they think the rebound of evil falls to their own smart'; the matter-of-fact astringency with which Sidney describes Timautus' way of winning support 'with those liberal protestations of friendship which men that care not for their word are wont to bestow' (p. 768); the throw-away similes, often occurring in contexts where cynicism has no relevance, as in the description of Amphialus' spaniel shaking the water from its coat 'as great men do their friends, now he had no further cause to use it' (p. 285) – all suggest a deep scepticism about human motives which is hostile to the heroic mode of the *Arcadia*. Sidney is remarkably ruthless in his presentation of life. In the battles, there is always a cowardly soldier at hand to stab the persons whom Amphialus has spared out of chivalry.

The explanation of this dichotomy lies in Sidney's theory of poetry. It is because the world of reality is brazen that the poet makes his a golden one. His heroes are not imitated from life but created to remind life of what it lacks. They represent the ideal reality which the all too fallen world must be wooed to love and hence to emulate, and which men are more likely to imprint in the tablet of memory when, in the words of the *Apology*, the Heroic poem presents virtue 'in her holiday apparel' (p. 119). The function of the Heroic poem is to provide the world with images of the virtues which it most needs, and the two levels of the *Arcadia* demonstrate this intention. Fielding's novels are still in the same tradition with their contrast between the good-hearted Tom Jones and the self-interest of Blifil or Black George or almost everybody he meets on his way, although Fielding was probably more sceptical about the efficacy of the moral example of the hero, and is beginning to blur the distinction between the two levels. For Sidney, the hero is the ultimate speaking picture: he belongs to poetry, not history.

## 6

I have emphasized the serious didactic purpose of the *Arcadia*, because Sidney's revisions suggest that this was his prime intention. It should be remembered, however, that he praises poetry not only for its 'teaching' but for its 'delightful teaching', and argues that the delight is what gives poetry its special power to penetrate, where the soberer precepts of the philosopher merely bounce off. By this means it is able to 'move men to take that goodness in hand, which without delight they would fly as from a stranger' (p. 103). The idea derives from Horace's phrase about mixing the useful with the pleasing, and is a commonplace of Renaissance literary theory. Undoubtedly, in Sidney's view, the greatest delight which poetry had to offer came from its power of story-telling, as his description of the poet in the *Apology* makes clear: 'with a tale forsooth he cometh unto you, with a tale which holdeth children from play and old men from the chimney corner. And, pretending no more, doth intend the winning of the mind from wickedness to virtue' (p. 113). The stronger didactic intention of the revised *Arcadia*, therefore, has a correspondingly greater virtuosity in narrative art to carry it, and the book attains a complexity in which the modern reader can easily lose himself.

Sidney begins his tale in the best traditional manner, *in medias res*, with the shipwreck of Musidorus near Arcadia. From this crucial point, he carries his story forward into the tangle of disguises, rebellions and elopements which compose the main action, and backwards into the sequence of events which brought the princes to Arcadia, by this means introducing characters such as Euarchus who will be used later when needed. Sidney had no technique of flashback at his disposal and so was forced to invent ingenious modes by which the past could be narrated without improbability. Musidorus, for example, can only establish his identity with Pamela by telling her his history; and through this we learn of his relationship with Euarchus and Pyrocles, of the first shipwreck as the princes start their journey home, and the first round of their adventures. Pyrocles in his turn, wishing to seal his love for Philoclea 'with the chief arms of his desire', is firmly kept at a distance and forced to tell his story instead; so that we get the later sequence of adventures which culminates in the second shipwreck off Arcadia. By page 375 we have worked back to page 64 where the story began; and the only gap in the saga concerns Plangus who is mentioned in the accounts of both princes. This in due course is filled in by the princesses who know this part of the story from another source. It is a brilliant narrative *tour de force*, as each step forward precipitates a further revelation of the past which in its turn allows the story to move forward again, and as the innumerable narrative pieces fit together, the total picture gradually emerges as from a gigantic jigsaw puzzle. Sidney has managed to combine the methods of traditional romance, derived from oral story-telling, as in The Thousand and One Nights, with those of the epic which traditionally has a sequence of narration as opposed to direct description in its middle stretches.

The whole sequence is given enormous variety by the alternation of exposition and action, of tragic and comic, and by endowing the sections which are recounted with a flavour which comes from the personality of the narrator. The huge structure, however, is kept under control by the establishment of narrative patterns and echoes based on parallel or contrasting sequences of action which form a commentary on each other and underline the common moral issues. The setting, too, plays an important part in this control, and Sidney's very firm grasp of the Greek world in which the story is located. The countries through which the princes wander are in their proper geographical places, and their

travels can be charted on the Elizabethan maps. The dynastic relationships are so close and so consistently developed that all the
main characters are related by blood or marriage either to Basilius
or Euarchus or the king of Iberia; and the more deeply we penetrate into the jungle of adventures, the more familiar the faces we
find there. The seemingly enormous world which Sidney has created is in the end a very small one based on a few interrelated
families, and the complex story is more easily digested because of
the solid base on which it stands.

The most impressive quality of Sidney's achievement, however,
is his astonishing control of detail, so that there are virtually no
loose ends in the *Arcadia*. Like a good novelist, he always has his
eye on the future, and even the most insignificant incidents, however casually introduced, are picked up again often two or three
hundred pages later. Early in the first book, for example, Pyrocles
disappears and Musidorus goes off in search of him. On the way
he discovers some pieces of armour lying on the ground, which he
tries on and finds too big for him; and immediately afterwards, he
is attacked by the servants of a beautiful queen who arrives in her
chariot. We discover that it is Queen Helen searching for her
beloved Amphialus who has mysteriously gone away, and that
the armour is his. Soon Amphialus' page arrives and mentions a
spaniel which Amphialus had with him, and we learn how he
came by the dog and why he has thrown away his armour.
Sidney is thus working backwards from the present situation
to uncover what has led up to it; but at the same time he is
introducing details which will be taken up in due course. The
little dog, for example, appears later when the princesses are bathing, and steals a book belonging to Philoclea which contains, inci-
dentally, the account of Plangus. And when Pyrocles follows the
dog to retrieve the book, it leads him to its master, Amphialus,
who has come secretly to Arcadia because he, too, is in love with
Philoclea, and that is why Helen cannot find him. The large size of
the armour is not forgotten but appears again three hundred pages
later when, in his fight with Musidorus, Amphialus is the taller
man, Musidorus 'something the lower' (p. 539). Last of all, when
Amphialus lies dying, Queen Helen catches up with him in time
to bear away his body and bring the cycle to its close. Nothing is

wasted and everything serves the larger narrative purpose, however merely decorative it may appear at the time. The tourney which Phalantus holds in Book One to prove that his mistress, Artesia, is the most beautiful of all women, and the pageant of the knights with the pictures of their ladies who come in response to his challenge, are commonplaces of the romance tradition. There is, however, one difference. Most of the ladies appear elsewhere in the story, and at our first glimpse of them here, Sidney describes them in seemingly casual terms which are yet very relevant to what is to come. Artesia herself enters in a chariot 'drawn by four winged horses with artificial flaming mouths and fiery wings, as if she had newly borrowed them of Phoebus' (p. 157). The reference is, of course, to Phaethon's ill-fated attempt to handle the horses of the sun, which made him the archetype of ambition in Renaissance mythology. Artesia in like manner is to suffer for her ambition later in the story. Andromana, we are told, had 'exceeding red hair' (p. 158), a feature traditionally associated with the lechery which later dominates her actions. Artaxia, though beautiful in detail, has features which together 'seemed not to make up that harmony that Cupid delights in, the reason whereof might seem a mannish countenance ...' (p. 158). Her appearance is a warning of the aggression which makes her a notable source of disharmony in the next book. Baccha, with her breasts 'over-familiarly laid open' (p. 158) is obviously a fitting destiny for Pamphilus, the professional philanderer. Sidney has turned what is usually a piece of conventional decoration into an organic sequence, a sort of dumb show of what is to come. By this kind of control he avoids the casual flow of events which makes up the normal romance.

What establishes the inner logic of the tale most effectively, however, and gives a kind of probability to the wildest adventures, is Sidney's unremitting attention to his characters. Things happen in the *Arcadia* because the actors are what they are, and plot is simply character in action. Sidney inherits a mass of traditional romance situations, but he takes great pains to justify them in terms of credible human motive and behaviour. Pyrocles falls in love with Philoclea's picture before he ever sees her in the flesh, for example, and this is a traditional enough motif. But Sidney provides a rational explanation by revealing later in the story that

Philoclea bears a marked resemblance to the maiden Zelmane who loved and, indeed, died of love for Pyrocles before he came to Arcadia. The tenderness which this engendered in the hero transfers itself to the picture and explains not only his sudden love but also why he adopted the name of Zelmane and took on the Amazonian disguise. The original Zelmane had disguised herself as a man for Pyrocles' sake, and he does the equivalent for her. The characters, though often complex, have clear identities and act consistently according to their natures in whatever they do. Basilius, having sworn never to marry, marries the young Gynecia in his middle age and, more unfittingly, would marry the young Amazon if he could, twenty years later. Similarly he makes precisely the same misjudgement of Clinias as he has earlier made with regard to Dametas. Cecropia's egotism fills every corner of her personality, and colours even her happy vision of the joys of possessing children: 'If you could conceive what a heart-tickling joy it is to see your own little ones with aweful love come running to your lap, and like little models of yourself still carry you about them ...' (p. 460). There are psychological perceptions of a subtlety which anticipates those of Shakespeare by almost two decades – as in the shrewd analysis of the relationship between Phalantus and Artesia (p. 155), for example, or of the vanity which is the motive for Dido's revenge (p. 338), or in the whole study of Gynecia's guilty conscience which provokes her prophetic surrealist dream (p. 376), and inhibits her from referring to her own daughter, Philoclea, for whom she feels so guilty a hatred: 'Is the being the mother of Pamela become an odious name unto you?' she says, when she upbraids Basilius for his attempted infidelity to her (p. 726).

The most elaborate character studies in the book are those of Pamela and Philoclea, whom Sidney conceived in terms of sense and sensibility, an Elizabethan Eleanor and Marianne Dashwood. Pamela has rational virtue, knowing good from evil and consciously choosing the former: 'She in whose mind virtue governed with the sceptre of knowledge' (p. 520). Philoclea knows nothing of evil but has a natural and instinctive innocence which is purer and yet more vulnerable than that of her sister. The difference between the rational self-control of the one and the impulsive instinctive generosity of the other is pointed in every detail of their actions. When Cecropia's wild beasts are let loose, Philoclea runs away in panic, whereas Pamela, keeping her head, lies down and feigns death, on the common assumption that a wild beast will not touch a dead body. When Musidorus tells his tale to her, Pamela is careful to test its truth by searching questions and roundabout inquiries, whereas Philoclea accepts Pyrocles' story out of instinct and love, without checking. Again, when the two sisters are imprisoned by Cecropia, Philoclea gives way to her grief, letting her clothes became dishevelled and her hair untidy; whereas Pamela takes extra care to be neat and unruffled, which in fact brings trouble on herself from Cecropia who cannot concieve of such self-respect and assumes, therefore, that Pamela cannot be unhappy in her imprisonment. Philoclea's innocence throughout manifests itself in a more free and careless attitude to her clothes than that of her sister – what Pyrocles calls her 'nymph-like apparel, so near nakedness as one might well discern part of her perfections' (p. 146). Because of this he allows her to continue her flight from the lion long after the beast is dead, since in flight her clothes reveal more of her beauty than usual 'which made Zelmane follow not over-hastily, lest she should too soon deprive herself of that pleasure' (p. 176). It is this carelessness about decorum in dress which is to be her undoing when Pyrocles finds her in her chamber in the *Old Arcadia*: she is destined by her very innocence to give herself in virtuous love when she is only betrothed. In the revised version, Sidney shows her in process of growing up through her love for Pyrocles and able, gently yet firmly, to resist his advances; but too much of her innocent sexuality still survives from the first version for this to be wholly credible. I suspect that Sidney would have carried out a few more revisions in this area if he had lived to complete the work. Philoclea is the most fully developed character of the book and the portrayal of her relations with Pyrocles while she still thinks him to be the Amazon, Zelmane, is a very remarkable piece of characterization. Zelmane makes her feelings for Philoclea only too apparent, but Philoclea, who is almost too young for love, at first feels only a tenderness which leads her to return Zelmane's kisses without understanding their import. When she finds herself

awakened to love, she is in utter confusion, distraught by the fact
that her desires can have no satisfaction yet obscurely comforted
by her observations that her mother appears to share the same
feelings. Sidney handles the relationship with great subtlety and
without any trace of prurience: it is a serious, moving and yet
extremely funny sequence.

This humour is the final aspect of the work to which I would
draw attention. In spite of its great cargo of didacticism, both moral
and political, the *Arcadia* is a very witty, very amusing book. It
covers the whole spectrum of comic situations, from the slapstick
of Dametas' family life, to the very sophisticated comedy of Zelmane, pursued by Basilius who thinks he is a woman, and by
Gynecia who knows he is a man. After his rescue of Philoclea
from the lion, Basilius compares the supposed Amazon to 'another
Pallas with the spoils of Gorgon', but the shrewder Gynecia likens
him to 'the young Hercules killing the Nemean lion' (p. 180). As
Zelmane can take advantage of her position as a woman to kiss
Philoclea as much as she likes, so she is open to the same treatment
from Gynecia. The tone, too, ranges from the gentlest irony to a
tartness worthy of Jane Austen. 'She was a queen and therefore
beautiful' is Sidney's comment on one of the ladies whose claims
to beauty are being defended at the tourney; and there is great
delicacy in the irony with which he describes Pamela's behaviour
on receiving a letter from Musidorus whom she has just banished
from her presence for trying to kiss her (p. 438):

But when she saw the letter, her heart gave her from whence it
came; and therefore clapping it to again she went away from it as if it
had been a contagious garment of an infected person ... 'Shall I,' said
she, 'second his boldness so far as to read his presumptuous letters?
And yet,' said she, 'he sees me not now, to grow the bolder thereby:
and how can I tell whether they be presumptuous?' ... At last, she
concluded it were not much amiss to look it over, that she might out
of his words pick some further quarrel against him.

Sidney is capable, however, of a masculine ruthlessness, which,
from the nature of the situations in which it occurs, is more sav-
agely funny than anything in Jane Austen. When, for example,
Basilius has spent the night with his wife Gynecia, thinking all

the time that he is with Zelmane, he wakens up in the darkness, savouring the adulterous pleasure which he imagines himself to have enjoyed. His comment on the situation is profoundly revealing of the human powers of self-deception: 'O,' says he, 'who would have thought there could have been such difference betwixt women!' (p. 725). While making the assignation earlier in the day, he has already protested that his wife shall not prevent him from enjoying Zelmane's favours: 'What,' said he, 'shall my wife become my mistress' (p. 673). The morning light reveals that this has indeed been the case. It is a sequence which would be at home in Jacobean drama.

## A NOTE ON THE TEXT

The basis of this text is the Countess of Pembroke's edition of 1593, but it has been emended in the light of the 1590 revised *Arcadia* and the 1598 Folio, and checked against Feuillerat's collation of the later editions. I have made use of Feuillerat's text of the *Old Arcadia* and Miss Robertson's recent edition of the same work in the parts which are relevant. The textual notes to Miss Robertson's *Arcadia* and to Professor Ringler's edition of the poem's have been invaluable. I have used as my copy text the modernized version edited by Ernest Baker (1907, reprinted 1921). Baker based his text on the editions of 1638 and 1674, both poor texts into which he introduced a considerable number of new errors. The copy text has therefore had to be heavily emended.

This is a modernized text, but the term needs some qualification. I have made no attempt to modernize the vocabulary since Sidney himself used deliberately archaic language appropriate to the decorum of a Romance and designed to raise the style above the colloquial level in accordance with the best Heroic theory. Spenser followed the same pattern for the same reason in the medievalisms of *The Faerie Queene*. I have kept, therefore, all the word forms traditional to the medieval romance, which were archaic in Sidney's own time – brake, spake, gat, damosel, etc., and have left unchanged all those Elizabethan words which have evolved modern forms over the intervening centuries – not only out of fidelity to the text but also because the modern form rarely carries quite the same significance as its earlier equivalent. 'Shame-facedness' is not identical in meaning with Sidney's 'shamefastness' nor is 'lecherous' the precise equivalent of 'lickerous', nor 'steadiness' the same as 'stayedness'. For this reason, although I have normally modernized the spelling, I have retained Sidney's form where to change it would have been to distort the meaning. He frequently uses the word 'travail' meaning either to travel or to labour or to travel laboriously. I use both forms therefore, keeping 'travail' wherever any element of labour is implied. Similarly I retain 'aweful' to remind the modern reader of the stronger force which this debased word originally carried. A modern edition continually presents the editor with minor dilemmas of this kind, since the freer Elizabethan spelling happily encouraged multiple meanings and enriched the language with complex effects which our own more precise distinctions have destroyed. When in the Third Eclogue, for example, Thyrsis wooes Kala, he does so with 'Poesyes' of spring flowers wrapped up in green silk (p. 690) which we can only reproduce as 'posies', although by so doing we throw away the pleasant pun on poetical offerings and the language of flowers. In the same way, when Philoclea sees what pains Gynecia is taking to separate her from Zelmane, 'the more jealous her mother was, the more she thought the jewel precious which was with so many locks guarded' (p. 240). The word 'locks' does not appear in the text until 1598: the editions of 1590 and 1593 both have 'lookes', and Sidney is, of course, punning. The locks with which Gynecia tries to guard the prince are her angry looks, and the two words are interchangeable. The modern editor is forced to separate what the Elizabethans sought to fuse.

It is more difficult to modernize the punctuation of a style and syntax which are essentially unmodern. Like that of *Paradise Lost*, the heroic style of the *Arcadia* is heavily latinate, and organized into enormous unbroken paragraphs in which subordinate clauses and ablative absolutes are woven around the main clause to give patterns of great syntactical complexity. Neither Sidney nor, perhaps, the nature of the English language is capable of keeping the strict grammatical control of such structures which is possible in an inflected language like Latin. Unrelated participles abound; the main clause sometimes gets lost, the subject changes, and pronouns which form the object of one sentence find themselves the subject of the next: 'But the watch gave a quick alarum to the soldiers within, whom practice already having prepared, began each ... to look to their charge ...' (p. 466). Yet in a style where grammar is so essentially the servant and not the master, such irregularities are of no consequence. Sidney's meaning is rarely ambiguous through lack of strict grammar, and the sense forces itself triumphantly through all obstacles. It demands, however, alertness, effort and cooperation from the reader. One cannot read the *Arcadia* passively; its pleasures and rewards come only from an active use of the intelligence, and a constant awareness of the context.

The original Elizabethan punctuation is of great help in meeting these demands. The punctuation of the *Arcadia* is that of Sidney's scribes or compositors and not his own, but it is clearly organic to the style of the work. Its most obvious features are a heavy use of the colon – especially valuable in starting off a new sentence with a relative pronoun which refers back to the previous sentence – and above all, the very frequent use of brackets which enclose the subordinate clauses and guide the reader along the high road of the main clause as by a row of signposts. No other Elizabethan prose work uses brackets so extensively, and it would seem to be an idiosyncrasy of Sidney himself. By means of brackets he can include a running commentary on the matter which he is relating, or he can exaggerate the rhetorical patterns so as to turn a dramatic statement into an exquisitely formal piece of art. When Pyrocles tells Philoclea of his relationship with Zelmane, his embarrassment is conveyed in a series of digressions and qualifications the purpose of which is emphasized by the use of brackets (pp. 350–51). In the same way the heavy flattery and deceit of Clinias towards Basilius are made more obvious, as they are meant to be (p. 392). It is impossible to reproduce such passages in any form without retaining the elaborate structure of brackets, and it seems likely, indeed, that the visual patterns on the page made possible by the printing, were consciously exploited by the author as one of the pleasures which reading can afford.

The *Old Arcadia* and the folios from 1593 onwards were divided into books, but in the 1590 quarto, the 'overseer of the print' in

49

addition broke up the text into chapters 'for the more ease of the Readers', prefacing each one with a brief summary of the contents. It is a pity that the Countess of Pembroke saw fit to eliminate these chapter divisions, even though they lacked the authority of Sidney himself, and I have restored them, though not the summaries, which are not always helpful. For the sake of uniformity as well as for ease of reference, I have carried on the division into chapters for the rest of the work. My own begin with Chapter 30 of Book Three, page 602.

In conclusion, a word must be said about the Eclogues between the separate books. Sidney himself seems to have been responsible for their order in the *Old Arcadia*, but in his revisions he incorporated some of them into the text itself, making necessary, therefore, a new pattern which his death prevented him from establishing. The eclogues of the 1590 volume were chosen by the overseer of the print, possibly with some informed direction by Fulke Greville. In the edition of 1593, the Countess reverted as far as she could to Sidney's own order of the first version although in the interim the story line had been radically changed; and she restored – presumably out of sentiment – some of the eclogues sung by Philisides, the pseudonym which Sidney chose for himself, in the *Old Arcadia* but which were omitted in the New. She also incorporated a number of Sidney's other poems not included in any of the previous *Arcadias* and never intended to be so. For this reason, the Eclogues of 1593 have no authority; and yet sufficient of their original intention can still be perceived to make them worth reading. The modern reader may ignore them without in any way losing the thread of the story: yet they do elaborate upon it; and they embody in verse the same instinct to experiment, the same deliberate art and the same dramatic impulse as the rest of the *Arcadia*. The work is all of a piece and all its parts illuminate each other.

The end notes aim to elucidate mythological references and difficult points of meaning, and I have included relevant passages from the *Old Arcadia* to indicate the degree and nature of the changes which the revision involved.

# Editions to which reference is made

## I. *The Arcadia*

### (A) ORIGINAL EDITIONS
(referred to throughout as '90, '93 and '98.)

(1) *The Countesse of Pembrokes Arcadia* written by Sir Philippe Sidnei. London. Printed for William Ponsonbie. Anno Domini 1590

(2) *The Countesse of Pembrokes Arcadia*. Written by Sir Philip Sidney Knight. Now since the first edition augmented and ended. London. Printed for William Ponsonbie. Anno Domini. 1593

(3) *The Countesse of Pembrokes Arcadia*. Written by Sir Philip Sidney Knight. Now the third time published, with sundry new additions of the same Author. London. Imprinted for William Ponsonbie. Anno Domini. 1598

(4) *The Countesse of Pembrokes Arcadia*. Written by Sir Philip Sidney Knight. Now the fift time published, with some new Additions. Also a supplement of a defect in the third part of this History. By Sir W. Alexander. Dublin, Printed by the Societie of Stationers. 1621. Cum Privilegio.

### (B) MODERN EDITIONS

(1) *The Old Arcadia* (referred to as O A)

*The Countess of Pembroke's* Arcadia, *being the original version,* ed. A Feuillerat, *Prose Works of Sidney*, vol. IV, CUP, 1970.
*The Countess of Pembroke's* Arcadia, ed. Jean Robertson, Oxford, 1973 (Robertson).

(2) *The Revised Arcadia*

*The Countesse of Pembrokes* Arcadia. London. 1590, ed. A. Feuillerat, *Prose Works of Sidney*, vol. I, CUP, 1969.

*The Last Part of the Countesse of Pembroke's* Arcadia (1593), ed. A. Feuillerat, *Prose Works of Sidney*, vol. II, CUP, 1968.

## EDITIONS TO WHICH REFERENCE IS MADE

(3) *The Complete Arcadia*

*The Countess of Pembroke's* Arcadia, by Sir Philip Sidney, ed. Ernest A. Baker, Routledge, 1907 (reprinted 1921).

II. *The Poems of Sir Philip Sidney*, ed. William A. Ringler jr, Oxford, 1962 (Ringler).
*An Apology for Poetry*, ed. Geoffrey Shepherd, Nelson, 1965.

III. *Other Texts*

HOMER, *The Iliad*, translated by E. V. Rieu, Penguin Books, 1950.
  *The Odyssey*, translated by E. V. Rieu, Penguin Books, 1946.
OVID, *Metamorphoses*, translated by Mary M. Innes, Penguin Books, 1955.
VIRGIL, *The Aeneid*, translated by W. F. Jackson Knight, Penguin Books, 1956.

# List of principal characters

AMPHIALUS, son of Cecropia, nephew to Basilius

ANAXIUS, a proud, brutal and very formidable knight, ally of Amphialus

ANDROMANA, lecherous queen of Iberia; mother of Palladius

ANTIPHILUS, low-born husband of Erona

ARGALUS, a noble knight: husband of Parthenia.

ARTAXIA, militant queen of Armenia, and enemy of Musidorus and Pyrocles

ARTESIA, brought up in the household of Cecropia and corrupted by her

BASILIUS, king of Arcadia

CECROPIA, sister-in-law to Basilius; mother of Amphialus

CLAIUS AND STREPHON, two virtuous shepherds

CLINIAS, cowardly and corrupt servant of Cecropia

CLITOPHON, son of Kalander; 'The Knight of the Pole'

DAIPHANTUS, name assumed by Zelmane when disguised as a page in the service of Pyrocles

DAMETAS, illiterate herdsman in whose care Basilius places his daughters

ERONA, queen of Lycia, loved by Plangus

EUARCHUS, king of Macedonia; father of Pyrocles and uncle of Musidorus

GYNECIA, wife of Basilius

HELEN, queen of Corinth, in love with Amphialus

KALANDER, Arcadian nobleman

KING OF IBERIA, father of Plangus and Palladus. Husband of Andromana

LEONATUS, virtuous son of the king of Paphlagonia: half-brother of Plexirtus

LYCURGUS, brother of Anaxius

MISO, wife of Dametas

MOPSA, daughter of Dametas

MUSIDORUS, prince of Thessalia, nephew of Euarchus. After Palladius' death he assumes his name to conceal his own identity while seeking adventure (see Palladius). In Arcadia he disguises himself as a shepherd, Dorus

PALLADIUS, son of King of Iberia by Andromana; friend and follower of Musidorus and Pyrocles: in love with Zelmane

PAMELA, elder daughter of Basilius

PARTHENIA, wife of Argalus; 'The Knight of the Tomb'

PHALANTUS, of Corinth; half-brother of Helen

PHILANAX, chief nobleman and adviser to Basilius

PHILISIDES, a shepherd; later 'The Knight of the Sheep'. Sidney's own pseudonym

PHILOCLEA, younger daughter of Basilius

PLANGUS, son of king of Iberia by his first marriage; in love with Erona

PLEXIRTUS, bastard son of king of Paphlagonia and half-brother to Leonatus. Father of Zelmane

PYROCLES, prince of Macedon and son of Euarchus. After the death of Zelmane, he assumes the name of Daiphantus to disguise his identity while seeking adventure (see Daiphantus). He later takes on the name of Zelmane when he disguises himself as an Amazon (see Zelmane)

STREPHON, see Claius

TIRIDATES, king of Armenia and brother of Artaxia. In love with Erona

TIMAUTUS, corrupt Arcadian nobleman

URANIA, noble shepherdess beloved of Claius and Strephon

ZELMANE, daughter of Plexirtus, in love with Pyrocles

ZOILUS, brother of Anaxius

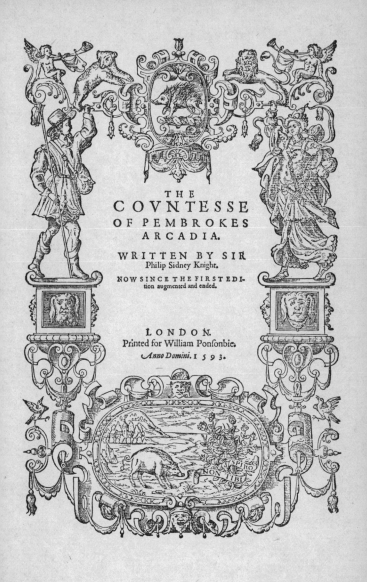

# THE
# COVNTESSE
## OF PEMBROKES
### ARCADIA.

WRITTEN BY SIR
Philip Sidney Knight.

NOW SINCE THE FIRST EDI-
tion augmented and ended.

LONDON.
Printed for William Ponsonbie.
*Anno Domini.* 1 5 9 3.

SPIRO
NON
TIBI

# THE COUNTESS OF PEMBROKE[1]

Here now have you (most dear, and most worthy to be most dear lady) this idle work of mine, which, I fear, like the spider's web, will be thought fitter to be swept away than worn to any other purpose. For my part, in very truth (as the cruel fathers among the Greeks were wont to do to the babes they would not foster) I could well find in my heart to cast out in some desert of forgetfulness this child which I am loth to father. But you desired me to do it, and your desire to my heart is an absolute commandment. Now it is done only for you, only to you: if you keep it to yourself or to such friends who will weigh errors in the balance of goodwill, I hope, for the father's sake, it will be pardoned, perchance made much of, though in itself it have deformities. For indeed, for severer eyes it is not, being but a trifle, and that triflingly handled. Your dear self can best witness the manner, being done in loose sheets of paper, most of it in your presence; the rest by sheets sent unto you as fast as they were done. In sum, a young head, not so well stayed* as I would it were (and shall be when God will) having many many fancies begotten in it, if it had not been in some way delivered, would have grown a monster; and more sorry might I be that they came in than that they gat out. But his chief safety shall be the not walking abroad; and his chief protection, the bearing the livery of your name, which (if much much goodwill do not deceive me) is worthy to be a sanctuary for a greater offender. This say I, because I know the virtue so; and this say I, because it may be ever so, or, to say better, because it will be ever so. Read it, then, at your idle times, and the follies your good judgement will find in it blame not, but laugh at. And so, looking for no better stuff than as in a haberdasher's shop, glasses or feathers, you will continue to love the writer, who doth exceed-

---

* *stayed*: governed.

ingly love you, and most heartily prays you may long live to be a principal ornament to the family of the Sidneys. Your loving brother,

PHILIP SIDNEY

# To the Reader[2]

The disfigured face, gentle reader, wherewith this work not long since appeared to the common view,[3] moved that noble lady to whose honour consecrated, to whose protection it was committed, to take in hand the wiping away those spots wherewith the beauties thereof were unworthily blemished. But as often in repairing a ruinous house the mending of some old part occasioneth the making of some new, so here her honourable labour, begun in correcting the faults, ended in supplying the defects, by the view of what was ill done guided to the consideration of what was not done. Which part with what advice entered into, with what success it hath been passed through (most by her doing, all by her directing), if they may be entreated not to define which are unfurnished of means to discern, the rest, it is hoped, will favourably censure. But this they shall for their better satisfaction understand, that though they find not here what might be expected, they may find nevertheless as much as was intended, the conclusion, not the perfection of Arcadia, and that no further than the author's own writings or known determinations could direct. Whereof who sees not the reason must consider there may be reason which he sees not. Albeit I dare affirm he either sees or, from wiser judgements than his own, may hear that Sir Philip Sidney's writings can no more be perfected without Sir Philip Sidney than Apelles' pictures without Apelles.[4] There are that think contrary, and no wonder. Never was Arcadia free from the cumber* of such cattle. 'To us,' say they, 'the pastures are not pleasant; and as for the flowers – such as we light on we take no delight in, but the greater part grow not within our reach.' Poor souls! What talk they of flowers! They are roses[5] not flowers must do them good, which, if they find not here, they shall do well to go feed elsewhere: any place will better like them; for without Arcadia* nothing grows in more plenty than lettuce suitable to their

*cumber: encumbrance. without Arcadia: outside.

lips.[6] If it be true that likeness is a great cause of liking and that contraries infer contrary consequences, then is it true that the worthless reader can never worthily esteem of so worthy a writing; and as true that the noble, the wise, the virtuous, the courteous, as many as have had any acquaintance with true learning and knowledge, will with all love and dearness entertain it, as well for affinity with themselves as being child to such a father. Whom albeit it do not exactly and in every lineament represent, yet considering the father's untimely death prevented the timely birth of the child, it may happily seem a thank-worthy labour that the defects being so few, so small and in no principal part, yet the greatest unlikeness is rather in defect than in deformity. But howsoever it is, it is now by more than one interest The Countess of Pembroke's Arcadia – done, as it was, for her; as it is, by her. Neither shall these pains be the last (if no unexpected accident cut off her determination) which the everlasting love of her excellent brother will make her consecrate to his memory.

H.S.

# The Countess of Pembroke's *Arcadia*
## written by Sir Philip Sidney

## The First Book

### CHAPTER 1

It was in the time that the earth begins to put on her new apparel against the approach of her lover, and that the sun, running a most even course, becomes an indifferent arbiter between the night and the day, when the hopeless shepherd Strephon was come to the sands which lie against the island of Cithera; where viewing the place with a heavy kind of delight, and sometimes casting his eyes to the isleward, he called his friendly rival, the pastor* Claius, unto him; and setting first down in his darkened countenance a doleful copy of what he would speak,

'O my Claius,' said he, 'hither we are now come to pay the rent for which we are so called unto by over-busy remembrance – remembrance, restless remembrance, which claims not only this duty of us but for it will have us forget ourselves. I pray you, when we were amid our flock, and that of other shepherds some were running after their sheep strayed beyond their bounds, some delighting their eyes with seeing them nibble upon the short and sweet grass, some medicining their sick ewes, some setting a bell* for an ensign of a sheepish squadron, some with more leisure inventing new games of exercising their bodies and sporting their wits; did remembrance grant us any holiday either for pastime or devotion – nay either for necessary food or natural rest – but that still it forced our thoughts to work upon this place where we last (alas, that the word *last* should so long last) did graze our eyes upon her ever-flourishing beauty? Did it not still cry within us "Ah, you base-minded wretches, are your thoughts so deeply bemired in the trade or ordinary worldeings, as for respect of gain

* *pastor*: shepherd. *setting a bell*: tying a bell on the leader of the flock.

some paltry wool may yield you, to let so much time pass without knowing perfectly her estate, especially in so troublesome a season; to leave that shore unsaluted from whence you may see to the island where she dwelleth; to leave those steps unkissed wherein Urania printed the farewell of all beauty?"

'Well, then, remembrance commanded; we obeyed, and here we find that as our remembrance came ever clothed unto us in the form of this place, so this place gives new heat to the fever of our languishing remembrance. Yonder, my Claius, Urania lighted. The very horse, methought, bewailed to be so disburdened. And as for thee, poor Claius, when thou wentest to help her down, I saw reverence and desire so divide thee that thou didst at one instant both blush and quake, and instead of bearing her wert ready to fall down thyself. There she sat, vouchsafing* my cloak (then most gorgeous) under her. At yonder rising of the ground she turned herself, looking back towards her wonted abode, and because of her parting, bearing much sorrow in her eyes, the lightsomeness whereof had yet so natural a cheerfulness as it made even sorrow seem to smile. At that turning she spake to us all, opening the cherry of her lips, and Lord, how greedily mine ears did feed upon the sweet words she uttered! And here she laid her hand over thine eyes, when she saw the tears springing in them, as if she would conceal them from other and yet herself feel some of thy sorrow. But woe is me, yonder, yonder, did she put her foot into the boat, at that instant, as it were, dividing her heavenly beauty between the earth and the sea. But when she was embarked, did you not mark how the winds whistled and the seas danced for joy, how the sails did swell with pride, and all because they had Urania? O Urania, blessed be thou, Urania, the sweetest fairness and fairest sweetness!'

With that word his voice brake so with sobbing that he could say no further, and Claius thus answered:

'Alas, my Strephon,' said he, 'what needs this score to reckon up only our losses? What doubt is there but that the sight of this place doth call our thoughts to appear at the court of affection,* held by that racking* steward remembrance? As well may sheep

---

* *vouchsafing*: graciously accepting. *affection*: passion. *racking*: torturing.

forget to fear when they spy wolves as we can miss such fancies when we see any place made happy by her treading. Who can choose that saw her but think where she stayed, where she walked, where she turned, where she spoke? But what is all this? Truly no more but as this place served us to think of those things, so those things serve as places to call to memory more excellent matters.[1] No, no, let us think with consideration, and consider with acknowledging, and acknowledge with admiration, and admire with love, and love with joy in the midst of all woes. Let us in such sort think, I say, that our poor eyes were so enriched as to behold, and our low hearts so exalted as to love, a maid who is such that as the greatest thing the world can shew is her beauty, so the least thing that may be praised in her is her beauty. Certainly as her eye-lids are more pleasant to behold than two white kids climbing up a fair tree and browsing on its tenderest branches, and yet are nothing compared to the day-shining stars contained in them; and as her breath is more sweet than a gentle south-west wind which comes creeping over flowery fields and shadowed waters in the extreme heat of summer, and yet is nothing compared to the honey-flowing speech that breath doth carry; no more all that our eyes can see of her (though when they have seen her, what else they shall ever see is but dry stubble after clover-grass) is to be matched with the flock of unspeakable virtues laid up delightfully in that best-builded fold. But indeed, as we can better consider the sun's beauty by marking how he gilds these waters and mountains than by looking upon his own face, too glorious for our weak eyes, so it may be our conceits* (not able to bear her sun-staining excellency) will better weigh it by her works upon some meaner subject employed. And alas, who can better witness that than we, whose experience is grounded upon feeling? Hath not the only love* of her made us, being silly ignorant shepherds, raise up our thoughts above the ordinary level of the world, so as great clerks* do not disdain our conference? Hath not the desire to seem worthy in her eyes made us, when others were sleeping, to sit viewing the course of the heavens; when others were running at Base,* to run over learned writings; when others

* *conceits:* understandings. *the only love:* love alone. *clerks:* scholars. *running at Base:* the country game of Prisoners' Base.

mark their sheep, we to mark ourselves? Hath not she thrown reason upon our desires and, as it were, given eyes unto Cupid?* Hath in any but in her, love-fellowship maintained friendship between rivals, and beauty taught the beholders chastity?'

He was going on with his praises, but Strephon bade him stay and look: and so they both perceived a thing which floated, drawing nearer and nearer to the bank, but rather by the favourable working of the sea than by any self-industry. They doubted a while what it should be till it was cast up even hard before them, at which time they fully saw that it was a man. Whereupon running for pity's sake unto him, they found his hands (as it should appear, constanter friends to his life than his memory) fast gripping upon the edge of a square small coffer which lay all under his breast: else in himself no show of life, so as the board seemed to be but a bier to carry him a-land to his sepulchre. So drew they up a young man of so goodly shape and well-pleasing favour that one would think death had in him a lovely countenance, and that, though he were naked, nakedness was to him an apparel. That sight increased their compassion, and their compassion called up their care; so that lifting his feet above his head, making a great deal of salt water come out of his mouth, they laid him upon some of their garments and fell to rub and chafe* him till they brought him to recover both breath, the servant, and warmth, the companion, of living. At length opening his eyes, he gave a great groan (a doleful note, but a pleasant ditty, for by that they found not only life but strength of life in him). They therefore continued on their charitable office until, his spirits being well returned, he – without so much as thanking them for their pains – gat up, and looking round about to the uttermost limits of sight, and crying upon the name of Pyrocles, nor seeing nor hearing cause of comfort:

'What,' said he, 'and shall Musidorus live after Pyrocles' destruction?'

Therewithal he offered wilfully to cast himself again into the sea: a strange sight to the shepherds, to whom it seemed that before, being in appearance dead had yet saved his life, and now, coming to his life should be a cause to procure his death; but they

*Cupid: traditionally blind. chafe: warm.

ran unto him, and pulling him back (then too feeble for them) by force stickled* that unnatural fray.

'I pray you,' said he, 'honest men, what such right have you in me as not to suffer me to do with myself what I list,* and what policy* have you to bestow a benefit where it is counted an injury?'

They hearing him speak in Greek (which was their natural language) became the more tender-hearted towards him, and considering by his calling and looking that the loss of some dear friend was great cause of his sorrow, told him they were poor men that were bound by course of humanity to prevent so great a mischief; and that they wished him, if opinion of some body's perishing bred such desperate anguish in him, that he should be comforted by his own proof, who had lately escaped as apparent danger as any might be.

'No, no,' said he, 'it is not for me to attend so high a blissfulness: but since you take care of me, I pray you find means that some barque may be provided that will go out of the haven, that if it be possible we may find the body, far, far too precious a food for fishes: and for the hire,' said he, 'I have within this casket of value sufficient to content them.'

Claius presently went to a fisherman, and having agreed with him, and provided some apparel for the naked stranger, he embarked, and the shepherds with him; and were no sooner gone beyond the mouth of the haven but that some way into the sea they might discern, as it were, a stain of the water's colour, and by times some sparks and smoke mounting thereout. But the young man no sooner saw it but that beating his breast he cried that there was the beginning of his ruin, entreating them to bend their course as near unto it as they could; telling how that smoke was but a small relique of a great fire which had driven both him and his friend rather to commit themselves to the cold mercy of the sea than to abide the hot cruelty of the fire; and that therefore, though they both had abandoned the ship, that he was (if anywhere) in that course to be met withal.

They steered therefore as near thither-ward as they could; but when they came so near as their eyes were full masters of the

* *stickled*: stopped. *list*: desire. *policy*: wisdom.

object, they saw a sight full of piteous strangeness: a ship, or rather the carcase of the ship, or rather some few bones of the carcase hulling* there, part broken, part burned, part drowned – death having used more than one dart to that destruction. About it floated great store of very rich things and many chests which might promise no less. And amidst the precious things were a number of dead bodies, which likewise did not only testify both elements' violence, but that the chief violence was grown of human inhumanity; for their bodies were full of grisly wounds, and their blood had (as it were) filled the wrinkles of the sea's visage, which it seemed the sea would not wash away that it might witness it is not always his fault when we condemn his cruelty. In sum, a defeat where the conquered kept both field and spoil; a shipwreck without storm or ill-footing,* and a waste of fire in the midst of water.

But a little way off they saw the mast, whose proud height now lay along, like a widow having lost her mate of whom she held her honour: but upon the mast they saw a young man – at least if he were a man – bearing show of about eighteen years of age, who sat as on horse back, having nothing upon him but his shirt which, being wrought with blue silk and gold, had a kind of resemblance to the sea on which the sun (then near his western home) did shoot some of his beams. His hair (which the young men of Greece used to wear very long) was stirred up and down with the wind, which seemed to have a sport to play with it as the sea had to kiss his feet; himself full of admirable beauty, set forth by the strangeness both of his seat and gesture. For holding his head up full of unmoved majesty, he held a sword aloft with his fair arm, which often he waved about his crown as though he would threaten the world in that extremity.

But the fishermen, when they came so near him that it was time to throw out a rope by which hold they might draw him, their simplicity bred such amazement and their amazement such a superstition that (assuredly thinking it was some God begotten between Neptune and Venus that had made all this terrible slaughter), as they went under sail by him, held up their hands

* *hulling:* drifting. *ill-footing:* running on the rocks.

and made their prayers. Which when Musidorus saw, though he were almost as much ravished with joy as they with astonishment, he leaped to the mariner and took the rope out of his hand, and saying, 'Dost thou live, and art thou well!' who answered, 'Thou canst tell best, since most of my well-being stands in thee', threw it out.

But already the ship was passed beyond Pyrocles; and therefore Musidorus could do no more but persuade the mariners to cast about again, assuring them that he was but a man although of most divine excellencies, and promising great rewards for their pain.

And now they were already come upon the stays,* when one of the sailors descried a galley which came with sails and oars directly in the chase of them, and straight perceived it was a well-known pirate who hunted not only for goods but for bodies of men which he employed either to be his galley-slaves or to sell at the best market. Which when the master understood, he commanded forthwith to set on all the canvas they could and fly homeward, leaving in that sort* poor Pyrocles so near to be rescued. But what did not Musidorus say, what did he not offer to persuade them to venture the fight! But fear standing at the gates of their ears put back all persuasions, so that he had nothing wherewith to accompany Pyrocles but his eyes, nor to succour him but his wishes. Therefore praying for him, and casting a long look that way, he saw the galley leave the pursuit of them and turn to take up the spoils of the other wreck. And lastly* he might well see them lift up the young man; and 'Alas,' said he to himself, 'dear Pyrocles, shall that body of thine be enchained? Shall those victorious hands of thine be commanded to base offices? Shall virtue become a slave to those that be slaves to viciousness? Alas, better had it been thou hadst ended nobly thy noble days. What death is so evil as unworthy servitude?'

But that opinion soon ceased when he saw the galley setting upon another ship which held long and strong fight with her; for then he began afresh to fear the life of his friend and to wish well to the pirates whom before he hated, lest in their ruin he might

* *come upon the stays*: turned about. *in that sort*: in that way. *lastly*: last of all.

67

perish. But the fishermen made such speed into the haven that they absented his eyes from beholding the issue; where being entered, he could procure neither them nor any other as then* to put themselves into the sea: so that being as full of sorrow for being unable to do anything as void of counsel how to do anything, besides that sickness grew something upon him, the honest shepherds Strephon and Claius (who being themselves true friends did the more perfectly judge the justness of his sorrow) advised him that he should mitigate somewhat of his woe since he had gotten an amendment in fortune, being come from assured persuasion of his death to have no cause to despair of his life – as one that had lamented the death of his sheep should after know they were but strayed would receive pleasure, though readily he knew not where to find them.

## CHAPTER 2

'Now, Sir,' said they, 'thus for ourselves it is. We are in profession but shepherds and in this country of Laconia little better than strangers, and therefore neither in skill nor ability of power greatly to stead* you. But what we can present unto you is this: Arcadia, of which country we are, is but a little way hence; and even upon the next confines there dwelleth a gentleman, by name Kalander, who vouchsafeth much favour unto us: a man who for his hospitality is so much haunted* that no news stirs but comes to his ears; for his upright dealing so beloved of his neighbours that he hath many ever ready to do him their uttermost service; and by the great goodwill our prince bears him, may soon obtain the use of his name and credit, which hath a principal sway not only in his own Arcadia but in all these countries of Peloponnesus: and – which is worth all – all these things give him not so much power as his nature gives him will to benefit, so that it seems no music is so sweet to his ears as deserved thanks. To him we will bring you, and there you may recover again your health, without which you cannot be able to make any diligent search for your friend, and therefore you must labour for it. Besides, we are sure the comfort of courtesy and ease of wise counsel shall not be wanting.'

* *as then:* at that time. *stead:* be of use to. *haunted:* frequented.

Musidorus (who, besides he was merely unacquainted in the country, had his wits astonished with sorrow) gave easy consent to that from which he saw no reason to disagree: and therefore (defraying* the mariners with a ring bestowed upon them) they took their journey together through Laconia; Claius and Strephon by course* carrying his chest for him, Musidorus only bearing in his countenance evident marks of a sorrowful mind supported with a weak body; which they perceiving, and knowing that the violence of sorrow is not, at the first, to be striven withal (being like a mighty beast, sooner tamed with following than overthrown by withstanding) they gave way unto it for that day and the next; never troubling him either with asking questions or finding fault with his melancholy, but rather fitting to his dolour dolorous discourses of their own and other folks' misfortunes. Which speeches, though they had not a lively entrance to his senses shut up in sorrow, yet like one half asleep he took hold of much of the matters spoken unto him, so as a man may say, ere sorrow was aware, they made his thoughts bear away something else beside his own sorrow; which wrought so in him that at length he grew content to mark their speeches, then to marvel at such wit in shepherds, after to like their company, and lastly to vouchsafe conference. So that the third day after, in the time that the morning did strew roses and violets in the heavenly floor against the coming of the sun, the nightingales (striving one with the other which could in most dainty variety recount their wrong-caused sorrow)[1] made them put off their sleep, and rising from under a tree (which that night had been their pavilion) they went on their journey, which by and by welcomed Musidorus' eyes, wearied with the wasted soil of Laconia, with delightful prospects.

There were hills which garnished their proud heights with stately trees; humble valleys whose base estate seemed comforted with refreshing of silver rivers; meadows enamelled with all sorts of eye-pleasing flowers; thickets, which, being lined with most pleasant shade, were witnessed so to by the cheerful deposition* of many well-tuned birds; each pasture stored with sheep feeding with sober security, while the pretty lambs with bleating oratory craved the dams' comfort; here a shepherd's boy piping as though

* *defraying:* reimbursing. *by course:* in turn. *deposition:* testimony.

he should never be old; there a young shepherdess knitting and withal singing, and it seemed that her voice comforted her hands to work and her hands kept time to her voice's music. As for the houses of the country – for many houses came under their eye – they were all scattered, no two being one by the other, and yet not so far off as that it barred mutual succour: a show, as it were, of an accompanable* solitariness and of a civil* wildness.

'I pray you,' said Musidorus, then first unsealing his long silent lips, 'what countries be these we pass through which are so divers in show, the one wanting no store, the other having no store but of want?'

'The country,' answered Claius, 'where you were cast ashore and now are passed through is Laconia, not so poor by the barrenness of the soil (though in itself not passing fertile) as by a civil war, which being these two years within the bowels of that estate between the gentlemen and the peasants (by them named Helots) hath in this sort as it were disfigured the face of nature, and made it so unhospital* as now you have found it: the towns neither of the one side nor the other willingly opening their gates to strangers, nor strangers willingly entering for fear of being mistaken.

'But this country where now you set your foot is Arcadia; and even hard by is the house of Kalander whither we lead you: this country being thus decked with peace and (the child of peace) good husbandry. These houses you see so scattered are of men as we two are that live upon the commodity of their sheep, and therefore in the division of the Arcadian estate are termed shepherds: a happy people, wanting little because they desire not much.'

'What cause then,' said Musidorus, 'made you venture to leave this sweet life and put yourself in yonder unpleasant and dangerous realm?'

'Guarded with poverty,' answered Strephon, 'and guided with love.'

'But now,' said Claius, 'since it hath pleased you to ask anything of us, whose baseness is such as the very knowledge is darkness, give us leave to know something of you and of the young

---

* *accomparable:* sociable. *civil:* civilized. *unhospital:* inhospitable.

man you so much lament, that at least we may be the better instructed to inform Kalander, and he the better know how to proportion his entertainment.'

Musidorus, according to the agreement between Pyrocles and him to alter their names, answered that he called himself Palladius and his friend Daiphantus; 'but till I have him again,' said he, 'I am indeed nothing, and therefore my story is of nothing. His entertainment (since so good a man he is) cannot be so low as I account my estate; and in sum, the sum of all his courtesy may be to help me by some means to seek my friend.'

They perceived he was not willing to open himself further, and therefore without further questioning brought him to the house; about which they might see (with fit consideration both of the air, the prospect, and the nature of the ground) all such necessary additions to a great house as might well show Kalander knew that provision is the foundation of hospitality and thrift the fuel of magnificence. The house itself was built of fair and strong stone, not affecting so much any extraordinary kind of fineness as an honourable representing of a firm stateliness. The lights, doors and stairs rather directed to the use of the guest than to the eye of the artificer; and yet as the one chiefly heeded, so the other not neglected; each place handsome without curiosity* and homely without loathsomeness; not so dainty* as not to be trod on, nor yet slubbered up* with good fellowship; all more lasting than beautiful but that the consideration of the exceeding lastingness made the eye believe it was exceeding beautiful. The servants, not so many in number as cleanly in apparel and serviceable in behaviour, testifying even in their countenances that their master took as well care to be served as of them that did serve. One of them was forthwith ready to welcome the shepherds as men whom, though they were poor, their master greatly favoured; and understanding by them that the young man with them was to be much accounted of,* for that they had seen tokens of more than common greatness (howsoever now eclipsed with fortune) he ran to his master; who came presently* forth, and pleasantly wel-

---

*curiosity: excessive refinement. *dainty*: over-fine. *slubbered up*: slovenly with too much freedom. *accounted of*: valued. *presently*: immediately.

coming the shepherds, but especially applying him to Musidorus, Strephon privately told him all what he knew of him, and particularly that he found this stranger was loth to be known.

'No,' said Kalander speaking aloud, 'I am no herald to inquire of men's pedigrees; it sufficeth me if I know their virtues, which (if this young man's face be not a false witness) do better apparel his mind than you have done his body.'

While he was thus speaking, there came a boy in show like a merchant's prentice who, taking Strephon by the sleeve, delivered him a letter written jointly both to him and Claius from Urania, which they no sooner had read but that with short leave taking of Kalander (who quickly guessed and smiled at the matter) and once again, though hastily, recommending the young man unto him, they went away, leaving Musidorus even loth to part with them for the good conversation he had of them and obligation he accounted himself tied in unto them. And therefore, they delivering his chest unto him, he opened it and would have presented them with two very rich jewels, but they absolutely refused them, telling him that they were more than enough rewarded in the knowing of him; and without hearkening unto a reply (like men whose hearts disdained all desires but one) gat speedily away, as if the letter had brought wings to make them fly. But by that sight Kalander soon judged that his guest was of no mean calling; and therefore the more respectfully entertaining him, Musidorus found his sickness (which the fight, the sea and late travel had laid upon him) grow greatly, so that fearing some sudden accident, he delivered the chest to Kalander, which was full of most precious stones gorgeously and cunningly set in divers manners, desiring him he would keep those trifles, and if he died, he would bestow so much of it as was needful to find out and redeem a young man naming himself Daiphantus, as then in the hands of Laconia pirates.

But Kalander, seeing him faint more and more, with careful speed conveyed him to the most commodious lodging in his house, where being possessed with an extreme burning fever he continued some while with no great hope of life. But youth at length got the victory of sickness, so that in six weeks the excellency of his returned beauty was a credible ambassador of his health, to the great joy of Kalander who, as in this time he had by certain friends of his that dwelt near the sea in Messenia set forth a ship and a galley to seek and succour Daiphantus, so at home did he omit nothing which he thought might either profit or gratify Palladius.

For having found in him (besides his bodily gifts beyond the degree of admiration) by daily discourses which he delighted himself to have with him, a mind of most excellent composition, a piercing wit quite void of ostentation, high erected thoughts seated in a heart of courtesy, an eloquence as sweet in the uttering as slow to come to the uttering, a behaviour so noble as gave a majesty to adversity, and all in a man whose age could not be above one and twenty years, the good old man was even enamoured with a fatherly love towards him, or rather became his servant by the bonds such virtue laid upon him: once* he acknowledged himself so to be by the badge of diligent attendance.

## CHAPTER 3

But Palladius having gotten his health, and only staying there to be in place where he might hear answer of the ships set forth, Kalander one afternoon led him abroad to a well-arrayed ground he had behind his house, which he thought to show him before his going as the place himself more than in any other delighted. The backside of the house was neither field, garden nor orchard, or rather it was both field, garden and orchard; for as soon as the descending of the stairs had delivered them down, they came into a place cunningly set with trees of the most taste-pleasing fruits; but scarcely they had taken that into their consideration but that they were suddenly stept into a delicate green; of each side of the green a thicket, and behind the thickets again new beds of flowers, which being under the trees, the trees were to them a pavilion* and they to the trees a mosaical floor, so that it seemed that Art therein would needs be delightful by counterfeiting his enemy Error and making order in confusion.

In the midst of all the place was a fair pond whose shaking crystal was a perfect mirror to all the other beauties, so that it bare show of two gardens; one in deed, the other in shadows. And in

* *once:* at once. *pavilion:* canopy.

one of the thickets was a fine fountain made thus: a naked Venus of white marble, wherein the graver had used such cunning, that the natural blue veins of the marble were framed in fit places to set forth the beautiful veins of her body. At her breast she had her babe Aeneas, who seemed, having begun to suck, to leave that to look upon her fair eyes which smiled at the babe's folly, meanwhile the breast running.[1]

Hard by was a house of pleasure built for a summer retiring-place; whither Kalander leading him, he found a square room full of delightful pictures made by the most excellent workman of Greece. There was Diana when Actaeon saw her bathing, in whose cheeks the painter had set such a colour as was mixed between shame and disdain; and one of her foolish nymphs, who weeping and withal louring, one might see the workman meant to set forth tears of anger. In another table* was Atalanta, the posture of whose limbs was so lively expressed, that if the eyes were the only judges as they be the only seers, one would have sworn the very picture had run. Besides many more, as of Helena, Omphale, Iole: but in none of them all beauty seemed to speak so much as in a large table which contained a comely old man, with a lady of middle-age but of excellent beauty; and more excellent would have been deemed, but that there stood between them a young maid whose wonderfulness took away all beauty from her but that which it might seem she gave her back again by her very shadow. And such difference (being known that it did indeed counterfeit a person living) was there between her and all the other (though goddesses) that it seemed the skill of the painter bestowed on the other new beauty, but that the beauty of her bestowed new skill of* the painter. Though he thought inquisitiveness an uncomely guest, he could not choose but ask who she was that, bearing show of one being in deed,[2] could with natural gifts go beyond the reach of invention. Kalander answered that it was made by Philoclea,[3] the younger daughter of his prince who also with his wife were contained in that table, the painter meaning to represent the present condition of the young lady, who stood watched by an over-curious eye of her parents; and that he would also have drawn her eldest sister (esteemed her match for beauty)

*table: picture. new skill of: i.e. 'on'.

in her shepherdish attire, but that the rude clown her guardian would not suffer it; neither durst he ask leave of the prince for fear of suspicion. Palladius perceived that the matter was wrapped up in some secrecy, and therefore would for modesty demand no further; but yet his countenance could not but with dumb eloquence desire it.

Which Kalander perceiving, 'Well,' said he, 'my dear guest, I know your mind and I will satisfy it. Neither will I do it like a niggardly answerer, going no further than the bounds of the question; but I will discover unto you as well that wherein my knowledge is common with others as that which by extraordinary means is delivered unto me, knowing so much in you (though not long acquainted) that I shall find your ears faithful treasurers.' So then sitting down in two chairs and sometimes casting his eye to the picture, he thus spake:

'This country Arcadia among all the provinces of Greece hath ever been had in singular reputation; partly for the sweetness of the air and other natural benefits, but principally for the well-tempered minds of the people who (finding that the shining title of glory, so much affected by other nations, doth indeed help little to the happiness of life) are the only people which, as by their justice and providence give neither cause nor hope to their neighbours to annoy them, so are they not stirred with false praise to trouble others' quiet, thinking it a small reward for the wasting of their own lives in ravening* that their posterity should long after say they had done so. Even the Muses seem to approve their good determination by choosing this country for their chief repairing place, and by bestowing their perfections so largely here that the very shepherds have their fancies lifted to so high conceits that the learned of other nations are content both to borrow their names and imitate their cunning.

'Here dwelleth and reigneth this prince (whose picture you see) by name Basilius; a prince of sufficient skill to govern so quiet a country, where the good minds of the former princes had set down good laws, and the well-bringing up of the people did serve as a most sure bond to hold them. But to be plain with you, he excels in nothing so much as in the zealous love of his people, wherein

*ravening: plundering.*

he doth not only pass all his own foregoers but, as I think, all the princes living. Whereof the cause is that though he exceed not in the virtues which get admiration, as depth of wisdom, height of courage and largeness of magnificence, yet is he notable in those which stir affection, as truth of word, meekness, courtesy, mercifulness and liberality.

'He, being already well stricken in years, married a young princess named Gynecia, daughter to the king of Cyprus, of notable beauty as by her picture you see: a woman of great wit, and in truth of more princely virtues than her husband; of most unspotted chastity, but of so working a mind and so vehement spirits as a man may say it was happy she took a good course, for otherwise it would have been terrible.

'Of these two are brought into the world two daughters, so beyond measure excellent in all the gifts allotted to reasonable creatures that we may think they were born to show that nature is no stepmother to that sex, how much soever some men, sharp-witted only in evil speaking, have sought to disgrace them. The elder is named Pamela, by many men not deemed inferior to her sister. For my part, when I marked them both, methought there was (if at least such perfections may receive the word of more) more sweetness in Philoclea but more majesty in Pamela: methought love played in Philoclea's eyes and threatened in Pamela's; methought Philoclea's beauty only persuaded, but so persuaded as all hearts must yield; Pamela's beauty used violence, and such violence as no heart could resist. And it seems that such proportion is between their minds: Philoclea so bashful, as though her excellencies had stolen into her before she was aware; so humble, that she will put all pride out of countenance; in sum, such proceeding as will stir hope but teach hope good manners. Pamela of high thoughts, who avoids not pride with not knowing her excellencies, but by making that one of her excellencies to be void of pride; her mother's wisdom, greatness, nobility, but – if I can guess aright – knit with a more constant temper. Now then, our Basilius – being so publicly happy as to be a prince, and so happy in that happiness as to be a beloved prince, and so in his private blessed as to have so excellent a wife and so over-excellent children – hath of late taken a course which yet makes him more spoken of than all these blessings. For, having made a journey to Delphos and safely returned, within short space he brake up his court and retired himself, his wife and children, into a certain forest hereby which he calleth his desert; wherein, besides a house appointed for stables and lodgings for certain persons of mean calling who do all household services, he hath builded two fine lodges. In the one of them himself remains with his younger daughter Philoclea – which was the cause they three were matched together in this picture – without having any other creature living in that lodge with him.

'Which though it be strange, yet not strange as the course he hath taken with the princess Pamela whom he hath placed in the other lodge; but how think you accompanied? Truly with none other but one Dametas, the most arrant doltish clown that I think ever was without the privilege of a bauble,* with his wife Miso and daughter Mopsa, in whom no wit can devise anything wherein they may pleasure her but to exercise her patience and to serve for a foil of her perfections. This loutish clown is such that you never saw so ill-favoured a vizor;* his behaviour such that he is beyond the degree of ridiculous; and for this apparel, even as I would wish him: Miso his wife, so handsome a beldam* that only her face* and her splay-foot have made her accused for a witch; only one good point she hath, that she observes decorum, having a froward* mind in a wretched body. Between these two personages (who never agreed in any humour, but in disagreeing) is issued forth mistress Mopsa, a fit woman to participate of both their perfections: but because a pleasant fellow of my acquaintance set forth her praises in verse, I will only repeat them and spare mine own tongue, since she goes for a woman. The verses are these, which I have so often caused to be sung that I have them without book.[4]

What length of verse can serve brave Mopsa's good to show,
Whose virtues strange, and beauties such, as no man them may
    know?
Thus shrewdly burden'd then, how can my Muse escape?

* *bauble*: jester's baton. *vizor*: appearance. *beldam*: hag. *only her face*: her face alone. *froward*: perverse.

The Gods must help, and precious things must serve to shew
  her shape:
Like great God Saturn fair, and like fair Venus chaste:
As smooth as Pan, as Juno mild, like Goddess Iris fast.
With Cupid she foresees, and goes God Vulcan's pace:
And for a taste of all these gifts, she steals God Momus' grace.
Her forehead Jacinth-like, her cheeks of Opal hue,
Her twinkling eyes bedeck'd with Pearl, her lips as Sapphire
  blue:
Her hair like Crapal stone;* her mouth O heav'nly wide!
Her skin like burnished gold, her hands like silver ore untry'd.*
As for her parts unknown, which hidden sure are best:
Happy be they which well believe, and never seek the rest.

'Now truly having made these descriptions unto you, methinks
you should imagine that I rather feign some pleasant device than
recount a truth, that a prince not banished from his own wits
could possibly make so unworthy a choice. But truly, dear guest,
so it is that princes (whose doings have been often smoothed*
with good success) think nothing so absurd which they cannot
make honourable. The beginning of his credit was by the prince's
straying out of the way one time he hunted, where meeting this
fellow and asking him the way, and so falling into other questions, he found some of his answers (as a dog sure, if he could
speak, had wit enough to describe his kennel) not unsensible, and
all uttered with such rudeness, which he interpreted plainness –
though there be great difference between them – that Basilius,
conceiving a sudden delight, took him to his court with apparent
show of his good opinion: where the flattering courtier had no
sooner taken the prince's mind but that there were straight
reasons to confirm the prince's doing and shadows of virtues found
for Dametas. His silence grew wit, his bluntness integrity, his
beastly ignorance virtuous simplicity; and the prince (according to
the nature of great persons, in love with what he had done himself) fancied that his weakness with his presence would much be
mended. And so like a creature of his own making, he liked him
more and more; and thus having first given him the office of prin-

* *Crapal stone*: toad-stone. *untry'd*: unrefined. *smoothed*: ('98 text)
'90, '93, 'soothed'.

cipal herdsman, lastly,* since he took this strange determination, he hath in a manner put the life of himself and his children into his hands. Which authority, like too great a sail for so small a boat, doth so oversway poor Dametas that, if before he was a good fool in a chamber, he might be allowed it now in a comedy; so as I doubt me (I fear me indeed) my master will in the end with his cost find that his office is not to make men but to use men as men are, no more than a horse will be taught to hunt, or an ass to manage. But in sooth I am afraid I have given your ears too great a surfeit with the gross discourses of that heavy piece of flesh. But the zealous grief I conceive to see so great an error in my lord hath made me bestow more words than I confess so base a subject deserveth.

## CHAPTER 4

'Thus much now that I have told you is nothing more than in effect any Arcadian knows. But what moved him to this strange solitariness hath been imparted, as I think, but to one person living. Myself can conjecture, and indeed more than conjecture, by this accident that I will tell you. I have an only son, by name Clitophon, who is now absent, preparing for his own marriage, which I mean shortly shall be here celebrated. This son of mine, while the prince kept his court, was of his bed-chamber; now since the breaking up thereof returned home and showed me, among other things he had gathered, the copy which he had taken of a letter which, when the prince had read, he had laid in a window, presuming nobody durst look in his writings; but my son not only took a time to read it but to copy it. In truth I blamed Clitophon for the curiosity which made him break his duty in such a kind, whereby kings' secrets are subject to be revealed; but since it was done, I was content to take so much profit as to know it. Now here is the letter that I ever since, for my good liking, have carried about me: which before I read unto you, I must tell you from whom it came. It is a nobleman of this country, named Philanax, appointed (by the prince) regent in this time of his retiring, and most worthy so to be; for there lives no man whose excellent wit

* *lastly*: latterly.

more simply embraceth integrity, besides his unfeigned love to his master, wherein never yet any could make question saving whether he loved Basilius or the prince* better: a rare temper, while most men either servilely yield to all appetites, or, with an obstinate austerity looking to that they fancy good, in effect neglect the prince's person. This then being the man whom of all other (and most worthy) the prince chiefly loves, it should seem – for more than the letter I have not to guess by – that the prince upon his return from Delphos (Philanax then lying sick) had written unto him his determination rising, as evidently appears, upon some oracles he had there received: whereunto he wrote this answer:

## Philanax' letter to Basilius

Most redoubted and beloved prince, if as well it had pleased you at your going to Delphos, as now, to have used my humble service, both I should in better season and to better purpose have spoken, and you (if my speech had prevailed) should have been at this time, as no way more in danger, so much more in quietness. I would then have said that wisdom and virtue be the only destinies appointed to man to follow, whence we ought to seek all our knowledge, since they be such guides as cannot fail; which, besides their inward comfort, do lead so direct a way of proceeding as either prosperity must ensue, or, if the wickedness of the world should oppress it, it can never be said that evil happeneth to him who falls accompanied with virtue. I would then have said the heavenly powers to be reverenced and not searched into, and their mercies rather by prayers to be sought than their hidden counsels by curiosity. These kinds of sooth-sayings (since they have left us in ourselves sufficient guides) to be nothing but fancy, wherein there must either be vanity or infallibleness, and so either not to be respected, or not to be prevented. But since it is weakness too much to remember what should have been done, and that your commandment stretcheth to know what is to be done, I do, most dear Lord, with humble boldness say that the manner of your determination doth in no sort better please me than the cause of your going. These thirty years you have so governed this region that neither your subjects have wanted justice in you, nor you obedience in them; and your neighbours have found you so hurtlessly strong

* *Basilius or the prince:* as a man or as a prince.

that they thought it better to rest in your friendship than to make new trial of your enmity. If this then have proceeded out of the good constitution of your state and out of a wise providence generally to prevent all those things which might encumber your happiness, why should you now seek new courses, since your own example comforts you to continue, and that it is to me most certain (though it please you not to tell me the very words of the oracle) that yet no destiny nor influence whatsoever can bring man's wit to a higher point than wisdom and goodness? Why should you deprive yourself of government for fear of losing your government, like one that should kill himself for fear of death? Nay, rather, if this oracle be to be accounted of, arm up your courage the more against it, for who will stick to him that abandons himself? Let your subjects have you in their eyes. Let them see the benefits of your justice daily more and more, and so must they needs rather like of present sureties than uncertain changes. Lastly, whether your time call you to live or die, do both like a prince.

Now for your second resolution, which is to suffer no worthy prince to be a suitor to either of your daughters, but while you live to keep them both unmarried and, as it were, to kill the joy of posterity which in your time you may enjoy, moved perchance by a misunderstood oracle: what shall I say, if the affection of a father to his own children cannot plead sufficiently against such fancies? Once certain* it is, the God which is God of nature doth never teach unnaturalness; and even the same mind hold I touching your banishing them from company, lest I know not what strange loves should follow. Certainly, Sir, in my ladies, your daughters, nature promiseth nothing but goodness, and their education by your fatherly care hath been hitherto such as hath been most fit to restrain all evil, giving their minds virtuous delights, and not grieving them for want of well-ruled liberty. Now to fall to a sudden straitening* them, what can it do but argue suspicion – a thing no more unpleasant than unsure for the preserving of virtue. Leave women's minds, the most untamed that way of any. See whether any cage can please a bird, or whether a dog grow not fiercer with tying. What doth jealousy but stir up the mind to think what it is from which they are restrained? For they are treasures or things of great delight which men use to hide for the aptness they have to catch men's fancies;[1] and the thoughts once awaked to that, harder sure it is to keep those thoughts from accomplishment than it had been before to have kept the mind (which

---

*Once certain:* absolutely certain. *straitening:* restricting.

being the chief part, by this means is defiled) from thinking. Lastly, for the recommending of so principal a charge of the princess Pamela (whose mind goes beyond the governing of many thousands such) to such a person as Dametas is (besides that the thing in itself is strange) it comes of a very evil ground that ignorance should be the mother of faithfulness. Oh no, he cannot be good that knows not why he is good, but stands so far good as his fortune may keep him unassayed; but coming once to that, his rude simplicity is either easily changed or easily deceived; and so grows that to be the last excuse of his fault which seemed to have been the first foundation of his faith. Thus far hath your commandment and my zeal drawn me; which I, like a man in a valley that may discern hills, or like a poor passenger that may spy a rock, so humbly submit to your gracious consideration, beseeching you again to stand wholly upon your own virtue as the surest way to maintain you in that you are, and to avoid any evil which may be imagined.

'By the contents of this letter you may perceive that the cause of all hath been the vanity which possesseth many who (making a perpetual mansion of this poor baiting-place* of man's life) are desirous to know the certainty of things to come, wherein there is nothing so certain as our continual uncertainty. But what in particular points the oracle was, in faith I know not, neither – as you may see by one place of Philanax's letter – he himself distinctly knew. But this experience shews us that Basilius' judgement, corrupted with a prince's fortune, hath rather heard than followed the wise (as I take it) counsel of Philanax. For having left the stern* of his government, with much amazement to the people, among whom many strange bruits* are received for current,* and with some appearance of danger in respect of the valiant Amphialus his nephew, and much envy in the ambitious number of the nobility against Philanax to see Philanax so advanced – though (to speak simply) he deserve more than as many of us as there be in Arcadia – the prince himself hath hidden his head in such sort as I told you, not sticking plainly to confess that he means not while he breathes that his daughters shall have any husband, but keep them thus solitary with him: where he gives no other body leave to visit him at any time but a certain priest, who

* *baiting-place*: a place for temporary rest, an inn. *stern*: steering. *bruits*: rumours. *for current*: for truth.

being excellent in poetry, he makes him write out such things as he best likes – he being no less delightful in conversation than needful for devotion – and about twenty specified shepherds in whom (some for exercises and some for eclogues) he taketh greater recreation.

'And now you know as much as myself; wherein if I have held you over-long, lay hardly the fault upon my old age, which in the very disposition of it is talkative: whether it be,' said he smiling, 'that nature loves to exercise that part most which is least decayed, and that is our tongue; or that knowledge being the only thing whereof we poor old men can brag, we cannot make it known but by utterance; or that mankind, by all means seeking to eternize himself so much the more as he is near his end, doth it not only by the children that come of him, but by speeches and writings recommended to the memory of hearers and readers. And yet thus much I will say for myself, that I have not laid these matters either so openly or largely to any as yourself; so much, if I much fail not, do I see in you which makes me both love and trust you.'

'Never may he be old,' answered Palladius, 'that doth not reverence that age whose heaviness, if it weigh down the frail and fleshly balance, it as much lifts up the noble and spiritual part; and well might you have alleged another reason, that their wisdom makes them willing to profit others. And that have I received of you, never to be forgotten but with ungratefulness. But among many strange conceits you told me, which have shewed effects in your prince, truly even the last, that he should conceive such pleasure in shepherds' discourses, would not seem the least unto me, saving that you told me at the first that this country is notable in those wits, and that indeed myself, having been brought not only to this place but to my life by Strephon and Claius, in their conference found wits as might better become such shepherds as Homer speaks of,[2] that be governors of peoples, than such senators who hold their council in a sheep-cote.'

'For them two,' said Kalander, 'especially Claius, they are beyond the rest by so much as learning commonly doth add to nature: for, having neglected their wealth in respect of their knowledge, they have not so much impaired the meaner as they bettered the better. Which all notwithstanding, it is a sport to hear how they impute to* love, which hath indued their thoughts, say they, with such a strength. But certainly all the people of this country, from high to low, is given to those sports of the wit, so as you would wonder to hear how soon even children will begin to versify. Once,* ordinary it is among the meanest sort to make songs and dialogues in metre, either love whetting their brain, or long peace having begun it, example and emulation amending it. Not so much, but* the clown Dametas will stumble sometimes upon some songs that might become a better brain: but no sort of people so excellent in that kind as the pastors, for their living standing but upon the looking to their beasts, they have ease, the nurse of poetry. Neither are our shepherds such as, I hear, they be in other countries, but they are the very owners of the sheep to which either themselves look, or their children give daily attendance. And then truly, it would delight you under some tree or by some river's side, when two or three of them meet together, to hear their rural muse,[8] how prettily it will deliver out sometimes joys, sometimes lamentations, sometimes challengings one of the other, sometimes under hidden forms uttering such matters as otherwise they durst not deal with. Then have they most commonly one who judgeth the prize to the best doer, of which they are no less glad than great princes are of triumphs; and his part is to set down in writing all that is said, save that it may be his pen with more leisure doth polish the rudeness of an unthought-on song.

Now the choice of all, as you may well think, either for goodness of voice or pleasantness of wit, the prince hath: among whom also there are two or three strangers, whom inward melancholies having made weary of the world's eyes, have come to spend their lives among the country people of Arcadia, and their conversation being well approved, the prince vouchsafeth them his presence, and not only by looking on but by great courtesy and liberality animates the shepherds the more exquisitely to labour for his good liking. So that there is no cause to blame the prince for sometimes hearing them; the blame-worthiness is that to hear them he rather goes to solitariness than makes them come to company. Neither do I accuse my master for advancing a country-man, as Dametas is,

---

* *impute to:* attribute it to. *Once:* to sum up. *Not so much, but:* not extraordinary that even.

since God forbid but where worthiness is – as truly it is among divers of that fellowship – any outward lowness should hinder the highest rising; but that he would needs make election of one the baseness of whose mind is such that it sinks a thousand degrees lower than the basest body could carry the most base fortune: which although it might be answered for the prince that it is rather a trust he hath in his simple plainness than any great advancement, being but chief herdman, yet all honest hearts feel that the trust of their lord goes beyond all advancement. But I am ever too long upon him when he crosseth the way of my speech, and by the shadow of yonder tower I see it is a fitter time with our supper to pay the duties we owe to our stomachs than to break the air with my idle discourses: and more wit I might have learned of Homer,[4] whom even now you mentioned, who never entertained either guests or hosts with long speeches till the mouth of hunger were thoroughly stopped.'

So withal he rose, leading Palladius through the garden again to the parlour where they used to sup; Palladius assuring him he had already been more fed to his liking than he could be by the skilfullest trencher-men* of Media.[5]

## CHAPTER 5

But being come to the supping-place, one of Kalander's servants rounded in his ear, at which his colour changing, he retired himself into his chamber, commanding his men diligently to wait upon Palladius, and to excuse his absence with some necessary business he had presently to dispatch: which they accordingly did, for some few days forcing themselves to let no change appear: but, though they framed their countenances never so cunningly, Palladius perceived there was some ill-pleasing accident fallen out. Whereupon, being again set alone at supper, he called to the steward and desired him to tell him the matter of his sudden alteration: who, after some trifling excuses, in the end confessed unto him that his master had received news that his son, before the day of his near marriage, chanced to be at a battle which was to be fought between the gentlemen of Lacedaemon and the Helots,

* *trencher-men*: cooks.

who winning the victory, he was there made prisoner going to deliver a friend of his, taken prisoner by the Helots: that the poor young gentleman had offered great ransom for his life; but that the hate those peasants conceived against all gentlemen was such that every hour he was to look for nothing but some cruel death, which hitherto had only been delayed by the captain's vehement dealing for him, who seemed to have a heart of more manly pity than the rest. Which loss had stricken the old gentleman with such sorrow, as if abundance of tears did not seem sufficiently to witness it, he was alone retired, tearing his beard and hair and cursing his old age that had not made his grave to stop his ears from such advertisements: but that his faithful servants had written in his name to all his friends, followers, and tenants (Philanax the governor refusing to deal in it, as a private cause, but yet giving leave to seek their best redress so as they wronged not the state of Lacedaemon) of whom there were now gathered upon the frontiers good forces that he was sure would spend their lives by any way to redeem or revenge Clitophon.

'Now Sir,' said he, 'this is my master's nature, though his grief be such as to live is a grief unto him and that even his reason is darkened with sorrow, yet the laws of hospitality (long and holily observed by him) gave still such a sway to his proceeding that he will no way suffer the stranger lodged under his roof to receive, as it were, any infection of his anguish, especially you, towards whom I know not whether his love or admiration be greater.'

But Palladius could scarce hear out his tale with patience, so was his heart torn in pieces with compassion of the case, liking of Kalander's noble behaviour, kindness for his respect to him-ward, and desire to find some remedy, besides the image of his dearest friend Daiphantus, whom he judged to suffer either a like or a worse fortune. Therefore rising from the board, he desired the steward to tell him particularly the ground and event of this accident, because by knowledge of many circumstances there might perhaps some way of help be opened. Whereunto the steward easily in this sort condescended.

'My Lord,' said he, 'when our good king Basilius, with better success than expectation, took to wife even in his more than decaying years the fair young princess Gynecia, there came with her a young lord, cousin german to herself, named Argalus, led hither partly with the love and honour of his noble kinswoman, partly with the humour of youth which ever thinks that good whose goodness he sees not. And in this court he received so good increase of knowledge, that after some years spent he so manifested a most virtuous mind in all his actions that Arcadia gloried such a plant was transported unto them, being a gentleman in deed most rarely accomplished, excellently learned, but without all vain glory; friendly without factiousness; valiant, so as for my part I think the earth hath no man that hath done more heroical acts than he, howsoever now of late the fame flies of the two princes of Thessalia and Macedon, and hath long done of our noble prince Amphialus, who indeed in our parts is only accounted likely to match him. But I say for my part, I think no man for valour of mind and ability of body to be preferred, if equalled to Argalus; and yet so valiant as he never durst do anybody injury: in behaviour, some will say, ever sad, surely sober, and somewhat given to musing, but never uncourteous; his word ever led by his thought and followed by his deed; rather liberal than magnificent, though the one wanted not and the other had ever good choice of the receiver. In sum (for I perceive I shall easily take a great draught of his praises, whom both I and all this country love so well) such a man was – and I hope is – Argalus as hardly the nicest* eye can find a spot in, if the over-vehement constancy of yet spotless affection may not in hard-wrested constructions be counted a spot: which in this manner began that work in him which hath made both him, and itself in him, over all this country famous.

My master's son Clitophon (whose loss gives the cause to this discourse, and yet gives me cause to begin with Argalus, since his loss proceeds from Argalus) being a young gentleman as of great birth, being our king's sister's son, so truly of good nature and one that can see good and love it, haunted more the company of this worthy Argalus than of any other; so as if there were not a friendship (which is so rare as it is to be doubted whether it be a thing in deed or but a word) at least there was such a liking and friendliness as hath brought forth the effects which you shall hear. About two years since, it so fell out that he brought him to a great

*nicest:* most critical.

lady's house, sister to my master, who had with her her only daughter, the fair Parthenia; fair indeed (fame, I think, itself daring not to call any fairer, if it be not Helena, queen of Corinth, and the two incomparable sisters of Arcadia) and that which made her fairness much the fairer was that it was but a fair ambassador of a most fair mind; full of wit, and a wit which delighted more to judge itself than to shew itself: her speech being as rare as precious; her silence without sullenness; her modesty without affectation; her shamefastness* without ignorance: in sum, one that to praise well, one must first set down with himself what it is to be excellent, for so she is.

'I think you think that these perfections, meeting, could not choose but find one another and delight in that they found; for likeness of manners is likely in reason to draw liking with affection: men's actions do not always cross with* reason. To be short, it did so indeed. They loved, although for a while the fire thereof (hope's wings being cut off) were blown by the bellows of despair, upon this occasion:

'There had been a good while before, and so continued, a suitor to this same lady, a great noble man, though of Laconia yet near neighbour to Parthenia's mother, named Demagoras; a man mighty in riches and power and proud thereof, stubbornly stout, loving nobody but himself and, for his own delight's sake, Parthenia: and pursuing vehemently his desire, his riches had so gilded over all his other imperfections that the old lady, though contrary to my lord her brother's mind, had given her consent; and using a mother's authority upon her fair daughter had made her yield thereunto, not because she liked her choice but because her obedient mind had not yet taken upon it to make choice. And the day of their assurance drew near, when my young lord Clitophon brought this noble Argalus, perchance principally to see so rare a sight, as Parthenia by all well-judging eyes was judged.

'But though few days were before the time of assurance appointed, yet love, that saw he had a great journey to make in short time, hasted so himself that before her word could tie her to Demagoras, her heart hath vowed her to Argalus with so grateful

* *shamefastness*: bashfulness. *cross with*: run counter to.

a receipt in mutual affection that if she desired above all things to have Argalus, Argalus feared nothing but to miss Parthenia. And now Parthenia had learned both liking and misliking, loving and loathing, and out of passion began to take the authority of judgement; insomuch that when the time came that Demagoras, full of proud joy, thought to receive the gift of herself, she, with words of resolute refusal though with tears showing she was sorry she must refuse, assured her mother she would first be bedded in her grave than wedded to Demagoras. The change was no more strange than unpleasant to the mother who, being determinately (lest I should say of a great lady, wilfully) bent to marry her to Demagoras, tried all ways which a witty and hard-hearted mother could use upon so humble a daughter in whom the only resisting power was love. But the more she assaulted, the more she taught Parthenia to defend; and the more Parthenia defended, the more she made her mother obstinate in the assault: who at length finding that Argalus standing between them was it that most eclipsed her affection from shining upon Demagoras, she sought all means how to remove him, so much the more as he manifested himself an unremovable suitor to her daughter: first, by employing him in as many dangerous enterprises as ever the evil stepmother[1] Juno recommended to the famous Hercules. But the more his virtue was tried, the more pure it grew, while all the things she did to overthrow him did set him up upon the height of honour enough to have moved her heart, especially to a man every way so worthy as Argalus: but she struggling against all reason, because she would have her will and shew her authority in matching her with Demagoras, the more virtuous Argalus was, the more she hated him, thinking herself conquered in his conquests, and therefore still employing him in more and more dangerous attempts. In the meanwhile she used all extremities possible upon her fair daughter to make her give over herself to her direction. But it was hard to judge whether he in doing or she in suffering shewed greater constancy of affection; for, as to Argalus the world sooner wanted occasions than he valour to go through them, so to Parthenia malice sooner ceased than her unchanged patience. Lastly, by treasons Demagoras and she would have made away with Argalus, but he with providence and courage so passed over all that the mother took such a spiteful grief at it that her heart brake withal, and she died.

'But then Demagoras, assuring himself that now Parthenia was her own she would never be his, and receiving as much by her own determinate answer; not more desiring his own happiness than envying Argalus, whom he saw with narrow eyes even ready to enjoy the perfection of his desires; strengthening his conceit with all the mischievous counsels which disdained love and envious pride could give unto him, the wicked wretch (taking a time that Argalus was gone to his country to fetch some of his principal friends to honour the marriage which Parthenia had most joyfully consented unto) the wicked Demagoras, I say, desiring to speak with her, with unmerciful force (her weak arms in vain resisting) rubbed all over her face a most horrible poison, the effect whereof was such that never leper looked more ugly than she did: which done, having his men and horses ready, departed away in spite of her servants, as ready to revenge as they could be in such an unexpected mischief. But the abominableness of this fact being come to my L. Kalander, he made such means, both by our king's intercession and his own, that by the king and senate of Lacedaemon, Demagoras was upon pain of death banished the country: who, hating the punishment where he should have hated the fault, joined himself, with all the powers he could make, unto the Helots, lately in rebellion against that state: and they, glad to have a man of such authority among them, made him their general, and under him have committed divers the most outrageous villanies that a base multitude full of desperate revenge can imagine.

'But within a while after this pitiful fact committed upon Parthenia, Argalus returned, poor Gentleman, having her fair image in his heart, and already promising his eyes the uttermost of his felicity when they (nobody else daring to tell it him) were the first messengers to themselves of their own misfortune. I mean not to move passions with telling you the grief of both when he knew her, for at first he did not; nor at first knowledge could possibly have virtue's aid so ready as not even weakly to lament the loss of such a jewel, so much the more as that skilful men in that art assured it was unrecoverable. But within a while, truth of love (which still held the first face in his memory) a virtuous constancy, and even a delight to be constant, faith given, and inward worthiness shining through the foulest mists, took so full hold of the noble Argalus, that not only in such comfort which witty arguments may bestow upon adversity, but even with the most abundant kindness that an eye-ravished lover can express, he laboured both to drive the extremity of sorrow from her and to hasten the celebration of their marriage: whereunto he unfeignedly shewed himself no less cheerfully earnest than if she had never been disinherited of that goodly portion which nature had so liberally bequeathed unto her; and for that cause deferred his intended revenge upon Demagoras, because he might continually be in her presence, shewing more humble serviceableness and joy to content her than ever before.

'But as he gave this rare example (not to be hoped for of any other but of another Argalus) so of the other side, she took as strange a course in affection; for where she desired to enjoy him more than to live, yet did she overthrow both her own desire and his and in no sort would yield to marry him: with a strange encounter of love's affects* and effects; that he by an affection sprung from excessive beauty should delight in horrible foulness, and she of a vehement desire to have him should kindly* build a resolution never to have him; for truth is, that so in heart she loved him as she could not find in her heart he should be tied to what was unworthy of his presence.

'Truly, Sir, a very good orator might have a fair field to use eloquence in, if he did but only repeat the lamentable and truly affectionated* speeches, while he conjured her by remembrance of her affection and true oaths of his own affection not to make him so unhappy as to think he had not only lost her face but her heart; that her face, when it was fairest, had been but as a marshal to lodge the love of her in his mind, which now was so well placed as it needed no further help of any outward harbinger;* beseeching her, even with tears, to know that his love was not so superficial as to go no further than the skin, which yet now to him was most fair since it was hers: how could he be so ungrateful as to love her

* *affects*: passions. *kindly*: out of the nature of her love. *affectionated*: impassioned. *harbinger*: purveyor of lodgings.

the less for that which she had only received for his sake; that he never beheld it, but therein he saw the loveliness of her love towards him; protesting unto her that he would never take joy of his life if he might not enjoy her for whom principally he was glad he had life. But (as I heard by one that overheard them) she, wringing him by the hand, made no other answer but this:

' "My Lord," said she, "God knows I love you. If I were princess of the whole world and had, withal, all the blessings that ever the world brought forth, I should not make delay to lay myself and them under your feet; or if I had continued but as I was, though, I must confess, far unworthy of you, yet would I (with too great a joy for my heart to think of) have accepted your vouchsafing me to be yours, and with faith and obedience would have supplied all other defects. But first let me be so much more miserable than I am ere I match Argalus to such a Parthenia. Live happy, dear Argalus, I give you full liberty, and I beseech you take it; and I assure you I shall rejoice (whatsoever become of me) to see you so coupled as may be fit both for your honour and satisfaction." With that she burst out crying and weeping, not able longer to contain herself from blaming her fortune and wishing her own death.

'But Argalus, with a most heavy heart still pursuing his desire, she fixed of mind to avoid further intreaty, and to fly all company which, even of him, grew unpleasant unto her; one night she stole away: but whither as yet is unknown or indeed, what is become of her.

'Argalus sought her long, and in many places; at length (despairing to find her, and the more he despaired, the more enraged) weary of his life, but first determining to be revenged of Demagoras, he went alone disguised into the chief town held by the Helots, where coming into his presence, guarded about by many of his soldiers, he could delay his fury no longer for a fitter time, but setting upon him, in despite of a great many that helped him, gave him divers mortal wounds, and himself (no question) had been there presently murdered, but that Demagoras himself desired he might be kept alive, perchance with intention to feed his own eyes with some cruel execution to be laid upon him. But death came sooner than he looked for, yet having had leisure to appoint his successor, a young man not long before delivered out of the prison of the king of Lacedaemon, where he should have suffered death for having slain the king's nephew: but him he named, who at that time was absent making inroads upon the Lacedaemonians. But being returned, the rest of the Helots, for the great liking they conceived of that young man (especially because they had none among themselves to whom the others would yield) were content to follow Demagoras' appointment. And well hath it succeeded with them, he having since done things beyond the hope of the youngest heads; of whom I speak the rather because he hath hitherto preserved Argalus alive, under pretence to have him publicly and with exquisite torments executed after the end of these wars, of which they hope for a soon and prosperous issue.

'And he hath likewise hitherto kept my young lord Clitophon alive, who, to redeem his friend, went with certain other noble men of Laconia and forces gathered by them, to besiege this young and new successor: but he issuing out, to the wonder of all men defeated the Laconians, slew many of the noblemen, and took Clitophon prisoner, whom with much ado he keepeth alive, the Helots being villainously cruel. But he tempereth them so, sometimes by following their humour, sometimes by striving with it, that hitherto he hath saved both their lives, but in different estates; Argalus being kept in a close and hard prison, Clitophon at some liberty. And now, Sir, though (to say the truth) we can promise ourselves little of their safeties while they are in the Helots' hands, I have delivered all I understand touching the loss of my lord's son, and the cause thereof: which though it was not necessary to Clitophon's case to be so particularly old, yet the strangeness of it made me think it would not be unpleasant unto you.'

## CHAPTER 6

Palladius thanked him greatly for it, being even passionately delighted with hearing so strange an accident of a knight so famous over the world as Argalus, with whom he had himself a long desire to meet: so had fame poured a noble emulation in him towards him.

But then, well bethinking himself, he called for armour, desiring them to provide him of horse and guide, and armed all saving the head, he went up to Kalander, whom he found lying upon the ground, having ever since banished both sleep and food as enemies to the mourning which passion persuaded him was reasonable.

But Palladius raised him up, saying unto him: 'No more, no more of this, my L. Kalander: let us labour to find, before we lament the loss. You know myself miss one who, though he be not my son, I would disdain the favour of life after him: but while there is a hope left, let not the weakness of sorrow make the strength of it languish. Take comfort, and good success will follow.'

And with those words, comfort seemed to lighten in his eyes, and that in his face and gesture was painted victory. Once,* Kalander's spirits were so revived withal that, receiving some sustenance and taking a little rest, he armed himself and those few of his servants he had left unsent, and so himself guided Palladius to the place upon the frontiers where already there were assembled between three and four thousand men; all well disposed for Kalander's sake to abide any peril, but like men disused with a long peace, more determinate to do than skilful how to do: lusty bodies, and brave armours; with such courage as rather grew of despising their enemies, whom they knew not, than of any confidence for anything which in themselves they knew; but neither cunning* use of their weapons nor art showed in their marching or encamping. Which Palladius soon perceiving, he desired to understand (as much as could be delivered unto him) the estate of the Helots.

And he was answered by a man well acquainted with the affairs of Laconia, that they were a kind of people who, having been of old freemen and possessioners, the Lacedaemonians had conquered them and laid not only tribute, but bondage upon them; which they had long borne, till of late, the Lacedaemonians through greediness growing more heavy than they could bear, and through contempt less careful how to make them bear, they had with a general consent (rather springing by the generalness of the cause than of any artificial practice) set themselves in arms, and whetting their courage with revenge, and grounding their resolution upon despair, they had proceeded with unlooked-for success,

*Once: straightway. cunning: skilful.

having already taken divers towns and castles, with the slaughter of many of the gentry, for whom no sex nor age could be accepted for an excuse. And that although at the first they had fought rather with beastly fury than any soldierly discipline, practice had now made them comparable to the best of the Lacedaemonians, and more of late than ever; by reason, first of Demagoras, a great lord, who had made himself of their party, and since his death, of another captain they had gotten, who had brought up their ignorance and brought down their fury to such a mean of good government, and withal led them so valorously that (besides the time wherein Clitophon was taken) they had the better in some other great conflicts: in such wise that the estate of Lacedaemon had sent unto them, offering peace with most reasonable and honourable conditions. Palladius having gotten this general knowledge of the party against whom, as he had already of the party for whom, he was to fight, he went to Kalander and told him plainly that by plain force there was small appearance of helping Clitophon; but some device was to be taken in hand wherein no less discretion than valour was to be used.

Whereupon, the counsel of the chief men was called, and at last this way Palladius (who by some experience, but specially by reading histories, was acquainted with stratagems) invented, and was by all the rest approved: that all the men there should dress themselves like the poorest sort of the people in Arcadia, having no banners, but bloody shirts hanged upon long staves, with some bad bag-pipes instead of drum and fife: their armour they should, as well as might be, cover, or at least make them look so rustily and ill-favouredly as might well become such wearers; and this the whole number should do, saving two hundred of the best chosen gentlemen for courage and strength, whereof Palladius himself would be one, who should have their arms chained, and be put in carts like prisoners.

This being performed according to the agreement, they marched on towards the town of Cardamila where Clitophon was captive; and being come two hours before sunset within view of the walls, the Helots already descrying their number and beginning to sound the alarm, they sent a cunning fellow (so much the cunninger as that he could mask it under rudeness) who, with such a kind of rhetoric as weeded out all flowers of rhetoric,[1] delivered unto the Helots assembled together that they were country-people of Arcadia, no less oppressed by their lords and no less desirous of liberty than they, and therefore had put themselves in the field and had already, besides a great number slain, taken nine or ten score gentlemen prisoners whom they had there well and fast chained. Now because they had no strong retiring place in Arcadia and were not yet of number enough to keep the field against their prince's forces, they were come to them for succour; knowing that daily more and more of their quality would flock unto them, but that in the meantime, lest their prince should pursue them or the Lacedaemonian king and nobility for the likeness of the cause fall upon them, they desired that if there were not room enough for them in the town, that yet they might encamp under the walls, and for surety have their prisoners (who were such men as were ever able to make their peace) kept within the town.

The Helots made but a short consultation, being glad that their contagion had spread itself into Arcadia, and making account that if the peace did not fall out between them and their king, that it was the best way to set fire in all the parts of Greece; besides their greediness to have so many gentlemen in their hands in whose ransoms they already meant to have a share; to which haste of concluding, two things well helped: the one, that their captain, with the wisest of them, was at that time absent about confirming or breaking the peace with the state of Lacedaemon: the second, that over-many good fortunes began to breed a proud recklessness in them. Therefore sending to view the camp, and finding that by their speech they were Arcadians, with whom they had had no war, never suspecting a private man's credit could have gathered such a force, and that all other tokens witnessed them to be of the lowest calling (besides the chains upon the gentlemen) they granted not only leave for the prisoners but for some others of the company, and to all, that they might harbour under the walls. So opened they the gates and received in the carts; which being done, and Palladius seeing fit time, he gave the sign, and shaking off their chains (which were made with such art that though they seemed most strong and fast, he that ware them might easily loose them) drew their swords hidden in the carts, and so setting upon the ward,* made them to fly either from the place or from their bodies, and so give entry to all the force of the Arcadians before the Helots could make any head to resist them.

But the Helots, being men hardened against dangers, gathered as well as they could together in the market-place, and thence would have given a shrewd welcome to the Arcadians but that Palladius (blaming those that were slow, heartening them that were forward, but especially with his own example leading them) made such an impression into the squadron of the Helots that at first the great body of them beginning to shake and stagger, at length every particular body recommended the protection of his life to his feet. Then Kalander cried to go to the prison where he thought his son was; but Palladius wished him, first scouring the streets, to house* all the Helots and make themselves masters of the gates.

But ere that could be accomplished, the Helots had gotten new heart, and with divers sorts of shot, from corners of streets and house-windows, galled* them; which courage was come unto them by the return of their captain, who, though he brought not many with him (having dispersed most of his companies to other of his holds) yet meeting a great number running out of the gate, not yet possessed by the Arcadians, he made them turn face, and with banners displayed, his trumpet gave the loudest testimony he could of his return: which once heard, the rest of the Helots, which were otherwise scattered, bent thitherward with a new life of resolution, as if their captain had been a root out of which as into branches their courage had sprung. Then began the fight to grow most sharp and the encounters of more cruel obstinacy: the Arcadians fighting to keep that they had won, the Helots to recover what they had lost; the Arcadians as in an unknown place, having no succour but in their hands; the Helots as in their own place, fighting for their lives, wives and children. There was victory and courage against revenge and despair, safety of both sides being no otherwise to be gotten but by destruction.

At length, the left wing of the Arcadians began to lose ground; which Palladius feeling, he straight thrust himself with his choice band against the throng that oppressed them, with such an

* ward: guard. house: drive into their houses. galled: harassed.

overflowing of valour that the captain of the Helots (whose eyes soon judged of that wherewith themselves were governed) saw that he alone was worth all the rest of the Arcadians: which he so wondered at, that it was hard to say whether he more liked his doings, or misliked the effects of his doings. But determining that upon that cast the game lay, and disdaining to fight with any other, sought only to join with him: which mind was no less in Palladius, having easily marked that he was as the first mover of all the other hands. And so their thoughts meeting in one point, they consented (though not agreed) to try each other's fortune: and so drawing themselves to be the uttermost* of the one side, they began a combat which was so much inferior to the battle in noise and number as it was surpassing it in bravery of fighting, and, as it were, delightful terribleness. Their courage was guided with skill, and their skill was armed with courage; neither did their hardiness darken their wit, nor their wit cool their hardiness: both valiant, as men despising death; both confident, as un-wonted* to be overcome, yet doubtful by their present feeling, and respectful by what they had already seen: their feet steady, their hands diligent, their eyes watchful, and their hearts resolute. The parts either not armed or weakly armed were well known, and according to the knowledge should have been sharply visited but that the answer was as quick as the objection. Yet some lighting, the smart bred rage and the rage bred smart again; till both sides beginning to wax faint, and rather desirous to die accompanied than hopeful to live victorious, the captain of the Helots with a blow whose violence grew of fury not of strength, or of strength proceeding of fury, struck Palladius upon the side of the head that he reeled astonished; and withal the helmet fell off, he remaining bare-headed, but other of the Arcadians were ready to shield him from any harm might rise of that nakedness.

But little needed it, for his chief enemy, instead of pursuing that advantage, kneeled down, offering to deliver the pommel of his sword in token of yielding; withal speaking aloud unto him that he thought it more liberty to be his prisoner than any other's general. Palladius standing upon himself and misdoubting some

* *the uttermost:* as far as possible. *unwonted:* unaccustomed.

craft, and the Helots that were next their captain, wavering between looking for some stratagem or fearing treason:

'What,' said the captain, 'hath Palladius forgotten the voice of Daiphantus?'

By that watch-word Palladius knew that it was his only friend Pyrocles whom he had lost upon the sea, and therefore both, most full of wonder so to be met if they had not been fuller of joy than wonder, caused the retreat to be sounded, Daiphantus by authority, and Palladius by persuasion: to which helped well the little advantage that was of either side, and that of the Helots' party their captain's behaviour had made as many amazed as saw or heard of it, and of the Arcadian side the good old Kalander, striving more than his old age could achieve, was newly taken prisoner. But indeed the chief parter of the fray was the night which with her black arms pulled their malicious sights one from the other. But he that took Kalander meant nothing less than to save him, but only so long as the captain might learn the enemies' secrets; towards whom he led the old gentleman, when he caused the retreat to be sounded, looking for no other delivery from that captivity but by the painful taking away of all pain, when whom should he see next to the captain (with good tokens how valiantly he had fought that day against the Arcadians) but his son Clitophon!

But now the captain had caused all the principal Helots to be assembled, as well to deliberate what they had to do as to receive a message from the Arcadians; among whom Palladius' virtue (besides the love Kalander bare him) having gotten principal authority, he had persuaded them to seek rather by parley to recover the father and the son than by the sword; since the goodness of the captain assured him that way to speed, and his value (wherewith he was of old acquainted) made him think any other way dangerous. This therefore was done in orderly manner, giving them to understand that as they came but to deliver Clitophon, so offering to leave the footing they already had in the town, to go away without any further hurt, so as they might have the father and the son without ransom delivered.

Which conditions being heard and conceived by the Helots,

Daiphantus persuaded them without delay to accept them. 'For first,' said he, 'since the strife is within our own home, if you lose, you lose all that in this life can be dear unto you: if you win, it will be a bloody victory with no profit but the flattering in ourselves that same bad humour of revenge. Besides, it is like to stir Arcadia upon us, which now, by using these persons well, may be brought to some amity. Lastly, but especially, lest the king and nobility of Laconia, with whom now we have made a perfect peace, should hope by occasion of this quarrel to join the Arcadians with them, and so break off the profitable agreement already concluded. In sum, as in all deliberations, weighing the profit of the good success with the harm of the evil success, you shall find this way most safe and honourable.'

The Helots, as much moved by his authority as persuaded by his reasons, were content therewith. Whereupon Palladius took order that the Arcadians should presently march out of the town, taking with them their prisoners, while the night with mutual diffidence might keep them quiet, and ere day came they might be well on of their way, and so avoid those accidents which in late enemies a look, a word, or a particular man's quarrel might engender. This being on both sides concluded on, Kalander and Clitophon, who now with infinite joy did know each other, came to kiss the hands and feet of Daiphantus: Clitophon telling his father how Daiphantus, not without danger to himself, had preserved him from the furious malice of the Helots; and even that day going to conclude the peace, lest in his absence he might receive some hurt, he had taken him in his company and given him armour, upon promise he should take the part of the Helots; which he had in this fight performed, little knowing that it was against his father; 'But,' said Clitophon, 'here is he who (as a father) hath new-begotten me and (as a god) hath saved me from many deaths which already laid hold on me,' which Kalander with tears of joy acknowledged (besides his own deliverance) only his benefit.

But Daiphantus, who loved doing well for itself and not for thanks, brake off those ceremonies, desiring to know how Palladius – for so he called Musidorus – was come into that company, and what his present estate was; whereof receiving a brief declaration of Kalander, he sent him word by Clitophon that he should not as now come unto him, because he held himself not so sure a master of the Helots' minds that he would adventure him in their power, who was so well known with an unfriendly acquaintance; but that he desired him to return with Kalander, whither also he within few days, having dispatched himself of the Helots, would repair. Kalander would need kiss his hand again for that promise, protesting he would esteem his house more blessed than a temple of the gods, if it had once received him. And then desiring pardon for Argalus, Daiphantus assured them that he would die but he would bring him (though till then kept in close prison, indeed for his safety, the Helots being so animated against him as else he could not have lived) and so taking their leave of him, Kalander, Clitophon, Palladius, and the rest of the Arcadians swearing that they would no further in any sort molest the Helots, they straightway marched out of the town, carrying both their dead and wounded bodies with them; and by morning were already within the limits of Arcadia.

## CHAPTER 7

The Helots, of the other side, shutting their gates, gave themselves to bury their dead, to cure their wounds and rest their wearied bodies; till, the next day bestowing the cheerful use of the light upon them, Daiphantus, making a general convocation, spake unto them in this manner:

'We are first,' said he, 'to thank the gods that, further than we had either cause to hope or reason to imagine, have delivered us out of this gulf of danger wherein we were already swallowed. For all being lost, had they not directed my return so just as they did, it had been too late to recover that which, being had, we could not keep. And had I not happened to know one of the principal men among them, by which means the truce began between us, you may easily conceive what little reason we have to think but that either by some supply out of Arcadia, or from the nobility of this country (who would have made fruits of wisdom grow out of this occasion) we should have had our power turned to ruin, our pride to repentance and sorrow. But now the storm as it fell, so it ceased: and the error committed, in retaining Clitophon more hardly than his age or quarrel deserved, becomes a sharply learned experience, to use in other times more moderation.

'Now have I to deliver unto you the conclusion between the kings, with the nobility of Lacedaemon, and you; which is in all points as ourselves desired, as well for that you would have granted as for the assurance of what is granted. The towns and forts you presently have are still left unto you, to be kept either with or without garrison, so as you alter not the laws of the country, and pay such duties as the rest of the Laconians do. Yourselves are made by public decree free men, and so capable both to give and receive voice in election of magistrates. The distinction of names between Helots and Lacedaemonians to be quite taken away, and all indifferently to enjoy both names and privileges of Laconians. Your children to be brought up with theirs in the Spartan discipline: and so you, framing yourselves to be good members of that estate, to be hereafter fellows and no longer servants.

'Which conditions you see carry in themselves no more contention than assurance; for this is not a peace which is made with them, but this a peace by which you are made of them. Lastly a forgetfulness decreed of all what is past, they showing themselves glad to have so valiant men as you are joined with them, so that you are to take minds of peace, since the cause of war is finished; and as you hated them before like oppressors, so now to love them as brothers; to take care of their estate because it is yours, and to labour by virtuous doing that the posterity may not repent your joining. But now one article only they stood upon, which in the end I with your commissioners have agreed unto, that I should no more tarry here; mistaking perchance my humour, and thinking me as seditious as I am young; or else it is the king Amiclas' procuring, in respect that it was my ill hap to kill his nephew Eurileon; but howsoever it be, I have condescended.'

'But so will not we,' cried almost the whole assembly, counselling one another rather to try the uttermost event than to lose him by whom they had been victorious. But he, as well with general orations as particular dealing with the men of most credit, made them thoroughly see how necessary it was to prefer such an opportunity before a vain affection; but yet could not prevail till openly he sware that he would (if at any time the Lacedaemonians brake this treaty) come back again, and be their captain.

So, then, after a few days, setting them in perfect order, he took his leave of them, whose eyes bade him farewell with tears, and mouths with kissing the places where he stepped, and after, making temples unto him as to a demi-god, thinking it beyond the degree of humanity to have a wit so far over-going his age, and such dreadful terror proceed from so excellent beauty. But he for his sake obtained free pardon for Argalus, whom also (upon oath never to bear arms against the Helots) he delivered; and taking only with him certain principal jewels of his own, he would have parted alone with Argalus (whose countenance well showed, while Parthenia was lost, he counted not himself delivered) but that the whole multitude would needs guard him into Arcadia; where again leaving them all to lament his departure, he by enquiry got to the well-known house of Kalander. There was he received with loving joy of Kalander; with joyful love of Palladius; with humble, though doleful, demeanour of Argalus (whom specially both he and Palladius regarded); with grateful serviceableness of Clitophon, and honourable admiration of all. For being now well viewed to have no hair of his face to witness him a man, who had done acts beyond the degree of a man, and to look with a certain almost bashful kind of modesty as if he feared the eyes of men, who was unmoved with sight of the most horrible countenances of death, and, as if nature had mistaken her work, to have a Mars' heart in a Cupid's body; all that beheld him (and all that might behold him, did behold him) made their eyes quick messengers to their minds that there they had seen the uttermost that in mankind might be seen. The like wonder Palladius had before stirred but that Daiphantus, as younger and newer come, had gotten now the advantage in the moist and fickle impression of eye-sight. But while all men, saving poor Argalus, made the joy of their eyes speak for their hearts towards Daiphantus, fortune (that belike was bid to that banquet, and meant then to play the good-fellow) brought a pleasant adventure among them.

It was that as they had newly dined, there came in to Kalander a messenger that brought him word a young noble lady, near kinswoman to the fair Helen, queen of Corinth, was come thither, and desired to be lodged in his house. Kalander, most glad of such an occasion, went out, and all his other worthy guests with him saving only Argalus who remained in his chamber, desirous that this company were once broken up, that he might go in his solitary quest after Parthenia. But when they met this lady, Kalander straight thought he saw his niece Parthenia, and was about in such familiar sort to have spoken unto her, but she, in grave and honourable manner giving him to understand that he was mistaken, he, half ashamed, excused himself with the exceeding likeness was between them, though indeed it seemed that this lady was of the more pure and dainty complexion. She said it might very well be, having been many times taken one for another. But as soon as she was brought into the house, before she would rest her, she desired to speak with Argalus publicly who, she heard, was in the house. Argalus came hastily, and as hastily thought as Kalander had done, with sudden changes of joy into sorrow. But she, when she had stayed their thoughts with telling them her name and quality, in this sort spake unto him:

'My Lord Argalus,' said she, 'being of late left in the court of queen Helen of Corinth as chief in her absence, she being upon some occasion gone thence, there came unto me the lady Parthenia, so disfigured as I think Greece hath nothing so ugly to behold. For my part, it was many days before with vehement oaths and some good proofs she could make me think that she was Parthenia. Yet at last finding certainly it was she and greatly pitying her misfortune, so much the more as that all men had ever told me, as now you do, of the great likeness between us, I took the best care I could of her, and of her understood the whole tragical history of her undeserved adventure; and therewithal of that most noble constancy in you, my lord Argalus, which whosoever loves not, shows himself to be a hater of virtue and unworthy to live in the society of mankind. But no outward cherishing could salve the inward sore of her mind; but a few days since she died, before her death earnestly desiring and persuading me to think of no husband but of you, as of the only man in the world worthy to be loved. Withal she gave me this ring to deliver you, desiring you, and by the authority of love commanding you, that the affection you bare her you should turn to me, assuring you that nothing can please her soul more than to see you and me matched together. Now my lord, though this office be not, perchance, suitable to my estate nor sex, who should rather look to be desired, yet an extraordinary desert requires an extraordinary proceeding; and therefore I am come, with faithful love built upon your worthiness, to offer myself, and to beseech you to accept the offer: and if these noble gentlemen present will say it is great folly, let them withal say, it is great love.'

And then she stayed, earnestly attending Argalus' answer; who, first making most hearty sighs do such obsequies as he could to Parthenia, thus answered her:

'Madam,' said he, 'infinitely am I bound unto you for this no more rare than noble courtesy; but most bound for the goodness I perceive you showed to the lady Parthenia'; (with that the tears ran down his eyes, but he followed on) 'and as much as so unfortunate a man, fit to be the spectacle of misery, can do you a service, determine you have made a purchase of a slave, while I live, never to fail you. But this great matter you propose unto me, wherein I am not so blind as not to see what happiness it should be unto me: excellent lady, know that if my heart were mine to give, you before all other should have it. But Parthenia's it is, though dead. There I began: there I end all matter of affection. I hope I shall not long tarry after her, with whose beauty if I had only been in love, I should be so with you who have the same beauty. But it was Parthenia's self I loved and love, which no likeness can make one, no commandment dissolve, no foulness defile, nor no death finish.'

'And shall I receive,' said she, 'such disgrace as to be refused?'

'Noble lady,' said he, 'let not that hard word be used, who know your exceeding worthiness far beyond my desert; but it is only happiness I refuse, since of the only happiness I could and can desire, I am refused.'

He had scarce spoken those words, when she ran to him and embracing him, 'Why then Argalus,' said she, 'take thy Parthenia.' And Parthenia it was indeed. But because sorrow forbade him too soon to believe, she told him the truth, with all circumstances: how being parted alone, meaning to die in some solitary place, as she happened to make her complaint, the queen Helen of

Corinth (who likewise felt her part of miseries) being then walking lonely in that lovely place, heard her and never left till she had known the whole discourse. Which the noble queen greatly pitying, she sent her to a physician of hers, the most excellent man in the world, in hope he could help her; which in such sort as they saw he had performed; and she, taking with her of the queen's servants, thought yet to make this trial whether he would quickly forget his true Parthenia or no. Her speech was confirmed by the Corinthian gentlemen who before had kept her counsel, and Argalus easily persuaded to what more than ten thousand years of life he desired; and Kalander would needs have the marriage celebrated in his house, principally the longer to hold his dear guests, towards whom he was now, besides his own habit of hospitality, carried with love and duty, and therefore omitted no service that his wit could invent and power minister.

## CHAPTER 8

But no way he saw he could so much pleasure them as by leaving the two friends alone; who being shrunk aside to the banqueting-house where the pictures were, there Palladius recounted unto him that after they had both abandoned the burning ship and either of them taken something under him the better to support him to the shore, he knew not how, but either with over-labouring in the fight and sudden cold or the too much receiving of salt-water, he was past himself: but yet holding fast (as the nature of dying men is to do) the chest that was under him, he was cast on the sands, where he was taken up by a couple of shepherds, and by them brought to life again and kept from drowning himself when he despaired of his safety. How after having failed to take him into the fisher-boat, he had by the shepherds' persuasion come to this gentleman's house; where being dangerously sick, he had yielded to seek the recovery of health only for that he might the sooner go seek the delivery of Pyrocles; to which purpose Kalander by some friends of his in Messenia had already set a ship or two abroad, when this accident of Clitophon's taking had so blessedly procured their meeting. Then did he set forth unto him the noble entertainment and careful cherishing of Kalander towards him, and so upon occasion of the pictures present, delivered with the frankness of a friend's tongue, as near as could be, word by word what Kalander had told him touching the strange story (with all the particularities belonging) of Arcadia; which did in many sorts so delight Pyrocles to hear that he would needs have much of it again repeated, and was not contented till Kalander himself had answered him divers questions.

But first at Musidorus' request, though in brief manner, his mind much running upon the strange story of Arcadia, he did declare by what course of adventures he was come to make up their mutual happiness in meeting.

'When, cousin,' said he, 'we had stripped ourselves, and were both leaped into the sea, and swam a little towards the shore, I found by reason of some wounds I had that I should not be able to get the land, and therefore turned back again to the mast of the ship where you found me, assuring myself that if you came alive to shore, you would seek me; if you were lost, as I thought it as good to perish as to live, so that place as good to perish in as another. There I found my sword among some of the shrouds, wishing, I must confess, if I died, to be found with that in my hand, and withal waving it about my head that sailors by might have the better glimpse of me. There you missing me, I was taken up by pirates, who putting me under board prisoner, presently set upon another ship and maintaining a long fight, in the end put them all to the sword. Amongst whom I might hear them greatly praise one young man who fought most valiantly, whom (as love is careful, and misfortune subject to doubtfulness) I thought certainly to be you. And so holding you as dead, from that time till the time I saw you, in truth I sought nothing more than a noble end, which perchance made me more hardy than otherwise I would have been.

'Trial whereof came within two days after; for the kings of Lacedaemon having set out some galleys under the charge of one of their nephews to scour the sea of the pirates, they met with us, where our captain, wanting men, was driven to arm some of his prisoners, with promise of liberty for well fighting: among whom I was one; and being boarded by the admiral, it was my fortune to kill Eurileon the king's nephew. But in the end they prevailed and we were all taken prisoners, I not caring much what became of me, only keeping the name of Daiphantus, according to the resolution you know is between us.

'But being laid in the jail of Tenaria, with special hate to me for the death of Eurileon, the popular sort of that town conspired with the Helots and so by night opened them the gates; where entering and killing all of the genteel and rich faction, for honesty-sake brake open all prisons and so delivered me: and I, moved with gratefulness and encouraged with carelessness of life, so behaved myself in some conflicts they had in few days, that they barbarously thinking unsensible wonders of me, and withal so much the better trusting me as they heard I was hated of the king of Lacedaemon – their chief captain (being slain, as you know, by the noble Argalus) who helped thereunto by his persuasion, having borne a great affection unto me; and to avoid the dangerous emulation which grew among the chief who should have the place; and also affected* as rather to have a stranger than a competitor – they elected me (God wot little proud of that dignity!) restoring unto me such things of mine as, being taken first by the pirates and then by the Lacedaemonians, they had gotten in the sack of the town. Now being in it, so good was my success with many victories that I made a peace for them to their own liking, the very day that you delivered Clitophon whom I, with much ado, had preserved. And in my peace the king Amiclas of Lacedaemon would needs have me banished and deprived of the dignity whereunto I was exalted: which (and you may see how much you are bound to me) for your sake I was content to suffer, a new hope rising in me that you were not dead, and so meaning to travail over the world to seek you. And now here, my dear Musidorus, you have me.'

And with that, embracing and kissing each other, they called Kalander, of whom Daiphantus desired to hear the full story which before he had recounted to Palladius, and to see the letter of Philanax, which he read and well marked.

But within some days after, the marriage between Argalus and the fair Parthenia being to be celebrated, Daiphantus and Palladius, selling some of their jewels, furnished themselves of very

* *affected*: desirous.

fair apparel, meaning to do honour to their loving host, who, as much for their sakes as for the marriage, set forth each thing in most gorgeous manner. But all the cost bestowed did not so much enrich, nor all the fine deckings so much beautify, nor all the dainty devices so much delight, as the fairness of Parthenia, the pearl of all the maids of Mantinea; who as she went to the temple to be married, her eyes themselves seemed a temple wherein love and beauty were married. Her lips though they were kept close with modest silence, yet with a pretty kind of natural swelling they seemed to invite the guests that looked on them; her cheeks blushing and withal, when she was spoken unto, a little smiling, were like roses when their leaves are with a little breath stirred; her hair, being laid at the full length down her back, bare show as, if the vaward* failed, yet that would conquer.

Daiphantus marking her, 'O Jupiter!' said he speaking to Palladius, 'how happens it that beauty is only confined to Arcadia?'[1] But Palladius not greatly attending his speech, some days were continued in the solemnizing the marriage, with all conceits* that might deliver delight to men's fancies.

CHAPTER 9

But such a change was grown in Daiphantus that (as if cheerfulness had been tediousness, and good entertainment were turned to discourtesy) he would ever get himself alone, though almost when he was in company he was alone, so little attention he gave to any that spake unto him. Even the colour and figure of his face began to receive some alteration, which he shewed little to heed; but every morning early going abroad either to the garden or to some woods towards the desert, it seemed his only comfort was to be without a comforter. But long it could not be hid from Palladius, whom true love made ready to mark and long knowledge able to mark; and therefore being now grown weary of his abode in Arcadia, having informed himself fully of the strength and riches of the country, of the nature of the people and manner of their laws; and, seeing the court could not be visited, prohibited to all men but to certain shepherdish people, he greatly desired a speedy return to his own country after the many mazes of fortune

* *vaward*: vanguard, front. *conceits*: fanciful inventions.

he had trodden. But perceiving this great alteration in his friend, he thought first to break with him thereof and then to hasten his return, whereto he found him but smally inclined: whereupon one day taking him alone with certain graces and countenances, as if he were disputing with the trees, began in this manner to say unto him:

'A mind well trained and long exercised in virtue, my sweet and worthy cousin, doth not easily change any course it once undertakes but upon well-grounded and well-weighed causes; for being witness to itself of its own inward good, it finds nothing without it of so high a price for which it should be altered. Even the very countenance and behaviour of such a man doth shew forth images of the same constancy, by maintaining a right harmony betwixt it and the inward good, in yielding itself suitable to the virtuous resolution of the mind. This speech I direct to you, noble friend Pyrocles, the excellency of whose mind and well chosen course in virtue if I do not sufficiently know, having seen such rare demonstrations of it, it is my weakness, and not your unworthiness: but as indeed I know it, and knowing it, most dearly love both it and him that hath it, so must I needs say that since our late coming into this country, I have marked in you, I will not say an alteration, but a relenting truly, and a slackening of the main career you had so notably begun and almost performed, and that in such sort as I cannot find sufficient reason in my great love toward you how to allow it: for (to leave off other secreter arguments which my acquaintance with you makes me easily find) this in effect to any man may be manifest, that whereas you were wont in all places you came to give yourself vehemently to the knowledge of those things which might better your mind, to seek the familiarity of excellent men in learning and soldiery, and lastly, to put all these things in practice, both by continual wise proceding and worthy enterprises as occasion fell for them; you now leave all these things undone: you let your mind fall asleep: beside your countenance troubled, which surely comes not of virtue, for virtue, like the clear heaven, is without clouds: and lastly, you subject yourself to solitariness, the sly enemy that doth most separate a man from well doing.'

Pyrocles' mind was all this while so fixed upon another devotion that he no more attentively marked his friend's discourse than the child that hath leave to play marks the last part of his lesson, or the diligent pilot in a dangerous tempest doth attend the unskilful words of a passenger: yet the very sound having imprinted the general point of his speech in his heart, pierced with any mislike of so dearly an esteemed friend, and desirous by degrees to bring him to a gentler consideration of him, with a shamefast look, witnessing he rather could not help than did not know his fault, answered him to this purpose:

'Excellent Musidorus, in the praise you gave me in the beginning of your speech I easily acknowledge the force of your good will unto me; for neither could you have thought so well of me if extremity of love had not made your judgement partial, nor could you have loved me so entirely if you had not been apt to make so great, though undeserved, judgements of me; and even so must I say to those imperfections to which, though I have ever through weakness been subject, yet you by the daily mending of your mind have of late been able to look into them, which before you could not discern; so that the change you speak of falls not out by my impairing but by your bettering. And yet under the leave of your better judgement, I must needs say thus much, my dear cousin, that I find not myself wholly to be condemned because I do not with continual vehemency follow those knowledges, which you call the bettering of my mind; for both the mind itself must, like other things, sometimes be unbent, or else it will be either weakened or broken; and these knowledges, as they are of good use, so are they not all the mind may stretch itself unto. Who knows whether I feed not my mind with higher thoughts? Truly, as I know not all the particularities, so yet I see the bounds of all these knowledges: but the workings of the mind I find much more infinite than can be led unto by the eye, or imagined by any that distract their thoughts without themselves. And in such contemplation or, as I think, more excellent, I enjoy my solitariness, and my solitariness perchance is the nurse of these contemplations. Eagles we see fly alone, and they are but sheep which always herd together. Condemn not therefore my mind sometime to enjoy itself, nor blame not the taking of such times as serve most fit for it. And alas, dear Musidorus, if I be sad, who knows better than you the just causes I have of sadness?'

And here Pyrocles suddenly stopped, like a man unsatisfied in himself, though his wit might well have served to have satisfied another. And so looking with a countenance as though he desired he should know his mind without hearing him speak, and yet desirous to speak, to breathe out some part of his inward evil, sending again new blood to his face, he continued his speech in this manner:

'And Lord, dear cousin,' said he, 'doth not the pleasantness of this place carry in itself sufficient reward for any time lost in it? Do you not see how all things conspire together to make this country a heavenly dwelling? Do you not see the grass, how in colour they excel the emeralds, every one striving to pass his fellow, and yet they are all kept of an equal height? And see you not the rest of these beautiful flowers, each of which would require a man's wit to know and his life to express? Do not these stately trees seem to maintain their flourishing old age with the only happiness of their seat, being clothed with a continual spring, because no beauty here should ever fade? Doth not the air breathe health, which the birds, delightful both to ear and eye, do daily solemnize with the sweet consent of their voices? Is not every echo thereof a perfect music? And these fresh and delightful brooks, how slowly they slide away, as loth to leave the company of so many things united in perfection, and with how sweet a murmur they lament their forced departure? Certainly, certainly, cousin, it must needs be that some goddess inhabiteth this region, who is the soul of this soil: for neither is any less than a goddess worthy to be shrined in such a heap of pleasures, nor any less than a goddess could have made it so perfect a plot of the celestial dwellings.'

And so ended with a deep sigh, ruefully casting his eye upon Musidorus, as more desirous of pity than pleading.

But Musidorus had all this while held his look fixed upon Pyrocles' countenance, and with no less loving attention marked how his words proceeded from him; but in both these he perceived such strange diversities that they rather increased new doubts than gave him ground to settle any judgement. For besides his eyes sometimes even great with tears, the oft changing of his colour, with a kind of shaking unstaidness* over all his body, he

* *unstaidness*: agitation.

might see in his countenance some great determination mixed with fear, and might perceive in him store of thoughts rather stirred than digested; his words interrupted continually with sighs (which served as a burthen* to each sentence) and the tenor of his speech (though of his wonted phrase) not knit together to one constant end, but rather dissolved in itself as the vehemency of the inward passion prevailed: which made Musidorus frame his answer nearest to that humour which should soonest put out the secret.

For having in the beginning of Pyrocles' speech, which defended his solitariness, framed in his mind a reply against it in the praise of honourable action, in showing that such a kind of contemplation is but a glorious title to idleness; that in action a man did not only better himself but benefit others; that the gods would not have delivered a soul into the body which hath arms and legs, only instruments of doing, but that it were intended the mind should employ them; and that the mind should best know his own good or evil by practice, which knowledge was the only way to increase the one and correct the other; besides many other arguments which the plentifulness of the matter yielded to the sharpness of his wit: when he found Pyrocles leave that and fall into such an affected praising of the place, he left it likewise and joined with him therein, because he found him in that humour utter more store of passion: and even thus kindly embracing him, he said:

'Your words are such, noble cousin, so sweetly and strongly handled in the praise of solitariness, as they would make me likewise yield myself up into it but that the same words make me know it is more pleasant to enjoy the company of him that can speak such words than by such words to be persuaded to follow solitariness. And even so do I give you leave, sweet Pyrocles, ever to defend solitariness, so long as to defend it, you ever keep company. But I marvel at the excessive praises you give to this country. In truth it is not unpleasant, but yet if you would return into Macedon you should either see many heavens, or find this no more than earthly. And even Tempe in my Thessalia (where you and I, to my great happiness, were brought up together) is nothing inferior unto it. But I think you will make me see that the vigour of your wit can

*burthen: refrain.

show itself in any subject: or else you feed sometimes your solitariness with the conceits of the poets, whose liberal pens can as easily travel over mountains as molehills and so, like well-disposed* men, set up everything to the highest note; especially, when they put such words in the mouths of one of these fantastical, mind-infected people that children and musicians call "Lovers".'

This word 'Lover' did no less pierce poor Pyrocles than the right tune of music toucheth him that is sick of the Tarantula.[1] There was not one part of his body that did not feel a sudden motion, while his heart with panting seemed to dance to the sound of that word. Yet after some pause, lifting up his eyes a little from the ground, and yet not daring to place them in the eyes of Musidorus, armed with the very countenance of the poor prisoner at the bar whose answer is nothing but 'Guilty', with much ado he brought forth this question:

'And alas,' said he, 'dear cousin, what if I be not so much the poet (the freedom of whose pen can exercise itself in anything) as even that miserable subject of his cunning whereof you speak?'

'Now the eternal gods forbid,' mainly* cried out Musidorus, 'that ever my ear should be poisoned with so evil news of you. O let me never know that any base affection should get any lordship in your thoughts.'

But as he was speaking more, Kalander came and brake off their discourse with inviting them to the hunting of a goodly stag, which being harboured in a wood thereby, he hoped would make them good sport, and drive away some part of Daiphantus' melancholy. They condescended, and so going to their lodgings, furnished themselves as liked them, Daiphantus writing a few words which he left sealed in a letter against their return.

## CHAPTER 10

Then went they together abroad, the good Kalander entertaining them with pleasant discoursing how well he loved the sport of hunting when he was a young man; how much in the comparison thereof he disdained all chamber-delights; that the sun (how great a journey soever he had to make) could never prevent* him with

* *well-disposed*: favourably disposed. *mainly*: with vigour. *prevent*: come before.

earliness, nor the moon with her sober countenance dissuade him from watching till midnight for the deer feeding.

'O,' said he, 'you will never live to my age without you keep yourselves in breath with exercise and in heart with joyfulness. Too much thinking doth consume the spirits, and oft it falls out that while one thinks too much of his doing, he leaves to do the effect of his thinking.'

Then spared he not to remember how much Arcadia was changed since his youth; activity and good fellowship being nothing in the price it was then held in, but, according to the nature of the old-growing world, still worse and worse. Then would he tell them stories of such gallants as he had known: and so with pleasant company beguiled the time's haste and shortened the way's length, till they came to the side of the wood, where the hounds were in couples staying their coming, but with a whining accent craving liberty, many of them in colour and marks so resembling, that it shewed they were of one kind. The huntsmen handsomely attired in their green liveries as though they were children of summer,[1] with staves in their hands to beat the guiltless earth when the hounds were at a fault,[2] and with horns about their necks to sound an alarm upon a silly* fugitive. The hounds were straight uncoupled, and ere long the stag thought it better to trust to the nimbleness of his feet than to the slender fortification of his lodging: but even his feet betrayed him, for howsoever they went, they themselves uttered themselves to the scent of their enemies, who (one taking it of another, and sometimes believing the wind's advertisements, sometimes the view of their faithful counsellors, the huntsmen) with open mouths then denounced war when the war was already begun; their cry being composed of so well-sorted* mouths that any man would perceive therein some kind of proportion, but the skilful woodmen did find a music. Then delight and variety of opinion drew the horsemen sundry ways, yet cheering their hounds with voice and horn, kept still, as it were, together. The wood seemed to conspire with them against his own citizens, dispersing their noise through all his quarters; and even the nymph Echo[3] left* to bewail the loss of Narcissus and became a hunter. But the stag was in the end so hotly pur-

---

* *silly*: poor. *well-sorted*: well-matched. *left*: left off.

sued that, leaving his flight, he was driven to make courage of
despair, and so, turning his head, made the hounds with change of
speech to testify that he was at a bay, as if from hot pursuit
of their enemy they were suddenly come to a parley.

But Kalander, by his skill of coasting the country, was among
the first that came in to the besieged deer; whom when some of the
younger sort would have killed with their swords, he would not
suffer, but with a cross-bow sent a death to the poor beast, who
with tears showed the unkindness he took of man's cruelty.

But by the time that the whole company was assembled and
that the stag had bestowed himself liberally among them that had
killed him, Daiphantus was missed, for whom Palladius carefully
inquiring, no news could be given him but by one that said he
thought he was returned home, for that he marked him, in the
chief of* the hunting, take a bye-way which might lead to Kalander's house. That answer for the time satisfying, and they
having performed all duties as well for the stag's funeral as the
hounds' triumph, they returned; some talking of the fatness of the
deer's body; some of the fairness of his head; some of the hounds'
cunning; some of their speed, and some of their cry; till coming
home, about the time that the candles begin to inherit the sun's
office, they found Daiphantus was not to be found. Whereat Palladius greatly marvelling, and a day or two passing while neither
search nor inquiry could help him to knowledge, at last he lighted
upon the letter which Pyrocles had written before he went a hunting, and left in his study among other of his writings. The letter
was directed to Palladius himself and contained these words:

My only friend, violence of love leads me into such a course,
whereof your knowledge may much more vex you than help me.
Therefore pardon my concealing it from you, since, if I wrong you, it
is in the respect I bear you. Return into Thessalia, I pray you, as full
of good fortune as I am of desire; and if I live, I will in a short time
follow you; if I die, love my memory.

This was all, and this Palladius read twice or thrice over. 'Ah,'
said he, 'Pyrocles, what means this alteration? What have I deserved of thee to be thus banished of thy counsels? Heretofore I

*in the chief of: at the height of.

have accused the sea, condemned the pirates, and hated my evil fortune that deprived me of thee; but now thyself is the sea which drowns my comfort; thyself is the pirate that robs thyself from me; thy own will becomes my evil fortune.'

Then turned he his thoughts to all forms of guesses that might light upon the purpose and course of Pyrocles, for he was not sure by his words that it was love as he was doubtful where the love was. One time he thought some beauty in Laconia had laid hold of his eyes; another time he feared that it might be Parthenia's excellency which had broken the bands of all former resolution. But the more he thought, the more he knew not what to think, armies of objections rising against any accepted opinion.

Then as careful he was what to do himself: at length determined never to leave seeking him till his search should be either by meeting accomplished or by death ended. Therefore (for all the unkindness, bearing tender respect that his friend's secret determination should be kept from any suspicion in others) he went to Kalander and told him that he had received a message from his friend, by which he understood he was gone back again into Laconia about some matters greatly importing the poor men whose protection he had undertaken, and that it was in any sort fit for him to follow him, but in such private wise as not to be known, and that therefore he would as then bid him farewell; arming himself in a black armour as either a badge or prognostication of his mind, and taking only with him a good store of money and a few choice jewels, leaving the greatest number of them and most of his apparel with Kalander – which he did partly to give the more cause to Kalander to expect their return, and so to be the less curiously inquisitive after them – and partly to leave those honourable thanks unto him for his charge and kindness, which he knew he would no other way receive.

The good old man, having neither reason to dissuade nor hope to persuade, received the things with mind of a keeper not of an owner; but before he went, desired he might have the happiness fully to know what they were, which, he said, he had ever till then delayed, fearing to be anyway importune; but now he could not be so much an enemy to his desires as any longer to imprison them in silence. Palladius told him that the matter was not secret but that so worthy a friend deserved the knowledge, and should have it as soon as he might speak with his friend, without whose consent – because their promise bound him otherwise – he could not reveal it; but bade him hold for most assured that if they lived but a while, he should find that they which bore the names of Daiphantus and Palladius would give him and his cause to think his noble courtesy well employed. Kalander would press him no further; but desiring that he might have leave to go, or at least to send his son and servants with him, Palladius brake off all ceremonies by telling him his case stood so that his greatest favour should be in making least ado of his parting. Wherewith Kalander, knowing it to be more cumber than courtesy to strive, abstained from further urging him, but not from hearty mourning the loss of so sweet a conversation.

Only Clitophon by vehement importunity obtained to go with him to come again to Daiphantus, whom he named and accounted his lord. And in such private guise departed Palladius, though having a companion to talk withal yet talking much more with unkindness. And first they went to Mantinea, whereof because Parthenia was, he suspected there might be some cause of his abode. But, finding there no news of him, he went to Tegea, Ripa, Enispae, Stimphalus and Pheneus, famous for the poisonous Stygian water, and through all the rest of Arcadia, making their eyes, their ears and their tongues serve almost for nothing but that enquiry. But they could know nothing but that in none of those places he was known. And so went they, making one place succeed to another in like uncertainty to their search, many times encountering strange adventures worthy to be registered in the rolls of fame; but this may not be omitted. As they passed in a pleasant valley (of either side of which high hills lifted up their beetle-brows as if they would overlook the pleasantness of their under-prospect) they were by the daintiness of the place and the weariness of themselves invited to light from their horses; and pulling off their bits that they might something refresh their mouths upon the grass (which plentifully grew, brought up under the care of those well-shading trees) they themselves laid them down hard by the murmuring music of certain waters which spouted out of the side of the hills, and in the bottom of the valley made of many springs a pretty brook, like a commonwealth of many families.

But when they had a while hearkened to the persuasion of sleep, they rose and walked onward in that shady place, till Clitophon espied a piece of armour and, not far off, another piece; and so the sight of one piece teaching him to look for more, he at length found all, with head-piece and shield, by the device* whereof he straight knew it to be the armour of his cousin, the noble Amphialus. Whereupon (fearing some inconvenience happened unto him) he told both his doubt and cause of doubt to Palladius who, considering thereof, thought best to make no longer stay but to follow on, lest perchance some violence were offered to so worthy a knight whom the fame of the world seemed to set in balance with any knight living. Yet with a sudden conceit, having long borne great honour to the name of Amphialus, Palladius thought best to take that armour, thinking thereby to learn by them that should know that armour some news of Amphialus, and yet not hinder him in the search of Daiphantus too. So he, by the help of Clitophon, quickly put on that armour, whereof there was no one piece wanting, though hacked in some places, betraying some fight not long since passed. It was something too great, but yet served well enough.

And so, getting on their horses, they travelled but a little way when, in the opening of the mouth of the valley into a fair field, they met with a coach drawn with four milk-white horses furnished all in black, with a black-a-moor boy upon every horse, they all apparelled in white, the coach itself very richly furnished in black and white. But before they could come so near as to discern what was within, there came running upon them above a dozen horsemen who cried to them to yield themselves prisoners or else they should die. But Palladius, not accustomed to grant over the possession of himself upon so unjust titles, with sword drawn gave them so rude an answer that divers of them never had breath to reply again: for being well backed by Clitophon, and having an excellent horse under him, when he was overpressed by some he avoided them, and ere the other thought of it, punished in him his fellow's faults, and so either with cunning or with force,

* *device*: heraldic design on shield.

or rather with a cunning force, left none of them either living or able to make his life serve to others' hurt. Which being done, he approached the coach, assuring the black boys they should have no hurt, who were else ready to have run away; and looking into the coach, he found in the one end a lady of great beauty, and such a beauty as showed forth the beams both of wisdom and good nature, but all as much darkened as might be with sorrow. In the other, two ladies (who by their demeanour showed well they were but her servants) holding before them a picture in which was a goodly gentleman (whom he knew not) painted, having in their faces a certain waiting sorrow, their eyes being infected with their mistress' weeping.

But the chief lady having not so much as once heard the noise of this conflict (so had sorrow closed up all the entries of her mind, and love tied her senses to that beloved picture) now the shadow of him falling upon the picture made her cast up her eye; and seeing the armour which too well she knew, thinking him to be Amphialus, the lord of her desires (blood coming more freely into her cheeks as though it would be bold, and yet there, growing new again pale for fear) with a pitiful look, like one unjustly condemned,

'My Lord Amphialus,' said she, 'you have enough punished me. It is time for cruelty to leave you, and evil fortune me. If not, I pray you (and to grant my prayer fitter time nor place you can have) accomplish the one even now, and finish the other.'

With that, sorrow impatient to be slowly uttered in her often-staying speeches poured itself so fast in tears that Palladius could not hold her longer in error, but pulling off his helmet, 'Madam,' said he, 'I perceive you mistake me. I am a stranger in these parts, set upon without any cause given by me by some of your servants, whom, because I have in my just defence evil entreated,* I came to make my excuse to you, whom seeing such as I do, I find greater cause why I should crave pardon of you.'

When she saw his face and heard his speech she looked out of the coach, and seeing her men, some slain, some lying under their dead horses and striving to get from under them, without making more account of the matter, 'Truly,' said she, 'they are well served

* *entreated:* treated.

that durst lift up their arms against that armour. But, Sir Knight,'
said she, 'I pray you tell me, how came you by this armour? For if
it be by the death of him that owned it, then have I more to say
unto you.'

Palladius assured her it was not so, telling her the true manner
how he found it.

'It is like enough,' said she, 'for that agrees with the manner he
hath lately used. But I beseech you, Sir,' said she, 'since your
prowess hath bereft me of my company, let it yet so far heal the
wounds itself hath given as to guard me to the next town.'

'How great soever my business be, fair lady,' said he, 'it shall
willingly yield to so noble a cause. But first, even by the favour
you bear to the lord of this noble armour, I conjure you to tell me
the story of your fortune herein, lest hereafter, when the image of
so excellent a lady in so strange a plight come before mine eyes, I
condemn myself of want of consideration in not having demanded thus much. Neither ask I it without protestation that
wherein my sword and faith may avail you they shall bind themselves to your service.'

'Your conjuration, fair knight,' said she, 'is too strong for my
poor spirit to disobey, and that shall make me (without any other
hope, my ruin being but by one unrelievable) to grant your will
herein; and to say the truth, a strange niceness* were it in me to
refrain that from the ears of a person representing so much
worthiness which I am glad even to rocks and woods to utter.'

## CHAPTER 11

'Know you then that my name is Helen, queen by birth, and hitherto possessor of the fair city and territory of Corinth. I can say no
more of myself but beloved of my people, and may justly say
beloved, since they are content to bear with my absence and folly.
But I being left by my father's death, and accepted by my people
in the highest degree that country could receive; as soon, or rather,
before that my age was ripe for it, my court quickly swarmed full
of suitors: some, perchance, loving my state, others my person; but
once* I know all of them, howsoever my possessions were in their

* *niceness*: over-scrupulosity. *once*: in short.

hearts, my beauty, such as it is, was in their mouths: many strangers of princely and noble blood, and all of mine own country to whom either birth or virtue gave courage to avow so high a desire.

'Among the rest, or rather, before the rest, was the lord Philoxenus, son and heir to the virtuous nobleman, Timotheus; which Timotheus was a man both in power, riches, parentage, and (which passed all these) goodness, and (which followed all these) love of the people, beyond any of the great men of my country. Now this son of his, I must say truly not unworthy of such a father, bending himself by all means of serviceableness to me, and setting forth of himself to win my favour, won thus far of me that in truth I less misliked him than any of the rest, which, in some proportion, my countenance delivered unto him – though, I must confess, it was a very false ambassador if it delivered at all any affection, whereof my heart was utterly void, I as then esteeming myself born to rule and thinking foul scorn willingly to submit myself to be ruled.

'But while Philoxenus in good sort pursued my favour and perchance nourished himself with overmuch hope, because he found I did in some sort acknowledge his value, one time among the rest he brought with him a dear friend of his.' With that she looked upon the picture before her and straight sighed, and straight tears followed, as if the idol of duty ought to be honoured with such oblations; and then her speech stayed the tale, having brought her to that look, but that look having quite put her out of her tale.

But Palladius, greatly pitying so sweet a sorrow in a lady whom by fame he had already known and honoured, besought her for her promise sake to put silence so long unto her moaning, till she had recounted the rest of this story.

'Why,' said she, 'this is the picture of Amphialus. What need I say more to you? What ear is so barbarous but hath heard of Amphialus? Who follows deeds of arms, but everywhere finds monuments of Amphialus? Who is courteous, noble, liberal, but he that hath the example before his eyes of Amphialus? Where are all heroical parts but in Amphialus? O Amphialus, I would thou were not so excellent, or I would I thought thee not so excellent, and yet would I not that I would so.'

With that she wept again, till he again soliciting the conclusion of her story: 'Then must you,' said she, 'know the story of Amphialus, for his will is my life, his life my history; and indeed in what can I better employ my lips than in speaking of Amphialus.

'This knight, then, whose figure you see, but whose mind can be painted by nothing but by the true shape of virtue, is brother's son to Basilius, King of Arcadia, and in his childhood esteemed his heir, till Basilius, in his old years marrying a young and a fair lady, had of her those two daughters, so famous for their perfection in beauty, which put by their young cousin from that expectation. Whereupon his mother (a woman of an haughty heart, being daughter to the King of Argos) either disdaining or fearing that her son should live under the power of Basilius, sent him to that lord Timotheus, between whom and her dead husband there had passed straight bands of mutual hospitality, to be brought up in company with his son Philoxenus.

'A happy resolution for Amphialus, whose excellent nature was by this means trained on with as good education as any prince's son in the world could have, which otherwise it is thought his mother, far unworthy of such a son, would not have given him, the good Timotheus no less loving him than his own son. Well they grew in years; and shortly occasions fell aptly to try Amphialus, and all occasions were but steps for him to climb fame by. Nothing was so hard but his valour overcame; which yet still he so guided with true virtue that although no man was in our parts spoken of but he for his manhood, yet, as though therein he excelled himself, he was commonly called the courteous Amphialus. An endless thing it were for me to tell how many adventures, terrible to be spoken of, he achieved; what monsters, what giants, what conquests of countries, sometimes using policy, sometimes force, but always virtue well followed; and but followed by Philoxenus, between whom and him so fast a friendship by education was knit that at last Philoxenus, having no greater matter to employ his friendship in than to win me, therein desired and had his uttermost furtherance.

'To that purpose brought he him to my court, where truly I may justly witness with him that what his wit could conceive (and his wit can conceive as far as the limits of reason stretch) was all

directed to the setting forward the suit of his friend Philoxenus:
my ears could hear nothing from him but touching the worthiness
of Philoxenus, and of the great happiness it would be unto me to
have such a husband, with many arguments which, God knows, I
cannot well remember because I did not much believe. For why
should I use many circumstances to come to that where already I
am, and ever while I live must continue? In few words, while he
pleaded for another, he won me for himself – if at least' (with that
she sighed) 'he would account it a winning, for his fame had so
framed the way to my mind that his presence, so full of beauty,
sweetness and noble conversation, had entered there before he
vouchsafed to call for the keys. O lord, how did my soul hang at
his lips while he spake! O when he in feeling manner would describe the love of his friend, how well, thought I, doth love between those lips! When he would with daintiest eloquence stir
pity in me toward Philoxenus, 'Why sure,' said I to myself,
'Helen, be not afraid; this heart cannot want pity': and when he
would extol the deeds of Philoxenus – who indeed had but waited
of* him therein – alas, thought I, good Philoxenus, how evil doth
it become thy name to be subscribed to his letter! What should I
say? Nay, what should I not say, noble knight, who am not
ashamed, nay am delighted thus to express mine own passions?

'Days passed, his eagerness for his friend never decreased, my
affection to him ever increased. At length, in way of ordinary
courtesy, I obtained of him, who suspected no such matter, this
his picture, the only Amphialus, I fear, that I shall ever enjoy; and
grown bolder, or madder, or bold with madness, I discovered my
affection unto him. But lord, I shall never forget how anger and
courtesy at one instant appeared in his eyes when he heard that
motion; how with his blush he taught me shame. In sum, he left
nothing unassayed which might disgrace himself to grace his
friend, in sweet terms making me receive a most resolute refusal of
himself. But when he found that his presence did far more persuade for himself than his speech could do for his friend, he left
my court, hoping that forgetfulness (which commonly waits upon
absence) would make room for his friend, to whom he would not

* *waited of:* been a follower of.

utter thus much, I think, for a kind fear not to grieve him; or perchance, though he cares little for me, of a certain honourable gratefulness not yet to discover* so much of my secrets; but, as it should seem, meant to travel into far countries until his friend's affection either ceased or prevailed. But within a while, Philoxenus came to see how onward the fruits were of his friend's labour, when – as in truth I cared not much how he took it – he found me sitting, beholding this picture I know not with how affectionate countenance but I am sure with a most affectionate mind. I straight found jealousy and disdain took hold of him; and yet the forward pain of mine own heart made me so delight to punish him whom I esteemed the chiefest let* in my way, that when he with humble gesture and vehement speeches sued for my favour, I told him that I would hear him more willingly if he would speak for Amphialus as well as Amphialus had done for him. He never answered me, but pale and quaking went straight away; and straight my heart misgave me some evil success. And yet, though I had authority enough to have stayed him (as in these fatal things it falls out that the high-working powers make second causes unwittingly accessory to their determinations) I did no further but sent a footman of mine, whose faithfulness to me I well knew, from place to place to follow him and bring me word of his proceedings, which, alas, have brought forth that which I fear I must ever rue.

'For he had travelled scarce a day's journey out of my country but that, not far from this place, he overtook Amphialus who, by succouring a distressed lady, had been here stayed, and by and by called him to fight with him, protesting that one of them two should die. You may easily judge how strange it was to Amphialus, whose heart could accuse itself of no fault but too much affection toward him, which he (refusing to fight with him) would fain have made Philoxenus understand. But, as my servant since told me, the more Amphialus went back, the more he followed, calling him traitor and coward, yet never telling the cause of this strange alteration.

' "Ah Philoxenus," said Amphialus, "I know I am no traitor,

* *discover*: reveal. *let*: obstacle.

and thou well knowest I am no coward: but I pray thee content thyself with this much, and let this satisfy thee that I love thee, since I bear thus much of thee."

'But he, leaving words, drew his sword and gave Amphialus a great blow or two which, but for the goodness of his armour, would have slain him; and yet so far did Amphialus contain himself, stepping aside, and saying to him,

' "Well, Philoxenus, and thus much villainy am I content to put up, not any longer for thy sake (whom I have no cause to love since thou dost injure me and wilt not tell me the cause) but for thy virtuous father's sake to whom I am so much bound. I pray thee go away and conquer thy own passions and thou shalt make me soon yield to be thy servant."

'But he would not attend to his words, but still strake so fiercely at Amphialus that in the end, nature prevailing above determination, he was fain to defend himself, and withal so to offend him that by an unlucky blow the poor Philoxenus fell dead at his feet, having had time only to speak some words whereby Amphialus knew it was for my sake: which when Amphialus saw, he forthwith gave such tokens of true-felt sorrow that, as my servant said, no imagination could conceive greater woe but that by and by an unhappy occasion made Amphialus pass* himself in sorrow. For Philoxenus was but newly dead, when there comes to the same place the aged and virtuous Timotheus, who, having heard of his son's sudden and passionate manner of parting from my court, had followed him as speedily as he could, but, alas, not so speedily but that he found him dead before he could overtake him. Though my heart be nothing but a stage for tragedies, yet, I must confess, it is even unable to bear the miserable representation thereof, knowing Amphialus and Timotheus as I have done. Alas, what sorrow, what amazement, what shame was in Amphialus when he saw his dear foster-father find him the killer of his only son! In my heart, I know he wished mountains had lain upon him to keep him from that meeting. As for Timotheus, sorrow of his son and, I think principally, unkindness of Amphialus so devoured his vital spirits that, able to say no more but "Amphialus, Amphialus, have I – " he sank to the earth and presently died.

* *pass:* exceed.

'But not my tongue, though daily used to complaints; no, nor if my heart (which is nothing but sorrow) were turned to tongues, durst it undertake to show the unspeakableness of his grief. But (because this serves to make you know my fortune) he threw away his armour, even this which you have now upon you, which at the first sight I vainly hoped he had put on again; and then, as ashamed of the light, he ran into the thickest of the woods, lamenting, and even crying out so pitifully that my servant, though of a fortune not used to much tenderness, could not refrain weeping when he told it me. He once overtook him; but Amphialus drawing his sword, which was the only part of his arms (God knows to what purpose) he carried about him, threatened to kill him if he followed him, and withal bade him deliver this bitter message, that he well enough found I was the cause of all this mischief, and that if I were a man, he would go over the world to kill me; but bade me assure myself that of all creatures in the world he most hated me. Ah, Sir knight (whose ears I think by this time are tired with the rugged ways of these misfortunes) now weigh my case, if at least you know what love is. For this cause have I left my country, putting in hazard how my people will in time deal by me, adventuring what perils or dishonours might ensue, only to follow him who proclaimeth hate against me, and to bring my neck unto him, if that may redeem my trespass and assuage his fury. And now, Sir,' said she, 'you have your request: I pray you take pains to guide me to the next town, that there I may gather such of my company again as your valour hath left me.'

Palladius willingly condescended; but ere they began to go, there came Clitophon who, having been something hurt by one of them, had pursued him a good way: at length overtaking him and ready to kill him, understood they were servants to the fair queen Helen, and that the cause of this enterprise was for nothing but to make Amphialus prisoner whom they knew their mistress sought, for she concealed her sorrow nor cause of her sorrow from nobody. But Clitophon, very sorry for this accident, came back to comfort the queen, helping such as were hurt in the best sort that he could, and framing friendly constructions of this rashly undertaken enmity; when in comes another, till that time unseen, all armed, with his beaver down, who first looking round about upon the company, as soon as he spied Palladius, he drew his sword, and making no other prologue, let fly at him. But Palladius, sorry for so much harm as had already happened, sought rather to retire and ward, thinking he might be someone that belonged to the fair queen whose case in his heart he pitied. Which Clitophon seeing, stepped between them, asking the new-come knight the cause of his quarrel, who answered him that he would kill that thief who had stolen away his master's armour, if he did not restore it. With that Palladius looked upon him and saw that he of the other side had Palladius' own armour upon him.

'Truly,' said Palladius, 'if I have stolen this armour, you did not buy that; but you shall not fight with me upon such a quarrel. You shall have this armour willingly, which I did only put on to do honour to the owner.'

But Clitophon straight knew by his words and voice that it was Ismenus, the faithful and diligent page of Amphialus; and therefore telling him that he was Clitophon, and willing him to acknowledge his error to the other, who deserved all honour, the young gentleman pulled off his head-piece and, lighting, went to kiss Palladius' hands, desiring him to pardon his folly caused by extreme grief, which easily might bring forth anger.

'Sweet gentleman,' said Palladius, 'you shall only make me this amends, that you shall carry this your lord's armour from me to him, and tell him from an unknown knight, who admires his worthiness, that he cannot cast a greater mist over his glory than by being unkind to so excellent a princess as this queen is.'

Ismenus promised he would, as soon as he durst find his master; and with that went to do his duty to the queen, whom in all these encounters astonishment made hardy. But as soon as she saw Ismenus, looking to her picture, 'Ismenus,' said she, 'here is my lord; where is yours? Or come you to bring me some sentence of death from him? If it be so, welcome be it. I pray you speak, and speak quickly.'

'Alas, Madam,' said Ismenus, 'I have lost my lord;' – with that tears came into his eyes – 'for as soon as the unhappy combat was concluded with the death both of father and son, my master, casting off his armour, went his way, forbidding me upon pain of death to follow him. Yet divers days I followed his steps, till lastly* I found him, having newly met with an excellent spaniel belonging to his dead companion Philoxenus. The dog straight fawned on my master for old knowledge, but never was there thing more pitiful than to hear my master blame the dog for loving his master's murderer, renewing afresh his complaints with the dumb counsellor, as if they might comfort one another in their miseries. But my lord, having spied me, rase up in such rage that in truth I feared he would kill me: yet as then he said only, if I would not displease him, I should not come near him till he sent for me: too hard a commandment for me to disobey. I yielded, leaving him only waited on by his dog, and, as I think, seeking out the most solitary places that this or any other country can grant him: and I, returning where I had left his armour, found another instead thereof, and (disdaining, I must confess, that any should bear the armour of the best knight living) armed myself therein to play the fool, as even now I did.'

'Fair Ismenus,' said the queen, 'a fitter messenger could hardly be to unfold my tragedy. I see the end, I see my end.'

With that, sobbing, she desired to be conducted to the next town, where Palladius left her to be waited on by Clitophon, at Palladius' earnest entreaty, who desired alone to take that melancholy course of seeking his friend; and therefore changing armours again with Ismenus, who went withal to a castle belonging to his master, he continued his quest for his friend Daiphantus.

## CHAPTER 12

So directed he his course to Laconia, as well among the Helots as Spartans. There indeed he found his fame flourishing,* his monuments engraved in marble, and yet more durably in men's memories; but the universal lamenting his absented presence assured him of his present absence. Thence into the Elean province, to see whether at the Olympian games there celebrated he might in such concourse bless his eyes with so desired an encounter: but that huge and sportful assembly grew to him a tedious loneliness, es-

* *lastly:* eventually, *his fame flourishing:* i.e. Pyrocles' fame.

teeming nobody found, since Daiphantus was lost. Afterwards he passed through Achaia and Sicyonia, to the Corinthians, proud of their two seas, to learn whether by the strait of that Isthmus it were possible to know of his passage. But finding every place more dumb than other to his demands, and remembering that it was late-taken love which had wrought this new course, he returned again, after two months travel in vain, to make a fresh search in Arcadia; so much the more as then first he bethought himself of the picture of Philoclea which, resembling her he had once loved,[1] might perhaps awake again that sleeping passion. And having already passed over the greatest part of Arcadia, one day coming under the side of the pleasant mountain Maenalus, his horse, nothing guilty of his inquisitiveness, with flat tiring taught him that discreet stays* make speedy journeys: and therefore lighting down and unbridling his horse, he himself went to repose himself in a little wood he saw thereby; where lying under the protection of a shady tree, with intention to make forgetting sleep comfort a sorrowful memory, he saw a sight which persuaded and obtained of his eyes that they would abide yet a while open. It was the appearing of a lady who, because she walked with her side toward him, he could not perfectly see her face, but so much he might see of her that was a surety for the rest that all was excellent.

Well might he perceive the hanging of her hair in fairest quantity in locks, some curled and some as it were forgotten, with such a careless care and an art so hiding art that she seemed she would lay them for a pattern whether nature simply or nature helped by cunning* be the more excellent: the rest whereof was drawn into a coronet of gold richly set with pearl, and so joined all over with gold wires and covered with feathers of divers colours that it was not unlike to an helmet, such a glittering show it bare, and so bravely it was held up from the head. Upon her body she ware a doublet of sky-colour satin, covered with plates of gold and, as it were, nailed with precious stones that in it she might seem armed. The nether part of her garment was so full of stuff and cut after such a fashion, that though the length of it reached to the ankles, yet in her going one might sometimes discern the small of her leg,

* *discreet stays*: timely rests. *cunning*: knowledge and art.

which with the foot was dressed in a short pair of crimson velvet
buskins,* in some places open, as the ancient manner was, to
show the fairness of the skin. Over all this she ware a certain
mantle made in such manner, that coming under her right arm
and covering most of that side, it had no fastening on the left side
but only upon the top of her shoulder, where the two ends met
and were closed together with a very rich jewel: the device[2]
whereof, as he after saw, was this: a Hercules made in little form,
but set with a distaff in his hand, as he once was by Omphale's
commandment, with a word in Greek but thus to be interpreted,
'Never more valiant.' On the same side, on her thigh she ware a
sword which, as it witnessed her to be an Amazon or one following that profession, so it seemed but a needless weapon, since
her other forces were without withstanding.[3]

But this lady walked out-right* till he might see her enter into a
fine close arbour. It was of trees, whose branches so lovingly interlaced one the other that it could resist the strongest violence of
eyesight; but she went into it by a door she opened, which moved
him, as warily as he could, to follow her; and by and by he might
hear her sing this song with a voice no less beautiful to his ears
than her goodliness was full of harmony to his eyes:

> Transform'd in show, but more transform'd in mind,
>     I cease to strive, with double conquest foil'd:
> For, woe is me, my powers all I find
>     With outward force, and inward treason, spoil'd.
>
> For from without came to mine eyes the blow,
>     Whereto mine inward throughts did faintly yield;
> Both these conspir'd poor reason's overthrow;
>     False in myself, thus have I lost the field.
>
> Thus are my eyes still captive to one sight;
>     Thus all my thoughts are slaves to one thought still:
> Thus reason to his servants* yields his right;
>     Thus is my power transformed to your will.
>         What marvel then I take a woman's hue,
>         Since what I see, think, know, is all but you?

*buskins: ancient Greek footwear. out-right: straight on. to his
servants: i.e. the senses.

This ditty gave him some suspicion, but the voice gave him almost assurance who the singer was; and therefore boldly thrusting open the door and entering into the arbour, he perceived indeed that it was Pyrocles thus disguised: wherewith not receiving so much joy to have found him as grief so to have found him, amazedly looking upon him (as Apollo is painted when he saw Daphne suddenly turned into a laurel) he was not able to bring forth a word; so that Pyrocles (who had as much shame as Musidorus had sorrow) rising to him, would have formed a substantial excuse, but his insinuation[4] being of blushing and his division of sighs, his whole oration stood upon a short narration what was the cause of this metamorphosis. But by that time Musidorus had gathered his spirits together, and yet casting a ghastful* countenance upon him as if he would conjure some strange spirit, he thus spake unto him:

'And is it possible that this is Pyrocles, the only young prince in the world formed by nature and framed by education to the true exercise of virtue? Or is it indeed some Amazon that hath counterfeited the face of my friend in this sort to vex me? For likelier sure I would have thought it that any outward face might have been disguised than that the face of so excellent a mind could have been thus blemished. O sweet Pyrocles, separate yourself a little, if it be possible, from yourself, and let your own mind look upon your own proceedings; so shall my words be needless and you best instructed. See with yourself how fit it will be for you in this your tender youth, born so great a prince, and of so rare not only expectation but proof, desired of your old father, and wanted of your native country, now so near your home to divert your thoughts from the way of goodness to lose, nay, to abuse your time. Lastly to overthrow all the excellent things you have done, which have filled the world with your fame; as if you should drown your ship in the long desired haven, or, like an ill player, should mar the last act of his tragedy. Remember (for I know you know it) that if we will be men, the reasonable part of our soul is to have absolute commandment, against which, if any sensual weakness arise, we are to yield all our sound forces to the overthrowing of so unnatural a rebellion; wherein how can we want

* *ghastful:* horror-stricken.

courage, since we are to deal against so weak an adversary that in itself is nothing but weakness? Nay, we are to resolve that if reason direct it, we must do it; and if we must do it, we will do it; for, to say "I cannot," is childish, and "I will not," womanish.

'And see how extremely every way you can endanger your mind: for to take this womanish habit, without you frame your behaviour accordingly, is wholly vain; your behaviour can never come kindly* from you but as the mind is proportioned unto it: so that you must resolve, if you will play your part to any purpose, whatsoever peevish imperfections are in that sex, to soften your heart to receive them – the very first down-step to all wickedness. For do not deceive yourself, my dear cousin, there is no man suddenly either excellently good or extremely evil, but grows either as he holds himself up in virtue or lets himself slide to viciousness.

'And let us see what power is the author of all these troubles: forsooth love, love, a passion, and the basest and fruitlessest of all passions. Fear breedeth wit; anger is the cradle of courage; joy openeth and enableth* the heart; sorrow, as it closeth, so it draweth it inward to look to the correcting of itself; and so all of them generally have power towards some good by the direction of reason. But this bastard Love (for indeed the name of love is most unworthily applied to so hateful humour) as it is engendered betwixt lust and idleness; as the matter it works upon is nothing but a certain base weakness which some gentle fools call a gentle heart; as his adjoined companions be unquietness, longings, fond comforts, faint discomforts, hopes, jealousies, ungrounded rages, causeless yieldings; so is the highest end it aspires unto a little pleasure with much pain before and great repentance after. But that end, how endless it runs to infinite evils, were fit enough for the matter we speak of; but not for your ears, in whom, indeed, there is so much true disposition to virtue.

'Yet thus much of his worthy effects in yourself is to be seen, that (besides your breaking laws of hospitality with Kalander and of friendship with me) it utterly subverts the course of nature in making reason give place to sense, and man to woman. And truly I think hereupon it first gat the name of love: for indeed the true love hath that excellent nature in it, that it doth transform the

* *kindly:* naturally. *enableth:* strengthens.

very essence of the lover into the thing loved, uniting and, as it were, incorporating it with a secret and inward working. And herein do these kinds of love imitate the excellent; for as the love of heaven makes one heavenly, the love of virtue, virtuous, so doth the love of the world make one become worldly: and this effeminate love of a woman doth so womanize a man that, if he yield to it, it will not only make him an Amazon, but a launder,* a distaff-spinner* or whatsoever other vile occupation their idle heads can imagine and their weak hands perform.

'Therefore, to trouble you no longer with my tedious but loving words, if either you remember what you are, what you have been, or what you must be; if you consider what it is that moved you, or by what kind of creature you are moved, you shall find the cause so small, the effect so dangerous, yourself so unworthy to run into the one or to be driven by the other, that I doubt not I shall quickly have occasion rather to praise you for having conquered it than to give you further counsel how to do it.'

But in Pyrocles this speech wrought no more but that he who (before he was espied) was afraid, after (being perceived) was ashamed, now (being hardly rubbed upon*) left both fear and shame and was moved to anger. But the exceeding good will he bare to Musidorus striving with it, he thus (partly to satisfy him, but principally to loose the reins to his own motions*) made him answer:

'Cousin, whatsoever good disposition nature hath bestowed upon me, or howsoever that disposition hath been by bringing up confirmed, this must I confess, that I am not yet come to that degree of wisdom to think light of the sex of whom I have my life, since if I be anything (which your friendship rather finds than I acknowledge) I was, to come to it, born of a woman and nursed of a woman. And certainly (for this point of your speech doth nearest touch me) it is strange to see the unmanlike cruelty of mankind, who, not content with their tyrannous ambition to have brought the other's virtuous patience under them, like childish masters think their masterhood nothing without doing injury to them who (if we will argue by reason) are framed of nature with

* *launder*: washer-woman. *distaff-spinner*: flax-spinner. *hardly rubbed upon*: put under pressure. *loose* ... *motions*: relieve his own feelings.

the same parts of the mind for the exercise of virtue as we are. And for example, even this estate of Amazons (which I now for my greatest honour do seek to counterfeit) doth well witness that if generally the sweetness of their disposition did not make them see the vainness of these things which we account glorious, they neither want valour of mind, nor yet doth their fairness take away their force. And truly we men and praisers of men should remember that if we have such excellencies, it is reason to think them excellent creatures of whom we are, since a kite never brought forth a good flying hawk. But to tell you true, as I think it superfluous to use any words of such a subject which is so praised in itself as it needs no praises, so withal, I fear lest my conceit (not able to reach unto them) bring forth words which for their unworthiness may be a disgrace to them I so inwardly honour. Let this suffice, that they are capable of virtue: and virtue, you yourselves say, is to be loved, and I too, truly. But this I willingly confess, that it likes me much better when I find virtue in a fair lodging than when I am bound to seek it in an ill-favoured creature, like a pearl in a dung-hill. As for my fault of being an uncivil guest to Kalander, if you could feel what an inward guest myself am host unto, you would think it very excusable, in that I rather perform the duties of an host than the ceremonies of a guest. And for my breaking the laws of friendship with you, which I would rather die than effectually do, truly I could find in my heart to ask you pardon for it but that your now handling of me gives me reason to confirm my former dealing.'

And here Pyrocles stayed as to breathe himself, having been transported with a little vehemency, because it seemed him Musidorus had over-bitterly glanced against the reputation of womankind: but then quieting his countenance as well as out of an unquiet mind it might be, he thus proceeded on:

'And poor Love,' said he, 'dear cousin, is little beholding unto you, since you are not contented to spoil it of the honour of the highest power of the mind which notable men have attributed unto it; but you deject it below all other passions, in truth somewhat strangely, since, if love receive any disgrace, it is by the company of these passions you prefer before it. For those kinds of bitter objections (as that lust, idleness, and a weak heart should

be, as it were, the matter and form of love) rather touch me, dear
Musidorus, than love; but I am good witness of mine own imperfections, and therefore will not defend myself. But herein I must
say you deal contrary to yourself: for if I be so weak, then can you
not with reason stir me up as you did by remembrance of my own
virtue; or if indeed I be virtuous, then must you confess that love
hath his working in a virtuous heart; and so no doubt hath it,
whatsoever I be: for, if we love virtue, in whom shall we love it
but in a virtuous creature – without your meaning be,* I should
love this word "Virtue" where I see it written in a book! Those
troublesome effects you say it breeds be not the faults of love but
of him that loves, as an unable* vessel to bear such a liquor; like
evil eyes not able to look on the sun, or like a weak brain, soonest
overthrown with the best wine. Even that heavenly love you
speak of is accompanied in some hearts with hopes, griefs,
longings and despairs. And in that heavenly love, since there are
two parts – the one the love itself, the other the excellency of the
thing loved – I, not able at the first leap to frame both in me, do
now, like a diligent workman, make ready the chief instrument
and first part of that great work, which is love itself; which when
I have a while practised in this sort, then you shall see me turn it
to greater matters. And thus gently you may, if it please you,
think of me. Neither doubt you because I wear a woman's apparel
I will be the more womanish, since I assure you, for all my apparel, there is nothing I desire more than fully to prove myself a
man in this enterprise. Much might be said in my defence, much
more for love, and most of all for that divine creature which hath
joined me and love together. But these disputations are fitter for
quiet schools than my troubled brains, which are bent rather in
deeds to perform than in words to defend the noble desire that
possesseth me.'

'O lord,' said Musidorus, 'how sharp-witted you are to hurt
yourself!'

'No,' answered he, 'but it is the hurt you speak of which makes
me so sharp-witted.'

* *without your meaning be:* unless you mean. *unable:* unfit.

'Even so,' said Musidorus, 'as every base occupation makes one sharp in that practice and foolish in all the rest.'

'Nay rather,' answered Pyrocles, 'as each excellent thing, once well-learned, serves for a measure of all other knowledges.'

'And is that become,' said Musidorus, 'a measure for other things which never received measure in itself?'

'It is counted without measure,' answered Pyrocles, 'because the workings of it are without measure; but otherwise, in nature it hath measure, since it hath an end allotted unto it.'

'The beginning being so excellent,' said Musidorus, 'I would gladly know the end.'

'Enjoying,' answered Pyrocles with a deep sigh.

'O,' said Musidorus, 'now set you forth the baseness of it, since if it end in enjoying, it shows all the rest was nothing.'

'You mistake me,' answered Pyrocles, 'I spake of the end to which it is directed; which end ends not, no sooner than the life.'

'Alas, let your own brain disenchant you,' said Musidorus.

'My heart is too far possessed,' said Pyrocles.

'But the head gives you direction, 'said Musidorus.

'And the heart gives me life,' answered Pyrocles.

But Musidorus was so grieved to see his well-beloved friend obstinate, as he thought, to his own destruction, that it forced him with more than accustomed vehemency to speak these words.

'Well, well,' said he, 'you list to abuse yourself. It was a very white and red virtue which you could pick out of a painterly gloss* of a visage.⁵ Confess the truth, and you shall find the utmost was but beauty, a thing, which though it be in as great excellency in yourself as may be in any, yet I am sure you make no further reckoning of it than of an outward fading benefit Nature bestowed upon you. And yet such is your want of a true grounded virtue, which must be like itself in all points, that what you wisely account a trifle in yourself, you fondly become a slave unto in another. For my part I now protest I have left nothing unsaid which my wit could make me know, or my most entire friendship to you requires of me. I do now beseech you even for the love betwixt us (if this other love have left any in you towards

* *gloss*: deceptive appearance.

me) and for the remembrance of your old careful father (if you can remember him that forget yourself) lastly, for Pyrocles' own sake (who is now upon the point of falling or rising) to purge yourself of this vile infection. Otherwise give me leave to leave off this name of friendship as an idle title of a thing which cannot be where virtue is abolished.'

The length of these speeches before had not so much cloyed Pyrocles, though he were very impatient of long deliberations, as this last farewell of him he loved as his own life did wound his soul. For thinking himself afflicted, he was the apter to conceive unkindness deeply; insomuch that shaking his head, and delivering some show of tears, he thus uttered his griefs:

'Alas,' said he, 'Prince Musidorus, how cruelly you deal with me. If you seek the victory, take it, and, if you list, the triumph. Have you all the reason of the world, and with me remain all the imperfections, yet such as I can no more lay from me than the crow can be persuaded by the swan to cast off all his black feathers. But truly you deal with me like a physician that, seeing his patient in a pestilent fever, should chide him instead of ministering help, and bid him be sick no more; or rather like such a friend that, visiting his friend condemned to perpetual prison and laden with grievous fetters, should will him to shake off his fetters or he would leave him. I am sick, and sick to the death. I am prisoner, neither is there any redress but by her to whom I am a slave. Now, if you list, leave him that loves you in the highest degree: but remember ever to carry this with you, that you abandon your friend in his greatest extremity.'

And herewith the deep wound of his love, being rubbed afresh with this new unkindness, began, as it were, to bleed again in such sort that he was unable to bear it any longer; but gushing out abundance of tears, and crossing his arms over his woeful heart, as if his tears had been out-flowing blood, his arms an over-pressing burden, he sunk down to the ground. Which sudden trance went so to the heart of Musidorus that, falling down by him and kissing the weeping eyes of his friend, he besought him not to make account of his speech which, if it had been over-vehement, yet was it to be borne withal, because it came out of a love much more vehement: that he had not thought fancy could have received so deep a wound; but now finding in him the force of it, he would no further contrary it but employ all his service to medicine it in such sort as the nature of it required. But even this kindness made Pyrocles the more melt in the former unkindness, which his manlike tears well showed, with a silent look upon Musidorus, as who should say: 'And is it possible that Musidorus should threaten to leave me?'; and this struck Musidorus' mind and senses so dumb, too, that for grief being not able to say anything, they rested with their eyes placed one upon another, in such sort as might well paint out the true passion of unkindness to be never aright but betwixt them that most dearly love.

And thus remained they a time, till at length Musidorus, embracing him, said 'And will you thus shake off your friend?'

'It is you that shake me off,' said Pyrocles, 'being for my unperfectness unworthy of your friendship.'

'But this,' said Musidorus, 'shows you more unperfect, to be cruel to him that submits himself unto you. But since you are unperfect,' said he, smiling, 'it is reason you be governed by us wise and perfect men. And that authority will I begin to take upon me with three absolute commandments: the first, that you increase not your evil with further griefs: the second, that you love her with all the powers of your mind: and the last commandment shall be, you command me to do what service I can towards the attaining of your desires.'

Pyrocles' heart was not so oppressed with the two mighty passions of love and unkindness but that it yielded to some mirth at this commandment of Musidorus that he should love; so that something clearing his face from his former shows of grief: 'Well,' said he, 'dear cousin, I see by the well choosing of your commandments that you are far fitter to be a prince than a counsellor, and therefore I am resolved to employ all my endeavour to obey you, with this condition, that the commandments you command me to lay upon you shall only be, that you continue to love me, and look upon my imperfections with more affection than judgement.'

'Love you?' said he. 'Alas, how can my heart be separated from the true embracing of it without it burst by being too full of it? But,' said he, 'let us leave off these flowers of new begun friendship: and now I pray you again tell me, but tell it me fully, omitting no circumstance, the story of your affections, both beginning and proceeding, assuring yourself that there is nothing so great which I will fear to do for you, nor nothing so small which I will disdain to do for you. Let me, therefore, receive a clear understanding, which many times we miss while those things we account small, as a speech or a look, are omitted, like as a whole sentence may fail of his congruity by wanting one particle. Therefore between friends all must be laid open, nothing being superfluous nor tedious.'

'You shall be obeyed,' said Pyrocles, 'and here are we in as fit a place for it as may be; for this arbour nobody offers to come into but myself, I using it as my melancholy retiring place, and therefore that respect is borne unto it. Yet if by chance any should come, say that you are a servant sent from the queen of the Amazons to seek me, and then let me alone for the rest.' So sat they down, and Pyrocles thus said.

## CHAPTER 13

'Cousin,' said he, 'then began the fatal overthrow of all my liberty when, walking among the pictures in Kalander's house, you yourself delivered unto me what you had understood of Philoclea; who much resembling (though I must say much surpassing) the lady Zelmane whom so well I loved, there were mine eyes infected, and at your mouth did I drink my poison. Yet alas, so sweet was it unto me, that I could not be contented till Kalander had made it more and more strong with his declaration. Which the more I questioned, the more pity I conceived of her unworthy fortune; and when with pity once my heart was made tender, according to the aptness of the humour, it received quickly a cruel impression of that wonderful passion which to be defined is impossible, because no words reach to the strange nature of it. They only know it, which inwardly feel it: it is called love.

'Yet did I not, poor wretch, at first know my disease, thinking it only such a wonted kind of desire to see rare sights, and my pity to be no other but the fruits of a gentle nature. But even this arguing with myself came of further thoughts, and the more I argued the more my thoughts increased. Desirous I was to see the place where she remained, as though the architecture of the lodges would have been much for my learning; but more desirous to see herself, to be judge, forsooth, of the painter's cunning – for thus at the first did I flatter myself, as though my wound had been no deeper. But when within short time I came to the degree of uncertain wishes and that those wishes grew to unquiet longings; when I could fix my thoughts upon nothing but that within little varying they should end with Philoclea; when each thing I saw seemed to figure out some part of my passions; when even Parthenia's fair face became a lecture to me of Philoclea's imagined beauty; when I heard no word spoken but that methought it carried the sound of Philoclea's name; then, indeed, then I did yield to the burden, finding myself prisoner before I had leisure to arm myself, and that I might well, like the spaniel, gnaw upon the chain that ties him, but I should sooner mar my teeth than procure liberty.

'Yet I take to witness the eternal spring of virtue that I had never read, heard nor seen anything, I had never any taste of philosophy nor inward feeling in myself which for a while I did not call to my succour. But, alas, what resistance was there, when ere long my very reason was, you will say, corrupted – I must confess, conquered – and that methought even reason did assure me that all eyes did degenerate from their creation which did not honour such beauty? Nothing in truth could hold any plea with it but the reverend friendship I bare unto you. For as it went against my heart to break anyway from you, so did I fear, more than any assault, to break it to you; finding (as it is indeed) that to a heart fully resolute, counsel is tedious but reprehension is loathsome, and that there is nothing more terrible to a guilty heart than the eye of a respected friend. This made me determine with myself (thinking it a less fault in friendship to do a thing without your knowledge than against your will) to take this secret course: which conceit was most builded up in me the last day of my parting and speaking with you, when upon your speech with me and my but naming love, when else perchance I would have gone further, I saw your voice and countenance so change as it assured me my revealing it should but purchase your grief with my cumber;* and therefore, dear Musidorus, even ran away from thy well-known chiding. For having written a letter, which I know not whether you found or no, and taking my chief jewels with me, while you were in the midst of your sport I got a time, as I think, unmarked by any, to steal away I cared not whither so I might escape you.

'And so came I to Ithonia in the province of Messenia, where, lying secret, I put this in practice which before I had devised. For remembering by Philanax's letter and Kalander's speech how obstinately Basilius was determined not to marry his daughters, and therefore fearing lest any public dealing should rather increase her captivity than further my love, love (the refiner of invention) had put in my head thus to disguise myself that under that mask I might, if it were possible, get access; and what access could bring forth commit to fortune and industry, determining to bear the countenance of an Amazon. Therefore in the closest manner I could, naming myself Zelmane for that dear lady's sake to whose memory I am so much bound, I caused this apparel to be made, and bringing it near the lodges which are hard at hand, by night thus dressed myself, resting till occasion might make me to be found by them whom I sought; which the next morning happened as well as my own plot could have laid it. For after I had run over the whole pedigree of my thoughts, I gave myself to sing a little, which, as you know, I ever delighted in, so now especially – whether it be the nature of this clime to stir up poetical fancies, or rather as I think, of love, whose scope, being pleasure, will not so much as utter his griefs but in some form of pleasure.

'But I had sung very little, when (as I think, displeased with my bad music) comes master Dametas with a hedging bill in his hand, chafing* and swearing by the pantable* of Pallas and such other oaths as his rustical bravery could imagine; and when he saw me, I assure you my beauty was no more beholding to him than my harmony; for leaning his hands upon his bill and his chin upon his hands, with the voice of one that playeth Hercules in a play but never had his fancy in his head, the first word he spake to me was, "Am not I Dametas? Why, am not I Dametas?"

'He needed not name himself, for Kalander's description had set

* *cumber*: distress. *chafing*: fuming. *pantable*: slipper.

such a note upon him as made him very notable unto me; and therefore the height of my thoughts would not descend so much as to make him any answer, but continued on my inward discourses; which he (perchance witness of his own unworthiness, and therefore the apter to think himself contemned)* took in so heinous manner, that standing upon his tiptoes, and staring as if he would have had a mote pulled out of his eye, "Why," said he, "thou woman, or boy, or both, whatsoever thou be, I tell thee here is no place for thee, get thee gone. I tell thee it is the prince's pleasure; I tell thee it is Dametas' pleasure."

'I could not choose but smile at him, seeing him look so like an ape that had newly taken a purgation; yet taking myself with the manner,[1] spake these words to myself: "O spirit," said I, "of mine, how canst thou receive any mirth in the midst of thine agonies? And thou, mirth, how darest thou enter into a mind so grown of late thy professed enemy?"

' "Thy spirit!" said Dametas, "Dost thou think me a spirit? I tell thee I am Basilius' officer, and have charge of him and his daughters."

' "O only pearl," said I, sobbing, "that so vile an oyster should keep thee!"

' "By the comb case of Diana," sware Dametas, "this woman is mad. Oysters and pearls! Dost thou think I will buy oysters? I tell thee once again, get thee packing," and with that lifted up his bill to hit me with the blunt end of it; but indeed that put me quite out of my lesson, so that I forgot all Zelmaneship, and drawing out my sword, the baseness of the villain yet made me stay my hand; and he – who, as Kalander told me, from his childhood ever feared the blade of a sword – ran backward with his hands above his head at least twenty paces, gaping and staring with the very grace, I think, of the clowns that by Latona's prayers were turned into frogs.[2]

'At length staying, finding himself without the compass* of blows, he fell to a fresh scolding, in such mannerly manner as might well show he had passed through the discipline of a tavern. But seeing me walk up and down without marking what he said, he went his way, as I perceived after, to Basilius; for within a

* *contemned*: despised. *compass*: range.

while he came unto me, bearing indeed shows in his countenance of an honest and well-minded gentleman, and with as much courtesy as Dametas with rudeness saluting me:

' "Fair lady," said he, "it is nothing strange that such a solitary place as this should receive solitary persons, but much do I marvel how such a beauty as yours is should be suffered to be thus alone."

'I, that now knew it was my part to play, looking with a grave majesty upon him, as if I found in myself cause to be reverenced, "They are never alone," said I, "that are accompanied with noble thoughts."

' "But those thoughts," replied Basilius, "cannot in this your loneliness neither warrant you from suspicion in others nor defend you from melancholy in yourself."

'I then showing a mislike that he pressed me so far, "I seek no better warrant," said I, "than my own conscience, nor no greater pleasure than my own contentation."*

' "Yet virtue seeks to satisfy others," said Basilius.

' "Those that be good," said I, "and they will be satisfied as long as they see no evil."

' "Yet will the best in this country," said Basilius, "suspect so excellent beauty being so weakly guarded."

' "Then are the best but stark naught," answered I, "for open suspecting others comes of secret condemning themselves. But in my country, whose manners I am in all places to maintain and reverence, the general goodness which is nourished in our hearts makes every one think the strength of virtue in another whereof they find the assured foundation in themselves."

' "Excellent lady," said he, "you praise so greatly, and yet so wisely, your country that I must needs desire to know what the nest is out of which such birds do fly."

' "You must first deserve it," said I, "before you may obtain it."

' "And by what means," said Basilius, "shall I deserve to know your estate?"

' "By letting me first know yours," answered I.

' "To obey you," said he, "I will do it; although it were so much more reason yours should be known first, as you do deserve in all points to be preferred. Know you, fair lady, that my name is

* *contentation*: satisfaction.

144

Basilius, unworthily lord of this country. The rest, either fame hath already brought to your ears or (if it please you to make this place happy by your presence) at more leisure you shall understand of me."

'I that from the beginning assured myself it was he, but would not seem I did so, to keep my gravity the better, making a piece of reverence unto him, "Mighty prince," said I, "let my not knowing you serve for the excuse of my boldness; and the little reverence I do you, impute it to the manner of my country, which is the invincible land of the Amazons: myself niece to Senicia, queen thereof, lineally descended of the famous Penthesilea slain by the bloody hand of Pyrrhus. I, having in this my youth determined to make the world see the Amazons' excellencies as well in private as in public virtue, have passed some dangerous adventures in divers countries till the unmerciful sea deprived me of my company; so that shipwreck casting me not far hence, uncertain wandering brought me to this place."

'But Basilius (who now began to taste of that, which since he hath swallowed up, as I will tell you) fell to more cunning entreating my abode than any greedy host would use to well-paying passengers.* I thought nothing could shoot righter at the mark of my desires; yet had I learned already so much, that it was against my womanhood to be forward in my own wishes. And therefore he (to prove whether intercessions in fitter mouths might better prevail) commanded Dametas to bring forthwith his wife and daughters thither; three ladies, although of diverse, yet all of excellent beauty.

'His wife in grave matron-like attire, with countenance and gesture suitable and of such fairness (being in the strength of her age) as (if her daughters had not been by) might with just price have purchased admiration; but they being there, it was enough that the most dainty eye would think her a worthy mother of such children. The fair Pamela, whose noble heart I find doth greatly disdain that the trust of her virtue is reposed in such a lout's hands as Dametas, had yet, to show an obedience, taken on shepherdish apparel, which was but of russet-cloth cut after their fashion, with a straight body, open breasted, the nether part full

*passengers: travellers.*

of pleats, with long and wide sleeves: but believe me she did apparel her apparel, and with the preciousness of her body made it most sumptuous. Her hair at the full length wound about with gold lace, only by the comparison to show how far her hair doth excel in colour: betwixt her breasts, which sweetly rase up like two fair mountainets in the pleasant vale of Tempe, there hung a very rich diamond set but in a black horn; the word I have since read is this: "Yet still myself."[3] And thus particularly have I described them, because you may know that mine eyes are not so partial but that I marked them too.

'But when the ornament of the earth, the model of heaven, the triumph of Nature, the life of beauty,* the queen of love, young Philoclea appeared in her nymph-like apparel, so near nakedness as one might well discern part of her perfections, and yet so apparelled as did show she kept best store of her beauty to herself: her hair (alas, too poor a word! Why should I not rather call them her beams!) drawn up into a net, able to have caught Jupiter when he was in the form of an eagle;[4] her body (O sweet body!) covered with a light taffeta garment, so cut as the wrought smock came through it in many places, enough to have made your restrained imagination have thought what was under it: with the cast of her black eyes – black indeed, whether nature so made them that we might be the more able to behold and bear their wonderful shining, or that she, goddess-like, would work this miracle with herself in giving blackness the price above all beauty – then, I say, indeed methought the lilies grew pale for envy; the roses methought blushed to see sweeter roses in her cheeks, and the apples methought fell down from the trees to do homage to the apples of her breast. Then the clouds gave place that the heavens might more freely smile upon her – at the least the clouds of my thoughts quite vanished, and my sight, then more clear and forcible than ever, was so fixed there that, I imagine, I stood like a well-wrought image with some life in show but none in practice. And so had I been like enough to have stayed long time but that Gynecia stepping between my sight and the only Philoclea, the change of object made me recover my senses so that I could with reasonable good manner receive the salutation of her and of the Princess

* life of beauty: '93 text. '90, 'light'.

Pamela, doing them yet no further reverence than one princess useth to another. But when I came to the never-enough praised Philoclea, I could not but fall down on my knees, and taking by force her hand and kissing it, I must confess, with more than womanly ardency, "Divine lady," said I, "let not the world nor these great princesses marvel to see me, contrary to my manner, do this especial honour unto you, since all, both men and women, do owe this to the perfection of your beauty."

'But she, blushing like a fair morning in May at this my singularity, and causing me to rise, "Noble lady," said she, "it is no marvel to see your judgement much mistaken in my beauty, since you begin with so great an error as to do more honour unto me than to them to whom I myself owe all service."

' "Rather," answered I with a bowed down countenance, "that shows the power of your beauty which forced me to do such an error, if it were an error."

' "You are so well acquainted," said she sweetly, most sweetly smiling, "with your own beauty that it makes you easily fall into the discourse of beauty."

' "Beauty in me?" said I, truly sighing, "Alas, if there be any it is in my eyes, which your blessed presence hath imparted unto them."

'But then, as I think, Basilius willing her so to do, "Well," said she, "I must needs confess I have heard that it is a great happiness to be praised of hem hat are mos praiseworthy; and well I find that you are an invincible Amazon since you will overcome, though in a wrong matter. But if my beauty be anything, then let it obtain thus much of you, that you will remain some while in this company to ease your own travail and our solitariness."

' "First let me die," said I, "before any word spoken by such a mouth should come in vain."

'And thus with some other words of entertaining was my staying concluded, and I led among them to the lodge: truly a place for pleasantness, not unfit to flatter solitariness; for it being set upon such an unsensible* rising of the ground as you are come to a pretty height before almost you perceive that you ascend, it gives the eye lordship over a good large circuit, which according to the

* *unsensible*: imperceptible.

nature of the country, being diversified between hills and dales, woods and plains, one place more clear, another more darksome, it seems a pleasant picture of nature, with lovely lightsomeness and artificial shadows. The lodge is of a yellow stone, built in the form of a star, having round about a garden framed into like points; and beyond the garden, ridings* cut out, each answering the angles of the lodge. At the end of one of them is the other smaller lodge but of like fashion, where the gracious Pamela liveth, so that the lodge seemeth not unlike a fair comet, whose tail stretcheth itself to a star of less greatness.'

## CHAPTER 14

'So Gynecia herself bringing me to my lodging, anon* after, I was invited and brought down to sup with them in the garden, a place not fairer in natural ornaments than artificial inventions, wherein is a banqueting-house among certain pleasant trees, whose heads seemed curled with the wrappings about of vine branches. The table was set near to an excellent water-work; for by the casting of the water in most cunning manner, it makes, with the shining of the sun upon it, a perfect rainbow, not more pleasant to the eye than to the mind so sensibly to see the proof of the heavenly Iris.[1] There were birds also made so finely that they did not only deceive the sight with their figure, but the hearing with their songs which the watery instruments did make their gorge deliver. The table at which we sat was round, which being fast to the floor whereon we sat, and that divided from the rest of the buildings, with turning a vice* – which Basilius at first did to make me sport – the table and we about the table did all turn round by means of water which ran under and carried it about as a mill. But alas, what pleasure did it to me to make divers times the full circle round about, since Philoclea, being also set, was carried still in equal distance from me, and that only my eyes did overtake her, which (when the table was stayed and we began to feed) drank much more eagerly of her beauty than my mouth did of any other liquor. And so was my common sense[2] deceived, being chiefly bent to her, that as I

* *ridings*: tracks cut out of woodland. *anon*: straightway. *vice*: mechanical device.

148

drank the wine and withal stole a look on her, me seemed I tasted her deliciousness. But alas, the one thirst was much more inflamed than the other quenched. Sometimes my eyes would lay themselves open to receive all the darts she did throw, sometimes close up with admiration, as if with a contrary fancy they would preserve the riches of that sight they had gotten, or cast my lids as curtains over the image of beauty her presence had painted in them. True it is that my reason, now grown a servant to passion, did yet often tell his master that he should more moderately use his delight. But he, that of a rebel was become a prince, disdained almost to allow him the place of a counsellor; so that my senses' delights being too strong for any other resolution, I did even loose the reins unto them, hoping that going for a woman, my looks would pass either unmarked or unsuspected.

'Now thus I had, as methought, well played my first act, assuring myself that under that disguisement I should find opportunity to reveal myself to the owner of my heart. But who would think it possible (though I feel it true) that in almost eight weeks' space I have lived here (having no more company but her parents, and I being familiar as being a woman, and watchful as being a lover) yet could never find opportunity to have one minute's leisure of private conference: the cause whereof is as strange as the effects are to me miserable. And, alas, this it is.

'At the first sight that Basilius had of me (I think Cupid having headed his arrows with my misfortune) he was stricken (taking me to be such as I profess) with great affection towards me, which since is grown to such a doting love that till I was fain to get this place sometimes to retire unto freely, I was even choked with his tediousness. You never saw four score years dance up and down more lively in a young lover, now as fine in his apparel as if he would make me in love with a cloak, and verse for verse with the sharpest-witted lover in Arcadia. Do you not think that this is a sallet of wormwood* while mine eyes feed upon the ambrosia of Philoclea's beauty?

'But this is not all; no, this is not the worst: for he, good man, were easy enough to be dealt with; but (as I think) love and mischief, having made a wager which should have most power in me,

* *sallet of wormwood*: bitter-tasting salad.

have set Gynecia also on such a fire towards me as will never, I fear, be quenched but with my destruction. For she, being a woman of excellent wit and of strong-working thoughts, whether she suspected me by my over-vehement shows of affection to Philoclea (which love forced me unwisely to utter, while hope of my mask foolishly encouraged me) or that she hath taken some other mark of me that I am not a woman, or what devil it is hath revealed it unto her, I know not; but so it is, that all her countenances, words, and gestures are even miserable portraitures of a desperate affection. Whereby a man may learn that these avoidings of company do but make the passions more violent when they meet with fit subjects. Truly it were a notable dumb show* of Cupid's kingdom to see my eyes, languishing with over-vehement longing, direct themselves to Philoclea; and Basilius, as busy about me as a bee and indeed as cumbersome,* making such vehement suits to me, who neither could if I would nor would if I could, help him; while the terrible wit of Gynecia, carried with the beer* of violent love, runs through us all. And so jealous is she of my love to her daughter that I could never yet begin to open my mouth to the unevitable* Philoclea but that her unwished presence gave my tale a conclusion before it had a beginning.

'And surely, if I be not deceived, I see such shows of liking and, if I be acquainted with passions, of almost a passionate liking in the heavenly Philoclea towards me, that I may hope her ears would not abhor my discourse. And for good Basilius, he thought it best to have lodged us together, but that the eternal hatefulness of my destiny made Gynecia's jealousy stop that and all other my blessings. Yet must I confess that one way her love doth me pleasure, for since it was my foolish fortune or unfortunate folly to be known by her, that keeps her from betraying me to Basilius. And thus, my Musidorus, you have my tragedy played unto you by myself, which I pray the gods may not indeed prove a tragedy.' And therewith he ended, making a full point* of a hearty sigh.

Musidorus recommended to his best discourse,* all which Pyrocles had told him, but therein he found such intricateness that

* *notable dumbshow:* pageant demonstrating Cupid's power. *cumbersome:* troublesome. *beer:* birr, force. *unevitable:* irresistible. *full point:* full stop. *recommended . . .discourse:* pondered deeply.

he could see no way to lead him out of the maze. Yet perceiving his affection so grounded that striving against it did rather anger than heal the wound, and rather call his friendship in question than give place to any friendly counsel, 'Well,' said he, 'dear cousin, since it hath pleased the gods to mingle your other excellencies with this humour of love, yet happy it is that your love is employed upon so rare a woman; for certainly a noble cause doth ease much a grievous case. But as it stands now, nothing vexeth me so much as that I cannot see wherein I can be serviceable unto you.'

'I desire no greater service of you,' answered Pyrocles, 'than that you remain secretly in this country, and sometimes come to this place, either late in the night or early in the morning, where you shall have my key to enter, because as my fortune either amends or impairs, I may declare it unto you and have your counsel and furtherance. And hereby I will of purpose lead her, that is the praise and yet the stain of all womankind, that you may have so good a view as to allow my judgement; and as I can get the most convenient time, I will come unto you; for, though by reason of yonder wood you cannot see the lodge, it is hard at hand. But now,' said she, 'it is time for me to leave you, and towards evening we will walk out of purpose hitherward: therefore keep yourself close* in that time.'

But Musidorus, bethinking himself that his horse might happen to betray them, thought it best to return for that day to a village not far off, and dispatching his horse in some sort, the next day early to come a foot thither, and so to keep that course afterwards, which Pyrocles very well liked of.

'Now farewell, dear cousin,' said he, 'from me, no more Pyrocles nor Daiphantus now, but Zelmane. Zelmane is my name; Zelmane is my title; Zelmane is the only hope of my advancement.' And with that word going out and seeing that the coast was clear, Zelmane dismissed Musidorus, who departed as full of care to help his friend as before he was to dissuade him.

*close: hidden.

## CHAPTER 15

Zelmane returned to the lodge, where (inflamed by Philoclea, watched by Gynecia, and tired by Basilius) she was like a horse desirous to run and miserably spurred, but so short reined as he cannot stir forward. Zelmane sought occasion to speak with Philoclea, Basilius with Zelmane, and Gynecia hindered them all. If Philoclea happened to sigh (and sigh she did often) as if that sigh were to be waited on, Zelmane sighed also; whereto Basilius and Gynecia soon made up four parts* of sorrow. Their affection increased their conversation, and their conversation increased their affection. The respect borne bred due ceremonies, but the affection shined so through them that the ceremonies seemed not ceremonious. Zelmane's eyes were (like children before sweetmeat) eager, but fearful of their ill-pleasing governors. Time, in one instant, seeming both short and long unto them: short, in the pleasingness of such presence; long, in the stay of their desires.

But Zelmane failed not to entice them all many times abroad because she was desirous her friend Musidorus (near whom of purpose she led them) might have full sight of them; sometimes angling to a little river near hand, which, for the moisture it bestowed upon the roots of some flourishing trees, was rewarded with their shadow. There would they sit down, and pretty wagers be made between Pamela and Philoclea which could soonest beguile silly fishes, while Zelmane protested that the fit prey for them was hearts of princes. She also had an angle* in her hand, but the taker was so taken that she had forgotten taking. Basilius in the meantime would be the cook himself of what was so caught, and Gynecia sit still, but with no still pensiveness. Now she brought them to see a seeled* dove, who, the blinder she was, the higher she strave.[1] Another time a kite, which having a gut cunningly pulled out of her and so let fly, called all the kites in that quarter, who (as oftentimes the world is deceived) thinking her prosperous when indeed she was wounded, made the poor kite find that opinion of riches* may well be dangerous.

*four parts*: as in a song for four voices. *angle*: fishing-rod. *seeled*: with eyelids stitched together. *opinion of riches*: reputation of being rich.

But these recreations were interrupted by a delight of a more gallant show; for one evening, as Basilius returned from having forced his thoughts to please themselves in such small conquests, there came a shepherd who brought him word that a gentleman desired leave to do a message from his lord unto him. Basilius granted; whereupon the gentleman came, and after the dutiful ceremonies observed in his master's name, told him that he was sent from Phalantus of Corinth to crave licence that, as he had done in many other courts, so he might in his presence defy all Arcadian knights in the behalf of his mistress' beauty who would, besides, herself in person be present to give evident proof what his lance should affirm. The conditions of his challenge were that the defendant should bring his mistress' picture, which being set by the image of Artesia (so was the mistress of Phalantus named), who in six courses should have better of the other in the judgement of Basilius, with him both the honours and the pictures should remain. Basilius, though he had retired himself into that solitary dwelling with intention to avoid rather than to accept any matters of drawing company, yet because he would entertain Zelmane that she might not think the time so gainful to him loss to her, granted him to pitch his tents for three days not far from the lodge, and to proclaim his challenge that what Arcadian knight (for none else but upon his peril was licensed to come) would defend what he honoured against Phalantus should have the like freedom of access and return.

This obtained and published, Zelmane being desirous to learn what this Phalantus was, having never known him further than by report of his good jousting, in so much as he was commonly called 'The fair man of arms'; Basilius told her that he had had occasion by one very inward with him to know in part the discourse* of his life, which was, that he was bastard brother to the fair Helen queen of Corinth, and dearly esteemed of her for his exceeding good parts, being honourably courteous and wronglessly valiant, considerately pleasant in conversation, and an excellent courtier without unfaithfulness; who (finding his sister's unpersuadable melancholy through the love of Amphialus) had for a time left her court and gone into Laconia, where, in the war

* *discourse:* course.

153

against the Helots, he had gotten the reputation of one that both durst and knew.[2] But as it was rather choice than nature that led him to matters of arms, so as soon as the spur of honour ceased, he willingly rested in peaceable delights, being beloved in all companies for his lovely qualities and (as a man may term it) winning cheerfulness; whereby to the prince and court of Laconia, none was more agreeable than Phalantus: and he, not given greatly to struggle with his own disposition, followed the gentle current of it, having a fortune sufficient to content, and he content with a sufficient fortune.

'But in that court he saw and was acquainted with this Artesia whose beauty he now defends; became her servant; said himself (and perchance thought himself) her lover. But certainly,' said Basilius, 'many times it falls out that these young companions make themselves believe they love at the first liking of a likely beauty; loving, because they will love for want of other business, not because they feel indeed that divine power which makes the heart find a reason in passion, and so, God knows, as inconstantly leave upon the next chance that beauty casts before them. So therefore taking love upon him like a fashion, he courted this lady Artesia, who was as fit to pay him in his own money as might be: for she, thinking she did wrong to her beauty if she were not proud of it, called her disdain of him chastity, and placed her honour in little setting by* his honouring her; determining never to marry but him whom she thought worthy of her, and that was one in whom all worthinesses were harboured. And to this conceit not only nature had bent her, but the bringing-up she received at my sister-in-law Cecropia had confirmed her; who, having in her widowhood taken this young Artesia into her charge because her father had been a dear friend of her dear husband's, had taught her to think that there is no wisdom but in including both heaven and earth in oneself; and that love, courtesy, gratefulness, friendship, and all other virtues are rather to be taken on than taken in oneself.[3] And so good a disciple she found of her that, liking the fruits of her own planting, she was content (if so her son could have liked of it) to have wished her in marriage to my nephew Amphialus. But I think that desire hath lost some of his heat since

* *little setting by*: setting little value on.

she hath known that such a queen as Helen is doth offer so great a price as a kingdom to buy his favour; for, if I be not deceived in my good sister Cecropia, she thinks no face so beautiful as that which looks under a crown.

'But Artesia indeed liked well of my nephew Amphialus – for I can never deem that love which in haughty hearts proceeds of a desire only to please and, as it were, peacock themselves: but yet she hath showed vehemency of desire that way, I think, because all her desires be vehement, insomuch that she hath both placed her only brother (a fine youth called Ismenus) to be his 'squire, and herself is content to wait upon my sister till she may see the uttermost what she may work in Amphialus: who being of a melancholy (though, I must say, truly courteous and noble) mind, seems to love nothing less than love; and of late, having through some adventure or inward miscontentment withdrawn himself from anybody's knowledge where he is, Artesia the easier condescended to go to the court of Laconia, whither she was sent for by the king's wife to whom she is somewhat allied.

'And there, after the war of the Helots, this knight Phalantus, at least for tongue-delight, made himself her servant, and she, so little caring as not to show mislike thereof, was content only to be noted to have a notable servant. For truly one in my court, nearly* acquainted with him, within these few days made me a pleasant description of their love, while he with cheerful looks* would speak sorrowful words, using the phrase of his affection in so high a style that Mercury* would not have wooed Venus with more magnificent eloquence; but else, neither in behaviour nor action accusing in himself any great trouble in mind whether he spde or no. And she, of the other side, well finding how little it was and not caring for more, yet taught him that often it falleth out but a foolish wittiness to speak more than one thinks.

'For she made earnest benefit of his jest, forcing him in respect of his profession to do her such services as were both cumbersome and costly unto him, while he still thought he went beyond her because his heart did not commit the idolatry. So that lastly she, I think, having in mind to make the fame of her beauty an orator

---

* *nearly*: closely. *while he with cheerful looks*: i.e. Phalantus. *Mercury*: patron of eloquence and plausible speech.

for her to Amphialus (persuading herself, perhaps, that it might fall out in him as it doth in some that have delightful meat before them, and have no stomach to it before other folks praise it) she took the advantage one day, upon Phalantus' unconscionable praisings of her and certain cast-away vows how much he would do for her sake, to arrest his word as soon as it was out of his mouth, and by the virtue thereof to charge him to go with her through all the courts of Greece, and with the challenge now made to give her beauty the principality over all other. Phalantus was entrapped, and saw round about him but could not get out. Exceedingly perplexed he was, as he confessed to him that told me the tale, not for doubt he had of himself (for indeed he had little cause, being accounted, with his lance especially, whereupon the challenge is to be tried, as perfect as any that Greece knoweth) but because he feared to offend his sister Helen; and withal, as he said, he could not so much believe his love but that he must think in his heart (whatsoever his mouth affirmed) that both she,* my daughters, and the fair Parthenia (wife to a most noble gentleman, my wife's near kinsman) might far better put in their claim for that prerogative.* But his promise had bound him prentice, and therefore it was now better with willingness to purchase thanks than with a discontented doing to have the pain and not the reward; and therefore went on as his faith rather than love did lead him.

'And now hath he already passed the courts of Laconia, Elis, Argos, and Corinth. And, as many times it happens that a good pleader makes a bad cause to prevail, so hath his lance brought captives to the triumph of Artesia's beauty such as, though Artesia be among the fairest, yet in that company were to have the pre-eminence: for in those courts many knights that had been in other far countries defended such as they had seen and liked in their travel; but their defence had been such as they had forfeited the pictures of their ladies to give a forced false testimony to Artesia's excellency. And now, lastly, is he come hither, where he hath leave to try his fortune. But I assure you, if I thought it not in due and true consideration an injurious service and churlish

* *both she:* i.e. Helen. *for that prerogative:* i.e. to be more beautiful than Artesia.

courtesy to put the danger of so noble a title in the deciding of such a dangerless combat, I would make young master Phalantus know that your eyes can sharpen a blunt lance, and that age (which my grey hairs, only gotten by the loving care of others, make seem more than it is) hath not diminished in me the power to protect an undeniable verity.'

With that he bustled up himself, as though his heart would fain have walked abroad. Zelmane with an inward smiling gave him outward thanks, desiring him to reserve his force for worthier causes.

## CHAPTER 16

So passing their time according to their wont,* they waited for the coming of Phalantus, who the next morning, having already caused his tents to be pitched near to a fair tree hard by the lodge, had upon the tree made a shield to be hanged up, which the defendant should strike that would call him to the maintaining his challenge. The impresa in the shield was a heaven full of stars, with a speech signifying that it was the beauty which gave it the praise.* Himself came in next after a triumphant chariot made of carnation-velvet enriched with purl* and pearl, wherein Artesia sat, drawn by four winged horses with artificial flaming mouths and fiery wings, as if she had newly borrowed them of Phoebus. Before her marched, two after two, certain footmen pleasantly attired, who between them held one picture after another of them that by Phalantus' well running* had lost the prize in the race of beauty, and at every pace they stayed, turning the pictures to each side so leisurely that with perfect judgement they might be discerned.

The first that came in, following the order of the time wherein they had been won, was the picture of Andromana, queen of Iberia, whom a Laconian knight (having some time and with special favour served, though some years since returned home) with more gratefulness than good fortune defended. But therein Fortune had borrowed wit; for indeed she was not comparable to

* wont: custom. impresa ... speech: heraldic device and motto carried at tournaments. purl: gold embroidery. well running: victorious jousting.

Artesia, not because she was a good deal older (for time had not yet been able to impoverish her store thereof) but an exceeding red hair with small eyes did, like ill companions, disgrace the other assembly of most commendable beauties.

Next after her was borne the counterfeit of the Princess of Elis, a lady that taught the beholders no other point of beauty but this: that as liking is not always the child of beauty, so whatsoever liketh* is beautiful; for in that visage there was neither majesty, grace, favour, nor fairness; yet she wanted not a servant that would have made her fairer than the fair Artesia. But he wrote her praises with his helmet in the dust, and left her picture to be as true a witness of his overthrow as his running was of her beauty.

After her was the goodly Artaxia, great queen of Armenia, a lady upon whom nature bestowed and well placed her most delightful colours, and, withal, had proportioned her without any fault quickly to be discovered by the senses; yet all together seemed not to make up that harmony that Cupid delights in; the reason whereof might seem a mannish countenance which overthrew that lovely sweetness, the noblest power of womankind, far fitter to prevail by parley than by battle.

Of a far contrary consideration was the representation of her that next followed, which was Erona queen of Lycia, who though of so brown a hair as no man should have injured it to have called it black, and that in the mixture of her cheeks the white did so much overcome the red – though what was, was very pure – that it came near to paleness, and that her face was a thought longer than the exact symmetrians* perhaps would allow; yet love played his part so well in every part that it caught hold of the judgement before it could judge, making it first love, and after acknowledge it fair; for there was a certain delicacy which in yielding conquered, and with a pitiful look made one find cause to crave help himself.

After her came two ladies of noble but not of royal birth. The former was named Baccha, who though very fair, and of a fatness rather to allure than to mislike, yet her breasts over-familiarly laid

---

* *liketh*: is loved. *symmetrians*: lovers of symmetry.

open, with a made countenance* about her mouth between simpering and smiling, her head bowed somewhat down, seemed to languish with over-much idleness, and with an inviting look cast upward dissuaded with too much persuading, while hope might seem to overrun desire.

The other, whose name was written Leucippe, was of a fine daintiness of beauty, her face carrying in it a sober simplicity like one that could do much good and meant no hurt, her eyes having in them such a cheerfulness as nature seemed to smile in them; though her mouth and cheeks obeyed to that pretty demureness which the more one marked the more one would judge the poor soul apt to believe, and therefore the more pity to deceive her.

Next came the queen of Laconia, one that seemed born in the confines* of beauty's kingdom; for all her lineaments were neither perfect possessioners* thereof, nor absolute strangers* thereto: but she was a queen and therefore beautiful.

But she that followed conquered indeed with being conquered, and might well have made all the beholders wait upon her triumph while herself were led captive. It was the excellently fair queen Helen, whose jacinth hair, curled by nature but intercurled by art (like a fine brook through golden sands) had a rope of fair pearl which now hiding, now hidden by the hair, did as it were play at fast and loose* each with other, mutually giving and receiving richness. In her face so much beauty and favour expressed as (if Helen had not been known) some would rather have judged it the painter's exercise to show what he could do than the counterfeiting of any living pattern; for no fault the most faultfinding wit could have found, if it were not that to the rest of the body the face was somewhat too little. But that little was such a spark of beauty as was able to inflame a world of love; for everything was full of a choice fineness, that if it wanted anything in majesty, it supplied it with increase in pleasure; and if at the first it strake not admiration, it ravished with delight. And no indifferent soul there was, which if it could resist from subjecting

---

* *a made countenance:* an affected expression. *in the confines:* born there but not a native of it. *possessioners:* permanent occupiers. *strangers:* foreigners. *fast and loose:* a cheating game whose aim is to deceive the eye.

itself to make it his princess, that would not long to have such a playfellow. As for her attire, it was costly and curious;* though the look (fixed with more sadness than it seemed nature had bestowed to any that knew her fortune) betrayed that as she used those ornaments not for herself but to prevail with another, so she feared that all would not serve.

Of a far differing, though esteemed equal, beauty was the fair Parthenia who next waited on Artesia's triumph though far better she might have sat in the throne. For in her everything was goodly and stately, yet so, that it might seem that great-mindedness was but the ensign-bearer to the humbleness. For her great grey eye, which might seem full of her own beauty, a large and exceedingly fair forehead, with all the rest of her face and body cast in the mould of nobleness, was yet so attired as might show the mistress thought it either not to deserve, or not to need any exquisite decking, having no adorning but cleanliness; and so far from all art that it was full of carelessness, unless that carelessness itself, in spite of itself, grew artificial. But Basilius could not abstain from praising Parthenia as the perfect picture of a womanly virtue and wifely faithfulness, telling withal Zelmane how he had understood that when in the court of Laconia her picture, maintained by a certain Sycionian knight, was lost through want rather of valour than justice, her husband, the famous Argalus, would in a chafe* have gone and redeemed it with a new trial. But she, more sporting than sorrowing for her undeserved champion, told her husband she desired to be beautiful in nobody's eye but his, and that she would rather mar her face as evil as ever it was than that it should be a cause to make Argalus put on armour. Then would Basilius have told Zelmane that which she already knew of the rare trial of that coupled affection: but the next picture made their mouths give place to their eyes.

It was of a young maid which sat pulling out a thorn out of a lamb's foot, with her look so attentive upon it, as if that little foot could have been the circle of her thoughts; her apparel so poor, as it had nothing but the inside to adorn it; a sheep-hook lying by her with a bottle upon it. But with all that poverty, beauty played the prince and commanded as many hearts as the greatest queen

*curious: chosen with skill. chafe: anger.

there did. Her beauty and her estate made her quickly to be known to be the fair shepherdess Urania, whom a rich knight called Lacemon, far in love with her, had unluckily defended.

The last of all in place, because last in the time of her being captive, was Zelmane, daughter to the King Plexirtus, who at the first sight seemed to have some resembling of Philoclea; but with more marking* (comparing it to the present Philoclea, who indeed had no paragon but her sister) they might see it was but such a likeness as an unperfect glass doth give, answerable enough in some features and colours, but erring in others. But Zelmane sighing, turning to Basilius, 'Alas, Sir,' said she, 'here be some pictures which might better become the tombs of their mistresses than the triumph of Artesia.'[1]

'It is true, sweetest lady,' said Basilius, 'some of them be dead, and some other captive; but that hath happened so late as it may be the knights that defended their beauty knew not so much; without* we will say (as in some hearts I know it would fall out) that death itself could not blot out the image which love hath engraven in them. But divers besides those,' said Basilius, 'hath Phalantus won, but he leaves the rest, carrying only such who either for greatness of estate or of beauty may justly glorify the glory of Artesia's triumph.'

## CHAPTER 17

Thus talked Basilius with Zelmane, glad to make any matter subject to speak of with his mistress, while Phalantus, in this pompous* manner, brought Artesia with her gentlewomen into one tent, by which he had another; where they both waited who would first strike upon the shield, while Basilius, the judge, appointed sticklers* and trumpets* to whom the other should obey. But none that day appeared, nor the next, till already it had consumed half his allowance of light; but then there came in a knight, protesting himself as contrary to him in mind as he was in apparel. For Phalantus was all in white, having in his bases and caparison* embroidered a waving water, at each side whereof he

* *with more marking*: after a closer look. *without*: unless. *pompous*: ceremonious. *sticklers*: umpires. *trumpets*: trumpeters. *bases and caparison*: ornamental skirt and saddle cloth to drape on a horse.

had nettings cast over, in which were divers fishes naturally made, and so prettily that as the horse stirred, the fishes seemed to strive and leap in the net.

But the other knight, by name Nestor, by birth an Arcadian, and in affection vowed to the fair shepherdess, was all in black, with fire burning both upon his armour and horse. His impresa in his shield was a fire made of juniper,* with this word, 'More easy and more sweet.' But this hot knight was cooled with a fall which at the third course he received of Phalantus, leaving this picture to keep company with the other of the same stamp; he going away remedilessly chafing at his rebuke. The next was Polycetes, greatly esteemed in Arcadia for deeds he had done in arms, and much spoken of for the honourable love he had long borne to Gynecia, which Basilius himself was content not only to suffer but to be delighted with, he carried it in so honourable and open plainness, setting to his love no other mark* than to do her faithful service. But neither her fair picture nor his fair running could warrant him from overthrow and her from becoming as then the last of Artesia's victories; a thing Gynecia's virtues would little have recked* at another time, nor then, if Zelmane had not seen it. But her champion went away as much discomforted as discomfited. Then Telamon for Polixena, and Eurileon for Elpine, and Leon for Zoana, all brave knights, all fair ladies, with their going down lifted up the balance of his praise for activity and hers for fairness.

Upon whose loss, as the beholders were talking, there comes into the place where they ran a shepherd stripling (for his height made him more than a boy, and his face would not allow him a man) brown of complexion, whether by nature or by the sun's familiarity, but very lovely withal[1]*; for the rest so perfectly proportioned that Nature showed she doth not like men who slubber up* matters of mean account.[2] And well might his proportion be judged, for he had nothing upon him but a pair of slops,* and upon his body a goat skin which he cast over his shoulder, doing all things with so pretty a grace that it seemed ignorance could not make him do amiss because he had a heart to do well. Holding

---

* *junipers*: burns with a sweet smell. *setting no other mark*: aiming at no other target. *recked*: cared about. *withal*: none the less. *slubber up*: deal carelessly with. *slops*: loose trousers.

in his right hand a long staff, and so coming with a look full of amiable fierceness, as in whom choler* could not take away the sweetness, he came towards the king, and making a reverence, which in him was comely because it was kindly,*

'My liege lord,' said he, 'I pray you hear a few words, for my heart will break if I say not my mind to you. I see here the picture of Urania which, I cannot tell how nor why, these men when they fall down they say is not so fair as yonder gay woman. But pray God I may never see my old mother alive if I think she be any more match to Urania than a goat is to a fine lamb, or than the dog that keeps our flock at home is like your white greyhound that pulled down the stag last day. And therefore I pray you let me be dressed as they be, and my heart gives me I shall tumble him on the earth; for indeed he might as well say that a cowslip is as white as a lily. Or else I care not, let him come with his great staff, and I with this in my hand, and you shall see what I can do to him.'

Basilius saw it was the fine shepherd Lalus, whom once he had afore him in pastoral sports, and had greatly delighted in his wit full of pretty simplicity; and therefore laughing at his earnestness, he bade him be content, since he saw the pictures of so great queens were fain to follow their champions' fortune. But Lalus, even weeping ripe,* went among the rest, longing to see somebody that would revenge Urania's wrong, and praying heartily for everybody that ran against Phalantus, then beginning to feel poverty that he could not set himself to that trial.

But by and by, even when the sun, like a noble heart, began to show his greatest countenance in his lowest estate, there came in a knight called Phebilus, a gentleman of that country, for whom hateful fortune had borrowed the dart of love to make him miserable by the sight of Philoclea. For he had even from her infancy loved her, and was stricken by her before she was able to know what quiver of arrows her eyes carried; but he loved and despaired, and the more he despaired, the more he loved. He saw his own unworthiness, and thereby made her excellency have more terrible aspect upon him. He was so secret therein as not daring to be open, that to no creature he ever spake of it; but his heart made

* *choler:* anger, the hot humour. *kindly:* natural. *weeping ripe:* almost in tears.

such silent complaints within itself that, while all his senses were attentive thereto, cunning judges might perceive his mind, so that he was known to love though he denied, or rather, was the better known because he denied it. His armour and his attire was of a sea colour; his impresa, the fish called Sepia, which being in the net casts a black ink about itself, that in the darkness thereof it may escape: his word was, 'Not so.'³ Philoclea's picture with almost an idolatrous magnificence was borne in by him. But straight jealousy was a harbinger for disdain in Zelmane's heart when she saw any but herself should be avowed a champion for Philoclea; insomuch that she wished his shame till she saw him shamed. For at the second course he was stricken quite from out of the saddle, so full of grief and rage withal that he would fain with the sword have revenged it, but that being contrary to the order set down, Basilius would not suffer; so that wishing himself in the bottom of the earth, he went his way, leaving Zelmane no less angry with his loss than she would have been with his victory. For if she thought before a rival's praise would have angered her, her lady's disgrace did make her much more forget what she then thought, while that passion reigned so much the more as she saw a pretty blush in Philoclea's cheeks betray a modest discontentment. But the night commanded truce for those sports, and Phalantus, though entreated, would not leave Artesia, who in no case would come into the house, having, as it were, sucked of Cecropia's breath a mortal mislike against Basilius.

But the night, measured by the short ell* of sleep, was soon passed over, and the next morning had given the watchful stars leave to take their rest, when a trumpet summoned Basilius to play his judge's part; which he did, taking his wife and daughters with him, Zelmane having locked her door so as they would not trouble her for that time: for already there was a knight in the field ready to prove Helen of Corinth had received great injury, both by the erring judgement of the challenger and the unlucky weakness of her former defender. The new knight was quickly known to be Clitophon (Kalander's son of Basilius' sister) by his armour which, all gilt, was so well handled that it showed like a glittering sand and gravel interlaced with silver rivers. His device he had put in

* *ell*: measure.

the picture of Helen which he defended: it was the Ermion* with a speech that signified, 'Rather dead than spotted.' But in that armour since he had parted from Helen, who would no longer his company finding him to enter into terms of affection,* he had performed so honourable actions, still seeking for his two friends by the names of Palladius and Daiphantus, that though his face were covered, his being was discovered. Which yet Basilius, who had brought him up in his court, would not seem to do,* but glad to see trial of him of whom he had heard very well, he commanded the trumpets to sound: to which the two brave knights obeying, they performed their courses, breaking their six staves* with so good both skill in the hitting and grace in the manner that it bred some difficulty in the judgement. But Basilius in the end gave sentence against Clitophon, because Phalantus had broken more staves upon the head, and that once Clitophon had received such a blow that he had lost the reins of his horse with his head well-nigh touching the crupper of the horse. But Clitophon was so angry with the judgement, wherein he thought he had received wrong, that he omitted his duty to his prince and uncle, and suddenly went his way, still in the quest of them whom as then he had left by seeking,* and so yielded the field to the next comer.

Who, coming in about two hours after, was no less marked than all the rest before, because he had nothing worth the marking. For he had neither picture nor device; his armour of as old a fashion, besides the rusty poorness, that it might better seem a monument of his grandfather's courage. About his middle he had, instead of bases, a long cloak of silk, which as unhandsomely (as it needs must) became the wearer, so that all that looked on measured his length on the earth already, since he had to meet one who had been victorious of so many gallants. But he went on towards the shield and with a sober grace strake it; but as he let his sword fall upon it, another knight, all in black, came rustling in* who strake the shield almost as soon as he, and so strongly that he brake the shield in two. The ill-appointed knight (for so the beholders called

---

* *Ermion:* ermine, noted for its white fur. *terms of affection:* fall in love. *would not seem to do:* i.e. recognize him. *staves:* lances. *left by seeking:* because the princes were at the tourney. *rustling in:* rushing in hastily.

him) angry with that (as he accounted) insolent injury to himself, hit him such a sound blow that they that looked on said it well became a rude arm. The other answered him again in the same case, so that lances were put to silence, the swords were so busy.

But Phalantus, angry of this defacing his shield, came upon the black knight and with the pommel of his sword set fire to his eyes, which presently was revenged not only by the black but the ill-apparelled knight, who disdained another should enter into his quarrel; so as who ever saw a matachin* dance to imitate fighting, this was a fight that did imitate the matachin: for they being but three that fought, everyone had two adversaries, striking him who struck the third, and revenging perhaps that of him which he had received of the other. But Basilius, rising himself, came to part them, the sticklers' authority scarcely able to persuade choleric hearers; and part them he did.

But before he could determine, comes in a fourth, halting on foot, who complained to Basilius, demanding justice on the black knight for having by force taken away the picture of Pamela from him, which in little form he ware in a tablet, and covered with silk had fastened it to his helmet, purposing, for want of a bigger, to paragon* the little one with Artesia's length, not doubting but even in that little quantity the excellency of that would shine through the weakness of the other as the smallest star doth through the whole element of fire.[4] And by the way he had met with this black knight who had, as he said, robbed him of it. The injury seemed grievous, but when it came fully to be examined, it was found that the halting knight meeting the other, asking the cause of his going thitherward and finding it was to defend Pamela's divine beauty against Artesia's, with a proud jollity commanded him to leave that quarrel only for him who was only worthy to enter into it. But the black knight obeying no such commandments, they fell to such a bickering that he gat a halting and lost his picture. This understood by Basilius, he told him he was now fitter to look to his own body than another's picture, and so, uncomforted therein, sent him away to learn of Aesculapius* that he was not fit for Venus.

* *matachin*: sword dance. *paragon*. match. *Aesculapius*: god of medicine.

But then the question arising, who should be the former against Phalantus of the black or the ill-apparelled knight (who now had gotten the reputation of some sturdy lout, he had so well defended himself); of the one side, was alleged the having a picture which the other wanted;* of the other side, the first striking the shield: but the conclusion was that the ill-apparelled knight should have the precedence, if he delivered the figure of his mistress to Phalantus; who asking him for it:

'Certainly,' said he, 'her liveliest picture, if you could see it, is in my heart, and the best comparison I could make of her is of the sun and all the other heavenly beauties. But because perhaps all eyes cannot taste the divinity of her beauty, and would rather be* dazzled than taught by the light, if it be not clouded by some meaner thing, know you then that I defend that same lady whose image Phebilus so feebly lost yesternight, and, instead of another, if you overcome me, you shall have me your slave to carry that image in your mistress' triumph.' Phalantus easily agreed to the bargain, which already he made his own.

But when it came to the trial, the ill-apparelled knight, choosing out the greatest staves in all the store, at the first course gave his head such a remembrance that he lost almost his remembrance, he himself receiving the encounter of Phalantus without any extraordinary motion; and at the second, gave him such a counterbluff, that because Phalantus was so perfect a horseman as not to be driven from the saddle, the saddle with broken girths was driven from the horse; Phalantus remaining angry and amazed, because now being come almost to the last of his promised enterprise, that disgrace befell him which he had never before known.

But the victory being by the judges given, and the trumpets witnessed to the ill-apparelled knight, Phalantus' disgrace was ingrieved* in lieu of comfort of Artesia, who telling him she never looked for other, bade him seek some other mistress. He excusing himself, and turning over the fault to Fortune, 'Then let that be your ill fortune too,' said she, 'that you have lost me.'

'Nay, truly madam,' said Phalantus, 'it shall not be so, for I think the loss of such a mistress will prove a great gain,' and so

* *wanted*: lacked. *would rather be*: would more probably be. *ingrieved*: because a source of grievance rather than of sympathy.

concluded, to the sport of Basilius to see young folks' love, that came in masked with so great pomp, go out with so little constancy. But Phalantus, first professing great service to Basilius for his courteous intermitting his solitary course for his sake, would yet conduct Artesia to the castle of Cecropia whither she desired to go, vowing in himself that neither heart nor mouth-love should ever any more entangle him. And with that resolution he left the company.

Whence all being dismissed (among whom the black knight went away repining at his luck that had kept him from winning the honour, as he knew he should have done, to the picture of Pamela) the ill-apparelled knight (who was only desired to stay because Basilius meant to show him to Zelmane) pulled off his helmet and then was known himself to be Zelmane, who that morning, as she told, while the others were busy, had stolen out to the prince's stable, which was a mile off from the lodge, had gotten a horse – they knowing it was Basilius' pleasure she should be obeyed – and borrowing that homely armour for want of a better, had come upon the spur to redeem Philoclea's picture which, she said, she could not bear (being one of that little wilderness-company) should be in captivity, if the cunning she had learned in her country of the noble Amazons could withstand it. And under that pretext fain she would have given a secret passport to her affection. But this act painted at one instant redness in Philoclea's face and paleness in Gynecia's, but brought forth no other countenances but of admiration, no speeches but of commendations; all these few, besides love, thinking they honoured themselves in honouring so accomplished a person as Zelmane, whom daily they sought with some or other sports to delight; for which purpose Basilius had, in a house not far off, servants who, though they came not uncalled, yet at call were ready.

## CHAPTER 18

And so many days were spent and many ways used, while Zelmane was like one that stood in a tree waiting a good occasion to shoot, and Gynecia a blancher* which kept the dearest deer from

* *blancher:* one who heads back the deer.

her. But the day being come on which, according to an appointed course, the shepherds were to assemble and make their pastoral sports afore Basilius, Zelmane, (fearing lest many eyes, and coming divers ways, might hap to spy Musidorus) went out to warn him thereof.

But before she could come to the arbour, she saw walking from her-ward a man in shepherdish apparel, who being in the sight of the lodge, it might seem he was allowed there. A long cloak he had on, but that cast under his right arm, wherein he held a sheep hook so finely wrought that it gave a bravery to poverty; and his raiments, though they were mean, yet received they hand-someness by the grace of the wearer, though he himself went but a kind of languishing pace, with his eyes sometimes cast up to heaven (as though his fancies strove to mount higher) sometimes thrown down to the ground (as if the earth could not bear the burden of his sorrows). At length, with a lamentable tune, he sung these few verses.

Come shepherd's weeds,* become* your master's mind:
    Yield outward show what inward change he tries:
Nor be abash'd, since such a guest you find,
    Whose strongest hope in your weak comfort lies.

Come shepherd's weeds, attend my woeful cries:
    Disuse* yourselves from sweet Menalcas' voice:[1]
For other be those tunes which sorrow ties
    From those clear notes which freely may rejoice.
      Then pour out plaint, and in one word say this:
      Helpless his plaint who spoils* himself of bliss.

And having ended, he struck himself on the breast, saying, 'O miserable wretch, whither do thy destinies guide thee?'

The voice made Zelmane hasten her pace to overtake him, which having done, she plainly perceived that it was her dear friend Musidorus; whereat marvelling not a little, she demanded of him whether the goddess of those woods had such a power to transform every body, or whether, as in all enterprises else he had done, he meant thus to match her in this new alteration.

* *weeds:* cloths. *become:* be fitting to. *Disuse:* disaccustom. *spoils:* robs himself of the possibility of.

'Alas,' said Musidorus, 'what shall I say, who am loth to say, and yet fain would have said? I find, indeed, that all is but lip-wisdom which wants experience. I now (woe is me) do try what love can do. O Zelmane, who will resist it must either have no wit, or put out his eyes. Can any man resist his creation? Certainly by love we are made, and to love we are made. Beasts only cannot discern beauty, and let them be in the roll of beasts that do not honour it.'

The perfect friendship Zelmane bare him, and the great pity she, by good trial, had of such cases, could not keep her from smiling at him, remembering how vehemently he had cried out against the folly of lovers; and therefore a little to punish him, 'Why, how now dear cousin,' said she, 'you that were last day so high in the pulpit against lovers, are you now become so mean an auditor? Remember that love is a passion, and that a worthy man's reason must ever have the masterhood.'

'I recant, I recant,' cried Musidorus, and withal falling down prostrate, 'O thou celestial, or infernal spirit of love, or what other heavenly or hellish title thou list* to have (for effects of both I find in myself) have compassion of me, and let thy glory be as great in pardoning them that be submitted to thee as in conquering those that were rebellious.'

'No, no,' said Zelmane, 'I see you well enough you make but an interlude* of my mishaps, and do but counterfeit thus to make me see the deformity of my passions. But take heed that this jest do not one day turn to earnest.'

'Now I beseech thee,' said Musidorus, taking her fast by the hand, 'even for the truth of our friendship (of which, if I be not altogether an unhappy man, thou hast some remembrance) and by those secret flames* which I know have likewise nearly* touched thee, make no jest of that which hath so earnestly pierced me through, nor let that be light to thee which is to me so burdenous that I am not able to bear it.'

Musidorus, both in words and behaviour, did so lively deliver out his inward grief that Zelmane found indeed he was thoroughly wounded: but there rose a new jealousy in her mind, lest it might be with Philoclea, by whom, as Zelmane thought, in

* *thou list:* it pleases you. *interlude:* comic play. *secret flames:* '93 text. '90, 'sacred'. *nearly:* very closely.

right all hearts and eyes should be inherited. And therefore desirous to be cleared of that doubt, Musidorus shortly, as in haste and full of passionate perplexedness, thus recounted his case unto her.

'The day,' said he, 'I parted from you, I being in mind to return to a town from whence I came hither, my horse (being before tired) would scarce bear me a mile hence; where being benighted,* the light of a candle I saw a good way off guided me to a young shepherd's house, by name Menalcas, who, seeing me to be a straying stranger, with the right honest hospitality which seems to be harboured in the Arcadian breasts, and, though not with curious costliness, yet with cleanly sufficiency, entertained me. And having by talk with him found the manner of the country something more in particular than I had by Kalander's report, I agreed to sojourn with him in secret, which he faithfully promised to observe. And so hither to your arbour divers times repaired; and here by your means had the sight – O that it had never been so! Nay, O that it might ever be so! – of the goddess who in a definite compass* can set forth infinite beauty.'

All this while Zelmane was racked with jealousy. But he went on, 'For,' said he, 'I lying close, and in truth thinking of you, and saying thus to myself, "O sweet Pyrocles, how art thou bewitched! Where is thy virtue? Where is the use of thy reason? How much am I inferior to thee in the state of mind, and yet know I that all the heavens cannot bring me to such a thraldom!" Scarcely, think I, had I spoken this word when the ladies came forth; at which sight, I think the very words returned back again to strike my soul: at least, an unmeasurable sting I felt in myself that I had spoken such words.'

'At which sight?' said Zelmane, not able to bear him any longer.

'O,' said Musidorus, 'I know your suspicion. No, no, banish all such fear; it was, it is, and must be Pamela.'

'Then all is safe,' said Zelmane. 'Proceed, dear Musidorus.'

'I will not,' said he, 'impute it to my late solitary life, which yet is prone to affections, nor to the much thinking of you (though that called the consideration of love into my mind, which before I

* *benighted*: overtaken by night. *in a definite compass*: through a limited form.

ever neglected) nor to the exaltation of Venus, nor revenge of Cupid; but even to her who is the planet, nay, the goddess, against which the only shield must be my sepulchre. When I first saw her, I was presently* stricken, and I (like a foolish child that, when anything hits him, will strike himself again upon it) would needs look again, as though I would persuade mine eyes that they were deceived. But alas, well have I found that love to a yielding heart is a king, but to a resisting, is a tyrant. The more with arguments I shaked the stake which he had planted in the ground of my heart, the deeper still it sank into it. But what mean I to speak of the causes of my love, which is as impossible to describe as to measure the back-side of heaven? Let this word suffice: I love. And that you may know I do so, it was I that came in black armour to defend her picture, where I was both prevented and beaten by you. And so I that waited here to do you service have now myself most need of succour.'

'But whereupon got you yourself this apparel?' said Zelmane.

'I had forgotten to tell you,' said Musidorus, 'though that were one principal matter of my speech; so much am I now master of my own mind. But thus it happened. Being returned to Menalcas' house full of tormenting desire, after a while fainting under the weight, my courage stirred up my wit to seek for some relief before I yielded to perish. At last this came into my head, that very evening* that I had to no purpose last used my horse and armour. I told Menalcas that I was a Thessalian gentleman who, by mischance having killed a great favourite of the prince of that country, was pursued so cruelly that in no place but either by favour or corruption they would obtain my destruction; and that therefore I was determined, till the fury of my persecutors might be assuaged, to disguise myself among the shepherds of Arcadia and, if it were possible, to be one of them that were allowed the prince's presence; because if the worst should fall that I were discovered, yet having gotten the acquaintance of the prince, it might happen to move his heart to protect me. Menalcas, being of an honest disposition, pitied my case, which my face through my inward torment made credible; and so (I giving him largely for it)

* *presently*: immediately. *that very evening*: i.e. the evening of the tourney when he missed fighting Phalanteus.

let me have this raiment, instructing me in all the particularities touching himself or myself which I desired to know. Yet not trusting so much to his constancy as that I would lay my life, and life of my life upon it, I hired him to go into Thessalia to a friend of mine, and to deliver him a letter from me; conjuring him to bring me as speedy an answer as he could, because it imported me greatly to know whether certain of my friends did yet possess any favour, whose intercessions I might use for my restitution.

He willingly took my letter, which being well sealed, indeed contained other matter. For I wrote to my trusty servant Kalodulus, whom you know, that as soon as he had delivered the letter, he should keep him prisoner in his house, not suffering him to have conference with any body till he knew my further pleasure; in all other respects that he should use him as my brother. And thus is Menalcas gone, and I here a poor shepherd; more proud of this estate than of any kingdom, so manifest it is that the highest point outward things can bring one unto is the contentment of the mind with which no estate, without which, all estates be miserable. Now have I chosen this day because, as Menalcas told me, the other shepherds are called to make their sports, and hope that you will with your credit find means to get me allowed among them.

'You need not doubt,' answered Zelmane, 'but that I will be your good mistress. Marry, the best way of dealing must be by Dametas, who – since his blunt brain hath perceived some favour the prince doth bear unto me (as without doubt the most servile flattery is lodged most easily in the grossest capacity, for their ordinary conceit draweth a yielding to their greaters, and then have they not wit to discern the right degrees of duty) – is much more serviceable unto me than I can find any cause to wish him. And therefore despair not to win him, for every present occasion will catch his senses, and his senses are masters of his silly mind. Only reverence him, and reward him, and with that bridle and saddle you shall well ride him.'

'O heaven and earth,' said Musidorus, 'to what a pass are our minds brought that from the right line of virtue are wried* to these crooked shifts! But O love, it is thou that does it; thou

* *wried*: contorted.

changest name upon name; thou disguisest our bodies, and disfigurest our minds. But indeed thou hast reason, for though the ways be foul, the journey's end is most fair and honourable.'

## CHAPTER 19

'No more, sweet Musidorus,' said Zelmane, 'of these philosophies, for here comes the very person of Dametas.' And so he did indeed, with a sword by his side, a forest-bill on his neck, and a chopping-knife under his girdle, in which well provided sort he had ever gone since the fear Zelmane had put him in. But he no sooner saw her, but with head and arms he laid his reverence afore her enough to have made any man forswear all courtesy. And then in Basilius' name he did invite her to walk down to the place where that day they were to have the pastorals.

But when he spied Musidorus to be none of the shepherds allowed in that place, he would fain have persuaded himself to utter some anger but that he durst not. Yet muttering and champing, as though his cud troubled him, he gave occasion to Musidorus to come near him and feign this tale of his own life: that he was a younger brother of the shepherd Menalcas, by name Dorus, sent by his father in his tender age to Athens, there to learn some cunning more than ordinary that he might be the better liked of the prince; and that after his father's death, his brother Menalcas (lately gone thither to fetch him home) was also deceased, where, upon his death, he had charged him to seek the service of Dametas, and to be wholly and ever guided by him as one in whose judgement and integrity the prince had singular confidence. For token whereof he gave to Dametas a good sum of gold in ready coin, which Menalcas had bequeathed unto him upon condition he should receive this poor Dorus into his service that his mind and manners might grow the better by his daily example.

Dametas, that of all manner of style could best conceive of golden eloquence, being withal tickled by Musidorus' praises, had his brain so turned that he became slave to that which he that sued to be his servant offered to give him; yet for countenance sake, he seemed very squeamish in respect of the charge he had of the princess Pamela. But such was the secret operation of the gold, helped with the persuasion of the Amazon, Zelmane (who said it was pity so handsome a young man should be anywhere else than with so good a master) that in the end he agreed, if that day he behaved himself so to the liking of Basilius as he might be contented, that then he would receive him into his service.

And thus went they to the lodge, where they found Gynecia and her daughters ready to go to the field, to delight themselves there a while until the shepherds' coming: whither also taking Zelmane with them, as they went Dametas told them of Dorus, and desired he might be accepted there that day instead of his brother Menalcas. As for Basilius, he stayed behind to bring the shepherds, with whom he meant to confer, to breed the better Zelmane's liking (which he only regarded)* while the other beautiful band came to the fair field appointed for the shepherdish pastimes. It was indeed a place of delight; for through the midst of it there ran a sweet brook which did both hold the eye open with her azure streams, and yet seek to close the eye with the purling noise it made upon the pebble stones it ran over: the field itself being set in some places with roses, and in all the rest constantly preserving a flourishing green. The roses added such a ruddy show unto it, as though the field were bashful at his own beauty. About it, as if it had been to enclose a theatre, grew such sort of trees as either excellency of fruit, stateliness of growth, continual greenness, or poetical fancies, have made at any time famous. In most part of which there had been framed by art such pleasant arbours, that, one answering another, they became a gallery aloft from tree to tree almost round about, which below gave a perfect shadow; a pleasant refuge then from the choleric look of Phoebus.*

In this place while Gynecia walked hard by them, carrying many unquiet contentions about her, the ladies sat them down, inquiring diverse questions of the shepherd Dorus; who, keeping his eye still upon Pamela, answered with such a trembling voice and abashed countenance and oftentimes so far from the matter, that it was some sport to the young ladies, thinking it want of education which made him so discountenanced with unwonted presence. But Zelmane that saw in him the glass of her own

* which he only regarded: which was his only concern. the choleric look of Phoebus: the heat of the sun.

misery, taking the hand of Philoclea, and with burning kisses setting it close to her lips (as if it should stand there like a hand in the margin of a book to note some saying worthy to be marked[1]) began to speak these words: 'O love, since thou art so changeable in men's estates, how art thou so constant in their torments?' – when suddenly there came out of a wood a monstrous lion, with a she-bear not far from him of a little less fierceness, which, as they guessed, having been hunted in forests far off, were by chance come thither where before such beasts had never been seen. Then care not fear, or fear not for themselves altered something the countenances of the two lovers, but so as any man might perceive was rather an assembling of powers than dismayedness of courage.

Philoclea no sooner espied the lion but that, obeying the commandment of fear, she leaped up and ran to the lodge-ward* as fast as her delicate legs could carry her, while Dorus drew Pamela behind a tree, where she stood quaking like the partridge on which the hawk is even ready to seize. But the lion, seeing Philoclea run away, bent his race to her-ward, and was ready to seize himself on the prey when Zelmane (to whom danger then was a cause of dreadlessness, all the composition of her elements being nothing but fiery[2]) with swiftness of desire crossed him, and with force of affection strake him such a blow upon his chine that she opened all his body: wherewith the valiant beast turning upon her with open jaws, she gave him such a thrust through his breast that all the lion could do was with his paw to tear off the mantle and sleeve of Zelmane with a little scratch rather than a wound, his death-blow having taken away the effect of his force.

But therewithal he fell down, and gave Zelmane leisure to take off his head to carry it for a present to her lady Philoclea: who all this while, not knowing what was done behind her, kept on her course like Arethusa when she ran from Alpheus;[3] her light apparel being carried up with the wind, that much of those beauties she would at another time have willingly hidden was presented to the sight of the twice wounded Zelmane. Which made Zelmane not follow her over-hastily, lest she should too soon deprive herself of that pleasure; but carrying the lion's head in her

* to the lodge-ward: towards the lodge.

hand, did not fully overtake her till they came to the presence of Basilius. Neither were they long there but that Gynecia came thither also, who had been in such a trance of musing, that Zelmane was fighting with the lion before she knew of any lion's coming.

But then affection resisting, and the soon ending of the fight preventing all extremity of fear, she marked Zelmane's fighting: and when the lion's head was off, as Zelmane ran after Philoclea, so she could not find in her heart but run after Zelmane: so that it was a new sight Fortune had prepared to those woods, to see those great personages thus run one after the other, each carried forward with an inward violence; Philoclea with such fear that she thought she was still in the lion's mouth; Zelmane with an eager and impatient delight; Gynecia with wings of love, flying she neither knew nor cared to know whither. But now, being all come before Basilius amazed with this sight, and fear having such possession in the fair Philoclea that her blood durst not yet to come to her face to take away the name of paleness from her most pure whiteness, Zelmane kneeled down, and presenting the lion's head unto her:

'Only lady,' said she, 'here see you the punishment of that unnatural beast which, contrary to his own kind, would have wronged prince's blood,[4] guided with such traitorous eyes as durst rebel against your beauty.'

'Happy am I, and my beauty both,' answered the sweet Philoclea then blushing (for fear had bequeathed his room to his kinsman bashfulness) 'that you, excellent Amazon, were there to teach him good manners.'

'And even thanks to that beauty,' answered Zelmane, 'which can give an edge to the bluntest swords.'

There Philoclea told her father how it had happened; but as she had turned her eyes in her tale to Zelmane she perceived some blood upon Zelmane's shoulder, so that starting with the lovely grace of pity, she showed it to her father and mother, who (as the nurse sometimes with over-much kissing may forget to give the babe suck) so had they with too much delighting, in beholding and praising Zelmane, left off to mark whether she needed succour. But then they ran both unto her, like a father and mother to an only child, and (though Zelmane assured them it was nothing) would needs see it, Gynecia having skill in surgery, an art in those days much esteemed because it served to virtuous courage which even ladies would, ever with the contempt of cowards, seem to cherish. But looking upon it – which gave more inward bleeding wounds to Zelmane, for she might sometimes feel Philoclea's touch whiles she helped her mother – she found it was indeed of no importance; yet applied she a precious balm unto it of power to heal a greater grief.

But even then, and not before, they remembered Pamela; and therefore Zelmane, thinking of her friend Dorus, was running back to be satisfied, when they might all see Pamela coming between Dorus and Dametas, having in her hand the paw of a bear which the shepherd Dorus had newly presented unto her, desiring her to accept it as of such a beast which though she deserved death for her presumption, yet was her wit to be esteemed since she could make so sweet a choice. Dametas for his part came piping and dancing, the merriest man in a parish: but when he came so near as he might be heard of Basilius, he would needs break through his ears with this joyful song of their good success.

> Now thanked be the great god Pan,
>   Which thus preserves my loved life:
> Thanked be I that keep a man,
>   Who ended hath this bloody strife:
> For if my Man must praises have,
>   What then must I, that keep the knave?
>
> For as the Moon the eye doth please,
>   With gentle beams not hurting sight:
> Yet hath Sir Sun the greatest praise,
>   Because from him doth come her light:
> So if my man must praises have,
>   What then must I, that keep the knave?

Being all now come together, and all desirous to know each other's adventures, Pamela's noble heart would needs gratefully make known the valiant means of her safety, which, directing her speech to her mother, she did in this manner:

'As soon,' said she, 'as ye were all run away and that I hoped to be in safety, there came out of the same woods a foul horrible bear, which (fearing belike to deal while the lion was present) as soon as he was gone came furiously towards the place where I was, and this young shepherd left alone by me. I truly (not guilty of any wisdom, which since they lay to my charge, because they say it is the best refuge against that beast, but even pure fear bringing forth that effect of wisdom) fell down flat on my face, needing not counterfeit being dead, for indeed I was little better. But this young shepherd with a wonderful courage, having no other weapon but that knife you see, standing before the place where I lay, so behaved himself that the first sight I had, when I thought myself already near Charon's ferry,[5] was the shepherd showing me his bloody knife in token of victory.'

'I pray you,' said Zelmane, speaking to Dorus whose valour she was careful to have manifested, 'in what sort, so ill weaponed, could you achieve this enterprise?'

'Noble lady,' said Dorus, 'the manner of these beasts fighting with any man is to stand up upon their hinder feet; and so this did, and being ready to give me a shrewd embracement, I think the god Pan, ever careful of the chief blessing of Arcadia, guided my hand so just to the heart of the beast that neither she could once touch me nor (which is the only matter in this worthy remembrance) breed any danger to the princess. For my part, I am rather with all subjected humbleness to thank her excellencies, since the duty thereunto gave me heart to save myself, than to receive thanks for a deed which was her only inspiring.'

And this Dorus spake, keeping affection as much as he could back from coming into his eyes and gestures. But Zelmane, that had the same character in her heart, could easily decipher it, and therefore to keep him the longer in speech, desired to understand the conclusion of the matter, and how the honest Dametas was escaped.

'Nay,' said Pamela, 'none shall take that office from myself, being so much bound to him as I am for my education.' And with that word, scorn borrowing the countenance of mirth, somewhat she smiled, and thus spake on: 'When,' said she, 'Dorus made me assuredly perceive that all cause of fear was passed, the truth is I was ashamed to find myself alone with this shepherd: and therefore looking about me if I could see anybody, at length we both perceived the gentle Dametas, lying with his head and breast as far as he could thrust himself into a bush, drawing up his legs as close unto him as he could; for like a man of a very kind nature, soon to take pity of himself he was fully resolved not to see his own death. And when this shepherd pushed him, bidding him to be of good cheer, it was a great while ere we could persuade him that Dorus was not the bear, so that he was fain to pull him out by the heels and show him the beast as dead as he could wish it, which, you may believe me, was a very joyful sight unto him. But then he forgat all courtesy, for he fell upon the beast, giving it many a manful wound, swearing by much it was not well such beasts should be suffered in a commonwealth. And then my governor, as full of joy as before of fear, came dancing and singing before, as even now you saw him.'

'Well, well,' said Basilius, 'I have not chosen Dametas for his fighting, nor for his discoursing but for his plainness and honesty, and therein I know he will not deceive me.'

But then he told Pamela – not so much because she should know it as because he would tell it – the wonderful act Zelmane had performed, which Gynecia likewise spake of, both in such extremity of praising as was easy to be seen the construction of their speech might best be made by the grammar rules of affection. Basilius told with what a gallant grace she ran with the lion's head in her hand, like another Pallas with the spoils of Gorgon.[6] Gynecia sware she saw the very face of the young Hercules killing the Nemean lion;[7] and all with a grateful assent confirmed the same praises. Only poor Dorus, though of equal desert yet not proceeding of equal estate, should have been forgotten, had not Zelmane again with great admiration begun to speak of him, asking whether it were the fashion or no in Arcadia that shepherds should perform such valorous enterprises.

This Basilius, having the quick sense of a lover, took as though his mistress had given him a secret reprehension that he had not showed more gratefulness to Dorus; and therefore, as nimbly as he could, inquired of his estate, adding promise of great rewards; among the rest, offering to him (if he would exercise his courage in soldiery) he would commit some charge unto him under his lieutenant Philanax. But Dorus (whose ambition climbed by another stair) having first answered touching his estate that he was brother to the shepherd Menalcas, who among others was wont to resort to the prince's presence, and excused his going to soldiery by the unaptness he found in himself that way; he told Basilius that his brother in his last testament had willed him to serve Dametas, and therefore, for due obedience thereunto, he would think his service greatly rewarded if he might obtain by that means to live in the sight of the prince and yet practise his own chosen vocation. Basilius, liking well his goodly shape and handsome manner, charged Dametas to receive him like a son into his house, saying, that his valour and Dametas' truth would be good bulwarks against such mischiefs, as, he sticked not to say, were threatened to his daughter Pamela.

Dametas, no whit out of countenance with all that had been said (because he had no worse to fall into than his own) accepted Dorus; and withal telling Basilius that some of the shepherds were come, demanded in what place he would see their sports. Who first curious to know whether it were not more requisite for Zelmane's hurt to rest than sit up at those pastimes, and she (that felt no wound but one) earnestly desiring to have the Pastorals, Basilius commanded it should be at the gate of the lodge: where the throne of the prince being, according to the ancient manner, he made Zelmane sit between him and his wife therein (who thought herself between drowning and burning) and the two young ladies of either side the throne; and so prepared their eyes and ears to be delighted by the shepherds.

But before all of them were assembled to begin their sports, there came a fellow who, being out of breath, or seeming so to be for haste, with humble hastiness told Basilius that his mistress, the lady Cecropia, had sent him to excuse the mischance of her beasts ranging in that dangerous sort, being happened by the folly of the keeper, who, thinking himself able to rule them, had carried them abroad and so was deceived: whom yet, if Basilius would punish for it, she was ready to deliver. Basilius made no other answer but that his mistress, if she had any more such beasts, should cause them to be killed: and then he told his wife and

Zelmane of it, because they should not fear those woods as though they harboured such beasts where the like had never been seen. But Gynecia took a further conceit* of it, mistrusting greatly Cecropia, because she had heard much of the devilish wickedness of her heart, and that particularly she did her best to bring up her son Amphialus (being brother's son to Basilius) to aspire to the crown as next heir male after Basilius; and therefore saw no reason but that she might conjecture it proceeded rather of some mischievous practice than of misfortune. Yet did she only utter her doubt to her daughters, thinking, since the worst was past, she would attend a further occasion,* lest overmuch haste might seem to proceed of the ordinary mislike between sisters-in-law. Only they marvelled that Basilius looked no further into it, who, good man, thought so much of his late conceived commonwealth, that all other matters were but digressions unto him. But the shepherds were ready, and with well handling themselves, called their senses to attend their pastimes.

## THE FIRST ECLOGUES

Basilius, because Zelmane so would have it, used the artificial day of torches to lighten the sports their inventions could minister; and because many of the shepherds were but newly come, he did in a gentle manner chastise their negligence with making them, for that night, the torch bearers; and the others he willed with all freedom of speech and behaviour to keep their accustomed method. Which while they prepared to do, Dametas, who much disdained (since his late authority) all his old companions, brought his servant Dorus in good acquaintance and allowance of them, and himself stood like a director over them, with nodding, gaping, winking, or stamping, showing how he did like or mislike those things he did not understand. The first sports the shepherds showed were full of such leaps and gambols as, being accorded to the pipe (which they bore in their mouths even as they danced) made a right picture of their chief god Pan and his companions the Satyrs. Then would they cast away their pipes, and holding hand

---

*conceit: conception. *attend a further occasion: wait for another attempt before taking action.

in hand, dance as it were in a brawl* by the only cadence* of their voices, which they would use in singing some short couplets, whereto the one half beginning, the other half should answer. As the one half, saying:

> We love, and have our loves rewarded,
> The others would answer,
> We love, and are no whit regarded.
> The first again,
> We find most sweet affection's snare.
> With like tune it should be as in a choir sent back again,
> That sweet,* but sour, despairful care.
> A third time likewise thus:
> Who can despair, whom hope doth bear?
> The answer,
> And who can hope that feels despair?

Then all joining their voices and dancing a faster measure, they would conclude with some such words:

> As without breath no pipe doth move,
> No music kindly without love.

Having thus varied both their songs and dances into divers sorts of inventions, their last sport was one of them to provoke another to a more large expressing of his passions: which Thyrsis (accounted one of the best singers amongst them) having marked in Dorus' dancing no less good grace and handsome behaviour than extreme tokens of a troubled mind, began first with his pipe and then with his voice thus to challenge Dorus, and was by him answered in the under-written sort.[1]

### THYRSIS · DORUS

THYRSIS: Come Dorus, come, let songs thy sorrows signify;
    And if for want of use thy mind ashamed is,
That very shame with love's high title dignify.
    No style is held for base where love well named is:
Each ear sucks up the words a true-love scattereth,
And plain speech oft than quaint phrase better framed is.

* *brawl:* French dance. *by the only cadence:* to the music of their voices alone. *That sweet:* i.e. affection.

DORUS: Nightingales seldom sing, the pye still chattereth,
  The wood cries most, before it throughly kindled be,
Deadly wounds inward bleed, each slight sore mattereth.
  Hardly they herd, which by good hunters singled be:[2]
Shallow brooks murmur most, deep, silent slide away,
Nor true-love loves his loves with others mingled be.*

THYRSIS: If thou wilt not be seen, thy face go hide away,
  Be none of us, or else maintain our fashion:
Who frowns at others' feasts doth better bide away.
  But if thou hast a love, in that love's passion,
I challenge thee by show of her perfection,
Which of us two deserveth most compassion.

DORUS: Thy challenge great, but greater my protection:
  Sing then, and see (for now thou hast inflamed me)
Thy health too mean a match for my infection.
  No, though the heavens for high attempts have blamed me,
Yet high is my attempt.[3] O Muse historify
Her praise, whose praise to learn your skill hath framed me.

THYRSIS: Muse hold your peace; but thou, my god Pan, glorify
  My Kala's gifts, who with all good gifts filled is.
Thy pipe, O Pan, shall help, though I sing sorrily.
  A heap of sweets she is, where nothing spilled is;
Who though she be no Bee, yet full of honey is:
A Lily-field, with plough of Rose which tilled is:
  Mild as a lamb, more dainty than a coney* is:
Her eyes my eye-sight is, her conversation
  More glad to me than to a miser money is.
What coy* account she makes of estimation:
  How nice* to touch! How all her speeches peized* be!
A nymph thus turned, but mended in translation.[4]

DORUS: Such Kala is: but ah my fancies raised be
  In one, whose name to name were high presumption,[3]
Since virtues all, to make her title, pleased be.
  O happy gods, which by inward assumption[5]

* *with others mingled be*: to mingle with others. *coney*: rabbit. *coy*:
modest. *nice*: delicate. *peized*: well-weighed.

Enjoy her soul, in body's fair possession,
And keep it joined, fearing your seat's consumption.
　　How oft with rain of tears skies make confession
Their dwellers rapt with sight of her perfection
From heav'nly throne to her heav'n use digression?[6]
Of best things then what world can yield confection*
　　To liken her? Deck yours with your comparison:
She is herself of best things the collection.

THYRSIS: How oft my doleful sire cry'd to me, 'Tarry son,'
　　When first he spied my love! How oft he said to me,
'Thou art no soldier fit for Cupid's garrison.
　　My son, keep this, that my long toil hath laid to me:
Love well thine own: methinks wool's whiteness passeth all:
　　I never found long love such wealth hath paid to me.'
This wind he spent: but when my Kala glasseth* all
My sight in her fair limbs, I then assure myself,
Not rotten sheep, but high crowns she surpasseth all.
　　Can I be poor, that her gold hair procure myself?
Want I white wool, whose eyes her white skin garnished?
'Till I get her, shall I to keep* enure* myself?

DORUS: How oft, when reason saw love of her harnished*
　　With armour of my heart, he cried, 'O vanity,
To set a pearl in steel so meanly varnished!
　　Look to thyself; reach not beyond humanity.
Her mind, beams, state, far from thy weak wings banished;
　　And love which lover hurts is inhumanity.'
Thus reason said: but she came, reason vanished;
Her eyes so mastering me, that such objection
　　Seemed but to spoil the food of thoughts long famished.
Her peerless height my mind to high erection
　　Draws up; and if hope-failing end life's pleasure,
Of fairer death how can I make election?

THYRSIS: Once my well-waiting eyes espied my treasure,

* confection: mixture. glasseth: makes a looking-glass of. keep: take
care of sheep. enure: accustom. harnished: armed and equipped.

185

With sleeves turn'd up, loose hair, and breast enlarged,*
Her father's corn (moving her fair limbs) measure.
'O,' cried I, 'of so mean work be discharged:
Measure my case, how by thy beauty's filling,
With seed of woes my heart brim-full is charged.
Thy father bids thee save, and chides for spilling;
Save then my soul, spill not my thoughts well heaped;
No lovely praise was ever got by killing.'
These bold words she did hear, this fruit I reaped,
That she, whose look alone might make me blessed,
Did smile on me, and then away she leaped.

DORUS: Once, O sweet once, I saw with dread oppressed
Her whom I dread, so that with prostrate lying⁷
Her length the earth in love's chief clothing dressed.
I saw that riches fall, and fell a crying:
'Let not dead earth enjoy so dear a cover,
But deck therewith my soul for your sake dying.
Lay all your fear upon your fearful lover:
Shine eyes on me, that both our lives be guarded;
So I your sight, you shall yourselves recover.'
I cried, and was with open rays rewarded:
But straight they fled, summoned by cruel honour,
Honour, the cause desert is not regarded.

THYRSIS: This maid, thus made for joys, O Pan, bemoan her,
That without love she spends her years of love:
So fair a field would well become an owner.
And if enchantment can a hard heart move,
Teach me what circle may acquaint her sprite
Affection's charms in my behalf to prove.
The circle is my round-about-her sight;
The power I will invoke dwells in her eyes;
My charm should be, she haunt me day and night.

DORUS: Far other care, O Muse, my sorrow tries,
Bent to such one in whom, myself must say,
Nothing can mend one point that in her lies.

* *enlarged*: unbound.

What circle then in so rare force bears sway?
  Whose sprite all sprites can foil, raise, damn, or save,
No charm holds her, but well possess she may;
    Possess she doth, and makes my soul her slave:
My eyes the bands, my thoughts the fatal knot.
No thrall like them that inward bondage have.

THYRSIS: Kala, at length, conclude my lingering lot:
    Disdain me not, although I be not fair.
Who is an heir of many hundred sheep
Doth beauties keep which never sun can burn,
Nor storms do turn: fairness serves oft to wealth.
Yet all my health I place in your good will;
Which if you will (O do) bestow on me,
Such as you see, such still you shall me find,
Constant and kind: my sheep your food shall breed,
Their wool your weed; I will you music yield
In flowery field; and as the day begins,
With twenty gins* we will the small birds take,
And pastimes make, as Nature things hath made.
But when in shade we meet of myrtle boughs,
Then love allows, our pleasures to enrich,
The thought of which doth pass all worldly pelf.

DORUS: Lady yourself, whom neither name I dare,
  And titles are but spots to such a worth,
Hear plaints come forth from dungeon of my mind.
The noblest kind rejects not others' woes.
I have no shows of wealth: my wealth is you,
My beauty's hue your beams, my health your deeds;
My mind for weeds your virtue's livery wears.
My food is tears; my tunes waymenting* yield;
Despair my field; the flowers, spirit's wars:
My day new cares; my gins my daily sight,[8]
In which do light small birds of thoughts o'erthrown:
My pastimes none: time passeth on* my fall:
Nature made all, but me of dolours made.
I find no shade, but where my sun doth burn:

* gins: traps. waymenting: lamenting. passeth on: passes sentence on.

No place to turn; without, within it fries:
Nor help by life or death, who living dies.

THYRSIS: But if my Kala thus my suit denies,
 Which so much reason bears,
Let crows pick out mine eyes, which too much saw.
 If she still hate love's law,
My earthy mould doth melt in watery tears.

DORUS: My earthy mould doth melt in watery tears,
 And they again resolve
To air of sighs, sighs to the heart's fire turn,
 Which doth to ashes burn.
Thus doth my life within itself dissolve.

THYRSIS: Thus doth my life within itself dissolve
 That I grow like the beast,
Which bears the bit a weaker force doth guide,
 Yet patient must abide.
Such weight it hath, which once is full possessed.

DORUS: Such weight it hath, which once is full possessed,
 That I become a vision,
Which hath in others' head his only being,
 And lives in fancy's seeing.
O wretched state of man in self-division!

THYRSIS: O wretched state of man in self-division!
 O well thou say'st! A feeling declaration
Thy tongue hath made of Cupid's deep incision.
 But now hoarse voice doth fail this occupation,
And others long to tell their loves' condition:
Of singing thou hast got the reputation.[9]

DORUS: Of singing thou hast got the reputation,
 Good Thyrsis mine; I yield to thy ability;
My heart doth seek another estimation.
 But ah, my Muse, I would thou had'st facility
To work my Goddess so by thy invention,
 On me to cast those eyes where shine nobility:
Seen and unknown; heard, but without attention.

Dorus did so well in answering Thyrsis that everyone desired to hear him sing something alone. Seeing therefore a lute lying under the Princess Pamela's feet, glad to have such an errand to approach her, he came, but came with a dismayed grace, all his blood stirred betwixt fear and desire; and playing upon it with such sweetness as everybody wondered to see such skill in a shepherd, he sang unto it with a sorrowing voice these elegiac[10] verses:

DORUS: Fortune, Nature, Love, long have contended about me,
    Which should most miseries cast on a worm that I am.
Fortune thus gan say; 'Misery and misfortune is all one,
    And of misfortune, Fortune hath only the gift.
With strong foes on land, on seas with contrary tempests
    Still do I cross this wretch, what so he taketh in hand.'
'Tush, tush,' said Nature, 'this is all but a trifle; a man's self
    Gives haps or mishaps, even as he ordereth his heart,
But so his humour I frame, in a mould of choler adusted,*
    That the delights of life shall be to him dolorous.'

Love smiled, and thus said; 'Want joined to Desire is unhappy:
    But if he nought do desire, what can *Heraclitus* ail?[11]
None but I works by Desire: by Desire have I kindled in his soul
    Infernal agonies unto a beauty divine.
Where thou, poor Nature, left'st all thy due glory to Fortune,
    Her vertue is sovereign,* Fortune a vassal of hers.'
Nature abash'd went back: Fortune blush'd; yet she replied thus:
    'And even in that love shall I reserve him a spite.'
Thus, thus, alas, woeful in Nature, unhappy by Fortune,
    But most wretched I am, now Love awakes my Desire.

Dorus when he had sung this, having had all the while a free beholding of the fair Pamela (who could well have spared such honour, and defended the assault he gave unto her face with bringing a fair stain of shamefastness unto it) let fall his arms, and remained so fastened in his thoughts as if Pamela had grafted him there to grow in continual imagination. But Zelmane espying it and fearing he should too much forget himself, she came to him,

* *choler adusted:* dried up with the heat of choler, the 'hot' humour.
*Her vertue is sovereign:* i.e. Desire's.

and took out of his hand the lute, and laying fast hold of Philoclea's face with her eyes, she sung these Sapphics, speaking as it were to her own hope:

> If mine eyes can speak to do hearty errand,
> Or mine eyes' language she do hap to judge of,
> So that eyes' message be of her received,
>> Hope, we do live yet.
> But if eyes fail then, when I most do need them,
> Or if eyes' language be not unto her known,
> So that eyes' message do return rejected,
>> Hope, we do both die.
> Yet dying, and dead, do we sing her honour;
> So become our tombs monuments of her praise;
> So becomes our loss the triumph of her gain;
>> Hers be the glory.
> If the spheres senseless do yet hold a music,*
> If the swan's sweet voice* be not heard, but at death,
> If the mute timber when it hath the life lost
>> Yieldeth a lute's tune,
> Are then human minds privileg'd so meanly,
> As that hateful death can abridge them of power
> With the voice of truth to record to all worlds
>> That we be her spoils?
> Thus not ending ends the due praise of her praise:[12]
> Fleshly veil consumes; but a soul hath his life,
> Which is held in love; love it is that hath join'd
>> Life to this our soul.
> But if eyes can speak to do hearty errand,
> Or mine eyes' language she do hap to judge of,
> So that eyes' message be of her received
>> Hope, we do live yet.

Great was the pleasure of Basilius, and greater would have been Gynecia's but that she found too well it was intended to her daughter. As for Philoclea, she was sweetly ravished withal.

* *the spheres … music*: 'the music of the spheres'. *swan's sweet voice*: the 'swan song' of which swans were only capable when dying.

190

When Dorus, desiring in a secret manner to speak of their cases as perchance the parties intended might take some light of it, making low reverence to Zelmane, began this provoking song in Hexameter verse unto her; whereunto she soon finding whither his words were directed, in like tune and verse answered as followeth:

## DORUS · ZELMANE[13]

DORUS: Lady reserved by the heavens to do pastor's company honour,
Joining your sweet voice to the rural muse of a desert,
Here you fully do find this strange operation of love,
How to the woods love runs as well as rides to the palace;
Neither he bears reverence to a prince, nor pity to a beggar,
But, like a point in midst of a circle, is still of a nearness;
All to a lesson he draws; neither hills nor caves can avoid him.

ZELMANE: Worthy shepherd by my song to myself all favour is happ'ned,
That to the sacred Muse* my annoys somewhat be revealed,
Sacred Muse, who in one contains what nine do in all them.
But O, happy be you, which safe from fiery reflection
Of Phoebus' violence in shade of sweet Cyparissus,*
Or pleasant myrtle, may teach the unfortunate Echo
In these woods to resound the renowned name of a goddess.
Happy be you that may to the saint, your only Idea,*
(Although simply attired) your manly affection utter.
Happy be those mishaps which, justly proportion holding,
Give right sound to the ears, and enter aright to the judgement:
But wretched be the souls which, veiled in a contrary subject,*
How much more we do love, so the less our loves be believed.
What skill salveth a sore of a wrong infirmity judged?
What can justice avail to a man that tells not his own case?
You though fears do abash, in you still possible hopes be:
Nature against we do seem to rebel, seem fools in a vain suit.

* sacred Muse: i.e. Philoclea. Cyparissus: cypress tree. Idea: the Platonic ideal. veiled in a contrary subject: dressed as a woman.

But so unheard, condemn'd, kept thence* we do seek to abide
in,
Self-lost in wand'ring, banished that place we do come from,
What mean is there, alas, we can hope our loss to recover?
What place is there left we may hope our woes to recomfort?
Unto the heav'ns? Our wings be too short: th' earth thinks us a
burden:
Air? We do still with sighs increase: to the fire? We do want
none:
And yet his outward heat our tears would quench, but an
inward
Fire no liquor can cool: Neptune's realm would not avail us.
Happy shepherd, with thanks to the Gods, still think to be
thankful,
That to thy advancement their wisdoms have thee abased.

DORUS: Unto the gods with a thankful heart all thanks I do
render,
That to my advancement their wisdoms have me abased.
But yet, alas, O but yet, alas, our haps be but hard haps,
Which must frame contempt to the fittest purchase of honour.
Well may a pastor plain,* but alas his plaints be not esteem'd:
Silly shepherd's poor pipe, when his harsh sound testifies
anguish,
Into the fair looker-on, pastime, not passion, enters.
And to the woods or brooks, who do make such dreary recital
What be the pangs they bear, and whence those pangs be de-
rived,
Pleas'd to receive that name by rebounding answer of Echo,
May hope thereby to ease their inward horrible anguish
When trees dance to the pipe, and swift streams stay by the
music,
Or when an Echo begins unmov'd to sing them a love-song.
Say then, what vantage do we get by the trade of a pastor,
(Since no estates be so base, but love vouchsafeth his arrow,
Since no refuge doth serve from wounds we do carry about us,
Since outward pleasures be but halting helps to decayed souls)

* *kept thence:* kept away from the place. *plain:* complain.

Save that daily we may discern what fire we do burn in?
Far more happy be you, whose greatness gets a free access,
Whose fair bodily gifts are fram'd most lovely to each eye.
Virtue you have, of virtue you have left proof to the whole
    world,
And virtue is grateful, with beauty and richness adorn'd.
Neither doubt you a whit, time will your passion utter.
Hardly* remains fire hid where skill is bent to the hiding,
But in a mind that would his flames should not be repressed,
Nature worketh enough with a small help for the revealing.
Give therefore to the Muse great praise, in whose very likeness
You do approach to the fruit your only desires be to gather.

ZELMANE: First shall fertile grounds not yield increase of a good
    seed,
First the rivers shall cease to repay their floods to the ocean,
First may a trusty greyhound transform himself to a tiger,
First shall virtue be vice, and beauty be counted a blemish,
Ere that I leave with song of praise her praise to solemnize,
Her praise, whence to the world all praise hath his only be-
    ginning:
But yet well I do find each man most wise in his own case.
None can speak of a wound with skill, if he have not a wound
    felt.
Great to thee my state seems, thy state is blest by my judge-
    ment:
And yet neither of us great or blest deemeth his own self.
For yet (weigh this, alas) great is not great to the greater.
What judge you doth a hillock show by the lofty Olympus?
Such my minute greatness doth seem compar'd to the greatest.
When cedars to the ground fall down by the weight of an
    emmot,*
Or when a rich ruby's price be the worth of a walnut,
Or to the sun for wonders seem small sparks of a candle,
Then by my high cedar, rich ruby, and only shining sun,
Virtue, richess, beauties of mine shall great be reputed.
Oh, no, no, worthy shepherd, worth can never enter a title,

* *hardly*: with difficulty. *emmot*: ant.

Where proofs justly do teach, thus match'd, such worth to be
    nought worth.
Let not a puppet abuse thy sprite; kings' crowns do not help
    them
From the cruel headache, nor shoes of gold do the gout heal,
And precious couches full oft are shak'd with a fever.
If then a bodily evil in a bodily gloss* be not hidden,
Shall such morning dews be an ease to the heat of a love's fire?

DORUS: O glittering miseries of man, if this be the fortune
    Of those fortune lulls, so small rest rests in a kingdom,
    What marvel tho' a prince transform himself to a pastor,
    Come from marble bowers, many times the gay harbour of
        anguish,
    Unto a silly cabin, though weak, yet stronger against woes?
    Now by thy words I begin, most famous lady, to gather
    Comfort into my soul. I do find, I do find what a blessing
    Is chanced to my life, that from such muddy abundance
    Of carking* agonies to estates which still be adherent,*
    Destiny keeps me aloof: for if all this estate to thy virtue
    Join'd, by thy beauty adorn'd, be no means those griefs to abol-
        ish;
    If neither by that help, thou canst climb up to thy fancy,
    Nor yet fancy so dress'd do receive more plausible hearing,
    Then do I think indeed that better it is to be private
    In sorrow's torments, than, tied to the pomps of a palace,
    Nurse inward maladies, which have not scope to be breath'd
        out,
    But perforce digest all bitter juices of horror
    In silence, from a man's own self with company robbed.
    Better yet do I live, that though by my thoughts I be plunged
    Into my life's bondage, yet may I disburden a passion
    (Oppress'd with ruinous conceits) by the help of an out-cry:
    Not limited to a whispering note, the lament of a courtier,
    But sometimes to the woods, sometimes to the heav'n do
        decipher

*gloss: appearance. *carking:* worrying. *to estates ... adherent:* belonging to high estate.

With bold clamour unheard, unmark'd, what I seek, what I
suffer:
And when I meet these trees, in the earth's fair livery clothed,
Ease I do feel (such ease as falls to one wholly diseased)
For that I find in them part of my state represented.
Laurel shows what I seek;[14] by the myrrh is showed how I seek
it;
Olive paints me the peace that I must aspire to by conquest:
Myrtle makes my request; my request is crown'd with a willow.
Cypress promiseth help, but a help where comes no recomfort:
Sweet juniper saith this, 'Though I burn, yet I burn in a sweet
fire.'
Yew doth make me think what kind of bow the boy* holdeth,
Which shoots strongly without any noise, and deadly without
smart.
Fir-trees great and green, fix'd on a high hill but a barren,
Like to my noble thoughts, still new, well plac'd, to me fruitless.
Fig that yields most pleasant fruit, his shadow is hurtful:
Thus be her gifts most sweet, thus more danger to be near her.
But in a palm when I mark how he doth rise under a burden,
And may I not (say I then) get up though griefs be so weighty?
Pine is a mast to a ship: to my ship shall hope for a mast serve?
Pine is high, hope is as high; sharp leav'd, sharp yet be my
hope's buds.
Elm embrac'd by a vine, embracing fancy reviveth:
Poplar changeth his hue from a rising sun to a setting:
Thus to my sun do I yield, such looks her beams do afford me.
Old aged oak cut down of new works serves to the building:
So my desires by my fear cut down, be the frames of her honour.
Ash makes spears which shields do resist; her force no repulse
takes.
Palms do rejoice to be join'd by the match of a male to a female,
And shall sensive* things be so senseless as to resist sense?
Thus be my thoughts dispers'd, thus thinking nurseth a think-
ing.
Thus both trees and each thing else be the books of a fancy.
But to the cedar, queen of woods, when I lift my be-tear'd eyes,

* *the boy*: Cupid. *sensive*: capable of feeling.

Then do I shape to myself that form which reigns so within me,
And think there she do dwell and hear what plaints I do utter:
When that noble top doth nod, I believe she salutes me;
When by the wind it maketh a noise, I do think she doth
　　answer.
Then kneeling to the ground, oft thus do I speak to that image:
'Only jewel, O only jewel, which only deservest
That men's hearts be thy seat, and endless fame be thy servant,
O descend for a while, from this great height to behold me,
But nought else do behold (else is nought worth the beholding)
Save what a work by thyself is wrought: and since I am alter'd
Thus by thy work, disdain not that which is by thyself done.
In mean caves oft treasure abides; to an hostry* a king comes.
And so behind foul clouds full oft fair stars do lie hidden.

ZELMANE: Hardy shepherd, such as thy merits, such may be her
　　insight
Justly to grant thee reward, such envy I bear to thy fortune.
But to myself what wish can I make for a salve to my sorrows,
Whom both nature seems to debar from means to be helped,
And if a mean were found, fortune th' whole course of it
　　hinders?
Thus plagu'd how can I frame to my sore any hope of amend-
　　ment?
Whence may I show to my mind any light of possible escape?
Bound, and bound by so noble bands, as loth to be unbound,
Jailer I am to myself, prison and prisoner to mine own self.
Yet be my hopes thus plac'd, here fix'd lives all my recomfort,
That that dear diamond, where wisdom holdeth a sure seat,
Whose force had such force so to transform, nay to reform me,
Will at length perceive those flames by her beams to be
　　kindled,
And will pity the wound festered so strangely within me.
O be it so, grant such an event, O gods, that event give,
And for a sure sacrifice I do daily oblation offer
Of mine own heart, where thoughts be the temple, sight is an
　　altar.

* *hostry*: inn.

But cease worthy shepherd, now cease we to weary the hearers
With moanful melodies; for enough our griefs be revealed,
If the parties meant* our meanings rightly be marked,
And sorrows do require some respite unto the senses.

What exclaiming praises Basilius gave to this Eclogue any man
may guess that knows love is better than a pair of spectacles to
make everything seem greater which is seen through it, and then
is never tongue-tied where fit commendation (whereof womankind
is so lickerous) is offered unto it. But before any other came in to
supply the place, Zelmane, having heard some of the shepherds by
chance name Strephon and Claius, supposing thereby they had
been present, was desirous both to hear them for the fame of their
friendly love and to know them for their kindness towards her
best loved friend. Much grieved was Basilius that any desire of his
mistress should be unsatisfied, and therefore to represent them
unto her (as well as in their absence it might be) he commanded
on Lamon, who had at large set down their country pastimes and
first love to Urania, to sing the whole discourse, which he did in
this manner:[15]

A shepherd's tale no height of style desires,[16]
    To raise in words what in effect is low:
A plaining song plain-singing voice requires,
For warbling notes from inward cheering flow.
I then, whose burd'ned breast but thus aspires
Of shepherds two the silly* case to show,
    Need not the stately Muse's help invoke
    For creeping rhymes, which often sighings choke.
But you, O you, that think not tears too dear
    To spend for harms, although they touch you not,
And deign to deem your neighbours' mischief near,
    Although they be of meaner parents got,
You I invite with easy ears to hear
    The poor-clad truth of love's wrong-order'd lot.
        Who may be glad, be glad you be not such:
        Who share in woe, weigh others have as much.

* *the parties meant*: i.e. the two princesses. *lickerous*: greedy. *silly*:
sorry.

There was (O seldom blessed word of was!)
  A pair of friends, or rather one call'd two,
Train'd in the life which on short-bitten grass
  In shine or storm must set the clouted* shoe:
He, that the other in some years did pass,
  And in those gifts that years distribute do,
    Was Claius call'd (ah, Claius, woeful wight*!)
    The later born, yet too soon, Strephon hight.*
Epirus high was honest Claius' nest,
  To Strephon Aeoles' land first breathing lent:
But east and west were join'd by friendship's hest.*
  As Strephon's ear and heart to Claius bent,
So Claius' soul did in his Strephon rest.
  Still both their flocks flocking together went,
    As if they would of owners'* humour be,
    And eke their pipes did well, as friends, agree.
Claius for skill of herbs and shepherd's art
  Among the wisest was accounted wise,
Yet not so wise as of unstained heart:
  Strephon was young, yet marked with humble eyes
How elder rul'd their flocks and cur'd their smart,
  So that the grave did not his words despise.
    Both free of mind, both did clear dealing love,
    And both had skill in verse their voice to move.
Their cheerful minds, 'till poison'd was their cheer,
  The honest sports of earthy lodging prove;
Now for a clod-like hare in form they peer,
  Now bolt* and cudgel squirrels' leap do move:
Now the ambitious lark with mirror clear
  They catch,[17] while he (fool!) to himself makes love:
    And now at keels* they try a harmless chance,
    And now their cur they teach to fetch and dance.
When merry May first early calls the morn,
  With merry maids a maying they do go:
Then do they pull from sharp and niggard thorn

---

*clouted: hob-nailed. wight: person. high: was called. hest: command. of owners': of their owners'. bolt: arrow. keels: nine-pins.

The plenteous sweets* (can sweets so sharply grow?)
Then some green gowns are by the lasses worn[18]
　In chastest plays, 'till home they walk a row,
　　While dance about the may-pole is begun,
　　When, if need were, they could at Quintain* run.
While thus they ran a low but levell'd race,
　While thus they liv'd (this was indeed a life)
With nature pleas'd, content with present case,
　Free of proud fears, brave begg'ry, smiling strife
Of climb-fall court, the envy hatching place;
　While those restless desires in great men rife,
　　To visit so low folks did much disdain,
　　This while, though poor, they in themselves did reign.
One day (O day, that shin'd to make them dark!)
　While they did ward* sun-beams with shady bay,*
And Claius taking for his younglings cark,*
　(Lest greedy eyes to them might challenge lay)
Busy with oker did their shoulders mark,
　(His mark a pillar was devoid of stay,[19]
　　As bragging that free of all passions' moan,
　　Well might he others bear, but lean to none)
Strephon with leafy twigs of laurel tree
　A garland made on temples for to wear,
For he then chosen was the dignity
　Of village lord that Whitsuntide to bear;
And full, poor fools, of boyish bravery,
　With triumph's shows would show he nought did fear.
　　But fore-accounting oft makes builders miss:
　　They found, they felt, they had no lease of bliss.
For ere that either had his purpose done,
　Behold (beholding well it doth deserve)
They saw a maid who thitherward did run
　To catch her Sparrow which from her did swerve,
As she a black-silk cap on him begun
　To set for foil of his milk-white to serve.

* *plenteous sweets*: may blossoms. *Quintain*: tilting at a post with lances or poles. *ward*: guard themselves from. *bay*: laurel branch. *cark*: care.

She chirping ran, he peeping flew away,
  'Till hard by them both he and she did stay.
Well for to see, they kept themselves unseen,
  And saw this fairest maid of fairer mind,
By fortune mean, in nature born a queen,
  How well apaid* she was her bird to find:
How tenderly her tender hands between
  In ivory cage she did the micher* bind:
    How rosy moist'ned lips about his beak
    Moving, she seem'd at once to kiss, and speak.
Chast'ned but thus, and thus his lesson taught,
  The happy wretch she put into her breast,
Which to their eyes the bowls[20] of Venus brought,
  For they seem'd made even of sky metal best,
And that the bias of her blood was wrought.
Betwixt them two the peeper* took his nest,
    Where snugging well he well appear'd content
    So to have done amiss, so to be shent.*
This done, but done with captive-killing grace,
  Each motion seeming shot from beauty's bow,
With length laid down, she deck'd the lonely place.
  Proud grew the grass that under her did grow,
The trees spread out their arms to shade her face,
  But she on elbow lean'd, with sighs did show
    No grass, no trees, nor yet her sparrow might
    To long-perplexed mind breed long delight.
She troubled was (alas that it might be!)
  With tedious brawlings of her parents dear,
Who would have her in will and word agree
  To wed Antaxius their neighbour near.
A herdman rich, of much account was he,
  In whom no evil did reign, nor good appear.
    In some such one she lik'd not his desire,
    Fain would be free, but dreadeth parents' ire.
Kindly, sweet soul, she did unkindness take
  That bagged baggage of a miser's mud

* *apaid:* pleased. *micher:* truant. *peeper:* the sparrow, chirping and looking. *shent:* punished.

Should price of her, as in a market, make;
  But gold can gild a rotten piece of wood.
To yield she found her noble heart to ache:
  To strive she fear'd how it with virtue stood.
    These doubting clouds o'ercasting heav'nly brain,
    At length in rows of kiss-cheek tears they rain.
Cupid the wag, that lately conquer'd had
  Wise counsellors, stout captains, puissant kings,
And tied them fast to lead his triumph bad,
  Glutted with them, now plays with meanest things.
So oft in feasts with costly changes clad
  To crammed maws a sprat new stomach brings:
    So lords, with sport of stag and heron full,
    Sometimes we see small birds from nests do pull.
So now for prey these shepherds two he took,
  Whose metal stiff he knew he could not bend
With hear-say pictures, or a window-look;
  With one good dance, or letter finely penn'd
That were in court a well proportion'd hook,
  Where piercing wits do quickly apprehend:
    Their senses rude plain objects only move,
    And so must see great cause before they love.
Therefore love arm'd in her now takes the field,
  Making her beams his bravery and might:
Her hands which pierc'd the soul's sev'n-double shield,
  Were now his darts, leaving his wonted fight.
Brave crest to him her scorn-gold hair did yield,
  His complete harness was her purest white;
    But fearing lest all white might seem too good,
    In cheeks and lips the tyrant threatens blood.
Besides this force, within her eyes he kept
  A fire, to burn the prisoners he gains,
Whose boiling heat increased as she wept:
  For ev'n in forge, cold water fire maintains.
Thus proud and fierce unto the hearts he stepp'd
  Of them, poor souls; and cutting reason's reins,
    Made them his own before they had it wist.*

* *wist:* known.

But if they had, could sheep-hooks this resist?
Claius straight felt, and groaned at the blow,
    And call'd, now wounded, purpose* to his aid:
Strephon, fond boy, delighted, did not know
    That it was love that shin'd in shining maid:
But lickerous, poison'd,* fain to her would go,
    If him new-learned manners had not stay'd.
        For then Urania homeward did arise,
        Leaving in pain their well-fed hungry eyes.
She went, they stay'd, or rightly for to say,
    She stay'd in them, they went in thought with her:
Claius indeed would fain have pull'd away
    This mote from out his eye, this inward bur,
And now, proud rebel, 'gan for to gainsay
    The lesson which but late he learn'd too far;
        Meaning with absence to refresh the thought
        To which her presence such a fever brought.
Strephon did leap with joy and jollity,
    Thinking it just more therein to delight
Than in good dog, fair field, or shading tree.
    So have I seen trim books in velvet dight,*
With golden leaves and painted babery,*
    Of silly boys please unacquainted sight;
        But when the rod began to play his part,
        Fain would, but could not, fly from golden smart.
He quickly learn'd Urania was her name,
    And straight, for failing, grav'd it in his heart:
He knew her haunt, and haunted in the same,
    And taught his sheep her sheep in food to thwart,
Which soon as it did bateful* question frame,
    He might on knees confess his faulty part,
        And yield himself unto her punishment,
        While nought but game the self-hurt wanton meant.
Nay, even unto her home he oft would go,
    Where bold and hurtless many plays he tries,
Her parents liking well it should be so,

* *purpose*: resolution. *lickerous, poison'd*: greedy for more poison.
*dight*: clad. *babery*: ornamentation. *bateful*: causing debate.

For simple goodness shined in his eyes.
There did he make her laugh in spite of woe,
  So as good thoughts of him in all arise,
    While into none doubt of his love did sink,
    For not himself to be in love did think.
But glad desire, his late embosom'd guest
  Yet but a babe, with milk of sight he nurst:
Desire the more he suck'd, more sought the breast,
  Like dropsy-folk still drink to be athirst.
'Till one fair ev'n an hour ere sun did rest,
  Who then in Lion's cave* did enter first,
    By neighbours pray'd, she went abroad thereby,
    At Barley-brake[21] her sweet swift foot to try.
Never the earth on his round shoulders bare
  A maid train'd up from high or low degree,
That in her doings better could compare
  Mirth with respect, few words with courtesy,
A careless comeliness with comely care,
  Self-guard with mildness, sport with majesty:
    Which made her yield to deck this shepherd's band,
    And still,* believe me, Strephon was at hand.
A-field they go, where many lookers be,
  And thou, seek-sorrow Claius, them among:
Indeed thou said'st it was thy friend to see,
  Strephon, whose absence seem'd unto thee long,
While most with her he less did keep with thee.
  No, no, it was in spite of wisdom's song
    Which absence wish'd: love play'd a victor's part:
    The heav'n-love lode-stone drew thy iron heart.
Then couples three be straight allotted there,
  They of both ends the middle two do fly;
They two that in mid-place, Hell called were,
  Must strive with waiting foot, and watching eye
To catch of them, and them to hell to bear,
  That they, as well as they, hell may supply:
    Like some which seek to salve their blotted name
    With others' blot, 'till all do taste of shame.

    *Lion's cave: the sun entering Leo, July. still: ever.

There may you see, soon as the middle two
 Do coupled towards either couple make,
They false and fearful do their hands undo,
 Brother his brother, friend doth friend forsake,
Heeding himself, cares not how fellow do,
 But of a stranger mutual help doth take:
  As perjur'd cowards in adversity
  With sight of fear, from friends to fremd* do fly.
These sports shepherds devis'd such faults to show.
 Geron, though old yet gamesome, kept one end
With Cosma, for whose love Pas passed in woe.
 Fair Nous with Pas the lot to hell did send:
Pas thought it hell while he was Cosma fro.
 At other end Uran did Strephon lend
  Her happy-making hand, of whom one look
  From Nous and Cosma all their beauty took.
The play began: Pas durst not Cosma chase,
 But did intend next bout with her to meet,
So he with Nous to Geron turn'd their race,
 With whom to join fast ran Urania sweet:
But light legg'd Pas had got the middle space.
 Geron strove hard, but aged were his feet,
  And therefore finding force now faint to be,
  He thought gray hair safforded subtlety.
And so when Pas hand-reached him to take,
 The fox on knees and elbows tumbled down;
Pas could not stay, but over him did rake,
 And crown'd the earth with his first touching crown:
His heels grown proud did seem at heav'n to shake,
 But Nous that slipp'd from Pas, did catch the clown.
  So laughing all, yet Pas to ease somedel,*
  Geron with Uran were condemn'd to hell.
Cosma this while to Strephon safely came,
 And all to second Barley-brake are bent:
The two in hell did toward Cosma frame,*
 Who should to Pas, but they would her prevent.

* *fremd:* stranger. *somedel:* in some degree. *frame:* shape their
course.

Pas mad with fall, and madder with the shame,
　Most mad with beams* which he thought Cosma sent,
　　With such mad haste he did to Cosma go,
　　That to her breast he gave a noisome blow.
She quick and proud, and who did Pas despise,
　Up with her fist, and took him on the face;
'Another time,' quoth she, 'become more wise.'
　Thus Pas did kiss her hand with little grace,
And each way luckless, yet in humble guise
　Did hold her fast for fear of more disgrace,
　　While Strephon might with pretty Nous have met,
　　But all this while another course he fet.*
For as Urania after Cosma ran,
　He, ravished with sight how gracefully
She mov'd her limbs and drew the aged man,
　Left Nous to coast the loved beauty nigh.
Nous cry'd and chaf'd, but he no other can.
　'Till Uran seeing Pas to Cosma fly,
　　And Strephon single, turn'd after him:
　　Strephon so chas'd did seem in milk to swim.
He ran, but ran with eye o'er shoulder cast,
　More marking her than how himself did go,
Like Numid lions by the hunters chas'd,
　Though they do fly, yet backwardly do glow*
With proud aspect, disdaining greatest haste:
　What rage in them, that love in him did show.
　　But God gives them instinct the man to shun,
　　And he by law of Barley-brake must run.
But as his heat with running did augment,
　Much more his sight increas'd his hot desire:
So is in her the best of Nature spent,
　The air her sweet race mov'd doth blow the fire.
Her feet be pursuivants* from Cupid sent,
　With whose fine steps all loves and joys conspire.
　　The hidden beauties seem'd in wait to lie,
　　To down proud hearts that would not willing die.
Thus, fast he fled from her he follow'd sore,

* *beams:* glances. *fet:* took. *glow:* glare. *pursuivants:* messengers.

Still shunning Nous to lengthen pleasing race,
'Till that he spied old Geron could no more,
  Then did he slack his love-instructed pace.
So that Uran, whose arm old Geron bore,
  Laid hold on him with most lay-holding grace.
    So caught, him seem'd he caught of joys the bell,*
    And thought it heav'n so to be drawn to hell.
To hell he goes, and Nous with him must dwell.
  Nous sware it was no right; for his default
Who would be caught, that she should go to hell:
  But so she must. And now the third assault
Of Barley-brake among the six befell.
  Pas Cosma match'd, yet angry with his fault,
    The other end Geron with Uran guard:
    I think you think Strephon bent thitherward.
Nous counsell'd Strephon Geron to pursue,
  For he was old, and easily would be caught:
But he drew her as love his fancy drew,
  And so to take the gem Urania sought,
While Geron old came safe to Cosma true,
  Though him to meet at all she stirred nought.
    For Pas, whether it were for fear or love,
    Mov'd not himself, nor suffer'd her to move.
So they three did together idly stay,
  While dear Uran, whose course was Pas to meet,
(He staying thus) was fain abroad to stray
  With larger round, to shun the following feet.
Strephon, whose eyes on her back parts did play,
  With love drawn on, so fast with pace unmeet
    Drew dainty Nous, that she not able so
    To run, brake forth his hands, and let him go.
He single thus hop'd soon with her to be,
  Who nothing earthly, but of fire and air,
Though with soft legs, did run as fast as he.
  He thrice reach'd, thrice deceiv'd, when her to bear
He hopes, with dainty turns she doth him flee.
  So on the Downs we see, near Wilton fair,[22]

    *caught ... the bell: carried off the prize.

A hasten'd hare from greedy greyhound go,
  And past all hope his chaps to frustrate so.
But this strange race more strange conceits did yield:
  Who victor seem'd was to his ruin brought:
Who seem'd o'erthrown was mistress of the field:
  She fled, and took; he followed and was caught.
So have I heard to pierce pursuing shield,
  By parents train'd, the Tartars wild are taught,
    With shafts shot out from their back-turned bow.
    But ah! Her darts did far more deeply go.
As Venus' bird, the white, swift, lovely Dove,
  (O happy Dove that art compar'd to her!)
Doth on her wings her utmost swiftness prove,
  Finding the gripe of Falcon fierce not far;
So did Uran: the nar,* the swifter move,
  (Yet beauty still as fast as she did stir)
    'Till with long race dear she was breathless brought,
    And then the Phoenix feared to be caught.
Among the rest that there did take delight
  To see the sports of double shining day,
And did the tribute of their wond'ring sight
  To Nature's heir, the fair Urania, pay,
I told you Claius was the hapless wight,
  Who earnest found what they accounted play.
    He did not there do homage of his eyes,
    But on his eyes his heart did sacrifice.
With gazing looks, short sighs, unsettled feet,
  He stood, but turn'd, as Gyrosol,* to sun:
His fancies still did her in half-way meet,
  His soul did fly as she was seen to run.
In sum, proud Boreas* never ruled fleet
  (Who Neptune's web on danger's distaff spun)
    With greater power than she did make them wend
    Each way, as she, that age's praise, did bend.
'Till 'spying well she well nigh weary was,
  And surely taught by his love-open eye,
His eye, that ev'n did mark her trodden grass,

* *nar*: nearer. *Gyrosol*: sunflower. *Boreas*: god of the north wind.

That she would fain the catch of Strephon fly,
Giving his reason passport for to pass
    Whither it would, so it would let him die;
      He that before shunn'd her, to shun such harms,
      Now runs, and takes her in his clipping arms.
For with pretence from Strephon her to guard,
  He met her full, but full of warefulness,*
With inbowed* bosom well for her prepar'd,
  When Strephon cursing his own backwardness,
Came to her back, and so with double ward
  Imprison her who both them did possess
    As heart-bound slaves: and happy then embrace
    Virtue's proof, fortune's victor, beauty's place.
Her race did not her beauty's beams augment,
  For they were ever in the best degree,
But yet a setting forth it someway lent,
  As rubies lustre when they rubbed be.
The dainty dew on face and body went
  As on sweet flower, when morning's drops we see.
    Her breath, then short, seem'd loth from home to pass,
    Which more it mov'd, the more it sweeter was.
Happy, O happy! if they so might bide
  To see her eyes, with how true humbleness
They looked down to triumph over pride;
  With how sweet saws* she blam'd their sauciness;
To feel the panting heart, which through her side,
  Did beat their hands, which durst so near to press;
    To see, to feel, to hear, to taste, to know
    More than, besides her, all the earth could show.
But never did Medea's golden weed
    On Creon's child his poison sooner throw,[23]
Than those delights through all their sinews breed
  A creeping serpent-like of mortal woe,
'Till she brake from their arms (although indeed
  Going from them, from them she could not go)
    And fare-welling the flock, did homeward wend,

* *warefulness*: caution. *inbowed*: curved in (so as not to bruise her).
*saws*: commands.

And so that even the Barley-brake did end.
It ended, but the others' woe began,
  Began at least to be conceiv'd as woe,
For then wise Claius found no absence can
  Help him who can no more her sight forgo.
He found man's virtue is but part of man,
  And part must follow where whole man doth go.
    He found that reason's self now reasons found
    To fasten knots, which fancy first had bound.
So doth he yield, so takes he on his yoke,
  Not knowing who did draw with him therein;
Strephon, poor youth, because he saw no smoke,
  Did not conceive what fire he had within:
But after this to greater rage it broke,
  'Till of his life it did full conquest win,
    First killing mirth, then banishing all rest,
    Filling his eyes with tears, with sighs his breast.
Then sports grew pains, all talking tedious:
  On thoughts he feeds, his looks their figure change,
The day seems long, but night is odious,
  No sleeps, but dreams; no dreams, but visions strange,
'Till finding still his evil increasing thus,
  One day he with his flock abroad did range:
    And coming where he hop'd to be alone,
    Thus on a hillock set, he made his moan:
'Alas! what weights are these that load my heart!
  I am as dull as winter-starved sheep,
Tir'd as a jade in over-laden cart,
  Yet thoughts do fly, though I can scarcely creep.
All visions seem, at every bush I start:
  Drowsy am I, and yet can rarely sleep.
    Sure I bewitched am, it is even that:
    Late near a cross I met an ugly cat.
For, but by charms, how fall these things on me,
  That from those eyes, where heav'nly apples been,
Those eyes, which nothing like themselves can see,
  Of fair Urania, fairer than a green,
Proudly bedeck'd in April's livery,

A shot unheard gave me a wound unseen?
 He was invisible that hurt me so,
  And none invisible, but spirits can go.
When I see her, my sinews shake for fear,
 And yet, dear soul, I know she hurteth none:
Amid my flock with woe my voice I tear,
 And, but bewitch'd, who to his flock would moan?
Her cherry lips, milk hands, and golden hair
 I still do see, though I be still alone.
  Now make me think that there is not a fiend,
  Who hid in angel's shape my life would end.
The sports wherein I wonted to do well,
 Come she, and sweet the air with open breast,
Then so I fail, when most I would do well,
 That at me so amaz'd my fellows jest:
Sometimes to her news of myself to tell
 I go about, but then is all my best
  Wry words, and stammering, or else doltish dumb:
  Say then, can this but of enchantment come?
Nay each thing is bewitched to know my case:
 The Nightingales for woe their songs refrain:
In river as I look'd my pining face,
 As pin'd a face as mine I saw again.
The courteous mountains, griev'd at my disgrace,
 Their snowy hair tear off in melting pain.
  And now the dropping trees do weep for me,
  And now fair evenings blush my shame to see.
But you my pipe, whilom my chief delight,
 'Till strange delight, delight to nothing wear;
And you my flock, care of my careful sight,
 While I was I, and so had cause to care;
And thou my dog, whose truth and valiant might
 Made wolves (not inward wolves) my ewes to spare;
  Go you not from your master in his woe,
  Let it suffice that he himself forgo.
For though like wax this magic makes me waste,
 Or like a lamb, whose dam away is fet,*

     * fet: taken.

(Stolen from her young by thieves' unchoosing haste)
    He treble baas for help, but none can get;
Though thus, and worse, though now I am at last,
    Of all the games that here ere now I met,
        Do you remember still you once were mine,
        'Till my eyes had their curse from blessed eyne.
Be you with me while I unheard do cry,
    While I do score my losses on the wind,
While I in heart my will write ere I die.
    In which, by will, my will and wits I bind
Still to be hers, about her aye to fly,
    As this same sprite about my fancies blind
        Doth daily haunt, but so, that mine become
        As much more loving, as less cumbersome.
Alas, a cloud hath overcast mine eyes:
    And yet I see her shine amid the cloud.
Alas, of ghosts I hear the ghastly cries:
    Yet there, me seems, I hear her singing loud.
This song she sings in most commanding wise:
    "Come shepherd's boy, let now thy heart be bow'd
        To make itself to my least look a slave:
        Leave sleep, leave all, I will no piecing* have."
I will, I will, alas, alas, I will:
    Wilt thou have more? More have, if more I be.
Away ragg'd rams, care I what murrain kill!
        Out shrieking pipe made of some witched tree!
Go bawling cur, thy hungry maw go fill
    On yond foul flock, belonging not to me!'
        With that his dog he henc'd,* his flock he curs'd,
        With that, yet kissed first, his pipe he burst.
This said, this done, he rose, even tir'd with rest,
    With heart as careful, as with careless grace,
With shrinking legs, but with a swelling breast,
    With eyes which threat'ned they would drown his face,
Fearing the worst, not knowing what were best,
    And giving to his sight a wand'ring race,*

* *piecing*: patching, i.e. no half measures. *henc'd*: drove away. *race*:
course.

He saw behind a bush where Claius sat,
  His well-known friend, but yet his unknown mate:
Claius the wretch, who lately yielden was
  To bear the bonds which time nor wit could break,
(With blushing soul at sight of judgement's glass,
  While guilty thoughts accus'd his reason weak)
This morn alone to lonely walk did pass,
  Within himself of her dear self to speak,
    'Till Strephon's plaining voice him nearer drew,
    Where by his words his self-like cause he knew.
For hearing him so oft with words of woe
  Urania name, whose force he knew so well,
He quickly knew what witchcraft gave the blow,
  Which made his Strephon think himself in hell.
Which when he did in perfect image show
  To his own wit, thought upon thought did swell,
    Breeding huge storms within his inward part,
    Which thus breath'd out, with earth-quake of his heart.

As Lamon would have proceeded, Basilius, knowing by the wasting of the torches that the night also was far wasted, and withal remembering Zelmane's hurt, asked her whether she thought it not better to reserve the complaint of Claius till another day. Which she, perceiving the song had already worn out much time, and not knowing when Lamon would end, being even now stepping over to a new matter, though much delighted with what was spoken, willingly agreed unto. And so of all sides they went to recommend themselves to the elder brother of death.*

* *the elder brother of death:* i.e. sleep.

THE END OF THE FIRST BOOK

# The Second Book of the Countess of Pembroke's Arcadia

## CHAPTER 1

In these pastoral pastimes a great number of days were sent to follow their flying predecessors, while the cup of poison* (which was deeply tasted of this noble company) had left no sinew of theirs without mortally searching into it; yet never manifesting his venomous work, till once that the night (parting away angry that she could distil no more sleep into the eyes of lovers) had no sooner given place to the breaking out of the morning light and the sun bestowed his beams upon the tops of the mountains, but that the woeful Gynecia (to whom rest was no ease) had left her loathed lodging and gotten herself into the solitary places those deserts were full of, going up and down with such unquiet motions as a grieved and hopeless mind is wont to bring forth. There appeared unto the eyes of her judgement the evils she was like to run into, with ugly infamy waiting upon them: she felt the terrors of her own conscience; she was guilty of a long exercised virtue which made this vice the fuller of deformity. The uttermost of the good she could aspire unto was a mortal wound to her vexed spirits; and lastly, no small part of her evils was that she was wise to see her evils. Insomuch that, having a great while thrown her countenance ghastly about her (as if she had called all the powers of the world to be witness of her wretched estate) at length casting up her watery eyes to heaven:

'O sun,' said she, 'whose unspotted light directs the steps of mortal mankind, art thou not ashamed to impart the clearness of thy presence to such a dust-creeping worm as I am? O you heavens, which continually keep the course allotted unto you, can none of your influences prevail so much upon the miserable Gynecia as to make her preserve a course so long embraced by her? O deserts, deserts, how fit a guest am I for you, since my heart can

* *the cup of poison:* love.

213

people you with wild ravenous beasts, which in you are wanting! O virtue, where dost thou hide thyself? What hideous thing is this which doth eclipse thee? Or is it true that thou wert never but a vain name and no essential thing, which hast thus left thy professed servant when she had most need of thy lovely presence? O imperfect proportion of reason which can too much foresee and too little prevent! Alas, alas,' said she, 'if there were but one hope for all my pains or but one excuse for all my faultiness! But wretch that I am, my torment is beyond all succour, and my evil deserving doth exceed my evil fortune. For nothing else did my husband take this strange resolution to live so solitarily. For nothing else have the winds delivered this strange guest to my country. For nothing else have the destinies reserved my life to this time, but that only I, most wretched I, should become a plague to myself and a shame to womankind. Yet if my desire, how unjust soever it be, might take effect, though a thousand deaths followed it and every death were followed with a thousand shames, yet should not my sepulchre receive me without some contentment. But alas, though sure I am that Zelmane is such as can answer my love, yet as sure I am that this disguising must needs come for some foretaken conceit. And then, wretched Gynecia, where canst thou find any small ground-plot for hope to dwell upon? No, no, it is Philoclea his heart is set'upon; it is my daughter I have borne to supplant me. But if it be so, the life I have given thee, ungrateful Philoclea, I will sooner with these hands bereave thee of than my birth shall glory she hath bereaved me of my desires. In shame there is no comfort but to be beyond all bounds of shame.'

Having spoken thus, she began to make a piteous war with her fair hair, when she might hear not far from her an extremely doleful voice, but so suppressed with a kind of whispering note that she could not conceive the words distinctly. But as a lamentable tune is the sweetest music to a woeful mind, she drew thither near-away* in hope to find some companion of her misery; and as she paced on she was stopped with a number of trees so thickly placed together that she was afraid she should, with rushing through, stop the speech of the lamentable party which she was so

* *near-away*: near to it: cf. far away.

desirous to understand. And therefore sitting her down as softly as she could (for she was now in distance to hear) she might first perceive a lute excellently well played upon, and then the same doleful voice accompanying it with these verses:

> In vain, mine eyes, you labour to amend
>   With flowing tears your fault of hasty sight;
> Since to my heart her shape you so did send,
>   That her I see, though you did lose your light.
>
> In vain, my heart, now you with sight are burn'd,
>   With sighs you seek to cool your hot desire;
> Since sighs, into mine inward furnace turn'd,
>   For bellows serve to kindle more the fire.
>
> Reason in vain, now you have lost my heart,
>   My head you seek, as to your strongest fort;
> Since there mine eyes have play'd so false a part,
>   That to your strength your foes have sure resort.
>     Then since in vain I find were all my strife,
>     To this strange death I vainly yield my life.

The ending of the song served but for a beginning of new plaints, as if the mind, oppressed with too heavy a burden of cares, was fain to discharge itself of all sides and, as it were, paint out the hideousness of the pain in all sorts of colours. For the woeful person (as if the lute had evil joined with the voice) threw it to the ground with such like words:

'Alas, poor lute, how much art thou deceived to think that in my miseries thou could'st ease my woes, as in my careless times thou wast wont to please my fancies! The time is changed, my lute, the time is changed; and no more did my joyful mind then receive everything to a joyful consideration than my careful* mind now makes each thing taste like the bitter juice of care. The evil is inward, my lute, the evil is inward; which all thou dost doth serve but to make me think more freely of, and the more I think, the more cause I find of thinking, but less of hoping. And alas, what is then thy harmony but the sweet-meats of sorrow? The discord of

* *careful*: full of care.

215

my thoughts, my lute, doth ill agree to the concord of thy strings; therefore be not ashamed to leave thy master, since he is not afraid to forsake himself.'

And thus much spoken, instead of a conclusion was closed up with so hearty a groaning that Gynecia could not refrain to show herself, thinking such griefs could serve fitly for nothing but her own fortune. But as she came into the little arbour of this sorrowful music, her eyes met with the eyes of Zelmane which was the party that thus had indited herself of misery, so that either of them remained confused with a sudden astonishment, Zelmane fearing lest she had heard some part of those complaints which she had risen up that morning early of purpose to breathe out in secret to herself. But Gynecia a great while stood still with a kind of dull amazement, looking steadfastly upon her. At length returning to some use of herself, she began to ask Zelmane what cause carried her so early abroad. But, as if the opening of her mouth to Zelmane had opened some great flood-gate of sorrow whereof her heart could not abide the violent issue, she sank to the ground with her hands over her face, crying vehemently, 'Zelmane, help me, O Zelmane have pity on me!'

Zelmane ran to her, marvelling what sudden sickness had thus possessed her; and beginning to ask her the cause of her pain and offering her service to be employed by her, Gynecia opening her eyes wildly upon her, pricked with the flames of love and the torments of her own conscience, 'O Zelmane, Zelmane,' said she, 'dost thou offer me physic, which art my only poison? Or wilt thou do me service which hast already brought me into eternal slavery?'

Zelmane then knowing well at what mark she shot, yet loth to enter into it: 'Most excellent lady,' said she, 'you were best retire yourself into your lodging that you the better may pass this sudden fit.'

'Retire myself?' said Gynecia, 'If I had retired myself into myself when thou (to me unfortunate guest) camest to draw me from myself, blessed had I been, and no need had I had of this counsel. But now alas, I am forced to fly to thee for succour whom I accuse of all my hurt, and make thee judge of my cause, who art the only author of my mischief.'

Zelmane the more astonished, the more she understood her, 'Madam,' said she, 'whereof do you accuse me that I will not clear myself? Or wherein may I stead* you that you may not command me?'

'Alas!' answered Gynecia, 'What shall I say more? Take pity of me, O Zelmane, but not as Zelmane, and disguise not with me in words, as I know thou dost in apparel.'

Zelmane was much troubled with that word, finding herself brought to this strait. But as she was thinking what to answer her, they might see old Basilius pass hard by them without ever seeing them, complaining likewise of love very freshly, and ending his complaint with this song, love having renewed both his invention and voice:

> Let not old age disgrace my high desire;
>> O heavenly soul in human shape contain'd:
> Old wood inflam'd doth yield the bravest fire,
>> When younger doth in smoke his virtue spend,
>
> Ne let white hairs which on my face do grow
>> Seem to your eyes of a disgraceful hue,
> Since whiteness doth present the sweetest show,
>> Which makes all eyes do homage unto you.
>
> Old age is wise and full of constant truth;
>> Old age well stayed* from ranging humour lives;
> Old age hath known whatever was in youth;
>> Old age o'ercome, the greater honour gives.
>>> And to old age since you yourself aspire,
>>> Let not old age disgrace my high desire.

Which being done, he looked very curiously upon himself, sometimes fetching a little skip as if he had said his strength had not yet forsaken him.

But Zelmane, having in this time gotten some leisure to think for an answer, looking upon Gynecia as if she thought she did her some wrong: 'Madam,' said she, 'I am not acquainted with those words of disguising; neither is it the profession of an Amazon; neither are you a party with whom it is to be used. If my service

---

*stead: be of use. stayed: settled.

may please you, employ it, so long as you do me no wrong in misjudging of me.'

'Alas, Zelmane,' said Gynecia, 'I perceive you know full little how piercing the eyes are of a true lover. There is no one beam of those thoughts you have planted in me but is able to discern a greater cloud than you do go in. Seek not to conceal yourself further from me, nor force not the passion of love into violent extremities.'

Now was Zelmane brought to an exigent,* when the king, turning his eyes that way through the trees, perceived his wife and mistress together; so that framing the most lovely countenance he could, he came straightway towards them, and at the first word, thanking his wife for having entertained Zelmane, desired her she would now return into the lodge because he had certain matters of estate to impart to the Lady Zelmane. The queen, being nothing troubled with jealousy in that point, obeyed the king's commandment, full of raging agonies, and determinately bent that as she would seek all loving means to win Zelmane, so she would stir up terrible tragedies rather than fail of her intent. And so went she from them to the lodge-ward;* with such a battle in her thoughts and so deadly an overthrow given to her best resolutions that even her body (where the field was fought) was oppressed withal, making a languishing sickness wait upon the triumph of passion, which the more it prevailed in her, the more it made her jealousy watchful both over her daughter and Zelmane, having ever one of them entrusted to her own eyes.

But as soon as Basilius was rid of his wife's presence, falling down on his knees, 'O lady,' said he, 'which hast only had the power to stir up again those flames which had so long lain dead in me, see in me the power of your beauty, which can make old age come to ask counsel of youth, and a prince unconquered to become a slave to a stranger. And when you see that power of yours, love that at least in me, since it is yours, although of me you see nothing to be loved.'

'Worthy prince,' answered Zelmane, taking him up from his kneeling, 'both your manner and your speech are so strange unto me as I know not how to answer it better than with silence.'

*exigent: crisis. to the lodge-ward: towards the lodge.

'If silence please you,' said the king, 'it shall never displease me, since my heart is wholly pledged to obey you. Otherwise, if you would vouchsafe mine ears such happiness as to hear you, they shall convey your words to such a mind which is with the humblest degree of reverence to receive them.'

'I disdain not to speak to you, mighty prince,' said Zelmane, 'but I disdain to speak to any matter which may bring my honour into question.'

And therewith, with a brave counterfeited scorn she departed from the king, leaving him not so sorry for his short answer as proud in himself that he had broken the matter. And thus did the king, feeding his mind with those thoughts, pass great time in writing verses and making more of himself than he was wont to do, that, with a little help, he would have grown into a pretty kind of dotage.

But Zelmane, being rid of this loving but little loved company, 'Alas,' said she, 'poor Pyrocles, was there ever one but I that had received wrong and could blame nobody, that having more than I desire, am still in want of that I would? Truly, love, I must needs say thus much on thy behalf; thou hast employed my love there where all love is deserved, and for recompense hast sent me more love than ever I desired. But what wilt thou do, Pyrocles? Which way canst thou find to rid thee of thy intricate troubles? To her whom I would be known to, I live in darkness; and to her am I revealed from whom I would be most secret. What shift shall I find against the diligent love of Basilius? What shield against the violent passions of Gynecia? And if that be done, yet how am I the nearer to quench the fire that consumes me? Well, well, sweet Philoclea, my whole confidence must be builded in thy divine spirit which cannot be ignorant of the cruel wound I have received by you.'

## CHAPTER 2

But as sick folks when they are alone think company would relieve them, and yet having company, do find it noisome, changing willingly outward objects when indeed the evil is inward; so poor Zelmane was no more weary of Basilius than she was of herself when Basilius was gone; and ever the more, the more she turned her eyes to become her own judges. Tired wherewith, she longed to meet her friend Dorus that upon the shoulders of friendship she might lay the burden of sorrow; and therefore went toward the other lodge, where among certain beeches she found Dorus, apparelled in flannen,* with a goat's-skin cast upon him and a garland of laurel mix'd with cypress leaves[1] on his head, waiting on his master Dametas who at that time was teaching him how with his sheep-hook to catch a wanton lamb, and how with the same to cast a little clod at any one that strayed out of company. And while Dorus was practising, one might see Dametas holding his hand under his girdle behind him, nodding from the waist upwards, and swearing he never knew man go more awkwardly to work, and that they might talk of book-learning what they would but, for his part, he never saw more unfeatly* fellows than great clerks* were.

But Zelmane's coming saved Dorus from further chiding. And so she, beginning to speak with him of the number of his master's sheep and which province of Arcadia bare the finest wool, drew him on to follow her in such country-discourses; till (being out of Dametas' hearing) with such vehemency of passion as though her heart would climb into her mouth to take her tongue's office, she declared unto him upon what briars the roses of her affections grew; how time still seemed to forget her, bestowing no one hour of comfort upon her; she remaining still in one plight of ill fortune, saving* so much worse as continuance of evil doth in itself increase evil. 'Alas, my Dorus,' said she, 'thou seest how long and languishingly the weeks are passed over us since our last talking. And yet am I the same, miserable I, that I was, only stronger in longing and weaker in hoping.'

Then fell she to so pitiful a declaration of the insupportableness of her desires that Dorus' ears, not able to show what wounds that discourse gave unto them, procured his eyes with tears to give testimony how much they suffered for her suffering; till passion (a most cumbersome guest to itself) made Zelmane, the sooner to shake it off, earnestly entreat Dorus that he also with like freedom of discourse would bestow a map of his little world upon her that

* *flannen:* flannel. *unfeatly:* clumsy. *clerks:* scholars. *saving:* except.

she might see whether it were troubled with such unhabitable climes of cold despairs and hot rages as hers was.

And so walking under a few palm-trees (which being loving in their own nature seemed to give their shadow the willinglier because they held discourse of love)² Dorus thus entered to the description of his fortune.

'Alas,' said he, 'dear cousin, that it hath pleased the high powers to throw us to such an estate as the only intercourse of our true friendship must be a bartering of miseries. For my part, I must confess, indeed, that from a huge darkness of sorrows I am crept, I cannot say to a lightsomeness, but to a certain dawning, or rather peeping out of some possibility of comfort: but woe is me, so far from the mark of my desires that I rather think it such a light as comes through a small hole to a dungeon, that the miserable caitiff may the better remember the light of which he is deprived; or like a scholar who is only come to that degree of knowledge to find himself utterly ignorant. But thus stands it with me. After that by your means I was exalted to serve in yonder blessed lodge, for a while I had in the furnace of my agonies this refreshing: that, because of the service I had done in killing of the bear, it pleased the princess (in whom indeed stateliness shines through courtesy) to let fall some gracious look upon me; sometimes to see my exercises, sometimes to hear my songs. For my part, my heart would not suffer me to omit any occasion whereby I might make the incomparable Pamela see how much extraordinary devotion I bare to her service, and withal strave to appear more worthy in her sight, that small desert, joined to so great affection, might prevail something in the wisest lady. But too well, alas, I found that a shepherd's service was but considered of as from a shepherd, and the acceptation limited to no further proportion than of a good servant. And when my countenance had once given notice that there lay affection under it, I saw, straight, Majesty (sitting in the throne of beauty) draw forth such a sword of just disdain that I remained as a man thunderstricken, not daring – no not able – to behold that power.

'Now to make my estate known seemed again impossible by reason of the suspiciousness of Dametas, Miso and my young mistress Mopsa. For Dametas (according to the constitution of a dull head) thinks no better way to show himself wise than by suspecting everything in his way: which suspicion Miso (for the hoggish shrewdness* of her brain) and Mopsa (for a very unlikely envy she hath stumbled upon against the princess' unspeakable beauty) were very glad to execute. So that I, finding my service by this means lightly regarded, my affection despised, and myself unknown, remained no fuller of desire than void of counsel how to come to my desire; which, alas, if these trees could speak, they might well witness. For many times have I stood here, bewailing myself unto them. Many times have I, leaning to yonder palm, admired the blessedness of it that it could bear love without sense of pain. Many times, when my master's cattle came hither to chew their cud in this fresh place, I might see the young bull testify his love, but how? With proud looks and joyfulness.

' "O wretched mankind," said I then to myself, "in whom wit, which should be the governor of his welfare, becomes the traitor to his blessedness! These beasts, like children to nature, inherit her blessings quietly: we, like bastards, are laid abroad, even as foundlings to be trained up by grief and sorrow. Their minds grudge not at their bodies' comfort, nor their senses are letted* from enjoying their objects: we have the impediments of honour and the torments of conscience."

'Truly in such cogitations have I sometimes so long stood that methought my feet began to grow into the ground, with such a darkness and heaviness of mind that I might easily have been persuaded to have resigned over my very essence. But love (which one time layeth burdens, another time giveth wings) when I was at the lowest of my downward thoughts, pulled up my heart to remember that nothing is achieved before it be throughly attempted, and that lying still doth never go forward; and that therefore it was time, now or never, to sharpen my invention to pierce through the hardness of this enterprise, never ceasing to assemble all my conceits one after the other how to manifest both my mind and estate. Till at last I lighted and resolved on this way, which yet perchance you will think was a way rather to hide it.

'I began to counterfeit the extremest love towards Mopsa that might be; and as for the love, so lively it was indeed within me

*shrewdness: maliciousness. letted: hindered.

(although to another subject) that little I needed to counterfeit any notable demonstrations of it: and so making a contrariety the place of my memory,* in her foulness I beheld Pamela's fairness, still looking on Mopsa but thinking on Pamela, as if I saw my sun shine in a puddled water. I cried out of nothing but Mopsa: to Mopsa my attendance was directed: to Mopsa the best fruits I could gather were brought: to Mopsa it seemed still that mine eye conveyed my tongue. So that Mopsa was my saying; Mopsa was my singing; Mopsa (that is only suitable in laying a foul complexion upon a filthy favour,* setting forth* both in sluttishness) she was the lode-star of my life, she the blessing of mine eyes, she the overthrow of my desires, and yet the recompense of my overthrow; she the sweetness of my heart, even sweetening the death which her sweetness drew upon me. In sum, whatsoever I thought of Pamela, that I said of Mopsa; whereby as I gat my master's goodwill (who before spited me, fearing lest I should win the princess' favour from him) so did the same make the princess the better content to allow me her presence – whether indeed it were that a certain spark of noble indignation did rise in her not to suffer such a baggage to win away anything of hers, how meanly soever she reputed of it, or rather (as I think) my words being so passionate and shooting so quite contrary from the marks of Mopsa's worthiness, she perceived well enough whither they were directed; and therefore being so masked, she was contented as a sport of wit to attend them. Whereupon one day determining to find some means to tell, as of a third person, the tale of mine own love and estate, finding Mopsa (like a cuckoo by a nightingale) alone with Pamela, I came in unto them, and with a face, I am sure, full of cloudy fancies, took a harp and sung this song:

> Since so mine eyes are subject to your sight,
>     That in your sight they fixed have my brain;
> Since so my heart is filled with that light,
>     That only light doth all my life maintain;
>
> Since in sweet you, all goods so richly reign,
>     That where you are, no wished good can want;

* *place of my memory*: see Notes I.1. p. 849. *filthy favour*: countence. *setting forth*: showing off to the full.

Since so your living image lives in me,
That in myself yourself true love doth plant;
How can you him unworthy then decree,
In whose chief part your worths implanted be?

The song being ended, which I had often broken off in the midst
with grievous sighs which overtook every verse I sang, I let fall
my harp from me, and casting mine eyes sometimes upon Mopsa,
but settling my sight principally upon Pamela, "And is it the only
fortune, most beautiful Mopsa," said I, "of wretched Dorus that
Fortune must be the measure of his mind? Am I only he that
because I am in misery, more misery must be laid upon me? Must
that which should be cause of compassion become an argument of
cruelty against me? Alas, excellent Mopsa, consider that a virtuous prince requires the life of his meanest subject, and the
heavenly sun disdains not to give light to the smallest worm. O
Mopsa, Mopsa, if my heart could be as manifest to you as it is
uncomfortable to me, I doubt not the height of my thoughts
should well countervail the lowness of my quality. Who hath not
heard of the greatness of your estate? Who seeth not that your
estate is much excelled with that sweet uniting of all beauties
which remaineth and dwelleth with you? Who knows not that all
these are but ornaments of that divine spark within you which,
being descended from heaven, could not elsewhere pick out so
sweet a mansion? But if you will know what is the band that
ought to knit all these excellencies together, it is a kind mercifulness to such a one as is in his soul devoted to those perfections."

'Mopsa, who already had had a certain smackering* towards
me, stood all this while with her hands sometimes before her face,
but most commonly with a certain special grace of her own, wag-
ging her lips, and grinning instead of smiling: but all the words I
could get of her was (wrying* her waist and thrusting out her
chin) "In faith you jest with me. You are a merry man indeed."

'But the ever pleasing Pamela (that well found the comedy
would be marred if she did not help Mopsa to her part) was content to urge a little further of me. "Master Dorus," said the fair
Pamela, "methinks you blame your fortune very wrongfully, since

*smackering: longing. wrying: contorting.

the fault is not in Fortune but in you that cannot frame yourself to your fortune; and as wrongfully do require Mopsa to so great a disparagement as to her father's servant, since she is not worthy to be loved that hath not some feeling of her own worthiness."

'I stayed a good while after her words, in hope she would have continued her speech, so great a delight I received in hearing her; but seeing her say no further, with a quaking all over my body I thus answered her: "Lady, most worthy of all duty, how falls it out that you, in whom all virtue shines, will take the patronage of Fortune, the only rebellious handmaid against virtue? Especially, since before your eyes you have a pitiful spectacle of her wickedness, a forlorn creature which must remain not such as I am but such as she makes me, since she must be the balance of worthiness or disparagement.[3] Yet alas, if the condemned man, even at his death, have leave to speak, let my mortal wound purchase thus much consideration: since the perfections are such in the party I love as the feeling of them cannot come into any unnoble heart, shall that heart, which doth not only feel them but hath all the working of his life placed in them, shall that heart, I say, lifted up to such a height, be counted base? O let not an excellent spirit do itself such wrong as to think where it is placed, embraced and loved, there can be any unworthiness, since the weakest mist is not easlier driven away by the sun than that is chased away with so high thoughts."

' "I will not deny," answered the gracious Pamela, "but that the love you bear to Mopsa hath brought you to the consideration of her virtues, and that consideration may have made you the more virtuous and so the more worthy: but even that, then (you must confess) you have received of her, and so are rather gratefully to thank her than to press any further, till you bring something of your own whereby to claim it. And truly Dorus, I must in Mopsa's behalf say thus much to you, that if her beauties have so overtaken you, it becomes a true love to have your heart more set upon her good than your own, and to bear a tenderer respect to her honour than your satisfaction."

' "Now by my hallidame,[4] Madam," said Mopsa, throwing a great number of sheep's eyes upon me, "you have even touched mine own mind to the quick, forsooth."

'I (finding that the policy that I had used had at least-wise procured thus much happiness unto me as that I might, even in my lady's presence, discover* the sore which had deeply festered within me, and that she could better conceive my reasons applied to Mopsa than she would have vouchsafed them whilst herself was a party) thought good to pursue on my good beginning, using this fit occasion of Pamela's wit and Mopsa's ignorance. Therefore with an humble piercing eye, looking upon Pamela as if I had rather been condemned by her mouth than highly exalted by the other, turning myself to Mopsa, but keeping mine eye where it was:

' "Fair Mopsa," said I, "well do I find by the wise knitting together of your answer that any disputation I can use is as much too weak as I unworthy, I find my love shall be proved no love, without I leave to love,* being too unfit a vessel in whom so high thoughts should be engraved. Yet since the love I bear you hath so joined itself to the best part of my life as the one cannot depart but that the other will follow, before I seek to obey you in making my last passage, let me know which is my unworthiness, either of mind, estate, or both?"

'Mopsa was about to say in neither; for her heart I think tumbled with overmuch kindness, when Pamela, with a more favourable countenance than before, finding how apt I was to fall into despair, told me I might therein have answered myself; for besides that it was granted me that the inward feeling of Mopsa's perfections had greatly beautified my mind, there was none could deny but that my mind and body deserved great allowance. "But Dorus," said she, "you must be so far master of your love as to consider that since the judgement of the world stands upon matter of fortune, and that the sex of womankind of all other is most bound to have regardful eye to men's judgements, it is not for us to play the philosophers in seeking out your hidden virtues, since that which in a wise prince would be counted wisdom, in us will be taken for a light grounded affection: so is not one thing one, done by divers persons."[5]

'There is no man in a burning fever feels so great contentment

* discover: make known. without I leave to love: unless I leave off loving.

in cold water greedily received (which as soon as the drink ceaseth, the rage reneweth) as poor I found my soul refreshed with her sweetly pronounced words, and newly and more violently again inflamed as soon as she had closed up her delightful speech with no less well graced silence. But remembering in myself that as well the soldier dieth which standeth still as he that gives the bravest onset, and seeing that to the making up of my fortune there wanted nothing so much as the making known of mine estate, with a face well witnessing how deeply my soul was possessed, and with the most submissive behaviour that a thralled heart could express, even as my words had been too thick for my mouth, at length spoke to this purpose:

' "Alas, most worthy Princess," said I, "and do not then your own sweet words sufficiently testify that there was never man could have a juster action against filthy fortune than I, since all other things being granted me, her blindness is my only let?* O heavenly God, I would either she had such eyes as were able to discern my deserts, or I were blind not to see the daily cause of my misfortune. But yet," said I, "most honoured lady, if my miserable speeches have not already cloyed you, and that the very presence of such a wretch become not hateful in your eyes, let me reply thus much further against my mortal sentence by telling you a story which happened in this same country long since – for woes make the shortest time seem long6 – whereby you shall see that my estate is not so contemptible but that a prince hath been content to take the like upon him, and by that only hath aspired to enjoy a mighty princess." Pamela graciously harkened, and I told my tale in this sort.

## CHAPTER 3

' "In the country of Thessalia (alas, why name I that accursed country which brings forth nothing but matters for tragedies1 – but name it I must!) in Thessalia, I say, there was (well may I say there was) a prince (No, no prince, whom bondage wholly possessed) but yet accounted a prince, and named Musidorus. O

* let: obstacle.

Musidorus, Musidorus! But to what serve exclamations, where there are no ears to receive the sound? This Musidorus being yet in the tenderest age, his worthy father paid to nature, with a violent death, her last duties, leaving his child to the faith of his friends and the proof of time. Death gave him not such pangs as the foresightful care he had of his silly* successor. And yet if in his foresight he could have seen so much, happy was that good prince in his timely departure which barred him from the knowledge of his son's miseries, which his knowledge could neither have prevented nor relieved. The young Musidorus (being thus, as for the first pledge of the destinies' goodwill, deprived of his principal stay)* was yet for some years after, as if the stars would breathe themselves for a greater mischief, lulled up in as much good luck as the heedful love of his doleful mother and the flourishing estate of his country could breed unto him.

‘ "But when the time now came that misery seemed to be ripe for him, because he had age to know misery, I think there was a conspiracy in all heavenly and earthly things to frame fit occasions to lead him unto it. His people (to whom all foreign matters in foretime* were odious) began to wish in their beloved prince experience by travel: his dear mother, whose eyes were held open only with the joy of looking upon him, did now dispense with the comfort of her widowed life, desiring the same her subjects did, for the increase of her son's worthiness.

‘ "And hereto did Musidorus' own virtue (see how virtue can be a minister to mischief) sufficiently provoke him; for indeed thus much I must say for him (although the likeness of our mishaps makes me presume to pattern myself unto him) that well-doing was at that time his scope, from which no faint pleasure could withhold him. But the present occasion which did knit all this together was his uncle the king of Macedon who, having lately before gotten such victories as were beyond expectation, did at this time send both for the prince his son (brought up together, to avoid the wars, with Musidorus) and for Musidorus himself, that his joy might be the more full, having such partakers of it. But alas, to what a sea of miseries my plaintful tongue doth lead me!" – and thus out of breath rather with that I thought than that I

* *silly*: deserving of pity. *stay*: support. *in foretime*: previously.

said, I stayed my speech, till Pamela showing by countenance that such was her pleasure, I thus continued it:

' "These two young princes, to satisfy the king, took their way by sea towards Thrace, whither they would needs go with a navy to succour him, he being at that time before Bizantium with a mighty army besieging it, where at that time his court was. But when the conspired heavens had gotten this subject of their wrath upon so fit a place as the sea was, they straight began to breathe out in boisterous winds some part of their malice against him, so that with the loss of all his navy, he only with the prince his cousin were cast a-land far off from the place whither their desires would have guided them. O cruel winds, in your unconsiderate rages why either began you this fury, or why did you not end it in his end? But your cruelty was such, as you would spare his life for many deathful torments. To tell you what pitiful mishaps fell to the young prince of Macedon, his cousin, I should too much fill your ears with strange horrors; neither will I stay upon those laboursome adventures nor loathsome misadventures to which, and through which, his fortune and courage conducted him. My speech hasteneth itself to come to the full point of Musidorus' infortunes. For as we find the most pestilent diseases do gather into themselves all the infirmities with which the body before was annoyed, so did his last misery embrace in the extremity of itself all his former mischiefs.

' "Arcadia, Arcadia was the place prepared to be the stage of his endless overthrow. Arcadia was (alas, well might I say, it is) the charmed circle where all his spirits for ever should be enchanted. For here, and nowhere else, did his infected eyes make his mind know what power heavenly beauty hath to throw it down to hellish agonies. Here, here did he see the Arcadian king's eldest daughter, in whom he forthwith placed so all his hopes of joy and joyful parts of his heart that he left in himself nothing but a maze of longing and a dungeon of sorrow. But alas, what can saying make them believe whom seeing cannot persuade? Those pains must be felt before they can be understood: no outward utterance can command a conceit.* Such was as then the state of the king as it was no time by direct means to seek her. And such was the state

* *command a conceit:* force an understanding.

of his captivated will as he could delay no time of seeking her.

‘ "In this entangled case, he clothed himself in a shepherd's weed, that under the baseness of that form he might at least have free access to feed his eyes with that which should at length eat up his heart. In which doing, thus much without doubt he hath manifested that this estate is not always to be rejected, since under that veil there may be hidden things to be esteemed.[2] And if he might with taking on a shepherd's look cast up his eyes to the fairest princess Nature in that time created, the like, nay the same desire of mine need no more to be disdained or held for disgraceful. But now, alas, mine eyes wax dim, my tongue begins to falter and my heart to want force to help either, with the feeling remembrance I have in what heap of miseries the caitiff prince lay at this time buried. Pardon, therefore, most excellent princess, if I cut off the course of my dolorous tale, since, if I be understood, I have said enough for the defence of my baseness; and for that which after might befall to that pattern of ill fortune, the matters are too monstrous for my capacity: his hateful destinies must best declare their own workmanship."

'Thus having delivered my tale in this perplexed manner, to the end the princess might judge that he meant himself who spake so feelingly, her answer was both strange and in some respect comfortable. For would you think it? She hath heard heretofore of us both by means of the valiant prince Plangus, and particularly of our casting away, which she (following my own style) thus delicately brought forth:

‘ "You have told," said she, "Dorus, a pretty tale, but you are much deceived in the latter end of it. For the Prince Musidorus with his cousin Pyrocles did both perish upon the coast of Laconia, as a noble gentleman called Plangus, who was well acquainted with the history, did assure my father."

'O how that speech of hers did pour joys in my heart! O blessed name (thought I) of mine, since thou hast been in that tongue, and passed through those lips, though I can never hope to approach them.

‘ "As for Pyrocles," said I, "I will not deny it but that he is perished," – (which I said lest sooner suspicion might arise of your being here than yourself would have it, and yet affirmed no lie unto her, since I only said I would not deny it) – "But for Musidorus," said I, "I perceive indeed you have neither heard or read the story of that unhappy prince; for this was the very objection which that peerless princess did make unto him when he sought to appear such as he was before her wisdom: and thus, as I have read it fair written, in the certainty of my knowledge he might answer her: that indeed the ship wherein he came by a treason was perished, and therefore that Plangus might easily be deceived; but that he himself was cast upon the coast of Laconia, where he was taken up by a couple of shepherds, who lived in those days famous for that both loving one fair maid, they yet remained constant friends – one of whose songs not long since was sung before you by the shepherd Lamon – and brought by them to a nobleman's house near Mantinea, whose son had, a little before his marriage, been taken prisoner, and by the help of this prince Musidorus (though naming himself by another name) was delivered."

'Now these circumlocutions I did use, because of the one side I knew the princess would know well the parties I meant, and of the other, if I should have named Strephon, Claius, Kalander and Clitophon, perhaps it would have rubb'd some conjecture into the heavy head of mistress Mopsa.

' "And therefore," said I, "most divine lady, he justly was thus to argue against such suspicions, that the prince* might easily by those parties be satisfied that upon that wreck such a one was taken up, and therefore that Plangus might well err, who knew not of any's taking up* again: that he that was so preserved brought good tokens to be one of the two chief of that wrecked company; which two, since Plangus knew to be Musidorus and Pyrocles, he must needs be one of them, although, as I said, upon a fore-taken vow he was otherwise at that time called. Besides, the princess must needs judge that no less than a prince durst undertake such an enterprise, which, though he might get the favour of the princess, he could never defend with less than a prince's power against the force of Arcadia. Lastly, said he, for a certain demonstration, he presumed to show unto the princess a mark he had on his face, as I might," said I, "show this of my neck to the rare

* *prince*: Basilius. *taking up*: being rescued.

Mopsa," – and, withal, showed my neck to them both, where, as you know, there is a red spot bearing figure, as they tell me, of a lion's paw – "that she may ascertain herself that I am Menalcas' brother. And so did he, beseeching her to send someone she might trust into Thessalia, secretly to be advertised whether the age, the complexion, and particularly that notable sign did not fully agree with their prince Musidorus."

' "Do you not know further," said she (with a settled countenance not accusing* any kind of inward motion) "of that story?"

' "Alas, no," said I, "for even here the historiographer stopped, saying the rest belonged to astrology."*

'And therewith, thinking her silent imaginations began to work upon somewhat, to mollify them (as the nature of music is to do) and, withal, to show what kind of shepherd I was,[3] I took up my harp and sang these few verses:

My sheep are thoughts, which I both guide and serve,
　　Their pasture is fair hills of fruitless love:
On barren sweets they feed, and feeding starve:
　　I wail their lot, but will not other prove.
My sheep-hook is wan hope, which all upholds:
　　My weeds, desire, cut out in endless folds.
　　　　What wool my sheep shall bear, whiles thus they live,
　　　　In you it is, you must the judgement give.

'And then, partly to bring Mopsa again to the matter lest she should too much take heed to our discourses, but principally, if it were possible, to gather some comfort out of her answers, I kneeled down to the princess and humbly besought her to move Mopsa in my behalf that she would unarm her noble heart of that steely resistance against the sweet blows of love: that since all her parts were decked with some particular ornament – her face with beauty, her head with wisdom, her eyes with majesty, her countenance with gracefulness, her lips with loveliness, her tongue with victory – that she would make her heart the throne of pity,

* *acusing*: betraying. *astrology*: the science of knowing the future.

being the most excellent raiment of the most excellent part.

'Pamela, without show either of favour or disdain, either of heeding or neglecting what I had said, turned her speech to Mopsa, and with such a voice and action as might show she spake of a matter which little did concern her, "Take heed to yourself," said she, "Mopsa, for your shepherd can speak well: but truly, if he do fully prove himself such as he saith, I mean, the honest shepherd Menalcas' brother and heir, I know no reason why you should think scorn of him."

'Mopsa, though in my conscience she were even then far spent towards me, yet she answered her that for all my quaint speeches she would keep her honesty close enough; and that as for the way of matrimony, she would step never a foot further till my master, her father, had spoken the whole word himself, no she would not. But ever and anon turning her muzzle towards me, she threw such a prospect upon me as might well have given a surfeit to any weak lover's stomach. But, lord, what a fool am I to mingle that drivel's speeches among my noble thoughts – but because she was an actor in this tragedy, to give you a full knowledge and to leave nothing that I can remember unrepeated.

'Now the princess being about to withdraw herself from us, I took a jewel made in the figure of a crab-fish, which, because it looks one way and goes another, I thought it did fitly pattern out my looking to Mopsa but bending to Pamela. The word about it was, "By force, not choice"; and still kneeling, besought the princess that she would vouchsafe to give it Mopsa, and with the blessedness of her hand to make acceptable unto her that toy which I had found, following of late an acquaintance of mine at the plough. "For," said I, "as the earth was turned up, the plough-share lighted upon a great stone. We pull'd that up, and so found both that and some other pretty things which we had divided betwixt us."

'Mopsa was benumbed with joy when the princess gave it her; but in the princess I could find no apprehension of what I either said or did, but with a calm carelessness letting each thing slide justly, as we do by their speeches who neither in matter nor person do anyway belong unto us; which kind of cold temper, mix'd with that lightning of her natural majesty, is of all others most terrible unto me: for yet if I found she contemned* me, I would desperately labour both in fortune and virtue to overcome it: if she only misdoubted me I were in heaven, for quickly I would bring sufficient assurance: lastly, if she hated me, yet I should know what passion to deal with, and either with infiniteness of desert I would take away the fuel from that fire, or if nothing would serve, then I would give her my heart-blood to quench it. But this cruel quietness, neither retiring to mislike nor proceeding to favour; gracious, but gracious still after one manner; all her courtesies having this engraven in them, that what is done is for virtue's sake, not for the party's;* ever keeping her course like the sun who neither for our praises nor curses will spur or stop his horses: this, I say, heavenliness of hers (for howsoever my misery is, I cannot but so entitle it) is so impossible to reach unto that I almost begin to submit myself to the tyranny of despair, not knowing any way of persuasion where wisdom seems to be unsensible.* I have appeared to her eyes like myself, by a device I used with my master, persuading him that we two might put on certain rich apparel I had provided, and so practise something on horseback before Pamela, telling him it was apparel I had gotten for playing well the part of a king in a tragedy at Athens. My horse indeed was it I had left at Menalcas' house, and Dametas got one by friendship out of the prince's stable. But howsoever I show I am no base body, all I do is but to beat a rock and get foam.'

## CHAPTER 4

But as Dorus was about to tell further, Dametas (who came whistling, and counting upon his fingers how many load of hay his seventeen fat oxen eat up in a year) desired Zelmane from the king that she would come into the lodge where they stayed for her.

'Alas,' said Dorus, taking his leave, 'the sum is this, that you may well find you have beaten your sorrow against such a wall which, with the force of rebound, may well make your sorrow stronger.'

*contemned*: despised. *not for the party's*: not for personal considerations. *unsensible*: without feeling.

But Zelmane turning her speech to Dametas, 'I shall grow,' said she, 'skilful in country matters if I have often conference with your servant.'

'In sooth,' answered Dametas with a graceless scorn, 'the lad may prove well enough, if he oversoon think not too well of himself, and will bear away that he heareth of his elders.'

And therewith as they walked to the other lodge, to make Zelmane find she might have spent her time better with him he began with a wild method[1] to run over all the art of husbandry, especially employing his tongue about well dunging of a field, while poor Zelmane yielded her ears to those tedious strokes, not warding them so much as with any one answer, till they came to Basilius and Gynecia, who attended for her in a coach to carry her abroad to see some sports prepared for her.

Basilius and Gynecia, sitting in the one end, placed her at the other, with her left side to Philoclea. Zelmane was moved in her mind to have kissed their feet for the favour of so blessed a seat, for the narrowness of the coach made them join from the foot to the shoulders very close together; the truer touch whereof though it were barred by their envious apparel, yet as a perfect magnes* though put in an ivory box will through the box send forth his embracing virtue to a beloved needle, so this imparadised neighbourhood made Zelmane's soul cleave unto her both through the ivory case of her body and the apparel which did overcloud it: all the blood of Zelmane's body stirring in her, as wine will do when sugar is hastily put into it, seeking to suck the sweetness of the beloved guest; her heart like a lion new imprisoned, seeing him that restrains his liberty before the grate, not panting but striving violently (if it had been possible) to have leaped into the lap of Philoclea.

But Dametas, even then proceeding from being master of a cart to be doctor of a coach, not a little proud in himself that his whip at that time guided the rule of Arcadia, drave the coach, the cover whereof was made with such joints that as they might (to avoid the weather) pull it up close when they listed, so when they would they might put each end down and remain as discovered and open-sighted as on horseback: till upon the side of the forest

* *magnes*: magnet.

they had both greyhounds, spaniels and hounds, whereof the first might seem the lords, the second the gentlemen, and the last the yeomen of dogs. A cast of merlins there was besides, which, flying of a gallant height over certain bushes, would beat the birds that rose down into the bushes, as falcons will do wild-fowl over a river.

But the sport which for that day Basilius would principally show to Zelmane was the mounty* at a hern;* which, getting up on his waggling wings with pain till he was come to some height (as though the air next to the earth were not fit for his great body to fly through) was now grown to diminish the sight of himself, and to give example to great persons that the higher they be, the less they should show; when a jerfaulcon was cast off after her, who straight spying where the prey was, fixing her eye with desire and guiding her wing by her eye, used no more strength than industry.* For as a good builder to a high tower will not make his stair upright but winding almost the full compass about, that the steepness be the more unsensible;* so she, seeing the towering of her pursued chase, went circling and compassing* about, rising so with the less sense of rising: and yet finding that way scantly serve the greediness of her haste, as an ambitious body will go far out of the direct way to win to a point of height which he desires, so would she, as it were, turn tail to the heron and fly quite out another way; but all was to return in a higher pitch, which once gotten, she would either beat with cruel assaults the heron (who now was driven to the best defence of force since flight would not serve) or else clasping with him, come down together, to be parted by the over-partial* beholders.

Divers of which flights Basilius showing to Zelmane, thus was the riches of the time spent and the day deceased before it was thought of, till night like a degenerating successor made his departure the better remembered. And therefore, so constrained, they willed Dametas to drive homeward, who (half sleeping, half musing about the mending of a wine-press) guided the horses so ill that the wheel coming over a great stub of a tree, it overturned the

*mounty: hunting of high-flying quarry by falcons. hern: heron. industry: dexterity. more unsensible: less noticeable. compassing: circling. over-partial: not impartial.

coach; which though it fell violently upon the side where Zelmane and Gynecia sat, yet for Zelmane's part, she would have been glad of the fall which made her bear the sweet burden of Philoclea, but that she feared she might receive some hurt. But indeed neither she did, nor any of the rest, by reason they kept their arms and legs within the coach, saving Gynecia who with the only bruise of the fall had her shoulder put out of joint; which, though by one of the falconer's cunning it was set well again, yet with much pain was she brought to the lodge; and pain (fetching his ordinary companion, a fever, with him) drave her to entertain them both in her bed.

But neither was the fever of such impatient heat as the inward plague-sore of her affection, nor the pain half so noisome as the jealousy she conceived of her daughter Philoclea, lest this time of her sickness might give apt occasion to Zelmane, whom she misdoubted.* Therefore she called Philoclea to her, and though it were late in the night, commanded her in her ear to go to the other lodge and send Miso to her, with whom she would speak, and she to lie with her sister Pamela. The meanwhile Gynecia kept Zelmane with her because she would be sure she should be out of the lodge before she licensed* Zelmane. Philoclea, not skill'd in any thing better than obedience, went quietly down; and the moon then full (not thinking scorn to be a torch-bearer to such beauty) guided her steps whose motions bare a mind which bare in itself far more stirring motions. And alas, sweet Philoclea, how hath my pen till now forgot thy passions, since to thy memory principally all this long matter is intended! Pardon the slackness to come to those woes which, having caused in others, thou didst feel in thyself.

The sweet minded Philoclea was in their degree of well-doing to whom the not knowing of evil serveth for a ground of virtue, and hold their inward powers in better form with an unspotted simplicity than many who rather cunningly seek to know what goodness is than willingly take into themselves the following of it. But as that sweet and simple breath of heavenly goodness is the easier to be altered because it hath not passed through the worldly wickedness nor feelingly found the evil that evil carries with it, so now

* *misdoubted:* mistrusted. *licensed:* allowed to depart.

the lady Philoclea (whose eyes and senses had received nothing but according as the natural course of each thing required, whose tender youth had obediently lived under her parents' behests, without framing out of her own will the forechoosing of any thing) when now she came to appoint wherein her judgement was to be practised in knowing faultiness by his first tokens, she was like a young fawn who, coming in the wind of* the hunters, doth not know whether it be a thing or no to be eschewed; whereof at this time she began to get a costly experience.

For after that Zelmane had a while lived in the lodge with her and that her only being a noble stranger had bred a kind of heedful attention; her coming to that lonely place where she had nobody but her parents, a willingness of conversation, her wit and behaviour, a liking and silent admiration, at length the excellency of her natural gifts joined with the extreme shows she made of most devout honouring Philoclea (carrying thus, in one person, the only two bands of goodwill, loveliness and lovingness) brought forth in her heart a yielding to a most friendly affection; which when it had gotten so full possession of the keys of her mind that it would receive no message from her senses without that affection were the interpreter, then straight grew an exceeding delight still to be with her, with an unmeasurable liking of all that Zelmane did: matters being so turned in her that where at first, liking her manners did breed goodwill, now goodwill became the chief cause of liking her manners, so that within a while Zelmane was not prized for her demeanour but the demeanour was prized because it was Zelmane's.

Then followed that most natural effect of conforming herself to that which she did like, and not only wishing to be herself such another in all things, but to ground an imitation upon so much an esteemed authority; so that the next degree was to mark all Zelmane's doings, speeches, and fashions, and to take them into herself as a pattern of worthy proceeding. Which when once it was enacted not only by the commonalty* of passions but agreed unto by her most noble thoughts, and that reason itself (not yet experienced in the issues of such matters) had granted his royal assent, then friendship, a diligent officer, took care to see the statute

* *coming in the wind of*: scenting. *commonalty*: the common level.

thoroughly observed. Then grew on* that not only she did imitate the soberness of her countenance, the gracefulness of her speech, but even their particular gestures; so that as Zelmane did often eye her, she would often eye Zelmane; and as Zelmane's eyes would deliver a submissive but vehement desire in their look, she, though as yet she had not the desire in her, yet should her eyes answer in like piercing kindness of a look. Zelmane, as much as Gynecia's jealousy would suffer, desired to be near Philoclea; Philoclea, as much as Gynecia's jealousy would suffer, desired to be near Zelmane. If Zelmane took her hand and softly strained it, she also, thinking the knots of friendship ought to be mutual, would with a sweet fastness* show she was loth to part from it. And if Zelmane sighed, she should sigh also; when Zelmane was sad, she deemed it wisdom and therefore she would be sad too. Zelmane's languishing countenance, with crossed arms and sometimes cast up eyes, she thought to have an excellent grace, and therefore she also willingly put on the same countenance, till at the last, poor soul, ere she were aware, she accepted not only the badge but the service, not only the sign but the passion signified.

For whether it were that her wit in continuance did find that Zelmane's friendship was full of impatient desire having more than ordinary limits, and therefore she was content to second Zelmane though herself knew not the limits, or that in truth true love, well considered, have an infective power, at last she fell in acquaintance with love's harbinger,* wishing. First she would wish that they two might live all their lives together, like two of Diana's nymphs. But that wish she thought not sufficient, because she knew there would be more nymphs besides them who also would have their part in Zelmane. Then would she wish that she were her sister, that such a natural band might make her more special to her. But against that, she considered that, though being her sister, if she happened to be married she should be robbed of her. Then grown bolder, she would wish either herself or Zelmane a man, that there might succeed a blessed marriage betwixt them. But when that wish had once displayed his ensign in her mind, then followed whole squadrons of longings that so it might be,

* *grew on:* followed. *fastness:* holding fast. *harbinger:* forerunner.

with a main battle* of mislikings and repinings against their creation, that so it was not. Then dreams by night began to bring more unto her than she durst wish by day, whereout waking did make her know herself the better by the image of those fancies. But as some diseases, when they are easy to be cured they are hard to be known, but when they grow easy to be known they are almost impossible to be cured, so the sweet Philoclea, while she might prevent it, she did not feel it; now she felt it when it was past preventing, like a river, no rampires being built against it till already it have overflowed. For now indeed love pulled off his mask and showed his face unto her, and told her plainly that she was his prisoner. Then needed she no more paint her face with passions, for passions shone through her face: then her rosy colour was often increased with extraordinary blushing, and so another time, perfect whiteness descended to a degree of paleness; now hot, then cold, desiring she knew not what, nor how, if she knew what.

Then her mind (though too late) by the smart was brought to think of the disease, and her own proof taught her to know her mother's mind, which (as no error gives so strong assault as that which comes armed in the authority of a parent) so greatly fortified her desires to see that her mother had the like desires. And the more jealous her mother was, the more she thought the jewel precious which was with so many locks guarded. But that prevailing so far as to keep the two lovers from private conference, then began she to feel the sweetness of a lover's solitariness when freely with words and gestures, as if Zelmane were present, she might give passage to her thoughts and so, as it were, utter out some smoke of those flames wherewith else she was not only burned but smothered: as this night, that going from the one lodge to the other by her mother's commandment, with doleful gestures and uncertain paces, she did willingly accept the time's offer to be a while alone; so that going a little aside into the wood where many times before she had delighted to walk, her eyes were saluted with a tuft of trees so close set together as, with the shade the moon gave through it, it might breed a fearful kind of devotion to look upon it. But true thoughts of love banished all vain fancy of

*battle: army.

superstition. Full well she did both remember and like the place, for there had she often with their shade beguiled Phoebus* of looking upon her: there had she enjoyed herself often, while she was mistress of herself and had no other thoughts but such as might arise out of quiet senses.

But the principal cause that invited her remembrance was a goodly white marble stone that should seem had been dedicated in ancient time to the Sylvan gods; which she finding there a few days before Zelmane's coming, had written these words upon it as a testimony of her mind against the suspicion her captivity made her think she lived in. The writing was this:

You living powers enclos'd in stately shrine
   Of growing trees; you rural Gods that wield
Your sceptres here, if to your ears divine
   A voice may come, which troubled soul doth yield;
     This vow receive, this vow, O Gods, maintain;
     My virgin life no spotted thought shall stain.

Thou purest stone, whose pureness doth present
   My purest mind; whose temper hard doth show
My temper'd heart; by thee my promise sent
   Unto myself let after-livers know.
     No fancy mine, nor others' wrong suspect
     Make me, O virtuous shame, thy laws neglect.

O Chastity, the chief of heavenly lights,
   Which mak'st us most immortal shape to wear,
Hold thou my heart, establish thou my sprites:
   To only thee my constant course I bear.
     'Till spotless soul unto thy bosom fly,
     Such life to lead, such death I vow to die.

But now that her memory served as an accuser of her change and that her own handwriting was there to bear testimony against her fall, she went in among those few trees, so closed in the tops together as they might seem a little chapel; and there might she, by the help of the moon-light, perceive the goodly

*Phoebus: the sun.

stone which served as an altar in that woody devotion. But neither the light was enough to read the words, and the ink was already forworn and in many places blotted, which as she perceived, 'Alas,' said she, 'fair marble, which never received'st spot but by my writing, well do these blots become a blotted writer. But pardon her which did not dissemble then, although she have changed since. Enjoy, enjoy the glory of thy nature which can so constantly bear the marks of my inconstancy.' And herewith, hiding her eyes with her soft hand, there came into her head certain verses which, if she had had present commodity,* she would have adjoined as a retractation* to the other. They were to this effect.

> My words, in hope to blaze* my steadfast mind,
>   This marble chose, as of like temper known:
> But lo, my words defac'd, my fancies blind,
>   Blots to the stone, shames to myself I find:
>     And witness am, how ill agree in one
>     A woman's hand with constant marble stone.
>
> My words full weak, the marble full of might;
>   My words in store,* the marble all alone;
> My words black ink, the marble kindly* white;
>   My words unseen, the marble still in sight,
>     May witness bear how ill agree in one
>     A woman's hand with constant marble stone.

But seeing she could not see means to join as then this recantation to the former vow, laying all her fair length under one of the trees, for a while she did nothing but turn up and down, as if she had hoped to turn away the fancy that mastered her, and hid her face, as if she could have hidden herself from her own fancies.

At length with a whispering note to herself: 'O me unfortunate wretch,' said she, 'what poisonous heats be these which thus torment me? How hath the sight of this strange guest invaded my soul? Alas, what entrance found this desire, or what strength had it thus to conquer me?' Then a cloud passing between her sight

---

* *commodity*: means of writing. *retractation*: retraction. *blaze*: proclaim. *in store*: abundant. *kindly*: by nature.

and the moon, 'O Diana,'* said she, 'I would either the cloud that now hides the light of my virtue would as easily pass away as you will quickly overcome this let, or else that you were for ever thus darkened to serve for an excuse of my outrageous folly.'

Then looking to the stars, which had perfectly as then beautified the clear sky: 'My parents,' said she, 'have told me that in these fair heavenly bodies there are great hidden deities which have their working in the ebbing and flowing of our estates. If it be so, then, O you stars, judge rightly of me, and if I have with wicked intent made myself a prey to fancy, or if by any idle lusts I framed my heart fit for such an impression, then let this plague daily increase in me till my name be made odious to womankind. But if extreme and unresistable violence have oppressed me, who will ever do any of you sacrifice, O you stars, if you do not succour me? No, no, you will not help me. No, no, you cannot help me: sin must be the mother and shame the daughter of my affection. And yet are these but childish objections, simple Philoclea; it is the impossibility that doth torment me: for unlawful desires are punished after the effect of enjoying, but unpossible desires are punished in the desire itself. O then, O ten times unhappy that I am, since where in all other hope kindleth love, in me despair should be the bellows of my affection; and of all despairs the most miserable which is drawn from impossibility. The most covetous man longs not to get riches out of a ground which never can bear anything. Why? Because it is impossible. The most ambitious wight* vexeth not his wits to climb into heaven. Why? Because it is impossible. Alas, then, O love, why dost thou in thy beautiful sampler set* such a work for my desire to take out, which is as much impossible?

'And yet alas, why do I thus condemn my fortune before I hear what she can say for herself? What do I, silly wench, know what love hath prepared for me? Do I not see my mother as well, at least as furiously as myself, love Zelmane, and should I be wiser than my mother? Either she sees a possibility in that which I think impossible, or else impossible loves need not misbecome me. And do I not see Zelmane (who doth not think a thought which is not

* *Diana:* the goddess associated with the moon. *wight:* person. *set:* sew.

first weighed by wisdom and virtue) doth not she vouchsafe to love me with like ardour? I see it; her eyes depose* it to be true. What then? And if she can love poor me, shall I think scorn to love such a woman as Zelmane? Away then all vain examinations of why and how. Thou lovest me, excellent Zelmane, and I love thee.' And with that, embracing the very ground whereon she lay, she said to herself (for even to herself she was ashamed to speak it out in words) 'O my Zelmane, govern and direct me, for I am wholly given over unto thee.'

## CHAPTER 5

In this depth of muses and divers sorts of discourses would she ravingly have remained but that Dametas and Miso (who were round about to seek her, understanding she was to come to their lodge that night) came hard by her; Dametas saying that he would not deal in other body's matters, but for his part he did not like that maids should once stir out of their father's houses but if it were to milk a cow or save a chicken from a kite's foot or some such other matter of importance; and Miso swearing that if it were her daughter Mopsa, she would give her a lesson for walking so late that should make her keep within doors for one fortnight. But their jangling made Philoclea rise, and pretending as though she had done it but to sport with them, went with them (after she had willed Miso to wait upon her mother) to the lodge; where, being now accustomed (by her parents' discipline) as well as her sister to serve herself, she went alone up to Pamela's chamber: where, meaning to delight her eyes and joy her thoughts with the sweet conversation of her beloved sister, she found her (though it were in the time that the wings of night doth blow sleep most willingly into mortal creatures) sitting in a chair, lying backward, with her head almost over the back of it, and looking upon a wax candle which burnt before her; in one hand holding a letter, in the other her handkerchief which had lately drunk up the tears of her eyes, leaving instead of them crimson circles, like red flakes in the element* when the weather is hottest. Which Philoclea finding (for her eyes had learned to know the badges of sorrow) she earnestly

* *depose*: testify. *element*: atmosphere.

entreated to know the cause thereof, that either she might comfort or accompany her doleful humour. But Pamela, rather seeming sorry that she had perceived so much than willing to open any further:

'O my Pamela,' said Philoclea, 'who are to me a sister in nature, a mother in counsel, a princess by the law of our country, and (which name methinks of all other is the dearest) a friend by my choice and your favour, what means this banishing me from your counsels? Do you love your sorrow so well as to grudge me part of it? Or do you think I shall not love a sad Pamela so well as a joyful? Or be my ears unworthy, or my tongue suspected? What is it, my sister, that you should conceal from your sister, yea and servant Philoclea?'

These words won no further of Pamela but that telling her they might talk better as they lay together, they impoverished their clothes to enrich their bed which for that night might well scorn the shrine of Venus: and there, cherishing one another with dear though chaste embracements, with sweet though cold kisses, it might seem that love was come to play him there without dart, or that, weary of his own fires, he was there to refresh himself between their sweet breathing lips.

But Philoclea earnestly again entreated Pamela to open her grief; who, drawing the curtain that the candle might not complain of her blushing,[1] was ready to speak, but the breath, almost formed into words, was again stopped by her and turned into sighs. But at last, 'I pray you,' said she, 'sweet Philoclea, let us talk of some other thing: and tell me whether you did ever see anything so amended as our pastoral sports be since that Dorus came hither?'

O love, how far thou seest with blind eyes! Philoclea had straight found her, and therefore to draw out more, 'Indeed,' said she, 'I have often wondered to myself how such excellencies could be in so mean a person; but belike Fortune was afraid to lay her treasures where they should be stained with* so many perfections: only I marvel how he can frame himself to hide so rare gifts under such a block as Dametas.'

'Ah,' said Pamela, 'if you knew the cause: but no more do I

* *stained with*: eclipsed by.

neither; and to say the truth – but Lord, how are we fallen to talk of this fellow! And yet indeed if you were sometimes with me to mark him while Dametas reads his rustic lecture unto him how to feed his beasts before noon, where to shade them in the extreme heat, how to make the manger handsome for his oxen, when to use the goad and when the voice, giving him rules of a herdman though he pretend to make him a shepherd – to see all the while with what a grace (which seems to set a crown upon his base estate) he can descend to those poor matters, certainly you would – but to what serves this? No doubt we were better sleep than talk of these idle matters.'

'Ah my Pamela,' said Philoclea, 'I have caught you. The constancy of your wit was not wont to bring forth such disjointed speeches. You love. Dissemble no further.'

'It is true,' said Pamela, 'now you have it; and with less ado should, if my heart could have thought those words suitable for my mouth. But indeed, my Philoclea, take heed, for I think virtue itself is no armour of proof against affection. Therefore learn by my example.'

'Alas,' thought Philoclea to herself, 'your shears come too late to clip the bird's wings that already is flown away.' But then Pamela, being once set in the stream of her love, went away amain, withal telling her how his noble qualities had drawn her liking towards him, but yet ever weighing his meanness, and so held continually in due limits; till seeking many means to speak with her, and ever kept from it (as well because she shunn'd it, seeing and disdaining his mind, as because of her jealous jailors) he had at length used the finest policy that might be in counterfeiting love to Mopsa, and saying to Mopsa whatsoever he would have her know: and in how passionate manner he had told his own tale in a third person, making poor Mopsa believe that it was a matter fallen out many ages before.

'And in the end, because you shall know my tears come not neither of repentance nor misery, who, think you, is my Dorus fallen out to be? Even the Prince Musidorus, famous over all Asia for his heroical enterprises, of whom you remember how much good the stranger Plangus told my father; he not being drowned, as Plangus thought, though his cousin Pyrocles indeed perished. Ah my sister, if you had heard his words or seen his gestures when he made me know what and to whom his love was, you would have matched in yourself those two rarely matched together, pity and delight. Tell me, dear sister – for the gods are my witnesses I desire to do virtuously – can I without the detestable stain of ungratefulness abstain from loving him who (far exceeding the beautifulness of his shape with the beautifulness of his mind, and the greatness of his estate with the greatness of his acts) is content so to abase himself as to become Dametas' servant for my sake? You will say, but how know I him to be Musidorus, since the handmaid of wisdom is slow of belief? That consideration did not want in me, for the nature of desire itself is no easier to receive belief than it is hard to ground belief. For as desire is glad to embrace the first show of comfort, so is desire desirous of perfect assurance: and that have I had of him, not only by necessary arguments to any of common sense, but by sufficient demonstrations. Lastly, he would have me send to Thessalia; but truly I am not as now in mind to do my honourable love so much wrong as so far to suspect him: yet poor soul, knows he no other but that I do both suspect, neglect, yea, and detest him. For every day he finds one way or other to set forth himself unto me, but all are rewarded with like coldness of acceptation.

'A few days since, he and Dametas had furnished themselves very richly to run at the ring before me.[2] O how mad a sight it was to see Dametas, like rich tissue furred with lamb-skins! But O, how well it did with Dorus, to see with what a grace he presented himself before me on horseback, making majesty wait upon humbleness: how at the first, standing still with his eyes bent upon me, as though his motions were chained to my look, he so stayed till I caused Mopsa bid him do something upon his horse: which no sooner said but, with a kind rather of quick gesture than show of violence, you might see him come towards me beating the ground in so due time as no dancer can observe better measure. If you remember the ship we saw once when the sea went high upon the coast of Argos, so went the beast. But he, as if centaur-like he had been one piece with the horse, was no more moved than one is with the going of his own legs; and in effect so did he command him as his own limbs; for though he had both spurs and wand,* they seemed rather marks of sovereignty than instruments of punishment, his hand and leg with most pleasing grace commanding without threatening, and rather remembering* than chastising: at least if sometimes he did, it was so stolen as neither our eyes could discern it nor the horse with any change did complain of it; he ever going so just with the horse, either forth-right or turning, that it seemed as he borrowed the horse's body so he lent the horse his mind. In the turning one might perceive the bridle-hand something gently stir, but indeed so gently as it did rather distil virtue than use violence. Himself (which methinks is strange) showing at one instant both steadiness and nimbleness; sometimes making him turn close to the ground, like a cat when scratchingly she wheels about after a mouse; sometimes with a little more rising before, now like a raven leaping from ridge to ridge, then like one of Dametas' kids bound over the hillocks; and all so done as neither the lusty kind showed any roughness nor the easier any idleness; but still like a well-obeyed master, whose beck* is enough for a discipline, ever concluding each thing he did with his face to me-wards, as if thence came not only the beginning but ending of his motions.

The sport was to see Dametas, how he was tossed from the saddle to the mane of the horse and thence to the ground, giving his gay apparel almost as foul an outside as it had an inside. But as before he had ever said he wanted but horse and apparel to be as brave a courtier as the best, so now bruised with proof, he proclaimed it a folly for a man of wisdom to put himself under the tuition of a beast, so as Dorus was fain alone to take the ring. Wherein truly at least my womanish eyes could not discern but that taking his staff from his thigh, the descending it a little down, the getting of it up into the rest,* the letting of the point fall, and taking the ring, was but all one motion – at least, if they were divers motions, they did so stealingly slip one into another as the latter part was ever in hand before the eye could discern the former was ended. Indeed Dametas found fault that he showed no

* wand: switch. remembering: reminding. beck: nod. rest: shoulder-rest for butt of lance in jousting.

more strength in shaking of his staff; but to my conceit the fine cleanness of bearing it was exceeding delightful.

'But how delightful soever it was, my delight might well be in my soul, but it never went to look out of the window* to do him any comfort. But how much more I found reason to like him, the more I set all the strength of mind to suppress it or at least to conceal it. Indeed I must confess that, as some physicians have told me, when one is cold outwardly he is not inwardly, so truly the cold ashes laid upon my fire did not take the nature of fire from it. Full often hath my breast swollen with keeping my sighs imprisoned. Full often have the tears I drave back from mine eyes turned back to drown my heart. But alas, what did that help poor Dorus, whose eyes, being his diligent intelligencers,* could carry unto him no other news but discomfortable? I think no day passed but by some one invention he would appear unto me to testify his love. One time he danced the matachin dance in armour (O, with what a graceful dexterity!) I think to make me see that he had been brought up in such exercises.³ Another time he persuaded his master, to make my time seem shorter, in manner of a dialogue to play Priamus while he played Paris. Think, sweet Philoclea, what a Priamus we had: but truly, my Paris was a Paris and more than a Paris, who, while in a savage apparel, with naked neck, arms and legs, he made love to Oenone, you might well see by his changed countenance and true tears that he felt the part he played. Tell me, sweet Philoclea, did you ever see such a shepherd? Tell me, did you ever hear of such a prince? And then tell me if a small or unworthy assault have conquered me. Truly I would hate my life if I thought vanity led me. But since my parents deal so cruelly with me, it is time for me to trust something to my own judgement. Yet hitherto have my looks been as I told you, which, continuing after many of these his fruitless trials, have wrought such change in him as I tell you true,' – with that word she laid her hand upon her quaking side – 'I do not a little fear him.* See what a letter this is,' – then drew she the curtain and took the letter from under her pillow – 'which today, with an afflicted humbleness, he delivered me, pretending before Mopsa that I

*look out of the window: show itself outwardly. intelligencers: gatherers of intelligence. fear him: fear for him.

should read it unto her to mollify, forsooth, her iron stomach.'
With that she read the letter, containing thus much:

Most blessed paper, which shalt kiss that hand whereto all blessedness is in nature a servant, do not yet disdain to carry with thee the woeful words of a miser* now despairing: neither be afraid to appear before her, bearing the base title of the sender. For no sooner shall that divine hand touch thee but that thy baseness shall be turned to most high preferment. Therefore mourn boldly, my ink, for while she looks upon you, your blackness will shine. Cry out boldly my lamentation, for while she reads you, your cries will be music. Say then (O happy messenger of a most unhappy message) that the too soon born and too late dying creature, which dares not speak, no not look, no not scarcely think (as from his miserable self, unto her heavenly highness) only presumes to desire thee (in the time that her eyes and voice do exalt thee) to say, and in this manner to say, not from him – O no, that were not fit – but of him, thus much unto her sacred judgement: 'O you, the only honour to women, to men the only admiration; you that being armed by love, defy him that armed you, in this high estate wherein you have placed me, yet let me remember him to whom I am bound for bringing me to your presence; and let me remember him, who (since he is yours, how mean soever he be) it is reason you have an account of him. The wretch (yet your wretch) though with languishing steps, runs fast to his grave; and will you suffer a temple (how poorly built soever, but yet a temple of your deity) to be razed? But he dieth: it is most true, he dieth; and he in whom you live, to obey you, dieth. Whereof though he plain,* he doth not complain, for it is a harm but no wrong which he hath received. He dies, because in woeful language all his senses tell him that such is your pleasure: for since you will not that he live, alas, alas, what followeth of the most ruined Dorus but his end? End then, evil-destined Dorus, end; and end thou, woeful letter, end; for it sufficeth her wisdom to know that her heavenly will shall be accomplished.'

'O my Philoclea, is he a person to write these words? And are these words lightly to be regarded? But if you had seen, when with trembling hand he had delivered it, how he went away, as if he had been but the coffin that carried himself to his sepulchre. Two times, I must confess, I was about to take courtesy into

* *miser*: wretch. *plain*: laments.

mine eyes, but both times the former resolution stopped the entry of it, so that he departed without obtaining any further kindness. But he was no sooner out of the door but that I looked to the door kindly; and truly the fear of him ever since hath put me into such perplexity as now you found me.'

'Ah my Pamela,' said Philoclea, 'leave sorrow. The river of your tears will soon lose his fountain. It is in your hand as well to stitch up his life again as it was before to rent it.' And so, though with self-grieved mind, she comforted her sister, till sleep came to bathe himself in Pamela's fair weeping eyes.

Which when Philoclea found, wringing her hands, 'O me,' said she, 'indeed the only subject of the destinies' displeasure, whose greatest fortunateness is more unfortunate than my sister's greatest unfortunateness. Alas, she weeps because she would be no sooner happy: I weep because I can never be happy. Her tears flow from pity; mine from being too far lower than the reach of pity. Yet do I not envy thee, dear Pamela, I do not envy thee: only I could wish that being thy sister in nature, I were not so far off akin in fortune.'

## CHAPTER 6

But the darkness of sorrow overshadowing her mind as the night did her eyes, they were both content to hide themselves under the wings of sleep, till the next morning had almost lost his name before the two sweet sleeping sisters awaked from dreams which flattered them with more comfort than their waking could or would consent unto. For then, they were called up by Miso, who, having been with Gynecia, had received commandment to be continually with her daughters, and particularly not to let Zelmane and Philoclea have any private conference but that she should be present to hear what passed. Miso, having now her authority increased, came with scowling eyes to deliver a slavering good morrow to the two ladies, telling them it was a shame for them to mar their complexions, yea and conditions too, with long lying abed, and that when she was of their age, she trowed,* she would have made a handkerchief by that time a day. The two sweet

* *she trowed:* she was sure.

princesses with a smiling silence answered her entertainment and, obeying her direction, covered their dainty beauties with the glad clothes. But as soon as Pamela was ready – and sooner she was than her sister – the agony of Dorus giving a fit* to herself which the words of his letter (lively imprinted in her mind) still remembered her of, she called to Mopsa and willed her to fetch Dorus to speak with her because, she said, she would take further judgement of him before she would move Dametas to grant her in marriage unto him. Mopsa, as glad as of sweetmeat to go of such an errand, quickly returned with Dorus to Pamela, who intended both by speaking with him to give some comfort to his passionate heart and withal, to hear some part of his life past, which although fame had already delivered unto her, yet she desired in more particular certainties to have it from so beloved an historian. Yet the sweetness of virtue's disposition, jealous even over itself, suffered her not to enter abruptly into questions of Musidorus (whom she was half ashamed she did love so well, and more than half sorry she could love no better) but thought best first to make her talk arise of Pyrocles and his virtuous father: which thus she did.

'Dorus,' said she, 'you told me the last day that Plangus was deceived in that he affirmed the prince Musidorus was drowned: but, withal, you confessed his cousin Pyrocles perished; of whom certainly in that age there was a great loss, since, as I have heard, he was a young prince of whom all men expected as much as man's power could bring forth, and yet virtue promised for him their expectation should not be deceived.'

'Most excellent lady,' said Dorus, 'no expectation in others nor hope in himself could aspire to a higher mark than to be thought worthy to be praised by your judgment, and made worthy to be praised by your mouth. But most sure it is, that as his fame could by no means get so sweet and noble an air to fly in as in your breath, so could not you (leaving yourself aside) find in the world a fitter subject of commendation: as noble as a long succession of royal ancestors, famous and famous for victories, could make him; of shape most lovely, and yet of mind more lovely; valiant, courteous, wise – what should I say more? Sweet Pyrocles, excellent

* fit: shock.

Pyrocles, what can my words but wrong thy perfections, which I would to God in some small measure thou had'st bequeathed to him that ever must have thy virtues in admiration, that, masked at least in them, I might have found some more gracious acceptation.'

With that he imprisoned his look for a while upon Mopsa, who thereupon fell into a very wide smiling.

'Truly,' said Pamela, 'Dorus, I like well your mind that can raise itself out of so base a fortune as yours is, to think of the imitating so excellent a prince as Pyrocles was. Who shoots at the mid-day sun, though he be sure he shall never hit the mark, yet as sure he is he shall shoot higher than who aims but at a bush. But I pray you, Dorus,' said she, 'tell me, since I perceive you are well acquainted with that story, what prince was that Euarchus, father to Pyrocles, of whom so much fame goes for his rightly royal virtues, or by what ways he got that opinion. And then so descend to the causes of his sending first away from him, and then to him for that excellent son of his, with the discourse of his life and loss: and therein you may (if you list) say something of that same Musidorus his cousin, because they going together, the story of Pyrocles (which I only desire) may be the better understood.'

'Incomparable lady,' said he, 'your commandment doth not only give me the will but the power to obey you, such influence hath your excellency. And first, for that famous king Euarchus, he was, at this time you speak of, king of Macedon, a kingdom which in elder time had such a sovereignty over all the provinces of Greece that even the particular kings therein did acknowledge, with more or less degrees of homage, some kind of fealty thereunto, as among the rest, even this now most noble (and by you ennobled) kingdom of Arcadia. But he, when he came to his crown, finding by his latter ancestors' either negligence or misfortune that in some ages many of those duties had been intermitted, would never stir up old titles (how apparent soever) whereby the public peace, with the loss of many not guilty souls, should be broken; but contenting himself to guide that ship wherein the heavens had placed him, showed no less magnanimity in dangerless despising than others in dangerous affecting the multiplying of kingdoms, for the earth hath since borne enow bleeding witnesses that it was no want of true courage. Who as he was most wise to see what was best, and most just in the performing what he saw and temperate in abstaining from anything anyway contrary, so think I, no thought can imagine a greater heart to see and contemn danger, where danger would offer to make any wrongful threatening upon him. A prince that indeed especially measured his greatness by his goodness: and if for anything he loved greatness, it was because therein he might exercise his goodness. A prince of a goodly aspect, and the more goodly by a grave majesty wherewith his mind did deck his outward graces; strong of body, and so much the stronger as he by a well-disciplined exercise taught it both to do and suffer. Of age, so as he was about fifty years when his nephew Musidorus took on such shepherdish apparel for the love of the world's paragon as I now wear.

'This king, left orphan both of father and mother (whose father and grandfather likewise had died young) he found his estate (when he came to the age which allowed his authority) so disjointed even in the noblest and strongest limbs of government that the name of a king was grown even odious to the people, his authority having been abused by those great lords and little kings who in those between-times of reigning, by unjust favouring those that were partially theirs, and oppressing them that would defend their liberty against them, had brought in (by a more felt than seen manner of proceeding) the worst kind of Oligarchy: that is, when men are governed indeed by a few, and yet are not taught to know what those few be to whom they should obey.

'For they, having the power of kings but not the nature of kings, used the authority as men do their farms of which they see within a year they shall go out, making the king's sword strike whom they hated, the king's purse reward whom they loved; and (which is worst of all) making the royal countenance serve to undermine the royal sovereignty. For the subjects could taste no sweeter fruits of having a king than grievous taxations to serve vain purposes; laws made rather to find faults than to prevent faults; the court of prince rather deemed as a privileged place of unbridled licentiousness than as the abiding of him who, as a father, should give a fatherly example unto his people. Hence grew a very dissolution of all estates, while the great men (by the nature of ambition never satisfied) grew factious among themselves, and the underlings glad indeed to be underlings to them they hated least, to preserve them from such they hated most. Men of virtue suppressed, lest their shining should discover the others' filthiness; and at length virtue itself almost forgotten when it had no hopeful end whereunto to be directed: old men long nuzzled* in corruption, scorning them that would seek reformation: young men very fault-finding but very faulty, and so given to new-fangleness both of manners, apparel and each thing else, by the custom of self-guilty evil glad to change, though oft for a worse: merchandise abused, and so towns decayed for want of just and natural liberty: offices, even of judging souls, sold: public defences neglected; and in sum (lest too long I trouble you) all awry, and (which wried* it to the most wry course of all) wit abused rather to feign reason why it should be amiss than how it should be amended.

'In this, and a much worse plight than it is fit to trouble your excellent ears withal, did the king Euarchus find his estate when he took upon him the regiment:* which, by reason of the long stream of abuse, he was forced to establish by some even extreme severity, not so much for the very faults themselves (which he rather sought to prevent than to punish) as for the faulty ones, who, strong even in their faults, scorned his youth, and could not learn to digest that the man which they so long had used to mask their own appetites should now be the reducer of them into order. But so soon as some few (but indeed notable) examples had thundered a duty into the subjects' hearts, he soon showed no baseness of suspicion nor the basest baseness of envy could any whit rule such a ruler. But then shined forth indeed all love among them when an aweful* fear, engendered by justice, did make that love most lovely; his first and principal care being to appear unto his people such as he would have them be, and to be such as he appeared; making his life the example of his laws, and his laws, as it were, his axioms arising out of his deeds. So that within small time he won a singular love in his people and engraffed* singular confidence. For how could they choose but love him, whom they

* *nuzzled*: nurtured. *wried*: twisted. *regiment*: rule. *aweful*: full of awe. *engraffed*: implanted.

found so truly to love them? – he even in reason disdaining that they that have charge of beasts should love their charge and care for them, and that he that was to govern the most excellent creature should not love so noble a charge. And therefore, where most princes (seduced by flattery to build upon false grounds of government) make themselves, as it were, another thing from the people, and so count it gain what they get from them and (as if it were two counter-balances, that their estate goes highest when the people goes lowest) by a fallacy of argument thinking themselves most kings when the subject is most basely subjected; the contrariwise (virtuously and wisely acknowledging that he with his people made all but one politic body whereof himself was the head) even so cared for them as he would for his own limbs; never restraining their liberty without it stretched* to licentiousness, nor pulling from them their goods which they found were not employed to the purchase of a greater good; but in all his actions showing a delight in their welfare, brought that to pass that, while by force he took nothing, by their love he had all. In sum, peerless princess, I might as easily set down the whole art of government as to lay before your eyes the picture of his proceedings. But in such sort he flourished in the sweet comfort of doing much good, when, by an occasion of leaving his country, he was forced to bring forth his virtue of magnanimity, as before he had done of justice.

'He had only one sister, a lady (lest I should too easily fall to partial praises of her) of whom it may be justly said that she was no unfit branch to the noble stock whereof she was come. Her he had given in marriage to Dorilaus, prince of Thessalia, not so much to make a friendship as to confirm the friendship between their posterity, which between them, by the likeness of virtue, had been long before made; for certainly, Dorilaus could need no amplifier's mouth for the highest point of praise.'

'Who hath not heard,' said Pamela, 'of the valiant, wise and just Dorilaus whose unripe death doth yet, so many years since, draw tears from virtuous eyes? And indeed, my father is wont to speak of nothing with greater admiration than of the notable friendship (a rare thing in princes, more rare between princes) that so holily

* *without it stretched*: unless it went.

was observed to the last, of those two excellent men. But,' said she, 'go on, I pray you.'

'Dorilaus,' said he, 'having married his sister, had his marriage in short time blest (for so are folk wont to say, how unhappy soever the children after grow[1]) with a son, whom they named Musidorus, of whom I must needs first speak before I come to Pyrocles, because, as he was born first, so upon his occasion grew, as I may say, accidentally, the other's birth. For scarcely was Musidorus made partaker of this oft-blinding light, when there were found numbers of soothsayers who affirmed strange and incredible things should be performed by that child; whether the heavens at that time listed to play with ignorant mankind, or that flattery be so presumptuous as even at times to borrow the face of divinity. But certainly, so did the boldness of their affirmation accompany the greatness of what they did affirm (even descending to particularities, what kingdoms he should overcome) that the king of Phrygia, who over-superstitiously thought himself touched in the matter, sought by force to destroy the infant to prevent his after expectations, because a skilful man, having compared his nativity with the child, so told him. Foolish man, either vainly fearing what was not to be feared or not considering that if it were a work of the superior powers, the heavens at length are never children. But so he did, and by the aid of the kings of Lydia and Crete (joining together their armies) invaded Thessalia, and brought Dorilaus to some behind-hand of fortune, when his faithful friend and brother Euarchus came so mightily to his succour that, with some interchanging changes of fortune, they begat of just war the best child, Peace. In which time Euarchus made a cross-marriage also with Dorilaus' sister, and shortly left her with child of the famous Pyrocles, driven to return to the defence of his own country, which in his absence (helped with some of the ill-contented nobility) the mighty king of Thrace and his brother, king of Pannonia, had invaded.

'The success of those wars was too notable to be unknown to your ears, to which it seems all worthy fame hath glory to come unto. But there was Dorilaus, valiantly requiting his friend's help, in a great battle deprived of life, his obsequies being no more solemnized by the tears of his partakers than the blood of his enemies; with so piercing a sorrow to the constant heart of Euarchus that the news of his son's birth could lighten his countenance with no show of comfort, although all the comfort that might be in a child, truth itself in him forthwith delivered. For what fortune only soothsayers foretold of Musidorus, that, all men might see prognosticated in Pyrocles, both heavens and earth giving tokens of the coming forth of an heroical virtue. The senate house of the planets was at no time so set for the decreeing of perfection in a man, as at that time all folks skilful therein did acknowledge. Only love was threatened, and promised to him, and so to his cousin, as both the tempest and haven of their best years. But as death may have prevented Pyrocles, so unworthiness must be the death of Musidorus.

## CHAPTER 7

'But the mother of Pyrocles shortly after her childbirth dying was cause that Euarchus recommended the care of his only son to his sister, doing it the rather because the war continued in cruel heat betwixt him and those evil neighbours of his. In which meantime those young princes, the only comforters of that virtuous widow, grew on so that Pyrocles taught admiration to the hardest conceits, Musidorus (perchance because among his subjects) exceedingly beloved; and by the good order of Euarchus (well performed by his sister) they were so brought up that all the sparks of virtue which nature had kindled in them were so blown to give forth their uttermost heat, that, justly it may be affirmed, they inflamed the affections of all that knew them. For almost before they could perfectly speak, they began to receive conceits*[1] not unworthy of the best speakers, excellent devices being used, to make even their sports profitable: images of battles and fortifications being then delivered to their memory, which after, their stronger judgments might dispense; the delight of tales being converted to the knowledge of all the stories of worthy princes, both to move them to do nobly and teach them how to do nobly; the beauty of virtue still being set before their eyes, and that taught them with far more diligent care than grammatical rules; their bodies exercised in all

* *receive conceits*: take in conceptions.

abilities both of doing and suffering, and their minds acquainted by degrees with dangers; and in sum, all bent to the making up of princely minds: no servile fear used towards them, nor any other violent restraint, but still as to* princes, so that a habit of commanding was naturalized in them, and therefore the further from tyranny: Nature having done so much for them in nothing as that it made them lords of truth, whereon all the other goods were builded.

'Among which, nothing I so much delight to recount as the memorable friendship that grew betwixt the two princes, such as made them more like than the likeness of all other virtues, and made them more near one to the other than the nearness of their blood could aspire unto; which I think grew the faster, and the faster was tied between them by reason that Musidorus being elder by three or four years, it was neither so great a difference in age as did take away the delight in society, and yet by the difference there was taken away the occasion of childish contentions till they had both passed over the humour of such contentions. For Pyrocles bare reverence full of love to Musidorus, and Musidorus had a delight full of love in Pyrocles. Musidorus, what he had learned either for body or mind, would teach it to Pyrocles; and Pyrocles was so glad to learn of none as of Musidorus: till Pyrocles, being come to sixteen years of age, he seemed so to overrun his age in growth, strength and all things following it that not Musidorus, no nor any man living, I think, could perform any action, either on horse or foot, more strongly, or deliver that strength more nimbly, or become the delivery more gracefully, or employ all more virtuously. Which may well seem wonderful: but wonders are no wonders in a wonderful subject.

'At which time, understanding that the king Euarchus, after so many years' war and the conquest of all Pannonia and almost Thrace, had now brought the conclusion of all to the siege of Byzantium (to the raising of which siege great forces were made) they would needs fall to the practice of those virtues which they before learned. And therefore the mother of Musidorus nobly yielding over her own affects* to her children's good (for a mother she was in effect to them both) the rather that they might help her

* *still as to:* ever as to. *affects:* desires.

beloved brother, they brake off all delays; which Musidorus for his part thought already had devoured too much of his good time, but that he had once granted a boon (before he knew what it was) to his dear friend Pyrocles that he would never seek the adventures of arms until he might go with him, which having fast bound his heart (a true slave to faith) he had bid a tedious delay* of following his own humour for his friend's sake; till now being both sent for by Euarchus, and finding Pyrocles able every way to go through with that kind of life, he was as desirous for his sake as for his own to enter into it.

'So therefore preparing a navy, that they might go like themselves, and not only bring the comfort of their presence but of their power to their dear parent Euarchus, they recommended themselves to the sea, leaving the shore of Thessalia full of tears and vows, and were received thereon with so smooth and smiling a face as if Neptune had as then learned falsely to fawn on princes. The wind was like a servant, waiting behind them so just, that they might fill the sails as they listed;* and the best sailors, showing themselves less covetous of his liberality, so tempered it that they all kept together like a beautiful flock which so well could obey their master's pipe; without* sometimes, to delight the princes' eyes, some two or three of them would strive who could (either by the cunning of well spending the wind's breath, or by the advantageous building of their moving houses) leave their fellows behind them in the honour of speed: while the two princes had leisure to see the practice of that which before they had learned by books: to consider the art of catching the wind prisoner to no other end but to run away with it; to see how beauty and use can so well agree together that of all the trinkets* wherewith they are attired, there is not one but serves to some necessary purpose. And, O lord, to see the admirable power and noble effects of love, whereby the seeming insensible lodestone, with a secret beauty (holding the spirit of iron in it) can draw that hard-hearted thing unto it and, like a virtuous mistress, not only make it bow itself, but with it make it aspire to so high a love as of the

* *bid a tedious delay ... humour*: long delayed doing what he wanted. *listed*: wished. *without*: except when. *trinkets*: sails, tackle, etc.

heavenly poles, and thereby to bring forth the noblest deeds that the children of the earth can boast of. And so the princes delighting their conceits with confirming their knowledge, seeing wherein the sea-discipline differed from land-service, they had for a day and almost a whole night as pleasing entertainment as the falsest heart could give to him he means worst to.

'But by that the next morning began a little to make a gilden* show of a good meaning, there arose even with the sun a veil of dark clouds before his face, which shortly, like ink poured into water, had blacked over all the face of heaven, preparing, as it were, a mournful stage for a tragedy to be played on. For forthwith the winds began to speak louder and, as in a tumultuous kingdom, to think themselves fittest instruments of commandment; and blowing whole storms of hail and rain upon them, they were sooner in danger than they could almost bethink themselves of change. For then the traitorous sea began to swell in pride against the afflicted navy under which, while the heaven favoured them, it had lain so calmly, making mountains of itself over which the tossed and tottering ship should climb, to be straight carried down again to a pit of hellish darkness; with such cruel blows against the sides of the ship (that, which way soever it went, was still in his malice) that there was left neither power to stay nor way to escape. And shortly had it so dissevered the loving company which the day before had tarried together, that most of them never met again but were swallowed up in his never satisfied mouth. Some indeed, as since was known, after long wandering returned into Thessalia; others recovered* Byzantium, and served Euarchus in his war.

'But in the ship wherein the princes were (now left as much alone as proud lords be when fortune fails them) though they employed all industry to save themselves, yet what they did was rather for duty to nature than hope to escape. So ugly a darkness, as if it would prevent* the night's coming, usurped the day's right, which (accompanied sometimes with thunders, always with horrible noises of the chafing winds) made the master and pilots so astonished that they knew not how to direct, and if they knew, they could scarcely (when they directed) hear their own whistle.

* *gilden:* gilded. *recovered:* reached. *prevent:* anticipate.

For the sea strave with the winds which should be louder, and the shrouds of the ship, wih a ghastful* noise to them that were in it, witnessed that their ruin was the wager of the others' contention,[2] and the heaven roaring out thunders the more amazed them, as having those powers for enemies. Certainly there is no danger carries with it more horror than that which grows in those floating kingdoms.* For that dwelling place is unnatural to mankind; and then the terribleness of the continual motion, the desolation of the far-being from comfort, the eye and the ear having ugly images ever before it, doth still vex the mind, even when it is best armed against it.

'But thus the day passed (if that might be called a day) while the cunningest mariners were so conquered by the storm as they thought it best with stricken sails* to yield to be governed by it: the valiantest feeling inward dismayedness, and yet the fearfullest ashamed fully to show it, seeing that the princes (who were to part from the greatest fortunes) did in their countenances accuse* no point of fear; but encouraging them to do what might be done (putting their hands to every most painful office) taught them at one instant to promise themselves the best and yet to despise the worst. But so were they carried by the tyranny of the wind and the treason of the sea all that night, which the elder it was, the more wayward it showed itself towards them: till the next morning (known to be a morning better by the hour-glass than by the day's clearness) having run fortune as blindly as itself ever was painted, lest the conclusion should not answer to the rest of the play, they were driven upon a rock, which (hidden with those outrageous waves) did, as it were, closely dissemble his cruel mind, till, with an unbelieved* violence (but to them that have tried it) the ship ran upon it; and seeming willinger to perish than to have her course stayed, redoubled her blows till she had broken herself in pieces and, as it were, tearing out her own bowels to feed the sea's greediness, left nothing within it but despair of safety and expectation of a loathsome end.

'There was to be seen the divers manner of minds in distress:

* *ghastful:* fearful. *floating kingdoms:* '93 text. '90, 'flowing'. *stricken sails:* '93 text. '90, 'striking'. *accuse:* betray. *unbelieved:* unbelievable.

some sat upon the top of the poop weeping and wailing, till the sea swallowed them; someone, more able to abide death than fear of death, cut his own throat to prevent drowning; some prayed, and there wanted not of them which cursed, as if the heavens could not be more angry than they were. But a monstrous cry begotten of many roaring voices was able to infect with fear a mind that had not prevented it with the power of reason.

'But the princes (using the passions of fearing evil, and desiring to escape only to serve the rule of virtue, not to abandon one's self) leapt to a rib of the ship which, broken from his fellows, floated with more likelihood to do service than any other limb of that ruinous body; upon which there had gotten already two brethren, well known servants of theirs; and straight they four were carried out of sight, in that huge rising of the sea, from the rest of the ship. But the piece they were on sinking by little and little under them, not able to support the weight of so many, the brethren (the elder whereof was Leucippus, the younger Nelsus) showed themselves right faithful and grateful servants unto them. Grateful, I say, for this cause: those two gentlemen had been taken prisoners in the great war the king of Phrygia made upon Thessalia in the time of Musidorus' infancy; and having been sold into another country, though peace fell after between those realms, could not be delivered (because of their valour known) but for a far greater sum than either all their friends were able or the dowager willing to make, in respect of the great expenses herself and people had been put to in those wars; and so had they remained in prison about thirteen years, when the two young princes, hearing speeches of their good deserts, found means both by selling all the jewels they had of great price, and by giving under their hands great estates when they should come to be kings (which promises their virtue promised for them should be kept) to get so much treasure as redeemed them from captivity. This remembered, and kindly remembered by these two brothers, perchance helped by a natural duty to their princes' blood, they willingly left hold of the board, committing themselves to the sea's rage, and even when they meant to die, themselves praying for the princes' lives. It is true that neither the pain nor danger so moved the princes' hearts as the tenderness of that loving part, far from glory, having so few lookers on; far from hope of reward, since themselves were sure to perish.

## CHAPTER 8

'But now of all the royal navy they lately had, they had left but one little piece of one ship whereon they kept themselves, in all truth having interchanged their cares while either cared for other, each comforting and counselling how to labour for the better and to abide the worse. But so fell it out that as they were carried by the tide (which there, seconded by the storm, ran exceeding swiftly) Musidorus seeing, as he thought, Pyrocles not well upon the board, as he would with his right hand have helped him on better, he had no sooner unfastened his hold but that a wave forcibly spoiled his weaker hand of hold; and so for a time parted those friends, each crying to the other, but the noise of the sea drowned their farewell. But Pyrocles (then careless of death, if it had come by any means but his own) was shortly brought out of the sea's fury to the land's comfort when (in my conscience) I know that comfort was but bitter unto him: and bitter indeed it fell out even in itself to be unto him.

'For being cast on land much bruised and beaten both with the sea's hard farewell and the shore's rude welcome, and even almost deadly tired with the length of his uncomfortable labour, as he was walking up to discover somebody to whom he might go for relief, there came straight running unto him certain, who (as it was after known) by appointment* watched with many others in divers places along the coast; who laid hands on him, and without either questioning with him or showing will to hear him, like men fearful to appear curious, or (which was worse) having no regard to the hard plight he was in (being so wet and weak) they carried him some miles thence to a house of a principal officer of that country: who with no more civility (though with much more busyness than those under-fellows had showed) began in captious manner to put interrogatories unto him; to which he, unused to such entertainment, did shortly and plainly answer what he was and how he came thither. But that no sooner known, with

* *by appointment*: were appointed to watch.

numbers of armed men to guard him (for mischief, not from mischief) he was sent to the king's court, which as then was not above a day's journey off, with letters from that officer containing his own serviceable diligence in discovering so great a personage; adding withal more than was true of his conjectures, because he would endear his own service.

'This country whereon he fell was Phrygia, and it was to the king thereof to whom he was sent: a prince of a melancholy constitution both of body and mind; wickedly sad, ever musing of horrible matters; suspecting, or rather condemning all men of evil, because his mind had no eye to espy goodness; and therefore accusing sycophants, of all men, did best sort to* his nature; but therefore not seeming sycophants, because of no evil they said, they could bring any new or doubtful thing unto him but such as already he had been apt to determine, so as they came but as proofs of his wisdom: fearful, and never secure, while the fear he had figured in his mind had any possibility of event:* a toad-like retiredness and closeness of mind, nature teaching the odiousness of poison and the danger of odiousness. Yet while youth lasted in him, the exercises of that age, and his humour* (not yet fully discovered) made him something the more frequentable and less dangerous. But after that years began to come on with some, though more seldom, shows of a bloody nature, and that the prophecy of Musidorus' destiny came to his ears (delivered unto him, and received of him with the hardest interpretation, as though his subjects did delight in the hearing thereof), then gave he himself indeed to the full current of his disposition, especially after the war of Thessalia, wherein (though in truth wrongly) he deemed his unsuccess proceeded of their unwillingness to have him prosper. And then thinking himself contemned, knowing no countermine against contempt but terror, began to let nothing pass which might bear the colour of a fault, without sharp punishment: and when he wanted* faults, excellency grew a fault; and it was sufficient to make one guilty, that he had power to be guilty. And as there is no humour to which impudent poverty cannot make itself serviceable, so were there enow* of those of des-

*sort to: suit with. *event*: fulfilment. *humour*: temper of mind. *wanted*: failed to find. *enow*: enough.

perate ambition who would build their houses upon others' ruins, which after should fall by like practices; so as servitude came mainly upon that poor people, whose deeds were not only punished but words corrected and even thoughts by some mean or other pulled out of them, while suspicion bred the mind of cruelty, and the effects of cruelty stirred a new cause of suspicion. And in this plight, full of watchful fearfulness, did the storm deliver sweet Pyrocles to the stormy mind of that tyrant; all men that did such wrong to so rare a stranger (whose countenance deserved both pity and admiration) condemning themselves as much in their hearts as they did brag in their faces.

'But when this bloody king knew what he was, and in what order he and his cousin Musidorus (so much of him feared) were come out of Thessalia, assuredly thinking (because ever thinking the worst) that those forces were provided against him, glad of the perishing (as he thought) of Musidorus, determined in public sort to put Pyrocles to death. For having quite lost the way of nobleness, he strave to climb to the height of terribleness; and thinking to make all men a-dread to make such one an enemy who would not spare nor fear to kill so great a prince, and lastly, having nothing in him why to make him his friend, he thought he would take him away from being his enemy. The day was appointed, and all things appointed for that cruel blow, in so solemn an order as if they would set forth tyranny in most gorgeous decking: the princely youth, of invincible valour yet so unjustly subjected to such outrageous wrong, carrying himself in all his demeanour so constantly, abiding extremity, that one might see it was the cutting away of the greatest hope of the world and destroying virtue in his sweetest growth.

'But so it fell out that his death was prevented by a rare example of friendship in Musidorus who, being almost drowned, had been taken up by a fisherman belonging to the kingdom of Pontus; and being there, and understanding the full discourse – as fame was very prodigal of so notable an accident – in what case Pyrocles was; learning withal that his hate was far more to him than to Pyrocles, he found means to acquaint himself with a nobleman of that country, to whom largely discovering what he was, he found him a most fit instrument to effectuate his desire.

For this nobleman had been one who in many wars had served Euarchus, and had been so mind-stricken by the beauty of virtue in that noble king that, though not born his subject, he ever professed himself his servant. His desire therefore to him was to keep Musidorus in a strong castle of his, and then to make the king of Phrygia understand that if he would deliver Pyrocles, Musidorus would willingly put himself into his hands, knowing well that how thirsty soever he was of Pyrocles' blood, he would rather drink that of Musidorus.

'The nobleman was loth to preserve one by the loss of another, but time urging resolution, the importunity of Musidorus (who showed a mind not to over-live Pyrocles) with the affection he bare to Euarchus so prevailed that he carried this strange offer of Musidorus, which by that tyrant was greedily accepted.

'And so upon security of both sides, they were interchanged. Where I may not omit the work of friendship in Pyrocles, who both in speech and countenance to Musidorus well showed that he thought himself injured and not relieved by him; asking him what he had ever seen in him why he could not bear the extremities of mortal accidents as well as any man, and why he should envy him the glory of suffering death for his friend's cause, and, as it were, rob him of his own possession? But in this notable contention (where the conquest must be the conqueror's destruction, and safety the punishment of the conquered) Musidorus prevailed because he was a more welcome prize to the unjust king that wished none well, to them worse than others, and to him worst of all: and as cheerfully going towards as Pyrocles went frowardly fromward* his death, he was delivered to the king, who could not be enough sure of him without he fed his own eyes upon one whom he had begun to fear as soon as the other began to be.

'Yet because he would in one act both make ostentation of his own felicity (into whose hands his most feared enemy was fallen) and withal cut off such hopes from his suspected subjects (when they should know certainly he was dead) with much more skilful cruelty and horrible solemnity he caused each thing to be prepared for his triumph of tyranny. And so the day being come, he was led forth by many armed men, who often had been the

---

* *frowardly fromward*: unwillingly away from.

fortifiers of wickedness, to the place of execution; where coming with a mind comforted in that he had done such service to Pyrocles, this strange encounter he had.

'The excelling Pyrocles was no sooner delivered by the king's servants to a place of liberty than he bent his wit and courage – and what would they not bring to pass? – how either to deliver Musidorus or to perish with him. And finding he could get in that country no forces sufficient by force to rescue him, to bring himself to die with him (little hoping of better event) he put himself in poor raiment, and by the help of some few crowns he took of that nobleman (who, full of sorrow, though not knowing the secret of his intent, suffered him to go in such order from him) he – even he, born to the greatest expectation and of the greatest blood that any prince might be – submitted himself to be servant to the executioner that should put to death Musidorus: a far notabler proof of his friendship, considering the height of his mind, than any death could be. That bad officer, not suspecting him (being arrayed fit for such an estate and having his beauty hidden by many foul spots he artificially put upon his face) gave him leave not only to wear a sword himself but to bear his sword prepared for the justified murder.

'And so Pyrocles taking his time, when Musidorus was upon the scaffold (separated somewhat from the rest, as allowed to say something) he stepped unto him, and putting the sword into his hand, not bound* (a point of civility the officers used towards him because they doubted no such enterprise) "Musidorus," said he, "die nobly." In truth, never man, between joy before knowledge what to be glad of and fear after considering his case, had such a confusion of thoughts as I had, when I saw Pyrocles so near me.'

But with that Dorus blushed and Pamela smiled, and Dorus the more blushed at her smiling, and she the more smiled at his blushing, because he had, with the remembrance of that plight he was in, forgotten in speaking of himself to use the third person.

But Musidorus turned again her thoughts from his cheeks to his tongue in this sort: 'But,' said he, 'when they were with swords in hands, not turning backs one to the other (for there they knew was no place of defence) but making it a preservation in not

* *not bound*: i.e. Musidorus.

hoping to be preserved, and now acknowledging themselves subject to death, meaning only to do honour to their princely birth, they flew amongst them all (for all were enemies) and had quickly, either with flight or death, left none upon the scaffold to annoy* them: wherein Pyrocles, the excellent Pyrocles, did such wonders beyond belief as was able to lead Musidorus to courage, though he had been born a coward. But indeed just rage and desperate virtue did such effects that the popular sort of the beholders began to be almost superstitiously amazed as at effects beyond mortal power. But the king with angry threatenings from out a window (where he was not ashamed the world should behold him a beholder) commanded his guard and the rest of his soldiers to hasten their death. But many of them lost their bodies to lose their souls, when the princes grew almost so weary as they were ready to be conquered with conquering.

'But as they were still fighting with weak arms and strong hearts, it happened that one of the soldiers (commanded to go up after his fellows against the princes) having received a light hurt, more wounded in his heart, went back with as much diligence as he came up with modesty: which another of his fellows seeing, to pick a thank of the king, strake him upon the face, reviling him that (so accompanied)* he would run away from so few. But he (as many times it falls out) only valiant when he was angry, in revenge thrust him through, which with his death was straight revenged by a brother of his and that again requited by a fellow of the others. There began to be a great tumult amongst the soldiers; which seen and not understood by the people, used to fears but not used to be bold in them, some began to cry treason; and that voice straight multiplying itself, the king (O, the cowardice of a guilty conscience) before any man set upon him, fled away. Wherewith a bruit* (either by art of some well-meaning men, or by such chance as such things often fall out by) ran from one to the other that the king was slain: wherewith certain young men of the bravest minds cried with a loud voice, "Liberty"; and encouraging the other citizens to follow them, set upon the guard and soldiers as chief instruments of tyranny: and quickly, aided by

* *annoy*: harm. *so accompanied*: with so many on his side. *Wherewith a bruit*: because of which, a rumour.

the princes, they had left none of them alive, nor any other in the city who they thought had in any sort set his hand to the work of their servitude, and, god knows, by the blindness of rage killing many guiltless persons, either for affinity to the tyrant or enmity to the tyrant-killers. But some of the wiser (seeing that a popular licence is indeed the many-headed tyranny) prevailed with the rest to make Musidorus their chief; choosing one of them (because princes) to defend them, and him (because elder and most hated of the tyrant) and by him to be ruled; whom forthwith they lifted up – Fortune, I think, smiling at her work therein, that a scaffold of execution should grow to a scaffold of coronation.

'But by and by there came news of more certain truth, that the king was not dead but fled to a strong castle of his near hand, where he was gathering forces in all speed possible to suppress this mutiny. But now they had run themselves too far out of breath to go back again to the same career; and too well they knew the sharpness of his memory to forget such an injury. Therefore learning virtue of necessity, they continued resolute to obey Musidorus, who seeing what forces were in the city, with them issued against the tyrant while they were in this heat, before practices might be used to dissever them; and with them met the king, who likewise hoping little to prevail by time, knowing and finding his people's hate, met him with little delay in the field, where himself was slain by Musidorus after he had seen his only son ( a prince of great courage and beauty, but fostered in blood by his naughty father) slain by the hand of Pyrocles. This victory obtained with great and truly not undeserved honour to the two princes, the whole estates of the country with one consent gave the crown and all other marks of sovereignty to Musidorus, desiring nothing more than to live under such a government as they promised themselves of him.

'But he, thinking it a greater greatness to give a kingdom than get a kingdom, understanding that there was left of the blood royal and next to the succession an aged gentleman of approved goodness (who had gotten nothing by his cousin's power but danger from him and odiousness for him, having passed his time in modest secrecy and as much from intermeddling in matters of government as the greatness of his blood would suffer him) did, after having received the full power to his own hands, resign all to the nobleman; but with such conditions, and cautions of the conditions, as might assure the people (with as much assurance as worldly matters bear) that not only that governor, of whom indeed they looked for all good, but the nature of the government, should be no way apt to decline to tyranny.

## CHAPTER 9

'This doing set forth no less his magnificence than the other act did his magnanimity; so that greatly praised of all, and justly beloved of the new king who in all both words and behaviour protested himself their tenant and liegeman, they were drawn thence to revenge those two servants of theirs, of whose memorable faith I told you, most excellent princess, in willingly giving themselves to be drowned for their sakes: but drowned indeed they were not, but got with painful swimming upon a rock, from whence, after being come as near famishing as before drowning, the weather breaking up, they were brought to the mainland of Pontus, the same country upon which Musidorus also was fallen, but not in so lucky a place.

'For they were brought to the king of that country, a tyrant also, not through suspicion, greediness or revengefulness, as he of Phrygia, but, as I may term it, of a wanton cruelty: inconstant in his choice of friends, or rather never having a friend but a playfellow; of whom when he was weary, he could not otherwise rid himself than by killing them; giving sometimes prodigally, not because he loved them to whom he gave but because he lusted to give; punishing, not so much for hate or anger as because he felt not the smart of punishment; delighted to be flattered, at first for those virtues which were not in him, at length making his vices virtues worthy the flattering; with like judgement glorying when he had happened to do a thing well as when he had performed some notable mischief.

'He chanced at that time – for indeed long time none lasted with him – to have next in use about him a man of the most envious disposition that, I think, ever infected the air with his breath; whose eyes could not look right upon any happy man, nor ears bear the burden of anybody's praise; contrary to the natures of all other plagues, plagued with others' well being; making happiness the ground of his unhappiness and good news the argument of his sorrow: in sum, a man whose favour no man could win but by being miserable.

'And so because those two faithful servants of theirs came in miserable sort to that court, he was apt enough at first to favour them; and the king understanding of their adventure (wherein they had showed so constant a faith unto their lords) suddenly falls to take a pride in making much of them, extolling them with infinite praises, and praising himself in his heart in that he praised them. And by and by were they made great courtiers and in the way of minions;* when advancement (the most mortal offence to envy) stirred up their former friend to overthrow his own work in them, taking occasion upon the knowledge (newly come to the court) of the late death of the king of Phrygia destroyed by their two lords; who having been a near kinsman to this prince of Pontus, by this envious counsellor (partly with suspicion of practice, partly with glory of in part revenging his cousin's death) the king was suddenly turned (and every turn with him was a downfall) to lock them up in prison as servants to his enemies, whom before he had never known nor (till that time one of his own subjects had entertained and dealt for them) did ever take heed of. But now earnest in every present humour, and making himself brave in his liking, he was content to give them just cause of offence when they had power to make just revenge. Yet did the princes send unto him before they entered into war, desiring their servants' liberty. But he, swelling in their humbleness (like a bubble blown up with a small breath, broken with a great) forgetting, or never knowing humanity, caused their heads to be stricken off, by the advice of his envious counsellor, who now hated them so much the more as he foresaw their happiness in having such, and so fortunate masters; and sent them with unroyal reproaches to Musidorus and Pyrocles, as if they had done traitorously and not heroically in killing his tyrannical cousin.

'But that injury went beyond all degree of reconcilement; so that they making forces in Phrygia (a kingdom wholly at their

* *minions*: favourites.

commandment by the love of the people and gratefulness of the king) they entered his country; and wholly conquering it, with such deeds as at least fame said were excellent, took the king; and by Musidorus' commandment (Pyrocles' heart more inclining to pity) he was slain upon the tomb of their two true servants, which they caused to be made for them with royal expenses and notable workmanship to preserve their dead lives. For his wicked servant, he should have felt the like or worse, but that his heart brake even to death with the beholding the honour done to their dead carcasses. There might Pyrocles quietly have enjoyed that crown by all the desire of that people, most of whom had revolted unto him; but he, finding a sister of the late king's, (a fair and well esteemed lady) looking for nothing more than to be oppressed with her brother's ruins, gave her in marriage to the nobleman, his father's old friend, and endowed with them the crown of that kingdom. And not content with those public actions of princely and, as it were, governing virtue, they did, in that kingdom and some other near about, divers acts of particular trials, more famous because more perilous. For in that time those regions were full both of cruel monsters and monstrous men, all which in short time by private combats they delivered the countries of.

'Among the rest, two brothers of huge both greatness and force, therefore commonly called giants, who kept themselves in a castle seated upon the top of a rock, impregnable because there was no coming unto it but by one narrow path where one man's force was able to keep down an army. These brothers had a while served the king of Pontus, and in all his affairs (especially of war whereunto they were only apt)* they had showed as unconquered courage, so a rude faithfulness, being men indeed by nature apter to the faults of rage than of deceit; not greatly ambitious more than to be well and uprightly dealt with; rather impatient of injury than delighted with more than ordinary courtesies; and in injuries more sensible of smart or loss than of reproach or disgrace. These men being of this nature (and certainly jewels to a wise man, considering what indeed wonders they were able to perform) yet were discarded by that unworthy prince, after many notable deserts, as not worthy the holding; which was the more evident to them

*only apt: only skilful.

because it suddenly fell from an excess of favour which (many examples having taught them) never stopped his race till it came to an headlong overthrow.

'They full of rage, retired themselves unto this castle: where thinking nothing juster than revenge, nor more noble than the effects of anger (that, according to the nature* full of inward bravery and fierceness, scarcely in the glass of reason* thinking itself fair but when it is terrible) they immediately gave themselves to make all the country about them (subject to that king) to smart for their lord's folly, not caring how innocent they were, but rather thinking the more innocent they were, the more it testified their spite which they desired to manifest. And with use of evil growing more and more evil, they took delight in slaughter, and pleased themselves in making others' wrack* the effect of their power; so that where in the time that they obeyed a master, their anger was a serviceable power of the mind to do public good, so now, unbridled and blind judge of itself, it made wickedness violent, and praised itself in excellency of mischief almost to the ruin of the country, not greatly regarded* by their careless and loveless king. Till now these princes, finding them so fleshed in cruelty as not to be reclaimed, secretly undertook the matter alone, for accompanied they would not have suffered them to have mounted; and so those great fellows scornfully receiving them as foolish birds fallen into their net, it pleased the eternal justice to make them suffer death by their hands: and so they were manifoldly acknowledged the savers of that country.

'It were the part of a very idle orator to set forth the numbers of well-devised honours done unto them: but as high honour is not only gotten and born by pain and danger, but must be nursed by the like or else vanisheth as soon as it appears to the world, so the natural hunger thereof which was in Pyrocles suffered him not to account a resting seat of that which ever either riseth or falleth, but still to make one occasion beget another, whereby his doings might send his praise to others' mouths to rebound again true contentment to his spirit. And therefore having well established

* according to the nature: i.e. of anger. scarcely in the glass of reason: not as reason would show it. wrack: destruction. regarded: cared about.

those kingdoms under good governors, and rid them by their valour of such giants and monsters as before-time armies were not able to subdue, they determined in unknown order to see more of the world, and to employ those gifts, esteemed rare in them, to the good of mankind; and therefore would themselves (understanding that the king Euarchus was passed all the cumber of his wars) go privately to seek exercises of their virtue, thinking it not so worthy to be brought to heroical effects by fortune or necessity, like Ulysses and Aeneas, as by one's own choice and working. And so went they away from very unwilling people to leave them, making time haste itself to be a circumstance of their honour, and one place witness to another of the truth of their doings. For scarcely were they out of the confines of Pontus, but that as they rode alone armed – for alone they went, one serving the other – they met an adventure, which though not so notable for any great effect they performed, yet worthy to be remembered for the un-used* examples therein as well of true natural goodness as of wretched ungratefulness.

## CHAPTER 10

'It was in the kingdom of Galatia, the season being, as in the depth of winter, very cold and as then suddenly grown to so extreme and foul a storm that never any winter, I think, brought forth a fouler child; so that the princes were even compelled by the hail that the pride of the wind blew into their faces to seek some shrouding place, which a certain hollow rock offering unto them, they made it their shield against the tempest's fury. And so stay-ing there till the violence thereof was passed, they heard the speech of a couple who, not perceiving them, being hid within that rude canopy, held a strange and pitiful disputation, which made them step out, yet in such sort as they might see unseen. There they perceived an aged man and a young, scarcely come to the age of a man, both poorly arrayed, extremely weather-beaten; the old man blind, and the young man leading him; and yet through all those miseries, in both there seemed to appear a kind

* *unused*: unusual.

of nobleness not suitable to that affliction. But the first words they heard were these of the old man.

'"Well Leonatus," said he, "since I cannot persuade thee to lead me to that which should end my grief and thy trouble, let me now entreat thee to leave me. Fear not; my misery cannot be greater than it is, and nothing doth become me but misery. Fear not the danger of my blind steps, I cannot fall worse than I am. And do not, I pray thee, do not obstinately continue to infect thee with my wretchedness, but fly, fly from this region only worthy of me."

'"Dear father," answered he, "do not take away from me the only remnant of my happiness. While I have power to do you service, I am not wholly miserable."

'"Ah, my son," said he, and with that he groaned as if sorrow strave to break his heart, "how evil fits it me to have such a son, and how much doth thy kindness upbraid my wickedness!"

'These doleful speeches and some others to like purpose (well showing they had not been born to the fortune they were in) moved the princes to go out unto them and ask the younger what they were.

'"Sirs," answered he with a good grace, and made the more agreeable by a certain noble kind of piteousness, "I see well you are strangers that know not our misery, so well here known that no man dare know but that we must be miserable. Indeed our state is such as though nothing is so needful unto us as pity, yet nothing is more dangerous unto us than to make ourselves so known as may stir pity. But your presence promiseth that cruelty shall not over-run hate; and if it did, in truth our state is sunk below the degree of fear.

'"This old man whom I lead was lately rightful prince of this country of Paphlagonia, by the hard-hearted ungratefulness of a son of his deprived not only of his kingdom (whereof no foreign forces were ever able to spoil him) but of his sight, the riches which Nature grants to the poorest creatures: whereby and by other his unnatural dealings, he hath been driven to such grief as even now he would have had me to have led him to the top of this rock, thence to cast himself headlong to death; and so would have made me, who received my life of him, to be the worker of his destruction. But noble gentlemen," said he, "if either of you have a father and feel what dutiful affection is engraffed in a son's heart, let me entreat you to convey this afflicted prince to some place of rest and security. Amongst your worthy acts it shall be none of the least that a king of such might and fame, and so unjustly oppressed, is in any sort by you relieved."

'But before they could make him answer, his father began to speak: "Ah, my son," said he, "how evil an historian are you that leave out the chief knot of all the discourse, my wickedness, my wickedness! And if thou dost it to spare my ears (the only sense now left me proper for knowledge) assure thyself thou dost mistake me. And I take witness of that sun which you see," – with that he cast up his blind eyes as if he would hunt for light – "and wish myself in worse case than I do wish myself (which is as evil as may be) if I speak untruly, that nothing is so welcome to my thoughts as the publishing of my shame. Therefore know you, gentlemen (to whom from my heart I wish that it may not prove some ominous foretoken of misfortune to have met with such a miser* as I am) that whatsoever my son (O God, that truth binds me to reproach him with the name of my son) hath said is true. But besides those truths, this also is true, that having had in lawful marriage, of a mother fit to bear royal children, this son (such a one as partly you see and better shall know by my short declaration) and so enjoyed the expectations in the world of him till he was grown to justify their expectations (so as I needed envy no father for the chief comfort of mortality, to leave another oneself after me) I was carried by a bastard son of mine (if at least I be bound to believe the words of that base woman my concubine, his mother) first to mislike, then to hate, lastly to destroy, or to do my best to destroy this son (I think you think) undeserving destruction. What ways he used to bring me to it, if I should tell you, I should tediously trouble you with as much poisonous hypocrisy, desperate fraud, smooth malice, hidden ambition and smiling envy as in any living person could be harboured. But I list* it not: no remembrance of naughtiness delights me but mine own; and methinks, the accusing his traps might in some manner excuse my fault, which certainly I loath to do. But the conclusion is that I gave order to some servants of mine, whom I thought as

* *miser:* wretch. *list:* desire.

277

apt for such charities as myself, to lead him out into a forest and there to kill him.

'"But those thieves, better natured to my son than myself, spared his life, letting him go to learn to live poorly; which he did, giving himself to be a private soldier in a country hereby. But as he was ready to be greatly advanced for some noble pieces of service which he did, he heard news of me, who, drunk in my affection to that unlawful and unnatural son of mine, suffered myself so to be governed by him that all favours and punishments passed by him, all offices and places of importance distributed to his favourites; so that ere I was aware, I had left myself nothing but the name of a king. Which he shortly weary of, too, with many indignities – if anything may be called an indignity which was laid upon me – threw me out of my seat and put out my eyes, and then, proud in his tyranny, let me go, neither imprisoning nor killing me, but rather delighting to make me feel my misery: misery indeed, if ever there were any; full of wretchedness, fuller of disgrace, and fullest of guiltiness. And as he came to the crown by so unjust means, as unjustly he kept it by force of stronger soldiers in citadels, the nests of tyranny and murderers of liberty; disarming all his own countrymen, that no man durst show himself a well-willer of mine – to say the truth, I think, few of them being so, considering my cruel folly to my good son and foolish kindness to my unkind bastard. But if there were any who fell to pity of so great a fall, and had yet any sparks of unstained duty* left in them towards me, yet durst they not show it scarcely with giving me alms at their doors, which yet was the only sustenance of my distressed life, nobody daring to show so much charity as to lend me a hand to guide my dark steps.

'"Till this son of mine (God knows, worthy of a more virtuous and more fortunate father) forgetting my abominable wrongs, not recking danger, and neglecting the present good way he was in of doing himself good, came hither to do this kind office you see him perform towards me; to my unspeakable grief, not only because his kindness is a glass (even to my blind eyes) of my naughtiness, but that above all griefs, it grieves me he should desperately adventure the loss of his well-deserving life for mine that yet owe

* *unstained duty*: '90 text. '93, 'unslain'.

more to fortune for my deserts, as if he would carry mud in a chest of crystal. For well I know, he that now reigneth, how much soever and with good reason he despiseth me, of all men despised, yet he will not let slip any advantage to make away with him whose just title, ennobled by courage and goodness, may one day shake the seat of a never secure tyranny. And for this cause I craved of him to lead me to the top of this rock, indeed I must confess, with meaning to free him from so serpentine* a companion as I am. But he, finding what I purposed, only therein since he was born showed himself disobedient unto me. And now, gentlemen, you have the true story, which I pray you publish to the world, that my mischievous proceedings may be the glory of his filial piety, the only reward now left for so great a merit. And if it may be, let me obtain that of you which my son denies me: for never was there more pity in saving any than in ending me, both because therein my agonies shall end, and so shall you preserve this excellent young man, who else wilfully follows his own ruin."

'The matter in itself lamentable, lamentably expressed by the old prince (which needed not take to himself the gestures of pity since his face could not put off the marks thereof) greatly moved the two princes to compassion, which could not stay in such hearts as theirs without seeking remedy. But by and by the occasion was presented: for Plexirtus (so was the bastard called) came thither with forty horse only of purpose to murder his brother, of whose coming he had soon advertisement, and thought no eyes of sufficient credit in such a matter but his own, and therefore came himself to be actor and spectator. And as soon as he came, not regarding the weak (as he thought) guard but of two men, commanded some of his followers to set their hands to his* in the killing of Leonatus. But the young prince, though not otherwise armed but with a sword, how falsely soever he was dealt with by others, would not betray himself, but bravely drawing it out, made the death of the first that assailed him warn his fellows to come more warily after him. But then Pyrocles and Musidorus were quickly become parties, so just a defence deserving as much as old friendship, and so did behave them among that company

* *serpentine:* dangerous. *set their hands to his:* join him.

(more injurious* than valiant) that many of them lost their lives for their wicked master.

'Yet perhaps had the number of them at last prevailed if the king of Pontus (lately by them made so) had not come unlooked for to their succour: who (having had a dream which had fixed his imagination vehemently upon some great danger presently to follow those two princes whom he most dearly loved) was come in all haste, following as well as he could their track with a hundred horses in that country, which he thought (considering who then reigned) a fit place enough to make the stage of any tragedy.

'But then the match had been so ill made for Plexirtus that his ill-led life and worse-gotten honour should have tumbled together to destruction, had there not come in Tydeus and Telenor with forty or fifty in their suite, to the defence of Plexirtus. These two were brothers, of the noblest house of that country, brought up from their infancy with Plexirtus; men of such prowess as not to know fear in themselves and yet to teach it others that should deal with them; for they had often made their lives triumph over most terrible dangers, never dismayed, and ever fortunate; and truly no more settled in valour than disposed to goodness and justice, if either they had lighted on a better friend or could have learned to make friendship a child and not the father of virtue. But bringing up rather than choice having first knit their minds unto him (indeed crafty enough either to hide his faults, or never to show them but when they might pay home)* they willingly held out the course rather to satisfy him than all the world, and rather to be good friends than good men: so as though they did not like the evil he did, yet they liked him that did the evil; and though not counsellors of the offence, yet protectors of the offender. Now they, having heard of this sudden going out with so small a company in a country full of evil-wishing minds towards him (though they knew not the cause) followed him, till they found him in such case as they were to venture their lives or else he to lose his: which they did with such force of mind and body that truly I may justly say, Pyrocles and Musidorus had never till then found any that could make them so well repeat their hardest lesson in the feats of arms. And briefly so they did that

* *injurious*: wishing to do injury. *pay home*: do enough damage.

if they overcame not, yet were they not overcome, but carried away that ungrateful master of theirs to a place of security, howsoever the princes laboured to the contrary. But this matter being thus far begun, it became not the constancy of the princes so to leave it; but in all haste making forces both in Pontus and Phrygia, they had in few days left him but only that one strong place where he was. For fear having been the only knot that had fastened his people unto him, that once untied by a greater force, they all scattered from him like so many birds whose cage had been broken.

'In which season the blind king (having in the chief city of his realm set the crown upon his son Leonatus' head) with many tears both of joy and sorrow setting forth to the whole people his own faults and his son's virtue, after he had kissed him and forced his son to accept honour of him, as of his new-become subject, even in a moment died, as it should seem, his heart broken with unkindness and affliction, stretched so far beyond his limits with this excess of comfort as it was able no longer to keep safe his vital spirits. But the new king, having no less lovingly performed all duties to him dead than alive, pursued on the siege of his unnatural brother, as much for the revenge of his father as for the establishing of his own quiet. In which siege truly I cannot but acknowledge the prowess of those two brothers, than whom the princes never found in all their travel two of greater ability to perform, nor of abler skill for conduct.

'But Plexirtus, finding that if nothing else, famine would at last bring him to destruction, thought better by humbleness to creep where by pride he could not march. For certainly so had Nature formed him, and the exercise of craft conformed him to all turningness of sleights that, though no man had less goodness in his soul than he, no man could better find the places whence arguments might grow of goodness to another;[1] though no man felt less pity, no man could tell better how to stir pity; no man more impudent to deny, where proofs were not manifest; no man more ready to confess with a repenting manner of aggravating his own evil, where denial would but make the fault fouler. Now he took this way, that having gotten a passport for one (that pretended he would put Plexirtus alive into his hands) to speak with the king his brother, he himself (though much against the minds of the valiant brothers, who rather wished to die in brave defence) with a rope about his neck, bare-footed, came to offer himself to the discretion of Leonatus. Where what submission he used, how cunningly in making greater the fault he made the faultiness the less, how artificially he could set out the torments of his own conscience with the burdensome cumber he had found of his ambitious desires, how finely seeming to desire nothing but death as ashamed to live, he begged life in the refusing it, I am not cunning enough to be able to express. But so fell out of it that though at first sight Leonatus saw him with no other eye than as the murderer of his father, and anger already began to paint revenge in many colours; ere long he had not only gotten pity but pardon, and if not an excuse of the fault past, yet an opinion of a future amendment: while the poor villains (chief ministers of his wickedness, now betrayed by the author thereof) were delivered to many cruel sorts of death; he so handling it that it rather seemed he had more come into the defence of an unremediable mischief already committed than that they had done it at first by his consent.

'In such sort the princes left these reconciled brothers (Plexirtus in all his behaviour carrying him in far lower degree of service than the ever-noble nature of Leonatus would suffer him) and taking likewise their leaves of their good friend the king of Pontus, who returned to enjoy their benefit, both of his wife and kingdom, they privately went thence, having only with them the two valiant brothers who would needs accompany them through divers places, they four doing acts more dangerous though less famous, because they were but private chivalries. Till hearing of the fair and virtuous queen Erona of Lycia besieged by the puissant king of Armenia, they bent themselves to her succour, both because the weaker (and weaker as being a lady) and partly because they heard the king of Armenia had in his company three of the most famous men living, for matters of arms, that were known to be in the world: whereof one was the prince Plangus whose name was sweetened by your breath, peerless lady, when the last day it pleased you to mention him unto me. The other two were two great princes (though holding of him)* Barzanes and Euardes,

* *though holding of him:* bearing allegiance to.

men of giant-like both hugeness and force, in which two especially the trust the king had of victory was reposed. And of them, those brothers Tydeus and Telenor, sufficient judges in warlike matters, spake so high commendations that the two princes had even a youthful longing to have some trial of their virtue. And therefore as soon as they were entered into Lycia, they joined themselves with them that faithfully served the poor queen at that time besieged; and ere long animated in such sort their almost overthrown hearts, that they went by force to relieve the town, though they were deprived of a great part of their strength by the parting of the two brothers (who were sent for in all haste to return to their old friend and master Plexirtus) who, willingly hoodwinking themselves from seeing his faults, and binding themselves to believe what he said, often abused the virtue of courage to defend his foul vice of injustice. But now they were sent for to advance a conquest he was about, while Pyrocles and Musidorus pursued the delivery of the queen Erona.'

## CHAPTER 11

'I have heard,' said Pamela, 'that part of the story of Plangus when he passed through this country: therefore you may, if you list, pass over that war of Erona's quarrel lest, if you speak too much of war matters, you should wake Mopsa, which might haply* breed a great broil.'

He looked, and saw that Mopsa indeed sat swallowing of sleep with open mouth, making such a noise withal as nobody could lay the stealing of a nap to her charge. Whereupon, willing to use that occcasion, he kneeled down, and with humble heartedness and hearty earnestness printed in his graces:

'Alas,' said he, 'divine lady, who have wrought such miracles in me as to make a prince (none of the basest) to think all principalities base in respect of the sheephook which may hold him up in your sight; vouchsafe now at last to hear in direct words my humble suit, while this dragon* sleeps that keeps the golden fruit. If in my desire I wish, or in my hopes aspire, or in my imagination

* *haply:* perchance. *this dragon:* which guarded the golden apples of the Hesperides.

feign to myself anything which may be the least spot to that heavenly virtue which shines in all your doings, I pray the eternal powers that the words I speak may be deadly poisons while they are in my mouth, and that all my hopes, all my desires, all my imaginations may only work their own confusion. But if love, love of you, love of your virtues, seek only that favour of you which becometh that gratefulness which cannot misbecome your excellency, O do not – '

He would have said further, but Pamela calling aloud, 'Mopsa', she suddenly start up, staggering; and rubbing her eyes, ran first out of the door and then back to them, before she knew how she went out or why she came in again: till at length, being fully come to her little self, she asked Pamela why she had called her.

'For nothing,' said Pamela, 'but that you might hear some tales of your servant's telling: and therefore now,' said she, 'Dorus, go on.'

But as he (who found no so good sacrifice as obedience) was returning to the story of himself, Philoclea came in, and by and by after her, Miso, so as for that time they were fain to let Dorus depart. But Pamela, delighted even to preserve in her memory the words of so well a beloved speaker, repeated the whole substance to her sister; till their sober dinner being come and gone, to recreate themselves something (even tired with the noisomeness of Miso's conversation) they determined to go, while the heat of the day lasted, to bathe themselves (such being the manner of the Arcadian nymphs often to do) in the river of Ladon, and take with them a lute, meaning to delight them under some shadow. But they could not stir but that Miso with her daughter Mopsa was after them: and as it lay in their way to pass by the other lodge, Zelmane out of her window espied them and so stale down after them, which she might the better do because that Gynecia was sick, and Basilius (that day being his birth-day) according to his manner was busy about his devotions; and therefore she went after, hoping to find some time to speak with Philoclea. But not a word could she begin but that Miso would be one of the audience, so that she was driven to recommend thinking, speaking, and all, to her eyes, who diligently performed her trust, till they came to the river's side, which of all the rivers of Greece had the prize for excellent pureness and sweetness, insomuch as the very bathing in it was accounted exceeding healthful. It ran upon so fine and delicate a ground as one could not easily judge whether the river did more wash the gravel or the gravel did purify the river; the river not running forth right* but almost continually winding, as if the lower streams would return to their spring, or that the river had a delight to play with itself. The banks of either side seeming arms of the loving earth that fain would embrace it, and the river a wanton nymph which still would slip from it; either side of the bank being fringed with most beautiful trees, which resisted the sun's darts from over-much piercing the natural coldness of the river. There was the ...¹

But among the rest a goodly cypress, who bowing her fair head over the water, it seemed she looked into it, and dressed her green locks by that running river.

There the princesses determining to bathe themselves, though it was so privileged a place upon pain of death as nobody durst presume to come thither, yet for the more surety they looked round about, and could see nothing but a water-spaniel, who came down the river showing that he hunted for a duck, and with a snuffling grace disdaining that his smelling force could not as well prevail through the water as through the air; and therefore waiting with his eye to see whether he could espy the ducks getting up again, but then a little below them failing of his purpose, he got out of the river, and shaking off the water (as great men do their friends) now he had no further cause to use it, inweeded* himself so as the ladies lost the further marking his sportfulness. And inviting Zelmane also to wash herself with them, and she excusing herself with having taken a late cold, they began by piece-meal to take away the eclipsing of their apparel.

Zelmane would have put to her helping hand, but she was taken with such a quivering that she thought it more wisdom to lean herself to a tree and look on, while Miso and Mopsa, like a couple of foreswat melters,* were getting the pure silver of their bodies out of the ure* of their garments. But as the raiments went

* *forth right*: in a straight course. *inweeded*: hid in the weeds. *foreswat melters*: sweating metal refiners. *ure*: ore.

off to receive kisses of the ground, Zelmane envied the happiness of all, but of the smock was even jealous; and when that was taken away too, and that Philoclea remained – for her Zelmane only marked – like a diamond taken from out of the rock, or rather like the sun getting from under a cloud and showing his naked beams to the full view, then was the beauty too much for a patient sight, the delight too strong for a stayed conceit,* so that Zelmane could not choose but run to touch, embrace and kiss her. But conscience* made her come to herself and leave Philoclea who, blushing and withal smiling, making shamefulness pleasant and pleasure shamefaced, tenderly moved her feet, unwonted to feel the naked ground, till the touch of the cold water made a pretty kind of shrugging come over her body, like the twinkling of the fairest among the fixed stars. But the river itself gave way unto her, so that she was straight breast high, which was the deepest that thereabout she could be: and when cold Ladon had once fully embraced them, himself was no more so cold to those ladies, but as if his cold complexion had been heated with love, so seemed he to play about every part he could touch.

'Ah sweet, now sweetest Ladon,' said Zelmane, 'why dost thou not stay thy course to have more full taste of thy happiness? But the reason is manifest: the upper streams make such haste to have their part of embracing that the nether, though loathly,* must needs give place unto them. O happy Ladon, within whom she is, upon whom her beauty falls, through whom her eye pierceth: O happy Ladon which art now an unperfect mirror of all perfection, canst thou ever forget the blessedness of this impression? If thou do, then let thy bed be turned from fine gravel to weeds and mud. If thou do, let some unjust niggards* make weirs to spoil thy beauty. If thou do, let some greater river fall into thee to take away the name of Ladon. O Ladon, happy Ladon, rather slide than run by her, lest thou should'st make her legs slip from her; and then, O happy Ladon, who would then call thee but the most cursed Ladon?'

But as the ladies played them in the water, sometimes striking it with their hands, the water (making lines in his face) seemed to

* *stayed conceit*: unmoved perception. *conscience*: consciousness. *loathly*: unwillingly. *niggards*: miserly persons.

smile at such beating, and with twenty bubbles, not to be content to have the picture of their face in large upon him, but he would in each of these bubbles set forth the miniature of them.

But Zelmane, whose sight was gain-said* by nothing but the transparent veil of Ladon (like a chamber where a great fire is kept, though the fire be at one stay,* yet with the continuance continually hath his heat increased) had the coals of her affection so kindled with wonder and blown with delight that now all her parts grudged that her eyes should do more homage than they to the princess of them. Insomuch that taking up the lute, her wit began to be with a divine fury inspired; her voice would in so beloved an occasion second her wit; her hands accorded the lute's music to the voice; her panting heart danced to the music; while I think her feet did beat the time, while her body was the room where it should be celebrated, her soul the queen which should be delighted. And so together went the utterance and the invention[2] that one might judge it was Philoclea's beauty which did speedily write it in her eyes, or the sense thereof which did word by word indite it in her mind, whereto she (but as an organ) did only lend utterance. The song was to this purpose:[3]

> What tongue can her perfections tell,
> In whose each part all pens may dwell?
> Her hair fine threads of finest gold,
> In curled knots man's thought to hold:
> But that her forehead says, 'In me
> A whiter beauty you may see';
> Whiter indeed, more white than snow,
> Which on cold winter's face doth grow.
> That doth present those even brows
> Whose equal line their angles bows,
> Like to the moon when after change
> Her horned head abroad doth range;
> And arches be to heavenly lids,
> Whose wink each bold attempt forbids.
> For the black stars those spheres contain,
> The matchless pair, even praise doth stain.

* *gain-said*: obstructed. *one stay*: unchanging level.

No lamp whose light by art is got,
No sun which shines, and seeth not,
Can liken them without all peer,
Save one as much as other clear:
Which only thus unhappy be,
Because themselves they cannot see.
Her cheeks with kindly claret spread,
Aurora*-like new out of bed;
Or like the fresh queen-apple's* side,
Blushing at sight of Phoebus' pride.
Her nose, her chin pure ivory wears:
No purer than the pretty ears.
So that therein appears some blood,
Like wine and milk that mingled stood:
In whose incirclets if ye gaze,
Your eyes may tread a lover's maze.
But with such turns the voice to stray,
No talk untaught can find the way.
The tip no jewel needs to wear;
The tip is jewel of the ear.

But who those ruddy lips can miss,
Which blessed still themselves do kiss?
Rubies, cherries, and roses new,
In worth, in taste, in perfit* hue:
Which never part, but that they show
Of precious pearl the double row,
The second sweetly-fenced ward,
Her heavenly-dewed tongue to guard,
Whence never word in vain did flow.

Fair under these doth stately grow
The handle of this precious work,
The neck in which strange graces lurk.
Such be, I think, the sumptuous towers
Which skill doth make in princes' bowers.
So good a say* invites the eye
A little downward to espy

* *Aurora:* goddess of the dawn. *queen-apple:* early variety of apple.
*perfit:* perfect. *say:* foretaste.

The lovely clusters of her breasts,
Of Venus' babe the wanton nests:
Like pommels round of marble clear,
Where azur'd veins well mix'd appear,
With dearest tops of porphyry.

Betwixt these two a way doth lie,
A way more worthy beauty's fame,
Than that which bears the milken name.*
This leads into the joyous field,
Which only still doth lilies yield;
But lilies such whose native smell
The Indian odours doth excel.
Waist it is called, for it doth waste
Men's lives, until it be imbraced.

There may one see, and yet not see
Her ribs in white all armed be,
More white than Neptune's foamy face,
When struggling rocks he would embrace.

In those delights the wand'ring thought
Might of each side astray be brought,
But that her navel doth unite,
In curious circle, busy sight,
A dainty seal of virgin-wax,
Where nothing but impression lacks.

Her belly then glad sight doth fill,
Justly entitled Cupid's hill:
A hill most fit for such a master,
A spotless mine of alabaster,
Like alabaster fair and sleek,
But soft and supple, satin-like.
In that sweet seat the boy* doth sport:
Loth, I must leave his chief resort.
For such a use the world hath gotten,
The best things still must be forgotten.

Yet never shall my song omit
Her thighs, for Ovid's song more fit;
Which flanked with two sugared flanks,

* *the milken name*: the milky way. *the boy*: i.e. Cupid.

Lift up their stately swelling banks,
That Albion cliffs in whiteness pass;
With haunches smooth as looking-glass.
But bow all knees, now of her knees
My tongue doth tell what fancy sees.
The knots of joy, the gins* of love,
Whose motion makes all graces move:
Whose bought incaved* doth yield such sight
Like cunning painter shadowing white.[4]
The gartring place with child-like sign
Shows easy print in metal fine.
But then again the flesh doth rise
In her brave calves, like crystal skies,
Whose Atlas[5] is a smallest small,
More white than whitest bone of whale.*

Thereout steals out that round clean foot,
This noble cedar's precious root:
In show and scent pale violets,
Whose step on earth all beauty sets.

But back unto her back, my Muse,
Where Leda's swan his feathers mews,*[6]
Along whose ridge such bones are met,
Like comfits* round in marchpane* set.

Her shoulders be like two white doves,
Perching within square royal roofs,
Which leaded are with silver skin,[7]
Passing the hate-spot ermelin.*

And thence those arms derived are;
The Phoenix wings are not so rare
For faultless length, and stainless hue.

Ah woe is me, my woes renew.
Now course doth lead me to her hand,
Of my first love the fatal band;
Where whiteness doth for ever sit:
Nature herself enamell'd it.

---

\* *gins*: snares. (OA text. '90 and '93, 'gems'). *bought incaved*: bend
of the leg behind the knee. *whale*: (Ringler). '90, '93, 'all'. *mews*: sheds.
*comfits*: sweets. *marchpane*: marzipan. *ermelin*: ermine.

For there with strange compact* doth lie
Warm snow, moist pearl, soft ivory.
There fall those sapphire-coloured brooks,*
Which conduit-like* with curious crooks,*
Sweet islands make in that sweet land.
As for the fingers of the hand,
The bloody shafts of Cupid's war,
With amatists* they headed are.
   Thus hath each part his beauty's part:
But how the Graces do impart
To all her limbs a special grace,
Becoming every time and place,
Which doth even beauty beautify,
And most bewitch the wretched eye;
How all this is but a fair inn
Of fairer guests, which dwell within.
Of whose high praise, and praiseful bliss,
Goodness the pen, Heaven paper is,
The ink immortal fame doth lend.
As I began, so must I end.
    No tongue can her perfections tell,
    In whose each part all pens may dwell.

But as Zelmane was coming to the latter end of her song, she might see the same water-spaniel, which before had hunted, come and fetch away one of Philoclea's gloves, whose fine proportion showed well what a dainty guest was wont there to be lodged. It was a delight to Zelmane to see that the dog was therewith delighted, and so let him go a little way withal, who quickly carried it out of sight among certain trees and bushes which were very close together. But by and by he came again, and amongst the raiments – Miso and Mopsa being preparing sheets against their coming out – the dog lighted upon a little book of four or five leaves of paper and was bearing that away too. But then Zelmane (not knowing what importance it might be of) ran after the dog,

* *compact*: composition. *brooks*: i.e. her veins. *conduit-like*: like artificial channels. *crooks*: bends. *amatists*: amethysts, i.e. her fingernails.

who going straight to those bushes, she might see the dog deliver it to a gentleman who secretly lay there. But she hastily coming in, the gentleman rose up, and with a courteous though sad countenance presented himself unto her. Zelmane's eyes straight willed her mind to mark him, for she thought in her life she had never seen a man of a more goodly presence, in whom strong making took not away delicacy, nor beauty fierceness; being indeed such a right man-like man as Nature, often erring, yet shows she would fain make. But when she had a while, not without admiration, viewed him, she desired him to deliver back the glove and paper because they were the lady Philoclea's, telling him withal that she would not willingly let them know of his close lying in that prohibited place while they were bathing themselves, because she knew they would be mortally offended withal.

'Fair lady,' answered he, 'the worst of the complaint is already passed, since I feel of my fault in myself the punishment. But for these things, I assure you, it was my dog's wanton boldness, not my presumption.' With that he gave her back the paper: 'But for the glove,' said he, 'since it is my lady Philoclea's, give me leave to keep it, since my heart cannot persuade itself to part from it. And I pray you tell the lady (lady indeed of all my desires) that owns it, that I will direct my life to honour this glove with serving her.'

'O villain,' cried out Zelmane, maddened with finding an unlooked-for rival, and that he would make her a messenger. 'Dispatch,' said she, 'and deliver it, or by the life of her that owns it, I will make thy soul (though too base a price) pay for it': and with that drew out her sword, which, Amazon-like, she ever ware about her.

The gentleman retired himself into an open place from among the bushes, and then drawing out his too, he offered to deliver it unto her, saying, withal, 'God forbid I should use my sword against you, since, if I be not deceived, you are the same famous Amazon that both defended my lady's just title of beauty against the valiant Phalantus, and saved her life in killing the lion. Therefore I am rather to kiss your hands, with acknowledging myself bound to obey you.'

But this courtesy was worse than a bastinado* to Zelmane; so

* bastinado: beating.

that again with rageful eyes she bade him defend himself, for no less than his life should answer it.

'A hard case,' said he, 'to teach my sword that lesson, which hath ever used to turn itself to a shield in a lady's presence.'

But Zelmane, hearkening to no more words, began with such witty fury to pursue him with blows and thrusts, that nature and virtue commanded the gentleman to look to his safety. Yet still courtesy, that seemed incorporate in his heart, would not be persuaded by danger to offer any offence, but only to stand upon the best defensive guard he could; sometimes going back, being content in that respect to take on the figure of cowardice; sometimes with strong and well-met wards, sometimes cunning avoidings of his body, and sometimes feigning some blows which himself pull'd back before they needed to be withstood. And so with play did he a good while fight against the fight of Zelmane who (more spited with that courtesy, that one that did nothing should be able to resist her) burned away with choler any motions which might grow out of her own sweet disposition, determining to kill him if he fought no better; and so redoubling her blows, drave the stranger to no other shift than to ward and go back, at that time seeming the image of innocency against violence. But at length he found that both in public and private respects, who stands only upon defence stands upon no defence: for Zelmane seeming to strike at his head, and he going to ward it withal stepped back as he was accustomed, she stopped her blow in the air, and suddenly turning the point, ran full at his breast so as he was driven with the pommel of his sword (having no other weapon of defence) to beat it down: but the thrust was so strong that he could not so wholly beat it away but that it met with his thigh, through which it ran.

But Zelmane retiring her sword and seeing his blood, victorious anger was conquered by the before-conquered pity; and heartily sorry, and even ashamed with herself she was, considering how little he had done who well she found could have done more. Insomuch that she said, 'Truly I am sorry for your hurt, but yourself gave the cause, both in refusing to deliver the glove, and yet not fighting as I know you could have done. But,' said she, 'because I perceive you disdain to fight with a woman, it may be before a year come about, you shall meet with a near kinsman of mine, Pyrocles prince of Macedon, and I give you my word, he for me shall maintain this quarrel against you.'

'I would,' answered Amphialus, 'I had many more such hurts, to meet and know that worthy prince, whose virtue I love and admire, though my good destiny hath not been to see his person.'

But as they were so speaking, the young ladies came, to whom Mopsa (curious in anything but her own good behaviour) having followed and seen Zelmane fighting, had cried what she had seen, while they were drying themselves, and the water, with some drops, seemed to weep that it should part from such bodies. But they careful of Zelmane (assuring themselves that any Arcadian would bear reverence to them) Pamela with a noble mind and Philoclea with a loving (hastily hiding the beauties whereof Nature was proud and they ashamed) they made quick work to come to save Zelmane. But already they found them in talk, and Zelmane careful of his wound. But when they saw him, they knew it was their cousin-german, the famous Amphialus, whom yet with a sweet graced bitterness they blamed for breaking their father's commandment, especially while themselves were in such sort retired. But he craved pardon, protesting unto them that he had only been to seek solitary places, by an extreme melancholy that had a good while possessed him; and guided to that place by his spaniel, where, while the dog hunted in the river, he had withdrawn himself to pacify with sleep his over watched eyes, till a dream waked him, and made him see that whereof he had dreamed; and withal not obscurely signified that he felt the smart of his own doings. But Philoclea, that was even jealous of herself for Zelmane, would needs have her glove, and not without so mighty a lour* as that face could yield.

As for Zelmane when she knew it was Amphialus, 'Lord Amphialus,' said she, 'I have long desired to know you, heretofore, I must confess, with more goodwill, but still with honouring your virtue, though I love not your person: and at this time, I pray you, let us take care of your wound, upon condition you shall hereafter promise that a more knightly combat shall be performed between us.'

* lour: angry look.

Amphialus answered in honourable sort, but with such excusing himself that more and more accused his love to Philoclea and provoked more hate in Zelmane. But Mopsa had already called certain shepherds not far off, who knew and well observed their limits, to come and help to carry away Amphialus, whose wound suffered him not without danger to strain it: and so he leaving himself with them, departed from them, faster bleeding in his heart than at his wound, which, bound up by the sheets wherewith Philoclea had been wrapped, made him thank the wound and bless the sword for that favour.

## CHAPTER 12

He being gone, the ladies (with merry anger talking in what naked simplicity their cousin had seen them) returned to the lodge-ward; yet thinking it too early (as long as they had any day) to break off so pleasing a company with going to perform a cumbersome obedience, Zelmane invited them to the little arbour only reserved for her, which they willingly did: and there sitting, Pamela having a while made the lute in his language show how glad it was to be touched by her fingers, Zelmane delivered up the paper which Amphialus had at first yielded unto her; and seeing written upon the backside of it 'The complaint of Plangus', remembering what Dorus had told her, and desiring to know how much Philoclea knew of her estate, she took occasion in the presenting of it to ask whether it were any secret or no.

'No truly,' answered Philoclea, 'it is but even an exercise of my father's writing, upon this occasion: he was one day, somewhile before your coming hither, walking abroad, having us two with him, almost a mile hence; and crossing a highway which comes from the city of Megalopolis, he saw this gentleman whose name is there written, one of the properest and best-graced men that ever I saw, being of middle age and of a mean* stature. He lay as then under a tree, while his servants were getting fresh post-horses for him. It might seem he was tired with the extreme travel he had taken, and yet not so tired that he forced to take any rest, so hasty he was upon his journey; and withal so sorrowful that

* *mean*: middle.

the very face thereof was painted in his face, which with pitiful motions, even groans, tears, and passionate talking to himself, moved my father to fall in talk with him: who at first not knowing him, answered him in such a desperate phrase of grief that my father afterwards took a delight to set it down in such a form as you see: which if you read, what you doubt of my sister and I are able to declare unto you. Zelmane willingly opened the leaves and read it, being written dialogue-wise in this manner.

## PLANGUS · BASILIUS

PLANGUS: Alas, how long this pilgrimage doth last!
 What greater ills have now the heavens in store,
  To couple coming harms with sorrows past?
Long since my voice is hoarse, and throat is sore,
 With cries to skies, and curses to the ground,
  But more I plain, I feel my woes the more.
Ah, where was first that cruel cunning found,
 To frame of earth a vessel of the mind,
  Where it should be to self-destruction bound?
What needed so high sprites such mansions blind?
 Or wrapped in flesh, what do they here obtain
  But glorious name of wretched human kind?
Balls to the stars, and thralls to Fortune's reign;
 Turn'd from themselves, infected with their cage,
  Where death is fear'd, and life is held with pain;
Like players plac'd to fill a filthy stage,
 Where change of thoughts one fool to other shows,
  And all but jests, save only sorrow's rage.
The child feels that; the man that feeling knows,
 With cries first born, the presage of his life,
  Where wit but serves to have true taste of woes.
A shop of shame, a book where blots be rife
 This body is: this body so composed,
  As in itself to nourish mortal strife.
So divers be the elements disposed
 In this weak work, that it can never be
  Made uniform to any state reposed.

Grief only makes his wretched state to see
    (Even like a top which nought but whipping moves)
    This man, this talking beast, this walking tree.
Grief is the stone which finest judgement proves.*
    For who grieves not hath but a blockish* brain,
    Since cause of grief no cause from life removes.

BASILIUS: How long wilt thou with moanful music stain
    The cheerful notes these pleasant places yield,
    Where all good haps a perfect state maintain?

PLANGUS: Cursed be good haps, and cursed be they that build
    Their hopes on haps, and do not make despair
    For all these certain blows the surest shield.
Shall I that saw Erona's shining hair
    Torn with her hands, and those same hands of snow
    With loss of purest blood themselves to tear;
Shall I that saw those breasts, where beauties flow,
    Swelling with sighs, made pale with mind's disease,
    And saw those eyes, those suns, such showers to show;
Shall I, whose ears her mournful words did seize,
    Her words in syrup laid of sweetest breath,
    Relent* those thoughts which then did so displease?
No, no. Despair my daily lesson saith,
    And saith, although I seek my life to fly,
    Plangus must live to see Erona's death.
Plangus must live some help for her to try
    (Though in despair) for Love so forceth me;
    Plangus doth live, and shall Erona die?
Erona die? O heaven (if heaven there be)
    Hath all thy whirling course so small effect?
    Serve all thy starry eyes this shame to see?
Let dolts in haste some altars fair erect
    To those high powers, which idly sit above,
    And virtue do in greatest need neglect.

* *stone . . . proves*: touchstone for testing metals. *blockish*: senseless.
*relent*: relinquish.

BASILIUS: O man, take heed how thou the gods do move
    To cause-ful wrath, which thou canst not resist.
    Blasphemous words the speaker vain do prove.
Alas, while we are wrapped in foggy mist
    Of our self love (so passions do deceive)
    We think they hurt, when most they do assist.
To harm us worms should that high Justice leave
    His nature? Nay, himself? For so it is.
    What glory from our loss can he receive?
But still our dazzled eyes their way do miss,
    While that we do at his sweet scourge repine,
    The kindly way to beat us on to bliss.
If she must die then hath she passed the line
    Of loathsome days, whose loss how canst thou moan,
    That dost so well their miseries define?
But such we are with inward tempest blown
    Of winds quite contrary in waves of will:
    We moan that lost, which had, we did bemoan.

PLANGUS: And shall she die? Shall cruel fire spill
    Those beams that set so many hearts on fire?
    Hath she not force even death with love to kill?
Nay, even cold Death inflam'd with hot desire
    Her to enjoy, where joy itself is thrall,
    Will spoil the earth of his most rich attire.
Thus Death becomes a rival to us all,
    And hopes with foul embracements her to get,
    In whose decay Virtue's fair shrine must fall.
O Virtue weak, shall Death his triumph set
    Upon thy spoils, which never should lie waste?
    Let Death first die; be thou his worthy let.*
By what eclipse shall that sun be defac'd?
    What mine* hath erst thrown down so fair a tower?
    What sacrilege hath such a saint disgrac'd?
The world the garden is, she is the flower
    That sweetens all the place; she is the guest
    Of rarest price, both heaven and earth her bower.

       *his worthy let:* opposer. *mine:* explosive device.

And shall, O me, all this in ashes rest?
    Alas if you a Phoenix new will have
    Burnt by the sun, she first must build her nest.
But well you know, the gentle sun would save
    Such beams so like his own, which might have might
    In him the thoughts of Phaeton's dam to grave.[1]
Therefore, alas, you use vile Vulcan's spite,
    Which nothing spares, to melt that virgin wax,
    Which while it is, it is all Asia's light.
O Mars, for what doth serve thy armed axe?
    To let that wittol[2] beast consume in flames
    Thy Venus child, whose beauty Venus lacks?
O Venus, if her praise no envy frames
    In thy high mind, get her thy husband's grace.
    Sweet speaking oft a currish heart reclaims.
O eyes of mine, where once she saw her face,
    Her face which was more lively in my heart;
    O brain, where thought of her hath only place;
O hand, which touch'd her hand when we did part;
    O lips that kiss'd that hand with my tears sprent;*
    O tongue, then dumb, not daring tell my smart;
O soul, whose love in her is only spent,
    What ere you see, think, touch, kiss, speak, or love,
    Let all for her, and unto her be bent.

BASILIUS: Thy wailing words do much my spirits move,
    They uttered are in such a feeling fashion,
    That sorrow's work against my will I prove.
Methinks I am partaker of thy passion,
    And in thy case do glass* mine own debility:
    Self-guilty folk most prone to feel compassion.
Yet reason saith, 'Reason should have ability
    To hold these worldly things in such proportion,
    As let them come or go with even facility.'
But our desire's tyrannical extortion
    Doth force us there to set our chief delightfulness

* *sprent:* sprinkled. *glass:* see as in a glass.

Where but a baiting place* is all our portion.
But still, although we fail of perfect rightfulness,
    Seek we to tame these childish superfluities:
    Let us not wink* though void of purest sightfulness.
For what can breed more peevish incongruities*
    Than man to yield to female lamentations?
    Let us some grammar learn of more congruities.

PLANGUS: If through mine ears pierce any consolations,
    By wise discourse, sweet tunes, or poets' fiction;
    If aught I cease these hideous exclamations,
While that my soul, she, she lives in affliction;
    Then let my life long time on earth maintained be,
    To wretched me, the last worst malediction.
Can I, that know her sacred parts restrained be
    From any joy, know fortune's vile displacing her,
    In moral rules let raging woes contained be?[3]
Can I forget, when they in prison placing her,
    With swelling heart in spite and due disdainfulness
    She lay for dead, till I help'd with unlacing her?
Can I forget from how much mourning plainfulness*
    With diamond in window-glass she graved
    'Erona die, and end this ugly painfulness'?
Can I forget in how strange phrase she craved
    That quickly they would her burn, drown or smother,
    As if by death she only might be saved?
Then let me eke forget one hand from other:
    Let me forget that Plangus I am called:
    Let me forget I am son to my mother:
But if my memory must thus be thralled
    To that strange stroke which conquer'd all my senses,
    Can thoughts still thinking so rest unappalled?

BASILIUS: Who still doth seek against himself offences,
    What pardon can avail? Or who employs him
    To hurt himself, what shields can be defences?

* *baiting place*: resting place. *wink*: shut our eyes. *incongruities*: things unfitting. *plainfulness*: lamentation.

Woe to poor man; each outward thing annoys him
   In divers kinds; yet as he were not filled,
   He heaps in inward grief, that most destroys him.
Thus is our thought with pain for thistles tilled:
   Thus be our noblest parts dried up with sorrow:
   Thus is our mind with too much minding spilled.*
One day lays up stuff of grief for the morrow:
   And whose good haps do leave him unprovided,
   Condoling cause of friendship he will borrow.⁴
Betwixt the good and shade of good divided,
   We pity deem that which but weakness is:
   So are we from our high creation slided.
But Plangus, lest I may your sickness miss,
   Or rubbing, hurt the sore, I here do end.
   The ass did hurt when he did think to kiss.

When Zelmane had read it over, marvelling very much of the
speech of Erona's death, and therefore desirous to know further of
it, but more desirous to hear Philoclea speak, 'Most excellent lady,'
said she, 'one may be little the wiser for reading this dialogue,
since it neither sets forth what this Plangus is, nor what Erona is,
nor what the cause should be which threatens her with death and
him with sorrow. Therefore I would humbly crave to understand
the particular discourse thereof because, I must confess, something
in my travel I have heard of this strange matter, which I would be
glad to find by so sweet an authority confirmed.'

'The truth is,' answered Philoclea, 'that after he knew my father
to be prince of this country, while he hoped to prevail something
with him in a great request he made unto him, he was content to
open fully the estate both of himself and of that lady; which with
my sister's help,' said she, 'who remembers it better than I, I will
declare unto you. And first of Erona (being the chief subject of
this discourse) this story (with more tears and exclamations than I
list to spend about it) he recounted.'

              * *spilled*: destroyed.

## CHAPTER 13

'Of late there reigned a king in Lycia who had, for the blessing of his marriage, this only daughter of his, Erona; a princess worthy, for her beauty, as much praise as beauty may be praise-worthy. This princess Erona, being nineteen years of age, seeing the country of Lycia so much devoted to Cupid as that in every place his naked pictures and images were superstitiously adored (either moved thereunto by the esteeming that could be no god-head which could breed wickedness, or the shamefast consideration of such nakedness) procured so much of her father as utterly to pull down and deface all those statues and pictures: which how terribly he punished – for to that the Lycians impute it – quickly after appeared.

'For she had not lived a year longer, when she was stricken with most obstinate love to a young man but of mean parentage in her father's court named Antiphilus: so mean as that he was but the son of her nurse, and by that means (without other desert) became known of her. Now so evil could she conceal her fire and so wilfully persevered she in it, that her father offering her the marriage of the great Tiridates, king of Armenia, who desired her more than the joys of heaven, she for Antiphilus' sake refused it. Many ways tiphilus, whom he kept in prison. But neither she liked persuasions, sometimes threatenings; once, hiding Antiphilus, and giving her to understand that he was fled the country; lastly, making a solemn execution to be done of another under the name of Antiphilus, whom he kept in prison. But neither she liked persuasions, nor feared threatenings, nor changed for absence: and when she thought him dead, she sought all means, as well by poison as knife, to send her soul, at least, to be married in the eternal church with him. This so brake the tender father's heart that, leaving things as he found them, he shortly after died. Then forthwith Erona, being seized of the crown, and arming her will with authority, sought to advance her affection to the holy title of matrimony.

'But before she could accomplish all the solemnities, she was overtaken with a war the King Tiridates made upon her only for her person, towards whom, for her ruin, love had kindled his cruel

heart – indeed cruel and tyrannous. For being far too strong in the
field, he spared not man, woman and child; but (as though there
could be found no foil to set forth the extremity of his love but
extremity of hatred) wrote, as it were, the sonnets of his love in
the blood, and tuned them in the cries of her subjects – although
his fair sister Artaxia, who would accompany him in the army,
sought all means to appease his fury: till lastly, he besieged Erona
in her best city, vowing to win her or lose his life. And now had
he brought her to the point either of a woeful consent or a ruinous
denial, when there came thither (following the course which
virtue and fortune led them) two excellent young princes, Pyrocles and Musidorus, the one prince of Macedon, the other of
Thessalia: two princes as Plangus said (and he witnessed his
saying with sighs and tears) the most accomplished both in body
and mind that the sun ever looked upon.'

While Philoclea spake those words, 'O sweet words', thought
Zelmane to herself, "which are not only a praise to me, but a
praise to praise itself, which out of that mouth issueth.'

'Those two princes,' said Philoclea, 'as well to help the weaker
(especially being a lady) as to save a Greek people from being
ruined by such whom we call and count barbarous, gathering
together such of the honestest Lycians as would venture their lives
to succour their princess, giving order by a secret message they
sent into the city that they should issue with all force at an appointed time, they set upon Tiridates' camp with so well guided a
fierceness that being of both sides assaulted, he was like to be
overthrown, but that this Plangus (being general of Tiridates'
horsemen) especially aided by the two mighty men, Euardes and
Barzanes, rescued the footmen, even almost defeated: but yet could
not bar the princes (with their succours both of men and victual)
to enter the city.

'Which when Tiridates found would make the war long (which
length seemed to him worse than a languishing consumption) he
made a challenge of three princes in his retinue against those two
princes and Antiphilus: and that thereupon the quarrel should be
decided, with compact that neither side should help his fellow, but
of whose side the more overcame, with him the victory should remain. Antiphilus (though Erona chose rather to bide the brunt of

war than venture him) yet could not for shame refuse the offer, especially since the two strangers that had no interest in it did willingly accept it; besides that he saw it like enough that the people (weary of the miseries of war) would rather give him up, if they saw him shrink, than for his sake venture their ruin, considering that the challengers were of far greater worthiness than himself. So it was agreed upon; and against Pyrocles was Euardes king of Bithynia; Barzanes of Hircania against Musidorus – two men that thought the world scarce able to resist them; and against Antiphilus he placed this same Plangus, being his own cousin german and son to the king of Iberia. Now so it fell out that Musidorus slew Barzanes, and Pyrocles Euardes, which victory those princes esteemed above all that ever they had: but of the other side Plangus took Antiphilus prisoner; under which colour (as if the matter had been equal, though indeed it was not, the greater part being overcome of his side) Tiridates continued his war; and to bring Erona to a compelled yielding, sent her word that he would the third morrow after, before the walls of the town, strike off Antiphilus' head, without his suit in that space were granted; adding, withal, because he had heard of her desperate affection, that if in the meantime she did herself any hurt, what tortures could be devised should be laid upon Antiphilus.

'Then lo, if Cupid be a god, or that the tyranny of our own thoughts seem as a god unto us – but whatsoever it was, then it did set forth the miserableness of his effects, she being drawn to two contraries by one cause. For the love of him commanded her to yield to no other: the love of him commanded her to preserve his life; which knot might well be cut, but untied it could not be. So that love in her passions, like a right make-bate,* whispered to both sides arguments of quarrel.

' "What," said he (of the one side) "dost thou love Antiphilus, O Erona, and shall Tiridates enjoy thy body? With what eyes wilt thou look upon Antiphilus when he shall know that another possesseth thee? But if thou wilt do it, canst thou do it? Canst thou force thy heart? Think with thyself, if this man have thee, thou shalt never have more part of Antiphilus than if he were dead. But thus much more, that the affection shall be still gnawing, and

* *make-bate*: trouble-maker.

304

the remorse still present. Death perhaps will cool the rage of thy affection, where thus, thou shalt ever love, and ever lack. Think this beside: if thou marry Tiridates, Antiphilus is so excellent a man that long he cannot be from being in some high place married. Canst thou suffer that too? If another kill him, he doth him the wrong: if thou abuse thy body, thou dost him the wrong. His death is a work of nature, and either now or at another time he shall die. But it shall be thy work, thy shameful work, which is in thy power to shun, to make him live to see thy faith falsified and his bed defiled."

'But when love had well kindled that party of her thoughts, then went he to the other side. "What," said he, "O Erona, and is thy love of Antiphilus come to that point as thou dost now make it a question whether he shall die or no? O excellent affection which for too much love will see his head off! Mark well the reasons of the other side, and thou shalt see it is but love of thyself which so disputeth. Thou canst not abide Tiridates: this is but love of thyself. Thou shalt be ashamed to look upon him afterwards: this is but fear of shame and love of thyself. Thou shalt want him as much then: this is but love of thyself. He shall be married: if he be well, why should that grieve thee but for love of thyself? No, no, pronounce these words if thou canst, "Let Antiphilus die." '

Then the images of each side stood before her understanding. One time she thought she saw Antiphilus dying; another time she thought Antiphilus saw her by Tiridates enjoyed: twenty times calling for a servant to carry message of yielding, but before he came the mind was altered. She blushed when she considered the effect of granting: she was pale when she remembered the fruits of denying. For weeping, sighing, wringing her hands and tearing her hair were indifferent of both sides. Easily she would have agreed to have broken all disputations with her own death, but that the fear of Antiphilus' further torments stayed her. At length, even the evening before the day appointed of his death, the determination of yielding prevailed, especially growing upon a message of Antiphilus who with all the conjuring terms he could devise, besought her to save his life upon any conditions. But she had no sooner sent her messenger to Tiridates but her mind changed, and she went to the two young princes, Pyrocles and Musidorus, and falling down at their feet, desired them to try some way for her deliverance, showing herself resolved not to over-live Antiphilus nor yet to yield to Tiridates.

'They, that knew not what she had done in private, prepared that night accordingly; and as sometimes it falls out that what is inconstancy seems cunning, so did this change indeed stand in as good stead as a witty dissimulation. For it made the king as reckless as them diligent, so that in the dead time of the night the princes issued out of the town, with whom she would needs go, either to die herself or rescue Antiphilus, having no armour nor weapon but affection. And I cannot tell you how, by what device, though Plangus at large described it; the conclusion was, the wonderful valour of the two princes so prevailed that Antiphilus was succoured and the king slain. Plangus was then the chief man left in the camp; and therefore seeing no other remedy, conveyed in safety into her country Artaxia, now Queen of Armenia; who with true lamentations made known to the world that her new greatness did no way comfort her in respect of her brother's loss, whom she studied all means possible to revenge upon every one of the occasioners, having (as she thought) overthrown her brother by a most abominable treason. Insomuch that being at home, she proclaimed great rewards to any private man, and herself in marriage to any prince, that would destroy Pyrocles and Musidorus. But thus was Antiphilus redeemed and (though against the consent of all her nobility) married to Erona; in which case the two Greek princes, being called away by another adventure, left them.

## CHAPTER 14

'But now, methinks, as I have read some poets who, when they intend to tell some horrible matter, they bid men shun the hearing of it, so if I do not desire you to stop your ears from me, yet may I well desire a breathing time before I am to tell the execrable treason of Antiphilus that brought her to this misery; and withal wish you all that from all mankind indeed you stop your ears. O most happy were we if we did set our loves one upon another.' And as she spake that word, her cheeks in red letters writ more than her tongue did speak. 'And therefore since I have named Plangus, I pray you, sister,' said she, 'help me with the rest, for I have held the stage long enough; and if it please you to make his fortune known, as I have done Erona's, I will after take heart again to go on with his falsehood; and so between us both, my Lady Zelmane shall understand both the cause and parties of this lamentation.'

'Nay, I beshrew me then,' said Miso, 'I will none of that, I promise you, as long as I have the government. I will first have my tale; and then, my Lady Pamela, my Lady Zelmane, and my daughter Mopsa' (for Mopsa was then returned from Amphialus) 'may draw cuts, and the shortest cut speak first. For I tell you, and this may be suffered, when you are married, you will have first and last word of your husbands.'

The ladies laughed to see with what an eager earnestness she looked, having threatening not only in her ferret eyes, but while she spake her nose seeming to threaten her chin, and her shaking limbs one to threaten another. But there was no remedy, they must obey; and Miso, sitting on the ground with her knees up, and her hands upon her knees, tuning her voice with many a quavering cough, thus discoursed unto them.

'I tell you true,' said she, 'whatsoever you think of me, you will one day be as I am; and I, simple though I sit here, thought once my penny as good silver as some of you do: and if my father had not played the hasty fool (it is no lie I tell you) I might have had another-gains* husband than Dametas. But let that pass, God amend him; and yet I speak it not without good cause. You are full in your tittle-tattlings of Cupid: here is Cupid and there is Cupid. I will tell you now what a good old woman told me, what an old wise man told her, what a great learned clerk told him, and gave it him in writing; and here I have it in my prayer-book.'

'I pray you,' said Philoclea, 'let us see it and read it.'

'No haste but good,' said Miso, 'you shall first know how I came by it. I was a young girl of a seven and twenty years old, and I could not go through the street of our village but I might hear the young men talk: "O the pretty little eyes of Miso": "O the fine thin lips of Miso": "O the goodly fat hands of Miso": besides, how well

* *another-gains*: of another sort.

a certain wrying I had of my neck became me. Then the one would wink with one eye, and the other cast daisies at me.[1] I must confess, seeing so many amorous, it made me set up my peacock's tail with the highest. Which when this good old[2] woman perceived (O the good old woman; well may the bones rest of the good old woman) she called me to her into her house. I remember full well it stood in the lane as you go to the barber's shop. All the town knew her; there was a great loss of her. She called me to her, and taking first a sop of wine to comfort her heart – it was of the same wine that comes out of Candia, which we pay so dear for now-a-days, and in that good world was very good cheap – she called me to her: "Minion,"* said she (indeed I was a pretty one in those days, though I say it) "I see a number of lads that love you. Well," said she, "I say no more; do you know what love is?" With that she brought me into a corner, where there was painted a foul fiend I trow, for he had a pair of horns like a bull, his feet cloven, as many eyes upon his body as my grey mare hath dapples, and for all the world so placed. This monster sat like a hangman upon a pair of gallows. In his right hand he was painted holding a crown of laurel, in his left hand a purse of money; and out of his mouth hung a lace* of two fair pictures of a man and a woman, and such a countenance he showed as if he would persuade folks by those allurements to come thither and be hanged. I, like a tender-hearted wench, shrieked out for fear of the devil. "Well," said she, "this same is even love: therefore do what thou list with all those fellows one after another, and it recks not much what they do to thee, so it be in secret; but upon my charge, never love none of them." "Why mother," said I, "could such a thing come from the belly of fair Venus?"[3] – for a few days before, our priest (between him and me) had told me the whole story of Venus. "Tush," said she, "they are all deceived"; and therewith gave me this book which she said a great maker of ballads had given to an old painter, who, for a little pleasure, had bestowed both book and picture of her. "Read there," said she, "and thou shalt see that his mother was a cow, and the false Argus his father." And so she gave me this book, and there now you may read it.'

* *Minion:* my darling, pet, etc. *a lace:* a cord with two pictures hanging on it.

With that the remembrance of the good old woman made her make such a face to weep as, if it were not sorrow, it was the carcass of sorrow that appeared there. But while her tears came out, like rain falling upon dirty furrows, the latter end of her prayer-book was read among these ladies, which contained this:

Poor Painters oft with silly Poets join,
To fill the world with strange but vain conceits:
One brings the stuff, the other stamps the coin,
Which breeds nought else but glosses of deceits.[4]
  Thus painters Cupid paint, thus poets do,
  A naked god, blind, young, with arrows two.

Is he a god that ever flies the light?
Or naked he, disguis'd in all untruth?
If he be blind, how hitteth he so right?
How is he young that tam'd old Phoebus' youth?
  But arrows two, and tipped with gold or lead?
  Some hurt, accuse a third with horny head.[5]

No, nothing so; an old false knave he is,
By Argus got on Io, then a cow:[6]
What time for her* Juno her Jove did miss,
And charge of her to Argus did allow.
  Mercury kill'd his false sire* for this act,
  His dam,* a beast, was pardon'd beastly fact.

With father's death and mother's guilty shame,
With Jove's disdain at such a rival's seed;
The wretch compell'd a runagate* became,
And learn'd what ill a miser*-state doth breed:
  To lie, to steal, to pry, and to accuse,
  Nought in himself, each other to abuse.

Yet bears he still his parents' stately gifts,
A horned head, cloven feet, and thousand eyes,
Some gazing still, some winking wily shifts,
With long large ears, where never rumour dies.

* *what time for her*: when, because of her. *his false sire*: Argus. *His dam*: Io. *runagate*: fugitive. *miser*: wretched.

His horned head doth seem the heaven to spite;
His cloven foot doth never tread aright.

Thus half a man, with man he daily haunts,
Cloth'd in the shape which soonest may deceive:
Thus half a beast, each beastly vice he plants,
In those weak hearts that his advice receive.
    He prowls each place still in new colours decked,
    Sucking one's ill, another to infect.

To narrow breasts, he comes all wrapped in gain:
To swelling hearts, he shines in honour's fire:
To open eyes, all beauties he doth rain;
Creeping to each with flattering of desire.
    But for that love is worst which rules the eyes,
    Thereon his name, there his chief triumph lies.

Millions of years this old drivel* Cupid lives,
While still more wretch, more wicked he doth prove.
Till now at length that Jove him office gives,
(At Juno's suit, who much did Argus love)
    In this our world a hangman for to be
    Of all those fools that will have all they see.

The ladies made sport at the description and story of Cupid. But Zelmane could scarce suffer those blasphemies (as she took them) to be read, but humbly besought Pamela she would perform her sister's request of the other part of the story.

'Noble lady,' answered she, beautifying her face with a sweet smiling, and the sweetness of her smiling with the beauty of her face, 'since I am born a prince's daughter, let me not give example of disobedience. My governess will have us draw cuts, and therefore I pray you let us do so: and so perhaps it will light upon you to entertain this company with some story of your own; and it is reason our ears should be willinger to hear, as your tongue is abler to deliver.'

'I will think,' answered Zelmane, 'excellent princess, my tongue of some value if it can procure your tongue thus much to favour me.'

*drivel*: drudge.

But Pamela pleasantly persisting to have fortune their judge, they set their hands, and Mopsa (though at first for squeamishness going up and down with her head like a boat in a storm) put to* her golden gols* among them, and blind fortune (that saw not the colour of them) gave her the pre-eminence: and so being her time to speak (wiping her mouth, as there was good cause) she thus tumbled into her matter.

'In time past,' said she, 'there was a king, the mightiest man in all his country, that had by his wife the fairest daughter that ever did eat pap. Now this king did keep a great house, that everybody might come and take their meat freely. So one day, as his daughter was sitting in her window, playing upon a harp, as sweet as any rose, and combing her head with a comb all of precious stones, there came in a knight into the court upon a goodly horse, one hair of gold, and the other of silver; and so the knight casting up his eyes to the window did fall into such love with her that he grew not worth the bread he eat; till many a sorry day going over his head, with Daily Diligence and Grisly Groans he won her affection, so that they agreed to run away together. And so in May, when all true hearts rejoice, they stale out of the castle without staying so much as for their breakfast. Now forsooth, as they went together, often all to-kissing one another, the knight told her he was brought up among the water-nymphs, who had so bewitched him that if he were ever ask'd his name, he must presently vanish away; and therefore charged her upon his blessing, that she never ask him what he was nor whither he would. And so a great while she kept his commandment; till once, passing through a cruel wilderness as dark as pitch, her mouth so watered that she could not choose but ask him the question. And then he, making the grievousest complaints that would have melted a tree to have heard them, vanish'd quite away, and she lay down, casting forth as pitiful cries as any screech-owl. But having lain so, wet by the rain and burnt by the sun, five days and five nights, she gat up and went over many a high hill and many a deep river, till she came to an aunt's house of hers, and came and cried to her for help; and she for pity gave her a nut, and bade her never open her nut till she was come to the extremest misery that ever tongue could

* *put to:* put forth. *gols:* paws.

speak of. And so she went, and she went, and never rested the evening where she went in the morning, till she came to a second aunt, and she gave her another nut.'

'Now good Mopsa,' said the sweet Philoclea, 'I pray thee at my request keep this tale till my marriage-day, and I promise thee that the best gown I wear that day shall be thine.' Mopsa was very glad of the bargain, especially that it should grow a festival tale: so that Zelmane – who desired to find the uttermost what these ladies understood touching herself, and having understood the danger of Erona (of which before she had never heard) purposing with herself (as soon as this pursuit she now was in was brought to any effect) to succour her – entreated again that she might know as well the story of Plangus as of Erona. Philoclea referred it to her sister's perfecter remembrance, who with so sweet a voice and so winning a grace as in themselves were of most forcible eloquence to procure attention, in this manner to their earnest request soon condescended.

## CHAPTER 15

'The father of this prince Plangus as yet lives and is king of Iberia: a man (if the judgement of Plangus may be accepted) of no wicked nature, nor willingly doing evil, without himself* mistake the evil seeing it disguised under some form of goodness. This prince being married at the first to a princess (who both from her ancestors and in herself was worthy of him) by her had this son, Plangus. Not long after whose birth, the queen, as though she had performed the message for which she was sent into the world, returned again unto her maker. The king, sealing up all thoughts of love under the image of her memory, remained a widower many years after, recompensing the grief of that disjoining from her in conjoining in himself both a fatherly and a motherly care towards her only child Plangus, who being grown to man's age, as our own eyes may judge, could not but fertilely requite his father's fatherly education.

'This prince (while yet the errors in his nature were excused by the greenness of his youth which took all the fault upon itself) loved a private man's wife of the principal city of that kingdom –

* *without himself*: unless he himself.

if that may be called love, which he rather did take into himself willingly than by which he was taken forcibly. It sufficeth that the young man persuaded himself he loved her, she being a woman beautiful enough, if it be possible that the only outside* can justly entitle a beauty. But finding such a chase as only fled to be caught, the young prince brought his affection with her to that point which ought to engrave remorse in her heart and to paint shame upon her face. And so possessed he his desire without any interruption, he constantly favouring her, and she thinking that the enamelling of a prince's name might hide the spots of a broken wedlock. But as I have seen one that was sick of a sleeping disease could not be made wake but with pinching of him, so out of his sinful sleep his mind, unworthy so to be lost, was not to be called to itself but by a sharp accident.

'It fell out that his many-times leaving of the court in undue times began to be noted, and (as prince's ears be manifold) from one to another came unto the king; who, careful of his only son, sought and found by his spies (the necessary evil servants to a king) what it was whereby he was from his better delights so diverted. Whereupon the king, to give his fault the greater blow, used such means by disguising himself that he found them (her husband being absent) in her house together, which he did to make him the more feelingly ashamed of it. And that way he took, laying threatenings upon her, and upon him reproaches. But the poor young prince (deceived with that young opinion that if it be ever lawful to lie, it is for one's lover) employed all his wit to bring his father to a better opinion. And because he might bend him from that – as he counted it – crooked conceit of her, he wrested him, as much as he could possibly, to the other side, not sticking with prodigal protestations to set forth her chastity; not denying his own attempt, but thereby the more extolling her virtue. His sophistry prevailed, his father believed, and so believed, that ere long, though he were already stepped into the winter of his age, he found himself warm in those desires which were in his son far more excusable. To be short, he gave himself over unto it and, because he would avoid the odious comparison of a young rival, sent away his son with an army to the subduing of a province

* *the only outside:* the outside alone.

lately rebelled against him, which he knew could not be a less work than of three or four years. Wherein he behaved him so worthily as even to this country the fame thereof came long before his own coming; while yet his father had a speedier success, but in a far unnobler conquest. For while Plangus was away, the old man, growing only in age and affection, followed his suit with all means of unhonest servants, large promises, and each thing else that might help to countervail his own unloveliness.

'And she, whose husband about that time died, forgetting the absent Plangus, or at least not hoping of him to obtain so aspiring a purpose, left no art unused which might keep the line from breaking whereat the fish was already taken, not drawing him violently, but letting him play himself upon the hook which he had so greedily swallowed. For, accompanying her mourning garments with a doleful countenance, yet neither forgetting handsomeness in her mourning garments nor sweetness in her doleful countenance, her words were ever seasoned with sighs, and any favour she showed, bathed in tears, that affection might see cause of pity, and pity might persuade cause of affection. And being grown skilful in his humours, she was no less skilful in applying his humours; never suffering his fear to fall to a despair, nor his hope to hasten to an assurance. She was content he should think that she loved him, and a certain stolen look should sometimes (as though it were against her will) betray it: but if thereupon he grew bold, he straight was encountered with a mask of virtue. And that which seemeth most impossible unto me (for as near as I can I repeat it as Plangus told it) she could not only sigh when she would, as all can do, and weep when she would, as, they say, some can do; but, being most impudent in her heart, she could, when she would, teach her cheeks blushing, and make a shamefastness the cloak of shamelessness.

'In sum, to leave out many particularities which he recited, she did not only use so the spur that his desire ran on, but so the bit, that it ran on even in such a career as she would have it; that within a while the king, seeing with no other eyes but such as she gave him, and thinking no other thoughts but such as she taught him; having at the first liberal measure of favours, then shortened of them when most his desire was inflamed, he saw no other way but marriage to satisfy his longing and her mind (as he thought) loving, but chastely loving. So that by the time Plangus returned from being notably victorious of the rebels, he found his father not only married but already a father of a son and daughter by this woman. Which though Plangus (as he had every way just cause) was grieved at, yet did his grief never bring forth either contemning of her or repining at his father. But she (who, besides she was grown a mother and a step-mother, did read in his eyes her own fault and made his conscience her guiltiness) thought still that his presence carried her condemnation; so much the more as that she, unchastely attempting his wonted fancies, found, for the reverence of his father's bed, a bitter refusal: which breeding rather spite than shame in her, or if it were a shame, a shame not of the fault but of the repulse, she did not only (as hating him) thirst for a revenge, but (as fearing harm from him) endeavoured to do harm unto him.

'Therefore did she try the uttermost of her wicked wit how to overthrow him in the foundation of his strength, which was in the favour of his father; which because she saw strong both in nature and desert, it required the more cunning how to undermine it. And therefore, shunning the ordinary trade of hireling sycophants, she made her praises of him to be accusations, and her advancing him to be his ruin. For first, with words nearer admiration than liking she would extol his excellencies, the goodliness of his shape, the power of his wit, the valiantness of his courage, the fortunateness of his successes, so as the father might find in her a singular love towards him: nay she shunned not to kindle some few sparks of jealousy in him. Thus having gotten an opinion in his father that she was far from meaning mischief to the son, then fell she to praise him with no less vehemency of affection, but with much more cunning of malice. For then she sets forth the liberty of his mind, the high flying of his thoughts, the fitness in him to bear rule, the singular love the subjects bear him, that it was doubtful whether his wit were greater in winning their favours or his courage in employing their favours; that he was not born to live a subject life, each action of his bearing in it majesty, such a kingly entertainment, such a kingly magnificence, such a kingly heart for enterprises; especially remembering those virtues which in a successor are no more honoured by the subjects than suspected of the princes. Then would she, by putting off objections, bring in objections to her husband's head, already infected with suspicion.

' "Nay," would she say, "I dare take it upon my death that he is no such son as many of like* might have been, who loved greatness so well as to build their greatness upon their father's ruin. Indeed ambition, like love, can abide no lingering, and ever urgeth on his own successes, hating nothing but what may stop them. But the gods forbid we should ever once dream of any such thing in him, who perhaps might be content that you and the world should know what he can do: but the more power he hath to hurt, the more admirable is his praise, that he will not hurt."

'Then ever remembering to strengthen the suspicion of his estate with private jealousy of her love, doing him excessive honour when he was in presence, and repeating his pretty speeches and graces in his absence; besides, causing him to be employed in all such dangerous matters as either he should perish in them, or (if he prevailed) they should increase his glory, which she made a weapon to wound him; until she found that suspicion began already to speak for itself, and that her husband's ears were grown hungry of rumours, and his eyes prying into every accident.

'Then took she help to her of a servant near about her husband, whom she knew to be of a hasty ambition, and such a one who, wanting true sufficiency* to raise him, would make a ladder of any mischief. Him she useth to deal more plainly in alleging causes of jealousy, making him know the fittest times when her husband already was stirred that way. And so they two with divers ways nourished one humour, like musicians that, singing divers parts, make one music. He sometimes with fearful countenance would desire the king to look to himself, for that all the court and city were full of whisperings and expectation of some sudden change, upon what ground himself knew not. Another time he would counsel the king to make much of his son and hold his favour, for that it was too late now to keep him under. Now seeming to fear himself, because, he said, Plangus loved none of them that were great about his father. Lastly, breaking with him

* *many of like*: many of his condition. *sufficiency*: merit.

directly, making a sorrowful countenance and an humble gesture
bear false witness for his true meaning, that he found not only
soldiery but people weary of his government, and all their
affections bent upon Plangus. Both he and the queen concurring
in strange dreams, and each thing else that in a mind already
perplexed might breed astonishment; so that within a while, all
Plangus' actions began to be translated into the language of suspicion. Which though Plangus found, yet could he not avoid, even
contraries being driven to draw one yoke* of argument. If he were
magnificent, he spent much with an aspiring intent: if he spared,
he heaped much with an aspiring intent: if he spake courteously,
he angled the people's hearts: if he were silent, he mused upon
some dangerous plot. In sum, if he could have turned himself to as
many forms as Proteus,[1] every form should have been made
hideous.

'But so it fell out that a mere trifle gave them occasion of further
proceeding. The king one morning going to a vineyard that lay
along the hill whereupon his castle stood, he saw a vine-labourer
that, finding a bough broken, took a branch of the same bough for
want of another thing and tied it about the place broken. The king
asking the fellow what he did, "Marry," said he, "I make the son
bind the father." This word (finding the king already super-
stitious through suspicion) amazed him straight, as a presage
of his own fortune; so that returning and breaking with* his wife
how much he misdoubted his estate, she made such gainsaying*
answers as while they strave, strave to be ovecome. But even
while the doubts most boiled, she thus nourished them.

'She under-hand dealt with the principal men of that country,
that at the great parliament (which was then to be held) they
should in the name of all the estates persuade the king (being now
stepped deeply into old age) to make Plangus his associate in
government with him, assuring them that not only she would join
with them, but that the father himself would take it kindly;
charging them not to acquaint Plangus withal, for that perhaps it
might be harmful unto him if the king should find that he were a
party. They (who thought they might do it not only willingly,

* *draw one yoke:* pull in the same direction. *breaking with:* declaring to. *gainsaying:* contradictory.

because they loved him, and truly, because such indeed was the mind of the people, but safely, because she who ruled the king was agreed thereto) accomplished her counsel; she indeed keeping promise of vehement persuading the same; which the more she and they did, the more she knew her husband would fear, and hate the cause of his fear. Plangus found this, and humbly protested against such desire or will to accept. But the more he protested, the more his father thought he dissembled, accounting his integrity to be but a cunning face of falsehood: and therefore delaying the desire of his subjects, attended some fit occasion to lay hands upon his son, which his wife thus brought to pass.

'She caused that same minister of hers to go unto Plangus and (enabling* his words with great show of faith, and endearing them with desire of secrecy) to tell him that he found his ruin conspired by his stepmother with certain of the noblemen of that country, the king himself giving his consent, and that few days should pass before the putting it in practice; withal discovering the very truth indeed with what cunning his stepmother had proceeded. This, agreeing with Plangus' his own opinion, made him give him the better credit; yet not so far as to fly out of his country (according to the naughty fellow's persuasion) but to attend and to see further. Whereupon the fellow, by the direction of his mistress, told him one day that the same night, about one of the clock, the king had appointed to have his wife and those noblemen together to deliberate of their manner of proceeding against Plangus; and therefore offered him that if himself would agree, he would bring him into a place where he should hear all that passed, and so have the more reason both to himself and to the world to seek his safety. The poor Plangus, being subject to that only disadvantage of honest hearts, credulity, was persuaded by him; and arming himself, because of his late going, was closely conveyed into the place appointed. In the meantime, his stepmother making all her gestures cunningly counterfeit a miserable affliction, she lay almost grovelling on the floor of her chamber, not suffering anybody to comfort her; until they calling for her husband, and he held off with long inquiry, at length she told him (even almost crying out every word) that she was weary of her life, since she

* *enabling*: strengthening.

was brought to that plunge either to conceal her husband's murder or accuse her son, who had ever been more dear than a son unto her. Then with many interruptions and exclamations she told him that her son Plangus, soliciting her in the old affection between them, had besought her to put her helping hand to the death of the king, assuring her that, though all the laws in the world were against it, he would marry her when he were king.

'She had not fully said thus much, with many pitiful digressions, when in comes the same fellow that brought Plangus; and running himself out of breath, fell at the king's feet, beseeching him to save himself for that there was a man with a sword drawn in the next room. The king, affrighted, went out and called his guard, who entering the place, found indeed Plangus with his sword in his hand, but not naked, yet standing suspiciously enough to one already suspicious. The king, thinking he had put up his sword because of the noise, never took leisure to hear his answer, but made him prisoner, meaning the next morning to put him to death in the market-place.

'But the day had no sooner opened the eyes and ears of his friends and followers but that there was a little army of them who came and by force delivered him, although numbers on the other side, abused with the fine framing of their report, took arms for the king. But Plangus, though he might have used the force of his friends to revenge his wrong and get the crown, yet the natural love of his father, and hate to make their suspicion seem just, caused him rather to choose a voluntary exile than to make his father's death the purchase of his life: and therefore went he to Tiridates, whose mother was his father's sister, living in his court eleven or twelve years, ever hoping by his intercession and his own desert to recover his father's grace. At the end of which time, the war of Erona happened, which my sister with the cause thereof discoursed unto you.

'But his father had so deeply engraved the suspicion in his heart that he thought his flight rather to proceed of a fearful guiltiness than of an humble faithfulness, and therefore continued his hate with such vehemency that he did even hate his nephew Tiridates, and afterwards his niece Artaxia, because in their court he received countenance, leaving no means unattempted of destroying his son; among other, employing that wicked servant of his, who undertook to empoison him. But his cunning disguised him not so well but that the watchful servants of Plangus did discover him. Whereupon the wretch was taken and, before his well-deserved execution, by torture forced to confess the particularities of this, which in general I have told you.

'Which confession authentically set down, though Tiridates with solemn embassage sent it to the king, wrought no effect. For the king, having put the reins of the government into his wife's hand, never did so much as read it, but sent it straight by her to be considered, so as they rather heaped more hatred upon Plangus for the death of their servant. And now finding that his absence and their reports had much diminished the wavering people's affection towards Plangus, with advancing fit persons for faction, and granting great immunities to the commons, they prevailed so far as to cause the son of the second wife, called Palladius, to be proclaimed successor, and Plangus quite excluded: so that Plangus was driven to continue his serving Tiridates, as he did in the war against Erona, and brought home Artaxia, as my sister told you; when Erona by the treason of Antiphilus – '

But at that word she stopped. For Basilius, not able longer to abide their absence, came suddenly among them and with smiling countenance, telling Zelmane he was afraid she had stolen away his daughters, invited them to follow the sun's counsel in going then to their lodging, for indeed the sun was ready to set. They yielded, Zelmane meaning some other time to understand the story of Antiphilus' treason and Erona's danger, whose cause she greatly tendered. But Miso had no sooner espied Basilius but that as spitefully as her rotten voice could utter it she set forth the sauciness of Amphialus. But Basilius only attended what Zelmane's opinion was, who though she hated Amphialus, yet the nobility of her courage prevailed over it, and she desired he might be pardoned that youthful error, considering the reputation he had to be one of the best knights in the world, so as hereafter he governed himself as one remembering his fault. Basilius, giving the infinite terms of praises to Zelmane's both valour in conquering and pitifulness in pardoning, commanded no more words to be made of it, since such he thought was her pleasure.

BOOK TWO

## CHAPTER 16

So brought he them up to visit his wife, where, between her and him, the poor Zelmane received a tedious entertainment, oppressed with being loved almost as much as with loving. Basilius, not so wise in covering his passion, could make his tongue go almost no other pace but to run into those immoderate praises which the foolish lover thinks short of his mistress, though they reach far beyond the heavens. But Gynecia, whom womanly modesty did more outwardly bridle, yet did oftentimes use the advantage of her sex in kissing Zelmane as she sat upon her bed-side by her, which was but still more and more sweet incense to cast upon the fire wherein her heart was sacrificed. Once* Zelmane could not stir but that (as if they had been poppets,* whose motion stood only upon her pleasure) Basilius with serviceable steps, Gynecia with greedy eyes, would follow her. Basilius' mind Gynecia well knew, and could have found in her heart to laugh at, if mirth could have borne any proportion with her fortune. But all Gynecia's actions were interpreted by Basilius as proceeding from jealousy of his amorousness. Zelmane betwixt both, like the poor child whose father, while he beats him, will make him believe it is for love; or like the sick man, to whom the physician swears the ill-tasting wallowish* medicine he proffers is of a good taste. Their love was hateful, their courtesy troublesome, their presence cause of her absence thence where not only her light but her life consisted. 'Alas,' thought she to herself, 'dear Dorus, what odds is there between thy destiny and mine? For thou hast to do in thy pursuit but with shepherdish folks, who trouble thee with a little envious care and affected diligence; but I (besides that I have now Miso, the worst of thy devils, let loose upon me) am waited on by princes, and watched by the two wakeful eyes of love and jealousy. Alas, incomparable Philoclea, thou ever seest me, but dost never see me as I am. Thou hearest willingly all that I dare say, and I dare not say that which were most fit for thee to hear. Alas, who ever but I was imprisoned in liberty, and banished being still present? To whom but me have lovers been jailors, and honour a captivity?'

* *Once:* on any occasion. *poppets:* puppets. *wallowish:* nauseous.

321

But the night coming on with her silent steps upon them, they parted each from other (if at least they could be parted of whom every one did live in another) and went about to flatter sleep with their beds, that disdained to bestow itself liberally upon such eyes which by their will would ever be looking: and in least measure upon Gynecia, who (when Basilius after long tossing was gotten asleep, and the cheerful comfort of the lights removed from her) kneeling up in her bed, began with a soft voice and swollen heart to renew the curses of her birth; and then in a manner embracing her bed:

'Ah, chastest bed of mine,' said she, 'which never heretofore could'st accuse me of one defiled thought, how canst thou now receive this disastered changeling? Happy, happy be they only which be not; and thy blessedness only in this respect thou mayest feel that thou hast no feeling.' With that she furiously tare off great part of her fair hair: 'Take here, O forgotten virtue,' said she, 'this miserable sacrifice, while my soul was clothed with modesty, that was a comely ornament: now why should nature crown that head which is so wicked, as her only despair is she cannot be enough wicked?'

More she would have said but that Basilius, awaked with the noise, took her in his arms and began to comfort her, the good man thinking it was all for a jealous love of him; which humour if she would a little have maintained, perchance it might have weakened his new-conceived fancies. But he, finding her answers wandering from the purpose, left her to herself, glad the next morning to take the advantage of a sleep (which a little before day, overwatched with sorrow, her tears had as it were sealed up in her eyes) to have the more conference with Zelmane; who baited* on this fashion by those two lovers, and ever kept from any mean to declare herself, found in herself a daily increase of her violent desires, like a river, the more swelling, the more his current is stopped.

The chief recreation she could find in her anguish was sometime to visit that place where first she was so happy as to see the cause of her unhap. There would she kiss the ground and thank the trees, bless the air, and do dutiful reverence to everything that

* *baited*: harassed.

she thought did accompany her at their first meeting: then return again to her inward thoughts; sometimes despair darkening all her imaginations, sometimes the active passion of love cheering and clearing her invention how to unbar that cumbersome hindrance of her two ill-matched lovers. But this morning Basilius himself gave her good occasion to go beyond them. For having combed and tricked himself more curiously than any time forty winters before, coming where Zelmane was, he found her given over to her musical muses, to the great pleasure of the good old Basilius who retired himself behind a tree, while she with a most sweet voice did utter these passionate verses:

> Loved I am, and yet complain of love:
>> As loving not, accus'd, in love I die.
> When pity most I crave, I cruel prove:
>> Still seeking love, love found, as much I fly.
>>> Burnt in myself, I muse at other's fire;
>> What I call wrong, I do the same and more:
> Barr'd of my will, I have beyond desire;
>> I wail for want, and yet am chok'd with store.
>
>> This is thy work, thou god for ever blind:
>> Though thousands old, a boy entitled still.
> Thus children do the silly birds they find
>> With stroking hurt, and too much cramming kill.
>>> Yet thus much love, O love, I crave of thee:
>> Let me be lov'd, or else not loved be.

Basilius made no great haste from behind the tree, till he perceived she had fully ended her music. But then loth to lose the precious fruit of time, he presented himself unto her, falling down upon both his knees and holding up his hands, as the old governess of Danae is painted when she suddenly saw the golden shower,[1] 'O heavenly woman, or earthly goddess,' said he, 'let not my presence be odious unto you, nor my humble suit seem of small weight in your ears. Vouchsafe your eyes to descend upon this miserable old man, whose life hath hitherto been maintained but to serve as an increase of your beautiful triumphs. You only have overthrown me, and in my bondage consists my glory. Suffer not your own work to be despised of you, but look upon him with pity, whose life serves for your praise.'

Zelmane, keeping a countenance askance as she understood him not, told him it became her evil to suffer such excessive reverence of him, but that it worse became her to correct him to whom she owed duty; that the opinion she had of his wisdom was such as made her esteem greatly of his words, but that the words themselves sounded so as she could not imagine what they might intend.

'Intend?' said Basilius, proud that that was brought in question, 'What may they intend but a refreshing of my soul, and a swageing of my heat, and enjoying those your excellencies wherein my life is upheld and my death threatened?'

Zelmane, lifting up her face as if she had received a mortal injury of him, 'And is this the devotion your ceremonies have been bent unto?' said she: 'Is it the disdain of my estate or the opinion of my lightness that have emboldened such base fancies towards me? "Enjoying," quoth you! Now little joy come to them that yield to such enjoying.'

Poor Basilius was so appalled that his legs bowed under him; his eyes looked as though he would gladly hide himself, and his old blood going to his heart, a general shaking all over his body possessed him. At length, with a wan mouth, he was about to give a stammering answer, when it came into Zelmane's head by this device to make her profit of his folly; and therefore with a relented countenance thus said unto him, 'Your words, mighty Prince, were unfit either for me to hear or you to speak, but yet the large testimony I see of your affection makes me willing to suppress a great number of errors. Only thus much I think good to say, that the same words in my lady Philoclea's mouth, as from one woman to another, so as there were no other body by, might have had a better grace, and perchance have found a gentler receipt.'

Basilius (whose senses by desire were held open and conceit was by love quickened) heard scarcely half her answer out but that, as if speedy flight might save his life, he turned away and ran with all the speed his body would suffer him towards his daughter Philoclea, whom he found at that time dutifully watching by her mother, and Miso curiously watching her, having left Mopsa to do the like service to Pamela. Basilius forthwith calling Philoclea aside, with all the conjuring words which desire could indite and authority utter, besought her she would preserve his life in whom her life was begun, she would save his grey hairs from rebuke and his aged mind from despair; that if she were not cloyed with his company, and that she thought not the earth over-burdened with him, she would cool his fiery grief, which was to be done but by her breath: that in fine, whatsoever he was, he was nothing but what it pleased Zelmane, all the powers of his spirit depending of her; that if she continued cruel he could no more sustain his life than the earth remain fruitful in the sun's continual absence. He concluded, she should in one payment requite all his deserts; and that she needed not disdain any service, though never so mean, which was warranted by the sacred name of a father.

Philoclea, more glad than ever she had known herself that she might by this occasion enjoy the private conference of Zelmane, yet had so sweet a feeling of virtue in her mind that she would not suffer a vile colour to be cast over her fair thoughts, but with humble grace answered her father: that there needed neither promise nor persuasion to her to make her do her uttermost for her father's service; that for Zelmane's favour, she would in all virtuous sort seek it towards him; and that as she would not pierce further into his meaning than himself should declare, so would she interpret all his doings to be accomplished in goodness: and therefore desired (if otherwise it were) that he would not impart it to her, who then should be forced to begin, by true obedience, a show of disobedience; rather performing his general commandment (which had ever been to embrace virtue) than any new particular sprung out of passion and contrary to the former.

Basilius, content to take that since he could have no more, thinking it a great point, if, by her means, he could get but a more free access unto Zelmane, allowed her reasons and took her proffer thankfully, desiring only a speedy return of comfort. Philoclea was parting, and Miso straight behind her, like Alecto following Proserpina.[2] But Basilius forced her to stay though with much ado, she being sharp-set upon the fulfilling of a shrewd office in over-looking Philoclea; and so said to Basilius that she did as she was commanded, and could not answer it to Gynecia if she were any whit from Philoclea, telling him true that he did evil to take her charge from her. But Basilius, swearing he would put out her eyes if she stirred a foot to trouble his daughter, gave her a stop for that while.

## CHAPTER 17

So away departed Philoclea, with a new field of fancies for her travailing mind; for well she saw her father was grown her adverse party, and yet her fortune such as she must favour her rival; and the fortune of that fortune such, as neither that did hurt her nor any contrary mean help her.

But she walked but a little on, before she saw Zelmane lying upon a bank, with her face so bent over Ladon that (her tears falling into the water) one might have thought that she began meltingly to be metamorphosed to the under-running river. But by and by with speech she made known as well that she lived as that she sorrowed:

'Fair streams,' said she, 'that do vouchsafe in your clearness to represent unto me my blubbered face, let the tribute-offer of my tears unto you procure your stay a while with me, that I may begin yet at last to find something that pities me, and that all things of comfort and pleasure do not fly away from me. But if the violence of your spring command you to haste away to pay your duties to your great prince, the sea, yet carry with you these few words, and let the uttermost ends of the world know them. A love more clear than yourselves, dedicated to a love, I fear, more cold than yourselves, with the clearness lays a night of sorrow upon me, and with the coldness inflames a world of fire within me.'

With that she took a willow stick* and wrote in a sandy bank these few verses:

> Over these brooks trusting to ease mine eyes,
>     (Mine eyes even great in labour with their tears)
> I laid my face; my face wherein there lies
>     Clusters of clouds, which no sun ever clears.
>     In watery glass my watery eyes I see;
>     Sorrows ill eas'd, where sorrows painted be.

* *willow-stick:* emblem of unhappy love.

My thoughts imprison'd in my secret woes,
    With flamy breaths do issue oft in sound:
The sound to this strange air no sooner goes,
    But that it doth with Echoes' force rebound,
        And make me hear the plaints I would refrain:
        Thus outwards helps my inward grief maintain.

Now in this sand I would discharge my mind,
    And cast from me part of my burd'nous cares:
But in the sand my tales foretold I find,
    And see therein how well the writer fares.
        Since, stream, air, sand, mine eyes and ears conspire:
        What hope to quench, where each thing blows the fire?

And as soon as she had written them, a new swarm of thoughts
stinging her mind, she was ready with her foot to give the new-
born letters both death and burial. But Philoclea, whose delight of
hearing and seeing was before a stay from interrupting her, gave
herself to be seen unto her, with such a lightning of beauty upon
Zelmane that neither she could look on, nor would look off. At
last Philoclea, having a little mused how to cut the thread even
between her own hopeless affection and her father's unbridled
hope, with eyes, cheeks and lips (whereof each sang their part to
make up the harmony of bashfulness) began to say, 'My father, to
whom I owe myself, and therefore ...' when Zelmane (making a
womanish habit* to be the armour of her boldness, giving up her
life to the lips of Philoclea, and taking it again by the sweetness of
those kisses) humbly besought her to keep her speech for a while
within the paradise of her mind. For well she knew her father's
errand, who should soon receive a sufficient answer. But now she
demanded leave not to lose this long sought-for commodity of
time, to ease her heart thus far, that if in her agonies her destiny
was to be condemned by Philoclea's mouth, at least Philoclea
might know whom she had condemned. Philoclea easily yielded to
grant her own desire; and so making the green bank the situation,
and the river the prospect of the most beautiful buildings of
nature, Zelmane, doubting how to begin, though her thoughts

* *habit*: dress.

already had run to the end, with a mind fearing the unworthiness of every word that should be presented to her ears, at length brought it forth in this manner.

'Most beloved lady, the incomparable excellencies of yourself (waited on by the greatness of your estate) and the importance of the thing (whereon my life consisteth) doth require both many ceremonies before the beginning and many circumstances in the uttering my speech, both bold and fearful. But the small opportunity of envious occasion (by the malicious eye hateful love doth cast upon me) and the extreme bent of my affection (which will either break out in words or break my heart) compel me not only to embrace the smallest time but to pass by the respects due unto you, in respect of your poor caitiff's life, who is now or never to be preserved. I do therefore vow unto you hereafter never more to omit all dutiful form: do you only now vouchsafe to hear the matter of a mind most perplexed. If ever the sound of love have come to your ears, or if ever you have understood what force it hath had to conquer the strongest hearts and change the most settled estates, receive here an example of those strange tragedies – one, that in himself containeth the particularities of all those misfortunes; and from henceforth believe that such a thing may be, since you shall see it is. You shall see, I say, a living image and a present story of what love can do when he is bent to ruin.

'But alas, whither goest thou, my tongue, or how doth my heart consent to adventure the revealing his nearest touching secret? But peace, fear, thou comest too late when already the harm is taken. Therefore I say again, O only princess, attend here a miserable miracle of affection. Behold here before your eyes, Pyrocles, prince of Macedon, whom you only* have brought to this game of fortune and unused* metamorphosis, whom you only have made neglect his country, forget his father and lastly, forsake to be Pyrocles: the same Pyrocles who, you heard, was betrayed by being put in a ship, which being burned, Pyrocles was drowned. O most true presage! For these traitors, my eyes, putting me into a ship of desire which daily burneth – those eyes, I say, which betrayed me, will never leave till they have drowned me. But be not, be not, most excellent lady (you that Nature hath made to be

*you only: you alone. *unused*: unusual.

the lode-star of comfort) be not the rock of shipwreck. You whom virtue hath made the princess of felicity, be not the minister of ruin. You whom my choice hath made the goddess of my safety, O let not, let not from you be poured upon me destruction. Your fair face hath many tokens in it of amazement at my words. Think then what his amazement is from whence they come, since no words can carry with them the life of the inward feeling. I desire that my desire may be weighed in the balances of honour, and let virtue hold them. For if the highest love in no base person may aspire to grace, then may I hope your beauty will not be without pity. If otherwise you be (alas, but let it never be so) resolved, yet shall not my death be comfortless, receiving it by your sentence.'

The joy which wrought into Pygmalion's mind,[1] while he found his beloved image was softer and warmer in his folded arms till at length it accomplished his gladness with a perfect woman's shape (still beautified with the former perfections) was even such as, by each degree of Zelmane's words, creepingly entered into Philoclea, till her pleasure was fully made up with the manifesting of his being, which was such as in hope did overcome hope. Yet doubt would fain have played his part in her mind and called in question how she should be assured that Zelmane was Pyrocles. But love straight stood up and deposed that a lie could not come from the mouth of Zelmane. Besides, a certain spark of honour which rose in her well-disposed* mind made her fear to be alone with him with whom alone she desired to be, with all the other contradictions growing in those minds which neither absolutely climb the rock of virtue nor freely sink into the sea of vanity. But that spark* soon gave place,* or at least gave no more light in her mind than a candle doth in the sun's presence; but even sick with a surfeit of joy and fearful of she knew not what – as he that newly finds huge treasures doubts whether he sleep or no; or like a fearful deer, which then looks most about when he comes to the best feed – with a shrugging kind of tremor through all her principal parts, she gave these affectionate words for answer.

'Alas, how painful a thing it is to a divided mind to make a

---

* *well-disposed*: well-balanced. *that spark*: i.e. the doubts roused by her sense of honour. *gave place*: subsided.

well-joined answer! How hard it is to bring inward shame to out-ward confession! And what handsomeness, trow you, can be ob-served in that speech which is made one knows not to whom? Shall I say, "O Zelmane"? Alas, your words be against it. Shall I say "Prince Pyrocles"? Wretch that I am, your show is manifest against it. But this, this I may well say: if I had continued as I ought, Philoclea, you had either never been, or ever been Zelmane: you had either never attempted this change, set on with hope, or never discovered* it, stopped with despair. But I fear me, my be-haviour, ill governed, gave you the first comfort: I fear me, my affection, ill hid, hath given you this last assurance. I fear, indeed, the weakness of my government before, made you think such a mask would be grateful unto me; and my weaker government since, makes you to pull off the visor. What shall I do then? Shall I seek far-fetched inventions? Shall I labour to lay marble colours over my ruinous thoughts? Or rather, though the pureness of my virgin-mind be stained, let me keep the true simplicity of my word. True it is, alas, too true it is, O Zelmane (for so I love to call thee, since in that name my love first began, and in the shade of that name my love shall best lie hidden) that even while so thou wert (what eye bewitched me I know not) my passions were fitter to desire than to be desired. Shall I say then, I am sorry, or that my love must be turned to hate, since thou art turned to Pyrocles? How may that well be, since when thou wert Zelmane, the despair thou mightest not be thus did most torment me? Thou hast then the victory: use it with virtue. Thy virtue won me: with virtue preserve me. Dost thou love me? Keep me then still worthy to be beloved.'

Then held she her tongue and cast down a self-accusing look, finding that in herself she had, as it were, shot out of the bow of her affection a more quick opening of her mind than she minded to have done. But Pyrocles, so carried up with joy that he did not envy the gods' felicity, presented her with some jewels of right princely value, as some little tokens of his love and quality; and withal showed her letters from his father, King Euarchus, unto him, which even in the sea had amongst his jewels been preserved. But little needed those proofs to one who would have fallen out

* *discovered*: revealed.

with herself rather than make any contrary conjectures to Zelmane's speeches; so that with such embracements, as it seemed their souls desired to meet and their hearts to kiss as their mouths did, they passed the promise of marriage, which fain Pyrocles would have sealed with the chief arms of his desire, but Philoclea commanded the contrary.

And then at Philoclea's entreaty, who was willing to purloin* all occasions of remaining with Zelmane, she told her the story of her life from the time of their departing from Erona, for the rest she had already understood of her sister. 'For,' said she, 'I have understood how you first, in the company of your noble cousin Musidorus, parted from Thessalia, and of divers adventures which with no more danger than glory you passed through, till your coming to the succour of the queen Erona; and the end of that war you might perceive by myself I had understood of prince Plangus. But what since was the course of your doings until you came, after so many victories, to make a conquest of poor me, that I know not; the fame thereof having rather showed it by pieces than delivered any full form of it. Therefore, dear Pyrocles – for what can mine ears be so sweetly fed with as to hear you of you – be liberal unto me of those things which have made you indeed precious to the world; and now doubt not to tell of your perils, for since I have you here out of them, even the remembrance of them is pleasant.'

Pyrocles easily perceived she was content with kindness to put off occasion of further kindness, wherein love showed himself a cowardly boy that durst not attend for fear of offending. But rather love proved himself valiant that durst with the sword of reverent duty gain-stand the force of so many enraged desires. But so it was, that though he knew this discourse was to entertain him from a more straight parley,² yet he durst not but kiss his rod, and gladly make much of that entertainment which she allotted unto him: and therefore, with a desirous sigh chastening his breast for too much desiring:

'Sweet princess of my life,' said he, 'what trophies, what triumph, what monuments, what histories might ever make my fame yield so sweet a music to my ears, as that it pleaseth you to

*purloin: steal.

lend your mind to the knowledge of any thing touching Pyrocles, only therefore of value, because he is your Pyrocles? And therefore grow I now so proud as to think it worth the hearing, since you vouchsafe to give it the hearing. Therefore, only height of my hope, vouchsafe to know that after the death of Tiridates, and settling Erona in her government – for settled we left her – howsoever since (as I perceived by your speech the last day) the ungrateful treason of her ill-chosen husband overthrew her, a thing, in truth, never till this time by me either heard or suspected: for who could think, without having such a mind as Antiphilus, that so great a beauty as Erona's (indeed excellent) could not have held his affection, so great goodness could not have satisfied his ambition? But therefore true it is that wickedness may well be compared to a bottomless pit, into which it is far easier to keep one's self from falling than, being fallen, to give one's self any stay from falling infinitely. But for my cousin and me, upon this cause we parted from Erona.'

## CHAPTER 18

'Euardes, the brave and mighty prince, whom it was my fortune to kill in the combat for Erona, had three nephews, sons to a sister of his; all three set among the foremost ranks of fame, for great minds to attempt and great force to perform what they did attempt, especially the eldest, by name Anaxius, to whom all men would willingly have yielded the height of praise but that his nature was such as to bestow it upon himself before any could give it. For of so unsupportable a pride he was, that where his deeds might well stir envy, his demeanour did rather breed disdain. And if it be true that the giants ever made war against heaven,[1] he had been a fit ensign-bearer for that company. For nothing seemed hard to him, though impossible; and nothing unjust, while his liking was his justice. Now he in these wars had flatly refused his aid, because he could not brook that the worthy prince Plangus was by his cousin Tiridates preferred before him. For allowing no other weights but the sword and spear in judging of desert, how much he esteemed himself before Plangus in that, so much would he have had his allowance in his service.

'But now that he understood that his uncle was slain by me, I think rather scorn that any should kill his uncle than any kindness (an unused guest to an arrogant soul) made him seek his revenge, I must confess in manner gallant enough. For he sent a challenge unto me to meet him at a place appointed, in the confines of the kingdom of Lycia, where he would prove upon me that I had by some treachery overcome his uncle, whom else many hundreds such as I could not have withstood. Youth and success made me willing enough to accept any such bargain, especially because I had heard that your cousin Amphialus (who for some years hath universally borne the name of the best knight in the world) had divers times fought with him and never been able to master him, but so had left him that every man thought Anaxius in that one virtue of courtesy far short of him, in all other his match; Anaxius still deeming himself for his superior. Therefore to him I would go, and I would needs go alone because so, I understood for certain, he was; and, I must confess, desirous to do something without the company of the incomparable prince Musidorus, because in my heart I acknowledge that I owed more to his presence than to anything in myself, whatsoever before I had done. For of him indeed, as of any worldly cause, I must grant as received whatever there is or may be good in me. He taught me by word and best by example, giving me in him so lively an image of virtue as ignorance could not cast such mist over mine eyes as not to see and to love it; and all with such dear friendship and care as, O heaven, how can my life ever requite unto him? Which made me indeed find in myself such a kind of depending upon him as, without him, I found a weakness and a mistrustfulness of myself as one strayed from his best strength, when at any time I missed him. Which humour perceiving to over-rule me, I strave against it: not that I was unwilling to depend upon him in judgement, but by weakness I would not; which though it held me to him, made me unworthy of him. Therefore I desired his leave and obtained it, such confidence he had in me, preferring my reputation before his own tenderness; and so privately went from him, he determining, as after I knew, in secret manner not to be far from the place where we appointed to meet, to prevent any foul play that might be offered unto me. Full loth was Erona to let us depart from her, as it were, fore-feeling the harms which after fell to her. But I, (rid fully from those cumbers of kindness, and half a day's journey in my way towards Anaxius) met an adventure which, though in itself of small importance, I will tell you at large, because by the occasion thereof I was brought to as great cumber and danger as lightly any might escape.

'As I passed through a land, each side whereof was so bordered both with high timber trees and copses of far more humble growth, that it might easily bring a solitary mind to look for no other companions than the wild burgesses of the forest, I heard certain cries, which, coming by pauses to mine ears from within the wood of the right hand, made me well assured by the greatness of the cry it was the voice of a man, though it were a very unmanlike voice so to cry. But making mine ear my guide, I left not many trees behind me before I saw at the bottom of one of them a gentleman, bound with many garters hand and foot so as well he might tumble and toss, but neither run nor resist he could. Upon him, like so many eagles upon an ox, were nine gentlewomen, truly such as one might well enough say, they were handsome. Each of them held bodkins in their hands wherewith they continually pricked him, having been beforehand unarmed of any defence from the waist upward, but only of his shirt; so as the poor man wept and bled, cried and prayed, while they sported themselves in his pain and delighted in his prayers as the arguments of their victory.

'I was moved to compassion, and so much the more that he straight called to me for succour, desiring me at least to kill him to deliver him from those tormentors. But before myself could resolve, much less any other tell what I would resolve, there came in choleric haste towards me about seven or eight knights, the foremost of which willed me to get me away, and not to trouble the ladies while they were taking their due revenge; but with so overmastering a manner of pride as truly my heart could not brook it: and therefore, answering them that how I would have defended him from the ladies I knew not, but from them I would, I began to combat first with him particularly, and after his death with the others (that had less good manners) jointly. But such was the end of it that I kept the field with the death of some and flight of others. Insomuch as the women, afraid what angry victory would bring forth, ran all away, saving only one, who was so fleshed in malice that neither during nor after the fight she gave any truce to her cruelty, but still used the little instrument of her great spite, to the well-witnessed pain of the impatient patient; and was now about to put out his eyes (which all this while were spared, because they should do him the discomfort of seeing who prevailed over him) when I came in, and after much ado brought her to some conference – for some time it was before she would hearken, more before she would speak, and most before she would in her speech leave off the sharp remembrance of her bodkin. But at length when I pulled off my head-piece and humbly entreated her pardon, or knowledge why she was cruel, out of breath more with choler (which increased in his own exercise) than with the pain she took, much to this purpose she gave her grief unto my knowledge.

' "Gentleman," said she, "much it is against my will to forbear any time the executing of my just revenge upon this naughty* creature, a man in nothing but in deceiving women. But because I see you are young, and like enough to have the power, if you would have the mind, to do much more mischief than he, I am content upon this bad subject to read a lecture to your virtue. This man called Pamphilus in birth I must confess is noble (but what is that to him, if it shall be a stain to his dead ancestors to have left such an offspring?) in shape as you see, not uncomely (indeed the fit mask of his disguised falsehood) in conversation wittily pleasant and pleasantly gamesome; his eyes full of merry simplicity, his words, of hearty companionableness; and such a one whose head one would not think so stayed* as to think mischievously; delighted in all such things which by imparting their delight to others, makes the user thereof welcome, as music, dancing, hunting, feasting, riding, and such like. And to conclude, such an one as who can keep him at arms-end need never wish a better companion.

' "But under these qualities lies such a poisonous adder as I will tell you. For by those gifts of nature and fortune, being in all places acceptable, he creeps – nay, to say truly, he flies so into the

* *'naughty'*: of nought, hence 'in nothing'. *stayed*: changeable, fickle.

favour of poor silly women that I would be too much ashamed to confess, if I had not revenge in my hand as well as shame in my cheeks. For his heart being wholly delighted in deceiving us, we could never be warned, but rather one bird caught served for a stale* to bring in more. For the more he gat, the more still he showed that he, as it were, gave away to his new mistress when he betrayed his promises to the former. The cunning of his flattery, the readiness of his tears, the infiniteness of his vows, were but among the weakest threads of his net. But the stirring our own passions, and by the entrance of them to make himself lord of our forces, there lay his master's part of cunning, making us now jealous, now envious, now proud of what we had, desirous of more; now giving one the triumph, to see him, that was prince of many, subject to her; now with an estranged look making her fear the loss of that mind, which indeed could never be had: never ceasing humbleness and diligence till he had embarked us in some such disadvantage as we could not return dry-shod; and then suddenly a tyrant, but a crafty tyrant. For so would he use his imperiousness, that we had a delightful fear and an awe which made us loth to lose our hope. And, which is strangest, when sometimes with late repentance I think of it, I must confess even in the greatest tempest of my judgement was I never driven to think him excellent; and yet so could set my mind both to get and keep him, as though therein had laid my felicity: like them I have seen play at the ball grow extremely earnest who should have the ball, and yet every one knew it was but a ball.

' "But in the end the bitter sauce of the sport was that we had either our hearts broken with sorrow, or our estates spoiled with being at his direction, or our honours for ever lost, partly by our own faults, but principally by his faulty using of our faults. For never was there man that could with more scornful eyes behold her at whose feet he had lately lain, nor with a more unmanlike bravery use his tongue to her disgrace, which lately had sung sonnets of her praises; being so naturally inconstant; as I marvel his soul finds not some way to kill his body whereto it had been so long united. For so hath he dealt with us, unhappy fools, as we could never tell whether he made greater haste after he once liked,

*stale: decoy.

to enjoy, or after he once enjoyed, to forsake. But making a glory of his own shame, it delighted him to be challenged of unkindness; it was a triumph unto him to have his mercy called for, and he thought the fresh colours of his beauty were painted in nothing so well as in the ruins of his lovers: yet so far had we engaged ourselves, unfortunate souls, that we listed not complain, since our complaints could not but carry the greatest accusation to ourselves. But every of us, each for herself, laboured all means how to recover him, while he rather daily sent us companions of our deceit than ever returned in any sound and faithful manner. Till at length he concluded all his wrongs with betrothing himself to one, I must confess, worthy to be liked, if any worthiness might excuse so unworthy a changeableness, leaving us nothing but remorse for what was past and despair of what might follow. Then indeed the common injury made us all join in fellowship, who till that time had employed our endeavours one against the other; for we thought nothing was a more condemning of us than the justifying of his love to her by marriage. Then despair made fear valiant, and revenge gave shame countenance: whereupon we, that you saw here, devised how to get him among us alone; which he (suspecting no such matter of them whom he had by often abuses he thought made tame to be still abused) easily gave us opportunity to do.

' "And a man may see, even in this, how soon rulers grow proud, and in their pride foolish. He came with such an authority among us, as if the planets had done enough for us that by us once he had been delighted. And when we began in courteous manner, one after the other, to lay his unkindness unto him, he, seeing himself confronted by so many, like a resolute orator, went not to denial, but to justify his cruel falsehood, and all with such jests and disdainful passages that, if the injury could not be made greater, yet were our conceits made the apter to apprehend it.

' "Among other of his answers, forsooth, I shall never forget how he would prove it was no inconstancy to change from one love to another, but a great constancy; and contrary, that which we call constancy to be most changeable. 'For,' said he, 'I ever loved my delight, and delighted always in what was lovely: and wheresoever I found occasion to obtain that, I constantly followed it.

But these constant fools you speak of, though their mistress grow by sickness foul, or by fortune miserable, yet still will love her, and so commit the absurdest inconstancy that may be, in changing their love from fairness to foulness, and from loveliness to his contrary; like one not content to leave a friend, but will straight give over himself to his mortal enemy: where I (whom you call inconstant) am ever constant – to beauty, in others, and delight, in myself.' And so in this jolly scoffing bravery he went over us all, saying he left one because she was over-wayward; another, because she was too soon won; a third, because she was not merry enough; a fourth, because she was over gamesome; the fifth because she was grown with grief subject to sickness; the sixth, because she was so foolish as to be jealous of him; the seventh, because she had refused to carry a letter for him to another that he loved; the eighth, because she was not secret; the ninth, because she was not liberal: but to me, who am named Dido (and indeed have met with a false Aeneas²) to me, I say – O the ungrateful villainy – he could find no other fault to object but that, perdy, he met with many fairer.

' "But when he had thus played the careless prince, we (having those servants of ours in readiness, whom you lately so manfully overcame) laid hold of him, beginning at first but that trifling revenge in which you found us busy; but meaning afterwards to have mangled him so as should have lost his credit for ever abusing more. But as you have made my fellows fly away, so for my part the greatness of his wrong overshadows, in my judgement, the greatness of any danger. For was it not enough for him to have deceived me, and through the deceit abused me, and after the abuse forsaken me, but that he must now, of all the company, and before all the company, lay want of beauty to my charge? Many fairer? I trow even in your judgement, sir, if your eyes do not beguile me, not many fairer; and I know, whosoever says the contrary, there are not many fairer. And of whom should I receive this reproach, but of him who hath best cause to know there are not many fairer? And therefore howsoever my fellows pardon his injuries, for my part I will ever remember, and remember to revenge this scorn of all scorns." With that she to him afresh; and surely would have put out his eyes (who lay mute for shame if he did not sometimes cry for fear) if I had not leapt from my horse and mingling force with entreaty, stayed her fury.

'But while I was persuading her to meekness, comes a number of his friends, to whom he forthwith cried that they should kill that woman that had thus betrayed and disgraced him. But then I was fain to forsake the ensign under which I had before served, and to spend my uttermost force in the protecting of the lady: which so well prevailed for her that in the end there was a faithful peace promised of all sides. And so I, leaving her in a place of security, as she thought, went on my journey towards Anaxius, for whom I was fain to stay two days in the appointed place, he disdaining to wait for me till he was sure I was there.'

## CHAPTER 19

'I did patiently abide his angry pleasure till about that space of time he came (indeed, according to promise, alone) and – that I may not say too little, because he is wont to say too much – like a man whose courage was apt to climb over any danger. And as soon as ever he came near me, in fit distance for his purpose, he with much fury but with fury skilfully guided, ran upon me, which I, in the best sort I could, resisted, having kept myself ready for him, because I had understood that he observed few compliments in matters of arms but such as a proud anger did indite unto him. And so, putting our horses into a full career, we hit each other upon the head with our lances. I think he felt my blow. For my part, I must confess, I never received the like; but I think, though my senses were astonished, my mind forced them to quicken themselves because I had learned of him how little favour he is wont to show in any matter of advantage. And indeed he was turned and coming upon me with his sword drawn, both our staves having been broken at that encounter, but I was so ready to answer him that truly I know not who gave the first blow. But whosoever gave the first was quickly seconded by the second. And indeed, excellentest lady, I must say truly, for a time it was well fought between us; he undoubtedly being of singular valour – I would to God it were not abased by his too much loftiness. But as, by the occasion of the combat winning and losing ground, we changed places, his horse happened to come upon the point of the broken spear which (fallen to the ground) chanced to stand upward, so as it lighting upon his heart, the horse died. He, driven to dismount, threatened if I did not the like to do as much for my horse as fortune had done for his. But whether for that, or because I would not be beholding to fortune for any part of the victory, I descended.

'So began our foot-fight in such sort that we were well entered to blood of both sides, when there comes by that inconstant Pamphilus, whom I had delivered (easy to be known, for he was bare-faced) with a dozen armed men after him; but before him he had Dido, that lady who had most sharply punished him, riding upon a palfrey, he following her with most unmanlike cruelty, beating her with wands he had in his hand, she crying for sense of pain or hope of succour: which was so pitiful a sight unto me that it moved me to require Anaxius to defer our combat till another day, and now to perform the duties of knighthood in helping this distressed lady. But he that disdains to obey anything but his passion (which he calls his mind) bade me leave off that thought; but when he had killed me, he would then, perhaps, go to her succour. But I well finding the fight would be long between us, longing in my heart to deliver the poor Dido, giving him so great a blow as somewhat stayed him (to term it aright) I flatly ran away from him toward my horse, who trotting after the company, in mine armour I was put to some pain but that use made me nimble unto it. But as I followed my horse, Anaxius followed me; but his proud heart did so disdain that exercise that I had quickly over-run him and overtaken my horse, being, I must confess, ashamed to see a number of country folks who happened to pass thereby, who halloed and hooted after me as at the ar-rantest coward that ever showed his shoulders to his enemy. But when I had leapt on my horse (with such speedy agility that they all cried: "O see how fear gives him wings") I turned to Anaxius, and aloud promised him to return thither again as soon as I had relieved the injured lady. But he railing at me with all the base words angry contempt could indite, I said no more but "Anaxius, assure thyself I neither fear thy force nor thy opinion." And so using no weapon of a knight as at that time but my spurs, I ran (in my knowledge) after Pamphilus, but (in all their conceits) from Anaxius, which, as far as I could hear, I might well hear testified with such laughters and games that I was some few times moved to turn back again.

'But the lady's misery over-balanced my reputation, so that after her I went, and with six hours' hard riding (through so wild places as it was rather the cunning of my horse sometimes than of myself so rightly to hit the way) I overgat them a little before night, near to an old ill-favoured castle, the place where I perceived they meant to perform their unknightly errand. For there they began to strip her of her clothes, when I came in among them and running through the first with a lance, the justness of the cause so enabled me against the rest (false-hearted in their own wrong-doing) that I had, in as short time almost as I had been fighting with only Anaxius, delivered her from those injurious wretches, most of whom carried news to the other world that amongst men secret wrongs are not always left unpunished. As for Pamphilus, he, having once seen and, as it should seem, remembered me, even from the beginning began to be in the rearward, and before they had left fighting, he was too far off to give them thanks for their pains. But when I had delivered to the lady a full liberty, both in effect and in opinion – for some time it was before she could assure herself she was out of their hands who had laid so vehement apprehension of death upon her – she then told me how, as she was returning toward her father's, weakly accompanied as too soon trusting to the falsehood of reconcilement, Pamphilus had set upon her and, killing those that were with her, carried herself by such force and with such manner as I had seen to this place, where he meant in cruel and shameful manner to kill her in the sight of her own father, to whom he had already sent word of it, that out of his castle window (for this castle, she said, was his) he might have the prospect of his only child's destruction, if my coming (whom, she said, he feared as soon as he knew me by the armour) had not warranted her from the near-approaching cruelty. I was glad I had done so good a deed for a gentlewoman not unhandsome, whom before I had in like sort helped. But the night beginning to persuade some retiring place, the gentlewoman, even out of countenance before she began her speech, much after this manner invited me to lodge that night with her father.

'"Sir," said she, "how much I owe you can be but abased by words, since the life I have, I hold it now the second time of you; and therefore need not offer service unto you, but only to remember you that I am your servant: and I would my being so might any way yield any small contentment unto you. Now only I can but desire you to harbour yourself this night in this castle, because the time requires it; and in truth this country is very dangerous for murdering thieves, to trust a sleeping life among them. And yet I must confess that as the love I bear you makes me thus invite you, so the same love makes me ashamed to bring you to a place where you shall be so (not spoken by ceremony but by truth) miserably entertained."

'With that she told me that though she spake of her father, whom she named Chremes, she would hide no truth from me: which was in sum, that as he was of all that region the man of greatest possessions and riches, so was he, either by nature or an evil received opinion, given to sparing in so unmeasurable sort, that he did not only bar himself from the delightful, but almost from the necessary use thereof, scarcely allowing himself fit sustenance of life rather than he would spend of those goods for whose sake only he seemed to joy in life. Which extreme dealing, descending from himself upon her, had driven her to put herself with a great lady of that country, by which occasion she had stumbled upon such mischances as were little for the honour either of her or her family. But so wise had he showed himself therein, as while he found his daughter maintained without his cost, he was content to be deaf to any noise of infamy; which though it had wronged her much more than she deserved, yet she could not deny but she was driven thereby to receive more than decent favours. She concluded, that there at least I should be free from injuries, and should be assured to her-wards to abound as much in the true causes of welcomes as I should find want of the effects thereof.

'I, who had acquainted myself to measure the delicacy of food and rest by hunger and weariness, at that time well stored of both did not abide long entreaty but went with her to the castle, which I found of good strength, having a great moat round about it, the work of a noble gentleman of whose unthrifty son he had bought it: the bridge drawn up, where we were fain to cry a good while before we could have anwer, and to dispute a good while before answer would be brought to acceptance. At length a willingness rather than a joy to receive his daughter whom he had so lately seen so near death, and an opinion brought into his head by course because he heard himself called a father, rather than any kindness that he found in his own heart, made him take us in; for my part by that time grown so weary of such entertainment, that no regard of myself but only the importunity of his daughter made me enter. Where I was met with this Chremes, a drivelling old fellow, lean, shaking both of head and hands, already half earth and yet then most greedy of earth; who scarcely would give me thanks for what I had done, for fear, I suppose, that thankfulness might have an introduction of reward; but with a hollow voice giving me a false welcome, I might perceive in his eye to his daughter that it was hard to say whether the displeasure of her company did not overweigh the pleasure of her own coming.

'But on he brought me into so bare a house that it was the picture of miserable happiness and rich beggary, served only by a company of rustical villains, full of sweat and dust, not one of them other than a labourer: in sum, as he counted it, profitable drudgery; and all preparations both for food and lodging such as would make one detest niggardness, it is so sluttish a vice. His talk of nothing but of his poverty, for fear, belike, lest I should have proved a young borrower. In sum, such a man as any enemy could not wish him worse than to be himself. But there that night bid I the burden of being a tedious guest to a loathsome host, overhearing him sometimes bitterly warn his daughter of bringing such costly mates under his roof: which she grieving at, desired much to know my name, I think partly of kindness to remember who had done something for her, and partly because she assured herself I was such a one as would make even his miser-mind contented with what he had done. And accordingly, she demanded my name and estate, with such earnestness that I (whom love had not as then so robbed me of myself as to be other than I am) told her directly my name and condition; whereof she was no more glad than her father, as I might well perceive by some ill-favoured cheerfulness which then first began to wrinkle itself in his face.

'But the causes of their joys were far different. For as the shepherd and the butcher both may look upon one sheep with pleasing conceits, but the shepherd with mind to profit himself by preserving, the butcher with killing him; so she rejoiced to find that mine own benefits had tied me to be her friend who was a prince of such greatness, and lovingly rejoiced; but his joy grew, as I to my danger after perceived, by the occasion of the queen Artaxia's setting my head to sale for having slain her brother Tiridates; which being the sum of an hundred thousand crowns to whosoever brought me alive into her hands, that old wretch (who had over-lived all good nature) though he had lying idly by him much more than that, yet above all things loving money, for money's own sake determined to betray me (so well deserving of him) for to have that which he was determined never to use. And so knowing that the next morning I was resolved to go to the place where I had left Anaxius, he sent in all speed to a captain of a garrison near by, which though it belonged to the king of Iberia, yet knowing the captain's humour to delight so in riotous spending as he cared not how he came by the means to maintain it, doubted not that to be half with him in the gain he would play his quarter's part in the treason. And therefore that night agreeing of the fittest places where they might surprise me in the morning, the old caitiff was grown so ceremonious as he would needs accompany me some miles in my way; a sufficient token to me, if nature had made me apt to suspect, since a churl's courtesy rarely comes but either for gain or falsehood. But I suffered him to stumble into that point of good manner: to which purpose he came out with all his clowns, horsed upon such cart-jades, and so furnished as in good faith I thought with myself, if that were thrift, I wished none of my friends or subjects ever to thrive. As for his daughter, the gentle Dido, she would also (but in my conscience with a far better mind) prolong the time of farewell as long as he.

'And so we went on together: he so old in wickedness that he could look me in the face and freely talk with me, whose life he had already contracted for: till coming into the falling of a way which led us into a place, of each side whereof men might easily keep themselves undiscovered, I was encompassed suddenly by a great troop of enemies, both of horse and foot, who willed me to yield myself to the queen Artaxia. But they could not have used worse eloquence to have persuaded my yielding than that – I knowing the little goodwill Artaxia bare me. And therefore making necessity and justice my best sword and shield, I used the other weapons I had as well as I could – I am sure to the little ease of a good number, who trusting to their number more than to their valour, and valuing money higher than equity, felt that guiltlessness is not always with ease oppressed. As for Chremes, he withdrew himself, yet so gilding his wicked conceits with his hope of gain that he was content to be a beholder how I should be taken to make his prey.

'But I was grown so weary that I supported myself more with anger than strength, when the most excellent Musidorus came to my succour; who, having followed my trace as well as he could after he found I had left the fight with Anaxius, came to the niggard's castle, where he found all burned and spoiled by the country people, who bare mortal hatred to that covetous man and now took the time, when the castle was left almost without guard, to come in and leave monuments of their malice therein: which Musidorus not staying either to further or impeach, came upon the spur after me, because with one voice many told him that if I were in his company, it was for no good meant unto me, and in this extremity found me. But when I saw that cousin of mine, methought my life was doubled, and where before I thought of a noble death, I now thought of a noble victory. For who can fear that hath Musidorus by him? – who what he did there for me, how many he killed (not stranger for the number than for the strange blows wherewith he sent them to a well-deserved death) might well delight me to speak of, but I should so hold you too long in every particular. But in truth, there if ever, and ever, if ever any man, did Musidorus show himself second to none in able valour.

'Yet what the unmeasurable excess of their number would have done in the end I know not, but the trial thereof was cut off by the chanceable coming thither of the king of Iberia, that same father of the worthy Plangus whom it hath pleased you sometimes to mention; who (not yielding over to old age his country delights, especially of hawking) was at that time (following a merlin) brought to see this injury offered unto us; and having great numbers of courtiers waiting upon him, was straight known by the soldiers that assaulted us to be their king, and so most of them withdrew themselves.

'He, by his authority knowing of the captain's own constrained confession what was the motive of this mischievous practice, misliking much such violence should be offered in his country to men of our rank, but chiefly disdaining it should be done in respect of his niece whom (I must confess wrongfully) he hated because he interpreted that her brother and she had maintained his son Plangus against him, caused the captain's head presently to be stricken off, and the old bad Chremes to be hanged – though truly for my part, I earnestly laboured for his life, because I had eaten of his bread. But one thing was notable for a conclusion of his miserable life, that neither the death of his daughter, who (alas, poor gentlewoman) was by chance slain among his clowns, while she (over-boldly for her weak sex) sought to hold them from me, nor yet his own shameful end was so much in his mouth as he was led to execution, as the loss of his goods and burning of his house which often, with more laughter than tears of the hearers, he made pitiful exclamations upon.'

## CHAPTER 20

'This justice thus done and we delivered, the king indeed in royal sort invited us to his court not far thence, in all points entertaining us so as truly I must ever acknowledge a beholding-ness unto him, although the stream of it fell out not to be so sweet as the spring. For after some days being there (curing ourselves of such wounds as we had received) while I, causing diligent search to be made of Anaxius, could learn nothing but that he was gone out of the country, boasting in every place how he had made me run away, we were brought to receive the favour of acquaintance with this Queen Andromana, whom the princess Pamela did in so lively colours describe the last day as still methinks the figure thereof possesseth mine eyes, confirmed by the knowledge myself had.

'And therefore I shall need the less to make you know what

kind of woman she was; but this only, that first with the reins of affection, and after with the very use of directing, she had made herself so absolute a master of her husband's mind that awhile he would not, and after, he could not tell how to govern without being governed by her: but finding an ease in not understanding, let loose his thoughts wholly to pleasure, entrusting to her the entire conduct of all his royal affairs. A thing that may luckily fall out to him that hath the blessing to match with some heroical-minded lady. But in him it was neither guided by wisdom nor followed by fortune, but thereby was slipped insensibly into such an estate that he lived at her indiscreet discretion: all his subjects having by some years learned so to hope for good and fear of harm only from her, that it should have needed a stronger virtue than his to have unwound so deeply an entered vice. So that either not striving because he was contented, or contented because he would not strive, he scarcely knew what was done in his own chamber but as it pleased her instruments to frame the relation.

'Now we being brought known unto her, the time that we spent in curing some very dangerous wounds, after once we were acquainted – and acquainted we were sooner than ourselves expected – she continually almost haunted us, till (and it was not long a doing) we discovered a most violent bent of affection, and that so strangely that we might well see an evil mind in authority doth not only follow the sway of the desires already within it, but frames to itself new desires not before thought of. For, with equal ardour she affected us both; and so did her greatness disdain shamefastness that she was content to acknowledge it to both. For, having many times torn the veil of modesty, it seemed for a last delight that she delighted in infamy, which often she had used to her husband's shame, filling all men's ears but his with his reproach; while he, hoodwinked with kindness, least of all men knew who strake him. But her first degree was, by setting forth her beauties (truly in nature not to be misliked, but as much advanced to the eye as abased to the judgement by art) thereby to bring us, as willingly caught fishes, to bite at her bait. And thereto had she that scutcheon of her desires supported by certain badly-diligent ministers,[1] who often cloyed our ears with her praises, and would needs teach us a way of felicity by seeking her favour. But when she found that we were as deaf to them as dumb to her, then she listed no longer stay in the suburbs of her foolish desires but directly entered upon them, making herself an impudent suitor, authorizing herself very much with making us see that all favour and power in that realm so depended upon her, that now (being in her hands) we were either to keep or lose our liberty at her discretion; which yet awhile she so tempered as that we might rather suspect than she threaten.

'But when our wounds grew so as that they gave us leave to travel, and that she found we were purposed to use all means we could to depart thence, she, with more and more importunateness, craved that which in all good manners was either of us to be desired, or not granted. Truly, most fair and every way excellent lady, you would have wondered to have seen how before us she would confess the contention in her own mind between that lovely, indeed most lovely, brownness of Musidorus' face, and this colour of mine, which she, in the deceivable style of affection, would entitle beautiful: how her eyes wandered, like a glutton at a feast, from the one to the other; and how her words would begin half of the sentence to Musidorus and end the other half to Pyrocles: not ashamed, seeing the friendship between us, to desire either of us to be a mediator to the other, as if we should have played one request at tennis between us; and often wishing that she might be the angle where the lines of our friendship might meet, and be the knot which might tie our hearts together. Which proceeding of hers I do the more largely set before you, most dear lady, because by the foil thereof you may see the nobleness of my desire to you and the warrantableness of your favour to me.'

At that Philoclea smiled with a little nod. 'But,' said Pyrocles, 'when she perceived no hope by suit to prevail, then, persuaded by the rage of affection and encouraged by daring to do anything, she found means to have us accused to the King as though we went about some practice to overthrow him in his own estate. Which, because of the strange successes we had had in the kingdoms of Phrygia, Pontus and Galatia, seemed not unlikely to him who, but skimming anything that came before him, was disciplined to leave the thorough-handling of all to his gentle wife; who forthwith caused us to be put in prison, having, while we slept, deprived us of our arms: a prison, indeed injurious because a prison, but else well testifying affection, because in all respects as commodious as a prison might be: and indeed so placed as she might at all hours (not seen by many, though she cared not much how many had seen her) come unto us.

'Then fell she to sauce her desires with threatenings so that we were in a great perplexity, restrained to so unworthy a bondage, and yet restrained by love which (I cannot tell how) in noble minds by a certain duty claims an answering. And how much that love might move us, so much and more that faultiness of her mind removed us, her beauty being balanced by her shamelessness. But that which did, as it were, tie us in captivity was, that to grant had been wickedly injurious to him that had saved our lives; and to accuse a lady that loved us of her love unto us we esteemed almost as dishonourable: and but by one of those ways we saw no likelihood of going out of that place, where the words would be injurious to your ears which should express the manner of her suit; while yet many times earnestness dyed her cheeks with the colour of shamefastness, and wanton languishing borrowed of her eyes the down-cast look of modesty. But we in the meantime far from loving her, and often assuring her that we would not so recompense her husband's saving of our lives; to such a ridiculous degree of trusting her she had brought him that she caused him send us word that upon our lives we should do whatsoever she commanded us: good man, not knowing any other but that all her pleasures were directed to the preservation of his estate. But when that made us rather pity than obey his folly, then fell she to servile entreating us, as though force could have been the school of love, or that an honest courage would not rather strive against, than yield to injury. All which yet could not make us accuse her, though it made us almost pine away for spite to lose any of our time in so troublesome an idleness.

'But while we were thus full of weariness of what was past and doubt of what was to follow, love (that I think in the course of my life hath a sport sometimes to poison me with roses, sometimes to heal me with wormwood) brought forth a remedy unto us: which though it helped me out of that distress, alas, the conclusion was such that I must ever while I live think it worse than a wrack* so to have been preserved. This king by this queen had a son of tender age, but of great expectation, brought up in the hope of themselves and already acceptation of the inconstant people as successor of his father's crown, whereof he was as worthy (considering his parts) as unworthy in respect of the wrong was thereby done against the most noble Plangus: whose great deserts now either forgotten or ungratefully remembered, all men set their sails with the favourable wind which blew on the fortune of this young prince, perchance not in their hearts, but surely in their mouths; now giving Plangus (who some years before was their only champion) the poor comfort of calamity, pity.

'This youth therefore accounted prince of that region, by name Palladius, did with vehement affection love a young lady brought up in his father's court, called Zelmane, daughter to that mischievously unhappy prince Plexirtus (of whom already I have, and sometimes must make, but never honourable, mention) left there by her father, because of the intricate changeableness of his estate – he, by the mother's side, being half brother to this queen Andromana, and therefore the willinger committing her to her care. But as love, alas, doth not always reflect itself, so fell it out that this Zelmane, though truly reason there was enough to love Palladius, yet could not ever persuade her heart to yield thereunto, with that pain to Palladius as they feel that feel an unloved love. Yet loving indeed, and therefore constant, he used still the intercession of diligence and faith, ever hoping, because he would not put himself into that hell to be hopeless; until the time of our being come and captived there brought forth this end, which truly deserves of me a further degree of sorrow than tears.

'Such was therein my ill destiny, that this young lady Zelmane (like some unwisely liberal, that more delight to give presents than pay debts) she chose (alas the pity) rather to bestow her love (so much undeserved as not desired) upon me than to recompense him whose love (besides many other things) might seem (even in the court of honour) justly to claim it of her. But so it was (alas that so it was) whereby it came to pass that (as nothing doth more

* *wrack*: wreck.

naturally follow his cause than care to preserve and benefit doth follow unfeigned affection) she felt with me what I felt of my captivity, and straight laboured to redress my pain, which was her pain: which she could do by no better means than by using the help therein of Palladius, who (true lover) considering what, and not why, in all her commandments (and indeed she concealing from him her affection, which she intituled compassion) immediately obeyed to employ his uttermost credit to relieve us: which though as great as a beloved son with a mother, faulty otherwise, but not hard-hearted towards him, yet it could not prevail to procure us liberty. Wherefore he sought to have that by practice which he could not by prayer. And so being allowed often to visit us – for indeed our restraints were more or less, according as the ague of her passion was either in the fit or intermission – he used the opportunity of a fit time thus to deliver us.'

## CHAPTER 21

'The time of the marrying that queen was, every year, by the extreme love of her husband and the serviceable love of the courtiers, made notable by some public honours which did, as it were, proclaim to the world how dear she was to that people. Among other, none was either more grateful to the beholders or more noble in itself than jousts, both with sword and lance, maintained for a seven night together; wherein that nation doth so excel, both for comeliness and ableness, that from neighbour-countries they ordinarily come, some to strive, some to learn, some to behold.

'This day it happened that divers famous knights came thither from the court of Helen, Queen of Corinth; a lady whom fame at that time was so desirous to honour that she borrowed all men's mouths to join with the sound of her trumpet. For as her beauty hath won the prize from all women that stand in degree of comparison – for as for the two sisters of Arcadia, they are far beyond all conceit of comparison – so hath her government been such as hath been no less beautiful to men's judgements than her beauty to the eyesight. For being brought by right of birth, a woman, a young woman, a fair woman, to govern a people in nature mutinously proud, and always before so used to hard governors as they knew not how to obey without the sword were drawn; yet could she for some years so carry herself among them that they found cause, in the delicacy of her sex, of admiration, not of contempt: and which was notable, even in the time that many countries about her were full of wars (which for old grudges to Corinth were thought still would conclude there) yet so handled she the matter, that the threats ever smarted in the threateners: she using so strange and yet so well succeeding a temper that she made her people by peace, warlike; her courtiers by sports, learned; her ladies by love, chaste. For by continual martial exercises without blood, she made them perfect in that bloody art. Her sports were such as carried riches of knowledge upon the stream of delight: and such the behaviour both of herself and her ladies as builded their chastity not upon waywardness, but choice of worthiness, so as it seemed that court to have been the marriage-place of love and virtue, and that herself was a Diana apparelled in the garments of Venus.

And this which fame only delivered unto me – for yet I have never seen her – I am the willinger to speak of to you who, I know, know her better, being your near neighbour, because you may see by her example (in herself wise, and of others beloved) that neither folly is the cause of vehement love nor reproach the effect. For never, I think, was there any woman that with more unremovable determination gave herself to the counsel of love after she had once set before her mind the worthiness of your cousin Amphialus, and yet is neither her wisdom doubted of, nor honour blemished. For O God, what doth better become wisdom than to discern what is worthy the loving? What more agreeable to goodness than to love it, so discerned, and what to greatness of heart, than to be constant in it once loved? But at that time that love of hers was not so publicly known as the death of Philoxenus and her search of Amphialus hath made it; but then seemed to have such leisure to send thither divers choice knights of her court, because they might bring her at least the knowledge, perchance the honour, of that triumph.

'Wherein so they behaved themselves as for three days they carried the prize; which being come from so far a place to disgrace her servants, Palladius, who himself had never used arms, persuaded the queen Andromana to be content, for the honour sake

of her court, to suffer us two to have our horse and armour, that
he with us might undertake the recovery of their lost honour;
which she granted, taking our oath to go no further than her son,
nor ever to abandon him. Which she did not more for saving him
than keeping us: and yet not satisfied with our oath, appointed a
band of horsemen to have eye that we should not go beyond appointed limits. We were willing to gratify the young prince who,
we saw, loved us. And so the fourth day of that exercise we came
into the field: where, I remember, the manner was that the fore-
noon they should run at tilt, one after the other, the afternoon in
a broad field in manner of a battle, till either the strangers or that
country knights won the field.

'The first that ran was a brave knight, whose device was to
come in all chained, with a nymph leading him.[1] Against him
came forth an Iberian, whose manner of entering was with bag-
pipes instead of trumpets; a shepherd's boy before him for a page,
and by him a dozen apparelled like shepherds for the fashion,*
though rich in stuff,* who carried his lances, which though
strong to give a lancely blow indeed, yet so were they coloured
with hooks near the morne* that they prettily represented sheep-
hooks. His own furniture* was dressed over with wool, so enriched with jewels artificially placed that one would have thought
it a marriage between the lowest and the highest. His impresa was
a sheep marked with pitch, with this word, "Spotted to be
known." And because I may tell you out his conceit* (though
that were not done, till the running for that time was ended)
before the ladies departed from the windows – among whom there
was one, they say, that was the Star whereby his course was only
directed – the shepherds attending upon Philisides[2] went among
them and sang an eclogue; one of them answering another, while
the other shepherds pulling out recorders, which possessed the
place of pipes, accorded their music to the others' voice. The eclogue had great praise. I only remember six verses,* while* having
questioned one with the other of their fellow-shepherd's sudden

*for the fashion: in style. rich in stuff: made of rich material.
morne: blunted head of a tilting lance. furniture: equipment. conceit:
fanciful invention. verses: lines. while: which occur at the point
when.

growing a man of arms and the cause of his so doing, they thus said:

> Me thought some staves* he miss'd: if so, not much amiss;
> For where he most would hit, he ever yet did miss.
> One said he brake across;* full well it so might be:
> For never was there man more crossly crossed than he.
> But most cried, "O well broke"; O fool full gaily blest:
> Where failing is a shame, and breaking is his best.

'Thus I have digressed, because his manner liked me well; but when he began to run against Lelius, it had near grown (though great love had ever been betwixt them) to a quarrel.[3] For Philisides breaking his staves with great commendation, Lelius, who was known to be second to none in the perfection of that art, ran ever over his head but so finely, to the skilful eyes, that one might well see he showed more knowledge in missing than others did in hitting, for with so gallant a grace his staff came swimming close over the crest of the helmet, as if he would represent the kiss and not the stroke of Mars. But Philisides was much moved with it while he thought Lelius would show a contempt of his youth; till Lelius (who therefore would satisfy him because he was his friend) made him know that to such bondage he was for so many courses tied by her, whose disgraces to him were graced by her excellency, and whose injuries he could never otherwise return than honours.

'But so by Lelius' willing missing was the odds of the Iberian side, and continued so in the next by the excellent running of a knight, though fostered so by the Muses as many times the very rustic people left both their delights and profits to hearken to his songs, yet could he so well perform all armed sports as if he had never had any other pen than a lance in his hand. He came in like a wild man, but such a wildness as showed his eyesight had tamed him, full of withered leaves which, though they fell not, still threatened falling. His impresa was a mill-horse still bound to go in one circle, with this word, "Data fata secutus".* But after him the Corinthian knights absolutely prevailed, especially a great nobleman of Corinth, whose device was to come without any

---

* *staves:* lances. *across:* by a crooked blow. *'Data fata secutus':* 'following his destiny'.

device, all in white like a new knight (as indeed he was) but so new as his newness shamed most of the others' long exercise. Then another, from whose tent I remember a bird was made fly, with such art to carry a written embassage among the ladies, that one might say, if a live bird, how so taught; if a dead bird, how so made? Then he who hidden, man and horse, in a great figure lively representing the Phoenix, the fire took so artificially as it consumed the bird and left him to rise, as it were, out of the ashes thereof. Against whom was the fine frozen knight,[4] frozen in despair; but his armour so naturally representing ice, and all his furniture so lively answering thereto, as yet did I never see anything that pleased me better.

'But the delight of those pleasing sights have carried me too far into an unnecessary discourse. Let it then suffice, most excellent lady, that you know the Corinthians that morning in the exercise, as they had done the days before, had the better; Palladius neither suffering us nor himself to take in hand the party till the afternoon, when we were to fight in troops, not differing otherwise from earnest but that the sharpness of the weapons was taken away. But in the trial, Palladius (especially led by Musidorus, and somewhat aided by me) himself truly behaving himself nothing like a beginner, brought the honour to rest itself that night on the Iberian side: and the next day, both morning and afternoon being kept by our party,* he (that saw the time fit for the delivery he intended) called unto us to follow him, which we, both bound by oath and willing by goodwill, obeyed. And so the guard not daring to interrupt us, he commanding passage, we went after him upon the spur to a little house in a forest near by, which he thought would be the fittest resting place till we might go further from his mother's fury, whereat he was no less angry and ashamed than desirous to obey Zelmane.

'But his mother, as I learned since, understanding by the guard her son's conveying us away, forgetting her greatness, and resigning modesty to more quiet thoughts, flew out from her place and cried to be accompanied, for she herself would follow us. But what she did, being rather with vehemency of passion than conduct of reason, made her stumble while she ran, and by her own con-

* being kept by our party: the honours being retained by our side.

fusion hinder her own desires. For so impatiently she commanded as a good while nobody knew what she commanded, so as we had gotten so far the start as to be already past the confines of her kingdom before she overtook us. And overtake us she did in the kingdom of Bithynia, not regarding shame, or danger of having entered into another's dominions: but, having with her about a threescore horsemen, straight commanded to take us alive, and not to regard her son's threatening therein; which they attempted to do, first by speech, and then by force. But neither liking their eloquence nor fearing their might, we esteemed few swords in a just defence able to resist many unjust assaulters. And so Musidorus' incredible valour, beating down all lets, made both me and Palladius so good way that we had little to do to overcome weak wrong.

'And now had we the victory in effect without blood, when Palladius, heated with the fight and angry with his mother's fault, so pursued our assailers that one of them (who, as I heard since, had before our coming been a special minion of Andromana's and hated us for having dispossessed him of her heart) taking him to be one of us, with a traitorous blow slew his young prince: who falling down before our eyes whom he especially had delivered, judge, sweetest lady, whether anger might not be called justice in such a case. Once,* so it wrought in us, that many of his subjects' bodies we left there dead, to wait on him more faithfully to the other world.

'All this while disdain, strengthened by the fury of a furious love, made Andromana stay to the last of the combat; and when she saw us light down to see what help we might do to the helpless Palladius, she came running madly unto us, then no less threatening when she had no more power to hurt. But when she perceived it was her only son that lay hurt, and that his hurt was so deadly as that already his life had lost the use of the reasonable, and almost sensible* part, then only did misfortune lay his own ugliness upon her fault, and make her see what she had done and to what she was come; especially finding in us rather detestation than pity (considering the loss of that young prince) and resolution presently to depart, which still she laboured to stay. But de-

* *Once*: at once. *sensible*: involving the senses.

prived of all comfort, with eyes full of death, she ran to her son's dagger, and before we were aware of it (who else would have stayed it) struck herself a mortal wound. But then her love, though not her person, awaked pity in us, and I went to her, while Musidorus laboured about Palladius. But the wound was past the cure of a better surgeon than myself, so as I could but receive some few of her dying words, which were cursings of her ill-set affection, and wishing unto me many crosses and mischances in my love, whensoever I should love, wherein I fear, and only fear, that her prayer is from above granted. But the noise of this fight and issue thereof being blazed by the country people to some noblemen thereabouts, they came thither, and finding the wrong offered us, let us go on our journey, we having recommended those royal bodies unto them to be conveyed to the king of Iberia.'

With that Philoclea seeing the tears stand in his eyes with remembrance of Palladius, but much more of that which thereupon grew, she would needs drink a kiss from those eyes, and he suck another from her lips; whereat she blushed, and yet kissed him again to hide her blushing: which had almost brought Pyrocles into another discourse,* but that she with so sweet a rigour forbade him that he durst not rebel, though he found it a great war to keep that peace, but was fain to go on in his story, for so she absolutely bade him, and he durst not how to disobey.


## CHAPTER 22

'So,' said he, 'parting from that place before the sun had much abased himself of his greatest height, we saw sitting upon the dry sands (which yielded at that time a very hot reflection) a fair gentlewoman, whose gesture accused her of much sorrow and every way showed she cared not what pain she put her body to, since the better part, her mind, was laid under so much agony: and so was she dulled, withal, that we could come so near as to hear her speeches and yet she not perceive the hearers of her lamentation.

'But well we might understand her at times say, "Thou dost kill

* *discourse:* course.

357

me with thy unkind falsehood: and it grieves me not to die, but it grieves me that thou art the murderer. Neither doth mine own pain so much vex me as thy error. For God knows, it would not trouble me to be slain for thee, but much it torments me to be slain by thee. Thou art untrue, Pamphilus, thou art untrue, and woe is me therefore. How oft did'st thou swear unto me that the sun should lose his light, and the rocks run up and down like little kids, before thou would'st falsify thy faith to me? Sun, therefore, put out thy shining, and rocks, run mad for sorrow; for Pamphilus is false. But alas, the sun keeps his light, though thy faith be darkened; the rocks stand still, though thou change like a weather-cock. O fool that I am, that thought I could grasp water and bind the wind. I might well have known thee by others, but I would not; and rather wished to learn poison by drinking it myself, while my love helped thy words to deceive me. Well, yet I would thou had'st made a better choice when thou did'st forsake thy unfortunate Leucippe. But it is no matter; Baccha, thy new mistress, will revenge my wrongs. But do not, Baccha, let Pamphilus live happy, though I die."

'And much more to such like phrase she spake, but that I (who had occasion to know something of that Pamphilus) stepped to comfort her: and though I could not do that, yet I got thus much knowledge of her, that this being the same Leucippe to whom the unconstant Pamphilus had betrothed himself – which had moved the other ladies to such indignation as I told you – neither her worthiness (which in truth was great) nor his own suffering for her (which is wont to endear affection) could fetter his fickleness but that, before his marriage day appointed, he had taken to wife that Baccha[1] of whom she complained: one that in divers places I had heard before blazed as the most impudently unchaste woman of all Asia, and withal of such an imperiousness therein that she would not stick to employ them whom she made unhappy with her favour to draw more companions of their folly: in the multitude of whom she did no less glory than a captain would do of being followed by brave soldiers: waywardly proud; and therefore bold, because extremely faulty: and yet having no good thing to redeem both these and other unlovely parts but a little beauty, disgraced with wandering eyes and unweighed speeches. Yet had

Pamphilus, for her, left Leucippe and withal, left his faith: Leucippe, of whom one look, in a clear judgement, would have been more acceptable than all her kindnesses so prodigally bestowed. For myself, the remembrance of his cruel handling Dido, joined to this, stirred me to seek some revenge upon him but that I thought it should be a gain to him to lose his life, being so matched: and therefore, leaving him to be punished by his own election, we conveyed Leucippe to a house thereby, dedicated to Vestal nuns, where she resolved to spend all her years (which her youth promised should be many) in bewailing the wrong and yet praying for the wrong-doer.

'But the next morning, we (having striven with the sun's earliness) were scarcely beyond the prospect of the high turrets of that building, when there overtook us a young gentleman, for so he seemed to us: but indeed, sweet lady, it was the fair Zelmane, Plexirtus' daughter, whom unconsulting affection (unfortunately born to me-wards) had made borrow so much of her natural modesty as to leave her more-decent raiments, and taking occasion of Andromana's tumultuous pursuing us, had apparelled herself like a page; with a pitiful cruelty cutting off her golden hair, leaving nothing but the short curls to cover that noble head, but that she ware upon it a fair headpiece; a shield at her back, and a lance in her hand, else disarmed. Her apparel of white wrought upon with broken knots; her horse fair and lusty, which she rid so as might show a fearful boldness, daring to do that which she knew that she knew not how to do: and the sweetness of her countenance did give such a grace to what she did that it did make handsome the unhandsomeness, and make the eye force the mind to believe that there was a praise in that unskilfulness.

'But she straight approached me and with few words (which borrowed the help of her countenance to make themselves understood) she desired me to accept her into my service, telling me she was a nobleman's son of Iberia, her name Daiphantus who, having seen what I had done in that court, had stolen from her father to follow me. I enquired the particularities of the manner of Andromana's following me, which by her I understood, she hiding nothing (but her sex) from me. And still methought I had seen that face, but the great alteration of her fortune made her far distant from my memory: but liking very well the young gentleman – such I took her to be – admitted this Daiphantus about me, who well showed there is no service like his that serves because he loves. For though born of prince's blood, brought up with tenderest education, unapt to service (because a woman) and full of thoughts* (because in a strange estate) yet love enjoined such diligence that no apprentice – no, no bondslave could ever be by fear more ready at all commandments than that young princess was. How often, alas, did her eyes say unto me that they loved, and yet I, not looking for such a matter, had not my conceit open to understand them! How often would she come creeping to me, between gladness to be near me and fear to offend me! Truly I remember that then I marvelled to see her receive my commandments with sighs, and yet to do them with cheerfulness: sometimes answering me in such riddles as I then thought a childish inexperience, but since returning to my remembrance they have come more clear unto my knowledge. And pardon me, only dear lady, that I use many words, for her effection to me deserves of me an affectionate speech.

'But in such sort did she serve me in that kingdom of Bithynia, for two months' space; in which time we brought to good end a cruel war long maintained between the king of Bithynia and his brother. For my excellent cousin and I (dividing ourselves to either side) found means, after some trial we had made of ourselves,² to get such credit with them as we brought them to as great peace between themselves as love towards us for having made the peace. Which done, we intended to return through the kingdom of Galatia towards Thrace, to ease the care of our father and mother who, we were sure, first with the shipwreck, and then with the other dangers we daily passed, should have little rest in their thoughts till they saw us.

'But we were not entered into that kingdom when, by the noise of a great fight, we were guided to a pleasant valley which, like one of those circuses which in great cities somewhere doth give a pleasant spectacle of running horses, so of either side, stretching itself in a narrow length, was it hemmed in by woody hills, as if indeed Nature had meant therein to make a place for beholders.

* *thoughts*: anxieties.

And there we beheld one of the cruellest fights between two knights that ever hath adorned the most martial story, so as I must confess, a while we stood bewondered, another while delighted with the rare bravery thereof; till seeing such streams of blood as threatened a drowning of life, we galloped towards them to part them. But we were prevented by a dozen armed knights or rather villains, who, using this time of their extreme feebleness, all together set upon them. But common danger brake off particular discord so that, though with a dying weakness, with a lively courage they resisted, and by our help drave away or slew those murdering attempters: among whom we happed to take alive the principal. But going to disarm those two excellent knights, we found, with no less wonder to us than astonishment to themselves, that they were the two valiant, and indeed famous, brothers, Tydeus and Telenor, whose adventure – as afterwards we made that ungracious wretch confess – had thus fallen out.

'After the noble prince Leonatus had by his father's death succeeded in the kingdom of Galatia, he, forgetting all former injuries, had received that naughty Plexirtus into a strait* degree of favour, his goodness being as apt to be deceived as the other's craft was to deceive; till by plain proof, finding that the ungrateful man went about to poison him, yet would not suffer his kindness to be overcome, not by justice itself; but calling him to him, used words to this purpose.

' "Plexirtus," said he, "this wickedness is found by thee. No good deeds of mine have been able to keep it down in thee. All men counsel me to take away thy life, likely to bring forth nothing but as dangerous, as wicked, effects. But I cannot find it in my heart, remembering what father's son thou art. But since it is the violence of ambition which perchance pulls thee from thine own judgement, I will see whether the satisfying that may quiet the ill-working of thy spirits. Not far hence is the great city of Trebisond which, with the territory about it, anciently pertained unto this crown; now unjustly possessed, and as unjustly abused by those who have neither title to hold it, nor virtue to rule it. To the conquest of that for thyself I will lend thee force, and give thee

* strait: close.

my right. Go, therefore, and with less unnaturalness glut thy ambition there; and that done, if it be possible, learn virtue."

'Plexirtus, mingling forsworn excuses wih false-meant promises, gladly embraced the offer: and hastily sending back for those two brothers (who at that time were with us succouring the gracious queen Erona) by their virtue chiefly, if not only, obtained the conquest of that goodly dominion. Which indeed done by them gave them such an authority, that though he reigned, they in effect ruled, most men honouring them because they only deserved honour, and many thinking therein to please Plexirtus, considering how much he was bound unto them: while they likewise, with a certain sincere boldness of self-warranting friendship, accepted all openly and plainly, thinking nothing should ever by Plexirtus be thought too much in them, since all they were was his.

'But he (who by the rules of his own mind could construe no other end of men's doings but self-seeking) suddenly feared what they could do, and as suddenly suspected what they would do, and as suddenly hated them, as having both might and mind to do. But dreading their power, standing so strongly in their own valour and others' affection, he durst not take open way against them; and as hard it was to take a secret, they being so continually followed by the best and every way ablest of that region: and therefore used this devilish sleight* which I will tell you, not doubting, most wicked man, to turn their own friendship towards him to their own destruction. He (knowing that they well knew there was no friendship between him and the new king of Pontus, never since he succoured Leonatus and us, to his overthrow) gave them to understand that of late there had passed secret defiance between them, to meet privately at a place appointed. Which though not so fit a thing for men of their greatness, yet was his honour so engaged as he could not go back. Yet feigning to find himself weak by some counterfeit infirmity, the day drawing near, he requested each of them to go in his stead, making either of them swear to keep the matter secret, even each from other; delivering the self-same particularities to both, but that he told Tydeus the king would meet him in a blue armour, and Telenor

* *sleight:* cunning.

that it was a black armour: and with wicked subtlety, as if it had been so appointed, caused Tydeus to take a black armour, and Telenor a blue; appointing them ways how to go so as he knew they should not meet till they came to the place appointed, where each had promised to keep silence, lest the king should discover it was not Plexirtus. And there in await had he laid those murderers, that who overlived the other should by them be dispatched; he not daring trust more than those with that enterprise, and yet thinking them too few till themselves by themselves were weakened.

'This we learned chiefly by the chief of those way-beaters,* after the death of those two worthy brothers whose love was no less than their valour: but well we might find much thereof by their pitiful lamentation, when they knew their mismeeting, and saw each other (in despite of the surgery we could do unto them) striving who should run fastest to the goal of death: each bewailing the other, and more dying in the other than in himself; cursing their own hands for doing, and their breasts for not sooner suffering; detesting their unfortunately-spent time in having served so ungrateful a tyrant, and accusing their folly in having believed he could faithfully love who did not love faithfulness; wishing us to take heed how we placed our goodwill upon any other ground than proof of virtue, since length of acquaintance, mutual secrecies, nor height of benefits could bind a savage heart – no man being good to other that is not good in himself. Then, while any hope was, beseeching us to leave the care of him that besought, and only look to the other. But when they found by themselves, and us, no possibility, they desired to be joined; and so embracing and craving that pardon each of other which they denied to themselves, they gave us a most sorrowful spectacle of their death, leaving few in the world behind them their matches in anything, if they had soon enough known the ground and limits of friendship. But with woeful hearts we caused those bodies to be conveyed to the next town of Bithynia, where we learning thus much, as I have told you, caused the wicked historian* to conclude his history with his own well-deserved death.'

* *way-beaters*: felons. *the wicked historian*: i.e. the 'way-beater' who tells them the story.

## CHAPTER 23

'But then, I must tell you, I found such woeful countenances in
Daiphantus that I could not but much marvel (finding them continue beyond the first assault of pity) how the cause of strangers –
for further I did not conceive – could so deeply pierce. But the
truth indeed is that, partly with the shame and sorrow she took of
her father's faultiness, partly with the fear that the hate I conceived against him would utterly disgrace her in my opinion
whensoever I should know her, so vehemently perplexed her, that
her fair colour decayed, and daily and hastily grew into the very
extreme working of sorrowfulness, which oft I sought to learn and
help. But she, as fearful as loving, still concealed it; and so decaying still more and more in the excellency of her fairness, but that
whatsoever weakness took away, pity seemed to add. Yet still she
forced herself to wait on me with such care and diligence as might
well show had been taught in no other school but love.

'While we, returning again to embark ourselves for Greece,
understood that the mighty Otanes (brother to Barzanes, slain by
Musidorus in the battle of the six princes) had entered upon the
kingdom of Pontus, partly upon the pretences he had to the
crown, but principally because he would revenge upon him
(whom he knew we loved) the loss of his brother, thinking (as
indeed he had cause) that wheresoever we were, hearing of his
extremity, we would come to relieve him. In spite whereof he
doubted not to prevail, not only upon the confidence of his own
virtue and power, but especially because he had in his company
two mighty giants, sons to a couple whom we slew in the same
realm. They (having been absent at their father's death, and now
returned) willingly entered into his service, hating more than he
both us and that king of Pontus. We therefore with all speed went
thitherward, but by the way this fell out which, whensoever I
remember without sorrow, I must forget, withal, all humanity.

'Poor Daiphantus fell extreme sick, yet would needs conquer
the delicacy of her constitution and force herself to wait on me: till
one day going towards Pontus, we met one who in great haste
went seeking for Tydeus and Telenor, whose death as yet was not
known unto the messenger; who (being their servant, and know-

ing how dearly they loved Plexirtus) brought them word how, since their departing, Plexirtus was in present danger of a cruel death, if by the valiantness of one of the best knights of the world he were not rescued. We inquired no further of the matter, being glad he should now to his loss find what an unprofitable treason it had been unto him to dismember himself of two such friends, and so let the messenger part, not sticking to make him know his masters' destruction by the falsehood of Plexirtus.

'But the grief of that (finding a body already brought to the last degree of weakness) so overwhelmed the little remnant of the spirits left in Daiphantus, that she fell suddenly into deadly swoundings; never coming to herself but that withal she returned to make most pitiful lamentations; most strange unto us, because we were far from guessing the ground thereof. But finding her sickness such as began to print death in her eyes, we made all haste possible to convey her to the next town: but before we could lay her on a bed, both we and she might find in herself that the harbingers of over-hasty death had prepared his lodging in that dainty body, which she undoubtedly feeling, with a weak cheerfulness showed comfort therein; and then desiring us both to come near her, and that nobody else might be present, with pale and yet (even in paleness) lovely lips:

' "Now or never, and never indeed but now is it time for me," said she, "to speak: and I thank death which gives me leave to discover that, the suppressing whereof perchance hath been the sharpest spur that hath hasted my race to this end. Know then my lords, and especially you, my lord and master, Pyrocles, that your page Daiphantus is the unfortunate Zelmane, who for your sake caused my as unfortunate lover and cousin, Palladius, to leave his father's court, and consequently both him and my aunt, his mother, to lose their lives. For your sake myself have become of a princess, a page, and for your sake have put off the apparel of a woman, and (if you judge not more mercifully) the modesty."

'We were amazed at her speech, and then had, as it were, new eyes given us to perceive that which before had been a present stranger to our minds: for indeed we forthwith knew it to be the face of Zelmane, whom before we had known in the court of Iberia. And sorrow and pity laying her pain upon me, I comforted her the best I could by the tenderness of goodwill, pretending indeed better hope than I had of her recovery.

'But she that had inward ambassadors from the tyrant that shortly would oppress her: "No, my dear master," said she, "I neither hope nor desire to live. I know you would never have loved me," and with that word she wept, "nor, alas, had it been reason you should, considering many ways my unworthiness. It sufficeth me that the strange course I have taken shall to your remembrance witness my love; and yet this breaking of my heart, before I would discover my pain, will make you, I hope, think that I was not altogether unmodest. Think of me so, dear master, and that thought shall be my life." And with that, languishingly looking upon me, "And I pray you," said she, "even by these dying eyes of mine (which are only sorry to die because they shall lose your sight) and by these polled locks of mine (which, while they were long, were the ornament of my sex, now in their short curls, the testimony of my servitude) and by the service I have done you (which God knows hath been full of love) think of me after my death with kindness, though you cannot with love. And whensoever you shall make any other lady happy with your well-placed affection, if you tell her my folly, I pray you speak of it, not with scorn, but with pity."

'I assure you (dear princess of my life, for how could it be otherwise?) her words and her manner, with the lively consideration of her love, so pierced me, that though I had divers griefs before, yet methought I never felt till then how much sorrow enfeebleth all resolution: for I could not choose but yield to the weakness of abundant weeping; in truth with such grief, that I could willingly at that time have changed lives with her.

'But when she saw my tears, "O God," said she, "how largely am I recompensed for my losses! Why then," said she, "I may take boldness to make some requests unto you."

'I besought her to do, vowing the performance, though my life were the price thereof. She showed great joy.

' "The first," said she, "is this, that you will pardon my father the displeasure you have justly conceived against him, and for this once succour him out of the danger wherein he is: I hope he will amend: and I pray you, whensoever you remember him to be the faulty Plexirtus, remember withal that he is Zelmane's father. The second is, that when you come once into Greece, you will take unto yourself this name, though unlucky, of Daiphantus, and vouchsafe to be called by it; for so shall I be sure you shall have cause to remember me. And let it please your noble cousin to be called Palladius, that I may do that right to that poor prince, that his name yet may live upon the earth in so excellent a person: and so between you, I trust sometimes your unlucky page shall be, perhaps with a sigh, mentioned. Lastly, let me be buried here obscurely, not suffering my friends to know my fortune till, when you are safely returned to your own country, you cause my bones to be conveyed thither and laid. I beseech you, in some place where yourself vouchsafe sometimes to resort."

'Alas, small petitions for such a suitor; which yet she so earnestly craved that I was fain to swear the accomplishment. And then kissing me, and often desiring me not to condemn her of lightness, in mine arms she delivered her pure soul to the purest place, leaving me as full of agony as kindness, pity, and sorrow could make an honest heart. For I must confess for true that if my stars had not wholly reserved me for you, there else perhaps I might have loved, and – which had been most strange – begun my love after death: whereof let it be the less marvel, because somewhat she did resemble you, though as far short of your perfection as herself dying was of herself flourishing: yet something there was which, when I saw a picture of yours, brought again her figure into my remembrance, and made my heart as apt to receive the wound, as the power of your beauty with unresistible force to pierce.

'But we, in woeful and yet private manner burying her, performed her commandment: and then, enquiring of her father's estate, certainly learned that he was presently* to be succoured, or by death to pass the need of succour. Therefore we determined to divide ourselves; I (according to my vow) to help him, and Musidorus towards the king of Pontus, who stood in no less need than immediate succour: and even ready to depart one from the other, there came a messenger from him who after some inquiry found us, giving us to understand that he, trusting upon us two, had

*presently*: immediately.

appointed the combat between him and us against Otanes and the two giants. Now the day was so accorded as it was impossible for me both to succour Plexirtus, and be there where my honour was not only so far engaged, but (by the strange working of unjust fortune) I was to leave the standing by Musidorus, whom better than myself I loved, to go save him whom for just causes I hated. But my promise given, and given to Zelmane, and to Zelmane dying, prevailed more with me than my friendship to Musidorus, though certainly I may affirm, nothing had so great rule in my thoughts as that. But my promise carried me the easier, because Musidorus himself would not suffer me to break it. And so with heavy minds, more careful each of other's success than of our own, we parted; I toward the place where I understood Plexirtus was prisoner to an ancient lord, absolutely governing a goodly castle, with a large territory about it whereof he acknowledged no other sovereign but himself; whose hate to Plexirtus grew for a kinsman of his whom he maliciously had murdered, because in the time that he reigned in Galatia he found him apt to practise for the restoring of his virtuous brother Leonatus.

'This old knight, still thirsting for revenge, used as the way to it a policy which this occasion I will tell you prepared for him. Plexirtus in his youth had married Zelmane's mother, who dying of that only childbirth, he, a widower and not yet a king, haunted the court of Armenia where (as he was cunning to win favour) he obtained great good liking of Artaxia, which he pursued; till, being called home by his father, he falsely got his father's kingdom and then neglected his former love: till, thrown out of that by our means before he was deeply rooted in it, and by and by again placed in Trebisond, understanding that Artaxia by her brother's death was become queen of Armenia, he was hotter than ever in that pursuit.

'Which being understood by this old knight, he forged such a letter as might be written from Artaxia, entreating his present (but very privy*) repair thither, giving him faithful promise of present marriage – a thing far from her thought, having faithfully and publicly protested that she would never marry any but some such prince who would give sure proof that by his means we were

* *privy*: private.

destroyed. But he (no more witty to frame than blind to judge hopes) bit hastily at the bait and in private manner posted towards her; but by the way he was met by this knight, far better accompanied, who quickly laid hold of him and condemned him to a death, cruel enough, if anything may be both cruel and just. For he caused him to be kept in a miserable prison till a day appointed, at which time he would deliver him to be devoured by a monstrous beast of most ugly shape, armed like a rhinoceros, as strong as an elephant, as fierce as a lion, as nimble as a leopard, and as cruel as a tiger; whom he, having kept in a strong place from the first youth of it, now thought no fitter match than such a beastly monster with a monstrous tyrant: proclaiming yet withal that if any so well loved him as to venture their lives against his beast for him, if they overcame, he should be saved: not caring how many they were, such confidence he had in that monster's strength, but especially hoping to entrap thereby the great courages of Tydeus and Telenor, whom he no less hated because they had been principal instruments of the other's power.

'I dare say, if Zelmane had known what danger I should have passed, she would rather have let her father perish than me to have bidden that adventure. But my word was passed; and truly the hardness of the enterprise was not so much a bit as a spur unto me, knowing well that the journey of high honour lies not in plain ways. Therefore going thither, and taking sufficient security that Plexirtus should be delivered if I were victorious, I undertook the combat: and to make short, excellent lady, and not to trouble your ears with recounting a terrible matter, so was my weakness blessed from above that, without dangerous wounds, I slew that monster which hundreds durst not attempt; to so great admiration of many, who from a safe place might look on, that there was order given to have the fight, both by sculpture and picture, celebrated in most parts of Asia. And the old nobleman so well liked me that he loved me; only bewailing my virtue had been employed to save a worse monster than I killed, whom yet, according to faith given, he delivered; and accompanied me to the kingdom of Pontus whither I would needs in all speed go to see whether it were possible for me, if perchance the day had been delayed, to come to the combat. But that, before I came, had been thus finished.

'The virtuous Leonatus, understanding two so good friends of his were to be in that danger, would perforce be one himself; where he did valiantly, and so did the king of Pontus. But the truth is that both they being sore hurt, the incomparable Musidorus finished the combat by the death of both the giants, and the taking of Otanes prisoner. To whom as he gave his life, so he got a noble friend, for so he gave his word to be, and he is well known to think himself greater in being subject to that than in the greatness of his principality.

'But thither, understanding of our being there, flocked great multitudes of many great persons, and even of princes, especially those whom we had made beholding unto us: as, the kings of Phrygia, Bithynia, with those two hurt, of Pontus and Galatia, and Otanes, the prisoner by Musidorus set free; and thither came Plexirtus of Trebisond, and Antiphilus then king of Lycia; with as many mo* great princes, drawn either by our reputation, or by willingness to acknowledge themselves obliged unto us for what we had done for the others. So as in those parts of the world, I think, in many hundreds of years there was not seen so royal an assembly, where nothing was let pass to do us the highest honours which such persons (who might command both purses and inventions) could perform: all from all sides bringing unto us right royal presents, which we (to avoid both unkindness and importunity) liberally received; and not content therewith, would needs accept, as from us, their crowns, and acknowledge to hold them of us: with many other excessive honours which would not suffer the measure of this short leisure to describe unto you.'

CHAPTER 24

'But we, quickly aweary thereof, hasted to Greece-ward, led thither partly with the desire of our parents, but hastened principally because I understood that Anaxius with open mouth of defamation had gone thither to seek me, and was now come to Peloponnesus, where from court to court he made enquiry of me, doing yet himself so noble deeds as might hap to authorize an ill opinion of me. We therefore suffered but short delays, desiring to

* mo: more.

take this country in our way, so renowned over the world that no prince could pretend height, nor beggar lowness, to bar him from the sound thereof:[1] renowned indeed, not so much for the ancient praises attributed thereunto as for the having in it Argalus and Amphialus, two knights of such rare prowess as we desired especially to know; and yet by far not so much for that, as without suffering of comparison for the beauty of you and your sister, which makes all indifferent judges that speak thereof account this country as a temple of deities.

'But these causes indeed moving us to come by this land, we embarked ourselves in the next port, whither all those princes (saving Antiphilus, who returned, as he pretended, not able to tarry longer from Erona) conveyed us. And there found we a ship most royally furnished by Plexirtus, who had made all things so proper, as well for our defence as ease, that all the other princes greatly commended him for it: who, seeming a quite altered man, had nothing but repentance in his eyes, friendship in his gesture, and virtue in his mouth; so that we, who had promised the sweet Zelmane to pardon him, now not only forgave but began to favour, persuading ourselves with a youthful credulity that perchance things were not so evil as we took them and, as it were, desiring our own memory that it might be so. But so were we licensed from those princes, truly not without tears, especially of the virtuous Leonatus who, with the king of Pontus, would have come with us but that we (in respect of the one's young wife, and both their new settled kingdoms) would not suffer it. Then would they have sent whole fleets to guard us; but we, that desired to pass secretly into Greece, made them leave that motion when they found that more ships than one would be displeasing unto us. But so committing ourselves to the uncertain discretion of the wind, we (then determining as soon as we came to Greece to take the names of Daiphantus and Palladius, as well for our own promise to Zelmane as because we desired to come unknown into Greece) left the Asian shore full of princely persons, who even upon their knees recommended our safeties to the devotion of their chief desires; among whom none had been so officious (though I dare affirm, all quite contrary to his unfaithfulness) as Plexirtus.

'And so having sailed almost two days, looking for nothing but when we might look upon the land, a grave man (whom we had seen of great trust with Plexirtus and was sent as our principal guide) came unto us and, with a certain kind manner mixed with shame and repentance, began to tell us that he had taken such a love unto us (considering our youth and fame) that though he were a servant, and a servant of such trust about Plexirtus as that he had committed unto him even those secrets of his heart which abhorred all other knowledge,[2] yet he rather chose to reveal at this time a most pernicious counsel than by concealing it bring to ruin those whom he could not choose but honour. So went he on, and told us that Plexirtus (in hope thereby to have Artaxia, endowed with the great kingdom of Armenia, to his wife) had given him order, when we were near Greece to find some opportunity to murder us, bidding him to take us asleep, because he had seen what we could do waking.

' "Now, Sirs," said he, "I would rather a thousand times lose my life than have my remembrance, while I lived, poisoned with such a mischief; and therefore if it were only I that knew herein the king's order, then should my disobedience be a warrant of your safety. But to one more," said he, "namely the captain of the ship, Plexirtus hath opened so much touching the effect of murdering you, though I think laying the cause rather upon old grudge than his hope of Artaxia. And myself (before the consideration of your excellencies had drawn love and pity into mind) imparted it to such as I thought fittest for such a mischief. Therefore I wish you to stand upon your guard, assuring you that what I can do for your safety you shall see (if it come to the push) by me performed."

'We thanked him, as the matter indeed deserved, and from that time would no more disarm ourselves, nor the one sleep without his friend's eyes waked for him; so that it delayed the going forward of their bad enterprise, while they thought it rather chance than providence which made us so behave ourselves.

'But when we came within half a day's sailing of the shore, so that they saw it was speedily, or not at all to be done, then – and I remember it was about the first watch in the night – came the captain and whispered the counsellor in the ear: but he, as it should seem, dissuading him from it, the captain (who had been a pirate from his youth, and often blooded in it) with a loud voice sware that if Plexirtus bade him, he would not stick to kill God himself. And therewith called his mates, and in the King's name willed them to take us alive or dead, encouraging them with the spoil of us which he said (and indeed was true) would yield many exceeding rich jewels. But the counsellor, according to his promise, commanded them they should not commit such a villainy, protesting that he would stand between them and the king's anger therein. Wherewith the captain, enraged, "Nay," said he, "then we must begin with this traitor himself," and therewith gave him a sore blow upon the head, who honestly did the best he could to revenge himself.

'But then we knew it time rather to encounter than wait for mischief. And so against the captain we went, who straight was environed with most part of the soldiers and mariners. And yet the truth is, there were some whom either the authority of the counsellor, doubt of the king's mind, or liking of us, made draw their swords of our side, so that quickly it grew a most confused fight. For the narrowness of the place, the darkness of the time, and the uncertainty in such a tumult how to know friends from foes, made the rage of swords rather guide than be guided by their masters. For my cousin and me, truly I think we never performed less in any place, doing no other hurt than the defence of ourselves and succouring them who came for it drave us to: for not discerning perfectly who were for or against us, we thought it less evil to spare a foe than spoil a friend. But from the highest to the lowest part of the ship there was no place left without cries of murdering and murdered persons. The captain I happed a while to fight withal, but was driven to part with him by hearing the cry of the counsellor, who received a mortal wound, mistaken of one of his own side.

'Some of the wiser would call to parley and wish peace; but while the words of peace were in their mouths, some of their evil auditors gave them death for their hire. So that no man almost could conceive hope of living but by being last alive; and therefore every one was willing to make himself room by dispatching almost any other: so that the great number in the ship was reduced to exceeding few, when of those few the most part, weary of those troubles, leapt into the boat which was fast to the ship; but while they that were first were cutting off the rope that tied it, others came leaping in so disorderly that they drowned both the boat and themselves.

'But while even in that little remnant, like the children of Cadmus,[3] we continued still to slay one another, a fire which (whether by the desperate malice of some, or intention to separate, or accidentally, while all things were cast up and down) it should seem had taken a good while before, but never heeded of us (who only thought to preserve or revenge) now violently burst out in many places and began to master the principal parts of the ship. Then necessity made us see that a common enemy sets at one a civil war; for that little all we were (as if we had been waged* by one man to quench a fire) straight went to resist that furious enemy by all art and labour: but it was too late, for already it did embrace and devour from the stern to the waist of the ship; so as labouring in vain, we were driven to get up to the prow of the ship, by the work of nature seeking to preserve life as long as we could: while truly it was a strange and ugly sight to see so huge a fire, as it quickly grew to be, in the sea, and in the night, as if it had come to light us to death. And by and by it had burned off the mast, which all this while had proudly borne the sail (the wind, as might seem, delighted to carry fire and blood in his mouth) but now it fell overboard, and the fire growing nearer us, it was not only terrible in respect of what we were to attend, but insupportable through the heat of it.

'So that we were constrained to bide it no longer, but disarming and stripping ourselves, and laying ourselves upon such things as we thought might help our swimming to the land (too far for our own strength to bear us) my cousin and I threw ourselves into the sea. But I had swum a very little way when I felt, by reason of a wound I had, that I should not be able to bide the travail; and therefore seeing the mast, whose tackling had been burnt off, float clear from the ship, I swam unto it, and getting on it, I found mine own sword which by chance, when I threw it away, caught by a piece of canvas, had hung to the mast. I was glad because I loved it well, but gladder, when I saw at the other end the captain of the

* *waged*: hired.

ship and of all this mischief, who, having a long pike, belike had borne himself up with that till he had set himself upon the mast. But when I perceived him, "Villain," said I, "dost thou think to over-live so many honest men whom thy falsehood hath brought to destruction?" With that, bestriding the mast, I got by little and little towards him after such a manner as boys are wont, if ever you saw that sport, when they ride the wild mare. And he, perceiving my intention, like a fellow that had much more courage than honesty, set himself to resist: but I had in short space gotten within him and, giving him a sound blow, sent him to feed fishes. But there myself remained, until by pirates I was taken up, and among them again taken prisoner and brought into Laconia.'

'But what,' said Philoclea, 'became of your cousin Musidorus?'

'Lost,' said Pyrocles.

'Ah, my Pyrocles,' said Philoclea, 'I am glad I have taken you. I perceive you lovers do not always say truly. As though I knew not your cousin Dorus the shepherd!'

'Life of my desires,' said Pyrocles, 'what is mine, even to my soul, is yours, but the secret of my friend is not mine. But if you know so much, then I may truly say, he is lost since he is no more his own. But I perceive your noble sister and you are great friends, and well doth it become you so to be.'

'But go forward, dear Pyrocles, I long to hear out till your meeting me: for there to me-ward is the best part of your story.'

'Ah sweet Philoclea,' said Pyrocles, 'do you think I can think so precious leisure as this well spent in talking? Are your eyes a fit book, think you, to read a tale upon? Is my love quiet enough to be an historian? Dear princess, be gracious unto me.'

And then he fain would have remembered to have forgot himself. But she, with a sweetly disobeying grace, desired him that her desire, once for ever, might serve, that no spot might disgrace that love which shortly she hoped should be to the world warrantable. Fain he would not have heard, till she threatened anger; and then the poor lover durst not, because he durst not.

'Nay, I pray thee, dear Pyrocles,' said she, 'let me have my story.'

'Sweet princess,' said he, 'give my thoughts a little respite: and if it please you, since this time must so be spoiled, yet it shall suffer the less harm if you vouchsafe to bestow your voice, and let me know how the good queen Erona was betrayed into such danger, and why Plangus sought me. For indeed I should pity greatly any mischance fallen to that princess.'

'I will,' said Philoclea, smiling, 'so you give me your word your hands shall be quiet auditors.'

'They shall,' said he, 'because subject.'

Then began she to speak, but with so pretty and delightful a majesty, when she set her countenance to tell the matter, that Pyrocles could not choose but rebel so far as to kiss her. She would have pulled her head away and speak, but while she spake, he kissed, and it seemed he fed upon her words; but she gat away.

'How will you have your discourse,' said she, 'without you let my lips alone?'

He yielded, and took her hands. 'On this,' said he, 'will I revenge my wrong', and so began to make much of that hand, when her tale and his delight were interrupted by Miso who, taking her time while Basilius' back was turned, came unto them, and told Philoclea she deserved she knew what for leaving her mother (being evil at ease) to keep company with strangers. But Philoclea telling her that she was there by her father's commandment, she went away muttering that though her back and her shoulders and her neck were broken, yet as long as her tongue would wag, it should do her errand to her mother.

## CHAPTER 25

And so went up Miso to Gynecia, who was at that time miserably vexed with this manner of dream. It seemed unto her to be in a place full of thorns, which so molested her as she could neither abide standing still nor tread safely going forward. In this case she thought Zelmane (being upon a fair hill, delightful to the eye and easy in appearance) called her thither; whither with much anguish being come, Zelmane was vanished and she found nothing but a dead body like unto her husband; which seeming at the first with a strange smell to infect her as she was ready likewise within a while to die, the dead body, she thought, took her in his arms and said, 'Gynecia, leave all, for here is thy only rest.'

With that she awaked, crying very loud, 'Zelmane, Zelmane.'
But remembering herself, and seeing Basilius by (her guilty conscience more suspecting than being suspected) she turned her call
and called for Philoclea. Miso forthwith like a valiant shrew, looking at Basilius as though she would speak though she died for it,
told Gynecia that her daughter had been a whole hour together in
secret talk with Zelmane. 'And' says she, 'for my part I could not
be heard, your daughters are brought up in such awe, though I
told her of your pleasure sufficiently.'

Gynecia, as if she had heard her last doom pronounced against
her, with a side-look and changed countenance, 'O my lord,' said
she, 'what mean you to suffer those young folks together?'

Basilius, that aimed nothing at the mark of her suspicion, smil-
ingly took her in his arms: 'Sweet wife,' said he, 'I thank you for
your care of your child; but they must be youths of other metal
than Zelmane that can endanger her.'

'O but – ,' cried Gynecia, and therewith she stayed, for then
indeed she did suffer a right conflict betwixt the force of love and
rage of jealousy. Many times was she about to satisfy the spite of
her mind, and tell Basilius how she knew Zelmane to be far otherwise than the outward appearance. But those many times were all
put back by the manifold objections of her vehement love. Fain
she would have barred her daughter's hap, but loth she was to cut
off her own hope. But now, as if her life had been set upon a wager
of quick rising, as weak as she was, she gat up; though Basilius
(with a kindness flowing only from the fountain of unkindness,
being indeed desirous to win his daughter as much time as might
be) was loth to suffer it, swearing he saw sickness in her face, and
therefore was loth she should adventure the air.

But the great and wretched lady Gynecia, possessed with those
devils of love and jealousy, did rid herself from her tedious husband: and taking nobody with her, going towards them: 'O jealousy,' said she, 'the frenzy of wise folks, the well-wishing spite and
unkind carefulness; the self-punishment for other's fault and self-
misery in other's happiness; the cousin of envy, daughter of love,
and mother of hate, how could'st thou so quietly get thee a seat in
the unquiet heart of Gynecia – Gynecia,' said she sighing, 'thought
wise and once virtuous? Alas, it is thy breeder's power which

plants thee there: it is the flaming agony of affection that works the chilling access of thy fever, in such sort that nature gives place: the growing of my daughter seems the decay of myself; the blessings of a mother turn to the curses of a competitor, and the fair face of Philoclea appears more horrible in my sight than the image of death.'

Then remembered she this song, which she thought took a right measure of her present mind:

> With two strange fires of equal heat possessed,
>   The one of love, the other jealousy;
> Both still do work, in neither find I rest:
>   For both, alas, their strengths together tie:
> The one aloft doth hold the other high.
>     Love wakes the jealous eye, lest thence it moves:
>     The jealous eye, the more it looks, it loves.
>
> These fires increase; in these I daily burn;
>   They feed on me, and with my wings do fly:
> My lively joys to doleful ashes turn:
>   Their flames mount up, my powers prostrate lie;
> They live in force; I quite consumed die.
>     One wonder yet far passes my conceit:
>     The fuel small; how be the fires so great?

But her unleisured thoughts ran not over the ten first words; but going with a pace not so much too fast for her body as slow for her mind, she found them together, who after Miso's departure had left their tale and determined what to say to Basilius. But full abashed was poor Philoclea (whose conscience now began to know cause of blushing) for first salutation receiving an eye from her mother full of the same disdainful scorn which Pallas showed to poor Arachne[1] that durst contend with her for the prize of well weaving: yet did the force of love so much rule her that, though for Zelmane's sake she did detest her, yet for Zelmane's sake she used no harder words to her than to bid her go home and accompany her solitary father.

Then began she to display to Zelmane the store-house of her deadly desires; when suddenly the confused rumour of a mutinous multitude gave just occasion to Zelmane to break off any such conference (for well she found they were not friendly voices they heard) and to retire with as much diligence as conveniently they could towards the lodge. Yet before they could win the lodge by twenty paces, they were overtaken by an unruly sort of clowns and other rebels which, like a violent flood, were carried they themselves knew not whither. But as soon as they came within perfect discerning these ladies, like enraged beasts, without respect of their estates or pity of their sex, they began to run against them, as right villains thinking ability to do hurt to be a great advancement; yet so many as they were, so many almost were their minds,[2] all knit together only in madness. Some cried 'Take'; some 'Kill'; some, 'Save'; but even they that cried 'Save' ran for company with them that meant to kill. Everyone commanded; none obeyed; he only seemed chief captain that was most rageful.

Zelmane, whose virtuous courage was ever awake, drew out her sword, which upon those ill-armed churls giving as many wounds as blows, and as many deaths almost as wounds, lightning courage and thundering smart upon them, kept them at a bay, while the two ladies got themselves into the lodge, out of the which Basilius (having put on an armour long untried) came to prove his authority among his subjects, or at least to adventure his life with his dear mistress to whom he brought a shield, while the ladies tremblingly attended the issue of this dangerous adventure. But Zelmane made them perceive the odds between an eagle and a kite, with such a nimble steadiness and such an assured nimbleness that while one was running back for fear, his fellow had her sword in his guts.

And by and by was both her heart and help well increased by the coming in of Dorus who, having been making of hurdles for his master's sheep, heard the horrible cries of this mad multitude; and having straight represented before the eyes of his careful love the peril wherein the soul of his soul might be, he went to Pamela's lodge, but found her in a cave hard by, with Mopsa and Dametas, who at that time would not have opened the entry to his father. And therefore leaving them there as in a place safe, both for being strong and unknown, he ran as the noise guided him. But when he saw his friend in such danger among them, anger and contempt (asking no counsel but of courage) made him run among them with no other weapon but his sheep-hook, and with that overthrowing one of the villains, took away a two-hand sword from him, and withal helped him from ever being ashamed of losing it. Then lifting up his brave head, and flashing terror into their faces, he made arms and legs go complain to the earth how evil their masters had kept them. Yet the multitude still growing and the very killing wearying them, fearing lest in long fight they should be conquered with conquering, they drew back toward the lodge; but drew back in such sort that still their terror went forward; like a valiant mastiff, whom when his master pulls back by the tail from the bear with whom he hath already interchanged a hateful embracement, though his pace be backward, his gesture is forward, his teeth and eyes threatening more in the retiring than they did in the advancing: so guided they themselves homeward, never stepping step backward but that they proved themselves masters of the ground where they stepped.

Yet among the rebels there was a dapper fellow, a tailor by occupation who, fetching his courage only from their going back, began to bow his knees, and very fencer-like to draw near to Zelmane. But as he came within her distance, turning his sword very nicely about his crown, Basilius, with a side blow, strake off his nose. He (being a suitor to a seamster's daughter, and therefore not a little grieved for such a disgrace) stooped down, because he had heard that if it were fresh put to, it would cleave on again. But as his hand was on the ground to bring his nose to his head, Zelmane with a blow sent his head to his nose. That saw a butcher, a butcherly chuff* indeed (who that day was sworn brother to him in a cup of wine) and lifted up a great leaver,* calling Zelmane all the vile names of a butcherly eloquence. But she, letting slip the blow of the leaver, hit him so surely upon the side of the face that she left nothing but the nether jaw, where the tongue still wagged, as willing to say more if his master's remembrance had served. 'O,' said a miller that was half drunk, 'see the luck of a good-fellow,' and with that word ran with a pitchfork at Dorus; but the nimbleness of the wine carried his head so fast that it made it over-run his feet, so that he fell withal just between the

* *chuff*: churl. *leaver*: bar.

legs of Dorus, who, setting his foot on his neck (though he offered two milch kine and four fat hogs for his life) thrust his sword quite through from one ear to the other; which took it very unkindly, to feel such news before they heard of them, instead of hearing, to be put to such feeling. But Dorus, leaving the miller to vomit his soul out in wine and blood, with his two-hand sword strake off another quite by the waist who the night before had dreamed he was grown a couple, and, interpreting it that he should be married, had bragged of his dream that morning among his neighbours. But that blow astonished quite a poor painter who stood by with a pike in his hands. This painter was to counterfeit the skirmish between the Centaurs and Lapithes,[3] and had been very desirous to see some notable wounds, to be able the more lively to express them; and this morning, being carried by the stream of this company, the foolish fellow was even delighted to see the effect of blows. But this last, happening near him, so amazed him that he stood stock still, while Dorus, with a turn of his sword, strake off both his hands. And so the painter returned well skilled in wounds, but with never a hand to perform his skill.

## CHAPTER 26

In this manner they recovered* the lodge, and gave the rebels a face of wood of the outside. But they then (though no more furious, yet more courageous when they saw no resister) went about with pickaxe to the wall and fire to the gate to get themselves entrance. Then did the two ladies mix fear with love – especially Philoclea, who ever caught hold of Zelmane, so (by the folly of love) hindering the succour which she desired. But Zelmane seeing no way of defence nor time to deliberate (the number of those villains still increasing, and their madness still increasing with their number) thought it only the means to go beyond their expectation with an unused boldness and with danger to avoid danger, and therefore opened again the gate; and Dorus and Basilius standing ready for her defence, she issued again among them. The blows she had dealt before, though all in general were hasty, made each of them in particular take breath before they brought

* *recovered:* got back to.

them suddenly over-near her, so that she had time to get up to the judgement-seat of the prince which, according to the guise of that country, was before the court gate. There she paused a while, making sign with her hand unto them and, withal, speaking aloud that she had something to say unto them that would please them. But she was answered a while with nothing but shouts and cries, and some beginning to throw stones at her, not daring to approach her.

But at length a young farmer (who might do most among the country sort and was caught in a little affection towards Zelmane) hoping by this kindness to have some good of her, desired them if they were honest men to hear the woman speak.

'Fie fellows, fie,' said he, 'what will all the maids in our town say if so many tall men shall be afraid to hear a fair wench? I swear unto you by no little ones, I had rather give my team of oxen than we should show ourselves so uncivil wights. Besides, I tell you true, I have heard it of old men counted wisdom to hear much and say little.'

His sententious speech so prevailed that the most part began to listen. Then she (with such efficacy of gracefulness and such a quiet magnanimity represented in her face in this uttermost peril as the more the barbarous people looked, the more it fixed their looks upon her) in this sort began unto them:

'It is no small comfort unto me,' said she, 'having to speak something unto you for your own behoofs, to find that I have to deal with such a people who show indeed in themselves the right nature of valour, which, as it leaves no violence unattempted while the choler is nourished with resistance, so, when the subject of their wrath doth of itself unlooked-for offer itself into their hands, it makes them at least take a pause before they determine cruelty. Now then first (before I come to the principal matter) have I to say unto you that your prince Basilius himself in person is within this lodge, and was one of the three whom a few of you went about to fight withal; and' (this she said, not doubting but they knew it well enough, but because she would have them imagine that the prince might think that they did not know it) 'by him am I sent unto you as from a prince to his well-approved subjects, nay as from a father to beloved children, to know what it is that hath bred just quarrel among you, or who they be that have any way wronged you; what it is with which you are displeased or of which you are desirous. This he requires, and indeed (for he knows your faithfulness) he commands you presently to set down and choose among yourselves someone who may relate your griefs or demands unto him.'

This (being more than they hoped for from their prince) assuaged well their fury, and many of them consented, especially the young farmer helping on, who meant to make one of the demands that he might have Zelmane for his wife. But when they began to talk of their griefs, never bees made such a confused humming: the town dwellers demanding putting down of imposts;* the country fellows, laying out of commons:¹ some would have the prince keep his court in one place, some in another. All cried out to have new counsellors, but when they should think of any new, they liked them as well as any other that they could remember: especially they would have the treasure* so looked unto as that he should never need to take any more subsidies.* At length they fell to direct contrarieties. For the artisans, they would have corn and wine set at a lower price, and bound to be kept so still: the ploughmen, vine-labourers and farmers would none of that. The countrymen demanded that every man might be free in the chief towns: that could not the burgesses like of. The peasants would have all the gentlemen destroyed; the citizens (especially such as cooks, barbers, and those other that lived most on gentlemen) would but have them reformed. And of each side were like divisions, one neighbourhood beginning to find fault with another.

But no confusion was greater than of particular men's likings and dislikings: one dispraising such a one whom another praised, and demanding such a one to be punished whom the other would have exalted. No less ado was there about choosing him who should be their spokesman. The finer sort of burgesses, as merchants, prentices and cloth-workers, because of their riches disdaining the baser occupations, and they because of their number* as much disdaining them; all they scorning the countrymen's ig-

---

* *imposts:* taxes. *treasure:* exchequer. *subsidies:* levies of money. *they because of their number:* i.e. 'the baser sort'.

norance, and the countrymen suspecting* as much their cunning:* so that Zelmane (finding that their united rage was now grown not only to a dividing but to a crossing* of one another, and that the mislike grown among themselves did well allay the heat against her) made tokens again unto them (as though she took great care of their well-doing and were afraid of their falling out) that she would speak unto them. They now, grown jealous one of another (the stay* having engendered division and division having manifested their weakness) were willing enough to hear, the most part striving to show themselves willinger than their fellows: which Zelmane (by the acquaintance she had had with such kind of humours) soon perceiving, with an angerless bravery and an unabashed mildness, in this manner spake unto them.

'An unused* thing it is, and I think not heretofore seen, O Arcadians, that a woman should give public counsel to men, a stranger to the country people,* and that lastly in such a presence, by a private person the regal throne should be possessed. But the strangeness of your action makes that used for virtue which your violent necessity imposeth. For certainly, a woman may well speak to such men who have forgotten all man-like government; a stranger may with reason instruct such subjects that neglect due points of subjection; and is it marvel this place is entered into by another, since your own prince, after thirty years' government, dare not show his face unto his faithful people? Hear therefore, O Arcadians, and be ashamed.

'Against whom hath this zealous rage been stirred? Whither have been bent these manful weapons of yours? In this quiet harmless lodge there be harboured no Argians, your ancient enemies, nor Laconians, your now feared neighbours. Here be neither hard landlords nor biting usurers. Here lodge none but such as either you have great cause to love or no cause to hate: here being none, besides your prince, princess, and their children, but myself. Is it I then, O Arcadians, against whom your anger is armed? Am I the mark of your vehement quarrel?* If it be so that

* *suspecting*: mistrusting. *cunning*: know-how. *crossing*: opposing. *stay*: delay. *unused*: unusual. *a stranger ... people*: a foreigner to the peoples of the country. *quarrel*: bolt of a cross-bow. Sidney is making a pun.

innocency shall not be a stop for fury; if it be so that the law of hospitality (so long and holily observed among you) may not defend a stranger fled to your arms for succour; if, in fine, it be so that so many valiant men's courages can be inflamed to the mischief of one silly woman, I refuse not to make my life a sacrifice to your wrath. Exercise on me your indignation, so it go no further: I am content to pay the great favours I have received among you with my life, not ill-deserving: I present it here unto you, O Arcadians, if that may satisfy you, rather than you (called over the world the wise and quiet Arcadians) should be so vain as to attempt that alone which all the rest of your country will abhor; than you should show yourselves so ungrateful as to forget the fruit of so many years' peaceable government, or so unnatural as not to have with the holy name of your natural prince any fury overmastered. For such a hellish madness, I know, did never enter into your hearts as to attempt anything against his person; which no successor (though never so hateful) will ever leave (for his own sake) unrevenged.

'Neither can your wonted valour be turned to such a baseness, as instead of a prince, delivered unto you by so many royal ancestors, to take the tyrannous yoke of your fellow subject, in whom the innate meanness* will bring forth ravenous covetousness, and the newness of his estate, suspectful cruelty. Imagine, what could your enemies more wish unto you than to see your own estate with your own hands undermined? O what would your forefathers say if they lived at this time, and saw their offspring defacing such an excellent principality, which they with much labour and blood so wisely have established? Do you think them fools, that saw you should not enjoy your vines, your cattle, no not your wives and children without government? And that there could be no government without a magistrate, and no magistrate without obedience, and no obedience where everyone upon his own private passion may interpret the doings of the rulers? Let your wits make your present example a lesson to you. What sweetness, in good faith, find you in your present condition? What choice of choice find you, if you had lost Basilius? Under whose ensign would you go, if your enemies should invade you? If

* *meanness*: lowness of estate.

you cannot agree upon one to speak for you, how will you agree upon one to fight for you? But with this fear of I cannot tell what, one is troubled, and with that past wrong, another is grieved. And I pray you did the sun ever bring you a fruitful harvest but that it was more hot than pleasant? Have any of you children that be not sometimes cumbersome? Have any of you fathers that be not sometimes wearish?* What, shall we curse the sun, hate our children, or disobey our fathers? – but what need I use these words, since I see in your countenances, now virtuously settled, nothing else but love and duty to him by whom for your only sakes the government is embraced. For all what is done, he doth not only pardon you but thank you, judging the action by the minds and not the minds by the action. Your griefs and desires, whatsoever and whensoever you list, he will consider of, and to his consideration it is reason you should refer them. So then, to conclude: the uncertainty of his estate made you take arms. Now you see him well, with the same love lay them down. If now you end, as I know you will, he will make no other account of this matter but as of a vehement, I must confess, over vehement affection: the only* continuance might prove a wickedness. But it is not so, I see very well; you began with zeal and will end with reverence.

The action Zelmane used, being beautified by nature and apparelled with skill; her gestures being such that, as her words did paint out her mind, so they served as a shadow to make the picture more lively and sensible; with the sweet clearness of her voice rising and falling kindly* as the nature of the word and efficacy of the matter required – all together in such an admirable person (whose incomparable valour they had well felt, whose beauty did pierce through the thick dulness of their senses) gave such a way unto her speech through the rugged wilderness of their imaginations (who, besides they were stricken in admiration of her as of more than a human creature, were cooled with taking breath and had learned doubts out of leisure), that instead of roaring cries there was now heard nothing but a confused muttering whether her saying were to be followed, betwixt fear to pursue, and loathness to leave. Most of them could have been content it had never been begun, but how to end it (each afraid of his companion) they

* *wearish*: peevish. *the only*: only the. *kindly*: naturally.

knew not, finding it far easier to tie than to loose knots. But Zelmane thinking it no evil way in such mutinies to give the mutinous some occasion of such service as they might think, in their own judgement, would countervail their trespass, withal to take the more assured possession of their minds which she feared might begin to waver:

'Loyal Arcadians,' said she, 'now do I offer unto you the manifesting of your duties. All those that have taken arms for the prince's safety, let them turn their back to the gate, with their weapons bent against such as would hurt his sacred person.'

'O weak trust of the many-headed multitude whom inconstancy only doth guide to well-doing! Who can set confidence there where company takes away shame, and each may lay the fault on his fellow?' – so said a crafty fellow among them, named Clinias, to himself, when he saw the word no sooner out of Zelmane's mouth but that there were some shouts of joy, with, 'God save Basilius,' and divers of them with much jollity grown to be his guard that but little before meant to be his murderers.


CHAPTER 27

This Clinias in his youth had been a scholar so far as to learn rather words than manners, and of words rather plenty than order; and oft had used to be an actor in tragedies, where he had learned (besides a slidingness of language) acquaintance with many passions and to frame his face to bear the figure of them: long used to the eyes and ears of men, and to reckon no fault but shamefastness: in nature a most notable coward, and yet more strangely than rarely venturous in privy practices.

This fellow was become of near trust to Cecropia, Amphialus' mother, so that he was privy to all the mischievous devices wherewith she went about to ruin Basilius and his children, for the advancing of her son; and though his education had made him full of tongue, yet his love to be doing taught him in any evil to be secret, and had by his mistress been used, (ever since the strange retiring of Basilius), to whisper rumours into the people's ears: and this time, finding great aptness in the multitude, was one of the chief that set them in the uproar, though quite without the consent of Amphialus, who would not for all the kingdoms of the world so have adventured the life of Philoclea. But now perceiving the flood of their fury begun to ebb, he thought it policy to take the first of the tide, so that no man cried louder than he upon* Basilius. And some of the lustiest rebels not yet agreeing to the rest, he caused two or three of his mates that were at his commandment to lift him up, and then as if he had had a prologue to utter, he began with a nice* gravity to demand audience. But few attending what he said, with vehement gesture as if he would tear the stars from the skies, he fell to crying out so loud that not only Zelmane but Basilius might hear him:

'O unhappy men, more mad than the giants that would have plucked Jupiter out of heaven, how long shall this rage continue? Why do you not all throw down your weapons and submit yourselves to our good prince, our good Basilius, the Pelops of wisdom and Minos¹ of all good government? When will you begin to believe me, and other honest and faithful subjects, that have done all we could to stop your fury?'

The farmer that loved Zelmane could abide him no longer. For as at the first he was willing to speak of conditions, hoping to have gotten great sovereignties (and among the rest Zelmane) so now, perceiving that the people, once anything down the hill from their fury, would never stay till they came to the bottom of absolute yielding and so that he should be nearer fears of punishment than hopes of such advancement, he was one of them that stood most against the agreement: and to begin withal, disdaining this fellow should play the preacher who had been one of the chiefest make-bates,* strake him a great wound upon the face with his sword. The cowardly wretch fell down, crying for succour and, scrambling through the legs of them that were about him, got to the throne, where Zelmane took him and comforted him, bleeding for that was past and quaking for fear of more.

But as soon as that blow was given, as if Aeolus* had broke open the door to let all his winds out, no hand was idle, each one killing him that was next for fear he should do as much to him. For being divided in minds and not divided in companies, they

* *cried louder upon*: cried out in praise of. *nice*: careful. *make-bates*: trouble-makers. *Aeolus*: god of the winds.

that would yield to Basilius were intermingled with them that would not yield: these men thinking their ruin stood upon it; those men to get favour of their prince converted their ungracious motion into their own bowels, and by a true judgement grew their own punishers. None was sooner killed than those that had been leaders in the disobedience who, by being so, had taught them that they did lead, disobedience to the same leaders. And many times it fell out that they killed them that were of their own faction, anger whetting and doubt hastening their fingers. But then came down Zelmane, and Basilius with Dorus issued; and sometimes seeking to draw together those of their party, sometimes laying indifferently among them, made such havoc (among the rest Zelmane striking the farmer to the heart with her sword, as before she had done with her eyes) that in a while they of the contrary side were put to flight and fled to certain woods upon the frontiers, where feeding wildly and drinking only water, they were disciplined for their drunken riots; many of them being slain in the chase, about a score only escaping. But when these late rebels, now soldiers, were returned from the chase, Basilius, calling them together partly for policy's sake but principally because Zelmane before had spoken it (which was to him more than a divine ordinance) he pronounced their general pardon, willing them to return to their houses and thereafter be more circumspect in their proceedings, which they did, most of them with sharp marks of their folly. But imagining Clinias to be one of the chief that had bred this good alteration, he gave him particular thanks, and withal willed him to make him know how this frenzy had entered into the people.

Clinias purposing indeed to tell him the truth of all, saving what did touch himself or Cecropia, first dipping his hand in the blood of his wound:

'Now by this blood,' said he, 'which is more dear to me than all the rest that is in my body, since it is spent for your safety: this tongue (perchance unfortunate, but never false) shall not now begin to lie unto my prince, of me most beloved.'

Then stretching out his hand, and making vehement countenances the ushers to his speeches, in such manner of terms recounted this accident. 'Yesterday,' said he, 'being your birth-day, in the goodly green two mile hence before the city of Enispus, to do honour to the day were a four or five thousand people, of all conditions, as I think, gathered together, spending all the day in dancings and other exercises, and when night came, under tents and boughs making great cheer, and meaning to observe a wassailling watch all that night for your sake. Bacchus, the learned say, was begot with thunder:[2] I think that made him ever since so full of stir and debate. Bacchus indeed it was which sounded the first trumpet to this rude alarum. For that barbarous opinion being generally among them, to think with vice to do honour and with activity in beastliness to show abundance of love, made most of them seek to show the depth of their affection in the depth of their draught. But being once well chafed* with wine, having spent all the night and some piece of the morning in such revelling, and emboldened by your absented manner of living, there was no matter their ears had ever heard of that grew not to be a subject of their winey conference. I speak it by proof: for I take witness of the gods, who never leave perjuries unpunished, that I often cried out against their impudency and, when that would not serve, stopped mine ears because I would not be partaker of their blasphemies, till with buffets they forced me to have mine ears and eyes defiled. Public affairs were mingled with private grudges; neither was any man thought of wit that did not pretend some cause of mislike. Railing was counted the fruit of freedom, and saying nothing had his uttermost praise in ignorance.

'At the length, your sacred person (Alas, why did I live to hear it! Alas, how do I breathe to utter it! But your commandment doth not only enjoin obedience but give me force) your sacred person, I say, fell to be their table-talk; a proud word swelling in their stomachs, and disdainful reproaches against so great a greatness having put on the show of greatness in their little minds: till at length the very unbridled use of words having increased fire in their minds (which, God wot, thought their knowledge notable, because they had at all no knowledge to condemn their own want of knowledge) they descended (O never to be forgotten presumption!) to a direct mislike of your living from among them. Whereupon it were tedious to remember their far-fetched con-

* *chafed*: heated.

structions. But the sum was, you disdained them: and what were the pomps of your estate if their arms maintained you not? Who would call you a prince if you had not a people? When certain of them of wretched estates and worse minds, whose fortunes change could not impair, began to say that your government was to be looked into; how the great treasures you had levied among them had been spent; why none but great men and gentlemen could be admitted into counsel; that the commons, forsooth, were too plain-headed to say their opinions, but yet their blood and sweat must maintain all. Who could tell whether you were not betrayed in this place where you lived, nay, whether you did live or no? Therefore that it was time to come and see; and if you were here, to know (if Arcadia were grown loathsome in your sight) why you did not rid yourself of the trouble: there would not want those that would take so fair a cumber in good part. Since the country was theirs, and the government an adherent to the country, why should they not consider of the one as well as inhabit the other? "Nay rather," said they, "let us begin that which all Arcadia will follow. Let us deliver our prince from danger of practices, and ourselves from want of a prince. Let us do that which all the rest think. Let it be said that we only are not astonished with vain titles which have their force but in our force."

'Lastly, to have said and heard so much was as dangerous as to have attempted; and to attempt they had the glorious name of liberty with them. These words, being spoken, like a furious storm presently carried away their well inclined brains. What I and some other of the honester sort could do was no more than if with a puff of breath one should go about to make a sail go against a mighty wind, or, with one hand, stay the ruin of a mighty wall. So general grew this madness among them, there needed no drum, where each man cried, each spake to other that spake as fast to him, and the disagreeing sound of so many voices was the chief token of their unmeet* agreement. Thus was their banquet turned to a battle, their winey mirths to bloody rages, and the happy prayers for your life to monstrous threatening of your estate; the solemnizing your birth-day tended to have been the cause of your funeral.

* *unmeet*: unfitting.

'But as a drunken rage hath, besides his wickedness, that folly, that the more it seeks to hurt the less it considers how to be able to hurt, they never weighed how to arm themselves, but took up everything for a weapon that fury offered to their hands. Many swords, pikes, and bills there were; others took pitchforks and rakes, converting husbandry to soldiery*: some caught hold of spits, things serviceable for life, to be the instruments of death. And there was some such one who held the same pot wherein he drank to your health to use it, as he could, to your mischief. Thus armed, thus governed, forcing the unwilling and heartening the willing, adding fury to fury and increasing rage with running, they came headlong toward this lodge: no man, I dare say, resolved in his own heart what was the uttermost he would do when he came hither.

'But as mischief is of such nature that it cannot stand but with strengthening one evil by another, and so multiply in itself till it came to the highest and then fall with his own weight; so to their minds once past the bounds of obedience, more and more wickedness opened itself, so that they who first pretended to preserve you, then to reform you (I speak it in my conscience and with a bleeding heart) now thought no safety for them without murdering you. So as if the gods (who preserve you for the preservation of Arcadia) had not showed their miraculous power, and that they had not used for instruments both your own valour (not fit to be spoken of by so mean a mouth as mine) and some, I must confess, honest minds (whom, alas, why should I mention, since what we did reached not to the hundredth part of our duty?) our hands (I tremble to think of it) had destroyed all that for which we have cause to rejoice that we are Arcadians.'

With that the fellow did wring his hands, and wrung out tears, so as Basilius, that was not the sharpest piercer into masked minds, took a good liking to him; and so much the more as he had tickled him with praise in the hearing of his mistress. And therefore pitying his wound, willed him to get him home and look well into it, and make the best search he could to know if there were any further depth in this matter, for which he should be well

* *husbandry to soldiery*: the reverse of turning swords to ploughshares.

rewarded. But before he went away, certain of the shepherds being come (for that day was appointed for their pastorals) he sent one of them to Philanax and another to other principal noblemen and cities thereabouts, to make thorough inquiry of this uproar, and withal to place such garrisons in all the towns and villages near unto him, that he might thereafter keep his solitary lodge in more security, upon the making of a fire or ringing of a bell, having them in a readiness for him.

## CHAPTER 28

This, Clinias (having his ear one way when his eye was another) had perceived, and therefore hasted away with mind to tell Cecropia she was to take some speedy resolution, or else it were danger those examinations would both discover and ruin her; and so went his way, leaving that little company with embracements and praising of Zelmane's excellent proceeding, to show that no decking sets forth anything so much as affection. For as (while she stood at the discretion of those undiscreet rebels) every angry countenance any of them made seemed a knife laid upon their own throats, so unspeakable was now their joy that they saw (besides her safety and their own) the same wrought, and safely wrought by her means in whom they had placed all their delights. What examples Greece could ever allege of wit and fortitude were set in the rank of trifles, being compared to this action.

But as they were in the midst of those unfeigned ceremonies, a gittern* ill-played on, accompanied with a hoarse voice (who seemed to sing maugre* the Muses and to be merry in spite of fortune) made them look the way of the ill-noised* song. The song was this:

> A hateful cure with hate to heal:
> A bloody help with blood to save:
> A foolish thing with fools to deal.
> Let him be bob'd,* that bobs* will have.
> But who by means of wisdom high
> Hath sav'd his charge? It is even I.

* *gittern*: type of guitar. *maugre*: in defiance of. *ill-noised*: unmusical. *bob'd*: mocked. *bobs*: blows.

Let others deck their pride with scars,
  And of their wounds make brave lame shows:
First let them die, then pass the stars,
  When rotten fame will tell their blows:
    But eye from blade, and ear from cry,
    Who hath sav'd all? It is even I.

They had soon found it was Dametas, who came with no less
lifted up countenance than if he had passed over the bellies of all
his enemies; so wise a point he thought he had performed in using
the natural strength of the cave. But never was it his doing to
come so soon thence till the coast were more assuredly clear, for it
was a rule with him that after a great storm there ever fall a few
drops before it be fully finished. But Pamela, who had now experienced how much care doth solicit a lover's heart, used this occasion of going to her parents and sister, indeed as well for that
cause, as being unquiet till her eye might be assured how her
shepherd had gone through the danger.

But Basilius with the sight of Pamela (of whom almost his head,
otherwise occupied, had left the wonted* remembrance) was suddenly stricken into a devout kind of admiration, remembering the
oracle, which, according to the fawning humour of false hope, he
interpreted now his own to his own best, and with the willing
blindness of affection (because his mind ran wholly upon Zelmane) he thought the gods in their oracles did principally mind
her.

But as he was thinking deeply of the matter, one of the shepherds told him that Philanax was already come with a hundred
horse in his company. For having by chance rid not far off the
little desert,* he had heard of this uproar, and so was come upon
the spur, gathering a company of gentlemen as fast as he could, to
the succour of his master. Basilius was glad of it; but not willing
to have him, nor any other of the noblemen, see his mistress, he
himself went out of the lodge: and so giving order unto him of
placing garrisons and examining those matters; and Philanax with
humble earnestness beginning to entreat him to leave off this solitary course which already had been so dangerous unto him:

* *wonted:* accustomed. *desert:* uninhabited tract of land.

'Well,' said Basilius, 'it may be ere long I will condescend unto your desire. In the meantime, take you the best order you can to keep me safe in my solitariness. But,' said he, 'do you remember how earnestly you wrote unto me that I should not be moved by that oracle's authority which brought me to this resolution?'

'Full well, Sir,' answered Philanax, 'for though it pleased you not as then to let me know what the oracle's words were, yet all oracles holding, in my conceit, one degree of reputation, it sufficed me to know it was but an oracle which led you from your own course.'

'Well,' said Basilius, 'I will now tell you the words, which before I thought not good to do, because when all the events fall out, as some already have done, I may charge you with your incredulity.' So he repeated them in this sort:

Thy elder care shall from thy careful face
　　By princely mean be stolen, and yet not lost.
Thy younger shall with Nature's bliss embrace
　　An uncouth love, which Nature hateth most.
Both they themselves unto such two shall wed,
　　Who at thy bier, as at a bar, shall plead
　　Why thee (a living man) they had made dead.
In thine own seat a foreign state shall sit.
And ere that all these blows thy head do hit,
Thou, with thy wife adultery shall commit.

'For you, forsooth,' said he, 'when I told you that some supernatural cause sent me strange visions, which being confirmed with presagious* chances, I had gone to Delphos and there received this answer; you replied to me that the only supernatural causes were the humours of my body which bred such melancholy dreams, and that both they framed a mind full of conceits, apt to make presages of things which in themselves were merely chanceable: and withal, as I say, you remember what you wrote unto me touching the authority of the oracle: but now I have some notable trial of the truth thereof, which hereafter I will more largely communicate unto you. Only now, know that the thing I most feared is already performed – I mean, that a foreign state should

* *presagious*: ominous.

possess my throne. For that hath been done by Zelmane, but not, as I feared, to my ruin but to my preservation.'

But when he had once named Zelmane, that name was as good as a pulley to make the clock of his praises run on in such sort that (Philanax found) was more exquisite than the only admiration* of virtue breedeth: which his faithful heart inwardly repining at made him shrink away as soon as he could, to go about the other matters of importance which Basilius had enjoined unto him.

Basilius returned into the lodge, thus by himself construing the oracle: that in that he said his elder care should by princely mean be stolen away from him and yet not lost, it was now performed, since Zelmane had, as it were, robbed from him the care of his first begotten child; yet was it not lost, since in his heart the ground of it remained: that his younger should with Nature's bliss embrace the love of Zelmane, because he had so commanded her for his sake to do; yet should it be with as much hate of nature, for being so hateful an opposite to the jealousy he thought her mother had of him. The sitting in his seat he deemed by her already performed. But that which most comforted him was his interpretation of the adultery, which he thought he should commit with Zelmane, whom afterwards he should have to his wife. The point of his daughters' marriage, because it threatened his death withal, he determined to prevent with keeping them, while he lived, unmarried. But having, as he thought, gotten thus much understanding of the oracle, he determined for three days after to perform certain rites to Apollo; and even then began with his wife and daughters to sing this hymn, by them yearly used:

Apollo great, whose beams the greater world do light,
And in our little world do clear our inward sight,
Which ever shine, though hid from earth by earthly shade,
Whose lights do ever live, but in our darkness fade;
Thou god, whose youth was decked with spoil of Python's skin,
(So humble knowledge can throw down the snakish sin)
Latona's son,[1] whose birth in pain and travail long
Doth teach, to learn the good what travails do belong:

* *the only admiration*: the admiration of virtue alone.

In travail of our life, a short but tedious space,
While brickle* hour glass runs, guide thou our panting pace:
Give us foresightful minds: give us minds to obey
What foresight tells; our thoughts upon thy knowledge stay.
Let so our fruits grow up that nature be maintain'd:
But so our hearts keep down, with vice they be not stain'd.
Let this assured hold our judgements ever take,
That nothing wins the heaven, but what doth earth forsake.

As soon as he had ended his devotion (all the privileged shepherds being now come) knowing well enough he might lay all his care upon Philanax, he was willing to sweeten the taste of this past tumult with some rural pastimes. For which, while the shepherds prepared themselves in their best manner, Basilius took his daughter Philoclea aside, and with such haste, as if his ears hunted for words, desired to know how she had found Zelmane. She humbly answered him according to the agreement betwixt them, that thus much for her sake Zelmane was content to descend from her former resolution as to hear him whensoever he would speak; and further than that, she said, as Zelmane had not granted, so she neither did nor ever would desire. Basilius kissed her with more than fatherly thanks, and straight (like a hard-kept ward new come to his lands) would fain have used the benefit of that grant in laying his sickness before his only physician. But Zelmane (that had not yet fully determined with herself how to bear herself towards him) made him in a few words understand that the time, in respect of the company, was unfit for such a parley; and therefore to keep his brains the busier, letting him understand what she had learned of his daughters touching Erona's distress (whom in her travel she had known and been greatly beholding to) she desired him to finish the rest for so far as Plangus had told him; because, she said (and she said truly) she was full of care for that lady whose desert, only except an over-base choice, was nothing agreeable to misfortune. Basilius, glad that she would command him anything, but more glad that in excusing* the unfitness of that time she argued an intention to grant a fitter, obeyed her in this manner.

* *brickle*: brittle. *excusing*: using as an excuse.

## CHAPTER 29

'Madam,' said he, 'it is very true that since years enabled me to judge what is or is not to be pitied, I never saw anything that more moved me to justify a vehement compassion in myself than the estate of that prince whom, strong against all his own afflictions (which yet were great as I perceive you have heard) yet true and noble love had so pulled down as to lie under sorrow for another. Insomuch* as I could not temper my long idle pen* in that subject, which I perceive you have seen. But then to leave that unrepeated which I find my daughters have told you, it may please you to understand, since it pleaseth you to demand, that Antiphilus being crowned and so left by the famous princes Musidorus and Pyrocles (led thence by the challenge of Anaxius, who is now in these provinces of Greece, making a dishonourable enquiry after that excellent prince Pyrocles, already perished) – Antiphilus, I say, being crowned and delivered from the presence of those two, whose virtues (while they were present) like good schoolmasters suppressed his vanities, he had not strength of mind enough in him to make long delay of discovering what manner of man he was. But straight like one carried up to so high a place that he loseth the discerning of the ground over which he is, so was his mind lifted so far beyond the level of his own discourse, that remembering only that himself was in the high seat of a king, he could not perceive that he was a king of reasonable creatures who would quickly scorn follies and repine at injuries. But imagining no so true property of sovereignty as to do what he listed and to list whatsoever pleased his fancy, he quickly made his kingdom a tennis-court where his subjects should be the balls; not in truth cruelly but licentiously abusing them, presuming so far upon himself that what he did was liked of everybody, nay, that his disgraces were favours, and all because he was a king. For in nature not able to conceive the bounds of great matters, suddenly borne into an unknown ocean of absolute power, he was swayed withal, he knew not how, as every wind of passions puffed him. Whereto nothing helped him better than that poisonous sugar of flattery, which some used, out of the innate baseness of their

* *Insomuch*: to such an extent. *my long idle pen*: his poem, p. 296.

heart, straight like dogs fawning upon the greatest: others secretly hating him and disdaining his great rising so suddenly, so undeservedly, finding his humour, bent their exalting him only to his overthrow, like the bird that carries the shell-fish high to break him the easier with his fall. But his mind, being an apt matter to receive what form their amplifying speeches would lay upon it, danced so pretty a measure to their false music that he thought himself the wisest and worthiest and best beloved that ever gave honour to a royal title. And being but obscurely born, he had found out unblushing pedigrees that made him not only of the blood royal but true heir, though unjustly dispossessed by Erona's ancestors. And like the foolish bird that, when it so hides the head that it sees not itself, thinks nobody else sees it, so did he imagine that nobody knew his baseness, while he himself turned his eyes from it.

'Then vainness, a meagre friend to gratefulness, brought him so to despise Erona as of whom he had received no benefit, that within half a year's marriage he began to pretend barrenness; and making first an unlawful law of having more wives than one, he (still keeping Erona) under-hand, by messages sought Artaxia: who no less hating him than loving (as unlucky a choice) the naughty* king Plexirtus, yet to bring to pass what she purposed, was content to train him into false hopes, till already his imagination had crowned him king of Armenia and had made that but the foundation of more and more monarchies, as if fortune had only gotten eyes to cherish him. In which time a great assembly of most part of all the princes of Asia being to do honour to the never sufficiently praised Pyrocles and Musidorus, he would be one; not to acknowledge his obligation (which was as great as any of the others) but looking to have been "young-mastered"* among those great estates as he was among his abusing underlings. But so many valorous princes indeed far nearer to disdain him than otherwise, he was quickly (as standing upon no true ground inwardly) out of countenance with himself; till his seldom comfortless flatterers, persuading him it was envy and fear of his expected greatness, made him haste away from that company, and without further delay appointed the meeting with Artaxia, so incredibly

* *naughty*: worthless. '*Young-mastered*': addressed as a superior.

blinded with the over-bright shining of his royalty that he could think such a queen would be content to be joint-patent* with another to have such an husband. Poor Erona to all this obeyed, either vehemency of affection making her stoop to so over-base a servitude, or astonished with an unlooked for fortune, dull to any behooveful* resolution, or (as many times it falls out even in great hearts when they can accuse none but themselves) desperately bent to maintain it. For so went she on in that way of her love that, poor lady, to be beyond all other examples of ill-set affection, she was brought to write to Artaxia that she was content, for the public good, to be a second wife and yield the first place to her; nay to extol him, and even woo Artaxia for him.

'But Artaxia, mortally hating them both for her brother's sake, was content to hide her hate till she had time to show it; and pretending that all her grudge was against the two paragons of virtue, Musidorus and Pyrocles, even met them half-way in excusing her brother's murder, as not being principal actors, and of the other side, driven to what they did by the ever-pardonable necessity: and so well handled the matter as, though she promised nothing, yet Antiphilus promised himself all that she would have him think. And so a solemn interview was appointed. But, as the poets say, Hymen had not there his saffron-coloured coat.* For Artaxia laying men secretly (and easily they might be secret, since Antiphilus thought she over-ran him in love) when he came even ready to embrace her, showing rather a countenance of accepting than offering, they came forth and, having much advantage both in number, valour and fore-preparation, put all his company to the sword but such as could fly away. As for Antiphilus, she caused him and Erona both to be put in irons, hasting back toward her brother's tomb, upon which she meant to sacrifice them; making the love of her brother stand between her and all other motions of grace from which by nature she was alienated.

'But great diversity in them two quickly discovered itself for the bearing of that affliction. For Antiphilus, who had no greatness but outward, that taken away, was ready to fall faster than calamity could thrust him; with fruitless begging of life (where

---

*joint-patent: sharing legal possession. behooveful: fitting. Hymen ... coat: the god of marriage. See Ovid, Met. X, 1.

reason might well assure him his death was resolved) and weak bemoaning his fortune to give his enemies a most pleasing music, with many promises and protestations to as little purpose as from a little mind. But Erona, sad indeed, yet like one rather used than new fallen to sadness (as who had the joys of her heart already broken) seemed rather to welcome than to shun that end of misery; speaking little, but what she spake was for Antiphilus, remembering his guiltlessness, being at that time prisoner to Tiridates when the valiant princes slew him: to the disgrace of men, showing that there are women both more wise to judge what is to be expected and more constant to bear it when it is happened.

'But her wit endeared by her youth, her affliction by her birth, and her sadness by her beauty, made this noble prince Plangus, who (never almost from his cousin Artaxia) was now present at Erona's taking, to perceive the shape of loveliness more perfectly in woe than in joyfulness (as in a picture which receives greater life by the darkness of shadows than by more glittering colours) and seeing to like, and liking to love, and loving straight to feel the most incident effects of love, to serve and preserve. So borne by the hasty tide of short leisure, he did hastily deliver together his affection and affectionate care. But she (as if he had spoken of a small matter, when he mentioned her life, to which she had not leisure to attend) desired him if he loved her, to show it in finding some way to save Antiphilus. For her, she found the world but a wearisome stage unto her, where she played a part against her will; and therefore besought him not to cast his love in so unfruitful a place as could not love itself, but for a testimony of constancy and a suitableness to his word, to do so much comfort to her mind as that for her sake Antiphilus were saved.

'He told me how much he argued against her tendering him who had so ungratefully betrayed her and foolishly cast away himself. But perceiving she did not only bend her very good wits to speak for him against herself, but when such a cause could be allied to no reason, yet love would needs make itself a cause and bar her rather from hearing than yield that she should yield to such arguments, he likewise (in whom the power of love, as they say of spirits, was subject to the love in her) with grief consented, and though backwardly, was diligent to labour the help of Antiphilus, a man whom he not only hated as a traitor to Erona but envied as a possessor of Erona. Yet love sware his heart, in spite of his heart, should make him become a servant to his rival. And so did he, seeking all the means of persuading Artaxia which the authority of so near and so virtuous a kinsman could give unto him. But she, to whom the eloquence of hatred had given revenge the face of delight, rejected all such motions; but rather the more closely imprisoning them in her chief city, where she kept them with intention at the birthday of Tiridates (which was very near) to execute Antiphilus, and at the day of his death (which was about half a year after) to use the same rigour towards Erona. Plangus, much grieved because much loving, attempted* the humours of the Lycians, to see whether they would come in with forces to succour their princess. But there the next inheritor to the crown (with the true play that is used in the game of kingdoms) had no sooner his mistress in captivity but he had usurped her place, and making her odious to her people because of the unfit election she had made, had so left no hope there: but, which is worse, had sent to Artaxia, persuading the justicing her, because that unjustice might give his title the name of justice.

'Wanting that way, Plangus practised with some dear friends of his to save Antiphilus out of prison, whose day because it was much nearer than Erona's and that he well found she had twisted her life upon the same thread with his, he determined first to get him out of prison; and to that end having prepared all matters as well as in such case he could, where Artaxia had set many of Tiridates' old servants to have well marking eyes, he conferred with Antiphilus as, by the authority he had, he found means to do, and agreed with him of the time and manner how he should by the death of some of his jailors escape.

'But all being well ordered, and Plangus willingly putting himself into the greatest danger, Antiphilus (who like a bladder swelled ready to break while it was full of the wind of prosperity, that being out, was so abjected as apt to be trod on by everybody) when it came to the point that with some hazard he might be in apparent likelihood to avoid the uttermost harm, his heart fainted, and, weak fool, neither hoping nor fearing as he should, gat a

* *attempted*: tried to win over.

conceit that with betraying this practice he might obtain pardon:
and therefore even a little before Plangus should have come unto
him, opened the whole practice to him that had the charge, with
unpitied tears idly protesting he had rather die by Artaxia's commandment than against her will escape; yet begging life upon any
the hardest and wretchedest conditions that she would lay upon
him. His keeper provided accordingly, so that when Plangus came,
he was like, himself, to have been entrapped, but that finding with
a lucky insight that it was discovered, he retired, and calling his
friends about him, stood upon his guard as he had good cause. For
Artaxia (accounting him most ungrateful, considering that her
brother and she had not only preserved him against the malice of
his father but ever used him much liker his birth than his fortune)
sent forces to apprehend him. But he among the martial men had
gotten so great love that he could not only keep himself from her
malice, but work in their minds a compassion of Erona's adversity.

'But for the succour of Antiphilus he could get nobody to join
with him, the contempt of him having not been able to qualify the
hatred, so that Artaxia might easily upon him perform her will;
which was (at the humble suit of all the women of that city) to
deliver him to their censure, who mortally hating him for having
made a law of polygamy, after many tortures, forced him to throw
himself from a high pyramid which was built over Tiridates'
tomb, and so to end his false-hearted life which had planted no
strong thought in him but that he could be unkind.

'But Plangus well perceiving that Artaxia stayed only for the
appointed day that the fair Erona's body, consumed to ashes,
should make a notorious testimony how deeply her brother's
death was engraven in her breast, he assembled good numbers of
friends whom his virtue, though a stranger, had tied unto him, by
force to give her liberty. Contrariwise, Artaxia, to whom anger
gave more courage than her sex did fear, used her regal authority
the most she could to suppress that sedition and have her will,
which, she thought, is the most princely thing that may be. But
Plangus (who indeed, as all men witness, is one of the best captains, both for policy and valour, that are trained in the school of
Mars) in a conflict overthrew Artaxia's power though of far
greater number; and there took prisoner a base son of her brother's

whom she dearly affected, and then sent her word, that he should run the same race of fortune, whatsover it was, that Erona did; and happy was that threatening for her, for else Artaxia had hastened the day of her death in respect of those tumults.

'But now (some principal noblemen of that country interposing themselves) it was agreed that all persons else fully pardoned, and all prisoners, except Erona, delivered, she should be put into the hands of a principal nobleman who had a castle of great strength, upon oath, if by the day two years from Tiridates' death, Pyrocles and Musidorus did not in person combat and overcome two knights, whom she appointed to maintain her quarrel against Erona and them of having by treason destroyed her brother, that then Erona should be that same day burned to ashes: but if they came, and had the victory, she should be delivered; but upon no occasion neither freed nor executed till that day. And hereto of both sides, all took solemn oath, and so the peace was concluded; they of Plangus' party forcing him to agree, though he himself the sooner condescended, knowing the courtesy of those two excellent princes not to refuse so noble a quarrel, and their power such as two more (like the other two) were not able to resist. But Artaxia was more, and upon better ground, pleased with this action; for she had even newly received news from Plexirtus that upon the sea he had caused them both to perish, and therefore she held herself sure of the match.

'But poor Plangus knew not so much, and therefore seeing his party (as most times it falls out in like case) hungry of any conditions of peace, accepted them: and then obtained leave of the lord that indifferently* kept her to visit Erona, whom he found full of desperate sorrow, suffering neither his* unworthiness, nor his wrongs, nor his death (which is the natural conclusion of all worldly acts) either to cover with forgetfulness or diminish with consideration the affection she had borne him; but even glorying in affliction and shunning all comfort, she seemed to have no delight but in making herself the picture of misery. So that when Plangus came to her, she fell in deadly trances, as if in him she had seen the death of Antiphilus because he had not succoured him: and yet (her virtue striving) she did at one time acknowledge herself

* *indifferently*: impartially. *neither his*: i.e. Antiphilus'.

bound and profess herself injured; instead of allowing the conclusion* they had made, or writing to the princes as he wished her
to do, craving nothing but some speedy death to follow her (in
spite of just hate) beloved Antiphilus.

'So that Plangus, having nothing but a ravished* kiss from her
hand at their parting, went away towards Greece whitherward he
understood the princes were embarked. But by the way it was his
fortune to intercept letters written by Artaxia to Plexirtus,
wherein she signified her accepting him to her husband, whom she
had ever favoured, so much the rather as he had performed the
conditions of her marriage in bringing to their deserved end her
greatest enemies: withal thanking the sea, in such terms as he
might well perceive it was by some treason wrought in Plexirtus'
ship. Whereupon, to make more diligent search, he took ship himself and came into Laconia enquiring and by his enquiry finding,
that such a ship was indeed with fight and fire perished, none,
almost, escaping. But for Pyrocles and Musidorus, it was assuredly
determined that they were cast away, for the name of such
princes, especially in Greece, would quickly else have been a large
witness to the contrary.

'Full of grief with that, for the loss of such who left the world
poor of perfection, but more sorry for Erona's sake who now by
them could not be relieved, a new advertisement from Armenia
overtook him which multiplied the force of his anguish. It was a
message from the nobleman who had Erona in ward, giving him to
understand that since his departure, Artaxia, using the benefit of
time, had beseiged him in his castle, demanding present delivery of
her whom yet for his faith given he would not before the day
appointed, if possibly he could resist – which he foresaw long he
should not do for want of victual which he had not so wisely
provided, because he trusted upon the general oath taken for two
years' space: and therefore willed him to make haste to his succour, and come with no small forces, for all they that were of his
side in Armenia were consumed, and Artaxia had increased her
might by marriage of Plexirtus, who, now crowned king there,
sticked not to glory in the murder of Pyrocles and Musidorus, as

* *allowing the conclusions*: accepting the justice of. *ravished*: unwillingly granted.

having just cause thereto in respect of the deaths of his sister Andromana, her son, his nephew and his own daughter Zelmane, all whose loss he unjustly charged them withal, and now openly sticked not to confess what a revenge his wit had brought forth.

'Plangus, much astonished herewith, bethought himself what to do, for to return to Armenia was vain since his friends there were utterly overthrown. Then thought he of going to his father; but he had already, even since the death of his stepmother and brother, attempted the recovering his favour, and all in vain. For they that had before joined with Andromana to do him the wrong thought now no life for them if he returned, and therefore kept him still, with new forged suspicions, odious to his father. So that Plangus, reserving that for a work of longer time than the saving of Erona could bear, determined to go to the mighty and good king Euarchus; who lately having, to his eternal fame, fully not only conquered his enemies but established good government in their countries, he hoped he might have present succour of him, both for the justness of the cause and revenge of his children's death, by so heinous a treason murdered. Therefore with diligence he went to him, and by the way (passing through my country) it was my hap to find him, the most overthrown man with grief that ever I hope to see again. For still it seemed he had Erona at a stake before his eyes, such an apprehension he had taken of her danger, which in despite of all the comfort I could give him, he poured out in such lamentations that I was moved not to let him pass till he had made a full declaration, which by pieces my daughters and I have delivered unto you. Fain he would have had succour of myself, but the course of my life being otherwise bent, I only accompanied him with some that might safely guide him to the great Euarchus; for my part having had some of his speeches so feelingly in my memory that at an idle time, as I told you, I set them down dialogue-wise in such manner as you have seen.[1] And thus, excellent lady, I have obeyed you in this story; wherein if it well please you to consider what is the strange power of love and what is due to his authority, you shall exercise therein the true nobleness of your judgement, and do the more right to the unfortunate historian.'

Zelmane, sighing for Erona's sake, yet inwardly comforted in that she assured herself Euarchus would not spare to take in hand the just delivering of her joined with the just revenge of his children's loss, having now what she desired of Basilius, to avoid his further discourses of affection encouraged the shepherds to begin, whom she saw already ready for them.


### THE SECOND ECLOGUES

The rude tumult of the Enispians gave occasion to the honest shepherds to begin their Pastorals this day with a dance, which they called the skirmish betwixt Reason and Passion. For seven shepherds (which were named the reasonable shepherds) joined themselves; four of them making a square and the other two going a little wide of either side, like wings for the main battle, and the seventh man foremost, like the forlorn hope, to begin the skirmish. In like order came out the seven appassionated shepherds, all keeping the pace of their foot by their voice, and sundry consorted instruments they held in their arms. And first, the foremost of the Reasonable side began to sing:

REASON: Thou rebel vile, come, to thy master yield.

And the other that met with him answered:

PASSION: No, tyrant, no; mine, mine shall be the field.
R: Can Reason then a tyrant counted be?
P: If Reason will that Passions be not free.
R: But Reason will that Reason govern most.
P: And Passion will that Passion rule the roast.*
R: Your will is will, but Reason reason is.
P: Will hath his will when Reason's will doth miss.
R: Whom Passion leads unto his death is bent.
P: And let him die, so that he die content.
R: By nature you to Reason faith have sworn.
P: Not so, but fellow-like together born.
R: Who Passion doth ensue* lives in annoy.
P: Who Passion doth forsake lives void of joy.
R: Passion is blind, and treads an unknown trace.
P: Reason hath eyes to see his own ill case.

* *rule the roast:* be head of the table, i.e. be master. *ensue:* follow.

Then as they approached nearer, the two of Reason's side, as if they shot at the other, thus sang:

R: Dare Passions then abide in Reason's light?
P: And is not Reason dimmed with Passion's might?
R: O foolish thing, which glory doth destroy!
P: O glorious title of a foolish toy!
R: Weakness you are, dare you with our strength fight?
P: Because our weakness weakeneth all your might.
R: O sacred Reason, help our virtuous toils.
P: O Passion, pass on feeble Reason's spoils.
R: We with ourselves abide a daily strife.
P: We gladly use the sweetness of our life.
R: But yet our strife sure peace in end doth breed.
P: We now have peace, your peace we do not need.

Then did the two square battles meet, and instead of fighting, embrace one another, singing thus:

R: We are too strong: but Reason seeks not blood.
P: Who be too weak do feign they be too good.
R: Though we cannot o'ercome, our cause is just.
P: Let us o'ercome, and let us be unjust.
R: Yet Passion, yield at length to Reason's stroke.
P: What shall we win by taking Reason's yoke?
R: The joys you have shall be made permanent.
P: But so we shall with grief learn to repent.
R: Repent indeed, but that shall be your bliss.
P: How know we that, since present joys we miss?
R: You know it not; of Reason therefore know it.
P: No Reason yet had ever skill to show it.
R, P: Then let us both to heavenly rules give place,
    Which Passions kill, and Reason do deface.[1]

Then embraced they one another and came to the king, who framed his praises of them according to Zelmane's liking; whose unrestrained parts, the mind and eye, had their free course to the delicate Philoclea, whose look was not short in well requiting it although she knew it was a hateful sight to her jealous mother. But Dicus (that had in this time taken a great liking of Dorus for the good parts he found above his age in him) had a delight to taste the fruits of his wit, though in a subject which he himself most of all other despised; and so entered to speech with him in the manner of this following eclogue:

## DICUS · DORUS

DICUS: Dorus, tell me, where is thy wonted motion,
　To make those woods resound thy lamentation?
　Thy saint is dead, or dead is thy devotion.
　For who doth hold his love in estimation,
　To witness that he thinks his thoughts delicious,
　Seeks to make* each thing badge of his sweet passion.

DORUS: But what doth make thee, Dicus, so suspicious
　Of my due faith, which needs must be immutable?
　Who others' virtue doubt, themselves are vicious.
　Not so; although my metal were most mutable,
　Her beams have wrought therein most sure impression.
　To such a force soon change were nothing suitable.

DICUS: The heart well set doth never shun confession:
　If noble be thy bands, make them notorious:
　Silence doth seem the mask of base oppression:
　Who glories in his love doth make love glorious.
　　But who doth fear, or bideth mute wilfully,
　Shows guilty heart doth deem his state opprobrious.
　　Thou then, that fram'st both words and voice most skilfully,
　Yield to our ears a sweet and sound relation
　If love* took thee by force, or caught thee guilefully.

DORUS: If sunny beams shame heavenly habitation,
　If three-leav'd grass seem to the sheep unsavoury,
　　Then base and sour is love's most high vocation.
　Or if sheep's cries can help the sun's own bravery,
　　Then may I hope, my pipe may have ability
　To help her praise, who decks me in her slavery.
　　No, no; no words ennoble self-nobility.

* *seeks to make*: Ringler, OA, '90, '93: 'Thinks'. *if love*: whether love.

As for your doubts, her voice was it deceived me,
  Her eyes the force beyond my possibility.

DICUS: Thy words well voic'd, well grac'd, had almost heaved me
  Quite from myself, to love love's contemplation;
  Till of these thoughts thy sudden end bereaved me.
  Go on therefore, and tell us by what fashion,
  In thy own proof he gets so strange possession,
  And how, possessed, he strengthens his invasion.

DORUS: Sight is his root, in thought is his progression,
  His childhood wonder, prenticeship attention,
  His youth delight, his age the soul's oppression:
  Doubt is his sleep, he waketh in invention;
  Fancy his food, his clothing is of carefulness;
  Beauty his book, his play lovers' dissension:
  His eyes are curious search, but veiled with warefulness;
  His wings desire, oft clipped with desperation.
  Largess, his hands, could never skill of sparefulness.[2]
  But how he doth by might, or by persuasion
  To conquer, and his conquest how to ratify,
  Experience doubts, and schools hold disputation.

DICUS: But so thy sheep may thy good wishes satisfy
  With large increase, and wool of fine perfection,
  So she thy love, her eyes thy eyes may gratify
  As thou wilt give our souls a dear refection,*
  By telling how she was, how now she framed is
  To help, or hurt in thee her own infection.[3]

DORUS: Blest be the name wherewith my mistress named is:
  Whose wounds are salves,* whose yokes* please more than
      pleasure doth:
  Her stains are beams: virtue the fault she blamed is,
  The heart, eye, ear, here only find his treasure doth.
  All numbering arts her endless graces number not:
  Time, place, life, wit, scarcely her rare gifts measure doth.

* *refection*: recreation. *salves*: means of healing. *yokes*: burdens.

410

Is she in rage? So is the sun in summer hot,
Yet harvest brings. Doth she, alas, absent herself?
The sun is hid; his kindly shadows cumber not.
But when to give some grace she doth content herself,
O then it shines; then are the heavens distributed,
And Venus seems, to make up her, she spent herself.[4]
Thus then, I say, my mischiefs have contributed
A greater good by her divine reflection;
My harms to me, my bliss to her attributed.
Thus she is framed: her eyes are my direction,
Her love my life, her anger my instruction:*
Lastly, what so she is, that's my protection.

DICUS: Thy safety sure is wrapped in destruction,
For that construction thine own words do bear.
A man to fear a woman's moody eye,
Makes reason lie a slave to servile sense,
A weak defence where weakness is thy force:
So is remorse in folly dearly bought.

DORUS: If I had thought to hear blasphemous words,
My breast to swords, my soul to hell have sold
I rather would, than thus mine ears defile
With words so vile, which viler breath doth breed.
O herds take heed; for I a wolf* have found,
Who hunting round the strongest for to kill,
His breast doth fill with earth of others' woe,
And loaden so pulls down, pull'd down destroys.
O shepherds' boys, eschew those tongues of venom
Which do envenom both the soul and senses;
Our best defences are to fly these adders.
O tongues like ladders made to climb dishonour,
Who judge that honour which hath scope to slander!

DICUS: Dorus you wander far in great reproaches;
So love encroaches on your charmed reason,

*instruction: Ringler, OA. '90, '93, 'destruction'. wolf: for this
hunting habit of wolves see Pliny, Natural History, VIII, 34, on 'stag
wolves'.

But it is season for to end our singing,
Such anger bringing: as for me, my fancy
In sick-man's frenzy rather takes compassion
Than rage for rage: rather my wish I send to thee
Thou soon may have some help, or change of passion:
She oft her looks, the stars her favour bend to thee:
Fortune store, nature health, love grant persuasion.
A quiet mind none but thyself can lend to thee,
Thus I commend to thee all our former love.


DORUS: Well do I prove, error lies oft in zeal,
Yet it is seal,* though error of true heart.
Nought could impart such heats to friendly mind,
But for to find thy words did her disgrace,
Whose only face the little heaven is:
   Which who doth miss, his eyes are but delusions,
Barred from their chiefest object of delightfulness,
Thrown on this earth, the chaos of confusions.
   As for thy wish to my enraged spitefulness,
The lovely blow with rare reward, my prayer is
Thou may'st love her, that I may see thy sightfulness.
   The quiet mind (whereof myself impairer is,
As thou dost think) should most of all disquiet me
Without her love, than any mind who fairer is.[5]
   Her only cure from surfeit-woes can diet me:
She holds the balance of my contentation:
Her cleared eyes, nought else, in storms can quiet me.
   Nay rather than my ease discontentation
Should breed to her, let me for aye dejected be
From any joy, which might her grief occasion.
   With so sweet plagues my happy harms infected be:
Pain wills me die, yet will of death I mortify:
For though life irks, in life my loves protected be.
Thus for each change my changeless heart I fortify.


When they had ended, to the good pleasing of the assistants,*
especially of Zelmane, who never forgat to give due com-
      * seal: sigh. assistants: audience.

mendations to her friend Dorus, Basilius called Lamon to end his discourse of Strephon and Claius, wherewith the other day he marked Zelmane to have been exceedingly delighted. But him sickness had stayed from that assembly; which gave occasion to Histor and Damon, two young shepherds, taking upon them the two friendly rivals' names, to present Basilius with some other of their complaints eclogue-wise, and first with this double Sestine.

### STREPHON · CLAIUS[6]

STREPHON: Ye goat-herd gods, that love the grassy mountains,
  Ye nymphs that haunt the springs in pleasant valleys,
  Ye satyrs joy'd with free and quiet forests,
  Vouchsafe your silent ears to plaining music,
  Which to my woes gives still an early morning,
  And draws the dolour on till weary evening.

CLAIUS: O Mercury, foregoer* to the evening,
  O heavenly huntress* of the savage mountains,
  O lovely star,* entitled of the morning,
  While that my voice doth fill these woeful valleys,
  Vouchsafe your silent ears to plaining music
  Which oft hath Echo tired in secret forests.

STREPHON: I that was once free-burgess* of the forests,
  Where shade from sun, and sport I sought at evening,
  I that was once esteem'd for pleasant music,
  Am banish'd now among the monstrous mountains
  Of huge despair, and foul affliction's valleys,
  Am grown a screech-owl to myself each morning.

CLAIUS: I that was once delighted every morning,
  Hunting the wild inhabiters of forests:
  I that was once the music of these valleys
  So darken'd am, that all my day is evening;
  Heart-broken so, that molehills seem high mountains,
  And fill the vales with cries instead of music.

*foregoer: forerunner. *heavenly huntress*: Diana, the moon. *lovely star*: Lucifer, the morning star. *free-burgess*: a free citizen.

STREPHON: Long since, alas, my deadly swannish music[7]
   Hath made itself a crier of the morning:
   And hath with wailing strength climb'd highest mountains.
   Long since my thoughts more desert be than forests:
   Long since I see my joys come to their evening,
   And state thrown down to over-trodden valleys.

CLAIUS: Long since the happy dwellers of these valleys
   Have pray'd me leave my strange exclaiming music,
   Which troubles their day's work, and joys of evening:
   Long since I hate the night, more hate the morning:
   Long since my thoughts chase me like beasts in forests,
   And make me wish myself laid under mountains.

STREPHON: Me seems I see the high and stately mountains
   Transform themselves to low dejected valleys:
   Me seems I hear in these ill-changed forests,
   The Nightingales do learn of Owls their music:
   Me seems I feel the comfort of the morning,
   Turn'd to the mortal serene of an evening.

CLAIUS: Me seems I see a filthy cloudy evening,
   As soon as sun begins to climb the mountains:
   Me seems I feel a noisome scent, the morning
   When I do smell the flowers of these valleys:
   Me seems I hear, when I do hear sweet music,
   The dreadful cries of murder'd men in forests.

STREPHON: I wish to fire the trees of all these forests;
   I give the sun a last farewell each evening;
   I curse the fiddling finders out of music:
   With envy I do hate the lofty mountains;
   And with despite despise the humble valleys:
   I do detest night, evening, day and morning.

CLAIUS: Curse to myself my prayer is, the morning;
   My fire is more than can be made with forests;

My state more base than are the basest valleys:
I wish no evenings more to see, each evening;
Shamed I hate myself in sight of mountains,
And stop mine ears lest I grow mad with music.

STREPHON: For she whose parts maintain'd a perfect music,
Whose beauty shin'd more than the blushing morning,
Who much did pass in state the stately mountains,
In straightness pass'd the cedars of the forests,
Hath cast me, wretch, into eternal evening,
By taking her two suns* from these dark valleys.

CLAIUS: For she, with whom compar'd, the alps are valleys,
She, whose least word brings from the spheres their music,
At whose approach the sun rose in the evening,
Who, where she went, bare in her forehead morning,
Is gone, is gone, from those our spoiled forests,
Turning to deserts our best pastur'd mountains.

STREPHON: These mountains witness shall, so shall these
        valleys,
These forests eke,* made wretched by our music.

CLAIUS: Our morning hymn is this, and song at evening.

But as though all this had been but the taking of a taste of their
wailings, Strephon again began this Dizain which was answered
unto him in that kind of verse which is called the crown.[8]


STREPHON · CLAIUS

STREPHON: I joy in grief, and do detest all joys;
    Despise delight, am tir'd with thought of ease:
    I turn my mind to all forms of annoys,
    And with the change of them my fancy please.
    I study that which may me most displease,
    And in despite of that displeasure's might,

* *her two suns*: her eyes. *eke*: also.

Embrace that most, that most my soul destroys;
Blinded with beams, fell darkness is my sight;
Dwell in my ruins, feed with sucking smart;
I think from me, not from my woes to part.

CLAIUS: I think from me, not from my woes to part,
  And loath this time call'd life, nay think that life
  Nature to me for torment did impart;
  Think my hard haps have blunted death's sharp knife,
  Not sparing me,* in whom his works be rife:
  And thinking this, think Nature, Life and Death
  Place Sorrow's triumph on my conquered heart,
  Whereto I yield, and seek none other breath
  But from the scent of some infectious grave:
  Nor of my fortune aught but mischief crave.

STREPHON: Nor of my fortune aught but mischief crave,
  And seek to nourish that, which now contains
  All what I am: if I myself will save,
  Then must I save what in me chiefly reigns,
  Which is the hateful web of Sorrow's pains.
  Sorrow then cherish me, for I am Sorrow:
  No being now but Sorrow I can have:
  Then deck me as thine own; thy help I borrow,
  Since thou my riches art, and that thou hast
  Enough to make a fertile mind lie waste.

CLAIUS: Enough to make a fertile mind lie waste
  Is that huge storm, which pours itself on me:
  Hailstones of tears, of sighs a monstrous blast,
  Thunders of cries; lightning my wild looks be,
  The darkened heav'n my soul, which nought can see;
  The flying sprites which trees by roots uptear
  Be those despairs which have my hopes quite rased.
  The difference is: all folks those storms forbear,
  But I cannot; who then myself should fly,
  So close unto myself my wracks do lie.

  * *not sparing me*: i.e. not releasing me from torment, by death.

STREPHON: So close unto myself my wracks do lie,
 Both cause, effect, beginning, and the end
 Are all in me: what help then can I try?
 My ship, myself, whose course to Love doth bend,
 Sore beaten doth her mast of Comfort spend:
 Her cable, Reason, breaks from anchor Hope:
 Fancy, her tackling, torn away doth fly:
 Ruin, the wind, hath blown her from her scope:
 Bruised with waves of Cares, but broken is
 On rock Despair, the burial of my Bliss.

CLAIUS: On rock Despair, the burial of my Bliss,
 I long do plough with plough of deep Desire:
 The seed Fast-meaning is, no truth to miss:
 I harrow it with Thoughts, which all conspire
 Favour to make my chief and only hire.
 But woe is me, the year is gone about,
 And now I fain would reap, I reap but this,
 Hate fully grown, Absence new sprungen out.
 So that I see, although my sight impair,
 Vain is their pain, who labour in Despair.

STREPHON: Vain is their pain, who labour in Despair.
 For so did I, when with my angle, Will,
 I sought to catch the fish Torpedo fair.[9]
 Ev'n then Despair did Hope already kill:
 Yet Fancy would perforce employ his skill,
 And this hath got; the catcher now is caught.
 Lam'd with the angle, which itself did bear,
 And unto Death, quite drown'd in Dolors, brought
 To Death, as then disguis'd in her fair face:
 Thus, thus, alas, I had my loss in chase.*

CLAIUS: Thus, thus, alas, I had my loss in chase,
 When first that crowned Basilisk I knew,[10]
 Whose footsteps I with kisses oft did trace,
 Till by such hap, as I must ever rue,

    *in chase: while pursuing.

Mine eyes did light upon her shining hue,
And hers on me, astonish'd with that sight.
Since then my heart did lose his wonted place,
Infected so with her sweet poison's might,
That, leaving me for dead, to her it went:
But ah, her flight hath my dead reliques spent.*

STREPHON: But ah, her flight hath my dead reliques spent,
Her flight, from me, from me, though dead to me,
Yet living still in her, while her beams lent
Such vital spark, that her mine eyes might see.
But now those living lights absented be,
Full dead before, I now to dust should fall,
But that eternal pains my soul have hent,*
And keep it still within this body thrall,
That thus I must, while in this death I dwell,
In earthly fetters feel a lasting hell.

CLAIUS: In earthly fetters feel a lasting hell
Alas, I do; from which to find release,
I would the earth, I would the heavens sell.*
But vain it is to think those pains should cease,
Where life is death, and death cannot breed peace.
O fair, O only fair, from thee alas,
Those foul, most foul disasters to me fell;
Since thou from me (O me) O sun did'st pass.
Therefore esteeming all good blessings toys,
I joy in grief, and do detest all joys.

STREPHON: I joy in grief, and do detest all joys,
But now an end, O Claius, now an end,
For even the herbs our hateful music stroys,*
And from our burning breath the trees do bend.

So well were these wailful complaints accorded to the passions
of all the princely hearers, while every one made what he heard of

* *spent:* consumed. *hent:* seized. *sell:* Ringler, '93. OA, '90, 'fell'.
*stroys:* destroys.

another the balance of his own fortune, that they stood a long while stricken in sad and silent consideration of them. Which the old Geron no more marking than condemning in them, desirous to set forth what counsels the wisdom of age had laid up in store against such fancies, (as he thought) follies of youth, yet so as it might not appear that his words respected* them, bending himself to a young shepherd named Philisides[11] (who neither had danced nor sung with them, and had all this time lain upon the ground at the foot of a cypress tree, leaning upon his elbow with so deep a melancholy that his senses carried to his mind no delight from any of their objects) he strake him upon the shoulder with a right old man's grace that will seem livelier than his age will afford him. And thus began unto him this eclogue.

### GERON · PHILISIDES

GERON: Up, up, Philisides, let sorrows go,
  Who yields to woe, doth but increase his smart.
  Do not thy heart to plaintful custom bring,
  But let us sing; sweet tunes do passions ease;
  An old man hear who would thy fancies raise.

PHILISIDES: Who minds to please the mind drown'd in annoys
  With outward joys, which inly cannot sink,
  As well may think with oil to cool the fire;
  Or with desire to make such foe a friend,
  Who doth his soul to endless malice bend.

GERON: Yet sure an end to each thing time doth give;
  Though woes now live, at length thy woes must die.
  Then virtue try, if she can work in thee
  That which we see in many time hath wrought,
  And weakest hearts to constant temper brought.

PHILISIDES: Who ever taught a skilless* man to teach,
  Or stop a breach that never cannon saw?[12]
  Sweet virtue's law bars not a causeful moan.

*respected*: were directed at. *skilless*: ignorant.

Time shall in one my life and sorrows end,
And me perchance your constant temper lend.

GERON: What can amend where physick is refus'd?
The wits abused with will no counsel take.
Yet for my sake discover us thy grief.
Oft comes relief when most we seem in trap.
The stars thy state, fortune may change thy hap.

PHILISIDES: If fortune's lap became my dwelling place,
And all the stars conspired to my good,
Still were I one, this still should be my case,
Ruin's relique, care's web, and sorrow's food;
Since she, fair fierce, to such a state me calls,
Whose wit the stars, whose fortune fortune thralls.*

GERON: Alas what falls are fall'n unto thy mind,
That there where thou confessed thy mischief lies,
Thy wit dost use still still more harms to find.
Whom wit makes vain, or blinded with his eyes,
What counsel can prevail, or light give light,
Since all his force against himself he tries?
Then each conceit that enters in his sight
Is made, forsooth, a jurate* of his woes,
Earth, sea, air, fire, heaven, hell, and ghastly spright.
Then cries to senseless things, which neither knows
What aileth thee, and if they knew thy mind,
Would scorn in man, their king, such feeble shows.
Rebel, rebel; in golden fetters bind
This tyrant love; or rather do suppress
Those rebel-thoughts, which are thy slaves by kind.
Let not a glittering name thy fancy dress
In painted clothes; because they call it love:
There is no hate that can thee more oppress.
Begin (and half the work is done) to prove
By rising up, upon thyself to stand,
And think she is a she, that doth thee move.

* *thralls*: enslaves. *jurate*: sworn fitness.

He water ploughs, and soweth in the sand,
And hopes the flickering wind with net to hold,
Who hath his hopes laid up in woman's hand.
What man is he that hath his freedom sold?
Is he a manlike man that doth not know man
Hath power that sex with bridle to withhold?
A fickle sex, and true in trust to no man,
A servant sex, soon proud if they be coy'd:*
And to conclude, thy mistress is a woman.

PHILISIDES: O gods, how long this old fool hath annoy'd
My wearied ears! O gods, yet grant me this,
That soon the world of his false tongue be void.
O noble age who place their only bliss
In being heard until the hearer die,
Uttering a serpent's mind with serpent's hiss.
Then who will hear a well-authorized lie
(And patience hath) let him go learn of him
What swarms of virtues did in his youth fly;
Such hearts of brass, wise heads, and garments trim
Were in his days: which heard, one nothing hears,
If from his words the falsehood he do skim.
And herein most their folly vain appears,
That since they still allege, 'When they were young,'
It shows they fetch their wit from youthful years.
Like beast for sacrifice, where save the tongue
And belly, nought is left, such sure is he,
This live-dead man in this old dungeon flung.
Old houses are thrown down for new we see:
The oldest rams are culled from the flock:
No man doth wish his horse should aged be;
The ancient oak well makes a fired block:
Old men themselves do love young wives to choose:
Only fond youth admires a rotten stock.
Who once a white long beard well handle does
(As his beard him, not he his beard did bare)
Though cradle-witted, must not honour lose.

*coy'd: courted.

O when will men leave off to judge by hair,
And think them old that have the oldest mind,
With virtue fraught, and full of holy fear!

GERON: If that thy face were hid, or I were blind,
I yet should know a young man speaketh now,
Such wandering reasons in thy speech I find.
He is a beast, that beast's use will allow
For proof of man who, sprung of heav'nly fire,
Hath strongest soul when most his reins* do bow.
But fondlings fond know not your own desire,
Loth to die young, and when you must be old,
Fondly blame that to which yourselves aspire.
But this light choler that doth make you bold,
Rather to wrong than unto just defence,
Is past with me, my blood is waxen cold.
Thy words, though full of malapert* offence,
I weigh them not, but still will thee advise
How thou from foolish love mayest purge thy sense.
First think they err, that think them gaily wise
Who well can set a passion out to show:
Such sight have they that see with goggling eyes.
Passion bears high when puffing wit doth blow,
But is indeed a toy; if not a toy,
True cause of evils, and cause of causeless woe.
If once thou mayest that fancy gloss destroy
Within thyself, thou soon wilt be ashamed
To be a player of thine own annoy.
Then let thy mind with better books be tamed;
Seek to espy her faults as well as praise,
And let thine eyes to other sports be framed.
In hunting fearful beasts, do spend some days,
Or catch the birds with pit-falls or with lime,
Or train the fox that trains so crafty lays.
Lie but to sleep, and in the early prime
Seek skill of herbs in hills, haunt brooks near night,

*reins: loins. *malapert*: impudent.

And try with bait how fish will bite sometime.
Go graft again, and seek to graft them right,
Those pleasant plants, those sweet and fruitful trees,
Which both the palate and the eyes delight.
Cherish the hives of wisely painful bees;
Let special care upon thy flock be stayed;
Such active mind but seldom passion sees.

PHILISIDES: Hath any man heard what this old man said?
Truly not I, who did my thoughts engage
Where all my pains one look of her hath paid.

Geron was even out of countenance, finding the words he
thought were so wise win so little reputation at this young man's
hands; and therefore sometimes looking upon an old acquaintance
of his called Mastix (one of the repiningest fellows in the world,
and that beheld nobody but with a mind of mislike) saying still
the world was amiss but how it should be amended he knew not,
sometimes casting his eyes to the ground, even ashamed to see his
grey hairs despised; at last he spied his two dogs whereof the elder
was called Melampus and the younger Lelaps (indeed the jewels
he ever had with him) one brawling with another; which occasion
he took to restore himself to his countenance, and rating Melampus, he began to speak to his dogs as if in them a man should
find more obedience than in unbridled young men.

### GERON · MASTIX[13]

GERON: Down, down, Melampus; what? Your fellow bite?
I set you o'er the flock I dearly love,
Them to defend, not with yourselves to fight.
Do you not think this will the wolves remove
From former fear they had of your good minds,
When they shall such divided weakness prove?
What if Lelaps a better morsel finds
Than thou erst knew? Rather take part with him
Than jarl.* Lo, lo, even these how envy blinds.

* jarl: quarrel.

And thou, Lelaps, let not pride make thee brim*
Because thou hast thy fellow overgone,
But thank the cause; thou seest where he is dim.
Here Lelaps, here; indeed, against the foen*
Of my good sheep thou never truce-time took:
Be as thou art, but be with mine at one.
For though Melampus like a wolf do look
(For age doth make him of a wolfish hue)
Yet have I seen, when well a wolf he shook.
Fool that I am, that with my dogs speak Grew.*
Come near good Mastix, 'tis now full tway score
Of years, alas, since I good Mastix knew.
Thou heard'st even now a young man sneb* me sore,
Because I red* him, as I would my son.
Youth will have will; age must to age therefore.

MASTIX: What marvel if in youth such fault be done,
Since that we see our saddest* shepherds out,*
Who have their lesson so long time begun?
Quickly secure, and easily in doubt,
Either asleep be all, if nought assail,
Or all abroad if but a cub start out.
We shepherds are like them that under sail
Do speak high words, when all the coast is clear,
Yet to a passenger will bonnet vail.[14]*
'I con thee thank' to whom thy dogs be dear,[15]
But commonly like curs we them entreat,*
Save when great need of them perforce appear;
Then him we kiss, whom late before we beat
With such intemperance, that each way grows
Hate of the first, contempt of later feat.
And such discord 'twixt greatest shepherds flows,
That sport it is to see with how great art,
By justice' work they their own faults disclose:
Like busy boys, to win their tutor's heart,

* brim: fierce. foen: foes. Grew: Greek. sneb: snub. red: counselled.
saddest: soberest. out: wrong. bonnet vail: doff our caps. entreat: treat.

One saith, 'he mocks'; another saith, 'he plays',
The third his lesson missed, till all do smart.
As for the rest, how shepherds spend their days,
At blow-point,* hot-cockles, or else at keels,
While, 'Let us pass our time,' each shepherd says.
So small account of time the shepherd feels,
And doth not feel that life is nought but time,
And when that time is past, death holds his heels.
To age thus do they draw their youthful prime,
Knowing no more than what poor trial shows,
As fish sure trial hath of muddy slime.
This pattern good unto our children goes,
For what they see their parents love or hate
Their first-caught sense prefers to teachers' blows.
Those cocklings* cockered* we bewail too late,
When that we see our offspring gaily bent,
Women man-wood,* and men effeminate.

GERON: Fie man, fie man: what words hath thy tongue lent?
Yet thou art mickle* worse then ere was I;
Thy too much zeal, I fear thy brain hath spent.
We oft are angrier with the feeble fly
For business, where it pertains him not,
Than with the poisonous toads that quiet lie.
I pray thee what hath e'er the Parrot got
And yet they say he talks in great men's bowers?
   A cage, gilded perchance, is all his lot.
Who of his tongue the liquor gladly pours,
A good fool called with pain perhaps may be,
But even for that shall suffer mighty lours.
Let swan's example sicker* serve for thee,
Who once all birds in sweetly singing passed,*
But now to silence turned his minstrelsy.
For he would sing, that others were defaced:

*blow-point, etc., children's games. *cocklings:* young cockerels.
*cockered:* pampered. *man-wood:* as fierce as men. *mickle:* much.
*sicker:* surely. *passed:* surpassed.

The Peacock's pride, the Pie's* piled* flattery,
Cormorant's glut, Kite's spoil, Kingfisher's waste,
The Falcon's fierceness, Sparrow's lechery,
The Cuckoo's shame, the Goose's good intent,
Even Turtle touched he with hypocrisy,
And worse of other more; till by assent
Of all the birds, but namely* those were grieved,
Of fowls there called was a Parliament.
There was the Swan of dignity deprived,
And statute made he never should have voice,
Since when, I think, he hath in silence lived.
I warn thee therefore (since thou may'st have choice)
Let not thy tongue become a fiery match;
No sword so bites as that evil tool annoys.
Let our unpartial eyes a little watch
Our own demean, and soon we wonder shall
That, hunting faults, ourselves we did not catch.
Into our minds let us a little fall,
And we shall find more spots than Leopard's skin.
Then who makes us such Judges over all?
But farewell now, thy fault is no great sin,
Come, come my curs, 'tis late, I will go in.

And away with his dogs straight he went, as if he would be sure to have the last word; all the assembly laughing at the lustiness of the old fellow, who departed muttering to himself he had seen more in his days than twenty of them. But Basilius, who never before had heard Philisides,[16] though having seldom failed to be at these meetings, desired him he would begin some eclogue with some other of the shepherds, according to the accustomed guise. Philisides, though very unwilling, at the king's commandment offered to sing with Thyrsis. But he directly refused him, seeing he should within few days be married to the fair Kala; and since he had gotten his desire, he would sing no more. Then the king willed Philisides to declare the discourse of his own fortunes, unknown to them, as being a stranger in that country; but he prayed the king to pardon him, the time being far too

* *Pie:* magpie. *piled:* piled-on. *namely:* especially.

joyful to suffer the rehearsal of his miseries. But to satisfy Basilius some way, he began an eclogue betwixt himself and the Echo, framing his voice so in those desert places, as what words he would have the Echo reply unto, those he would sing higher than the rest; and so kindly framed a disputation betwixt himself and it, which with these Hexameters in the following order he uttered.

### PHILISIDES · ECHO

| PHILISIDES | ECHO |
|---|---|
| PHILISIDES Fair rocks, goodly rivers, sweet woods, when shall I see peace? | *Peace.* |
| Peace? What bars me my tongue? Who is it that comes me so nigh? | *I.* |
| Oh! I do know what guest I have met; it is Echo. | *'Tis Echo.* |
| Well met echo, approach: then tell me thy will too. | *I will too.* |
| Echo, what do I get yielding my sprite to my griefs? | *Griefs.* |
| What medicine may I find for a grief that draws me to death? | *Death.* |
| O poisonous medicine! What worse to me can be than it? | *It.* |
| In what state was I then, when I took this deadly disease? | *Ease.* |
| And what manner a mind which had to that humour a vein? | *Vain.* |
| Hath not reason enough vehemence the desire to reprove? | *Prove.* |
| Oft prove I: but what salve, when reason seeks to be gone? | *One.* |
| Oh, what is it, what is it that may be a salve to my love? | *Love.* |
| What do lovers seek for, long seeking for to enjoy? | *Joy.* |
| What be the joys, for which to enjoy they went to the pains? | *Pains.* |

| PHILISIDES | ECHO |
|---|---|
| Then to an earnest love what doth best victory lend? | *End.* |
| End? But I can never end; love will not give me leave. | *Leave.* |
| How be the minds dispos'd that cannot taste thy physick? | *Sick.* |
| Yet say again thy advice for the evils that I told thee. | *I told thee.* |
| Doth th' infected wretch of his harm th' extremity know? | *No.* |
| But if he know not his harms, what guides hath he while he be blind? | *Blind.* |
| What blind guides can he have that leans to a fancy? | *A fancy.* |
| Can fancies want eyes, or he fall that steppeth aloft? | *Oft.* |
| What causes first made these torments on me to light? | *Light.* |
| Can then a cause be so light that forceth a man to go die? | *Aye.* |
| Yet tell what light thing I had in me to draw me to die? | *Eye.* |
| Eye-sight made me to yield; but what first pierc'd to my eyes? | *Eyes.* |
| Eyes' hurters, eyes hurt; but what from them to me falls? | *Falls.* |
| But when I first did fall, what brought most fall to my heart? | *Art.* |
| Art? What can be that art that thou dost mean by thy speech? | *Speech.* |
| What be the fruits of speaking art? What grows by the words? | *Words.* |
| O much more than words: those words serv'd more me to bless. | *Less.* |
| O when shall I be known, where most to be known I do long? | *Long.* |

| PHILISIDES | ECHO |
|---|---|
| Long be thy woes for such news, but how recks she my thoughts? | *Oughts.\** |
| Then then what do I gain, since unto her will I do wind? | *Wind.* |
| Wind, tempests, and storms, yet in end what gives she desire? | *Ire.* |
| Silly reward! Yet among women hath she of virtue the most. | *Most.* |
| What great name may I give to so heav'nly a woman? | *A Woe-man.* |
| Woe but seems to me joy, that agrees to my thought so. | *I thought so.* |
| Think so, for of my desired bliss it is only the course. | *Curse.* |
| Curs'd be thyself for cursing that which leads me to joys. | *Toys.* |
| What be the sweet creatures where lowly demands be not heard? | *Hard.*[17] |
| What makes them be unkind? Speak for th' hast narrowly pry'd | *Pride.* |
| Whence can pride come there, since springs of beauty be thence? | *Thence.* |
| Horrible is this blasphemy unto the most holy. | *O lie.* |
| Thou liest false echo, their minds as virtue be just. | *Just.* |
| Mock'st thou those diamonds which only be match'd by the gods? | *Odds.* |
| Odds? What an odds is there since them to the heav'ns I prefer? | *Err.* |
| Tell yet again me the names of these fair form'd to do evils. | *Devils.* |
| Devils? If in hell such devils do abide, to the hells I do go. | *Go.* |

Philisides was commended for the placing of his echo; but little did he regard their praises, who had set the foundation of his

* *oughts: nothings.*

honour there where he was most despised: and therefore returning again to the train of his desolate pensiveness, Zelmane seeing nobody offer to fill the stage, as if her long restrained conceits did now burst out of prison, she thus (desiring her voice should be accorded to nothing but to Philoclea's ears) threw down the burden of her mind in Anacreon's* kind of verses.

> My muse, what ails this ardour,
> To blaze* my only secrets?
> Alas, it is no glory
> To sing my own decayed state;
> Alas, it is no comfort
> To speak without an answer;
> Alas, it is no wisdom
> To show the wound without cure.
>
> My muse, what ails this ardour?
> Mine eyes be dim, my limbs shake,
> My voice is hoarse, my throat scorched,
> My tongue to this my roof cleaves,
> My fancy amazed, my thoughts dulled,
> My heart doth ache, my life faints,
> My soul begins to take leave:
> So great a passion all feel
> To think a sore so deadly
> I should so rashly rip up.
>
> My muse, what ails this ardour?
> If that to sing thou art bent,
> Go sing the fall of old Thebes,
> The wars of ugly Centaurs,
> The life, the death of Hector:
> So may thy song be famous:
> Or if to love thou art bent,
> Recount the rape of Europe,
> Adonis' end, Venus' net,
> The sleepy kiss the moon stale:[18]
> So may thy song be pleasant.

* *Anacreon*: Greek writer of odes. *blaze*: proclaim.

My muse, what ails this ardour,
To blaze my only secrets?
Wherein do only flourish
The sorry fruits of anguish:
The song thereof a last will,
The tunes be cries, the words plaints,
The singer is the song's theme,
Wherein no ear can have joy,
Nor eye receive due object,
Ne pleasure here, ne fame get.

My muse, what ails this ardour?
'Alas,' she saith,* 'I am thine;
So are thy pains my pains too.
Thy heated heart my seat is,
Wherein I burn: thy breath is
My voice, too hot to keep in.
Besides, lo here the author*
Of all thy harms: lo here she,
That only can redress thee:
Of her I will demand help.

My muse, I yield: my muse, sing;
But all thy song herein knit.
The life we lead is all love;
The love we hold is all death;
Nor aught I crave to feed life,
Nor aught I seek to shun death,
But only that my goddess
My life, my death, do count hers.

Basilius, when she had fully ended her song, fell prostrate upon the ground and thanked the gods they had preserved his life so long as to hear the very music they themselves used in an earthly body. And then with like grace to Zelmane never left entreating her till she had (taking a lyre Basilius held for her) sung these Phaleuciacks:*

* *she saith*: i.e. the Muse. *the author*: i.e. Philoclea. *Phaleuciacks*: a metre used by Catullus.

431

Reason, tell me thy mind, if here be reason
In this strange violence, to make resistance,
Where sweet graces erect the stately banner
Of virtue's regiment, shining in harness
Of fortune's diadems, by beauty mustered:
Say then reason, I say, what is thy counsel?

Her loose hairs be the shot; the breasts the pikes be;
Scouts each motion is; the hands be horsemen;
Her lips are the riches the wars to maintain,
Where well couched abides a coffer of pearl;
Her legs carriage is of all the sweet camp:
Say then reason, I say, what is thy counsel?

Her cannons be her eyes; mine eyes the walls be,
Which at first volley gave too open entry,
Nor rampier* did abide; my brain was up blown,
Undermin'd with a speech, the piercer of thoughts.
Thus weakened by myself, no help remaineth;
Say then reason, I say, what is thy counsel?

And now fame, the herald of her true honour,
Doth proclaim with a sound made all by men's mouths,
That nature, sovereign of earthly dwellers,
Commands all creatures to yield obeisance
Under this, this her own, her only darling.
Say then reason, I say, what is thy counsel?

Reason sighs, but in end he thus doth answer:
'Nought can reason avail in heavenly matters.'
Thus, nature's diamond,* receive thy conquest;
Thus, pure pearl, I do yield my senses and soul,
Thus, sweet pain, I do yield what ere I can yield.
Reason look to thyself, I serve a goddess.

Dorus had long, he thought, kept silence from saying somewhat
which might tend to the glory of her in whom all glory (to his

---

* *rampier*: rampart. *nature's diamond, etc.*: i.e. Philoclea.

seeming) was included; but now he brake it, singing these verses
called Asclepiadiks.[19]

O sweet woods the delight of solitariness!
O how much I do like your solitariness!
Where man's mind hath a freed consideration
Of goodness to receive lovely direction:
Where senses do behold th' order of heav'nly host,
And wise thoughts do behold what the creator is:
Contemplation here holdeth his only seat:
Bounded with no limits, borne with a wing of hope,
Climbs even unto the stars; nature is under it.
Nought disturbs thy quiet, all to thy service yields;
Each sight draws on a thought, thought mother of science;*
Sweet birds kindly do grant harmony unto thee;
Fair trees' shade is enough fortification,
Nor dangers to thyself, if be not in thyself.

O sweet woods the delight of solitariness!
O how much do I like your solitariness!
Here nor treason is hid, veiled in innocence,
Nor envy's snaky eye finds any harbour here,
Nor flatterers' venomous insinuations,
Nor cunning humourists' puddled* opinions,
Nor courteous ruin of proffered usury,
Nor time prattled away, cradle of ignorance,
Nor causeless duty, nor cumber of arrogance,
Nor trifling title of vanity dazzleth us,
Nor golden manacles stand for a paradise.
Here wrong's name is unheard; slander a monster is.
Keep thy spirit from abuse, here no abuse doth haunt.
What man grafts in a tree dissimulation?

O sweet woods the delight of solitariness!
O how well I do like your solitariness!
Yet dear soil, if a soul clos'd in a mansion
As sweet as violets, fair as a lily is,
Straight as a cedar, a voice stains the canary birds',

* *science*: knowledge. *puddled*: muddied.

Whose shade safety doth hold, danger avoideth her,
Such wisdom, that in her lives Speculation,
Such goodness, that in her Simplicity triumphs,
Where envy's snaky eye winketh or else dieth,
Slander wants a pretext, flattery gone beyond –
Oh! if such a one have bent to a lonely life
Her steps, glad we receive, glad we receive her eyes.
And think not she doth hurt our solitariness,
For such company decks such solitariness.

The other shepherds were offering themselves to have continued the sports, but the night had so quietly spent the most part of herself among them that the king for that time licensed* them. And so bringing Zelmane to her lodging, who would much rather have done the same for Philoclea, of all sides they went to counterfeit a sleep in their bed, for a true one their agonies could not afford them. Yet there they lay (so might they be most solitary for the food of their thoughts) till it was near noon the next day, after which Basilius was to continue his Apollo devotions, and the other to meditate upon their private desires.

* *licensed*: dismissed.

THE END OF THE SECOND BOOK

# The Third Book of the Countess
of Pembroke's Arcadia

## CHAPTER 1

This last day's danger, having made Pamela's love discern what a loss it should have suffered if Dorus had been destroyed, bred such tenderness of kindness in her toward him that she could no longer keep love from looking out through her eyes and going forth in her words, whom before as a close prisoner she had to her heart only committed; so as finding not only by his speeches and letters, but by the pitiful oration of a languishing behaviour and the easily deciphered character of a sorrowful face, that despair began now to threaten him destruction, she grew content both to pity him and let him see she pitied him, as well by making her own beautiful beams to thaw away the former iciness of her behaviour, as by entertaining his discourses (whensoever he did use them) in the third person of Musidorus: to so far a degree, that in the end she said that if she had been the princess whom that disguised prince had virtuously loved, she would have requited his faith with faithful affection; finding in her heart that nothing could so heartily love as virtue, with many more words to the same sense of noble favour and chaste plainness.

Which when at the first it made that unexpected bliss shine upon Dorus, he was (like one frozen with extremity of cold overhastily brought to a great fire) rather oppressed than relieved with such a lightning of felicity. But after the strength of nature had made him able to feel the sweetness of joyfulness, that again, being a child of passion and never acquainted with mediocrity, could not set bounds upon his happiness, nor be content to give desire a kingdom but that it must be an unlimited monarchy. So that the ground he stood upon being over-high in happiness and slippery through affection, he could not hold himself from falling into such an error which with sighs blew all comfort out of his breast and washed away all cheerfulness of his cheer with tears.

For this favour filling him with hope, hope encouraging his desire, and desire considering nothing but opportunity; one time (Mopsa being called away by her mother, and he left alone with Pamela) the sudden occasion called Love, and that never stayed to ask reason's leave but made the too much loving Dorus take her in his arms, offering to kiss her, and, as it were, to establish a trophy of his victory.

But she, (as if she had been ready to drink a wine of excellent taste and colour which suddenly she perceived had poison in it, so did she put him away from her) looking first up to heaven, as amazed to find herself so beguiled in him; then laying the cruel punishment upon him of angry love and louring beauty, showing disdain, and a despising disdain: 'Away,' said she, 'unworthy man to love or to be loved! Assure thyself, I hate myself for being so deceived: judge then what I do thee for deceiving me. Let me see thee no more, the only fall of my judgement and stain of my conscience.'

With that she called Mopsa, not staying for any answer (which was no other but a flood of tears) which she seemed not to mark (much less to pity) and chid her for having so left her alone.

It was not an amazement, it was not sorrow, but it was even a death which then laid hold of Dorus: which certainly at that instant would have killed him but that the fear to tarry longer in her presence (contrary to her commandment) gave him life to carry himself away from her sight and to run into the woods, where, throwing himself down at the foot of a tree, he did not fall to lamentation (for that proceeded of pitying) or grieving for himself (which he did no way) but to curses of his life, as one that detested himself. For finding himself not only unhappy, but unhappy after being fallen from all happiness; and to be fallen from all happiness not by any misconceiving but by his own fault, and his fault to be done to no other but to Pamela, he did not tender* his own estate but despised it, greedily drawing into his mind all conceits which might more and more torment him. And so remained he two days in the woods, disdaining to give his body food or his mind comfort, loving in himself nothing but the love of her. And indeed that love only strave with the fury of his anguish,

* *tender*: feel pity for.

telling it that if it destroyed Dorus, it should also destroy the image of her that lived in Dorus: and when the thought of that was crept in unto him, it began to win of him some compassion to the shrine of that image, and to bewail not for himself (whom he hated) but that so notable a love should perish. Then began he only so far to wish his own good as that Pamela might pardon him the fault, though not the punishment; and the uttermost height he aspired unto was that after his death she might yet pity his error and know that it proceeded of love and not of boldness.

That conceit found such friendship in his thoughts that at last he yielded, since he was banished her presence, to seek some means by writing to show his sorrow and testify his repentance. Therefore getting him the necessary instruments of writing, he thought best to counterfeit his hand (fearing that as already she knew his, she would cast it away as soon as she saw it) and to put it in verse, hoping that would draw her on to read the more, choosing the elegiac as fittest for mourning. But never pen did more quakingly perform his office; never was paper more double-moistened with ink and tears; never words more slowly married together, and never the Muses more tired than now with changes and re-changes of his devices; fearing how to end before he had resolved how to begin, mistrusting each word, condemning each sentence. This word was not significant; that word was too plain: this would not be conceived; the other would be ill-conceived: here sorrow was not enough expressed; there he seemed too much for his own sake to be sorry: this sentence rather showed art than passion; that sentence rather foolishly passionate than forcibly moving.

At last, marring with mending and putting out better than he left, he made an end of it and being ended, was divers times ready to tear it, till his reason assuring him the more he studied the worse it grew, he folded it up, devoutly invoking good acceptation unto it; and watching his time, when they were all gone one day to dinner, saving Mopsa, to the other lodge, stale up into Pamela's chamber, and in her standish* (which first he kissed and craved of it a safe and friendly keeping) left it there to be seen at her next using her ink (himself returning again to be true prisoner to des-

*standish: inkstand.

perate sorrow) leaving her standish upon her beds-head to give her the more occasion to mark it; which also fell out.

For she, finding it at her afternoon return in another place than she left it, opened it. But when she saw the letter, her heart gave her from whence it came; and therefore clapping it to again she went away from it as if it had been a contagious garment of an infected person: and yet was not long away but that she wished she had read it, though she were loth to read it.

'Shall I,' said she, 'second his boldness so far as to read his presumptuous letters? And yet,' said she, 'he sees me not now, to grow the bolder thereby: and how can I tell whether they be presumptuous?' The paper came from him, and therefore not worthy to be received; and yet the paper, she thought, was not guilty. At last, she concluded it were not much amiss to look it over, that she might out of his words pick some further quarrel against him. Then she opened it, and threw it away, and took it up again, till (ere she were aware) her eyes would needs read it, containing this matter:

Unto a caitiff wretch, whom long affliction holdeth,
  And now fully believes help to be quite perished,
Grant yet, grant yet a look, to the last monument of his anguish,
  O you (alas, do I find) cause of his only ruin.
Dread not a whit (O goodly cruel) that pity may enter
  Into thy heart by the sight of this Epistle I send,
And so refuse to behold of these strange wounds the recital,
  Lest it might thee allure home to thyself to return –
(Unto thyself I do mean those graces dwell so within thee,
  Gratefulness, sweetness, holy love, hearty regard).
Such thing cannot I seek (despair hath giv'n me my answer,
  Despair most tragical clause to a deadly request);
Such thing cannot he hope, that knows thy determinate hardness,
  Hard like a rich marble; hard, but a fair diamond.
Can those eyes, that of eyes drown'd in most hearty flowing tears
  (Tears and tears of a man) had no return to remorse,
Can those eyes now yield to the kind conceit of a sorrow,
  Which ink only relates, but ne* laments ne replies?

* *ne:* nor.

Ah, that, that do I not conceive, though that to my bliss were
  More than Nestor's years, more than a King's diadem.
Ah, that, that do I not conceive. To the Heaven when a mouse
    climbs,
  Then may I hope to achieve grace of a heavenly tiger.
But, but alas, like a man condemned doth crave to be heard speak,
  Not that he hopes for amends of the disaster he feels,
But finding the approach of death with an inly relenting,
  Gives an adieu to the world, as to his only delight:
Right so my boiling heart, inflam'd with fire of a fair eye,
  Bubbling out doth breathe signs of his hugy dolours,
Now that he finds to what end his life and love be reserved,
  And that he thence must part, where to live only he liv'd.
O fair, O fairest, are such the triumphs to thy fairness?
  Can death beauty become? Must I be such a monument?
Must I be only the mark shall prove that virtue is angry,
  Shall prove that fierceness can with a white dove abide,
Shall to the world appear that faith and love be rewarded
  With mortal disdain, bent to unendly* revenge?
Unto revenge? O sweet, on a wretch wilt thou be revenged?
  Shall such high planets tend to the loss of a worm?
And to revenge who do bend would in that kind be revenged
  As th' offence was done, and go beyond if he can.[1]
All my offence was love: with love then must I be chastened;
  And with more, by the laws that to revenge do belong.
If that love be a fault, more fault in you to be lovely:
  Love never had me oppressed, but that I saw to be lov'd.
You be the cause that I lov'd. What Reason blameth a shadow
  That with a body 't goes, since by a body it is?
If that love you did hate, you should your beauty have hidden:
  You should those fair eyes have with a veil covered.
But fool, fool that I am, those eyes would shine from a dark cave:
  What veils then do prevail, but to a more miracle?
Or those golden locks, those locks which lock me to bondage,
  Torn you should disperse unto the blasts of a wind.
But fool, fool that I am, though I had but a hair of her head found,
  Ev'n as I am, so I should unto that hair be a thrall.

* *unendly*: endless.

Or with fair hands' nails (O hand which nails me to this death)
  You should have your face (since love is ill) blemished.
O wretch, what do I say? Should that fair face be defaced?
  Should my too-much sight cause so true a sun to be lost?
First let Cimmerian darkness² be my onl' habitation:
  First be mine eyes pull'd out, first be my brain perished,
Ere that I should consent to do so excessive a damage
  Unto the earth, by the hurt of this her heavenly jewel.
O not but* such love you say you could have afforded,
  As might learn temp'rance, void of a rage's events.
O sweet simplicity: from whence should love be so learned?
  Unto Cupid, that Boy, shall a pedant* be found?
Well, but faulty I was. Reason to my passion yielded,
  Passion unto my rage, rage to a hasty revenge.
But what's this for a fault, for which such faith be abolished,
  Such faith, so stainless, inviolate, violent?
Shall I not, O may I not thus yet refresh the remembrance,
  What sweet joys I had once, and what a place I did hold?
Shall I not once object, that you, you granted a favour
  Unto the man, whom now such miseries you award?
Bend your thoughts to the dear sweet words which then to me
    giv'n were:
  Think what a world is now, think who hath alt'red her heart.
What, was I then worthy such good, now worthy such evil?
  Now fled, then cherished? Then so nigh, now so remote?
Did not a rosed breath, from lips more rosy proceeding,
  Say that I well should find in what a care I was had,
With much more? Now what do I find, but care to abhor me?
  Care that I sink in grief, care that I live banished?
And banished do I live, nor now will seek a recovery,
  Since so she will, whose will is to me more than a law.
If then a man in most ill case may give you a farewell,
  Farewell, long farewell, all my woe, all my delight.

              * *not but*: only. *pedant*: schoolmaster.

## CHAPTER 2

What this would have wrought in her she herself could not tell, for before her reason could moderate the disputation between favour and faultiness, her sister and Miso called her down to entertain Zelmane who was come to visit the two sisters, about whom, as about two poles, the sky of beauty was turned; while Gynecia wearied her bed with her melancholy sickness, and made Miso's shrewdness* (who like a spirit set to keep a treasure, barred Zelmane from any further conference) to be the lieutenant of her jealousy; both she and her husband driving Zelmane to such a strait of resolution, either of impossible granting or dangerous refusing, as the best escape she had was (as much as she could) to avoid their company. So as this day, being the fourth day after the uproar (Basilius being with his sick wife, conferring upon such examinations as Philanax and other of his noblemen had made of this late sedition, all touching Cecropia, with vehement suspicion of giving either flame or fuel unto it) Zelmane came with her body to find her mind, which was gone long before her and had gotten his seat in Philoclea, who now with a bashful cheerfulness (as though she were ashamed that she could not choose but be glad) joined with her sister in making much of Zelmane.

And so as they sat devising how to give more feathers to the wings of time, there came to the lodge-door six maids, all in one livery of scarlet petticoats which were tucked up almost to their knees; the petticoats themselves being in many places garnished with leaves, their legs naked, saving that above the ankles they had little black silk laces upon which did hang a few silver bells, like which they had a little above their elbows upon their bare arms. Upon their hair they wore garlands of roses and gilliflowers, and the hair was so dressed as that came again above the garlands, interchanging a mutual covering so as it was doubtful whether the hair dressed the garlands, or the garlands dressed the hair. Their breasts liberal to the eye; the face of the foremost of them in excellency fair and of the rest lovely, if not beautiful; and beautiful might have been, if they had not suffered greedy Phoebus overoften and hard to kiss them.[1] Their countenances full of a graceful

* *shrewdness*: shrewishness.

gravity, so as the gesture matched with the apparel, it might seem a wanton modesty and an enticing soberness. Each of them had an instrument of music in their hands which, consorting* their well-pleasing tunes, did charge each ear with unsensibleness that did not lend itself unto them. The music entering alone into the lodge, the ladies were all desirous to see from whence so pleasant a guest was come; and therefore went out together, where, before they could take the pains to doubt, much less to ask the question of their quality, the fairest of them (with a gay, but yet discreet demeanour) in this sort spake unto them.

'Most excellent ladies (whose excellencies have power to make cities envy these woods, and solitariness to be accounted the sweetest company) vouchsafe our message your gracious hearing, which, as it comes from love, so comes it from lovely persons. The maids of all this coast of Arcadia, understanding the often access that certain shepherds of these quarters are allowed to have in this forbidden place, and that their rural sports are not disdained of you, have been stirred with emulation to them and affection to you, to bring forth something which might as well breed your contentment: and therefore hoping that the goodness of their intention, and the hurtlessness of their sex shall excuse the breach of the commandment in coming to this place unsent for, they chose out us to invite both your princely parents and yourselves to a place in the woods about half a mile hence, where they have provided some such sports as they trust your gracious acceptations will interpret to be delightful. We have been at the other lodge, but finding them there busied in weightier affairs, our trust is that you yet will not deny the shining of your eyes upon us.'

The ladies stood in some doubt whether they should go or not, lest Basilius might be angry withal. But Miso (that had been at none of the pastorals, and had a great desire to lead her old senses abroad to some pleasure) told them plainly they should nor will nor choose, but go thither, and make the honest country people know that they were not so squeamish as folks thought of them. The ladies, glad to be warranted by her authority, with a smiling humbleness obeyed her; Pamela only casting a seeking look whether she could see Dorus (who, poor wretch, wandered half

* *consorting*: sounding together.

mad for sorrow in the woods, crying for pardon of her who could not hear him) but indeed was grieved for his absence, having given the wound to him through her own heart. But so the three ladies and Miso went with those six Nymphs, conquering the length of the way with the force of music, leaving only Mopsa behind, who disgraced weeping with her countenance, because her mother would not suffer her to show her new-scoured face among them. But the place appointed, as they thought, met them half in their way, so well were they pleased with the sweet tunes and pretty conversation of their inviters. There found they in the midst of the thickest part of the wood a little square place, not burdened with trees, but with a board covered and beautified with the pleasantest fruits that sun-burned Autumn could deliver unto them. The maids besought the ladies to sit down and taste of the swelling grapes, which seemed great with child of Bacchus, and of the divers coloured plums, which gave the eye a pleasant taste before they came to the mouth. The ladies would not show to scorn their provision, but ate and drank a little of their cool wine, which seemed to laugh for joy to come to such lips,

But after the collation was ended and that they looked for the coming forth of such devices as were prepared for them, there rushed out of the woods twenty armed men, who round about environed them, and laying hold of Zelmane before she could draw her sword, and taking it from her, put hoods over the heads of all four, and so muffled, by force set them on horse-back, and carried them away; the sisters in vain crying for succour, while Zelmane's heart was rent in pieces with rage of the injury and disdain of her fortune. But when they had carried them a four or five mile further, they left Miso with a gag in her mouth and bound hand and foot, so to take her fortune, and brought the three ladies (by that time that the night seemed with her silence to conspire to their treason) to a castle about ten mile from the lodges, where they were fain to take a boat which waited for them, for the castle stood in the midst of a great lake upon a high rock, where partly by art, but principally by nature, it was by all men esteemed impregnable.

But at the castle-gate their faces were discovered,* and there

* *discovered:* uncovered.

were met with a great number of torches, after whom the sisters knew their aunt-in-law Cecropia. But that sight increased the deadly terror of the princesses, looking for nothing but death since they were in the power of the wicked Cecropia; who yet came unto them, making courtesy the outside of mischief, and desiring them not to be discomforted for they were in a place dedicated to their service. Philoclea (with a look where love shined through the mist of fear) besought her to be good unto them, having never deserved evil of her. But Pamela's high heart disdaining humbleness to injury, 'Aunt,' said she, 'what you have determined of us I pray you do it speedily. For my part I look for no service, where I find violence.'

But Cecropia, using no more words with them, conveyed them all three to several lodgings (Zelmane's heart so swelling with spite that she could not bring forth a word) and so left them; first taking from them their knives because they should do themselves no hurt, before she had determined of them: and then giving such order that they wanted nothing but liberty and comfort, she went to her son, who yet kept his bed because of his wound he had received of Zelmane, and told him whom now he had in his power. Amphialus was but even then returned from far countries where he had won immortal fame both of courage and courtesy, when he met with the princesses and was hurt by Zelmane, so as he was utterly ignorant of all his mother's wicked devices, to which he would never have consented, being (like a rose out of a briar) an excellent son of an evil mother: and now, when he heard of this, was as much amazed as if he had seen the sun fall to the earth. And therefore desired his mother that she would tell him the whole discourse, how all these matters had happened.

'Son,' said she, 'I will do it willingly, and since all is done for you I will hide nothing from you. And howsoever I might be ashamed to tell it strangers who would think it wickedness, yet what is done for your sake (how evil soever to others) to you is virtue. To begin then even with the beginning: this doting fool Basilius that now reigns, having lived unmarried until he was nigh threescore years old (and in all his speeches affirming, and in all his doings assuring, that he never would marry) made all the eyes of this country to be bent upon your father, his only brother, but younger by thirty years, as upon the undoubted successor; being indeed a man worthy to reign, thinking nothing enough for himself, where this goose (you see) puts down his head before there be anything near to touch him. So that he, holding place and estimation as heir of Arcadia, obtained me of my father, the king of Argos, his brother helping to the conclusion with protesting his bachelorly intention – for else, you may be sure, the king of Argos nor his daughter would have suffered their royal blood to be stained with the base name of subjection.

'So that I came into this country as apparent princess thereof, and accordingly was courted and followed of all the ladies of this country. My port and pomp did well become a king of Argos' daughter: in my presence their tongues were turned into ears, and their ears were captives unto my tongue. Their eyes admired my majesty, and happy was he or she on whom I would suffer the beams thereof to fall. Did I go to church, it seemed the very gods waited for me, their devotions not being solemnized till I was ready. Did I walk abroad to see any delight, nay, my walking was the delight itself, for to it was the concourse, one thrusting upon another who might show himself most diligent and serviceable towards me. My sleeps were inquired after, and my wakings never unsaluted: the very gate of my house full of principal persons, who were glad if their presents had received a grateful acceptation. And in this felicity wert thou born, the very earth submitting itself unto thee to be trodden on as by his prince; and to that pass had my husband's virtue (by my good help) within short time brought it, with a plot we laid, as we should not have needed to have waited the tedious work of a natural end of Basilius, when the heavens (I think envying my great felicity) then stopped thy father's breath, when he breathed nothing but power and sovereignty. Yet did not thy orphancy or my widowhood deprive us of the delightful prospect which the hill of honour doth yield, while expectation of thy succession did bind dependencies unto us.

'But before, my son, thou wert come to the age to feel the sweetness of authority, this beast (whom I can never name with patience) falsely and foolishly married this Gynecia, then a young girl, and brought her to sit above me in all feasts, to turn her shoulder to me-ward in all our solemnities. It is certain it is not so great a spite to be surmounted by strangers as by one's own allies. Think then what my mind was, since withal there is no question, the fall is greater from the first to the second than from the second to the undermost. The rage did swell in my heart so much the more as it was fain to be suppressed in silence and disguised with humbleness. But above all the rest, the grief of griefs was when with these two daughters, now thy prisoners, she cut off all hope of thy succession. It was a tedious thing to me that my eyes should look lower than anybody's, that (myself being by) another's voice than mine should be more respected. But it was insupportable unto me to think that not only I, but thou, should'st spend all thy time in such misery, and that the sun should see my eldest son less than a prince. And though I had been a saint I could not choose finding the change this change of fortune bred unto me; for now from the multitude of followers, silence grew to be at my gate and absence in my presence. The guess of my mind could prevail more before, than now many of my earnest requests.[2] And thou, my dear son, by the fickle multitude no more than an ordinary person (born of the mud of the people) regarded.

'But I (remembering that in all miseries weeping becomes fools, and practice wise folks) have tried divers means to pull us out of the mire of subjection. And though many times fortune failed me, yet did I never fail myself. Wild beasts I kept in a cave hard by the lodges, which I caused by night to be fed in the place of their pastorals – I as then living in my house hard by the place – and against the hour they were to meet (having kept the beasts without meat) then let them loose, knowing that they would seek their food there and devour what they found. But blind fortune, hating sharp-sighted inventions, made them unluckily to be killed. After, I used my servant Clinias to stir a notable tumult of country people; but those louts were too gross instruments for delicate conceits. Now lastly, finding Philanax's examinations grow dangerous, I thought to play double or quit, and with a sleight I used of my fine-witted wench Artesia, with other maids of mine, would have sent those goodly inheritrixes of Arcadia to have pleaded their cause before Pluto, but that over-fortunately for them, you made me know the last day how vehemently this childish passion of love doth torment you. Therefore I have brought them unto you, yet wishing rather hate than love in you. For hate often begetteth victory, love commonly is the instrument of subjection. It is true that I would also by the same practice have entrapped the parents, but my maids failed of it, not daring to tarry long about it. But this sufficeth, since (these being taken away) you are the undoubted inheritor, and Basilius will not long over-live this loss.'

'O mother,' said Amphialus, 'speak not of doing them hurt, no more than to mine eyes or my heart, or if I have anything more dear than eyes or heart unto me. Let others find what sweetness they will in ever fearing because they ever are feared. For my part, I will think myself highly entitled,* if I may be once by Philoclea accepted for a servant.'

'Well,' said Cecropia, 'I would I had born you of my mind as well as of my body: then should you not have sunk under these base weaknesses. But since you have tied your thoughts in so wilful a knot, it is happy my policy hath brought matters to such a pass as you may both enjoy affection, and upon that build your sovereignty.'

'Alas,' said Amphialus, 'my heart would fain yield you thanks for setting me in the way of felicity, but that fear kills them in me before they are fully born. For if Philoclea be displeased, how can I be pleased? If she count it unkindness, shall I give tokens of kindness? Perchance she condemns me of this action, and shall I triumph? Perchance she drowns now the beauties I love with sorrowful tears, and where is then my rejoicing?'

'You have reason,' said Cecropia with a feigned gravity. 'I will therefore send her away presently that her contentment may be recovered.'

'No, good mother,' said Amphialus, 'since she is here, I would not for my life constrain presence, but rather would I die than consent to absence.'

'Pretty intricate follies,' said Cecropia, 'but get you up and see how you can prevail with her, while I go to the other sister. For after, we shall have our hands full to defend ourselves if Basilius hap to besiege us.'

---

*entitled: given a title.

But remembering herself she turned back and asked him what he would have done with Zelmane, since now he might be revenged of his hurt. 'Nothing but honourably,' answered Amphialus, 'having deserved no other of me, especially being (as I hear) greatly cherished of Philoclea, and therefore I could wish they were lodged together.'

'O no,' said Cecropia, 'company confirms resolutions, and loneliness breeds a weariness of one's thoughts, and so a sooner consenting to reasonable proffers.'

## CHAPTER 3

But Amphialus (taking off his mother Philoclea's knives, which he kept as a relic since she had worn them) gat up, and calling for his richest apparel, nothing seemed sumptuous enough for his mistress' eyes; and that which was costly, he feared were not dainty; and though the invention were delicate, he misdoubted the making. As careful he was too of the colour, lest if gay, he might seem to glory in his injury and her wrong; if mourning, it might strike some evil presage unto her of her fortune. At length he took a garment more rich than glaring, the ground being black velvet, richly embroidered with great pearl and precious stones, but they set so among certain tufts of cypress* that the cypress was like black clouds through which the stars might yield a dark lustre. About his neck he ware a broad and gorgeous collar whereof the pieces interchangeably answering, the one was of diamonds and pearl set with a white enamel so as by the cunning of the workman it seemed like a shining ice, and the other piece being of rubies and opals, had a fiery glistering; which he thought pictured the two passions of fear and desire wherein he was enchained. His hurt, not yet fully well, made him a little halt, but he strave to give the best grace he could unto his halting.

And in that sort he went to Philoclea's chamber: whom he found (because her chamber was over-lightsome) sitting of that side of her bed which was from the window, which did cast such a shadow upon her as a good painter would bestow upon Venus, when under the trees she bewailed the murder of Adonis: her

* *cypress*: rich satin, originally from Cyprus.

hands and fingers (as it were) indented one within the other; her
shoulder leaning to her bed's head, and over her head a scarf
which did eclipse almost half her eyes, which under it fixed their
beams upon the wall by, with so steady a manner as if in that
place they might well change but not mend their object: and so
remained they a good while after his coming in, he not daring to
trouble her nor she perceiving him; till that (a little varying her
thoughts, something quickening her senses) she heard him as he
happed to stir his upper garment, and perceiving him, rose up
with a demeanour where, in the book of beauty, there was
nothing to be read but sorrow, for kindness was blotted out and
anger was never there.

But Amphialus, that had entrusted his memory with long and
forcible speeches, found it so locked up in amazement that he
could pick nothing out of it but the beseeching her to take what
was done in good part, and to assure herself there was nothing but
honour meant unto her person. But she, making no other answer,
but letting her hands fall one from the other which before were
joined (with eyes something cast aside, and a silent sigh) gave him
to understand that considering his doings, she thought his speech
as full of incongruity as her answer would be void of purpose:
whereupon he kneeling down and kissing her hand (which she
suffered with a countenance witnessing captivity but not kindness) he besought her to have pity of him whose love went beyond
the bounds of conceit, much more of uttering: that in her hands
the balance of his life or death did stand, whereto the least motion
of hers would serve to determine, she being indeed the mistress of
his life and he her eternal slave; and with true vehemency besought her that he might hear her speak: whereupon she suffered
her sweet breath to turn itself into these kind of words.

'Alas, cousin,' said she, 'what shall my tongue be able to do
which is informed by the ears one way and by the eyes another?
You call for pity and use cruelty; you say you love me, and yet do
the effects of enmity. You affirm your death is in my hands, but
you have brought me to so near a degree to death as when you
will, you may lay death upon me; so that while you say I am
mistress of your life, I am not mistress of mine own. You entitle
yourself my slave, but I am sure I am yours. If then violence,

injury, terror, and depriving of that which is more dear than life itself, liberty, be fit orators for affection, you may expect that I will be easily persuaded. But if the nearness of our kindred breed any remorse in you, or there be any such thing in you which you call love toward me, then let not my fortune be disgraced with the name of imprisonment: let not my heart waste itself by being vexed with feeling evil, and fearing worse. Let not me be a cause of my parents' woeful destruction; but restore me to myself, and so doing, I shall account I have received myself of you. And what I say for myself, I say for my dear sister, and my friend Zelmane, for I desire no well-being without they may be partakers.' With that her tears rained down from her heavenly eyes, and seemed to water the sweet and beautiful flowers of her face.

But Amphialus was like the poor woman who, loving a tame doe she had above all earthly things, having long played withal and made it feed at her hand and lap, is constrained at length by famine (all her flock being spent and she fallen into extreme poverty) to kill the deer to sustain her life. Many a pitiful look doth she cast upon it, and many a time doth she draw back her hand before she can give the stroke. For even so Amphialus by a hunger-starved affection was compelled to offer this injury, and yet the same affection made him with a tormenting grief think unkindness in himself that he could find in his heart any way to restrain her freedom. But at length, neither able to grant nor deny, he thus answered her:

'Dear lady,' said he, 'I will not say unto you (how justly soever I may do it) that I am neither author nor accessory unto this your withholding; for since I do not redress it, I am as faulty as if I had begun it. But this I protest unto you (and this protestation of mine let the heavens hear, and if I lie, let them answer me with a deadly thunderbolt) that in my soul I wish I had never seen the light, or rather, that I had never had a father to beget such a child, than that by my means those eyes should overflow their own beauties, than by my means the sky of your virtue should be overclouded with sorrow. But woe is me, most excellent lady, I find myself most willing to obey you: neither truly do mine ears receive the least word you speak with any less reverence than as absolute and unresistable commandments. But alas, that tyrant love (which now possesseth the hold of all my life and reason) will no way suffer it. It is love, it is love, not I which disobey you. What then shall I say, but that I, who am ready to lie under your feet, to venture, nay to lose my life at your least commandment, I am not the stay of your freedom, but love, love, which ties you in your own knots. It is you yourself that imprison yourself: it is your beauty which makes these castle-walls embrace you: it is your own eyes which reflect upon themselves this injury. Then is there no other remedy but that you some way vouchsafe to satisfy this love's vehemency which, since it grew in yourself, without question you shall find it (far more than I) tractable.'

But with these words Philoclea fell to so extreme a quaking, and her lively whiteness did degenerate to such a deadly paleness, that Amphialus feared some dangerous trance: so that taking her hand, and feeling that it (which was wont to be one of the chief fire-brands of Cupid) had all the sense of it wrapt up in coldness, he began humbly to beseech her to put away all fear, and to assure herself, upon the vow he made thereof unto God and herself, that the uttermost forces he would ever employ to conquer her affection should be desire and desert. That promise brought Philoclea again to herself, so that slowly lifting up her eyes upon him, with a countenance ever courteous but then languishing, she told him that he should do well to do so, if indeed he had ever tasted what true love was: for that where now she did bear him goodwill, she should, if he took any other way, hate and abhor the very thought of him; assuring him withal that though his mother had taken away her knives, yet the house of death had so many doors as she would easily fly into it if ever she found her honour endangered.

Amphialus, having the cold ashes of care cast upon the coals of desire, leaving some of his mother's gentlewomen to wait upon Philoclea, himself indeed a prisoner to his prisoner and making all his authority to be but a foot-stool to humbleness, went from her to his mother. To whom with words, which affection indited but amazement uttered, he delivered what had passed between him and Philoclea, beseeching her to try what her persuasions could do with her, while he gave order for all such things as were necessary against such forces as he looked daily Basilius would bring before his castle. His mother bade him quiet himself, for she doubted not to take fit times: but that the best way was first to let her own passion a little tire itself.

## CHAPTER 4

So they, calling Clinias and some other of their council, advised upon their present affairs. First, he dispatched private letters to all those principal lords and gentlemen of the country whom he thought either alliance or friendship to himself might draw with special motions from the general consideration of duty; not omitting all such whom either youthful age or youthlike minds did fill with unlimited desires, besides such whom any discontentment made hungry of change, or an overspended want made want a civil war: to each (according to the counsel of his mother) conforming himself after their humours. To his friends, friendliness; to the ambitious, great expectations; to the displeased, revenge; to the greedy, spoil: wrapping their hopes with such cunning as they rather seemed given over unto them as partakers than promises sprung of necessity. Then sent he to his mother's brother, the king of Argos; but he was as then so over-laid with war himself as from thence he could attend* small succour.

But because he knew how violently rumours do blow the sails of popular judgements, and how few there be that can discern between truth and truth-likeness, between shows and substance, he caused a justification of this his action to be written, whereof were sowed abroad many copies which, with some glosses of probability, might hide indeed the foulness of his treason, and from true common-places fetch down most false applications. For beginning how much the duty which is owed to the country goes beyond all other duties since in itself it contains them all, and that for the respect thereof, not only all tender respects of kindred or whatsoever other friendships are to be laid aside, but that even long-held opinions (rather builded upon a secret of government than any ground of truth) are to be forsaken; he fell by degrees to show that since the end whereto anything is directed is ever to be

* *attend:* expect.

of more noble reckoning than the thing thereto directed, that therefore the weal-public was more to be regarded than any person or magistrate that thereunto was ordained: the feeling consideration whereof had moved him (though as near of kin to Basilius as could be) yet to set principally before his eyes the good estate of so many thousands over whom Basilius reigned, rather than so to hood-wink himself with affection as to suffer the realm to run to manifest ruin. The care whereof did kindly appertain to those who, being subaltern magistrates and officers of the crown, were to be employed as from the prince, so for the people; and of all other, especially himself who being descended of the royal race and next heir male, Nature had no sooner opened his eyes, but that the soil whereupon they did look was to look for at his hands a continual carefulness: which as from his childhood he had ever carried, so now finding that his uncle had not only given over all care of government, but had put it into the hands of Philanax (a man neither in birth comparable to many, nor for his corrupt, proud, and partial dealing, liked of any) but beside, had set his daughters (in whom the whole estate, as next heirs thereunto, had no less interest than himself) in so unfit and ill-guarded a place, as it was not only dangerous for their persons but (if they should be conveyed to any foreign country) to the whole commonwealth pernicious: that therefore he had brought them into this strong castle of his, which way, if it might seem strange, they were to consider that new necessities require new remedies; but there they should be served and honoured as belonged to their greatness until by the general assembly of the estates it should be determined how they should to their best (both private and public) advantage be matched: vowing all faith and duty both to the father and children, never by him to be violated. But if in the meantime, before the estates could be assembled, he should be assailed, he would then for his own defence take arms; desiring all that either tendered the dangerous case of their country or in their hearts loved justice to defend him in this just action. And if the prince should command them otherwise, yet to know that therein he was no more to be obeyed than if he should call for poison to hurt himself withal; since all that was done was done for his service, howsoever he might (seduced by Philanax) interpret of it: he protesting that whatsoever he should do for his own defence should be against Philanax, and no way against Basilius.

To this effect, amplified with arguments and examples, and painted with rhetorical colours, did he sow abroad many discourses which, as they prevailed with some of more quick than sound conceit to run his fortune with him, so in many did it breed a coolness to deal violently against him, and a false-minded neutrality to expect* the issue. But besides the ways he used to weaken the adverse party, he omitted nothing for the strengthening of his own. The chief trust whereof (because he wanted men to keep the field) he reposed in the surety of his castle, which at least would win him much time, the mother of many mutations. To that therefore he bent both his outward and inward eyes, striving to make art strive with Nature to whether of them two that fortification should be most beholding. The seat Nature bestowed, but art gave the building which, as his rocky hardness would not yield to undermining force, so to open assaults he took counsel of skill how to make all approaches, if not impossible, yet difficult; as well at the foot of the castle as round about the lake, to give unquiet lodgings to them whom only enmity would make neighbours. Then omitted he nothing of defence, as well simple defence as that which did defend by offending, fitting instruments of mischief to places whence the mischief might be most liberally bestowed. Neither was his smallest care for victuals, as well for the providing that which should suffice, both in store and goodness, as in well preserving it and wary distributing it, both in quantity and quality, spending that first which would keep least.

But wherein he sharpened his wits to the piercingest point was touching his men, knowing them to be the weapon of weapons and master-spring, as it were, which makes all the rest to stir; and that therefore in the art of man stood the quintessence and ruling skill of all prosperous government, either peaceable or military. He chose in number as many as without pestering* (and so danger of infection) his victual would serve for two years to maintain; all of able bodies, and some few of able minds to direct, not seeking many commanders, but contenting himself that the multitude

* *expect*: await. *pestering*: overcrowding.

should have obeying wits, everyone knowing whom he should command and whom he should obey, the place where, and the matter wherein; distributing each office as near as he could to the disposition of the person that should exercise it, knowing no love, danger nor discipline can suddenly alter an habit in nature. Therefore would he not employ the still man to a shifting practice, nor the liberal man to be a dispenser of his victuals, nor the kind-hearted man to be a punisher; but would exercise their virtues in sorts where they might be profitable, employing his chief care to know them all particularly, and thoroughly regarding also the constitution of their bodies; some being able better to abide watching, some hunger, some labour; making his benefit of each ability, and not forcing beyond power.

Time to everything by just proportion he allotted, and as well in that as in everything else, no small error winked at, lest greater should be animated. Even of vices he made his profit, making the cowardly Clinias to have care of the watch, which he knew his own fear would make him very wakefully perform. And before the siege began, he himself caused rumours to be sowed and libels to be spread against himself, fuller of malice than witty persuasion; partly to know those that would be apt to stumble at such motions, that he might cull them from the faithfuller band, but principally, because in necessity they should not know (when any such thing were in earnest attempted) whether it were or not of his own invention. But even then (before the enemy's face came near to breed any terror) did he exercise his men daily in all their charges, as if danger had presently presented his most hideous presence: himself rather instructing by example than precept, being neither more sparing in travail nor spending in diet than the meanest soldier; his hand and body disdaining no base matters nor shrinking from the heavy.

The only odds was, that when others took breath, he sighed; and when others rested, he crossed his arms. For love, passing through the pikes of danger and tumbling itself in the dust of labour, yet still made him remember his sweet desire and beautiful image. Often when he had begun to command one, somewhat before half the sentence were ended, his inward guest did so entertain him that he would break it off, and a pretty while after end it when he had (to the marvel of the standers-by) sent himself in to talk with his own thoughts. Sometimes when his hand was lifted up to do something, as if with the sight of Gorgon's head he had been suddenly turned into a stone, so would he there abide with his eyes planted and hand lifted, till at length coming to the use of himself, he would look about whether any had perceived him. Then would he accuse and in himself condemn all those wits that durst affirm idleness to be the well-spring of love:

'O', would he say, 'all you that affect the title of wisdom by ungrateful scorning the ornaments of Nature, am I now piping in a shadow?* Or do slothful feathers now enwrap me? Is not hate before me and doubt behind me? Is not danger of the one side, and shame of the other? And do I not stand upon pain and travail, and yet over all, my affection triumphs? The more I stir about urgent affairs, the more methinks the very stirring breeds a breath to blow the coals of my love. The more I exercise my thoughts, the more they increase the appetite of my desires. O sweet Philoclea – ' (with that he would cast up his eyes, wherein some water did appear, as if they would wash themselves against they should see her) 'thy heavenly face is my astronomy; thy sweet virtue, my sweet philosophy: let me profit therein, and farewell all other cogitations. But alas, my mind misgives me, for your planets bear a contrary aspect unto me. Woe, woe is me, they threaten my destruction. And whom do they threaten this destruction? Even him that loves them; and by what means will they destroy, but by loving them? O dear though killing eyes, shall death head his dart with the gold of Cupid's arrow?* Shall death take his aim from the rest of beauty?* O beloved though hating Philoclea, how, if thou be'st merciful, hath cruelty stolen into thee? Or how, if thou be'st cruel, doth cruelty look more beautiful than ever mercy did? Or alas, is it my destiny that makes mercy cruel? Like an evil vessel which turns sweet liquor to sourness, so when thy grace falls upon me, my wretched constitution makes it become fierceness.'

Thus would he exercise his eloquence when she could not hear

* *piping in a shadow*: relaxing in the shade. *gold of Cupid's arrow*: see Notes, II. 14. 5. (p. 856). *rest of beauty*: support for fire-arm to ensure steady aim.

him, and be dumb-stricken when her presence gave him fit occasion of speaking; so that his wit could find out no other refuge but the comfort and counsel of his mother, desiring her, whose thoughts were unperplexed, to use for his sake the most prevailing manners of intercession.

## CHAPTER 5

Cecropia, seeing her son's safety depend thereon, though her pride much disdained the name of a desirer, took the charge upon her, not doubting the easy conquest of an unexpert virgin, who had already with subtilty and impudency begun to undermine a monarchy. Therefore, weighing Philoclea's resolutions by the counterpoise of her own youthful thoughts which she then called to mind, she doubted not at least to make Philoclea receive the poison distilled in sweet liquor which she with little disguising had drunk up thirstily. Therefore she went softly to Philoclea's chamber, and peeping through the side of the door, then being a little open, she saw Philoclea sitting low upon a cushion in such a given-over manner that one would have thought silence, solitariness and melancholy were come there under the ensign of mishap, to conquer delight and drive him from his natural seat of beauty. Her tears came dropping down like rain in sunshine, and she not taking heed to wipe the tears, they ran down upon her cheeks and lips as upon cherries which the dropping tree bedeweth. In the dressing of her hair and apparel, she might see neither a careful art nor an art of carelessness, but even left to a neglected chance, which yet could no more unperfect her perfections than a die any way cast could lose its squareness.

Cecropia, stirred with no other pity but for her son, came in, and haling* kindness into her countenance, 'What ails this sweet lady?' said she; 'Will you mar so good eyes with weeping? Shall tears take away the beauty of that complexion which the women of Arcadia wish for and the men long after? Fie of this peevish sadness: insooth it is untimely for your age. Look upon your own body and see whether it deserve to pine away with sorrow. See whether you will have these hands' (with that she took one of her

* *haling:* dragging.

hands and kissing it, looked upon it as if she were enamoured with it) 'fade from their whiteness which makes one desire to touch them, and their softness which rebounds again a desire to look on them, and become dry, lean and yellow, and make everybody wonder at the change and say that sure you had used some art before which now you had left, for if the beauties had been natural, they would never so soon have been blemished. Take a glass and see whether those tears become your eyes, although, I must confess, those eyes are able to make tears comely.'

'Alas, madam,' answered Philoclea, 'I know not whether my tears become mine eyes, but I am sure mine eyes thus beteared become my fortune.'

'Your fortune,' said Cecropia, 'if she could see to attire herself, would put on her best raiments. For I see, and I see it with grief and (to tell you true) unkindness, you misconstrue everything that only for your sake is attempted. You think you are offended, and are, indeed, defended: you esteem yourself a prisoner and are, in truth, a mistress: you fear hate, and shall find love. And truly, I had a thing to say to you, but it is no matter since I find you are so obstinately melancholy as that you woo his fellowship. I will spare my pains and hold my peace.' and so stayed indeed, thinking Philoclea would have had a female inquisitiveness of the matter. But she, who rather wished to unknow what she knew than to burden her heart with more hopeless knowledge, only desired her to have pity of her and if, indeed, she did mean her no hurt, then to grant her liberty, for else the very grief and fear would prove her unappointed executioners.

'For that,' said Cecropia, 'believe me upon the faith of a king's daughter, you shall be free, so soon as your freedom may be free of mortal danger, being brought hither for no other cause but to prevent such mischiefs as you know not of. But if you think, indeed, to win me to have care of you, even as of mine own daughter, then lend your ears unto me, and let not your mind arm itself with a wilfulness to be flexible to nothing. But if I speak reason, let reason have his due reward, persuasion. Then sweet niece,' said she, 'I pray you pre-suppose that now, even in the midst of your agonies which you paint unto yourself most horrible, wishing with sighs and praying with vows for a soon and safe delivery:

imagine niece (I say) that some heavenly spirit should appear unto
you and bid you follow him through the door that goes into the
garden, assuring you that you should thereby return to your dear
mother, and what other delights soever your mind esteems delights: would you (sweet niece) would you refuse to follow him,
and say that if he led you not through the chief gate, you would
not enjoy your over-desired liberty? Would you not drink the
wine you thirst for, without it were in such a glass as you especially fancied? Tell me (dear niece) – but I will answer for you,
because I know your reason and wit is such as must needs conclude that such niceness* can no more be in you, to disgrace such
a mind, than disgracefulness can have any place in so faultless a
beauty. Your wisdom would assuredly determine how the mark
were hit, not whether the bow were of yew or no wherein you
shot. If this be so, and thus sure (my dear niece) it is, then, I pray
you, imagine that I am that same good angel who, grieving in
your grief and, in truth, not able to suffer that bitter sighs should
be sent forth with so sweet a breath, am come to lead you, not
only to your desired and imagined happiness, but to a true and
essential happiness; not only to liberty, but to liberty with commandment. The way I will show you; which if it be not the gate
builded hitherto in your private choice, yet shall it be a door to
bring you through a garden of pleasures as sweet as this life can
bring forth; nay rather, which makes this life to be a life. My son
(let it be no blemish to him that I name him my son who was your
father's own nephew, for you know I am no small king's daughter) my son, I say, far passing the nearness of his kindred with
nearness of goodwill, and striving to match your matchless beauty
with a matchless affection, doth by me present unto you the full
enjoying of your liberty, so as with this gift you will accept a
greater, which is this castle, with all the rest which you know he
hath in honourable quantity, and will confirm his gift and your
receipt of both with accepting him to be yours. I might say much
both for the person and the matter, but who will cry out the sun
shines? It is so manifest a profit unto you as the meanest judgement must straight apprehend it; so far is it from the sharpness of
yours, thereof to be ignorant. Therefore, sweet niece, let your grate-

* *niceness*: over-fastidiousness.

fulness be my intercession and your gentleness my eloquence, and let me carry comfort to a heart which greatly needs it.'

Philoclea looked upon her and cast down her eye again: 'Aunt,' said she, 'I would I could be so much a mistress of my own mind as to yield to my cousin's virtuous request, for so I construe of it. But my heart is already set' (and staying a while on that word, she brought forth afterwards) 'to lead a virgin's life to my death; for such a vow I have in myself devoutly made.'

'The heavens prevent such a mischief,' said Cecropia. 'A vow, quoth you? No, no, my dear niece, Nature, when you were first born, vowed you a woman, and as she made you child of a mother, so to do your best to be mother of a child. She gave you beauty to move love: she gave you wit to know love: she gave you an excellent body to reward love: which kind of liberal rewarding is crowned with an unspeakable felicity. For this, as it bindeth the receiver, so it makes happy the bestower: this doth not impoverish but enrich the giver. O the sweet name of a mother! O the comfort of comforts to see your children grow up, in whom you are, as it were, eternized! If you could conceive what a heart-tickling joy it is to see your own little ones with aweful* love come running to your lap, and like little models of yourself still carry you about them, you would think unkindness in your own thoughts that ever they did rebel against the mean unto it. But perchance I set this blessedness before your eyes as captains do victory before their soldiers, to which they must come through many pains, griefs and dangers. No, I am content you shrink from this my counsel, if the way to come unto it be not most of all pleasant.'

'I know not,' answered the sweet Philoclea, fearing lest silence would offend for sullenness, 'what contentment you speak of; but I am sure the best you can make of it (which is marriage) is a burdenous yoke.'

'Ah, dear niece,' said Cecropia, 'how much you are deceived! A yoke, indeed, we all bear, laid upon us in our creation, which by marriage is not increased but thus far eased that you have a yoke-fellow to help to draw through the cloddy cumbers* of this world. O widow-nights, bear witness with me of the difference! How often, alas, do I embrace the orphan-side of my bed which was

*aweful: full of awe. *cloddy cumbers*: earthly troubles.

wont to be imprinted by the body of my dear husband, and with tears acknowledge that I now enjoy such a liberty as the banished man hath, who may, if he list, wander over the world, but is for ever restrained from his most delightful home: that I have now such a liberty as the seeled dove hath[1] which, being first deprived of eyes, is then by the falconer cast off. For believe me, niece, believe me, man's experience is woman's best eye-sight. Have you ever seen a pure rose-water kept in a crystal glass, how fine it looks, how sweet it smells while that beautiful glass imprisons it? Break the prison, and let the water take its own course; doth it not embrace dust and lose all his former sweetness and fairness? Truly so are we, if we have not the stay, rather than the restraint, of crystalline marriage. My heart melts to think of the sweet comforts I in that happy time received, when I had never cause to care but the care was doubled, when I never rejoiced, but that I saw my joy shine in another's eyes. What shall I say of the free delight which the heart might embrace without the accusing of the inward conscience or fear of outward shame? And is a solitary life as good as this? Then can one string make as good music as a consort:* then can one colour set forth a beauty. But it may be the general consideration of marriage doth not so much mislike you as the applying of it to him. He is my son: I must confess I see him with a mother's eyes, which if they do not much deceive me, he is no such one over whom contempt may make any just challenge. He is comely, he is noble, he is rich; but that which in itself should carry all comeliness, nobility and riches, he loves you; and he loves you who is beloved of others. Drive not away his affection, sweet lady, and make no other lady hereafter proudly brag that she hath robbed you of so faithful and notable a servant.'

Philoclea heard some pieces of her speeches no otherwise than one doth when a tedious prattler cumbers the hearing of a delightful music. For her thoughts had left her ears in that captivity, and conveyed themselves to behold (with such eyes as imagination could lend them) the estate of her Zelmane, for whom how well she thought many of those sayings might have been used with a far more grateful acceptation. Therefore listing* not to dispute in a matter whereof herself was resolved and desired not to inform

* *consort*: collection of instruments. *listing*: caring.

the other, she only told her that whilst she was so captivated, she could not conceive of any such persuasions (though never so reasonable) any otherwise than as constraints; and as constraints, must needs even in nature abhor them, which at her liberty, in their own force of reason, might more prevail with her; and so fain would have returned the strength of Cecropia's persuasions to have procured freedom.

## CHAPTER 6

But neither her witty words in an enemy, nor those words, made more than eloquent with passing through such lips, could prevail in Cecropia, no more than her persuasions could win Philoclea to disavow her former vow, or to leave the prisoner Zelmane for the commanding Amphialus. So that both sides being desirers, and neither granters, they brake off conference; Cecropia sucking up more and more spite out of her denial, which yet for her son's sake she disguised with a vizard of kindness, leaving no office unperformed which might either witness or endear her son's affection. Whatsoever could be imagined likely to please her was with liberal diligence performed: musics at her window, and especially such musics as might (with doleful embassage) call the mind to think of sorrow, and think of it with sweetness; with ditties so sensibly expressing Amphialus' case, that every word seemed to be but a diversifying of the name of Amphialus. Daily presents, as it were oblations to pacify an angry deity, sent unto her: wherein, if the workmanship of the form had striven with the sumptuousness of the matter, as much did the invention in the application contend to have the chief excellency; for they were as so many stories of his disgraces and her perfections; where the richness did invite the eyes, the fashion did entertain the eyes, and the device did teach the eyes the present misery of the presenter himself, awefully serviceable;* which was the more notable as his authority was manifest. And for the bondage wherein she lived, all means used to make known that if it were a bondage, it was a bondage only knit in love-knots.

But she in heart already understanding no language but one,

* *awefully serviceable*: serving with awe.

the music wrought, indeed, a dolefulness, but it was a dolefulness
to be in his power: the ditty intended for Amphialus he translated to Zelmane; the presents seemed so many tedious clogs* of a
thralled obligation; and his service, the more diligent it was, the
more it did exprobrate,* as she thought, unto her her unworthy
estate, that even he that did her service had authority of commanding her; only construing her servitude in his own nature,
esteeming it a right, and a right bitter servitude: so that all their
shots (how well soever levelled) being carried awry from the mark
by the storm of her mislike, the prince Amphialus affectionately
languished, and Cecropia, spitefully cunning, disdained at the barrenness of their success.

Which willingly Cecropia would have revenged, but that she
saw her hurt could not be divided from her son's mischief: wherefore she bethought herself to attempt Pamela, whose beauty being
equal, she hoped if she might be won, that her son's thoughts
would rather rest on a beautiful gratefulness than still be tormented with a disdaining beauty. Therefore giving new courage
to her wicked inventions, and using the more industry because she
had missed in this, and taking even precepts of prevailing in
Pamela by her failing in Philoclea, she went to her chamber, and
(according to her own ungracious method of subtle proceeding)
stood listening at the door, because that out of the circumstance of
her present behaviour there might kindly arise a fit beginning of
her intended discourse.

And so she might perceive that Pamela did walk up and down,
full of deep, though patient thoughts. For her look and countenance was settled, her pace soft and almost still of one measure,
without any passionate gesture or violent motion: till at length, as
it were, awaking and strengthening herself, 'Well,' said she, 'yet
this is the best, and of this I am sure, that howsoever they wrong
me, they cannot over-master God. No darkness blinds His eyes, no
jail bars Him out. To whom then else should I fly but to Him for
succour?' and therewith kneeling down even where she stood, she
thus said:

'O all-seeing light and eternal life of all things, to whom
nothing is either so great that it may resist, or so small that it is

* *clogs*: encumbrances. *exprobrate*: make a matter of reproach.

contemned; look upon my misery with Thine eye of mercy, and let Thine infinite power vouchsafe to limit out some proportion of deliverance unto me, as to Thee shall seem most convenient. Let not injury, O Lord, triumph over me, and let my faults by Thy hand be corrected, and make not mine unjust enemy the minister of Thy justice. But yet, my God, if in Thy wisdom, this be the aptest chastisement for my unexcusable folly; if this low bondage be fittest for my over-high desires; if the pride of my not-enough humble heart be thus to be broken, O Lord, I yield unto Thy will, and joyfully embrace what sorrow Thou wilt have me suffer. Only thus much let me crave of Thee (let my craving, O Lord, be accepted of Thee since even that proceeds from Thee) let me crave even by the noblest title which in my greatest affliction I may give myself (that I am Thy creature) and by Thy goodness (which is Thyself) that Thou wilt suffer some beam of Thy majesty so to shine into my mind, that it may still depend confidently upon Thee. Let calamity be the exercise, but not the overthrow of my virtue: let their power prevail, but prevail not to destruction: let my greatness be their prey: let my pain be the sweetness of their revenge: let them (if so it seem good unto Thee) vex me with more and more punishment. But, O Lord, let never their wickedness have such a hand, but that I may carry a pure mind in a pure body,' (and pausing awhile) 'And, O most gracious Lord,' said she, 'whatever become of me, preserve the virtuous Musidorus.'

The other part Cecropia might well hear, but this latter prayer for Musidorus, her heart held it as so jewel-like a treasure that it would scarce trust her own lips withal. But this prayer sent to heaven from so heavenly a creature, with such a fervent grace as if devotion had borrowed her body to make of itself a most beautiful representation; with her eyes so lifted to the skyward that one would have thought they had begun to fly thitherward to take their place among their fellow stars; her naked hands raising up their whole length and, as it were, kissing one another, as if the right had been the picture of Zeal, and the left of Humbleness, which both united themselves to make their suits more acceptable: lastly, all her senses being rather tokens than instruments of her inward motions – altogether had so strange a working power that even the hardhearted wickedness of Cecropia, if it found not a love of that goodness, yet it felt an abashment at that goodness; and if she had not a kindly remorse, yet had she an irksome accusation of her own naughtiness, so that she was put from the bias of her fore-intended lesson. For well she found there was no way at that time to take that mind but with some, at least, image of virtue; and what the figure thereof was her heart knew not.

Yet did she prodigally spend her uttermost eloquence, leaving no argument unprovided which might with any force invade her excellent judgement: the justness of the request being but for marriage; the worthiness of the suitor; then her own present fortune, which should not only have amendment but felicity; besides falsely making her believe that her sister would think herself happy if now she might have his love, which before she contemned; and obliquely touching what danger it should be for her if her son should accept Philoclea in marriage and so match the next heir apparent, she being in his power: yet plentifully perjuring how extremely her son loved her, and excusing the little shows he made of it with the dutiful respect he bare unto her, and taking upon herself that she restrained him since she found she could set no limits to his passions. And as she did to Philoclea, so did she to her, with the tribute of gifts seek to bring her mind into servitude; and all other means that might either establish a beholdingness or at least awake a kindness: doing it so, as by reason of their imprisonment, one sister knew not how the other was wooed but each might think that only she was sought. But if Philoclea with sweet and humble dealing did avoid their assaults, she with the majesty of virtue did beat them off.

### CHAPTER 7

But this day their speech was the sooner broken off, by reason that he who stood as watch upon the top of the Keep* did not only see a great dust arise (which the earth sent up as if it would strive to have clouds as well as the air) but might spy sometimes, especially when the dust (wherein the naked wind did apparel itself) was carried aside from them, the shining of armour, like flashing of lightning wherewith the clouds did seem to be with child; which

* *Keep*: central tower of castle.

the sun gilding with his beams, it gave a sight delightful to any but to them that were to abide the terror. But the watch gave a quick alarum to the soldiers within, whom practice already having prepared, began each with unabashed hearts, or at least countenances, to look to their charge or obedience which was allotted unto them.

Only Clinias and Amphialus did exceed the bounds of mediocrity, the one in his natural coldness of cowardice, the other in heat of courage. For Clinias (who was bold only in busy whisperings, and even in that whisperingness rather, indeed, confident in his cunning that it should not be betrayed than any way bold, if ever it should be betrayed) now that the enemy gave a dreadful aspect unto the castle, his eyes saw no terror nor ear heard any martial sound but that they multiplied the hideousness of it to his mated* mind. Before their coming he had many times felt a dreadful expectation, but yet his mind (that was willing to ease itself of the burden of fear) did sometimes feign unto itself possibility of let,* as the death of Basilius, the discord of the nobility; and (when other cause failed him) the nature of chance served as a cause unto him; and sometimes the hearing other men speak valiantly and the quietness of his unassailed senses would make himself believe that he durst do something. But now that present danger did display itself unto his eye and that a dangerous doing must be the only mean to prevent the danger of suffering, one that had marked him would have judged that his eyes would have run into him and his soul out of him, so unkindly did either take a scent of danger. He thought the lake was too shallow and the walls too thin: he misdoubted each man's treason, and conjectured every possibility of misfortune, not only forecasting likely perils but such as all the planets together could scarcely have conspired; and already began to arm himself, though it was determined he should tarry within doors; and while he armed himself, imagined in what part of the vault he would hide himself if the enemies won the castle. Desirous he was that everybody should do valiantly but himself, and therefore was afraid to show his fear, but for very fear would have hid his fear lest it should discomfort others; but the more he

* *mated*: daunted. *possibility of let*: anything which might prevent Basilius' attack.

sought to disguise it, the more the unsuitableness of a weak broken voice to high brave words, and of a pale shaking countenance to a gesture of animating, did discover him.

But quite contrarily Amphialus, who, before the enemies came, was careful, providently diligent and not sometimes without doubting of the issue, now the nearer danger approached (like the light of a glow-worm) the less still it seemed: and now his courage began to boil in choler and with such impatience to desire to pour out both upon the enemy, that he issued presently into certain boats he had of purpose, and carrying with him some choice men, went to the fortress he had upon the edge of the lake, which he thought would be the first thing that the enemy would attempt, because it was a passage which, commanding all that side of the country and being lost, would stop victuals or other supply that might be brought into the castle: and in that fortress having some force of horsemen, he issued out with two hundred horse and five hundred footmen; ambushed his footmen in the falling of a hill which was over-shadowed with a wood; he with his horsemen went a quarter of a mile further, aside-hand of which he might perceive the many troops of the enemy who came but to take view where best to encamp themselves.

But as if the sight of the enemy had been a magnes-stone* to his courage, he could not contain himself, but showing his face to the enemy and his back to his soldiers, used that action as his only oration, both of denouncing* war to the one and persuading help from the other: who faithfully following an example of such authority, they made the earth to groan under their furious burden, and the enemies to begin to be angry with them whom in particular they knew not. Among whom there was a young man, youngest brother to Philanax, whose face as yet did not betray his sex with so much as show of hair; of a mind having no limits of hope nor knowing why to fear; full of jollity in conversation, and lately grown a lover. His name was Agenor, of all that army the most beautiful: who having ridden in sportful conversation among the foremost, all armed, saving that his beaver was up to have his breath in more freedom, seeing Amphialus come a pretty way before his company, neither staying the commandment of the cap-

* *magnes-stone*: magnet. *denouncing*: proclaiming.

tain, nor recking* whether his face were armed or no, set spurs to his horse, and with youthful bravery casting his staff about his head, put it then in his rest* as careful of comely carrying it as if the mark had been but a ring[1] and the lookers-on ladies. But Amphialus' lance was already come to the last of his descending line, and began to make the full point of death against the head of this young gentleman, when Amphialus perceiving his youth and beauty, compassion so rebated* the edge of choler that he spared that fair nakedness, and let his staff fall to Agenor's vamplate:* so as both with brave breaking should hurtlessly have performed that match, but that the pitiless lance of Amphialus (angry with being broken) with an unlucky counterbuff, full of unsparing splinters, lighted upon that face, far fitter for the combats of Venus, giving not only a sudden, but a foul death, leaving scarcely any tokens of his former beauty; but his hands abandoning the reins and his thighs the saddle, he fell sideward from the horse. Which sight coming to Leontius, a dear friend of his, who in vain had lamentably cried unto him to stay when he saw him begin his career,* it was hard to say whether pity of the one or revenge against the other held as then the sovereignty in his passions. But while he directed his eye to his friend and his hand to his enemy, so wrongly-consorted* a power could not resist the ready-minded* force of Amphialus, who perceiving his ill-directed direction against him, so paid him his debt before it was lent, that he also fell to the earth, only happy that one place and one time did finish both their loves and lives together.

But by this time there had been a furious meeting of either side, where, after the terrible salutation of warlike noise, the shaking of hands was with sharp weapons. Some lances, according to the metal they met and skill of the guider, did stain themselves in blood; some flew up in pieces, as if they would threaten heaven because they failed on earth. But their office was quickly inherited, either by (the prince of weapons) the sword, or by some heavy mace or biting axe which, hunting still the weakest chase,

---

* *recking*: caring. *rest*: shoulder-socket in which butt end of lance is rested. *ring*: see Notes, II, 5.2 (p. 855). *rebated*: blunted. *vamplate*: armour plate fixed to butt of lance to protect the hand. *career*: charge. *wrongly-consorted*: divided. *ready-minded*: fully prepared.

sought ever to light there where smallest resistance might worse prevent mischief. The clashing of armour, the crushing of staves, the jostling of bodies, the resounding of blows, was the first part of that ill-agreeing music which was beautiful with the grisliness of wounds, the rising of dust, the hideous falls and groans of the dying. The very horses, angry in their masters' anger, with love and obedience brought forth the effects of hate and resistance, and with minds of servitude did as if they affected glory. Some lay dead under their dead masters, whom unknightly wounds had unjustly punished for a faithful duty. Some lay upon their lords by like accidents, and in death had the honour to be borne by them, whom in life they had borne. Some, having lost their commanding burdens, ran scattered about the field, abashed with the madness of mankind. The earth itself (wont to be a burial of men) was now, as it were, buried with men; so was the face thereof hidden with dead bodies, to whom death had come masked* in divers manners. In one place lay disinherited heads, dispossessed of their natural seignories; in another whole bodies to see to, but that their hearts, wont to be bound all over so close, were now with deadly violence opened: in others, fouler deaths had uglily displayed their trailing guts. There lay arms, whose fingers yet moved as if they would feel for him that made them feel; and legs, which contrary to common reason, by being discharged of their burden, were grown heavier. But no sword paid so large a tribute of souls to the eternal kingdom as that of Amphialus; who like a tiger from whom a company of wolves did seek to ravish a new gotten prey, so he (remembering they came to take away Philoclea) did labour to make valour, strength, choler and hatred to answer the proportion of his love which was infinite.

There died of his hands the old knight Aeschylus, who though by years might well have been allowed to use rather the exercises of wisdom than of courage, yet having a lusty body and a merry heart, he ever took the summons of time in jest, or else it had so creepingly stolen upon him that he had heard scarcely the noise of his feet, and therefore was as fresh in apparel and as forward in enterprises as a far younger man: but nothing made him bolder than a certain prophecy had been told him that he should die in

* *masked*: disguised.

the arms of his son, and therefore feared the less the arm of an enemy. But now when Amphialus' sword was passed through his throat, he thought himself abused but that before he died, his son, indeed, seeing his father begin to fall, held him up in his arms, till a pitiless soldier of the other side with a mace brained him, making father and son become twins in their never-again-dying birth.

As for Drialus, Memnon, Nisus and Polycrates; the first had his eyes cut out so as he could not see to bid the near-following death welcome: the second had met with the same prophet that old Aeschylus had, and having found many of his speeches true, believed this too, that he should never be killed but by his own companions: and therefore no man was more valiant than he against an enemy, no man more suspicious of his friends; so as he seemed to sleep in security when he went to a battle, and to enter into a battle when he began to sleep, such guards he would set about his person, yet mistrusting those very guards lest they would murder him. But now Amphialus helped to unriddle his doubts; for he overthrowing him from his horse, his own companions, coming with a fresh supply, pressed him to death. Nisus, grasping with Amphialus, was with a short dagger slain. And for Polycrates, while he shunned as much as he could, keeping only his place for fear of punishment, Amphialus with a memorable blow strake off his head; where, with the convulsions of death setting his spurs to his horse, he gave so brave a charge upon the enemy, as it grew a proverb that Polycrates was only valiant after his head was off.

But no man escaped so well his hands as Phebilus did: for he having long loved Philoclea, though for the meanness of his estate he never durst reveal it, now knowing Amphialus, setting the edge of a rival upon the sword of an enemy, he held strong fight with him. But Amphialus had already in the dangerousest places disarmed him, and was lifting up his sword to send him away from himself, when he thinking indeed to die, 'O Philoclea,' said he, 'yet this joys me that I die for thy sake.' The name of Philoclea first stayed his sword, and when he heard him out, though he abhorred him much worse than before, yet could he not vouchsafe him the honour of dying for Philoclea, but turned his sword another way, doing him no hurt for over-much hatred. But what good did that to poor Phebilus, if escaping a valiant hand, he was slain by a base soldier who, seeing him so disarmed, thrust him through?

## CHAPTER 8

Thus with the well-followed valour of Amphialus were the others almost overthrown, when Philanax, who was the marshal of the army, came in, with new force renewing the almost decayed courage of his soldiers. For crying to them, and asking them whether their backs or their arms were better fighters, he himself thrust into the press, and making force and fury wait upon discretion and government, he might seem a brave lion who taught his young lionets how, in taking a prey, to join courage with cunning. Then fortune, as if she had made chases enough of the one side of that bloody tennis-court,[1] went of the other side the line, making as many fall down of Amphialus' followers as before had done of Philanax's, they losing the ground as fast as before they had won it, only leaving them to keep it who had lost themselves in keeping it.* Then those that had killed inherited the lot of those that had been killed; and cruel death made them lie quietly together who most in their lives had sought to disquiet each other; and many of those first overthrown had the comfort to see their murderers over-run them to Charon's ferry.

Codrus, Ctesiphon and Milo lost their lives upon Philanax's sword. But nobody's case was more pitied than of a young esquire of Amphialus called Ismenus, who, never abandoning his master, and making his tender age aspire to acts of the strongest manhood, in this time that his side was put to the worst, and that Amphialus' valour was the only stay of them from delivering themselves over to a shameful flight, he saw his master's horse killed under him. Whereupon asking advice of no other thought but of faithfulness and courage, he presently lighted from his own horse, and with the help of some choice and faithful servants, gat his master up. But in the multitude that came of either side, some to succour, some to save Amphialus, he came under the hand of

* *who had lost themselves in keeping it*: i.e. died.

Philanax: and the youth perceiving he was the man that did most hurt to his party, desirous even to change his life for glory, strake at him as he rode by him, and gave him a hurt upon the leg that made Philanax turn towards him; but seeing him so young, and of a most lovely presence, he rather took pity of him, meaning to make him prisoner and then to give him to his brother Agenor to be his companion, because they were not much unlike, neither in years nor countenance. But as he looked down upon him with that thought, he spied where his brother lay dead, and his friend Leontius by him, even almost under the squire's feet. Then sorrowing not only his own sorrow, but the past-comfort sorrow which he foreknew his mother would take (who with many tears and misgiving sighs had suffered him to go with his elder brother, Philanax) blotted out all figures of pity out of his mind, and putting forth his horse (while Ismenus doubled two or three more valiant than well-set blows) saying to himself, 'Let other mothers bewail an untimely death as well as mine,' he thrust him through. And the boy fierce though beautiful, and beautiful though dying, not able to keep his failing feet, fell down to the earth, which he bit for anger, repining at his fortune and, as long as he could, resisting death, which might seem unwilling too, so long he was in taking away his young struggling soul.

Philanax himself could have wished the blow ungiven, when he saw him fall like a fair apple which some uncourteous body, breaking his bough, should throw down before it were ripe. But the case of his brother made him forget both that and himself; so as overhastily pressing upon the retiring enemies, he was (ere he was aware) further engaged than his own soldiers could relieve him; where being overthrown by Amphialus, Amphialus, glad of him, kept head against his enemies, while some of his men carried away Philanax.

But Philanax's men, as if with the loss of Philanax they had lost the fountain of their valour, had their courage so dried up in fear that they began to set honour at their backs and to use the virtue of patience in an untimely time; when into the press comes (as hard as his horse, more afraid of the spur than the sword, could carry him) a knight in armour as dark as blackness could make it, followed by none, and adorned by nothing; so far without authority that he was without knowledge.² But virtue quickly made him known, and admiration bred him such authority that though they of whose side he came knew him not, yet they all knew it was fit to obey him; and while he was followed by the valiantest, he made way for the vilest. For taking part with the besiegers, he made the Amphialians' blood serve for a caparison* to his horse and a decking to his armour. His arm no oftener gave blows, than the blows gave wounds, than the wounds gave deaths; so terrible was his force, and yet was his quickness more forcible than his force, and his judgement more quick than his quickness. For though his sword went faster than eyesight could follow it, yet his own judgement went still before it. There died of his hand Sarpedon, Plistonax, Strophilus and Hippolitus, men of great proof in wars, and who had that day undertaken the guard of Amphialus. But while they sought to save him, they lost the fortresses that Nature had placed them in. Then slew he Megalus, who was a little before proud to see himself stained in the blood of his enemies, but when his own blood came to be married to theirs, he then felt that cruelty doth never enjoy a good cheap glory. After him sent he Palemon who had that day vowed, with foolish bravery, to be the death of ten; and nine already he had killed, and was careful* to perform his (almost performed) vow, when the black knight helped him to make up the tenth himself.

And now the often-changing fortune began also to change the hue of the battles. For at the first, though it were terrible, yet terror was decked so bravely with rich furniture, gilt swords, shining armours, pleasant pencels* that the eye with delight had scarce leisure to be afraid: but now all universally defiled with dust, blood, broken armours, mangled bodies, took away the mask, and set forth horror in his own horrible manner. But neither could danger be dreadful to Amphialus' undismayable courage, nor yet seem ugly to him whose truly-affected* mind did still paint it over with the beauty of Philoclea: and therefore he (rather inflamed than troubled with the increase of dangers, and glad to find a worthy subject to exercise his courage) sought out this new knight, whom he might easily find: for he, like a wanton rich man

* *caparison*: decoration. *careful*: anxious. *pencels*: pennons. *truly-affected*: in the grip of passion.

that throws down his neighbours' houses to make himself the better prospect, so had his sword made him so spacious a room that Amphialus had more cause to wonder at the finding than labour for the seeking: which, if it stirred hate in him to see how much harm he did to the one side, it provoked as much emulation in him to perceive how much good he did to the other side. Therefore, they approaching one to the other, as in two beautiful folks love naturally stirs a desire of joining, so in their two courages hate stirred a desire of trial.

Then began there a combat between them worthy to have had more large lists* and more quiet beholders, for with the spur of courage and the bit of respect each so guided himself, that one might well see the desire to overcome made them not forget how to overcome. In such time and proportion they did employ their blows that none of Ceres' servants could more cunningly place his flail.[3] while the left foot spur set forward his own horse, the right set backward the contrary horse, even sometimes by the advantage of the enemy's leg, while the left hand (like him that held the stern)* guided the horse's obedient courage: all done in such order that it might seem the mind was a right prince indeed, who sent wise and diligent lieutenants into each of those well-governed parts. But the more they fought, the more they desired to fight; and the more they smarted, the less they felt the smart: and now were like to make a quick proof to whom fortune or valour would seem most friendly, when in comes an old governor of Amphialus, always a good knight and careful of his charge, who giving a sore wound to the black knight's thigh, while he thought not of him, with another blow slew his horse under him. Amphialus cried to him that he dishonoured him:

'You say well,' answered the old knight, 'to stand now like a private soldier, setting your credit upon particular fighting, while you may see Basilius with all his host is getting between you and your town.'

He looked that way and found that true indeed, that the enemy was beginning to encompass him about and stop his return: and therefore causing the retreat to be sounded, his governor led his men homeward, while he kept himself still hindmost, as if he had

* lists: space for jousting. *stern:* helm.

stood at the gate of a sluice to let the stream go with such proportion as should seem good unto him; and with so manful discretion performed it that (though with loss of many of his men) he returned in himself safe, and content that his enemies had felt how sharp the sword could bite of Philoclea's lover. The other party, being sorry for the loss of Philanax, was yet sorrier when the Black Knight could not be found: for he, having gotten a horse whom his dying master had bequeathed to the world, finding himself sore hurt, and not desirous to be known, had in the time of the enemies' retiring retired away also, his thigh not bleeding blood so fast as his heart bled revenge. But Basilius, having attempted in vain to bar the safe return of Amphialus, encamped himself as strongly as he could, while he, to his grief, might hear the joy was made in the town by his own subjects that he had that day sped no better. For Amphialus, being well beloved of that people, when they saw him not vanquished, they esteemed him as victorious, his youth setting a flourishing show upon his worthiness and his great nobility ennobling his dangers.

## CHAPTER 9

But the first thing Amphialus did, being returned, was to visit Philoclea, and first presuming to cause his dream to be sung unto her which he had seen the night before he fell in love with her, making a fine boy he had accord a pretty dolefulness unto it.

The song was this:[1]

Now was our heavenly vault deprived of the light
With sun's depart; and now the darkness of the night
Did light those beamy stars which greater light did dark:
Now each thing that enjoy'd that fiery quick'ning spark
(Which life is call'd) were mov'd their spirits to repose,
And wanting use of eyes, their eyes began to close.
A silence sweet each where with one consent embrac'd,
(A music sweet to one in careful musing plac'd);
And mother earth, now clad in mourning weeds, did breathe
A dull desire to kiss the image of our death;
When I, disgraced wretch, not wretched then, did give

My senses such relief as they which quiet live,
Whose brains boil not in woes, nor breasts with beatings ache,
With nature's praise are wont in safest home to take.
Far from my thoughts was aught whereto their minds aspire
Who under courtly pomps do hatch a base desire.
Free all my powers were from those captiving* snares
Which heav'nly purest gifts defile with muddy cares.
Ne could my soul itself accuse of such a fault
As tender conscience might with furious pangs assault.
But like the feeble flower (whose stalk cannot sustain
His weighty top) his top downward doth drooping lean,
Or as the silly bird in well-acquainted nest
Doth hide his head with cares, but only how to rest;
So I in simple course, and unentangled mind,
Did suffer drowsy lids mine eyes, then clear, to blind;
And laying down mine head, did nature's rule observe,
Which senses up doth shut the senses to preserve.
They first their youth forgot, then fancies lost their force,
Till deadly sleep at length possess'd my living corse.
A living corse I lay: but ah, my wakeful mind
(Which, made of heav'nly stuff, no mortal change doth blind)
Flew up with freer wings, of fleshly bondage free,
And having plac'd my thoughts, my thoughts thus placed me:
Methought, nay sure I was, I was in fairest wood
Of Samothea land, a land which whilom stood
An honour to the world, while honour was their end,
And while their line of years they did in virtue spend.
But there I was, and there my calmy thoughts I fed
On nature's sweet repast, as healthful senses led.
Her gifts my study was, her beauties were my sport,
My work her works to know, her dwelling my resort.
Those lamps of heav'nly fire to fixed motion bound,
The ever turning spheres, the never moving ground;[2]
What essence dest'ny hath; if fortune be or no;
Whence our immortal souls to mortal earth do flow:
What life it is, and how that all these lives do gather,

*captiving*: making captive.

With outward maker's force, or like an inward father.
Such thoughts, methought, I thought, and strain'd my single
  mind,
Then void of nearer cares, the depth of things to find,
When lo, with hugest noise, (such noise a tower makes
When it blown down with wind a fall of ruin takes,
Or, such a noise it was as highest thunders send,
Or cannons thunder-like, all shot together, lend),
The moon asunder rent, whereout with sudden fall
(More swift than falcon's stoop to feeding falconer's call)
There came a chariot fair, by doves and sparrows guided,
Whose storm-like course stay'd not till hard by me it bided.
I, wretch, astonished was, and thought the deathful doom
Of heaven, of earth, of hell, of time and place was come.
But straight there issued forth two ladies (ladies sure
They seemed to me) on whom did wait a virgin pure.
Strange were the ladies' weeds, yet more unfit than strange.
The first with clothes tucked up, as nymphs in woods do range,
Tucked up even with the knees, with bow and arrows prest:*
Her right arm naked was, discovered* was her breast.
But heavy was her pace, and such a meagre cheer,
As little hunting mind, God knows, did there appear.
The other had with art (more than our women know,
As stuff meant for the sale set out to glaring show)
A wanton woman's face, and with curl'd knots had twin'd
Her hair, which by the help of painters' cunning, shin'd.
When I such guests did see come out of such a house,
The mountains great with child I thought brought forth a
  mouse.[3]
But walking forth, the first thus to the second said,
'Venus, come on.' Said she,* 'Diana, you are obey'd.'
Those names abash'd me much, when those great names I heard,
Although their fame (me seem'd) from truth had greatly jarr'd.
As I thus musing stood, Diana call'd to her
The waiting nymph, a nymph that did excel as far

* *prest:* ready for action. *discovered:* uncovered. *Said she:* i.e. Venus
replies.

All things that erst I saw, as orient pearls exceed
That which their mother\* hight,\* or else their silly seed:\*
Indeed a perfect hew, indeed a sweet concent\*
Of all those Graces' gifts the heavens have ever lent.
And so she was attir'd as one that did not prize
Too much her peerless parts, nor yet could them despise.
But call'd, she came apace; a pace, wherein did move
The band of beauties all, the little world of love.
And bending humble eyes (O eyes, the sun of sight)
She waited mistress' will; who thus disclos'd her sprite:
'Sweet Mira mine,' quoth she, 'the pleasure of my mind,
In whom of all my rules the perfect proof I find,
To only thee, thou seest, we grant this special grace
Us to attend, in this most private time and place.
Be silent therefore now, and so be silent still
Of that thou seest; close up in secret knot thy will.'
She answered was with look, and well perform'd behest:
And Mira I admir'd; her shape sank in my breast.
But thus with ireful eyes and face that shook with spite,
Diana did begin, 'What mov'd me to invite
Your presence, sister dear, first to my moony sphere,
And hither now, vouchsafe to take with willing ear.
I know full well you know what discord long hath reign'd
Betwixt us two: how much that discord foul hath stain'd
Both our estates, while each the other did deprave,\*
Proof speaks too much to us that feeling trial have.
Our names are quite forgot, our temples are defac'd;
Our offerings spoil'd, our priests from priesthood are displac'd.
Is this the fruit of strife, those thousand churches high,
Those thousand altars fair now in the dust to lie?
In mortal minds, our minds but planets' names preserve;
No knees once bowed, forsooth, for them they say we serve.
Are we their servants grown? No doubt, a noble stay;\*
Celestial powers to worms, Jove's children serve to clay!
But such they say we be; this praise our discord bred,
While we for mutual spite a striving passion fed.

\* *their mother*: mother-of-pearl. *hight*: is called. *silly seed*: seed
pearls. *concent*: harmony. *deprave*: vilify. *stay*: state.

But let us wiser be; and what foul discord brake,
So much more strong again let fastest concord make.
Our years do it require; you see we both do feel
The weak'ning work of time's for ever whirling wheel.
Although we be divine, our grandsire Saturn is
With age's force decay'd, yet once the heaven was his.[4]
And now before we seek, by wise Apollo's skill,
Our young years to renew, for so he saith he will,
Let us a perfect peace between us two resolve;
Which, lest the ruinous want of government dissolve,
Let one the princess be, to her the other yield;
For vain equality is but contention's field.
And let her have the gifts that should in both remain;
In her let beauty both and chasteness fully reign.
So as if I prevail, you give your gifts to me;
If you, on you I lay what in my office be.
Now resteth only this, which of us two is she,
To whom precedence shall of both accorded be.
For that (so that you like) hereby doth lie a youth,'
(She beckoned unto me) 'as yet of spotless truth,
Who may this doubt discern: for better wit than lot,
Becometh us:[5] in us fortune determines not.
This crown of amber fair' (an amber crown she held)
'To worthiest let him give, when both he hath beheld;
And be it as he saith.' Venus was glad to hear
Such proffer made, which she well show'd with smiling cheer,
As though she were the same, as when by Paris' doom,[6]
She had chief goddesses in beauty overcome.
And smirkly* thus gan say, 'I never sought debate,
Diana dear; my mind to love and not to hate
Was ever apt; but you my pastimes did despise.
I never spited you, but thought you overwise.
Now kindness proferr'd is, none kinder is than I;
And so most ready am this mean of peace to try;
And let him be our judge: the lad doth please me well.
Thus both did come to me, and both began to tell
(For both together spake, each loth to be behind)

       *smirkly: with a smirk.

That they by solemn oath their deities would bind
To stand unto my will: their will they made me know.
I that was first aghast, when first I saw their show,
Now bolder wax'd, wax'd proud that I such sway must bear;
For near acquaintance doth diminish reverent fear.
And having bound them fast by Styx* they should obey
To all what I decreed, did thus my verdict say:
'How ill both you can rule well hath your discord taught;
Ne yet, for aught I see, your beauties merit aught.
To yonder Nymph therefore' (to Mira I did point)
'The crown above you both for ever I appoint.'
I would have spoken out, but out they both did cry,
'Fie, fie, what have we done? Ungodly rebel, fie!
But now we needs must yield to that our oaths require.
Yet thou shalt not go free,' quoth Venus. 'Such a fire
Her beauty kindle shall within thy foolish mind
That thou full oft shalt wish thy judging eyes were blind.'
'Nay then,' Diana said, 'the chasteness I will give
In ashes of despair, though burnt, shall make thee live.'
'Nay thou,' said both, 'shalt see such beams shine in her face,
That thou shalt never dare seek help of wretched case.'
And with that cursed curse away to heaven they fled,
First having all their gifts upon fair Mira spread.
The rest I cannot tell, for therewithal I wak'd,
And found with deadly fear that all my sinews shak'd.
Was it a dream? O dream, how hast thou wrought in me,
That I things erst unseen should first in dreaming see?
And thou, O traitor sleep, made for to be our rest,
How hast thou fram'd the pain wherewith I am oppress'd?
O coward Cupid, thus dost thou thy honour keep,
Unarm'd (alas) unwarn'd, to take a man asleep?

Laying not only the conquests, but the heart of the conqueror at
her* feet . . .⁷ But she receiving him after her wonted sorrowful
(but otherwise unmoved) manner, it made him think his good
success was but as a pleasant monument of a doleful burial, joy

* *Styx*: the river of Hell by which the gods took their oath. *her*:
Philoclea's.

itself seeming bitter unto him, since it agreed not to her taste.

Therefore, still craving his mother's help to persuade her, he himself sent for Philanax unto him, whom he had not only long hated but now had his hate greatly increased by the death of his squire Ismenus. Besides, he had made him as one of the chief causes that moved him to this rebellion, and therefore was inclined (to colour the better his action, and the more to embrew* the hands of his accomplices by making them guilty of such a trepass) in some formal sort to cause him to be executed, being also greatly egged thereunto by his mother and some other, who long had hated Philanax only because he was more worthy than they to be loved.

But while that deliberation was handled according rather to the humour than the reason of each speaker, Philoclea coming to knowledge of the hard plight wherein Philanax stood, she desired one of the gentlewomen appointed to wait upon her to go in her name and beseech Amphialus that, if the love of her had any power of persuasion in his mind, he would lay no further punishment than imprisonment upon Philanax. This message was delivered even as Philanax was entering to the presence of Amphialus, coming, according to the warning was given him, to receive a judgement of death. But when he, with manful resolution, attended the fruit of such a tyrannical sentence, thinking it wrong but no harm to him that should die in so good a cause, Amphialus turned quite the form of his pretended* speech, and yielded him humble thanks that by his means he had come to that happiness as to receive a commandment of his lady: and therefore he willingly gave him liberty to return in safety whither he would, quitting him not only of all former grudge, but assuring him that he would be willing to do him any friendship and service: only desiring thus much of him, that he would let him know the discourse and intent of Basilius' proceeding.

'Truly, my Lord,' answered Philanax, 'if there were any such known to me, secret in my master's counsel, as that the revealing thereof might hinder his good success, I should loathe the keeping of my blood with the loss of my faith, and would think the just name of a traitor a hard purchase of a few years' living. But since it is so that my master hath indeed no way of privy practice, but

* *embrew*: stain. *pretended*: intended.

means openly and forcibly to deal against you, I will not stick, in few words, to make your required declaration.'

Then told he him in what a maze of amazement both Basilius and Gynecia were when they missed their children and Zelmane; sometimes apt to suspect some practice of Zelmane, because she was a stranger; sometimes doubting some relics of the late mutiny, which doubt was rather increased than any wise satisfied by Miso, who, being found almost dead for hunger by certain country people, brought home word with what cunning they were trained out* and with what violence they were carried away. But that within a few days they came to knowledge where they were by Amphialus' own letters sent abroad to procure confederates in his attempts. That Basilius' purpose was never to leave the siege of this town till he had taken it, and revenged the injury done unto him. That he meant rather to win it by time and famine than by force of assault, knowing how valiant men he had to deal withal in the town: that he had sent order that supplies of soldiers, pioneers, and all things else necessary, should daily be brought unto him, so as, 'My Lord,' said Philanax, 'let me now, having received my life by your grace, let me give you your life and honour by my counsel; protesting unto you that I cannot choose but love you, being my master's nephew, and that I wish you well in all causes but this. You know his nature is as apt to forgive as his power is able to conquer. Your fault past is excusable, in that love persuaded and youth was persuaded. Do not urge the effects of angry victory, but rather seek to obtain that constantly by courtesy which you can never assuredly enjoy by violence.'

One might easily have seen in the cheer of Amphialus that disdainful choler would fain have made the answer for him, but the remembrance of Philoclea served for forcible barriers between anger and angry effects; so as he said no more, but that he would not put him to the trouble to give him any further counsel, but that he might return, if he listed, presently. Philanax glad to receive an uncorrupted liberty, humbly accepted his favourable convoy out of the town; and so departed, not visiting the princesses, thinking it might be offensive to Amphialus, and no way fruitful to them who were no way, but by force, to be rescued.

* *trained out*: decoyed away.

The poor ladies, indeed, not suffered either to meet together, or to have conference with any other but such as Cecropia had already framed to sing all their songs to her tune; she herself omitting no day, and catching hold of every occasion to move forward her son's desire and remove their own resolutions; using the same arguments to the one sister as to the other; determining that whom she could win first, the other should (without her son's knowledge) by poison be made away. But though the reasons were the same to both, yet the handling was diverse, according as she saw their humours to prepare a more or less aptness of apprehension: this day having used long speech to Philoclea, amplifying not a little the great dutifulness her son had showed in delivering Philanax; of whom she could get no answer but a silence sealed up in virtue, and so sweetly graced as that in one instant it carried with it both resistance and humbleness.

## CHAPTER 10

Cecropia, threatening in herself to run a more rugged race with her, went to her sister Pamela, who that day (having wearied herself with reading, and with the height of her heart disdaining to keep company with any of the gentlewomen appointed to attend her, whom she accounted her jailors) was working upon a purse certain roses and lilies, as by the fineness of the work one might see she had borrowed her wits of the sorrow that then owed* them, and lent them wholly to that exercise. For the flowers she had wrought carried such life in them that the cunningest painter might have learned of her needle, which with so pretty a manner made his careers to and fro through the cloth, as if the needle itself would have been loth to have gone fromward such a mistress but that it hoped to return thitherward very quickly again; the cloth looking with many eyes upon her, and lovingly embracing the wounds she gave it. The shears also were at hand to behead the silk that was grown too short: and if at any time she put her mouth to bite it off, it seemed that where she had been long in making of a rose with her hands, she would in an instant make roses with her lips, as the lilies seemed to have their

* *owed*: possessed.

whiteness rather of the hand that made them than of the matter whereof they were made, and that they grew there by the suns of her eyes, and were refreshed by the most in discomfort-comfortable air which an unwares sigh might bestow upon them. But the colours for the ground were so well chosen – neither sullenly dark nor glaringly lightsome, and so well proportioned as that, though much cunning were in it, yet it was but to serve for an ornament of the principal work – that it was not without marvel to see how a mind which could cast a careless semblant* upon the greatest conflicts of fortune could command itself to take care for so small matters. Neither had she neglected the dainty dressing of her self; but as if it had been her marriage time to affliction, she rather seemed to remember her own worthiness than the unworthiness of her husband. For well one might perceive she had not rejected the counsel of a glass, and that her hands had pleased themselves in paying the tribute of undeceiving skill to so high perfections of nature.

The sight whereof so diverse from her sister (who rather suffered sorrow to dress itself in her beauty than that she would bestow any entertainment of so unwelcome a guest) made Cecropia take a sudden assuredness of hope that she should obtain somewhat of Pamela; thinking, according to the squaring out of her own good nature, that beauty carefully set forth would soon prove a sign of an unrefusing harbour. Animated wherewith, she sat down by Pamela, and taking the purse, and with affected curiosity looking upon the work:

'Fully happy is he,' said she, 'at least if he knew his own happiness, to whom a purse in this manner, and by this hand wrought, is dedicated. In faith he shall have cause to account it not as a purse for treasure but as a treasure itself, worthy to be pursed up in the purse of his own heart.'

'And think you so indeed?' said Pamela, half smiling, 'I promise you I wrought it but to make some tedious hours believe that I thought not of them; for else I valued it but even as a very purse.'

'It is the right nature,' said Cecropia, 'of beauty to work unwitting effects of wonder.'

'Truly,' said Pamela, 'I never thought till now that this out-

* *cast . . . semblant*: appear indifferent to.

ward gloss, entitled beauty, which it pleaseth you to lay to my (as I think) unguilty charge, was but a pleasant mixture of natural colours, delightful to the eye as music is to the ear, without any further consequence, since it is a thing which not only beasts have, but even stones and trees, many of them, do greatly excel in it.'

'That other things,' answered Cecropia, 'have some portion of it takes not away the excellency of it where indeed it doth excel, since we see that even those beasts, trees and stones are in the name of beauty only highly praised. But that the beauty of human persons be beyond all other things there is great likelihood of reason, since to them only is given the judgement to discern beauty; and among reasonable wights, as it seems, that our sex hath the pre-eminence, so that in that pre-eminence Nature countervails* all other liberalities, wherein she may be thought to have dealt more favourably toward mankind. How do men crown, think you, themselves with glory for having either by force brought others to yield to their mind, or with long study and premeditated orations persuaded what they would have persuaded! And see, a fair woman shall not only command without authority but persuade without speaking. She shall not need to procure attention, for their own eyes will chain their ears unto it. Men venture lives to conquer; she conquers lives without venturing. She is served and obeyed, which is the most notable not because the laws so command it, but because they become laws to themselves to obey her;[1] not for her parents' sake, but for her own. She need not dispute whether to govern by fear or love since, without her thinking thereof, their love will bring forth fear, and their fear will fortify their love; and she need not seek offensive or defensive force, since her only lips may stand for ten thousand shields, and ten thousand unevitable* shot go from her eyes. Beauty, beauty, dear niece, is the crown of the feminine greatness which gift on whomsoever the heavens (therein most niggardly) do bestow, without question she is bound to use it to the noble purpose for which it is created; not only winning but preserving, since that indeed is the right happiness which is not only in itself happy but can also derive the happiness to another.'

* *countervails*: makes up for. *unevitable*: inescapable.

'Certainly, Aunt,' said Pamela, 'I fear me you will make me not only think myself fairer than ever I did, but think my fairness a matter of greater value than heretofore I could imagine it. For I ever, till now, conceived those conquests you speak of rather to proceed from the weakness of the conquered than from the strength of the conquering power; as they say, the Cranes overthrow whole battles* of Pygmies[2] not so much of their cranish courage as because the other are Pygmies; and that we see young babes think babies* of wonderful excellency, and yet the babies are but babies. But since your elder years and abler judgement find beauty to be worthy of so incomparable estimation, certainly, methinks, it ought to be held in dearness, according to the excellency, and no more than we would do of things which we account precious ever to suffer it to be defiled.'

'Defiled?' said Cecropia, 'Marry, God forbid that my speech should tend to any such purpose as should deserve so foul a title. My meaning is, to join your beauty to love, your youth to delight. For, truly, as colours should be as good as nothing if there were no eyes to behold them, so is beauty nothing, without the eye of love behold it: and therefore so far is it from defiling it that it is the only honouring of it, the only preserving of it; for beauty goes away, devoured by time, but where remains it ever flourishing but in the heart of a true lover? And such a one, if ever there were any, is my son, whose love is so subjected unto you, that rather than breed any offence unto you, it will not delight itself in beholding you.'

'There is no effect of his love,' answered Pamela, 'better pleaseth me than that: but as I have often answered you, so resolutely I say unto you, that he must get my parents' consent, and then he shall know further of my mind: for, without that I know I should offend God.'

'O sweet youth,' said Cecropia, 'how untimely subject it is to devotion! No, no, sweet niece, let us old folks think of such precise considerations: do you enjoy the heaven of your age, whereof you are sure; and like good householders which spend those things that will not be kept, so do you pleasantly enjoy that which else will bring an over-late repentance, when your glass shall accuse

* *battles*: armies. *babies*: dolls.

you to your face what a change there is in you. Do you see how
the spring-time is full of flowers, decking itself with them, and not
aspiring to the fruits of autumn? What lesson is that unto you,
but that in the April of your age you should be like April? Let not
some of them for whom already the grave gapeth, and perhaps
envy the felicity in you which themselves cannot enjoy, persuade
you to lose the hold of occasion while it may not only be taken,
but offers, nay sues to be taken; which, if it be not now taken, will
never hereafter be overtaken. Yourself know how your father hath
refused all offers made by the greatest princes about you; and will
you suffer your beauty to be hidden in the wrinkles of his peevish
thoughts?'

'If he be peevish,' said Pamela, 'yet is he my father; and how
beautiful soever I be, I am his daughter; so as God claims at my
hands obedience, and makes me no judge of his imperfections.'

These often replies upon conscience in Pamela made Cecropia
think that there was no righter way for her than, as she had (in
her opinion) set her in liking of beauty with persuasion not to
suffer it to be void of purpose, so if she could make her less feeling
of those heavenly conceits, that then she might easily wind her to
her crooked bias. Therefore employing the uttermost of her mischievous wit, and speaking the more earnestly because she spake
as she thought, she thus dealt with her.

'Dear niece, or rather, dear daughter (if my affection and wish
might prevail therein) how much doth it increase, trow you,* the
earnest desire I have of this blessed match to see these virtues of
yours knit fast with such zeal of devotion, indeed the best bond
which the most politic wits have found to hold man's wit in well
doing! For as children must first by fear be induced to know that
which after, when they do know, they are most glad of, so are
these bugbears of opinions brought by great clerks into the world
to serve as shewels* to keep them from those faults whereto else
the vanity of the world and weakness of senses might pull them.
But in you, niece, whose excellency is such as it need not to be
held up by the staff of vulgar opinions, I would not you should
love virtue servilely, for fear of I know not what which you see
not, but even for the good effects of virtue which you see. Fear,

* *trow you*: do you think. *shewels*: scarecrows.

and indeed, foolish fear, and fearful ignorance, was the first inventor of those conceits; for when they heard it thunder, not knowing the natural cause, they thought there was some angry body above that spake so loud; and ever the less they did perceive, the more they did conceive. Whereof they knew no cause, that grew straight a miracle; foolish folks not marking that the alterations be but upon particular accidents, the universality being always one. Yesterday was but as today, and tomorrow will tread the same footsteps of his foregoers: so as it is manifest enough that all things follow but the course of their own nature, saving only man, who while by the pregnancy of his imagination he strives to things supernatural, meanwhile he loseth his own natural felicity. Be wise, and that wisdom shall be a God unto thee. Be contented, and that is thy heaven: for else to think that those powers (if there be any such) above are moved either by the eloquence of our prayers or in a chafe* at the folly of our actions carries as much reason, as if flies should think that men take great care which of them hums sweetest, and which of them flies nimblest.'

She would have spoken further to have enlarged and confirmed her discourse, when Pamela, whose cheeks were dyed in the beautifullest grain* of virtuous anger, with eyes which glistered forth beams of disdain, thus interrupted her.

'Peace, wicked woman, peace, unworthy to breathe that dost not acknowledge the breath-giver; most unworthy to have a tongue which speaketh against him through whom thou speakest: keep your affection* to yourself which, like a bemired dog, would defile with fawning. You say yesterday was as today. O foolish woman, and most miserably foolish since wit makes you foolish! What doth that argue but that there is a constancy in the everlasting governor? Would you have an inconstant God, since we count a man foolish that is inconstant? He is not seen, you say: and would you think him a God who might be seen by so wicked eyes as yours? – which yet might see enough if they were not like such who, for sport's sake, willingly hoodwink* themselves to receive blows the easier. But though I speak to you without any hope of fruit in so rotten a heart, and there be nobody else here to

* *in a chafe*: in a rage. *grain*: colour. *affection*: disease. *hoodwink*: blindfold.

488

judge of my speeches, yet be thou my witness, O captivity, that my ears shall not be willingly guilty of my Creator's blasphemy.

'You say, because we know not the causes of things, therefore fear was the mother of superstition. Nay, because we know that each effect hath a cause, that hath engendered a true and lively devotion. For this goodly work of which we are, and in which we live, hath not his being by chance; on which opinion[3] it is beyond marvel by what chance any brain could stumble. For if it be eternal, as you would seem to conceive of it, eternity and chance are things unsufferable together. For that is chanceable which happeneth; and if it happen, there was a time before it happened when it might have not happened, or else it did not happen; and so, if chanceable, not eternal, as now being, then not being. And as absurd it is to think that if it had a beginning, his beginning was derived from chance: for chance could never make all things of nothing; and if there were substances before, which by chance should meet to make up this work, thereon follows another bottomless pit of absurdities. For then those substances must needs have been from ever, and so eternal: and that eternal causes should bring forth chanceable effects is as sensible as that the sun should be the author of darkness. Again, if it were chanceable, then was it not necessary; whereby you take away all consequents*. But we see in all things, in some respect or other, necessity of consequence: therefore in reason we must needs know that the causes were necessary.

'Lastly, chance is variable, or else it is not to be called chance: but we see this work is steady and permanent. If nothing but chance had glued those pieces of this All, the heavy parts would have gone infinitely downward, the light infinitely upward, and so never have met to have made up this goodly body. For before there was a heaven or earth, there was neither a heaven to stay* the height of the rising, nor an earth, which (in respect of the round walls of heaven) should become a centre.[4] Lastly, perfect order, perfect beauty, perfect constancy, if these be the children of chance, or Fortune the efficient* of these, let wisdom be counted the root of wickedness, and eternity the fruit of her inconstancy.[5]

*consequents: cause and effect. stay: halt. the efficient: the immediate cause.

'But, you will say, it is so by nature, as much as if you said, it is so because it is so. If you mean of many natures conspiring together as in a popular government to establish this fair estate, as if the elementish and ethereal parts should in their town-house set down the bounds of each one's office, then consider what follows: that there must needs have been a wisdom which made them concur; for their natures, being absolute contrary, in nature rather would have sought each others' ruin than have served as well consorted parts to such an unexpressible harmony. For that contrary things should meet to make up a perfection, without a force and wisdom above their powers, is absolutely impossible, unless you will fly to that hissed-out opinion of chance again. But you may, perhaps, affirm that one universal Nature, which hath been for ever, is the knitting together of these many parts to such an excellent unity. If you mean a Nature of wisdom, goodness and providence, which knows what it doth, then say you that which I seek of you, and cannot conclude* those blasphemies with which you defiled your mouth and mine ears. But if you mean a nature, as we speak of the fire which goeth upward, it knows not why; and of the nature of the sea, which in ebbing and flowing seems to observe so just a dance, and yet understands no music, it is but still the same absurdity superscribed with another title. For this word, One, being attributed to that which is All, is but one mingling of many, and many ones; as in a less matter, when we say one kingdom which contains many cities, or one city which contains many persons, wherein the under-ones (if there be not a superior power and wisdom) cannot by nature regard to* any preservation but of themselves: no more we see they do, since the water willingly quenches the fire and drowns the earth, so far are they from a conspired* unity, but that a right heavenly Nature indeed (as it were) unnaturing them, doth so bridle them.

'Again, it is as absurd in Nature that from an unity many contraries should proceed still kept in an unity, as that from the number of contrarieties an unity should arise. I say still, if you banish both a singularity and plurality of judgement from among them, then (if so earthly a mind can lift itself up so high) do but

* *conclude:* logically conclude in. *regard to:* have regard to. *conspired:* planned.

conceive how a thing whereto you give the highest and most excellent kind of being (which is eternity) can be of the base and vilest degree of being and next to a not-being, which is so to be as not to enjoy his own being. I will not here call all your senses to witness, which can hear nor see nothing which yields not most evident evidence of the unspeakableness of that wisdom; each thing being directed to an end, and an end of preservation, so proper effects of judgement, as speaking and laughing are of mankind.

'But what mad fury can ever so inveigle any conceit as to see our mortal and corruptible selves to have a reason, and that this universality (whereof we are but the least pieces) should be utterly devoid thereof; as if one should say that one's foot might be wise, and himself foolish? This heard I once alleged against such a godless mind as yours, who being driven to acknowledge this beastly absurdity that our bodies should be better than the whole world, if it had the knowledge whereof the other were void; he sought, (not able to answer directly) to shift it off in this sort: that if that reason were true, then must it follow also that the world must have in it a spirit that could write and read too, and be learned, since that was in us commendable. Wretched fool, not considering that books be but supplies of defects and so are praised because they help our want, and therefore cannot be incident to the eternal intelligence which needs no recording of opinions to confirm his knowledge, no more than the sun wants wax to be the fuel of his glorious lightfulness.

'This word therefore cannot otherwise consist but by a mind of wisdom which governs it; which whether you will allow to be the Creator thereof (as undoubtedly he is) or the soul and governor thereof, most certain it is, that whether he govern all, or make all, his power is above either his creatures or his government. And if his power be above all things, then consequently it must needs be infinite, since there is nothing above it to limit it; for beyond which there is nothing must needs be boundless and infinite. If his power be infinite, then likewise must his knowledge be infinite; for else there should be an infinite proportion of power which he should not know how to use, the unsensibleness* whereof I think even

* *unsensibleness*: senselessness.

you can conceive: and if infinite, then must nothing, no not the estate of flies (which you with so unsavoury scorn did jest at) be unknown unto him. For if it were, then there were his knowledge bounded, and so not infinite. If his knowledge and power be infinite, then must needs his goodness and justness march in the same rank; for infiniteness of power and knowledge, without like measure of goodness, must necessarily bring forth destruction and ruin, and not ornament and preservation.

'Since then there is a God, and an all-knowing God, so as he sees into the darkest of all natural secrets which is the heart of man; and sees therein the deepest dissembled thoughts, nay sees the thoughts before they be thought; since he is just to exercise his might, and mighty to perform his justice, assure thyself, most wicked woman (that hast so plaguily a corrupted mind as thou canst not keep thy sickness to thyself, but must most wickedly infect others) assure thyself, I say (for what I say depends of everlasting and unremovable causes) that the time will come when thou shalt know that power by feeling it; when thou shalt see His wisdom in the manifesting thy ugly shamefulness, and shalt only perceive him to have been a Creator in thy destruction.'

## CHAPTER 11

Thus she said, thus she ended, with so fair a majesty of unconquered virtue that captivity might seem to have authority over tyranny. So foully* was the filthiness of impiety discovered by the shining of her unstained goodness (so far as either Cecropia saw indeed, or else the guilty amazement of a self-accusing conscience made her eyes untrue judges of their natural object) that there was a light more than human which gave a lustre to her perfections. But Cecropia (like a bat which, though it have eyes to discern that there is a sun, yet hath so evil eyes that it cannot delight in the sun) found a truth but could not love it. But as great persons are wont to make the wrong they have done to be a cause to do the more wrong, her knowledge rose to no higher point but to envy a worthier; and her will was no otherwise bent but the more to hate, the more she found her enemy provided against her.

* *so foully:* in all its foulness.

Yet all the while she spake (though with eyes cast like a horse that would strike at the stirrup, and with colour which blushed through yellowness) she sat rather still than quiet, and after her speech rather muttered than replied; for the war of wickedness in herself brought forth disdainful pride to resist cunning dissimulation. So as, saying little more unto her but that she should have leisure enough better to bethink herself, she went away repining but not repenting, condemning greatly, as she thought, her son's over-feeble humbleness, and purposing to egg him forward to a course of violence: for herself, determining to deal with neither of them both any more in manner of a suitor, for what majesty of virtue did in the one, that did silent humbleness in the other. But finding her son over-apt to lay both condemnation and execution of sorrow upon himself, she sought to mitigate his mind with feigned delays of comfort, who (having this inward overthrow in himself) was the more vexed that he could not utter the rage thereof upon his outward enemies.

For Basilius, taught by the last day's trial what dangerous effects chosen courages can bring forth, rather used the spade than the sword, or the sword but to defend the spade, girding about the whole town with trenches; which beginning a good way off from the town, with a number of well directed pioneers* he still carried before him, till they came to a near distance, where he builded forts, one answering the other, in such sort as it was a pretty consideration in the discipline of war to see building used for the instrument of ruin, and the assailer entrenched as if he was besieged. But many sallies did Amphialus make to hinder their working. But they (exercising more melancholy than choler in their resolution)[1] made him find that if, by the advantage of place, few are able to defend themselves from many, that many must needs have power (making themselves strong in seat) to repel few, referring the revenge rather to the end than to a present requital. Yet oftentimes they dealt some blows in light skirmishes, each side having a strong retiring place, and rather fighting with many alarums to vex the enemy than for any hope of great success.

Which every way was a tedious cumber to the impatient courage of Amphialus: till the fame of this war bringing thither divers

* *pioneers*: trench-diggers.

both strangers and subjects, as well of princely as noble houses, the gallant Phalantus – who refrained his sportful delights as then, to serve Basilius (whom he honoured for received honours) – when he had spent some time in considering the Arcadian manner in marching, encamping and fighting, and had learned in what points of government and obedience their discipline differed from others, and so had satisfied his mind in the knowledges both for the cutting off the enemies' helps and furnishing one's self, which Basilius' orders could deliver unto him; his young spirits (weary of wanting cause to be weary) desired to keep his valour in know-ledge* by some private act, since the public policy restrained him – the rather, because his old mistress Artesia might see whom she had so lightly forsaken. And therefore demanding and obtaining leave of Basilius, he caused a herald to be furnished with apparel of his office and tokens of a peaceable message, and so sent him to the gate of the town to demand audience of Amphialus; who, understanding thereof, caused him both safely and courteously to be brought into his presence. Who, making lowly reverence unto him, presented his letters, desiring Amphialus that whatsoever they contained, he would consider that he was only the bearer and not the inditer.

Amphialus with noble gentleness assured him, both by honour-able speeches and a demeanour which answered for him, that his revenge, whensoever, should sort* unto itself a higher subject. But opening the letters, he found them to speak in this manner:

Phalantus of Corinth, to Amphialus of Arcadia, sendeth the greet-ing of a hateless enemy. The liking of martial matters without any mislike of your person hath brought me rather to the company than to the mind of your besiegers: where, languishing in idleness, I desire to refresh my mind with some exercise of arms which might make known the doers, with delight of the beholders. Therefore if there be any gentleman in your town that, either for the love of honour or honour of his love, will armed on horseback, with lance and sword, win another or lose himself, to be a prisoner at discretion of the conqueror, I will tomorrow morning by sunrising, with a trumpet and a squire only, attend him in like order furnished. The place I think fittest, the island within the lake, because it stands so well in

* *in knowledge:* publicly known. *sort:* choose.

view of your castle as that the ladies may have the pleasure of seeing the combat: which, though it be within the commandment of your castle, I desire no better security than the promise I make to myself of your virtue. I attend your answer, and wish you such success as may be to your honour, rather in yielding to that which is just than in maintaining wrong by violence.

Amphialus read it with cheerful countenance, and thinking but a little with himself, called for ink and paper, and wrote this answer:

Amphialus of Arcadia, to Phalantus of Corinth, wisheth all his own wishes, saving those which may be hurtful to another. The matter of your letters so fit for a worthy mind, and the manner so suitable to the nobleness of the matter, give me cause to think how happy I might account myself if I could get such a friend, who esteem it no small happiness to have met with so noble an enemy. Your challenge shall be answered, and both time, place, and weapon accepted. For your security from any treachery (having no hostage worthy to countervail you) take my word, which I esteem above all respects. Prepare therefore your arms to fight, but not your heart to malice, since true valour needs no other whetstone than desire of honour.

Having written and sealed his letter, he delivered it to the herald, and withal took a fair chain from off his own neck and gave it him. And so with safe convoy sent him away from out his city: and he being gone, Amphialus showed unto his mother and some other of his chief counsellors what he had received and how he had answered, telling them withal that he was determined to answer the challenge in his own person. His mother, with prayers authorized by motherly commandment; his old governor, with persuasions mingled with reprehensions, that he would rather affect the glory of a private fighter than of a wise general; Clinias with falling down at his feet and beseeching him to remember that all their lives depended upon his safety, sought all to dissuade him. But Amphialus (whose heart was inflamed with courage, and courage inflamed with affection) made an imperious resolution cut off the tediousness of replies, giving them in charge what they should do upon all occasions, and particularly to deliver the ladies, if otherwise than well happened unto him: only desiring his mother that she would bring Philoclea to a window, whence she might with ease perfectly discern the combat.

And so, as soon as the morning began to draw dew from the fairest greens to wash her face withal against the approach of the burning sun, he went to his stable, where himself chose out a horse whom (though he was near twenty year old) he preferred for a piece of sure service, before a great number of younger. His colour was of a brown bay, dappled thick with black spots; his forehead marked with a white star, to which, in all his body, there was no part suitable* but the left foot before; his mane and tail black and thick, of goodly and well proportioned greatness. He caused him to be trimmed with a sumptuous saddle of tawny* and gold enamel, enriched with precious stones. His furniture* was made into the fashion of the branches of a tree from which the leaves were falling; and so artificially were the leaves made that, as the horse moved, it seemed indeed that the leaves wagged as when the wind plays with them; and being made of a pale cloth of gold, they did bear the straw-coloured livery of ruin.[2] His armour was also of tawny and gold, but formed into the figure of flames darkened as when they newly break the prison of a smoky furnace. In his shield he had painted the Torpedo* fish. And so appointed,* he caused himself with his trumpet* and squire (whom he had taken since the death of Ismenus) to be ferried over into the island, a place well chosen for such a purpose. For it was so plain as there was scarcely any bush or hillock either to unlevel or shadow it; of length and breadth enough to try the uttermost both of lance and sword: and the one end of it facing the castle, the other extending itself towards the camp, and no access to it but by water, there could no secret treachery be wrought; and for manifest violence, either side might have time enough to succour their party.

But there he found Phalantus already waiting for him upon a horse, milk white but that upon his shoulder and withers he was freckled with red stains as when a few strawberries are scattered into a dish of cream. He had caused his mane and tail to be dyed in carnation; his reins were vine branches which, engendering one

---

* *suitable*: matching, *tawny*: orange-brown. *furniture*: trappings. *Torpedo*: see Notes, Second Eclogues, 9 (p. 859). *appointed*: equipped. *trumpet*: herald.

with the other, at the end, when it came to the bit, there for the boss brought forth a cluster of grapes, by the workman made so lively that it seemed as the horse champed on his bit, he chopped* for them and that it did make his mouth water to see the grapes so near him. His furniture behind was of vines, so artificially made as it seemed the horse stood in the shadow of the vine, so prettily were clusters of ruby grapes dispersed among the trappers* which embraced his sides. His armour was blue like the heaven, which a sun did with his rays (proportionately delivered) gild in most places. His shield was beautified with this device: a greyhound which over-running his fellow and taking the hare, yet hurts it not when it takes it. The word was, 'The glory, not the prey.'³

But as soon as Amphialus landed, he sent his squire to Phalantus to tell him that there was the knight ready to know whether he had anything to say to him. Phalantus answered that his answer now must be in the language of lances; and so each attended the warning of the trumpets, which were to sound at the appointment of four judges who, with consideration of the same, had divided the ground. Phalantus' horse, young and feeling the youth of his master, stood curvetting, which being well governed by Phalantus, gave such a glittering grace as when the sun in a clear day shines upon a waving water. Amphialus' horse stood pawing upon the ground with his further foot before, as if he would for his master's cause begin to make himself angry: till the trumpets sounding together, together they set spurs to their horses, together took their lances from their thighs, conveyed them up into their rests together, together let them sink downward, so as it was a delectable sight in a dangerous effect; and a pleasant consideration that there was so perfect agreement in so mortal disagreement, like a music made of cunning discords. But their horses, keeping an even line their masters had skilfully allotted unto them, passed one by another without encountering, although either might feel the angry breath of other. But the staves being come to a just descent but even* when the mark* was ready to meet them, Amphialus was run through the vam-

---

* *chopped*: snapped his jaws. *trappers*: skirt of armour or leather for horse. *but even*: at the exact moment when. *the mark*: the point aimed at.

plate* and under the arm, so as the staff appearing behind him, it seemed to the beholders he had been in danger. But he strake Phalantus just upon the gorget* so as he battered the lames* thereof, and made his head almost touch the back of his horse.

But either side having stayed the spur and used the bit to stop their horse's fury, casting away the truncheons* of their staves and drawing their swords, they attended the second summons of the death-threatening trumpet, which quickly followed; and they as soon making their horses answer their hands, with a gentle gallop set one toward the other: till being come in the nearness of little more than a stave's length, Amphialus, trusting more to the strength than to the nimbleness of his horse, put him forth with speedy violence, and making his head join to the other's flank, guiding his blow with discretion, and strengthening it with the course of his horse, strake Phalantus upon the head in such sort that his feeling sense did both dazzle his sight and astonish his hearing. But Phalantus (not accustomed to be ungrateful to such benefits) strake him upon the side of his face with such force that he thought his jaw had been cut asunder, though the faithfulness of his armour indeed guarded him from further damage. And so remained they awhile, rather angry with fighting than fighting for anger; till Amphialus' horse leaning hard upon the other and winning ground, the other horse, feeling himself pressed, began to rise a little before, as he was wont to do in his curvet, which advantage Amphialus taking, set forward his own horse with the further spur so as Phalantus' horse came over with his master under him. Which Amphialus seeing, lighted* with intention to help Phalantus. But his horse, that had faulted rather with untimely art than want of force,* gat up from burdening his burden, so as Phalantus (in the fall having gotten his feet free of the stirrup) could, though something bruised, arise; and seeing Amphialus near him, he asked him whether he had given him any help in removing his horse. Amphialus said 'No.'

'Truly,' said Phalantus, 'I asked it, because I would not wil-

---

* *vamplate*: armour plate fixed to butt of lance to protect the hand. *gorget*: armour covering the throat. *lames*: thin plates of overlapping metal. *truncheons*: broken pieces of lance. *lighted*: alighted. *force*: strength.

lingly have fought with him that had had my life in his mercy. But now,' said Phalantus, 'before we proceed further, let me know who you are, because never yet did any man bring me to the like fortune.'

Amphialus, listing to keep himself unknown, told him he was a gentleman to whom Amphialus that day had given armour and horse to try his valour, having never before been in any combat worthy remembrance.

'Ah,' said Phalantus in a rage, 'and must I be the exercise of your prentice age?' – and with that, choler took away either the bruise, or the feeling of the bruise, so as he entered afresh into the combat, and boiling into his arms the disdain of his heart, strake so thick upon Amphialus as if every blow would fain have been foremost. But Amphialus (that many like trials had taught great spending to leave small remnants) let pass the storm with strong wards* and nimble avoidings; till seeing his time fit, both for distance and nakedness, he strake him so cruel a blow on the knee that the poor gentleman fell down withal in a swoon.

But Amphialus, pitying approved valour made precious by natural courtesy, went to him, and taking off his headpiece to give him air, the young knight (disdaining to buy life with yielding) bade him use his fortune, for he was resolved never to yield.

'No more you shall,' said Amphialus, 'if it be not to my request that you will account yourself to have great interest in me.'

Phalantus, more overcome by his kindness than by his fortune, desired yet once again to know his name, who in his first beginning had showed such fury in his force, and yet such stay* in his fury. Amphialus then named himself, telling him withal he would think his name much bettered if it might be honoured by the title of his friend. But no balm could be more comfortable to his wound than the knowledge thereof was to his mind, when he knew his mishap should be excused by the renowned valour of the other. And so promising each to other assuredness of goodwill, Phalantus (of whom Amphialus would have no other ransom but his word of friendship) was conveyed into the camp, where he would but little remain among the enemies of Amphialus, but went to seek his adventures other-where.

*wards: parries. *stay*: control.

## CHAPTER 12

As for Amphialus, he was received with triumph into the castle, although one might see by his eyes (humbly lifted up to the window where Philoclea stood) that he was rather suppliant than victorious: which occasion Cecropia taking, who as then stood by Philoclea, and had lately left Pamela in another room whence also she might see the combat, 'Sweet lady,' said she, 'now you may see whether you have cause to love my son, who then lies under your feet when he stands upon the neck of his bravest enemies.'

'Alas,' said Philoclea, 'a simple service to me, methinks it is, to have those who come to succour me destroyed. If it be my duty to call it love, be it so; but the effects it brings forth, I confess I account hateful.'

Cecropia grew so angry with this unkind answer that she could not abstain from telling her that she was like them that could not sleep when they were softly laid; but that if her son would follow her counsel, he should take another course with her: and so flung away from her.

Yet, knowing the desperate melancholy of Amphialus in like cases, framed to him a very thankful message, powdering it* with some hope-giving phrases, which were of such joy to Amphialus that he (though against public respect and importunity of dissuaders) presently caused it to be made known to the camp that whatsoever knight would try the like fortune as Phalantus did, he should in like sort be answered. So as divers of the valiantest, partly of themselves, partly at the instigation of Basilius, attempted the combat with him; and according to everyone's humour, so were the causes of the challenge grounded: one laying treason to his charge; another preferring himself in the worthiness to serve Philoclea; a third exalting some lady's beauty beyond either of the sisters; a fourth laying disgrace to love itself, naming it the bewitcher of the wit, the rebel to reason, the betrayer of resolution, the defiler of thoughts, the underminer of magnanimity, the flatterer of vice, the slave to weakness, the infection of youth, the madness of age, the curse of life and reproach of death. A fifth, disdaining to cast at* less than at all, would make

* *powdering it*: scattering over it. *cast at*: let fly at (from hawking).

the cause of his quarrel the causers of love, and proclaim his blasphemies against womankind: that namely* that sex* was the oversight of nature, the disgrace of reasonableness, the obstinate cowards, the slave-born tyrants, the shops of vanities, the gilded weather cocks; in whom conscience is but peevishness, chastity waywardness, and gratefulness a miracle. But all these challenges (how well soever indited) were so well answered, that some by death taught others, though past learning themselves; and some by yielding gave themselves the lie for having blasphemed; to the great grief of Basilius so to see his rebel prevail and, in his own sight, to crown himself with deserved honour.

Whereupon thirsting for revenge, and else not hoping to prevail, the best of his camp being already overthrown, he sent a messenger to Argalus, in whose approved courage and force he had (and had cause) to have great confidence, with a letter requiring him to take this quarrel in hand, from which he had hitherto spared him in respect of his late marriage. But now his honour and (as he esteemed it) felicity standing upon it, he could no longer forbear to challenge of him his faithful service.

The messenger made speed, and found Argalus at a castle of his own, sitting in a parlour with the fair Parthenia, he reading in a book the stories of Hercules, she by him, as to hear him read; but while his eyes looked on the book, she looked on his eyes, and sometimes staying him with some pretty question, not so much to be resolved of the doubt as to give him occasion to look upon her. A happy couple: he joying in her, she joying in herself, but in herself, because she enjoyed him: both increasing their riches by giving to each other; each making one life double, because they made a double life one; where desire never wanted satisfaction, nor satisfaction ever bred satiety: he ruling, because she would obey, or rather because she would obey, she therein ruling.

But when the messenger came in with letters in his hand and haste in his countenance, though she knew not what to fear, yet she feared because she knew not; but she rose and went aside while he delivered his letters and message; yet afar off she looked, now at the messenger, and then at her husband: the same fear, which made her loth to have cause of fear, yet making her seek

*namely: in particular. that sex: women.

cause to nourish her fear. And well she found there was some serious matter; for her husband's countenance figured some resolution between loathness and necessity: and once his eye cast upon her, and finding hers upon him, he blushed, and she blushed because he blushed, and yet straight grew pale because she knew not why he had blushed. But when he had read, and heard, and dispatched away the messenger (like a man in whom honour could not be rocked asleep by affection) with promise quickly to follow, he came to Parthenia, and as sorry as might be for parting, and yet more sorry for her sorrow, he gave her the letter to read.

She with fearful slowness took it, and with fearful quickness read it; and having read it, 'Ah, my Argalus,' said she, 'and have you made such haste to answer? And are you so soon resolved to leave me?'

But he discoursing unto her how much it imported his honour (which, since it was dear to him, he knew it would be dear unto her) her reason, overclouded with sorrow, suffered her not presently to reply, but left the charge thereof to tears and sighs, which he, not able to bear, left her alone and went to give order for his present departure.

But by that time he was armed and ready to go, she had recovered a little strength of spirit again, and coming out, and seeing him armed and wanting nothing for his departure but her farewell, she ran to him, took him by the arm, and kneeling down without regard who either heard her speech or saw her demeanour,

'My Argalus, my Argalus,' said she, 'do not thus forsake me. Remember, alas, remember that I have interest in you, which I will never yield shall be thus adventured. Your valour is already sufficiently known. Sufficiently have you already done for your country: enow, enow there are beside you to lose less worthy lives. Woe is me, what shall become of me if you thus abandon me? Then was it time for you to follow those adventures, when you adventured nobody but yourself, and were nobody's but your own. But now pardon me, that now, or never, I claim mine own. Mine you are, and without me you can undertake no danger: and will you endanger Parthenia? Parthenia shall be in the battle* of

* *in the battle*: battle-front.

your fight: Parthenia shall smart in your pain, and your blood must be bled by Parthenia.'

'Dear Parthenia,' said he, 'this is the first time that ever you resisted my will. I thank you for it; but persevere not in it; and let not the tears of those most beloved eyes be a presage unto me of that which you would not should happen. I shall live, doubt not: for so great a blessing as you are was not given unto me so soon to be deprived of it. Look for me, therefore, shortly, and victorious; and prepare a joyful welcome, and I will wish for no other triumph.'

She answered not, but stood as it were thunder-stricken with amazement; for true love made obedience stand up against all other passions. But when he took her in his arms and sought to print his heart in her sweet lips, she fell in a swoon, so that he was fain to leave her to her gentlewomen; and carried away by the tyranny of honour, though with many a back-cast look and hearty groan, went to the camp. Where understanding the notable victories of Amphialus, he thought to give him some days' respite of rest, because he would not have his victory disgraced by the other's weariness. In which days, he sought by all means (having leave to parley with him) to dissuade him from his enterprise; and then imparting his mind to Basilius, because he found Amphialus was inflexible, wrote his defy* unto him in this manner.

Right famous Amphialus, if my persuasion in reason, or prayer in goodwill, might prevail with you, you should by better means be like to obtain your desire. You should make many brave enemies become your faithful servants, and make your honour fly up to heaven, being carried up by both the wings of valour and justice, whereof now it wants the latter. But since my suit nor counsel can get no place in you, disdain not to receive a mortal challenge, from a man so far inferior unto you in virtue as that I do not so much mislike of the deed, as I have the doer in admiration. Prepare therefore yourself, according to the noble manner you have used, and think not lightly of never so weak an arm which strikes with the sword of justice.

To this he quickly received this answer.

Much more famous Argalus, I, whom never threatenings could

* *defy*: challenge.

make afraid, am now terrified by your noble courtesy. For well I know from what height of virtue it doth proceed, and what cause I have to doubt such virtue bent to my ruin. But love, which justifieth the unjustice you lay unto me, doth also animate me against all dangers, since I come full of him by whom yourself have been (if I be not deceived) sometimes conquered. I will therefore attend your appearance in the isle, carrying this advantage with me, that as it shall be a singular honour if I get the victory, so there can be no dishonour in being overcome by Argalus.

The challenge thus denounced* and accepted, Argalus was armed in a white armour, which was all gilded over with knots of woman's hair, which came down from the crest of his head-piece and spread itself in rich quantity over all his armour. His furniture was cut out into the fashion of an eagle, whereof the beak (made into a rich jewel) was fastened to the saddle, the tail covered the crupper of the horse, and the wings served for trappers, which falling off each side, as the horse stirred, the bird seemed to fly. His peitrel* and reins were embroidered with feathers suitable unto it. Upon his right arm he wore a sleeve which his dear Parthenia had made for him to be worn in a joust, in the time that success was ungrateful to their well deserved love: it was full of bleeding hearts, though never intended to any bloody enterprise. In his shield (as his own device) he had two palm trees near one another, with a word signifying, 'In that sort of flourishing.'[1] His horse was of a fiery sorrel,* with black feet, and black list* on his back, who with open nostrils breathed war before he could see an enemy; and now up with one leg and then with another, seemed to complain of Nature that she had made him any whit earthy.

But he had scarcely viewed the ground of the island and considered the advantages (if any were) thereof, before the castle boat had delivered Amphialus, in all points provided to give a hard entertainment. And then sending each to other their squires in honourable manner to know whether they should attend any further ceremony, the trumpets sounding, the horses with smooth running, the staves with unshaked motion, obediently performed their choleric commandments. But when they drew near, Argalus'

* denounced: proclaimed. peitrel: armour covering the breast of a horse. sorrel: chestnut. list: stripe.

horse being hot, pressed in with his head, which Amphialus perceiving, knowing if he gave him his side it should be to his disadvantage, pressed in also with him, so as both the horses and men met shoulder to shoulder, so as the horses (hurt as much with the striking as being stricken) tumbled down to the earth, dangerously to their masters but that they, by strength nimble and by use skilful in the falling, shunned the harm of the fall, and without more respite drew out their swords with a gallant bravery, each striving to show himself the less endamaged, and to make known that they were glad they had now nothing else to trust to but their own virtue.

True it is that Amphialus was the sooner up, but Argalus had his sword out the sooner; and then fell they to the cruellest combat that any present eye had seen. Their swords first, like canons, battering down the walls of their armour, making breaches almost in every place for troops of wounds to enter. Among the rest, Argalus gave a great wound to Amphialus' disarmed face, though part of the force of it Amphialus warded upon his shield, and withal, first casting his eye up to Philoclea's window, as if he had fetched his courage thence, feigning to intend the same sort of blow, turned his sword and, with a mighty reverse, gave a cruel wound to the right arm of Argalus, the unfaithful armour yielding to the sword's strong-guided sharpness. But though the blood accused the hurt of Argalus, yet would he in no action of his confess it; but keeping himself in a lower ward, stood watching with timely thrusts to repair his loss, which quickly he did. For Amphialus, following his fawning fortune, laid on so thick upon Argalus that his shield had almost fallen piece-meal to the earth, when Argalus, coming in with his right foot, and something stooping to come under his armour, thrust him into the belly dangerously; and mortally it would have been, but that with the blow before, Amphialus had over-stricken himself so as he fell sideward down, and with falling saved himself from ruin, the sword by that means slipping aside and not piercing more deeply.

Argalus seeing him fall, threatening with voice and sword, bade him yield. But he striving without answer to rise, Argalus strake him with all his might upon his head. But his hurt arm, not able to master so sound a force, let the sword fall so as Amphialus, though astonished with the blow, could arise: which Argalus considering, ran in to grasp with him, and so closed together, falling so to the ground, now one getting above, and then the other. At length both, weary of so unlovely embracements, with a dissenting consent gat up and went to their swords, but happened each of his enemy's; where Argalus finding his foe's sword garnished in his blood, his heart rase with the same sword to revenge it, and on that blade to ally their bloods together. But his mind was evil waited on by his lamed force, so as he received still more and more wounds, which made all his armour seem to blush that it had defended his master no better. But Amphialus perceiving it, and weighing the small hatefulness of their quarrel with the worthiness of the knight, desired him to take pity of himself. But Argalus, the more repining the more he found himself in disadvantage, filling his veins with spite instead of blood, and making courage arise against faintness (like a candle, which a little before it goes out gives then the greatest blaze) so did he unite all his force, that casting away the little remnant of his shield, and taking his sword in both hands, he struck such a notable blow that he cleft his shield, armour, and arm almost to the bone.

But then Amphialus forgat all ceremonies, and with cruel blows made more of his best blood succeed the rest: till his hand being stayed by his ear, his ear filled with a pitiful cry, the cry guided his sight to an excellent fair lady who came running as fast as she could, and yet because she could not as fast as she would, she sent her lamentable voice before her: and being come, and being known to them both to be the beautiful Parthenia (who had that night dreamed she saw her husband in such estate as she then found him, which made her make such haste thither) they both marvelled. But Parthenia ran between them, fear of love making her forget the fear of nature, and then fell down at their feet, determining so to part them till she could get breath to sigh out her doleful speeches: and when her breath (which running had spent, and dismayedness made slow to return) had by sobs gotten into her sorrow-closed breast, for a while she could say nothing, but, 'O wretched eyes of mine, O wailful sight, O day of darkness!'

At length turning her eyes, wherein sorrow swam, to Amphialus, 'My Lord,' said she, 'it is said you love. In the power of that love, I beseech you to leave off this combat. As ever your heart may find comfort in his affection, even for her sake I crave it: or if you be mortally determined, be so pitiful unto me as first to kill me, that I may not see the death of Argalus.'

Amphialus was about to have answered, when Argalus, vexed with his fortune, but most vexed that she should see him in that fortune, 'Ah Parthenia,' said he, 'never until now unwelcome unto me, do you come to get my life by request? And cannot Argalus live but by request? Is that a life?'

With that he went aside for fear of hurting her, and would have begun the combat afresh. But Amphialus not only conjured by that which held the monarchy of his mind, but even in his noble heart melting with compassion at so passionate a sight, desired him to withhold his hands, for that he should strike one who sought his favour, and would not make resistance. A notable example of the wonderful effects of virtue, where the conqueror sought for friendship of the conquered, and the conquered would not pardon the conqueror: both indeed being of that mind to love each other for accepting, but not for giving mercy, and neither affected to over-live dishonour: so that Argalus, not so much striving with Amphialus (for if he had had him in the like sort, in like sort he would have dealt with him) as labouring against his own power (which he chiefly despised) set himself forward, stretching his strength to the uttermost. But the fire of that strife, blown with his inward rage, boiled out his blood in such abundance that he was driven to rest him upon the pommel of his sword: and then each thing beginning to turn round in the dance of death before his eyes, his sight both dazzled and dimmed, till, thinking to sit down, he fell in a swoon. Parthenia and Amphialus both hastily went unto him. Amphialus took off his helmet, and Parthenia laid his head in her lap, tearing off her linen sleeves and partlet* to serve about his wounds; to bind which she took off her hairlace, and would have cut off her fair hair herself, but that the squires and judges came in with fitter things for that purpose: while she bewailed herself with so lamentable sweetness as was

* *partlet*: neckerchief.

enough to have taught sorrow to the gladdest thoughts, and have engraved it in the minds of hardest metal.

'O Parthenia, no more Parthenia,' said she, 'what art thou? What seest thou? How is thy bliss in a moment fallen! How wert thou even now before all ladies the example of perfect happiness, and now the gazing-stock of endless misery! O God, what hath been my desert to be thus punished? Or if such have been my desert, why was I not in myself punished? O wandering life, to what wilderness wouldst thou lead me? But Sorrow, I hope thou art sharp enough to save my labour from other remedies. Argalus, Argalus, I will follow thee, I will follow thee.'

But with that Argalus came out of his swoon, and lifting up his languishing eyes (which a painful rest and iron sleep did seek to lock up) seeing her in whom, even dying, he lived, and himself seated in so beloved a place, it seemed a little cheerful blood came up to his cheeks, like a burning coal, almost dead, if some breath a little revive it: and forcing up, the best he could, his feeble voice,

'My dear, my dear, my better half,' said he, 'I find I must now leave thee: and by that sweet hand and fair eyes of thine I swear that death brings nothing with it to grieve me but that I must leave thee, and cannot remain to answer part of thy infinite deserts with being some comfort unto thee. But since so it pleaseth Him, whose wisdom and goodness guideth all, put thy confidence in Him, and one day we shall blessedly meet again, never to depart. Meanwhile live happily, dear Parthenia, and I persuade myself, it will increase the blessedness of my soul so to see thee. Love well the remembrance of thy loving, and truly loving Argalus: and let not,' (with that word he sighed) 'this disgrace of mine make thee one day think thou hadst an unworthy husband.'

They could scarcely understand the last words, for death began to seize himself of his heart; neither could Parthenia make answer, so full was her breast of anguish. But while the other sought to staunch his remediless wounds, she with her kisses made him happy; for his last breath was delivered into her mouth.

But when indeed she found his ghost was gone, then sorrow lost the wit of utterance and grew rageful and mad, so that she tare her beautiful face, and rent her hair, as though they could serve for nothing, since Argalus was gone: till Amphialus (so moved with pity of that sight as that he honoured his adversary's death with tears) caused her, with the help of her woman that came with her, partly by force to be conveyed into the boat, with the dead body of Argalus, from which she would not depart. And being come of the other side, there she was received by Basilius himself with all the funeral pomp of military discipline, trailing all their ensigns* upon the ground, making their warlike instruments sound doleful notes; and Basilius, with comfort in his mouth and woe in his face, sought to persuade some ease into Parthenia's mind. But all was as easeful to her as the handling of sore wounds; all the honour done being to her but the triumph of her ruin, she finding no comfort but in desperate yielding to sorrow, and rather determined to hate herself if ever she would find ease thereof. And well might she hear as she passed through the camp the great praises spoken of her husband, which all were records of her loss. But the more excellent he was, being indeed counted second to none in all Greece, the more did the breath of those praises bear up the wings of Amphialus' fame: to whom yet (such was his case) that trophy upon trophy still did but build up the monument of his thraldom; he ever finding himself in such favour of Philoclea that she was most absent when he was present with her, and ever sorriest when he had best success: which would have made him renounce all comfort but that his mother, with a diversity of devices, kept up his heart.

But while he allayed thus his outward glory with inward discomfort, he was like to have been overtaken with a notable treason, the beginning whereof (though merely ridiculous) had like to have brought forth unto him a weeping effect.

## CHAPTER 13

Among other that attended Basilius in this expedition, Dametas was one, whether to be present with him or absent from Miso; once, certain* it was without any mind to make his sword cursed by any widow. Now being in the camp, while each talk seemed injurious which did not acknowledge some duty to the fame of Amphialus, it fell out sometimes in communication that, as the

* *ensigns*: standards. *once, certain*: for sure.

speech of heaven doth often beget the mention of hell, so the admirable prowess of Amphialus (by a contrary) brought forth the remembrance of the cowardice of Clinias, insomuch as it grew almost to a proverb, 'As very a coward as Clinias'; describing him in such sort, that in the end Dametas began to think with himself that if he made a challenge unto him he would never answer it, and that then he should greatly increase the favourable conceit of Basilius.

This fancy of his he uttered to a young gentleman that waited upon Philanax, in whose friendship he had especial confidence because he haunted his company, laughing often merrily at his speeches, and not a little extolling the goodly dotes* of Mopsa. The young gentleman, as glad as if he had found a hare sitting, egged him on, breaking the matter with Philanax and then, for fear the humour* should quail in him, wrote a challenge himself for Dametas and brought it to him. But when Dametas read it, putting his head on his shoulder and somewhat smiling, he said it was pretty indeed, but that it had not a lofty style enough; and so would needs indite it in this sort.

O Clinias, thou Clinias, the wickedest worm that ever went upon two legs; the very fritter of fraud and seething pot of iniquity: I Dametas, chief governor of all the royal cattle, and also of Pamela (whom thy master most perniciously hath suggested* out of my dominion) do defy thee in a mortal affray from the bodkin to the pike upward. Which if thou dost presume to take in hand, I will, out of that superfluous body of thine, make thy soul to be evacuated.

The young gentleman seemed dumb-stricken with admiration, and presently took upon him to be the bearer thereof, while the heat of the fit lasted; and having gotten leave of Basilius (everybody helping on to ease his mind, overcharged with melancholy) he went into the town, according to the manner before time used, and, in the presence of Amphialus, delivered this letter to Clinias, desiring to have an answer which might be fit for his reputation. Clinias opened it, read it, and in the reading his blood, not daring to be in so dangerous a place, went out of his face and hid itself more inwardly, and his very words (as if they were afraid of

* *dotes*: natural gifts. *humour*: inclination. *suggested*: tempted away.

blows) came very slowly out of his mouth: but, as well as his panting breath would utter it, he bade him tell the lout that sent him that he disdained to have anything to do with him. But Amphialus, perceiving the matter, took him aside and very earnestly dealt with him not to shame himself, Amphialus only desirous to bring it to pass to make some sport to Philoclea: but not being able to persuade him, Amphialus licensed* the gentleman, telling him that by next morning he should have an answer.

The young gentleman, sorry he had sped no better, returned to Dametas, who had fetched many a sour-breathed sigh for fear Clinias would accept the challenge. But when he perceived by his trusty messenger that this delay was in effect a denial, there being no disposition in him to accept it, then lo, Dametas began to speak his loud voice, to look big, to march up and down, and in his march to lift his legs higher than he was wont, swearing by no mean devotions that the walls should not keep the coward from him but he would fetch him out of his coney-burrow:* and then was hotter than ever to provide himself of horse and armour, saying he would go to the island bravely addubed* and show himself to his charge Pamela. To this purpose many willing hands were about him, letting him have reins, peitrel* with the rest of the furniture, and very brave bases;* but all coming from divers houses, neither in colour nor fashion showing any kindred one with another: but that liked Dametas the better, for that, he thought, would argue that he was master of many brave furnitures.

Then gave he order to a painter for his device; which was a plough with the oxen loosed from it, a sword, with a great number of arms and legs cut off, and lastly, a great army of pen and ink-horns and books. Neither did he stick to tell the secret of his intent, which was that he had left off the plough to do such bloody deeds with his sword as many ink-horns and books should be employed about the historifying of them: and being asked why he set no word unto it, he said, that was indeed like the painter that saith in his picture, 'Here is the dog, and there is the hare', and with that he laughed so perfectly as was great consolation to the

* *licensed*: dismissed. *coney-burrow*: rabbit hole. *addubed*: equipped. *peitrel*: armour covering the breast of a horse. *bases*: skirt of mail.

beholders. Yet remembering that Miso would not take it well at his return if he forgat his duty to her, he caused in a border about to be written, 'Miso, mine own pigsnie, thou shalt hear news o Dametas.'[1]

Thus all things being condignly* ordered, with an ill-favoured impatiency he waited until the next morning, that he might make a muster of himself in the island, often asking them that very diligently waited upon him whether it were not pity that such a coward as Clinias should set his run-away feet upon the face of the earth.

But as he was by divers principal young gentlemen, to his no small glory, lifted up on horseback, comes me a page of Amphialus, who with humble smiling reverence delivered a letter unto him from Clinias; whom Amphialus had brought to this, first with persuasions (that for certain, if he did accept the combat, Dametas would never dare to appear and that then the honour should be his) but principally threatening him that if he refused it, he would turn him out of the town to be put to death for a traitor by Basilius: so as the present fear (ever to a coward most terrible) of being turned out of the town made him, though full unwillingly, undertake the other fear, wherein he had some show of hope that Dametas might hap either to be sick, or not to have the courage to perform the matter. But when Dametas heard the name of Clinias, very aptly suspecting what the matter might be, he bad the page carry back his letter like a naughty boy as he was, for he was in no humour, he told him, of reading letters. But Dametas' friend, first persuading him that for certain it was some submission, took upon him so much boldness as to open his letter, and to read it aloud, in this sort:

Filthy drivel, unworthy to have thy name set in any letter by a soldier's hand written, could thy wretched heart think it was timorousness that made Clinias suspend awhile his answer? No, caitiff, no: it was but as a ram, which goes back to return with the greater force. Know, therefore, that thou shalt no sooner appear (appear now if thou darest!) I say thou shalt no sooner appear in the island (O happy thou if thou do not appear!) but that I will come upon thee with all my force, and cut thee in pieces (mark what I say) joint after joint, to

*condignly: worthily.

the eternal terror of all presumptuous villains. Therefore look what thou dost; for I tell thee, horrible smart and pain shall be thy lot, if thou wilt needs be so foolish (I having given thee no such cause) as to meet with me.

These terrible words Clinias used, hoping they would give a cooling to the heat of Dametas' courage: and so indeed they did, that he did groan to hear the thundering of those threatenings. And when the gentleman had ended the reading of them, Dametas told them that in his opinion he thought this answer came too late, and that therefore he might very well go and disarm himself, especially considering the other had in courteous manner warned him not to come. But they, having him now on horseback, led him unto the ferry and so into the island; the clashing of his own armour striking miserable fear into him, and in his mind thinking great unkindness in his friend that he had brought him to a matter so contrary to his complexion. There stayed he but a little (the gentlemen that came with him teaching him how to use his sword and lance, while he cast his eye about to see which way he might run away, cursing all islands for being evil situated) when Clinias with a brave sound of trumpets landed at the other end: who came all the way debating with himself what he had deserved of Amphialus to drive him to those inconveniences. Sometimes his wit made him bethink himself what was best to be done: but fear did so corrupt his wit that whatsoever he thought was best, he still found danger therein; fearfulness (contrary to all other vices) making him think the better of another, the worse he found himself, rather imagining in himself what words he would use (if he were overcome) to get his life of Dametas, than how to overcome, whereof he could think with no patience: but oftentimes looking to the earth, pitifully complaining that a man of such sufficiency, as he thought himself, should in his best years be swallowed up by so base an element. Fain he would have prayed, but he had not heart enough to have confidence in prayer; the glittering of the armour and sounding of trumpets giving such an assault to the weak breach of his false senses that he grew from the degree of fear to an amazement, not almost to know what he did; till two judges (chosen for the purpose) making the trumpets cease, and taking the oath of these champions that they came without guile or witchcraft, set them at wonted distance one from the other.

Then the trumpets sounding, Dametas' horse (used to such causes) when he thought least of the matter, started out so lustily that Dametas was jogged back with head and body; and pulling withal his bridle-hand, the horse, that was tender of mouth, made half a stop and fell to bounding, so that Dametas threw away his lance and with both his hands held by the pommel, the horse half running, half leaping, till he met with Clinias: who fearing he should miss his rest, had put his staff therein before he began his career. Neither would he then have begun but that at the trumpets' warning, one (that stood behind) strake on his horse, who running swiftly, the wind took such hold of his staff that it crossed quite over his breast and in that sort gave a flat bastinado to Dametas who, half out of his saddle, went near to his old occupation of digging the earth, but with the crest of his helmet. Clinias, when he was past him, not knowing what he had done but fearing lest Dametas were at his back, turned with a wide turn; and seeing him on the ground, he thought then was his time, or never, to tread him under his horse's feet, and withal, if he could, hurt him with his lance which had not broken, the encounter was so easy. But putting forth his horse, what with the falling of the staff too low before the legs of the horse, and the coming upon Dametas, who was then scrambling up, the horse fell over and over, and lay upon Clinias. Which Dametas, who was gotten up, perceiving, drew out his sword, prying which way he might best come to kill Clinias behind. But the horse that lay upon him kept such a pawing with his feet that Dametas durst not approach but very leisurely, so as the horse, being lusty, gat up and withal fell to strike and leap that Dametas started back a good way and gave Clinias time to rise, but so bruised in body and broken in heart that he meant to yield himself to mercy; and with that intent drew out his sword, intending when he came nearer to present the pommel of it to Dametas. But Dametas, when he saw him come with his sword drawn, not conceiving of any such intent, went back as fast as his back and heels could lead him. But as Clinias found that, he began to think a possibility in the victory, and therefore followed with the cruel haste of a prevailing coward; laying upon Dametas, who did nothing but cry out to him to hold his hand, sometimes that he was dead, sometimes that he would complain to Basilius; but still bore the blows ungratefully, going back till at length he came into the water with one of his feet.

But then a new fear of drowning took him, so that not daring to go back, nor to deliberate (the blows still so lighted on him) nor to yield (because of the cruel threatenings of Clinias) fear being come to the extremity fell to a madness of despair; so that (winking* as hard as ever he could) he began to deal some blows, and his arm (being used to a flail in his youth) laid them on so thick that Clinias now began with lamentable eyes to see his own blood come out in many places; and before he had lost half an ounce, finding in himself that he fainted, cried out aloud to Dametas that he yielded.

'Throw away thy sword then,' said Dametas, 'and I will save thee,' but still laying on as fast as he could.

Clinias straight obeyed and humbly craved mercy, telling him his sword was gone. Then Dametas first opened his eyes and, seeing him indeed unweaponed, made him stand a good way off from it, and then willed him to lie down upon the earth as flat as he could. Clinias obeyed; and Dametas (who never could think himself safe till Clinias were dead) began to think with himself that if he strake at him with his sword, if he did not kill him at the first blow, that then Clinias might hap to arise and revenge himself. Therefore he thought best to kneel down upon him, and with a great whittle* he had (having disarmed his head) to cut his throat, which he had used so with calves as he had no small dexterity in it. But while he sought for his knife, which under his armour he could not well find out, and that Clinias lay with so sheepish a quietness, as if he would have been glad to have his throat cut for fear of more pain, the judges came in and took Dametas from off him, telling him he did against the law of arms, having promised life if he threw away his sword. Dametas was loth to consent, till they sware they would not suffer him to fight any more, when he was up; and then more forced than persuaded, he let him rise, crowing over him, and warning him to take heed how he dealt any more with any that came of his father's kindred.

*winking: with his eyes tightly shut. whittle: knife.

But thus this combat of cowards being finished, Dametas was with much mirth and melody received into the camp as victorious, never a page there failing to wait upon this triumph.

## CHAPTER 14

But Clinias, though he wanted heart to prevent shame, yet he wanted not wit to feel shame; not so much repining at it for the abhorring of shame as for the discommodities that to them that are shamed ensue. For well he deemed, it would be a great bar to his practice and a pulling on of injuries, when men needed not care how they used him. Insomuch, that Clinias (finding himself the scorning-stock of every company) fell with repining to hate the cause thereof; and hate in a coward's heart could set itself no other limits but death. Which purpose was well egged on by representing unto himself what danger he lately was in, which still kept no less ugly figure in his mind than when it was present; and quickly (even in his dissembling countenance) might be discerned a concealed grudge. For though he forced in himself a far more diligent officiousness towards Amphialus than ever before, yet a leering eye upon the one side at him, a countenance still framed to smiling before him (how little cause soever there was of smiling) and grumbling behind him at any of his commandments, with an uncertain manner of behaviour, his words coming out, though full of flattery, yet slowly, and hoarsely pronounced, might well have blazed* what arms his false heart bare. But despised because of his cowardliness, and not marked because despised, he had the freer scope of practice. Which he did the more desperately enter into, because the daily dangers Amphialus did submit himself unto made Clinias assuredly look for his overthrow, and for his own consequently, if he did not redeem his former treason to Basilius with a more treasonable falsehood towards Amphialus.

His chief care, therefore, was to find out, among all sorts of the Amphialians, whom either like fear, tediousness of the siege, or discontentment of some unsatisfied ambition would make apt to dig in the same mine that he did: and some already of wealthy weary folks and unconstant youths (who had not found such

* *blazed*: proclaimed.

sudden success as they had promised themselves) he had made stoop to his lure.* But of none he made so good account as of Artesia, sister to the late slain Ismenus and the chief of the six maids who had trained out* the princesses to their banquet of misery: so much did the sharpness of her wit countervail (as he thought) any other defects of her sex; for she had undertaken that dangerous practice by the persuasion of Cecropia, who assured her that the two princesses should be made away and then Amphialus would marry her, which she was the apter to believe by some false persuasion her glass had given her of her own incomparable excellencies, and by the great favour she knew he bare to her brother, Ismenus, which (like a self-flattering woman) she conceived was done for her sake.

But when she had achieved her attempt, and that she found the princesses were so far from their intended death as that the one of them was like to be her sovereign; and that neither her service had won of Amphialus much more than ordinary favour, nor her overlarge offering herself to a mind otherwise owed* had obtained a looked for acceptation; disdain to be disdained, spite of a frustrate hope, and perchance unquenched lust-grown rage made her unquiet thoughts find no other rest but malice; which was increased by the death of her brother, whom she judged neither succoured against Philanax, nor revenged upon Philanax. But all these coals were well blown by the company she especially kept with Zelmane all this time of her imprisonment. For finding her presence uncheerful to the mourning Philoclea and contemned of the high-hearted Pamela, she spent her time most with Zelmane who, though at the first hardly brooking the instrument of their misery, learning cunning in the school of adversity, in time framed herself to yield her acceptable entertainment.

For Zelmane, when she had by that unexpected mischief her body imprisoned, her valour over-mastered, her wit beguiled, her desires barred, her love eclipsed; assured of evil, fearing worse, able to know Philoclea's misfortune and not able to succour her, she was a great while before the greatness of her heart could descend to sorrow, but rather rose boiling up in spite and disdain, reason

* *stoop to his lure:* be attracted by his bait (from hawking). *trained out:* decoyed. *owed:* possessed.

hardly* making courage believe that it was distressed; but as if the walls would be afraid of her, so would her looks shoot out threatening upon them. But the fetters of servitude, growing heavier with wearing, made her feel her case, and the little prevailing of repining; and then grief gat a seat in her softened mind, making sweetness of past comforts by due title claim tears of present discomforts, and – since her fortune made her able to help as little as anybody, yet to be able to wail as much as anybody – solitary sorrow, with a continual circle in herself, going out at her own mouth to come in again at her own ears. Then was the name of Philoclea graved in the glass windows and, by the foolish idolatry of affection, no sooner written than adored, and no sooner adored than pitied: all the wonted praises she was wont to give unto her being now but figures of rhetoric to amplify[1] the injuries of misfortune; against which, being alone, she would often make invective declamations, methodized only by raging sorrow.

But when Artesia did insinuate herself into her acquaintance, she gave the government of her courage to wit and was content to familiarize herself with her; so much the rather as that she perceived in her certain flaws of ill-concealed discontentment. Insomuch that when Zelmane would sweeten her mouth with the praises of the sisters, especially setting forth their noble gratefulness in never forgetting well-intended services, and invoking the justice of the gods not to suffer such treasures to be wrongfully hidden, and sometimes, with a kind of unkindness, charging Artesia that she had been abused to abuse so worthy persons; Artesia (though falsely) would protest that she had been beguiled in it, never meaning other matter than recreation; and yet withal, by alleging how ungratefully she was dealt with, it was easy to be seen it was the unrewarding and not the evil employing her service which grieved her. But Zelmane, using her own bias* to bowl near the mistress* of her own thoughts, was content to lend her belief, and withal to magnify her desert, if willingly she would deliver whom unwillingly she had imprisoned; leaving no argument which might tickle ambition or flatter revenge. So that Ar-

* *hardly*: with difficulty. *bias*: the weight inserted into a bowl to make it take a curved course. *mistress*: the jack.

tesia, pushed forward by Clinias and drawn onward by Zelmane, bound herself to that practice; wherein Zelmane, for her part, desired no more but to have armour and weapons brought into her chamber, not doubting therewith to perform anything, how impossible soever, which longing love can persuade, and invincible valour dare promise.

But Clinias, whose faith could never comprehend the mysteries of courage, persuaded Artesia, while he by corruption had drawn the guard of one gate to open it (when he would appoint the time) to the enemy, that she should empoison Amphialus, which she might the easier do because she herself had used to make the broths when Amphialus, either wearied or wounded, did use such diet. And all things already were ready to be put in execution, when they thought best to break the matter with the two excellent sisters, not doubting of their consent in a thing so behoveful to themselves: their reasons being that the princesses, knowing their service, might be sure to preserve them from the fury of the entering soldiers, whereof Clinias, even so, could scarcely be sufficiently certain; and withal, making them privy to their action, to bind them afterwards to a promised gratefulness towards them. They went therefore at one time when they knew them to be alone, Clinias to Philoclea, and Artesia to Pamela; and Clinias, with no few words, did set forth what an exploit was intended for her service. But Philoclea, in whose clear mind treason could find no hiding-place, told him that she would be glad if he could persuade her cousin to deliver her, and that she would never forget his service therein; but that she desired him to lay down any such way of mischief, for that (for her part) she would rather yield to perpetual imprisonment than consent to the destroying her cousin, who, she knew, loved her, though wronged her. This unlooked-for answer amazed Clinias, so that he had no other remedy in his mind but to kneel down to Philoclea and beseech her to keep it secret, considering that the intention was for her service, and vowing, since she misliked it, to proceed no further therein. She comforted him with promise of silence, which she performed.

But that little availed; for Artesia having in like sort opened this device to Pamela, she, in whose mind virtue governed with the sceptre of knowledge, hating so horrible a wickedness, and straight judging what was fit to do:

'Wicked woman,' said she, 'whose unrepenting heart can find no way to amend treason but by treason, now the time is come that thy wretched wiles have caught thyself in thine own net. As for me, let the gods dispose of me as shall please them; but sure it shall be no such way nor way-leader by which I will come to liberty.'

This she spake something with a louder voice than she was wont to use, so as Cecropia heard the noise, who was (sooner than Artesia imagined she would) come up, to bring Pamela to a window where she might see a notable skirmish happened in the camp (as she thought) among themselves; and being a cunning fisher in troubled waters, straight found by their voices and gestures there was some matter of consequence, which she desired Pamela to tell her.

'Ask of her,' said Pamela, 'and learn to know that who do falsehood to their superiors teach falsehood to their inferiors.'

More she would not say. But Cecropia, taking away the each-way guilty Artesia, with fear of torture gat of her the whole practice; so as Zelmane was the more closely imprisoned, and Clinias, with the rest of his corrupted mates, according to their merits, executed: for as for Artesia, she was but locked up in her chamber, Amphialus not consenting, for the love he bare to Ismenus, that further punishment should be laid upon her.


CHAPTER 15

But the noise they heard in the camp was occasioned by the famous prince Anaxius, nephew to the giant Euardes, whom Pyrocles slew: a prince of body exceedingly strong; in arms so skilful and fortunate as no man was thought to excel him; of courage that knew not how to fear – parts worthy praise, if they had not been guided by pride and followed by injustice. For by a strange composition of mind, there was no man more tenderly sensible in anything offered to himself which in the furthest-fetched construction might be wrested to the name of wrong; no man that in his own actions could worse distinguish between valour and violence; so proud, as he could not abstain from a Thraso-like boasting,[1] and yet (so unlucky a lodging his virtues had gotten) he would never boast more than he would accomplish: falsely accounting an unflexible anger a courageous constancy; esteeming fear and astonishment righter causes of admiration than love and honour.

This man had four sundry times fought with Amphialus, but Mars had been so unpartial an arbiter that neither side got advantage of the other. But in the end, it happened that Anaxius found Amphialus, unknown, in great danger, and saved his life: whereupon, loving his own benefit, began to favour him, so much the more as (thinking so well of himself) he could not choose but like him whom he found a match for himself; which at last grew to as much friendship towards him as could by a proud heart be conceived. So as in this travail (seeking Pyrocles to be revenged of his uncle's death) hearing of this siege, never taking pains to examine the quarrel (like a man whose will was his god and his hand his law) taking with him his two brothers (men accounted little inferior to himself in martial matters) and two hundred chosen horsemen (with whom he thought himself able to conquer the world) yet commanding the rest of his forces to follow, he himself upon such an unexpected suddenness entered in upon the back of Basilius, that many with great unkindness took their death not knowing why nor how they were so murdered. There, if ever, did he make known the wonderfulness of his force. But the valiant and faithful Philanax with well governed speed made such head against him as would have showed how soon courage falls in the ditch which hath not the eye of wisdom, but that Amphialus at the same time issued out, and winning with abundance of courage one of the sconces* which Basilius had builded, made way for his friend Anaxius, with great loss of both sides but especially of the Basilians, such notable monuments had those two swords especially left of their master's redoubted worthiness.

There, with the respect fit to his estate, the honour due to his worthiness, and the kindness which accompanies friendship made fast by interchanged benefits, did Amphialus enforce himself (as

* *sconce*: small fort.

much as in a besieged town he could) to make Anaxius know that his succour was not so needful as his presence grateful. For causing the streets and houses of the town to witness his welcome, making both soldiers and magistrates in their countenances to show their gladness of him, he led him to his mother, whom he besought to entertain him with no less love and kindness than as one who once had saved her son's life, and now came to save both life and honour.

'Tush,' said Anaxius, speaking aloud, looking upon his brothers, 'I am only sorry there are not half-a-dozen kings more about you, that what Anaxius can do might be the better manifested.'

His brothers smiled, as though he had over-modestly spoken far underneath the pitch of his power. Then was he disarmed at the earnest request of Amphialus; for Anaxius boiled with desire to issue out upon the enemies, persuading himself that the sun should not be set before he had overthrown them. And having reposed himself Amphialus asked him whether he would visit the young princesses. But Anaxius whispered him in the ear, 'In truth,' said he, 'dear friend Amphialus, though I am none of those that love to speak of themselves, I never came yet in company of ladies but that they fell in love with me. And I that in my heart scorn them as a peevish paltry sex, not worthy to communicate with my virtues, would not do you the wrong, since, as I hear, you do debase yourself so much as to affect them.'

The courteous Amphialus could have been angry with him for those words; but knowing his humour, suffered him to dance to his own music; and gave himself to entertain both him and his brothers with as cheerful a manner as could issue from a mind whom unlucky love had filled with melancholy. For to Anaxius he yielded the direction of all. He gave the watch-word, and if any grace were granted, the means were to be made to Anaxius. And that night when supper was ended, wherein Amphialus would needs himself wait upon him, he caused in boats upon the lake an excellent music to be ordered; which, though Anaxius might conceive was for his honour, yet indeed he was but the brick-wall to convey it to the ears of the beloved Philoclea.[2]

The music was of cornets* whereof one answering the other, with a sweet emulation striving for the glory of music, and striking upon the smooth face of the quiet lake, was then delivered up to the castle walls, which with a proud reverberation spreading it into the air, it seemed before the harmony came to the ear that it had enriched itself in travel, the nature of those places adding melody to that melodious instrument. And when a while that instrument had made a brave proclamation to all unpossessed minds of attention,[3] an excellent concert* straight followed of five viols and as many voices; which all being but orators of their master's passions, bestowed this song upon her that thought upon another matter:

> The fire to see my wrongs for anger burneth;
> The air in rain for my affliction weepeth:
> The sea to ebb for grief his flowing turneth:
> The earth with pity dull his centre keepeth.
>> Fame is with wonder blazed;
>> Time runs away for sorrow:
>> Place standeth still amazed
> To see my night of evils, which hath no morrow.
>> Alas, alonely she no pity taketh
> To know my miseries, but chaste and cruel,
>> My fall her glory maketh;
> Yet still her eyes give to my flames their fuel.
>
> Fire, burn me quite, till sense of burning leave me:
> Air, let me draw thy breath no more in anguish:
> Sea, drown'd in thee, of tedious life bereave me;
> Earth, take this earth wherein my spirits languish.
>> Fame, say I was not born:
>> Time, haste my dying hour:
>> Place, see my grave uptorn:
> Fire, air, sea, earth, fame, time, place, show your power.
>> Alas from all their helps I am exiled,
> For hers am I, and Death fears her displeasure.
>> Fie Death thou art beguiled:
> Though I be hers, she makes of me no treasure.

*cornets: horns. concert: harmony.

But Anaxius, seeming a-weary before it was ended, told Amphialus that for his part he liked no music but the neighing of horses, the sound of trumpets, and the cries of yielding persons; and therefore desired that the next morning they should issue upon the same place where they had entered that day, not doubting to make them quickly a-weary of being the besiegers of Anaxius. Amphialus, who had no whit less courage, though nothing blown up with pride, willingly condescended: and so the next morning, giving false alarum to the other side of the camp, Amphialus at Anaxius' earnest request staying within the town to see it guarded, Anaxius and his brethren, Lycurgus and Zoilus, sallied out with the best chosen men. But Basilius, having been the last day somewhat unprovided, now had better fortified the overthrown sconce, and so well had prepared everything for defence that it was impossible for any valour from within to prevail. Yet things were performed by Anaxius beyond the credit of the credulous; for thrice, valiantly followed by his brothers, did he set up his banner upon the rampire of the enemy, though thrice again by the multitude and advantage of the place, but especially by the coming of three valiant knights, he were driven down again. Numbers there were that day whose deaths and overthrows were excused* by the well known sword of Anaxius; but the rest by the length of time and injury of historians have been wrapped up in dark forgetfulness. Only Tressenius is spoken of, because when all abandoned the place, he only made head to Anaxius; till having lost one of his legs yet not lost the heart of fighting, Lycurgus, second brother to Anaxius, cruelly murdered him, Anaxius himself disdaining any further to deal with him.

But so far had Anaxius at the third time prevailed that now the Basilians began to let their courage descend to their feet; Basilius and Philanax in vain striving with reverence of authority to bridle the flight of astonishment* and to teach fear discretion; so that Amphialus, seeing victory show such a flattering countenance to him, came out with all his force, hoping that day to end the siege.

But that fancy altered quickly by the sudden coming to the other side of three knights, whereof the one was in white armour,

* *excused*: extenuated. *astonishment*: panic.

the other in green, and the third, by his black armour and device, straight known to be the notable knight who the first day had given fortune so short a stop with his notable deeds and fighting hand to hand with the deemed invincible Amphialus. For the very cowards no sooner saw him, but as borrowing some of his spirit, they went like young eagles to the prey under the wing of their dam. For the three adventurers, not content to keep them from their rampire, leapt down among them and entered into a brave combat with the three valiant brothers. But to whether side fortune would have been partial could not be determined. For the Basilians, lightened with the beams of these strangers' valour, followed so thick that the Amphialians were glad with some haste to retire to the wall's ward;* though Anaxius, neither reason, fear, nor example could make him assuage the fury of his fight; until one of the Basilians (unworthy to have his name registered, since he did it cowardly, sideward, when he least looked that way) almost cut off one of his legs, so as he fell down, blaspheming heaven that all the influences thereof had power to overthrow him: and there death would have seized of his proud heart but that Amphialus took in hand the Black Knight, while some of his soldiers conveyed away Anaxius, so requiting life for life unto him.

And for the love and example of Amphialus, the fight began to enter into a new fit of heat, when Basilius (that thought enough to be done for that day) caused retreat to be sounded, fearing lest his men, following over-earnestly, might be the loss of those excellent knights whom he desired to know. The knights as soon as they heard the retreat (though they were eagerly set) knowing that courage without discipline is nearer beastliness than manhood, drew back their swords, though hungry of more blood: especially the Black Knight who, knowing Amphialus, could not refrain to tell him that this was the second time he escaped out of his hands, but that he would shortly bring him a bill of all the former accounts. Amphialus seeing it fit to retire also (most of his people being hurt both in bodies and hearts) withdrew himself with so well-seated a resolution that it was as far from anger as

* *ward:* protection.

from dismayedness, answering no other to the Black Knight's threats but that when he brought him his account, he should find a good paymaster.

<h2 style="text-align:center">CHAPTER 16</h2>

The fight being ceased and each side withdrawn within their strengths, Basilius sent Philanax to entertain the strange knights, and to bring them unto him that he might acknowledge what honour was due to their virtue. But they excused themselves, desiring to be known first by their deeds, before their names should accuse* their unworthiness: and though the other replied according as they deserved, yet (finding that unwelcome courtesy is a degree of injury) he suffered them to retire themselves to a tent of their own without the camp, where they kept themselves secret: Philanax himself being called away to another strange knight – strange not only by the unlooked-for-ness of his coming, but by the strange manner of his coming.

For he had before him four damosels, and so many behind him, all upon palfreys, and all apparelled in mourning weeds; each of them a servant of each side with like liveries of sorrow. Himself in an armour all painted over with such a cunning of shadow that it represented a gaping sepulchre: the furniture of his horse was all of cypress branches, wherewith in old time they were wont to dress graves. His bases, which he wore so long as they came almost to his ankle, were embroidered only with black worms, which seemed to crawl up and down, as ready already to devour him. In his shield, for impresa, he had a beautiful child, but having two heads, whereof the one showed that it was already dead; the other alive, but in that case, necessarily looking for death. The word was: 'No way to be rid from death, but by death.'

This Knight of the Tomb (for so the soldiers termed him) sent to Basilius to demand leave to send in a damosel into the town to call out Amphialus, according as before time some others had done. Which being granted (as glad any would undertake the charge, which nobody else in that camp was known willing to do) the damosel went in, and having with tears sobbed out a brave chal-

*accuse*: make known.

lenge to Amphialus from the Knight of the Tomb, Amphialus, honourably entertaining the gentlewoman, and desiring to know the knight's name (which the doleful gentlewoman would not discover) accepted the challenge, only desiring the gentlewoman to say thus much to the strange knight from him, that if his mind were like to his title, there were more cause of affinity than enmity between them. And therefore presently, according as he was wont, as soon as he perceived the Knight of the Tomb with his damosels and judge was come into the island, he also went over in accustomed manner; and yet, for the courtesy of his nature, desired to speak with him.

But the Knight of the Tomb, with silence and drawing his horse back, showed no will to hear nor speak; but with lance on thigh made him know it was fit for him to go to the other end of the career; whence waiting the start of the unknown knight, he likewise made his spurs claim haste of his horse. But when his staff was in his rest, coming down to meet with the knight, now very near him, he perceived the knight had missed his rest; wherefore the courteous Amphialus would not let his lance descend, but with a gallant grace ran over the head of his therein-friended enemy: and having stopped his horse, and with the turning of him blessed his sight with the window where he thought Philoclea might stand, he perceived the knight had lighted from his horse and thrown away his staff (angry with his misfortune as of having missed his rest) and drawn his sword, to make that supply his fellow's fault. He also lighted and drew his sword, esteeming victory by advantage rather robbed than purchased: and so the other coming eagerly toward him, he with his shield out and sword aloft, with more bravery than anger drew unto him, and straight made their swords speak for them a pretty while with equal fierceness.

But Amphialus, to whom the earth brought forth few matches, having both much more skill to choose the places, and more force to work upon the chosen, had already made many windows in his armour for death to come in at, when in the nobleness of his nature abhorring to make the punishment overgo the offence, he stepped a little back, and withal, 'Sir knight,' said he, 'you may easily see that it pleaseth God to favour my cause.

Employ your valour against them that wish you hurt: for my part I have not deserved hate of you.'

'Thou liest, false traitor,' said the other, with an angry, but weak voice; but Amphialus, in whom abused kindness became spiteful rage, 'Ah barbarous wretch,' said he, 'only courageous in discourtesy, thou shalt soon see whether thy tongue hath betrayed thy heart, or no': and with that, redoubling his blows, gave him a great wound upon his neck, and closing with him, overthrew him, and in the fall thrust him mortally into the body; and with that went to pull off his helmet, with intention to make him give himself the lie for having so said, or to cut off his head.

But the headpiece was no sooner off but that there fell about the shoulders of the overcome knight the treasure of fair golden hair which, with the face (soon known by the badge of excellency) witnessed that it was Parthenia, the unfortunately virtuous wife of Argalus; her beauty then, even in the despite of the passed sorrow or coming death, assuring all beholders that it was nothing short of perfection. For her exceeding fair eyes having with continual weeping gotten a little redness about them; her roundy sweetly swelling lips a little trembling, as though they kissed their neighbour death; in her cheeks the whiteness striving by little and little to get upon the rosiness of them; her neck, a neck indeed of alabaster, displaying the wound, which with most dainty blood laboured to drown his own beauties, so as here was a river of purest red, there an island of perfectest white, each giving lustre to the other; with the sweet countenance, God knows, full of an unaffected languishing: though these things to a grossly conceiving sense might seem disgraces, yet indeed were they but apparelling beauty in a new fashion which, all-looked-upon through the spectacles of pity, did even increase the lines of her natural fairness, so as Amphialus was astonished with grief, compassion and shame, detesting his fortune that made him unfortunate in victory.

Therefore putting off his headpiece and gauntlet, kneeling down unto her, and with tears testifying his sorrow, he offered his (by himself accursed) hands to help her, protesting his life and power to be ready to do her honour. But Parthenia, who had inward messengers of the desired death's approach, looking upon him, and straight turning away her feeble sight as from a delightless object, drawing out her words which her breath, loth to part from so sweet a body, did faintly deliver:

'Sir,' said she, 'I pray you, if prayers have place in enemies, to let my maids take my body untouched by you. The only honour I now desire by your means is that I have no honour of you. Argalus made no such bargain with you, that the hands which killed him should help me. I have of them (and I do not only pardon you, but thank you for it) the service which I desired. There rests nothing now but that I go live with him since whose death I have done nothing but die.'

Then pausing, and a little fainting, and again coming to herself:

'O sweet life, welcome,' said she. 'Now feel I the bands untied of the cruel death which so long hath held me. And O life, O death, answer for me, that my thoughts have not so much as in a dream tasted any comfort since they were deprived of Argalus. I come, my Argalus, I come: and, O God, hide my faults in thy mercies, and grant, as I feel thou dost grant, that in thy eternal love, we may love each other eternally. And this, O Lord' – but there Atropos* cut off her sentence: for with that, casting up both eyes and hands to the skies, the noble soul departed (one might well assure himself) to heaven, which left the body in so heavenly a demeanour.

But Amphialus, with a heart oppressed with grief, because of her request, withdrew himself: but the judges, as full of pity, had been all this while disarming her, and her gentlewomen with lamentable cries labouring to staunch the remediless wounds: and a while she was dead before they perceived it, death being able to divide the soul, but not the beauty from that body. But when the infallible tokens of death assured them of their loss, one of the women would have killed herself, but that the squire of Amphialus perceiving it, by force held her. Others that had as strong passion though weaker resolution, fell to cast dust upon their heads, to tear their garments; all falling upon the earth and crying upon their sweet mistress, as if their cries could persuade the soul to leave the celestial happiness, to come again into the elements of

* *Atropos:* the one of the three Fates whose task was to cut the thread of human life.

sorrow: one time calling to remembrance her virtue, chasteness, sweetness, goodness to them; another time accursing themselves that they had obeyed her, they having been deceived by her words, who assured them that it was revealed unto her that she should have her heart's desire in the battle against Amphialus, which they wrongly understood: then kissing her cold hands and feet, weary of the world, since she was gone who was their world. The very heavens seemed with a cloudy countenance to lour at the loss, and fame itself (though by nature glad to tell such rare accidents) yet could not choose but deliver it in lamentable accents; and in such sort went it quickly all over the camp: and, as if the air had been infected with sorrow, no heart was so hard but was subject to that contagion, the rareness of the accident matching together (the rarely matched together) pity with admiration.

Basilius himself came forth, and brought the fair Gynecia with him, who was come into the camp under colour of visiting her husband and hearing of her daughters: but indeed Zelmane was the saint to which her pilgrimage was intended, cursing, envying, blessing, and in her heart kissing the walls which imprisoned her. But both they, with Philanax and the rest of the principal nobility, went out to make honour triumph over death, conveying that excellent body (whereto Basilius himself would needs lend his shoulder) to a church a mile from the camp, where the valiant Argalus lay entombed; recommending to that sepulchre the blessed relics of faithful and virtuous love, giving order for the making of marble images to represent them, and each way enriching the tomb: upon which Basilius himself caused this epitaph to be written:

> His being was in her alone:
> And he not being, she was none.

> They joy'd one joy, one grief they griev'd,
> One love they lov'd, one life they liv'd.
> The hand was one, one was the sword
> That did his death, her death afford.

> As all the rest, so now the stone
> That tombs the two is justly one.

ARGALUS AND PARTHENIA

## CHAPTER 17

Then with eyes full of ears and mouths full of her praises returned they to the camp, with more and more hate against Amphialus, who, poor gentleman, had therefore greater portion of woe than any of them. For that courteous heart, which would have grieved but to have heard the like adventure, was rent with remembering himself to be the author; so that his wisdom could not so far temper his passion but that he took his sword, counted the best in the world (which with much blood he had once conquered of a mighty giant) and brake it into many pieces (which afterwards he had good cause to repent) saying, that neither it was worthy to serve the noble exercise of chivalry, nor any other worthy to feel that sword which had stroken so excellent a lady; and withal, banishing all cheerfulness of his countenance, he returned home, where he got him to his bed, not so much to rest his restless mind as to avoid all company, the sight whereof was tedious unto him.

And then melancholy, only rich in unfortunate remembrances, brought before him all the mishaps with which his life had wrestled, taking this not only as a confirming of the former but a presage of following misery; and to his heart, already overcome by sorrowfulness, even trifling misfortunes came to fill up the roll of a grieved memory, labouring only his wits to pierce further and further into his own wretchedness. So as all that night, in despite of darkness, he held his eyes open; and in the morning, when the light began to restore to each body his colour, then with curtains barred he himself from the enjoying of it, neither willing to feel the comfort of the day nor the ease of the night: until his mother (who never knew what love meant but only to him-ward) came to his bedside; and beginning with loving earnestness to lay a kind chiding upon him because he would suffer the weakness of sorrow to conquer the strength of his virtues, he did with a broken piece-meal speech (as if the tempest of passion unorderly blew out his words) remember the mishaps of his youth; the evils he had been cause of; his rebelling with shame, and that shame increased with shameful accidents; the deaths of Philoxenus and Parthenia, wherein he found himself hated of the ever-ruling powers; but especially (and so especially, as the rest seemed nothing when he came to that) his fatal love to Philoclea, to whom he had so governed himself as one that could neither conquer nor yield, being of the one side a slave, and of the other a jailor: and withal almost upbraiding unto his mother the little success of her large-hoping promises, he in effect finding Philoclea nothing mollified, and now himself so cast down as he thought himself unworthy of better.

But his mother, as she had plentiful cause, making him see that of his other griefs there was little or no fault in himself, and therefore there ought to be little or no grief in him; when she came to the head of the sore, indeed seeing that she could no longer patch up her former promises (he taking a desperate deafness to all delaying hopes) she confessed plainly that she could prevail nothing: but the fault was his own, who had marred the young girl by seeking to have that by prayer which he should have taken by authority: that as it were an absurd cunning to make high ladders to go in a plain way, so was it an untimely and foolish flattery, there to beseech where one might command, puffing them up, by being besought, with such a self-pride of superiority that it was not, forsooth, to be held out but by a denial.

'O God,' said Amphialus, 'how well I thought my fortune would bring forth this end of your labours! Assure yourself, mother, I will sooner pull out these eyes than they shall look upon the heavenly Philoclea but as upon a heaven whence they have their light, and to which they are subject. If they will pour down any influences of comfort, O happy I: but if by the sacrifice of a faithful heart they will not be called unto me, let me languish, and wither with languishing, and grieve with withering, but never so much as repine with never so much grieving. Mother, O Mother, lust may well be a tyrant, but true love where it is indeed, it is a servant. Accursed more than I am may I be, if ever I did approach her but that I freezed as much in a fearful reverence as I burned in a vehement desire. Did ever man's eye look through love upon the majesty of virtue shining through beauty, but that he became (as it well became him) a captive? And is it the style of a captive to write, "Our will and pleasure"?'

'Tush, tush, son,' said Cecropia. 'If you say you love but, withal, you fear, you fear lest you should offend. Offend? And how know you that you should offend? Because she doth deny? Deny! Now by my truth, if your sadness would let me laugh, I could laugh heartily to see that yet you are ignorant that "No" is no negative in a woman's mouth. My son, believe me, a woman speaking of women. A lover's modesty among us is much more praised than liked; or if we like it, so well we like it that for marring of his modesty he shall never proceed further. Each virtue hath his time. If you command your soldier to march foremost and he for courtesy put others before him, would you praise his modesty? Love is your general: he bids you dare. And will Amphialus be a dastard? Let examples serve. Do you think Theseus should ever have gotten Antiope[1] with sighing and crossing his arms? He ravished her, and ravished her that was an Amazon and therefore had gotten a habit of stoutness above the nature of a woman; but having ravished her, he got a child of her. And I say no more, but that, they say, is not gotten without consent of both sides. Iöle[2] had her own father killed by Hercules and herself ravished, by force ravished, and yet ere long this ravished and unfathered lady could sportfully put on the lion's skin upon her own fair shoulders, and play with the club with her own delicate hands: so easily had she pardoned the ravisher that she could not but delight in those weapons of ravishing. But above all mark Helen, daughter to Jupiter, who could never brook her mannerly-wooing Menelaus, but disdained his humbleness and loathed his softness. But so well she could like the force of enforcing Paris that for him she could abide what might be abidden. But what? Menelaus takes heart: he recovers her by force, by force carries her home, by force enjoys her; and she (who could never like him for serviceableness) ever after loved him for violence. For what can be more agreeable than upon force to lay the fault of desire, and in one instant to join a dear delight with a just excuse? Or rather the true cause is (pardon me, O woman-kind, for revealing to mine own son the truth of this mystery) we think there wants fire, where we find no sparkles at least of fury.

Truly I have known a great lady, long sought by most great, most wise, most beautiful, most valiant persons, never won, because they did over-superstitiously* solicit her: the same lady

* *over-superstitiously:* with too much reverence.

brought under by another, inferior to all them in all those qualities, only because he could use that imperious masterfulness which nature gives to men above women. For indeed, son, I confess unto you, in our very creation we are servants: and who prayeth* his servants shall never be well obeyed: but as a ready horse straight yields when he finds one that will have him yield, the same falls to bounds* when he feels a fearful horseman. Awake thy spirits, good Amphialus, and assure thyself that though she refuseth, she refuseth but to endear the obtaining. If she weep and chide and protest before it be gotten, she can but weep and chide and protest when it is gotten. Think she would not strive, but that she means to try thy force; and my Amphialus, know thyself a man, and show thyself a man; and, believe me upon my word, a woman is a woman.'

## CHAPTER 18

Amphialus was about to answer her, when a gentleman of his made him understand that there was a messenger come, who had brought a letter unto him from out of the camp: whom he presently calling for, took, opened and read the letter, importing this.

To thee Amphialus of Arcadia, the forsaken knight wisheth health and courage, that by my hand thou mayest receive punishment for thy treason, according to thine own offer which, wickedly occasioned, thou hast proudly begun, and accursedly maintained. I will presently (if thy mind faint thee not for his own guiltiness) meet thee in thy island, in such order as hath by the former been used: or if thou likest not the time, place, or weapon, I am ready to take thine own reasonable choice in any of them, so as thou do perform the substance. Make me such answer as may show that thou hast some taste of honour: and so I leave thee to live till I meet thee.

Amphialus read it, and with a deep sigh, according to the humour of inward affliction, seemed even to condemn himself, as though indeed his reproaches were true. But howsoever the dulness of melancholy would have languishingly yielded there-

* *prayeth*: begs favours of. (1613 text). '90, '93, 'praiseth'. *falls to bounds*: takes to leaping and rearing.

unto, his courage, unused to such injuries, desired help of anger to make him this answer:

Forsaken knight, though your nameless challenge might carry in itself excuse for a man of my birth and estate, yet herein set your heart at rest, you shall not be forsaken. I will, without stay, answer you in the wonted manner, and come both armed in your foolish threatenings, and yet the more fearless, expecting weak blows where I find so strong words. You shall not therefore long attend me in the island before proof teach you that of my life you have made yourself too large a promise. In the meantime, farewell.

This being written and delivered, the messenger told him that his lord would, if he liked the same, bring two knights with him to be his patrons. Which Amphialus accepted, and withal shaking off with resolution his mother's importunate dissuasions, he furnished himself for the fight, but not in his wonted furniture. For now, as if he would turn his inside outward, he would needs appear all in black; his decking both for himself and horse being cut out into the fashion of very rags, yet all so daintily joined together with precious stones, as it was a brave raggedness and a rich poverty: and so cunningly had the workman followed his humour in his armour that he had given it a rusty show, and yet so as any man might perceive was by art and not negligence, carrying at one instant a disgraced handsomeness and a new oldness. In his shield he bare for his device a Night, by an excellent painter excellently painted, with a sun with a shadow, and upon the shadow a speech signifying that it, only, was barred from enjoying that whereof it had his life, or 'From whose I am, banished.' In his crest he carried Philoclea's knives, the only token of her forced favour.

So passed he over into the island, taking with him the two brothers of Anaxius; where he found the forsaken knight attired in his own livery, as black as sorrow itself could see itself in the blackest glass: his ornaments of the same hue, but formed into the figure of ravens which seemed to gape for carrion: only his reins were snakes, which finely wrapping themselves one within the other, their heads came together to the cheeks and bosses of the bit, where they might seem to bite at the horse, and the horse, as he champed the bit, to bite at them, and that the white foam was engendered by the poisonous fury of the combat. His impresa was a Catoblepta,* which so long lies dead as the moon (whereto it hath so natural a sympathy) wants her light. The word signified, that the moon wanted not the light, but the poor beast wanted the moon's light. He had in his headpiece a whip, to witness a self-punishing repentance. Their very horses were coal black too, not having so much as one star to give light to their night of blackness; so as one would have thought they had been the two sons of sorrow and were come hither to fight for their birthright in that sorry inheritance.

Which alliance of passions so moved Amphialus, already tender-minded by the afflictions of love, that without staff or sword drawn, he trotted fairly to the forsaken knight, willing to have put off this combat to which his melancholy heart did (more than ever in like occasion) misgive him: and therefore saluting him.

'Good knight,' said he, 'because we are men, and should know reason why we do things, tell me the cause that makes you thus eager to fight with me.'

'Because I affirm,' answered the forsaken knight, 'that thou dost most rebellious injury to those ladies to whom all men owe service.'

'You shall not fight with me,' said Amphialus, 'upon that quarrel, for I confess the same too: but it proceeds from their own beauty, to enforce love to offer this force.'

'I maintain then,' said the forsaken knight, 'that thou art not worthy so to love.'

'And that confess I too,' said Amphialus, 'since the world is not so richly blessed as to bring forth anything worthy thereof. But no more unworthy than any other, since in none can be a more worthy love.'

'Yes, more unworthy than myself,' said the forsaken knight, 'for though I deserve contempt, thou deservest both contempt and hatred.'

But Amphialus by that thinking (though wrongly, each indeed mistaking other) that he was his rival, forgat all mind of reconciliation; and having all his thoughts bound up in choler,

* *Catoblepta*: a mythical beast out of Pliny's *Natural History*.

never staying either judge, trumpet or his own lance, drew out his sword, and saying, 'Thou liest, false villain,' unto him, his words and blows came so quick together as the one seemed a lightning of the other's thunder. But he found no barren ground of such seed; for it yielded him his own with such increase, that though reason and amazement go rarely together, yet the most reasonable eyes that saw it found reason to be amazed at the fury of their combat. Never game of death better played; never fury set itself forth in greater bravery. The courteous Vulcan, when he wrought (at his now more courteous wife's request) Aeneas an armour,[1] made not his hammer beget a greater sound than the swords of those noble knights did: they needed no fire to their forge, for they made the fire to shine at the meeting of their swords and armours, each side fetching still new spirit from the castle window, and careful of keeping their sight that way as a matter of greater consideration in their combat than either the advantage of sun or wind: which sun and wind, if the astonished eyes of the beholders were not by the astonishment deceived, did both stand still to be beholders of this rare match. For neither could their amazed eyes discern motion of the sun; and no breath of wind stirred, as if either for fear it would not come among such blows, or with delight had his eyes so busy as it had forgot to open his mouth.

This fight being the more cruel, since both Love and Hatred conspired to sharpen their humours, that hard it was to say whether Love with one trumpet, or Hatred with another, gave the louder alarum to their courages. Spite, Rage, Disdain, Shame, Revenge came waiting upon Hatred: of the other side came, with love-longing Desire, both invincible Hope and fearless Despair with rival-like Jealousy, which (although brought up within doors in the school of Cupid) would show themselves no less forward than the other dusty band of Mars, to make themselves notable in the notableness of this combat. Of either side confidence, unacquainted with loss, but assured trust to overcome, and good experience how to overcome: now seconding their terrible blows with cunning labouring the horses to win ground of the enemy; now unlooked-for parting one from the other to win advantage by an advantageous return. But force against force, skill against skill, so interchangeably encountered that it was not easy to determine whether enterprising or preventing came former: both sometimes at one instant doing and suffering wrong, and choler no less rising of the doing than of the suffering. But as the fire, the more fuel is put to it, the more hungry still it is to devour more, so the more they strake, the more unsatisfied they were with striking. Their very armour by piecemeal fell away from them; and yet their flesh abode the wounds constantly, as though it were less sensible of smart than the senseless armour: their blood in most places staining their black colour, as if it would give a more lively colour of mourning than black can do.

And so a long space they fought, while neither virtue nor fortune seemed partial of either side; which so tormented the unquiet heart of Amphialus, that he resolved to see a quick end: and therefore with the violence of courage, adding strength to his blow, he strake in such wise upon the side of the other's head that his remembrance left that battered lodging, so as he was quite from himself, casting his arms abroad and ready to fall down: his sword likewise went out of his hand, but that, being fast by a chain to his arm, he could not lose. And Amphialus used the favour of occasion, redoubling his blows; but the horse, weary to be beaten as well as the master, carried his master away, till he came unto himself. But then who could have seen him might well have discerned shame in his cheeks and revenge in his eyes: so as setting his teeth together with rage, he came running upon Amphialus, reaching out his arm, which had gathered up the sword, meaning with that blow to have cleaved Amphialus in two. But Amphialus, seeing the blow coming, shunned it with nimble turning his horse aside; wherewith the forsaken knight overstrake himself so, as almost he came down with his own strength. But the more hungry of his purpose, the more he was barred the food of it. Disdaining the resistance both of force and fortune, he returned upon the spur again, and ran with such violence upon Amphialus that his horse, with the force of the shock rose up before, almost overturned: which Amphialus perceiving, with rein and spur put forth his horse, and withal gave a mighty blow, in the descent of his horse, upon the shoulder of the forsaken knight, from whence sliding, it fell upon the neck of his horse so as horse and man fell to the ground: but he was scarce down before he was up on his feet again, with brave gesture showing rising of courage in the falling of fortune.

But the courteous Amphialus excused himself for having, against his will, killed his horse.

'Excuse thyself for viler faults,' answered the forsaken knight, 'and use this poor advantage the best thou canst, for thou shalt quickly find thou hast need of more.'

'Thy folly,' said Amphialus, 'shall not make me forget myself,' and therewith, trotting a little aside, alighted from his horse, because he would not have fortune come to claim any part of the victory. Which courteous act would have mollified the noble heart of the forsaken knight, if any other had done it besides the jailor of his mistress; but that was a sufficient defeasance* for the firmest bond of good nature; and therefore he was no sooner alighted but that he ran unto him, re-entering into as cruel a fight as eye did ever see, or thought could reasonably imagine; far beyond the reach of weak words to be able to express it. For what they had done on horseback was but as a morsel to keep their stomachs in appetite in comparison of that which now (being themselves) they did. Nor ever glutton by the change of dainty diet could be brought to fresh feeding (when he might have been satisfied before) with more earnestness, than those (by the change of their manner of fight) fell clean to a new fight, though any else would have thought they had had their fill already.

Amphialus, being the taller man, for the most part stood with his right leg before, his shield at the uttermost length of his arm, his sword high, but with the point towards his enemy. But when he strake, which came so thick, as if every blow would strive to be foremost, his arm seemed still a postilion* of death. The forsaken knight showed, with like skill, unlike gesture, keeping himself in continual motion, proportioning the distance between them to anything that Amphialus attempted: his eye guided his foot, and his foot conveyed his hand; and since nature had made him something the lower of the two, he made art follow and not strive with nature; shunning rather than warding his blows, like a cunning mastiff, who knows the sharpness of the horn and strength of the bull, fights low to get his proper advantage; answering mightiness

* *defeasance*: nullification. *postilion*: messenger.

with nimbleness, and yet at times employing his wonderful force wherein he was second to none. In sum, the blows were strong, the thrusts thick, and the avoidings cunning. But the forsaken knight (that thought it a degree of being conquered to be long in conquering) strake him so mighty a blow that he made Amphialus put knee to the ground without any humbleness. But when he felt himself stricken down and saw himself stricken down by his rival, then shame seemed one arm and disdain another, fury in his eyes, and revenge in his heart: skill and force gave place and they took the place of skill and force, with so unweariable a manner that the forsaken knight also was driven to leave the stern* of cunning and give himself wholly to be guided by the storm of fury; there being in both (because hate would not suffer admiration) extreme disdain to find themselves so matched.

'What,' said Amphialus to himself, 'am I Amphialus, before whom so many monsters and giants have fallen dead, when I only sought causeless adventures? And can one knight now withstand me in the presence of Philoclea, and fighting for Philoclea; or since I lost my liberty, have I lost my courage? Have I gotten the heart of a slave as well as the fortune? If an army were against me in the sight of Philoclea, could it resist me? O beast, one man resists thee: thy rival resists thee: or am I indeed Amphialus? Have not passions killed him, and wretched I, I know not how, succeeded into his place?'

Of the other side the forsaken knight with no less spite fell out with himself; 'Hast thou broken,' said he to himself, 'the commandment of thy only princess, to come now into her presence, and in her presence to prove thyself a coward? Doth Asia and Egypt set up trophies unto thee, to be matched here by a traitor? O noble Barsanes, how shamed will thy soul be, that he that slew thee should be resisted by this one man! O incomparable Pyrocles, more grieved wilt thou be with thy friend's shame than with thine own imprisonment, when thou shalt know how little I have been able to do for the delivery of thee and those heavenly princesses. Am I worthy to be friend to the most valorous prince that ever was entitled valorous, and show myself so weak a wretch? No, shamed Musidorus, worthy for nothing but to keep

*stern: guidance.

sheep, get thee a sheep-hook again, since thou canst use a sword no better.'

Thus at times did they, now with one thought then with another, sharpen their over-sharp humours, like the lion that beats himself with his own tail to make himself the more angry. These thoughts indeed not staying, but whetting their angry swords which now had put on the apparel of cruelty; they bleeding so abundantly, that everybody that saw them fainted for them; and yet they fainted not in themselves, their smart being more sensible to others' eyes than to their own feeling. Wrath and courage barring the common sense* from bringing any message of their case to the mind: pain, weariness, and weakness not daring to make known their case (though already in the limits of death) in the presence of so violent fury; which, filling the veins with rage instead of blood, and making the mind minister spirits to the body, a great while held out their fight, like an arrow shot upward by the force of the bow, though by his own nature he would go downward. The forsaken knight had the more wounds, but Amphialus had the sorer, which the other, watching time and place, had cunningly given unto him. Who ever saw a well-manned galley fight with a tall ship might make unto himself some kind of comparison of the difference of these two knights, a better couple than which the world could not brag of. Amphialus seemed to excel in strength, the forsaken knight in nimbleness; and yet did the one's strength excel in nimbleness, and the other's nimbleness excel in strength: but now strength and nimbleness were both gone, and excess of courage only maintained the fight. Three times had Amphialus with his mighty blows driven the forsaken knight to go staggering backward, but every one of those times he requited pain with smart, and shame with repulse. And now whether he had cause, or that over-much confidence (an over-forward scholar of unconquered courage) made him think he had cause, he began to persuade himself he had the advantage of the combat, though the advantage he took himself to have was only that he should be the later to die: which hope, hate (as unsecret as love) could not conceal, but drawing himself a little back from him, brake out in these manner of words.

* See Notes, I.14.2. (p. 851).

'Ah Amphialus,' said the forsaken knight, 'this third time thou shalt not escape me, but thy death shall satisfy thy injury and my malice, and pay for the cruelty thou showedst in killing the noble Argalus and the fair Parthenia.'

'In troth,' said Amphialus, 'thou art the best knight that ever I fought withal, which would make me willing to grant thee thy life, if thy wit were as good as thy courage, that (besides other follies) layest that to my charge which most against my will was committed. But whether my death be in thy power or no, let this tell thee', and upon the word waited a blow which parted his shield into two pieces and, despising the weak resistance of his already broken armour, made a great breach into his heart side, as if he would make a passage for his love to get out at.

But pain rather seemed to increase life than to weaken life in these champions. For the forsaken knight, coming in with his right leg and making it guide the force of the blow, strake Amphialus upon the belly so horrible a wound that his guts came out withal. Which Amphialus perceiving (fearing death, only because it should come with overthrow) he seemed to conjure all his strength for one moment's service; and so, lifting up his sword with both hands, hit the forsaken knight upon the head a blow, wherewith his sword brake. But, as if it would do a notable service before it died, it prevailed so, even in the instant of breaking, that the forsaken knight fell to the ground, quite for that instant forgetting both love and hatred: and Amphialus (finding himself also in such weakness as he looked for speedy death) glad of the victory though little hoping to enjoy it, pulled up his vizor, meaning with his dagger to give him death. But instead of death he gave him life; for the air so revived his spirits, that coming to himself and seeing his present danger, with a life conquering death he took Amphialus by the thigh, and together rose himself and overturned him. But Amphialus scrambled up again, both now so weak indeed as their motions rather seemed the after-drops to a storm than any matter of great fury.

But Amphialus might repent himself of his wilful breaking his good sword: for the forsaken knight (having with the extremity of justly-conceived hate and the unpitifulness of his own near-threatening death, blotted out all compliments of courtesy) let fly at him so cruelly, that though the blows were weak, yet weakness upon a weakened subject proved such strength that Amphialus, having attempted in vain once or twice to close with him, receiving wound upon wound, sent his whole burden to strike the earth with falling, since he could strike his foe no better in standing; giving no other tokens of himself than as of a man even ready to take his oath to be death's true servant.

Which when the hardy brothers of Anaxius perceived, not recking law of arms nor use of chivalry, they flew in to defend their friend or revenge their loss of him. But they were forthwith encountered with the two brave companions of the forsaken knight; whereof the one being all in green, both armour and furniture, it seemed a pleasant garden wherein grew orange trees which, with their golden fruits cunningly beaten in and embroidered, greatly enriched the eye-pleasing colour of green. In his shield was a sheep feeding in a pleasant field, with this word, 'Without fear or envy', and therefore was called the Knight of the Sheep.[2] The other knight was all in milk white, his attiring else all cut in stars, which, made of cloth of silver and silver spangles, each way seemed to cast many aspects. His device was the very pole itself, about which many stars stirring but the place itself left void. The word was, 'The best place yet reserved.'[3] But these four knights, inheriting the hate of their friends, began a most fierce combat; the forsaken knight himself not able to help his side, but was driven to sit him down with the extreme faintness of his more and more fainting body. But those valiant couples, seeking honour by dishonouring, and to build safety upon ruin, gave new appetites to the almost glutted eyes of the beholders; and now blood began to put sweat from the full possession of their outsides, no advantage being yet to be seen; only the knight of the sheep seeming most deliver,* and affecting most all that viewed him; when a company of soldiers sent by Cecropia came out in boats to the island, and all came running to the destruction of the three knights, whereof the one was utterly unable to defend himself.

But then did the other two knights show their wonderful courage and fidelity: for turning back to back, and both bestriding the black forsaken knight (who had fainted so long till he had lost the

* *deliver*: nimble.

feeling of faintness) they held play against the rest, though the two brothers unknightly helped them; till Philanax (who watchfully attended such traitorous practices) sent likewise over, both by boat and swimming, so choice a number as did put most of the other to the sword. Only the two brothers, with some of the bravest of them, carrying away the body of Amphialus, which they would rather have died than have left behind them.

So was the forsaken knight, laid upon cloaks, carried home to the camp. But his two friends knowing his earnest desire not to be known, covering him from anybody's eyes, conveyed him to their own tent: Basilius himself conquering his earnest desire to see him with fear to displease him, who had fought so notably in his quarrel. But fame set the honour upon his back, which he would not suffer to shine in his face; no man's mouth being barren of praises to the noble knight that had bettered the most esteemed knight in the world; everybody praying for his life, and thinking that therein they prayed for themselves. But he himself, when by the diligent care of friends and well applied cunning of surgeons he came to renew again the league between his mind and body, then fell he to a fresh war with his own thoughts, wrongfully condemning his manhood, laying cowardice to himself, whom the impudentest backbiter would not so have wronged. For his courage (used to use victory as an inheritance)* could brook no resistance at any time: but now that he had promised himself not only the conquest of him, but the scaling of the walls and delivery of Pamela, though he had done beyond all others' expectation, yet so short was he of his own that he hated to look upon the sun that had seen him do so weakly: and so much abhorred all visitation or honour (whereof he thought himself unworthy) that he besought his two noble friends to carry him away to a castle not far off, where he might cure his wounds and never be known till he made success excuse this (as he thought) want in him. They lovingly obeyed him, leaving Basilius and all the camp very sorry for the parting of these three unknown knights in whose prowess they had reposed the greatest trust of victory.

* *as an inheritance:* as his natural right.

## CHAPTER 19

But they being gone, Basilius and Philanax gave good order to the strengthening of the siege, fortifying themselves so as they feared no more any such sudden onset as that of Anaxius. And they within (by reason of Anaxius' hurt, but especially of Amphialus') gave themselves only to diligent watch and ward, making no sallies out, but committing the principal trust to Zoilus and Lycurgus. For Anaxius was yet forced to keep his chamber. And as for Amphialus, his body had such wounds, and he gave such wounds to his mind as easily it could not be determined whether death or he made the greater haste one to the other. For when the diligent care of cunning surgeons had brought life to the possession of his own right, Sorrow and Shame (like two corrupted servants) came waiting of it, persuading nothing but the giving over of itself to destruction. They laid before his eyes his present case, painting every piece of it in most ugly colours: they showed him his love wrapped in despair, his fame blotted by overthrow; so that if before he languished because he could not obtain his desiring, he now lamented because he durst not desire the obtaining.

'Recreant Amphialus,' would he say to himself, 'how darest thou entitle thyself the lover of Philoclea, that hast neither showed thyself a faithful coward nor a valiant rebel but both rebellious and cowardly, which no law can quit,* nor grave have pity of? Alas, life, what little pleasure thou dost me, to give me nothing but sense of reproach and exercise of ruin. I would, sweet Philoclea, I had died, before thy eyes had seen my weakness: and then perchance with some sigh thou wouldst have confessed thou hadst lost a worthy servant. But now, caitiff that I am, whatever I have done serves but to build up my rival's glory.'

To these speeches he would couple such gestures of vexation, and would fortify the gestures with such effects of fury, as sometimes offering to tear up his wounds, sometimes to refuse the sustenance of meat and counsel of physicians, that his perplexed mother was driven to make him by force to be tended, with extreme corsie* to herself and annoyance to him: till in the end he was contented to promise her he would attempt no violence upon

* *quit:* acquit. *corsie:* vexation.

himself, upon condition he might be troubled by nobody but only his physicians; his melancholy detesting all company, so as not the very surgeons nor servants durst speak unto him in doing him service. Only he had prayed his mother, as she tendered his life, she would procure him grace, and that without that she would never come at him more.

His mother, who had confined all her love only unto him, set only such about him as were absolutely at her commandment, whom she forbade to let him know anything that passed in the castle (till his wounds were cured) but as she from time to time should instruct them; she, for herself, being resolved, now she had the government of all things in her own hands, to satisfy her son's love by their yielding, or satisfy her own revenge in their punishment. Yet first, because she would be the freer from outward force, she sent a messenger to the camp to denounce* unto Basilius that if he did not presently raise his siege, she would cause the heads of the three ladies, prisoners, to be cut off before his eyes. And to make him the more fear a present performance, she caused his two daughters and Zelmane to be led unto the walls where she had made a scaffold, easy to be seen by Basilius; and there caused them to be kept as ready for the slaughter, till answer came from Basilius. A sight full of pity it was, to see those three (all excelling in all those excellencies wherewith Nature can beautify any body: Pamela giving sweetness to majesty; Philoclea enriching nobleness with humbleness; Zelmane setting in womanly beauty manlike valour) to be thus subjected to the basest injury of unjust fortune. One might see in Pamela a willingness to die rather than to have life at other's discretion; though sometimes a princely disdain would sparkle out of her princely eyes, that it should be in other's power to force her to die. In Philoclea a pretty fear came up to endamask* her rosy cheeks: but it was such a fear as rather seemed a kindly child to her innate humbleness than any other dismayedness: or if she were dismayed, it was more for Zelmane than for herself; or if more for herself, it was because Zelmane should lose her. As for Zelmane, as she went with her hands bound (for they durst not adventure on her well-known valour, especially among a people which perchance might be moved by

*_denounce_: threaten. _endamask_: bring a rosy blush to.

such a spectacle to some revolt) she was the true image of over-mastered courage, and of spite* that sees no remedy. For her breast swelled withal, the blood burst out at her nose, and she looked paler than accustomed, with her eyes cast on the ground, with such a grace as if she were fallen out with the heavens for suffering such an injury. The lookers on were so moved withal as they misliked what themselves did, and yet still did what themselves misliked. For some, glad to rid themselves of the dangerous annoyances of this siege; some, willing to shorten the way to Amphialus' succession (whereon they were dependants) some, and the greatest some, doing because others did and suffering because none durst begin to hinder, did in this sort set their hands to this (in their own conscience) wicked enterprise.

But when this message was brought to Basilius, and that this pitiful preparation was a sufficient letter of credit for him to believe it, he called unto him his chief counsellors: among which, those he chiefly trusted were Philanax, and Kalander, lately come to the camp at Basilius' commandment, and in himself weary of his solitary life, wanting his son's presence and never having heard from his beloved guests since they parted from him. Now in this doubt what he should do, he willed Kalander to give him his advice; who spake much to this purpose.

'You command me, Sir,' said he, 'to speak, rather because you will keep your wonted grave and noble manner to do nothing of importance without counsel, than that in this cause (which indeed hath but one way) your mind needs to have any counsel; so as my speech shall rather be to confirm what you have already determined than to argue against any possibility of other determination. For what sophistical scholar can find any question in this, whether you will have your incomparable daughters live or die, whether since you be here to cause their deliverance, you will make your being here the cause of their destruction? For nothing can be more unsensible than to think what one doth, and to forget the end why it is done. Do therefore, as I am sure you mean to do, remove the siege, and after seek by practice or other gentle means to recover that which by force you cannot: and thereof is indeed, when it pleaseth you, more counsel to be taken. Once,* in ex-

* *spite*: anger. *Once*: to sum up.

tremities the winning of time is the purchase of life, and worse by no means than their deaths can befall unto you. A man might use more words, if it were to any purpose to gild gold, or that I had any cause to doubt of your mind: but you are wise, and are a father.'

He said no more, for he durst not attempt to persuade the marrying of his daughter to Amphialus, but left that to bring in at another consultation. But Basilius made sign to Philanax who, standing a while in a maze as inwardly perplexed, at last thus delivered his opinion.

'If ever I could wish my faith untried and my counsel untrusted, it should be at this time, when in truth I must confess I would be content to purchase silence with discredit. But since you command, I obey. Only let me say thus much, that I obey not to these excellent ladies' father, but to my prince: and a prince it is to whom I give counsel. Therefore as to a prince I say that the grave and, I well know, true-minded counsel of my Lord Kalander had come in good time when you first took arms, before all your subjects got notice of your intention, before so much blood was spent, and before they were driven to seek this shift for their last remedy. But if now this force you away, why did you take arms, since you might be sure when ever they were in extremity they would have recourse to this threatening? And for a wise man to take in hand that which his enemy may with a word overthrow hath in my conceit great incongruity, and as great, not to forethink what his enemy in reason will do. But they threaten they will kill your daughters. What if they promised you, if you removed your siege, they would honourably send home your daughters? Would you be angled by* their promises? Truly no more ought you be terrified by their threatenings; for yet of the two, promise binds faith more than threatening.

'But indeed a prince of judgement ought not to consider what his enemies promise or threaten, but what the promisers and threateners in reason will do; and the nearest conjecture thereunto is what is best for their own behoof to do. They threaten if you remove not, they will kill your daughters: and if you do remove, what surety have you but that they will kill them, since if the

* *angled by*: caught.

purpose be to cut off all impediments of Amphialus' ambition, the same cause will continue when you are away; and so much the more encouraged, as the revenging power is absent, and they have the more opportunity to draw their factious friends about them? But if it be for their security only, the same cause will bring forth the same effect, and for their security they will preserve them. But it may be said, no man knows what desperate folks will do. It is true, and as true that no reason nor policy can prevent what desperate folks will do: and therefore they are among those dangers which wisdom is not to reckon. Only let it suffice to take away their despair, which may be by granting pardon for what is past, so as the ladies may be freely delivered. And let them that are your subjects trust you that are their prince: do not you subject yourself to trust them, who are so untrusty as to be manifest traitors. For if they find you so base-minded as, by their threatening, to remove your force, what indignity is it that they would not bring you unto still by the same threatening?

'Since, then, if love stir them, love will keep them from murdering what they love; and if ambition provoke them, ambitious they will be when you are away as well as while you are here, take not away your force, which bars not the one and bridles the other. For as for their shows and words, they are but fear-babes, not worthy once to move a worthy man's conceit, which must still consider what in reason they are like to do. Their despair, I grant, you shall do well to prevent: which as it is the last of all resolutions, so no man falls into it while so good a way as you may offer is open unto them. In sum, you are a prince, and a father of a people, who ought with the eye of wisdom, the hand of fortitude, and the heart of justice, to set down all private conceits in comparison of what for the public is profitable.'

He would have proceeded on, when Gynecia came running in, amazed for her daughter Pamela but mad for Zelmane; and falling at Basilius' feet, besought him to make no delay, using such gestures of compassion instead of stopped words[1] that Basilius (otherwise enough tender-minded) easily granted to raise the siege, which he saw dangerous to his daughters; but indeed more careful for Zelmane, by whose besieged person the poor old man was straitly besieged. So as to rid him of the famine of his mind, he went in speed away, discharging his soldiers. Only leaving the authority, as before, in Philanax's hands, he himself went with Gynecia to a strong castle of his, where he took counsel how first to deliver Zelmane, whom he called the poor stranger, as though only law of hospitality moved him; and for that purpose sent divers messengers to traffic with Cecropia.

## CHAPTER 20

Cecropia by this means rid of the present danger of the siege (desiring Zoilus and Lycurgus to take the care, till their brother recovered, of revictualling and furnishing the city, both with men and what else wanted, against any new occasion should urge them – she herself disdaining to hearken to Basilius, without he would grant his daughter in marriage to her son, which by no means he would be brought unto) bent all the sharpness of her malicious wit how to bring a comfortable grant to her son, whereupon she well found no less than his life depended. Therefore for a while she attempted all means of eloquent praying and flattering persuasion, mingling sometimes gifts, sometimes threatenings, as she had cause to hope that either open force or undermining would best win the castle of their resolution. And ever as much as she did to Philoclea, so much did she to Pamela, though in manner sometimes differing, as she found fit to level at the one's noble height and the other's sweet lowliness. For though she knew her son's heart had wholly given itself to Philoclea, yet seeing the equal gifts in Pamela, she hoped a fair grant would recover the sorrow of a fair refusal; cruelly intending the present empoisoning the one as soon as the other's affection were purchased.

But in vain was all her vain oratory employed. Pamela's determination was built upon so brave a rock that no shot of hers could reach unto it: and Philoclea (though humbly seated) was so environed with sweet rivers of clear virtue as could neither be battered nor undermined. Her witty persuasions had wise answers; her eloquence recompensed with sweetness; her threatenings repelled with disdain in the one, and patience in the other; her gifts either not accepted, or accepted to obey, but not to bind. So as Cecropia, in nature violent; cruel because ambitious; hateful,

for old rooted grudge to their mother, and now spiteful because she could not prevail with girls (as she counted them);
lastly, drawn on by her love to her son, and held up by a tyrannical authority, forthwith followed the bias of her own crooked
disposition, and doubling and redoubling her threatenings, fell to
confirm some of her threatened effects; first withdrawing all
comfort both of servants and service from them. But that those
excellent ladies had been used unto, even at home, and then found
in themselves how much good the hardness of education doth to
the resistance of misery. Then dishonourably using them both in
diet and lodging, by a contempt to pull down their thoughts to
yielding. But as before the consideration of a prison had disgraced
all ornaments, so now the same consideration made them attend*
all diseasefulness. Then still as she found those not prevail would
she go forward with giving them terrors, sometimes with noises of
horror, sometimes with sudden frightings in the night, when the
solitary darkness thereof might easier astonish the disarmed
senses. But to all, Virtue and Love resisted, strengthened one by
the other when each found itself over vehemently assaulted; Cecropia still sweetening her fierceness with fair promises, if they
would promise fair, that feeling evil and seeing a way far better,
their minds might the sooner be mollified. But they, that could not
taste her behaviour when it was pleasing in deed, could worse
now, when they had lost all taste by her injuries.

She, resolving all extremities rather than fail of conquest, pursued on her rugged way, letting no day pass without new and new
perplexing the poor ladies' minds and troubling their bodies: and
still swelling the more she was stopped, and growing hot with her
own doings, at length abominable rage carried her to absolute
tyrannies; so that taking with her certain old women (of wicked
dispositions, and apt for envy's sake to be cruel to youth and
beauty) with a countenance empoisoned with malice, flew to the
sweet Philoclea, as if so many kites should come about a white
dove; and matching violent gestures with mischievous threatenings, she having a rod in her hand (like a fury that should carry
wood to the burning of Diana's temple)[1] fell to scourge that most
beautiful body; love in vain holding the shield of beauty against

* *attend*: expect.

her blind cruelty. The sun drew clouds up to hide his face from so pitiful a sight, and the very stone walls did yield drops of sweat for agony of such a mischief: each senseless thing had sense of pity; only they that had sense were senseless. Virtue rarely found her worldly weakness* more than by the oppression of that day; and weeping Cupid told his weeping mother that he was sorry he was not deaf as well as blind, that he might never know so lamentable a work. Philoclea, with tearful eyes and sobbing breast (as soon as her weariness rather than compassion gave her respite) kneeled down to Cecropia, and making pity in her face honourable, and torment delightful, besought her since she hated her (for what cause she took God to witness she knew not) that she would at once take away her life, and not please herself with the tormenting of a poor gentlewoman.

'If,' said she, 'the common course of humanity cannot move you, nor the having me in your own walls cannot claim pity, nor womanly mercy, nor near alliance, nor remembrance (how miserable soever now) that I am a prince's daughter, yet let the love you have often told me your son bears me so much procure, that for his sake one death may be thought enough for me. I have not lived so many years but that one death may be able to conclude them. Neither have my faults, I hope, been so many, but that one death may satisfy them. It is no great suit to an enemy when but death is desired. I crave but that: and as for the granting your request, know for certain you lose your labours, being every day further-off-minded from becoming his wife who useth me like a slave.'

But that, instead of getting grace, renewed again Cecropia's fury, so that (excellent creature) she was newly again tormented by these hellish monsters: Cecropia using no other words but that she was a proud and ungrateful wench, and that she would teach her to know her own good, since of herself she would not conceive it. So that with silence and patience (like a fair gorgeous armour, hammered upon by an ill-favoured smith) she abode their pitiless dealing with her; till, rather reserving her for more than meaning to end, they left her to an uncomfortable leisure, to consider with herself her fortune, both helpless – herself being a prisoner – and

*worldly weakness: defencelessness.*

hopeless, since Zelmane was a prisoner. Who therein only was short of the bottom of misery, that she knew not how unworthily her angel by these devils was abused; but wanted, God wot, no stings of grief when those words did but strike upon her heart, that Philoclea was a captive and she not able to succour her. For well she knew the confidence Philoclea had in her, and well she knew Philoclea had cause to have confidence; and all trodden under foot by the wheel of senseless fortune. Yet if there be that imperious power in the soul as it can deliver knowledge to another without bodily organs, so vehement were the workings of their spirits as one met with the other, though themselves perceived it not, but only thought it to be the doubling of their own loving fancies. And that was the only worldly thing whereon Philoclea rested her mind, that she knew she should die beloved of Zelmane, and would die rather than be false to Zelmane. And so this most dainty nymph, easing the pain of her mind with thinking of another's pain, and almost forgetting the pain of her body through the pain of her mind, she wasted, even longing for the conclusion of her tedious tragedy.

But for a while she was unvisited, Cecropia employing her time in using the like cruelty upon Pamela, her heart growing not only to desire the fruit of punishing them but even to delight in the punishing them. But if ever the beams of perfection shined through the clouds of affliction, if ever virtue took a body to show his else-unconceivable beauty, it was in Pamela. For when reason taught her there was no resistance – for to just resistance first her heart was inclined – then with so heavenly a quietness and so graceful a calmness did she suffer the divers kinds of torments they used to her, that while they vexed her fair body, it seemed that she rather directed than obeyed the vexation. And when Cecropia ended and asked whether her heart would yield, she a little smiled, but such a smiling as showed no love and yet could not but be lovely.

And then, 'Beastly woman,' said she, 'follow on, do what thou wilt and canst upon me, for I know thy power is not unlimited. Thou mayest well wreck this silly body, but me thou canst never overthrow. For my part I will not do thee the pleasure to desire death of thee: but assure thyself, both my life and death shall triumph with honour, laying shame upon thy detestable tyranny.

And so, in effect, conquering their doing with her suffering, while Cecropia tried as many sorts of pains as might rather vex them than spoil them (for that she would not do while she were in any hope to win either of them for her son) Pamela remained almost as much content with trial in herself what virtue could do, as grieved with the misery wherein she found herself plunged: only sometimes her thoughts softened in her, when with open wings they flew to Musidorus. For then she would think with herself how grievously Musidorus would take this her misery; and she, that wept not for herself, wept yet Musidorus' tears which he would weep for her. For gentle love did easlier yield to lamentation than the constancy of virtue would else admit. Then would she remember the case wherein she had left her poor shepherd: and she, that wished death for herself, feared death for him; and she, that condemned in herself the feebleness of sorrow, yet thought it great reason to be sorry for his sorrow: and she that long had prayed for the virtuous joining themselves together, now thinking to die herself, heartily prayed that long time their fortunes might be separated.

'Live long, my Musidorus,' would she say, 'and let my name live in thy mouth, in thy heart my memory. Live long, that thou mayest love long the chaste love of thy dead Pamela.'

Then would she wish to herself that no other woman might ever possess his heart: and yet scarcely the wish was made a wish, when herself would find fault with it as being too unjust that so excellent a man should be banished from the comfort of life. Then would she fortify her resolution with bethinking the worst, taking the counsel of virtue and comfort of love.

## CHAPTER 21

So these diamonds of the world, whom Nature had made to be preciously set in the eyes of men to be the chief works of her workmanship, the chief ornaments of the world and princesses of felicity, by rebellious injury were brought to the uttermost distress that an enemy's heart could wish or a woman's spite invent;

Cecropia daily in one or other sort punishing them, still with her evil torments giving them fear of worse, making the fear itself the sorest torment of all, that in the end, weary of their bodies, they should be content to bestow them at her appointment.

But, as in labour, the more one doth exercise it, the more by the doing one is enabled to do, strength growing upon the work, so as what at first would have seemed impossible, after grows easy; so these princesses, second to none and far from any second, only to be matched by themselves, with the use of suffering their minds got the habit of suffering, so as all fears and terrors were to them but summons to a battle whereof they knew beforehand they should be victorious; and which in the suffering was painful, being suffered, was a trophy to itself: whereby Cecropia found herself still further off.

For where at first she might perchance have persuaded them to have visited her son and have given him some comfort in his sickness, drawing near to the confines of death's kingdom, now they protested that they would never otherwise speak to him than as to the enemy, of most unjust cruelty towards them that any time or place could ever make them know.

This made the poison swell in her cankered breast, perceiving that, as in water, the more she grasped the less she held; but yet now having run so long the way of rigour, it was too late in reason and too contrary to her passion to return to a course of meekness. And therefore, taking counsel of one of her old associates (who so far excelled in wickedness as that she had not only lost all feeling of conscience but had gotten a very glory in evil) in the end they determined that beating and other such sharp dealing did not so much pull down a woman's heart as it bred anger, and that nothing was more enemy to yielding than anger, making their tender hearts take on the armour of obstinacy (for thus did their wicked minds, blind to the light of virtue and owly-eyed in the night of wickedness, interpret of it) and that therefore was no more to be tried. And for fear of death (which, no question, would do most with them) they had been so often threatened as they began to be familiarly acquainted with it, and learned to esteem threatening words to be but words. Therefore the last, but best way now was that the one, seeing indeed the other's death, should perceive there was no dallying meant: and then there was no doubt that a woman's soul would do much, rather than leave so beautiful a body.

This being concluded, Cecropia went to Philoclea and told her that now she was to come to the last part of the play: for her part, though she found her hard-hearted obstinacy such that neither the sweetness of loving means nor the force of hard means could prevail with her, yet before she would pass to a further degree of extremity, she had sought to win her sister, in hope that her son might be with time satisfied with the love of so fair a lady: but finding her also rather more than less wilful, she was now minded that one of their deaths should serve for an example to the other that despising worthy folks was more hurtful to the despiser than the despised. That yet because her son especially affected her, and that in her own self she was more inclinable to pity her than she had deserved, she would begin with her sister, who that afternoon should have her head cut off before her face. If in the meantime one of them did not pull out their ill-wrought stitches of un-kindness, she bade her look for no other, nor longer time than she told her.

There was no assault given to the sweet Philoclea's mind that entered so far as this: for where to all pains and dangers of herself, foresight (with his lieutenant, resolution) had made ready defence, now with the love she bare her sister, she was driven to a stay,* before she determined. But long she stayed not before this reason did shine unto her, that since in herself she preferred death before such a base servitude, love did teach her to wish the same to her sister. Therefore crossing her arms, and looking sideward upon the ground:

'Do what you will,' said she, 'with us: for my part, heaven shall melt before I be removed. But if you will follow my counsel, for your own sake (for as for prayers for my sake, I have felt how little they prevail) let my death first serve for example to win her, who perchance is not so resolved against Amphialus; and so shall you not only justly punish me (who indeed do hate both you and your son) but, if that may move you, you shall do more virtuously in preserving one most worthy of life, and killing another most

* *stay:* hesitation.

desirous of death. Lastly, in winning her, instead of a peevish unhappy creature that I am, you shall bless your son with the most excellent woman in all praiseworthy things that the world holdeth.'

But Cecropia (who had already set down to herself what she would do) with bitter both terms and countenance told her that she should not need to woo death over-eagerly; for if her sister going before her did not teach her wit, herself should quickly follow. For since they were not to be gotten, there was no way for her son's quiet but to know that they were past getting. And so since no entreating nor threatening might prevail, she bade her prepare her eyes for a new play, which she should see within a few hours in the hall of that castle.

A place indeed over-fit for so unfit a matter: for being so stately made that the bottom of it being even with the ground, the roof reached as high as any part of the castle, at either end it had convenient lodgings. In the one end was, one storey from the ground, Philoclea's abode; in the other of even height, Pamela's, and Zelmane's in a chamber above her; but all so vaulted of strong and thickly built stone as one could no way hear the other. Each of these chambers had a little window to look into the hall, but because the sisters should not have so much comfort as to look one to another, there was, of the outsides, curtains drawn which they could not reach with their hands, so barring the reach of their sight. But when the hour came that the tragedy should begin, the curtains were withdrawn from before the windows of Zelmane and Philoclea: a sufficient challenge to call their eyes to defend themselves in such an encounter. And by and by came in at one end of the hall, with about a dozen armed soldiers, a lady, led by a couple, with her hands bound before her: from above her eyes to her lips muffled with a fair handkerchief, but from her mouth to the shoulders all bare: and so was led on to a scaffold raised a good deal from the floor, and all covered with crimson velvet. But neither Zelmane nor Philoclea needed to be told who she was: for the apparel she ware made them too well assured that it was the admirable Pamela; whereunto the rare whiteness of her naked neck gave sufficient testimony to their astonished senses. But the fair lady being come to the scaffold and then made to kneel down, and so left by her unkind supporters, as it seemed that she was about to speak somewhat (whereunto Philoclea, poor soul, earnestly listened, according to her speech even minding to frame her mind, her heart never till then almost wavering to save her sister's life) before the unfortunate lady could pronounce three words, the executioner cut off the one's speech and the other's attention with making his sword do his cruel office upon that beautiful neck. Yet the pitiless sword had such pity of so precious an object that at first it did but hit flat-long. But little availed that, since the lady falling down astonished* withal, the cruel villain forced the sword with another blow to divorce the fair marriage of the head and body.

And this was done so in an instant that the very act did overrun Philoclea's sorrow (sorrow not being able so quickly to thunderbolt her heart through her senses, but first only oppressed her with a storm of amazement). But when her eyes saw that they did see, as condemning themselves to have seen it they became weary of their own power of seeing, and her soul then drinking up woe with great draughts, she fell down to deadly trances: but her waiting jailors with cruel pity brought loathed life unto her; which yet many times took his leave, as though he would indeed depart: but when he was stayed by force, he kept with him deadly sorrow, which thus exercised her mourning speech:

'Pamela, my sister, my sister, Pamela, woe is me for thee, I would I had died for thee. Pamela never more shall I see thee; never more shall I enjoy thy sweet company and wise counsel. Alas, thou art gone to beautify heaven; and hast thou left me here, who have nothing good in me but that I did ever love thee, and ever will lament thee? Let this day be noted of all virtuous folks for most unfortunate. Let it never be mentioned but among curses; and cursed be they that did this mischief; and most accursed be mine eyes that beheld it. Sweet Pamela, that head is stricken off, where only wisdom might be spoken withal; that body is destroyed, which was the living book of virtue. Dear Pamela, how hast thou left me to all wretchedness and misery? Yet while thou livedst, in thee I breathed, of thee I hoped. O Pamela, how much did I for thy excellency honour thee more than my mother, and

* *astonished*: stunned.

love thee more than myself! Never more shall I lie with thee: never more shall we bathe in the pleasant river together: never more shall I see thee in thy shepherd apparel. But thou art gone, and where am I? Pamela is dead; and live I? O, my God' – and with that she fell again in a swoon so as it was a great while before they could bring her to herself again: but being come to herself: 'Alas,' said she, 'unkind women, since you have given me so many deaths, torment me not now with life: for God's sake let me go, and excuse your hands of more blood. Let me follow my Pamela whom ever I sought to follow. Alas, Pamela, they will not let me come to thee. But if they keep promise I shall tread thine own steps after thee. For to what am I born, miserable soul, but to be most unhappy in myself, and yet more unhappy in others? But O that a thousand more miseries had chanced unto me, so thou hadst not died: Pamela, my sister Pamela.'

And so, like lamentable Philomela,* complained she the horrible wrong done to her sister, which, if it stirred not in the wickedly closed minds of her tormentors a pity of her sorrow, yet bred it a weariness of her sorrow: so as only leaving one to prevent any harm she should do herself, the rest went away, consulting again with Cecropia how to make profit of this their late bloody act.

## CHAPTER 22

In the end, that woman that used most to keep company with Zelmane told Cecropia that she found, by many most sensible proofs in Zelmane, that there was never woman so loved another as she loved Philoclea, which was the cause that she (further than the commandment of Cecropia) had caused Zelmane's curtains to be also drawn, because having the same spectacle that Philoclea had, she might stand in the greater fear for her whom she loved so well: and that indeed she had hit the needle* in that device; for never saw she creature so astonished as Zelmane, exceedingly sorry for Pamela, but exceedingly exceeding that exceedingness in fear for Philoclea. Therefore her advice was, she should cause Zelmane to come and speak with Philoclea; for there being such vehemency

* Philomela: see Notes, I.2.1. (p. 849). hit the needle: scored a bulls-eye.

of friendship between them, it was most likely both to move Zelmane to persuade, and Philoclea to be persuaded. Cecropia liked well of the counsel, and gave order to the same woman to go deal therein with Zelmane, and to assure her with oath that Cecropia was determined Philoclea should pass the same way that Pamela had done, without she did yield to satisfy the extremity of her son's affection: which the woman did, adding thereunto many (as she thought) good reasons to make Zelmane think Amphialus a fit match for Philoclea.

But Zelmane (who had from time to time understood the cruel dealing they had used to the sisters, and now had her own eyes wounded with the sight of one's death) was so confused withal (her courage still rebelling against her wit, desiring still with force to do impossible matters) that as her desire was stopped with power, so her conceit* was darkened with a mist of desire. For blind love and invincible valour still would cry out that it could not be Philoclea should be in so miserable estate, and she not relieve her: and so while she haled her wit to her courage,[1] she drew it from his own limits. But now Philoclea's death (a word able to marshal all his thoughts in order) being come to so short a point either with small delay to be suffered, or by the giving herself to another to be prevented, she was driven to think and to desire some leisure of thinking, which the woman granted for that night unto her – a night that was not half so black as her mind, not half so silent as was fit for her musing thoughts. At last he that would fain have desperately lost a thousand lives for her sake could not find in his heart that she should lose any life for her own sake; and he that despised his own death in respect of honour yet could well nigh dispense with honour itself in respect of Philoclea's death; for once* the thought could not enter into his heart, nor the breath issue out of his mouth, which could consent to Philoclea's death for any bargain. Then how to prevent the next degree to death (which was her being possessed by another) was the point of his mind's labour: and in that he found no other way but that Philoclea should pretend a yielding unto Cecropia's request, and so by speaking with Amphialus, and making fair but delaying promises, procure liberty for Zelmane; who only wished but to come by a

* *conceit*: understanding. *for once*: for under any circumstances.

sword, not doubting then to destroy them all and deliver Philoclea, so little did both the men and their forces seem in her eyes, looking down upon them from the high top of affection's tower.

With that mind therefore, but first well bound, she was brought to Philoclea, having already plotted out in her conceit how she would deal with her: and so came she with heart and eyes which did each sacrifice either to love upon the altar of sorrow. And there had she the pleasing displeasing sight of Philoclea – Philoclea, whom already the extreme sense of sorrow had brought to a dulness therein, her face not without tokens that beauty had been by many miseries cruelly battered, and yet showed it most the perfection of that beauty, which could remain unoverthrown by such enemies. But when Zelmane was set down by her and the woman gone away (because she might be the better persuaded when nobody was by that had heard her say she would not be persuaded) then began first the eyes to speak and the hearts to cry out: sorrow a while would needs speak his own language, without using their tongues to be his interpreters. At last Zelmane brake silence, but spake with the only eloquence of amazement, for all her long methodized oration was inherited* only by such kind of speeches:

'Dear lady, in extreme necessities we must not – but alas, unfortunate wretch that I am that I live to see this day – And I take heaven and earth to witness, that nothing – ' and with that her breast swelled so with spite and grief, that her breath had not leisure to turn itself into words. But the sweet Philoclea, that had already died in Pamela, and of the other side had the heaviness of her heart something quickened in the most beloved sight of Zelmane, guessed somewhat at Zelmane's mind, and therefore spake unto her in this sort:

'My Pyrocles,' said she, 'I know this exceeding comfort of your presence is not brought unto me for any goodwill that is owed unto me, but, as I suppose, to make you persuade me to save my life with the ransom of mine honour. Although nobody should be so unfit a pleader in that cause as yourself, yet perchance you would have me live.'

'Your honour? God forbid,' said Zelmane, 'that ever, for any

*inherited: replaced.

cause, I should yield to any touch of it. But a while to pretend some affection, till time or my liberty might work something for your service – this, if my astonished senses would give me leave, I would fain have persuaded you.'

'To what purpose, my Pyrocles?' said Philoclea. 'Of a miserable time what gain is there? Hath Pamela's example wrought no more in me? Is a captive life so much worth? Can it ever go out of these lips that I love any other but Pyrocles? Shall my tongue be so false a traitor to my heart as to say I love any other but Pyrocles? And why should I do all this? To live? O Pamela, sister Pamela, why should I live? Only for thy sake, Pyrocles, I would live: but to thee I know too well I shall not live; and if not to thee, hath thy love so base alloy, my Pyrocles, as to wish me to live? For dissimulation, my Pyrocles, my simplicity is such, that I have hardly been able to keep a straight way: what shall I do in a crooked? But in this case there is no mean* of dissimulation, not for the cunningest: present answer is required, and present performance upon the answer. Art thou so terrible, O death? No, my Pyrocles; and for that I do thank thee, and in my soul thank thee: for I confess the love of thee is herein my chiefest virtue. Trouble me not therefore, dear Pyrocles, nor double not my death by tormenting my resolution. Since I cannot live with thee, I will die for thee. Only remember me, dear Pyrocles, and love the remembrance of me: and if I may crave so much of thee, let me be thy last love; for though I be not worthy of thee, who indeed art the worthiest creature living, yet remember that my love was a worthy love.'

But Pyrocles was so overcome with sorrow (which wisdom and virtue made just* in so excellent a lady's case, full of so excellent kindness) that words were ashamed to come forth, knowing how weak they were to express his mind and her merit: and therefore so stayed in a deadly silence, forsaken of hope, and forsaking comfort; till the appointed guardians came in, to see the fruits of Zelmane's labour. And then Zelmane, warned by their presence, fell again to persuade, though scarcely herself could tell what; but in sum, desirous of delays. But Philoclea, sweetly continuing constant, and in the end punishing her importunity with silence, Zelmane was fain to end. Yet craving another time's conference,

* *mean*: means. *just*: fitting.

she obtained it, and divers others; till at the last Cecropia found it was to no purpose, and therefore determined to follow her own way: Zelmane yet still desirous to win (by any means) respite, even wasted with sorrow, and uncertain whether in worse case in her presence or absence, being able to do nothing for Philoclea's succour but by submitting the greatest courage of the earth to fall at the feet of Cecropia, and crave stay of their sentence till the uttermost was seen what her persuasions might do.

Cecropia seemed much to be moved by her importunity, so as divers days were won of painful life to the excellent Philoclea; while Zelmane suffered some hope to cherish her mind, especially trusting upon the help of Musidorus, who, she knew, would not be idle in this matter. Till one morning a noise awaked Zelmane, from whose over-watchful mind the tired body had stolen a little sleep: and straight with the first opening of her eyes, care taking his wonted place, she ran to the window which looked into the hall (for that way the noise guided her) and there might she see (the curtain being left open ever since the last execution) seven or eight persons in a cluster upon the scaffold: who by and by retiring themselves, nothing was to be seen thereupon but a basin of gold pitifully enamelled with blood, and in the midst of it, the head of the most beautiful Philoclea. The horribleness of the mischief was such as Pyrocles could not at first believe his own senses, but bent his woeful eyes to discern it better; where too well he might see it was Philoclea's self, having no veil but beauty over the face, which still appeared to be alive: so did those eyes shine even as they were wont, and they were wont more than any other: and sometimes as they moved, it might well make the beholder think that death therein had borrowed her beauty, and not they any way disgraced by death, so sweet and piercing a grace they carried with them.

It was not a pity, it was not an amazement, it was not a sorrow which then laid hold on Pyrocles, but a wild fury of desperate agony, so that he cried out, 'O tyrant heaven, traitor earth, blind providence, no justice, how is this done? How is this suffered? Hath this world a government? If it have, let it pour out all his mischiefs upon me, and see whether it have power to make me more wretched than I am. Did she excel for this? Have I prayed for this? Abominable hand that did it: detestable devil that commanded it: cursed light that beheld it! And if the light be cursed, what are then mine eyes that have seen it? And have I seen Philoclea dead, and do I live? And have I lived not to help her, but to talk of her? And stand I still talking?' – and with that, carried with the madness of anguish, not having a readier way to kill himself, he ran as hard as ever he could with his head against the wall, with intention to brain himself. But the haste to do it made the doing the slower. For as he came to give the blow, his foot tripped so as it came not with the full force: yet forcible enough to strike him down, and withal to deprive him of his sense, so that he lay a while, comforted by the hurt in that he felt not his discomfort.

And when he came again to himself, he heard, or he thought he heard, a voice which cried, 'Revenge, Revenge,' unto him – whether indeed it were his good angel which used that voice to stay him from unnatural murdering of himself, or that his wandering spirits lighted upon that conceit, and by their weakness, subject to apprehensions, supposed they heard it. But that, indeed, helped with virtue and her valiant servant anger, stopped him from present destroying himself; yielding, in reason and manhood, first to destroy man, woman and child that were any way of kin to them that were accessory to this cruelty; then to raze the castle, and to build a sumptuous monument for her sister, and a most sumptuous for herself; and then himself to die upon her tomb. This determining in himself to do, and to seek all means how (for that purpose) to get out of prison, he was content a while to bear the thirst of death: and yet went he again to the window to kiss the beloved head with his eyes: but there saw he nothing but the scaffold all covered over with scarlet, and nothing but solitary silence to mourn this mischief. But then, sorrow having dispersed itself from his heart into all his noble parts, it proclaimed his authority in cries and tears, and with a more gentle dolefulness could pour out his inward evil.

'Alas,' said he, 'and is that head taken away too, so soon from my eyes? What, mine eyes, perhaps they envy the excellency of your sorrow? Indeed, there is nothing now left to become the eyes of all mankind but tears; and woe be to me, if any exceed me in woefulness. I do conjure you all, my senses, to accept no object but of sorrow: be ashamed, nay abhor to think of comfort. Unhappy eyes, you have seen too much, that ever the light should be welcome to you. Unhappy ears, you shall never hear the music of music in her voice. Unhappy heart that hast lived to feel these pangs. Thou hast done thy worst, world and cursed be thou, and cursed art thou, since to thine own self thou hast done the worst thou couldst do. Exiled Beauty, let only now thy beauty be blubbered faces. Widowed Music, let now thy tunes be roarings and lamentations. Orphan Virtue, get thee wings, and fly after her into heaven: here is no dwelling-place for thee. Why lived I, alas? Alas, why loved I? To die wretched, and to be the example of heaven's hate? And hate and spare not, for your worst blow is stricken. Sweet Philoclea, thou art gone, and hast carried with thee my love; and hast left thy love in me, and I, wretched man, do live: I live, to die continually, till thy revenge do give me leave to die; and then die I will, my Philoclea, my heart willingly makes this promise to itself. Surely he did not look upon thee that gave the cruel blow, for no eye could have abidden to see such beauty overthrown by such mischief. Alas, why should they divide such a head from such a body? No other body is worthy of that head; no other head is worthy of that body. O yet, if I had taken my last leave, if I might have taken a holy kiss from that dying mouth! Where art thou, Hope, which promisest never to leave a man while he liveth? Tell me, what canst thou hope for? Nay, tell me, what is there which I would willingly hope after? Wishing power, which is accounted infinite, what now is left to wish for? She is gone, and gone with her all my hope, all my wishing. Love, be ashamed to be called Love: cruel Hate, unspeakable Hate is victorious over thee. Who is there now left that can justify thy tyranny and give reason to thy passion? O cruel divorce of the sweetest marriage that ever was in Nature. Philoclea is dead, and dead is with her all goodness, all sweetness, all excellency. Philoclea is dead, and yet life is not ashamed to continue upon the earth. Philoclea is dead: O deadly word, which containeth in itself the uttermost of all misfortunes. But happy word when thou shalt be said of me, and long it shall not be before it be said.'

## CHAPTER 23

Then stopping his words with sighs, drowning his sighs in tears, and drying again his tears in rage, he would sit a while in a wandering muse which represented nothing but vexations unto him: then throwing himself sometimes upon the floor and sometimes upon the bed, then up again, till walking was wearisome and rest loathsome: and so neither suffering food nor sleep to help his afflicted nature, all that day and night he did nothing but weep Philoclea, sigh Philoclea, and cry out Philoclea; till as it happened (at that time upon his bed) toward the dawning of the day he heard one stir in his chamber, by the motion of garments, and with an angry voice asked who was there.

'A poor gentlewoman,' answered the party, 'that wish long life unto you.'

'And I soon death to you,' said he, 'for the horrible curse you have given me.'

'Certainly,' said she, 'an unkind answer, and far unworthy the excellency of your mind; but not unsuitable to the rest of your behaviour. For most part of this night I have heard you (being let into your chamber, you never perceiving it, so was your mind estranged from your senses) and have heard nothing of Zelmane in Zelmane, nothing but weak wailings, fitter for some nurse of a village than so famous a creature as you are.'

'O God,' cried out Pyrocles, 'that thou wert a man that usest these words unto me. I tell thee I am sorry: I tell thee I will be sorry, in despite of thee and all them that would have me joyful.'

'And yet,' replied she, 'perchance Philoclea is not dead, whom you so much bemoan.'

'I would we were both dead on that condition,' said Pyrocles.

'See the folly of your passion,' said she. 'As though you should be nearer to her, you being dead and she alive, than she being dead and you alive. And if she be dead, was she not born to die? What then do you cry out for? Not for her, who must have died one time or other, but for some few years; so as it is time and this world that seem so lovely things, and not Philoclea unto you.'

'O noble sisters,' cried Pyrocles, 'now you be gone who were the only exalters of all womankind, what is left in that sex, but babbling and busyness?'

'And truly,' said she, 'I will yet a little longer trouble you.'

'Nay, I pray you do,' said Pyrocles, 'for I wish for nothing in my short life but mischiefs and cumbers, and I am content you shall be one of them.'

'In truth,' said she, 'you would think yourself a greatly privileged person if, since the strongest building and lastingest monarchies are subject to end, only your Philoclea (because she is yours) should be exempted. But indeed you bemoan yourself who have lost a friend: you cannot her,* who hath in one act both preserved her honour and left the miseries of this world.'

'O woman's philosophy, childish folly,' said Pyrocles, 'as though if I do bemoan myself, I have not reason to do so, having lost more than any monarchy, nay than my life can be worth unto me.'

'Alas,' said she, 'comfort yourself. Nature did not forget her skill when she had made them: you shall find many their superiors, and perchance such as (when your eyes shall look abroad) yourself will like better.'

But that speech put all good manners out of the conceit of Pyrocles, insomuch that, leaping out of his bed, he ran to have stricken her; but coming near her (the morning then winning the field of darkness) he saw, or he thought he saw, indeed, the very face of Philoclea; the same sweetness, the same grace, the same beauty: with which carried into a divine astonishment, he fell down at her feet.

'Most blessed angel,' said he, 'well hast thou done to take that shape, since thou wouldst submit thyself to mortal sense; for a more angelical form could not have been created for thee. Alas, even by that excellent beauty, so beloved of me, let it be lawful for me to ask of thee what is the cause that she, that heavenly creature whose form you have taken, should by the heavens be destined to so unripe an end? Why should injustice so prevail? Why was she seen to the world, so soon to be ravished from us? Why was she not suffered to live, to teach the world perfection?'

'Do not deceive thyself,' answered she, 'I am no angel; I am

* *you cannot her:* i.e. bemoan her.

Philoclea, the same Philoclea, so truly loving you, so truly beloved of you.'

'If it be so,' said he, 'that you are indeed the soul of Philoclea, you have done well to keep your own figure, for no heaven could have given you a better. Then, alas, why have you taken the pains to leave your blissful seat to come to this place most wretched, to me who am wretchedness itself, and not rather obtain for me that I might come where you are, there eternally to behold and eternally to love your beauties? You know, I know, that I desire nothing but death, which I only stay to be justly revenged of your unjust murtherers.'

'Dear Pyrocles,' said she, 'I am thy Philoclea, and as yet living: not murdered as you supposed; and therefore be comforted,' and with that gave him her hand.

But the sweet touch of that hand seemed to his astrayed* powers so heavenly a thing that it rather for a while confirmed him in his former belief: till she, with vehement protestations (and desire that it might be so helping to persuade that it was so) brought him to yield, yet doubtfully to yield to this height of all comfort, that Philoclea lived: which witnessing with tears of joy, 'Alas,' said he, 'how shall I believe mine eyes any more? Or do you yet but appear thus unto me to stay me from some desperate end? For alas, I saw the excellent Pamela beheaded: I saw your head (the head, indeed, and chief part of all Nature's works) standing in a dish of gold, too mean a shrine, God wot, for such a relic. How can this be, my only dear, and you live? Or if this be not so, how can I believe mine own senses? And if I cannot believe them, why should I now believe these blessed tidings they bring me?'

'The truth is,' said she, 'my Pyrocles, that neither I, as you find, nor yet my dear sister is dead – although the mischievously subtle Cecropia used sleights to make either of us think so of other. For, having in vain attempted the furthest of her wicked eloquence to make either of us yield to her son; and seeing that neither it (accompanied with great flatteries and rich presents) could get any ground of us, nor yet the violent way she fell into, of cruelly tormenting our bodies, could prevail with us, at last she made either of us think the other dead and so hoped to have wrested

* *astrayed*: wandering.

our minds to the forgetting of virtue. And first she gave to mine eyes the miserable spectacle of my sister's (as I thought) death: but indeed it was not my sister; it was only Artesia, she who so cunningly brought us to this misery. Truly I am sorry for the poor gentlewoman, though justly she be punished for her double falsehood: but Artesia muffled so as you could not easily discern her, and in my sister's apparel (which they had taken from her under colour of giving her other) did they execute. And when I, for thy sake especially, dear Pyrocles, could by no force nor fear be won, they assayed the like with my sister, by bringing me down under the scaffold and (making me thrust my head up through a hole they had made therein) they did put about my poor neck a dish of gold whereout they had beaten the bottom, so as having set blood in it, you saw how I played the part of death (God knows, even willing to have done it in earnest). And so had they set me, that I reached but on tiptoes to the ground so as I scarcely could breathe, much less speak; and truly if they had kept me there any whit longer, they had strangled me instead of beheading me. But then they took me away, and seeking to see their issue of this practice, they found my noble sister (for the dear love she vouchsafeth to bear me) so grieved withal that she willed them to do their uttermost cruelty unto her, for she vowed never to receive sustenance of them that had been the causers of my murther. And finding both of us even given over, not like to live many hours longer, and my sister Pamela rather worse than myself – the strength of her heart worse bearing those indignities – the good woman Cecropia (with the same pity as folks keep fowl when they are not fat enough for their eating) made us know her deceit, and let us come one to another; with what joy you can well imagine who I know feel the like, saving that we only thought ourselves reserved to miseries, and therefore fitter for condoling than congratulating.

'For my part I am fully persuaded it is but with a little respite, to have a more feeling sense of the torments she prepares for us. True it is that one of my guardians would have me to believe that this proceeds of my gentle cousin Amphialus; who, having heard some inkling that we were evil entreated, had called his mother to his bedside, from whence he never rose since his last combat, and besought and charged her, upon all the love she bare him, to use us with all kindness: vowing with all the imprecations he could imagine that if ever he understood, for his sake, that I received further hurt than the want of my liberty, he would not live an hour longer. And the good woman sware to me that he would kill his mother if he knew how I had been dealt with, but that Cecropia keeps him from understanding things how they pass. Only having heard a whispering, and myself named, he had (of abundance, forsooth, of honourable love) given this charge for us, whereupon this enlargement of mine was grown. For my part, I know too well their cunning (who leave no money unoffered that may buy mine honour) to believe any word they say, but, my dear Pyrocles, even look for the worst, and prepare myself for the same.

'Yet I must confess, I was content to rob from death, and borrow of my misery the sweet comfort of seeing my sweet sister, and most sweet comfort of thee my Pyrocles. And so having leave, I came stealing into your chamber, where, O Lord, what a joy it was unto me to hear you solemnize the funerals of the poor Philoclea! That I myself might live to hear my death bewailed! And by whom? By my dear Pyrocles. That I saw death was not strong enough to divide thy love from me! O my Pyrocles, I am too well paid for my pains I have suffered: joyful is my woe for so noble a cause, and welcome be all miseries, since to thee I am so welcome. Alas, how I pitied to hear thy pity of me. And yet a great while I could not find in my heart to interrupt thee, but often had even pleasure to weep with thee: and so kindly came forth thy lamentations, that they enforced me to lament too, as if indeed I had been a looker on to see poor Philoclea die. Till at last I spake with you, to try whether I could remove thee from sorrow, till I had almost procured myself a beating.'

And with that she prettily smiled, which mingled with her tears, one could not tell whether it were a mourning pleasure or a delightful sorrow, but like when a few April drops are scattered by a gentle Zephirus among fine coloured flowers. But Pyrocles, who had felt (with so small distance of time) in himself the overthrow both of hope and despair, knew not to what key he should tune his mind, either of joy or sorrow. But finding perfect reason in neither, suffered himself to be carried by the tide of his imagination, and his imagination to be raised even by the sway which hearing or seeing might give unto them. He saw her alive; he was glad to see her alive: he saw her weep; he was sorry to see her weep: he heard her comfortable speeches, nothing more gladsome: he heard her prognosticating her own destruction; nothing more doleful. But when he had a little taken breath from the panting motion of such contrariety in passions, he fell to consider with her of her present estate; both comforting her that certainly the worst of this storm was past, since already they had done the worst which man's wit could imagine, and that if they had determined to have killed her, now they would have done it; and also earnestly counselling her and enabling* his counsels with vehement prayers, that she would so far second the hopes of Amphialus as that she might but procure him liberty; promising then as much to her as the liberality of loving courage durst promise to himself.

## CHAPTER 24

But who would lively describe the manner of these speeches should paint out the lightsome colours of affection shaded with the deepest shadows of sorrow, finding then between hope and fear a kind of sweetness in tears: till Philoclea, content to receive a kiss, and but a kiss, of Pyrocles, sealed up his moving lips and closed them up in comfort; and herself (for the passage was left between them open) went to her sister. With whom she had stayed but a while, fortifying one another (while Philoclea tempered Pamela's just disdain, and Pamela ennobled Philoclea's sweet humbleness) when Amphialus came unto them; who never since he had heard Philoclea named could be quiet in himself, although none of them about him (fearing more his mother's violence than his power) would discover what had passed; and many messages he sent to know her estate, which brought answers back according as it pleased Cecropia to indite them: till his heart (full of unfortunate affliction) more and more misgiving him, having impatiently borne the delay of the night's unfitness, this morning he gat up, and though full of wounds (which not without danger could suffer such exercise) he apparelled himself, and with a coun-

* *enabling*: reinforcing.

tenance that showed strength in nothing but in grief, he came where the sisters were, and weakly kneeling down, he besought them to pardon him if they had not been used in that castle according to their worthiness and his duty; beginning to excuse small matters, poor gentleman, not knowing in what sort they had been handled.

But Pamela's high heart, having conceived mortal hate for the injury offered to her and her sister, could scarcely abide his sight, much less hear out his excuses, but interrupted him with these words:

'Traitor,' said she, 'to thine own blood, and false to the profession of so much love as thou hast vowed, do not defile our ears with thy excuses, but pursue on thy cruelty that thou and thy godly mother have used towards us. For my part, assure thyself – and so do I answer for my sister, whose mind I know – I do not more desire mine own safety than thy destruction.'

Amazed with this speech he turned his eye, full of humble sorrowfulness, to Philoclea:

'And is this, most excellent lady, your doom of me also?'

She, sweet lady, sat weeping; for as her most noble kinsman she had ever favoured him and loved his love, though she could not be in love with his person; and now partly unkindness of his wrong, partly pity of his case made her sweet mind yield some tears before she could answer; and her answer was no other but that she had the same cause as her sister had. He replied no further, but delivering from his heart two or three untaught sighs, rose, and with most low reverence went out of their chamber: and straight, by threatening torture, learned of one of the women in what terrible manner those princesses had been used. But when he heard it, crying out, 'O God!' and then not able to say any more (for his speech went back to rebound woe upon his heart) he needed no judge to go upon* him; for no man could ever think any other worthy of greater punishment than he thought himself.

Full therefore of the horriblest despair which a most guilty conscience could breed, with wild looks promising some terrible issue, understanding his mother was upon the top of the leads,* he caught one of his servant's swords from him, and none of them

* *to go upon:* to pass judgement on. *the leads:* the leaded roof.

daring to stay him, he went up, carried by fury instead of strength; where she was at that time, musing how to go through with this matter, and resolving to make much of her nieces in show and secretly to empoison them; thinking since they were not to be won, her son's love would no otherwise be mitigated.

But when she saw him come in with a sword drawn, and a look more terrible than the sword, she straight was stricken with the guiltiness of her own conscience: yet the well-known humbleness of her son somewhat animated her, till he coming nearer her, and crying to her, 'Thou damnable creature, only fit to bring forth such a monster of unhappiness as I am', she fearing he would have stricken her (though indeed he meant it not, but only intended to kill himself in her presence) went back so far till, ere she were aware, she overthrew herself from over the leads, to receive her death's kiss at the ground: and yet was she not so happy as presently to die, but that she had time with hellish agony to see her son's mischief (whom she loved so well) before her end; when she confessed (with most desperate but not repenting mind) the purpose she had to empoison the princesses, and would then have had them murthered. But everybody, seeing, and glad to see her end, had left obedience to her tyranny.

And, if it could be, her ruin increased woe in the noble heart of Amphialus who, when he saw her fall, had his own rage stayed a little with the suddenness of her destruction.

'And was I not enough miserable before,' said he, 'but that before my end I must be the death of my mother, who, how wicked soever, yet I would she had received her punishment by some other! O Amphialus, wretched Amphialus, thou hast lived to be the death of thy most dear companion and friend, Philoxenus, and of his father, thy most careful foster-father. Thou has lived to kill a lady with thine own hands, and so excellent and virtuous a lady as the fair Parthenia was. Thou hast lived to see thy faithful Ismenus slain in succouring thee, and thou not able to defend him. Thou hast lived to show thyself such a coward, as that one unknown knight could overcome thee in thy lady's presence. Thou hast lived to bear arms against thy rightful prince, thine own uncle. Thou hast lived to be accounted, and justly accounted, a traitor, by the most excellent persons that this world holdeth.

Thou hast lived to be the death of her that gave thee life. But ah, wretched Amphialus, thou hast lived, for thy sake and by thy authority, to have Philoclea tormented. O heavens, in Amphialus' castle, where Amphialus commanded, tormented! Tormented? Torment of my soul, Philoclea tormented, and thou hast had such comfort in thy life as to live all this while! Perchance this hand, used only to mischievous acts, thinks it were too good a deed to kill me: or else, filthy hand, only worthy to kill women, thou art afraid to strike a man. Fear not, cowardly hand, for thou shalt kill but a cowardly traitor, and do it gladly, for thou shalt kill him whom Philoclea hateth.'

With that, furiously he tare open his doublet, and setting the pommel of the sword to the ground and the point to his breast, he fell upon it. But the sword more merciful than he to himself, with the slipping of the pommel, the point swerved and rased* him but upon the side: yet with the fall, his other wounds opened so as he bled in such extremity that Charon's boat might very well be carried in that flood, which yet he sought to hasten by this means. As he opened his doublet and fell, there fell out Philoclea's knives which Cecropia at the first had taken from her and delivered to her son, and he had ever worn them next his heart as the only relic he had of his saint. Now seeing them by him (his sword being so as weakness could not well draw it out from his doublet) he took the knives, and pulling one of them out and many times kissing it, and then, first with the passions of kindness and unkindness melting in tears:

'O dear knives, you are come in a good time to revenge the wrong I have done you all this while, in keeping you from her blessed side, and wearing you without your mistress' leave. Alas, be witness with me yet before I die (and well you may, for you have lain next my heart) that by my consent your excellent mistress should have had as much honour as this poor place could have brought forth for so high an excellency; and now I am condemned to die by her mouth. Alas, other, far other hope would my desire often have given me; but other event it hath pleased her to lay upon me. Ah Philoclea,' – with that his tears gushed out as though they would strive to overflow his blood – 'I would yet

*rased: scratched.

574

thou knewest how I love thee. Unworthy I am, unhappy I am, false I am; but to thee, alas, I am not false. But what a traitor am I any way to excuse him whom she condemneth! Since there is nothing left me wherein I may do her service but in punishing him who hath so offended her, dear knife, then do your noble mistress' commandment.'

With that, he stabbed himself into divers places of his breast and throat, until those wounds, with the old, freshly bleeding, brought him to the senseless gate of death.

By which time, his servants having, with fear of his fury, abstained a while from coming unto him, one of them (preferring dutiful affection before fearful duty) came in and there found him swimming in his own blood, giving a pitiful spectacle, where the conquest was the conqueror's overthrow, and self-ruin the only triumph of a battle fought between him and himself. The time full of danger, the person full of worthiness, the manner full of horror, did greatly astonish all the beholders: so as by and by all the town was full of it, and then of all ages came running up to see the beloved body; everybody thinking their safety bled in his wounds and their honour died in his destruction.

## CHAPTER 25

But when it came (and quickly it came) to the ears of his proud friend Anaxius, who by that time was grown well of his wound but never had come abroad, disdaining to abase himself to the company of any other but of Amphialus, he was exceedingly vexed either with kindness or (if a proud heart be not capable thereof) with disdain that he who had the honour to be called the friend of Anaxius should come to such an unexpected ruin. Therefore then coming abroad, with a face red in anger and engrained* in pride, with lids raised and eyes levelling from top to the toe of them that met him, treading as though he thought to make the earth shake under him, with his hand upon his sword; short speeches and disdainful answers, giving straight order to his two brothers to go take the oath of obedience, in his name, of all the soldiers and citizens in the town, and withal to swear them to

* *engrained*: dyed.

revenge the death of Amphialus upon Basilius; he himself went to see him, calling for all the surgeons and physicians there, spending some time in viewing the body, and threatening them all to be hanged if they did not heal him. But they (taking view of his wounds, and falling down at Anaxius' feet) assured him that they were mortal, and no possible means to keep him above two days alive: and he stood partly in doubt, to kill or save them, between his own fury and their humbleness, but vowing with his own hands to kill the two sisters as causers of his friend's death; when his brothers came to him, and told him they had done his commandment in having received the oath of allegiance, with no great difficulty: the most part terrified by their valour and force of their servants; and many that had been forward actors in the rebellion willing to do anything rather than come under the subjection of Basilius again; and such few as durst gainsay being cut off by present* slaughter.

But withal (as the chief matter of their coming to him) they told Anaxius that the fair queen Helen was come with an honourable retinue to the town; humbly desiring leave to see. Amphialus, whom she had sought in many places of the world; and lastly,* being returned into her own country, she heard together of the late siege and of his combat with the strange knight who had dangerously hurt him. Whereupon full of loving care (which she was content even to publish to the world, how ungratefully soever he dealt with her) she had gotten leave of Basilius to come by his frontiers, to carry away Amphialus with her to the excellentest surgeon then known, whom she had in her country, but so old as not able to travel; but had given her sovereign anointments to preserve his body withal till he might be brought unto him: and that Basilius had granted leave – either natural kindness prevailing over all the offences done, or rather glad to make any passage which might lead him out of his country and from his daughters. This discourse Lycurgus, understanding of Helen, delivered to his brother, with her vehement desire to see the body and take her last farewell of him. Anaxius, though he were fallen out with all womankind (in respect of the hate he bare the sisters, whom he accounted murderers of Amphialus) yet at his brother's

* *present*: immediate. *lastly*: recently.

request, granted her leave. And she, poor lady, with grievous expectation and languishing desire, carried her faint legs to the place where he lay, either not breathing, or in all appearance breathing nothing but death.

In which piteous plight when she saw him, though sorrow had set before her mind the pitifullest conceit thereof that it could paint, yet the present sight went beyond all former apprehensions: so that beginning to kneel by the body, her sight ran from her service rather than abide such a sight, and she fell in a swoon upon him, as if she could not choose but die of his wounds. But when her breath, aweary to be closed up in woe, broke the prison of her fair lips, and brought memory with his servant senses to his natural office, she yet made the breath convey these doleful words with it:

'Alas,' said she, 'Amphialus, what strange disasters be these, that having sought thee so long, I should be now sorry to find thee: that these eyes should look upon Amphialus, and be grieved withal: that I should have thee in my power without glory, and embrace thee without comfort! How often have I blest the means that might bring me near thee! Now, woe worth the cause that brings me so near thee! Often, alas, often hast thou disdained my tears: but now, my dear Amphialus, receive them: these eyes can serve for nothing else but to weep for thee: since thou wouldst never vouchsafe them thy comfort, yet disdain not them thy sorrow. I would they had been more dear unto thee, for then hadst thou lived. Woe is me that thy noble heart could love who hated thee, and hate who loved thee. Alas, why should not my faith to thee cover my other defects, who only sought to make my crown thy footstool, myself thy servant? That was all my ambition; and alas thou disdainedst it, to serve them by whom thy incomparable self wert disdained. Yet, O Philoclea, wheresoever you are — pardon me if I speak in the bitterness of my soul — excellent may you be in all other things (and excellent sure you are since he loved you) your want of pity, where the fault only was infiniteness of desert, cannot be excused. I would, O God, I would that you had granted his deserved suit of marrying you, and that I had been your serving-maid, to have made my estate the foil of your felicity, so he had lived. How many weary steps have I trodden after thee, while my only complaint was that thou wert unkind? Alas, I would now thou wert,* to be unkind. Alas, why wouldst thou not command my service, in persuading Philoclea to love thee? Who could, or (if everyone could) who would have recounted thy perfections so well as I? Who with such kindly passions could have stirred pity for thee as I, who should have delivered not only the words but the tears I had of thee; and so shouldst thou have exercised thy disdain in me, and yet used my service for thee.'

With that the body moving somewhat, and giving a groan full of death's music, she fell upon his face and kissed him, and withal cried out, 'O miserable I, that have only favour by misery,' and then would she have returned to a fresh career of complaints, when an aged and wise gentleman came to her, and besought her to remember what was fit for her greatness, wisdom, and honour: and withal, that it was fitter to show her love in carrying the body to her excellent surgeon, first applying such excellent medicines as she had received of him for that purpose, rather than only show herself a woman-lover in fruitless lamentations. She was straight warned with the obedience of an overthrown mind; and therefore leaving some surgeons of her own to dress the body, went herself to Anaxius, and humbling herself to him as low as his own pride could wish, besought him that since the surgeons there had utterly given him over, that he would let her carry him away in her litter with her, since the worst he could have should be to die, and to die in her arms that loved him above all things; and where he should have such monuments erected over him as were fit for her love and his worthiness: beseeching him withal, since she was in a country of enemies (where she trusted more to Anaxius' valour than Basilius' promise) that he would convey them safely out of these territories. Her reasons something moved him; but nothing thoroughly persuaded him but the last request of his help, which he straight promised, warranting all security as long as that sword had his master alive. She as happy therein as unhappiness could be, having received as small comfort of her own surgeons as of the others, caused yet the body to be easily conveyed into the litter; all the people then beginning to roar and cry as though never till

* I would now thou wert: i.e. alive.

then they had lost their lord. And if the terror of Anaxius had not kept them under, they would have mutinied rather than suffered his body to be carried away.

But Anaxius himself riding before the litter with the choice men of that place, they were afraid even to cry, though they were ready to cry for fear; but, because that they might do, everybody forced,* even with harming themselves, to do honour to him: some throwing themselves upon the ground, some tearing their clothes and casting dust upon their heads, and some even wounding themselves, and sprinkling their own blood in the air.

## CHAPTER 26

The general consort* of whose mourning performed so the natural tunes of sorrow,[1] that even to them (if any such were) that felt not the loss, yet others' grief taught them grief; having before their compassionate sense so passionate a spectacle of a young man, of great beauty, beautified with great honour, honoured by great valour, made of inestimable value by the noble using of it, to lie there languishing under the arrest of death, and a death where the manner could be no comfort to the discomfortableness of the matter. But when the body was carried through the gate, and the people (saving such as were appointed) not suffered to go further, then was such an universal cry as if they had all had but one life, and all received but one blow.

Which so moved Anaxius to consider the loss of his friend, that (his mind apter to revenge than tenderness) he presently giving order to his brothers to keep the prisoners safe and unvisited till his return from conveying Helen, he sent a messenger to the sisters to tell them this courteous message: that at his return, with his own hands he would cut off their heads, and send them for tokens to their father.

This message was brought unto the sisters as they sat at that time together with Zelmane, conferring how to carry themselves, having heard of the death of Amphialus. And as no expectation of death is so painful as where the resolution is hindered by the

* *forced:* did their uttermost. *consort:* group of voices and instruments.

intermixing of hopes, so did this new alarum though not remove, yet move somewhat the constancy of their minds which were so unconstantly dealt with. But within a while, the excellent Pamela had brought her mind again to his old acquaintance: and then as careful for her sister, whom most dearly she loved:

'Sister,' said she, 'you see how many acts our tragedy hath: fortune is not yet aweary of vexing us. But what? A ship is not counted strong for biding one storm. It is but the same trumpet of death which now perhaps gives the last sound: and let us make that profit of our former miseries, that in them we learned to die willingly.'

'Truly,' said Philoclea, 'dear sister, I was so beaten with the evils of life that though I had not virtue enough to despise the sweetness of it, yet my weakness bred that strength to be weary of the pains of it. Only I must confess that little hope, which by these late accidents was awaked in me, was at the first angry withal. But even in the darkness of that horror, I see a light of comfort appear; and how can I tread amiss, that see Pamela's steps? I would only (O that my wish might take place) that my school-mistress might live, to see me say my lesson truly.'

'Were that a life, my Philoclea?' said Pamela. 'No, no,' said she, 'let it come, and put on his worst face: for at the worst it is but a bugbear. Joy is it to me to see you so well resolved, and since the world will not have us, let it lose us. Only,' (with that she stayed a little and sighed) 'only my Philoclea,' (then she bowed down, and whispered in her ear, 'only Musidorus, my shepherd, comes between me and death, and makes me think I should not die, because I know he would not I should die.'

With that Philoclea sighed also, saying no more, but looking upon Zelmane who was walking up and down the chamber, having heard this message from Anaxius; and having in times past heard of his nature, thought him like enough to perform it, which winded her again into the former maze of perplexity. Yet debating with herself of the manner how to prevent it, she continued her musing humour, little saying, or indeed, little finding in her heart to say in a case of such extremity where peremptorily death was threatened. And so stayed they, having yet that comfort that they might tarry together: Pamela nobly, Philoclea sweetly, and Zelmane sadly and desperately; none of them entertaining sleep, which they thought should shortly begin never to awake.

But Anaxius came home, having safely conducted Helen: and safely he might well do it; for though many of Basilius' knights would have attempted something upon Anaxius by that means to deliver the ladies, yet Philanax, having received his master's commandment and knowing his word was given, would not consent unto it. And the Black Knight, who by then was able to carry abroad his wounds, did not know thereof, but was bringing forces, by force to deliver his lady. So as Anaxius, interpreting it rather fear than faith, and making even chance an argument of his virtue, returned: and as soon as he was returned, with a felon heart calling his brothers up with him, he went into the chamber where they were all three together, with full intention to kill the sisters with his own hands and send their heads for tokens to their father – though his brothers (who were otherwise inclined) dissuaded him, but his reverence stayed their persuasions.[2] But when he was come into the chamber, with the very words of choleric threatening climbing up his throat, his eyes first lighted upon Pamela; who hearing he was coming and looking for death, thought she would keep her own majesty in welcoming it; but the beams thereof so strake his eyes, with such a counterbuff* unto his pride, that if his anger could not so quickly love nor his pride so easily honour, yet both were forced to find a worthiness.

Which while it bred a pause in him, Zelmane (who had ready in her mind both what and how to say) stepped out unto him, and with a resolute steadiness, void either of anger, kindness, disdain, or humbleness, spake in this sort.

'Anaxius,' said she, 'if fame have not been over-partial to thee, thou art a man of exceeding valour. Therefore I do call thee even before that virtue, and will make it the judge between us. And now I do affirm that to the eternal blot of all the fair acts that thou hast done, thou dost weakly, in seeking without danger to revenge his death, whose life with danger thou mightest perhaps have preserved: thou dost cowardly, in going about by the death of these excellent ladies, to prevent the just punishment that hereafter they (by the powers which they, better than their father or

* *counterbuff*: rebuff.

any other, could make) might lay upon thee; and dost most basely, in once presenting thyself as an executioner, a vile office upon men and in a just cause;* beyond the degree of any vile word, in so unjust a cause and upon ladies, and such ladies. And therefore as a hangman, I say, thou art unworthy to be counted a knight, or to be admitted into the company of knights. Neither for what I say will I allege other reasons of wisdom or justice to prove my speech, because I know thou dost disdain to be tied to their rules; but even in thine own virtue, whereof thou so much gloriest, I will make my trial: and therefore defy thee, by the death of one of us two, to prove or disprove these reproaches. Choose thee what arms thou likest. I only demand that these ladies, whom I defend, may in liberty see the combat.'

When Zelmane began her speech, the excellency of her beauty and grace made him a little content to hear. Besides that, a new lesson he had read in Pamela had already taught him some regard. But when she entered into bravery of speech, he thought at first a mad and railing humour possessed her; till, finding the speeches hold well together and at length come to a flat challenge of combat, he stood leaning back with his body and head, sometimes with bent brows looking upon the one side of her, sometimes of the other, beyond marvel marvelling that he, who had never heard such speeches from any knight, should be thus rebuffed by a woman; and that marvel made him hear out her speech: which ended, he turned his head to his brother Zoilus and said nothing, but only lifting up his eyes, smiled.

But Zelmane finding his mind, 'Anaxius,' said she, 'perchance thou disdainest to answer me because, as a woman, thou thinkest me not fit to be fought withal. But I tell thee that I have been trained up in martial matters, with so good success that I have many times overcome braver knights than thyself; and am well known to be equal in feats of arms to the famous Pyrocles, who slew thy valiant uncle, the giant Euardes.'

The rembrance of his uncle's death something nettled him, so as he answered thus:

'Indeed,' said he, 'any woman may be as valiant as that coward and traitorly boy, who slew my uncle traitorously, and after ran

* *and in a just cause:* even in.

from me in the plain field. Five thousand such could not have overcome Euardes, but by falsehood. But I sought him all over Asia, following him still from one of his coney-holes to another; till coming into this country, I heard of my friend's being besieged, and so came to blow away the wretches that troubled him. But wheresoever the miserable boy fly, heaven nor hell shall keep his heart from being torn by these hands.'

'Thou liest in thy throat,' said Zelmane. 'That boy, wherever he went, did so noble acts as thy heart, as proud as it is, dares not think of, much less perform. But to please thee the better with my presence, I tell thee, no creature can be nearer of kin to him than myself: and so well we love, that he would not be sorrier for his own death than for mine; I being begotten by his father of an Amazon lady. And therefore, thou canst not devise to revenge thyself more upon him than by killing me: which, if thou darest do manfully, do it. Otherwise, if thou harm these incomparable ladies, or myself without daring to fight with me, I protest before these knights, and before heaven, and earth (that will reveal thy shame) that thou art the beggarliest dastardly villain that dishonoureth the earth with his steps: and if thou lettest me over-live them, so will I blaze thee.'

But all this could not move Anaxius, but that he only said, 'Evil should it become the terror of the world to fight, much less to scold with thee. But,' said he, 'for the death of these same,' pointing to the princesses, 'of my grace I give them life.' And withal going to Pamela, and offering to take her by the chin, 'And as for you, minion,' said he, 'yield but gently to my will, and you shall not only live, but live so happily' – he would have said further, when Pamela, displeased both with words, matter and manner, putting him away with her fair hand:

'Proud beast,' said she, 'yet thou playest worse thy comedy than thy tragedy. For my part, assure thyself, since my destiny is such that at each moment my life and death stand in equal balance, I had rather have thee, and think thee far fitter to be my hangman, than my husband.'

Pride and anger would fain have cruelly revenged so bitter an answer, but already Cupid had begun to make it his sport to pull his plumes: so that, unused to a way of courtesy, and put out of his bias of pride, he hastily went away, grumbling to himself, between threatening and wishing; leaving his brothers with them: the elder of whom, Lycurgus, liked Philoclea, and Zoilus would needs love Zelmane – or at least entertain themselves with making them believe so. Lycurgus, more braggart and near his brother's humour, began with setting forth their blood, their deeds, how many they had despised of most excellent women; how much they were bound to them that would seek that of them. In sum, in all his speeches more like the bestower than the desirer of felicity. Whom it was an excellent pastime (to those that would delight in the play of virtue) to see with what a witty ignorance she would not understand; and how, acknowledging his perfections, she would make that one of his perfections not to be injurious to ladies. But when he knew not how to reply, then would he fall to touching and toying, still viewing his graces in no glass but self-liking. To which Philoclea's shamefastness and humbleness were as strong resisters as choler and disdain: for though she yielded not, he thought she was to be overcome, and that thought a while stayed him from further violence. But Zelmane had eye to his behaviour, and set it in her memory upon the score of revenge, while she herself was no less attempted by Zoilus, who (less full of brags) was forwardest in offering, indeed, dishonourable violence.

## CHAPTER 27

But when after their fruitless labours they had gone away, called by their brother (who began to be perplexed between new conceived desires and disdain to be disdained) Zelmane (who with most assured quietness of judgement looked into their present estate) earnestly persuaded the two sisters that, to avoid the mischiefs of proud outrage, they would only so far suit their behaviour to their estates as they might win time, which, as it could not bring them to worse case than they were, so it might bring forth unexpected relief.

'And why,' said Pamela, 'shall we any longer flatter adversity? Why should we delight to make ourselves any longer balls to injurious fortune, since our own parents are content to be tyrants over us, since our own kin are content traitorously to abuse us?

Certainly, in mishap it may be some comfort to us that we are lighted in these fellows' hands, who yet will keep us from having cause of being miserable by our friends' means. Nothing grieves me more than that you, noble lady Zelmane, to whom the world might have made us able to do honour, should receive only hurt by the contagion of our misery. As for me and my sister, undoubtedly it becomes our birth to think of dying nobly, while we have done or suffered nothing which might make our soul ashamed at the parture* from these bodies. Hope is the fawning traitor of the mind, while under colour of friendship it robs it of his chief force of resolution.'

'Virtuous and fair lady,' said Zelmane, 'what you say is true, and that truth may well make up a part in the harmony of your noble thoughts. But yet the time (which ought always to be one)¹ is not tuned for it: while that may bring forth any good, do not bar yourself thereof; for then will be the time to die nobly, when you cannot live nobly.'

Then so earnestly she persuaded with them both to refer themselves to their father's consent (in obtaining whereof they knew some while would be spent) and by that means to temper the minds of their proud wooers, that in the end Pamela yielded to her because she spake reason, and Philoclea yielded to her reason, because she spake it.

And so when they were again solicited in that little pleasing petition, Pamela forced herself to make answer to Anaxius, that if her father gave his consent she would make herself believe that such was the heavenly determination, since she had no means to avoid it. Anaxius (who was the most frank promiser to himself of success) nothing doubted of Basilius' consent, but rather assured himself he would be his orator in that matter: and therefore he chose out an officious servant (whom he esteemed very wise, because he never found him but just of his opinion) and willed him to be his ambassador to Basilius, and to make him know that if he meant to have his daughter both safe and happy, and desired himself to have such a son-in-law as would not only protect him in his quiet course but (if he listed to accept it) would give him the monarchy of the world, that then he should receive Anaxius, who

* *parture:* separation.

never before knew what it was to pray anything. That if he did not, he would make him know that the power of Anaxius was in everything beyond his will, and yet his will not to be resisted by any other power. His servant, with smiling and cast-up look, desired God to make his memory able to contain the treasure of that wise speech; and therefore besought him to repeat it again that by the oftener hearing it his mind might be the better acquainted with the divineness thereof: and that being graciously granted, he then doubted not by carrying with him in his conceit the grace wherewith Anaxius spake it, to persuade rocky minds to their own harm; so little doubted he to win Basilius to that which he thought would make him think the heavens opened when he heard but the proffer thereof. Anaxius gravely allowed the probability of his conjecture; and therefore sent him away, promising him he should have the bringing up of his second son by Pamela.

The messenger with speed performed his lord's commandment to Basilius, who, by nature quiet and by superstition made doubtful, was loth to take any matter of arms in hand, wherein already he had found so slow success; though Philanax vehemently urged him thereunto, making him see that his retiring back did encourage injuries. But Basilius, betwixt the fear of Anaxius' might, the passion of his love, and jealousy of his estate, was so perplexed that, not able to determine, he took the common course of men, to fly only then to devotion when they want resolution. Therefore detaining the messenger with delays, he deferred the directing of his course to the counsel of Apollo, which because himself at that time could not well go to require, he entrusted the matter to his best trusted Philanax: who (as one in whom obedience was a sufficient reason unto him) went with diligence to Delphos; where being entered into the secret place of the temple and having performed the sacrifices usual, the spirit that possessed the prophesying woman, with a sacred fury, attended not his demand* but, as if it would argue him of* incredulity, told him (not in dark wonted speeches but plainly to be understood)[2] what he came for, and that he should return to Basilius and will him to deny his daughters to Anaxius and his brothers, for that they were re-

* *attended not his demand:* did not wait for his question. *argue him of:* accuse him of.

served for such as were better beloved of the Gods: that he should not doubt, for they should return unto him safely and speedily; and that he should keep on his solitary course till both Philanax and Basilius fully agreed in the understanding of the former prophecy: withal, commanding Philanax from thence forward to give tribute but not oblation to human wisdom.

Philanax, then finding that reason cannot show itself more reasonable than to leave reasoning in things above reason, returns to his lord, and like one that preferred truth before the maintaining of an opinion, hid nothing from him, nor from thenceforth durst any more dissuade him from that which he found by the celestial providence directed; but he himself looking to repair the government as much as in so broken an estate by civil dissension he might, and fortifying with notable art both the lodges so as they were almost made unapproachable, he left Basilius to bemoan the absence of his daughters, and to bewail the imprisonment of Zelmane. Yet wholly given holily to obey the Oracle, he gave a resolute negative unto the messenger of Anaxius who all this while had waited for it; yet in good terms desiring him to show himself in respect of his birth and profession so princely a knight, as without forcing him to seek the way of force, to deliver in noble sort these ladies unto him, and so should the injury have been in Amphialus and the benefit in him.

The messenger went back with this answer; yet having ever used to sugar anything which his master was to receive, he told him that when Basilius first understood his desires, he did overreach so far all his most hopeful expectations that he thought it were too great a boldness to hearken to such a man, in whom the heavens had such interest, without asking the Gods' counsel; and therefore had sent his principal counsellor to Delphos: who although he kept the matter ever so secret, yet his diligence, inspired by Anaxius' privilege over all worldly things, had found out the secret, which was that he should not presume to marry his daughter to one who already was enrolled among the demi-gods, and yet much less he should dare the attempting to take them out of his hands.

Anaxius, who till then had made fortune his creator and force his god, now began to find another wisdom to be above, that judged so rightly of him: and where in this time of his servant's waiting for Basilius' resolution, he and his brothers had courted their ladies as whom they vouchsafed to have for their wives, he resolved now to dally no longer in delays but to make violence his orator, since he had found persuasions had gotten nothing but answers. Which intention he opened to his brothers, who having all this while wanted nothing to take that way but his authority, gave spurs to his running; and, unworthy men, neither feeling virtue in themselves nor tendering it in others, they were head-long to make that evil consort of love and force, when Anaxius had word that from the tower there were descried some companies of armed men marching towards the town: wherefore he gave present order to his servants and soldiers to go to the gates and walls, leaving none within but himself and his brothers; his thoughts then so full of their intended prey that Mars' loudest trumpet could scarcely have awaked him.

## CHAPTER 28

But while he was directing what he would have done, his young-est brother Zoilus, glad that he had the commission, went in the name of Anaxius to tell the sisters that, since he had answer from their father that he and his brother Lycurgus should have them in what sort it pleased them, that they would now grant them no longer time but presently to determine whether they thought it more honourable comfort to be compelled or persuaded. Pamela made him answer, that in a matter whereon the whole state of her life depended, and wherein she had ever answered she would not lead but follow her parents' pleasure, she thought it reason she should, either by letter or particular messenger, understand some-thing from themselves, and not have her belief bound to the report of their partial* servant: and therefore, as to their words she and her sister had ever a simple and true resolution, so against their unjust force God, they hoped, would either arm their lives, or take away their lives.

'Well, ladies,' said he, 'I will leave my brothers, who by and by will come unto you, to be their own ambassadors. For my part I

* *partial*: biased.

must now do myself service.' And with that, turning up his mustachoes, and marching as if he would begin a pavan,* he went towards Zelmane.

But Zelmane (having had, all this while of the messenger's being with Basilius, much to do to keep those excellent ladies from seeking by the passport of death to escape those base dangers whereunto they found themselves subject) still hoping that Musidorus would find some means to deliver them; and therefore had often, both by her own example and comfortable reasons, persuaded them to overpass many insolent indignities of their proud suitors, who thought it was a sufficient favour not to do the uttermost injury; now come again to the strait she most feared for them, either of death or dishonour, if heroical courage would have let her, she had been beyond herself amazed:[1] but that yet held up her wit to attend the uttermost occasion which even then brought his hairy forehead unto her.[2] For Zoilus smacking his lips, as for the prologue of a kiss, and something advancing himself:

'Darling,' said he, 'let thy heart be full of joy, and let thy fair eyes be of counsel with it, for this day thou shalt have Zoilus, whom many have longed for, but none shall have him but Zelmane. And oh, how much glory I have to think what a race will be between us! The world, by the heavens, the world will be too little for them.'

And with that he would have put his arm about her neck, but she, withdrawing herself from him, 'My lord,' said she, 'much good may your thoughts do you: but that I may not dissemble with you, my nativity being cast by one that never failed in any of his prognostications, I have been assured that I should never be apt to bear children. But since you will honour me with so high favour, I must only desire that I may perform a vow which I made among my countrywomen, the famous Amazons, that I would marry none but such one as was able to withstand me in arms. Therefore, before I make mine own desire serviceable to yours, you must vouchsafe to lend me armour and weapons, that at least with a blow or two of the sword I may not find myself perjured to myself.'

But Zoilus, laughing with a hearty loudness, went by force to embrace her, making no other answer but since she had a mind to

* *pavan:* a stately dance.

try his knighthood, she should quickly know what a man of arms he was; and so, without reverence to the ladies, began to struggle with her.

But in Zelmane then disdain became wisdom, and anger gave occasion. For abiding no longer abode in the matter, she that had not put off (though she had disguised) Pyrocles, being far fuller of strong nimbleness, tripped up his feet so that he fell down at hers. And withal, meaning to pursue what she had begun, pulled out his sword which he ware about him: but before she could strike him withal, he gat up and ran to a fair chamber, where he had left his two brethren preparing themselves to come down to their mistresses. But she followed at his heels, and even as he came to throw himself into their arms for succour, she hit him with his own sword such a blow upon the waist that she almost cut him asunder: once,* she sundered his soul from his body, sending it to Proserpina, an angry goddess against ravishers.[3]

But Anaxius, seeing before his eyes the miserable end of his brother, fuller of despite than wrath, and yet fuller of wrath than sorrow, looking with a woeful eye upon his brother Lycurgus; 'Brother,' said he, 'chastise this vile creature, while I go down and take order lest further mischief arise,' and so went down to the ladies, whom he visited doubting there had been some further practice than yet he conceived. But finding them only strong in patience, he went and locked a great iron gate by which only anybody might mount to that part of the castle, rather to conceal the shame of his brother, slain by a woman, than for doubt of any other annoyance; and then went up to receive some comfort of the execution he was sure his brother had done of Zelmane.

But Zelmane no sooner saw those brothers, of whom reason assured her she was to expect revenge, but that she leaped to a target* as one that well knew the first mark of valour to be defence. And then accepting the opportunity of Anaxius' going away, she waited not the pleasure of Lycurgus, but without any words (which she ever thought vain, when resolution took the place of persuasion) gave her own heart the contentment to be the assailer. Lycurgus, who was in the disposition of his nature hazardous,* and by the lucky passing through many dangers grown

* *once*: straightway. *target*: shield. *hazardous*: reckless.

confident in himself, went toward her rather as to a spoil than to a fight, so far from fear, that his assuredness disdained to hope. But when her sword made demonstrations above all flattery of arguments, and that he found she pressed so upon him as showed that her courage sprang not from blind despair but was guarded both with cunning and strength, self-love then first in him divided itself from vain-glory, and made him find that the world of worthiness had not his whole globe comprised in his breast, but that it was necessary to have strong resistance against so strong assailing. And so between them, for a few blows, Mars himself might have been delighted to look on.

But Zelmane, who knew that in her case slowness of victory was little better than ruin, with the bellows of hate blew the fire of courage; and he striking a main blow at her head, she warded it with the shield, but so warded that the shield was cut in two pieces while it protected her: and withal she ran in to him, and thrusting at his breast, which he put by with his target, as he was lifting up his sword to strike again, she let fall the piece of her shield, and with her left hand catching his sword of the inside of the pommel, with nimble and strong sleight she had gotten his sword out of his hand before his sense could convey to his imagination what was to be doubted. And having now two swords against one shield, meaning not foolishly to be ungrateful to good fortune, while he was no more amazed with his being unweaponed than with the suddenness thereof, she gave him such a wound upon his head, in despite of the shield's over-weak resistance, that withal he fell to the ground astonished with the pain and aghast with fear. But seeing Zelmane ready to conclude her victory in his death, bowing up his head to her with a countenance that had forgotten all pride,

'Enough, excellent lady,' said he, 'the honour is yours; whereof you shall want the best witness if you kill me. As you have taken from men the glory of manhood, return so now again to your own sex for mercy. I will redeem my life of you with no small services, for I will undertake to make my brother obey all your commandments. Grant life, I beseech you, for your own honour, and for the person's sake that you love best.'

Zelmane repressed a while her great heart, either disdaining to be cruel, or pitiful and therefore not cruel: and now the image of the human condition began to be an orator unto her of compassion, when she saw, as he lifted up his arms with a suppliant's grace, about one of them, unhappily, tied a garter with a jewel which (given to Pyrocles by his aunt of Thessalia, and greatly esteemed by him) he had presented to Philoclea, and with inward rage promising extreme hatred, had seen Lycurgus with a proud force, and not without some hurt unto her, pull away from Philoclea because at entreaty she would not give it him. But the sight of that was like a cypher,* signifying all the injuries which Philoclea had of him suffered, and that remembrance, feeding upon wrath, trod down all conceits of mercy. And therefore saying no more, but, 'No villain, die. It is Philoclea that sends thee this token for thy love', with that she made her sword drink the blood of his heart, though he, wresting his body and with a countenance prepared to excuse, would fain have delayed the receiving of death's ambassadors.

But neither stayed Zelmane's hand, nor yet Anaxius' cry unto her; who having made fast the iron gate, even then came to the top of the stairs, when, contrary to all his imaginations, he saw his brother lie at Zelmane's mercy. Therefore crying, promising, and threatening to her to hold her hand, the last groan of his brother was the only answer he could get to his unrespected eloquence. But then pity would fain have drawn tears, which fury in their spring dried; and anger would fain have spoken, but that disdain sealed up his lips; but in his heart he blasphemed heaven that it could have such a power over him; no less ashamed of the victory he should have of her than of his brother's overthrow; and no more spited* that it was yet unrevenged, than that the revenge should be no greater than a woman's destruction. Therefore with no speech, but such a groaning cry as often is the language of sorrowful anger, he came running at Zelmane, use of fighting then serving instead of patient consideration what to do. Guided wherewith, though he did not with knowledge, yet did he according to knowledge, pressing upon Zelmane in such a well-defended manner, that in all combats that ever she had fought, she had never more need of quick senses and ready virtue. For being one of

* *cypher*: symbol. *spited*: angered.

the greatest men of stature then living, as he did fully answer that stature in greatness of might, so did he exceed both in greatness of courage, which, with a countenance formed by the nature both of his mind and body to an almost horrible fierceness, was able to have carried fear to any mind that was not privy to itself of a true and constant worthiness.

But Pyrocles, whose soul might well be separated from his body but never alienated from the remembering what was comely, if at the first he did a little apprehend the dangerousness of his adversary (whom once before he had something tried, and now perfectly saw as the very picture of forcible fury) yet was that apprehension quickly stayed in him, rather strengthening than weakening his virtue by that wrestling, like wine growing the stronger by being moved. So that they both, prepared in hearts and able in hands, did honour solitariness there with such a combat as might have demanded, as a right of fortune, whole armies of beholders. But no beholders needed there, where manhood blew the trumpet, and satisfaction did whet as much as glory. There was strength against nimbleness; rage against resolution; fury against virtue; confidence against courage; pride against nobleness: love, in both, breeding mutual hatred; and desire of revenging the injury of his brother's slaughter, to Anaxius, being like Philoclea's captivity to Pyrocles. Who had seen the one would have thought nothing could have resisted: who had marked the other would have marvelled that the other had so long resisted. But like two contrary tides, either of which are able to carry worlds of ships and men upon them with such swiftness as nothing seems able to withstand them, yet meeting one another, with mingling their watery forces and struggling together, it is long to say whether stream gets the victory; so between these, if Pallas had been there, she could scarcely have told whether she had nursed better in the feats of arms.[4] The Irish greyhound against the English mastiff; the sword-fish against the whale; the rhinoceros against the elephant, might be models, and but models of this combat.

Anaxius was better armed defensively; for (besides a strong casque* bravely covered, wherewith he covered his head) he had a

* casque: helmet.

huge shield, such, perchance, as Achilles showed to the pale walls of Troy, wherewithal that great body was covered. But Pyrocles, utterly unarmed for defence, to offend had the advantage, for in either hand he had a sword, and with both hands nimbly performed that office. And according as they were diversely furnished, so did they differ in the manner of fighting; for Anaxius most by warding, and Pyrocles oftenest by avoiding, resisted the adversary's assault. Both hasty to end, yet both often staying for advantage. Time, distance and motion, custom made them so perfect in that, as if they had been fellow counsellors and not enemies, each knew the other's mind, and knew how to prevent it: so as their strength failed them sooner than their skill, and yet their breath failed them sooner than their strength. And breathless indeed they grew before either could complain of any loss of blood.

## CHAPTER 29

So consenting by the mediation of necessity to a breathing time of truce, being withdrawn a little one from the other, Anaxius stood leaning upon his sword with his grim eye so settled upon Zelmane as is wont to be the look of an earnest thought. Which Zelmane marking and, according to the Pyroclean nature, fuller of gay bravery in the midst than in the beginning of danger:

'What is it,' said she, 'Anaxius, that thou so deeply musest on? Doth thy brothers' example make thee think of thy fault past, or of thy coming punishment?'

'I think,' said he, 'what spiteful god it should be who, envying my glory, hath brought me to such a wayward case, that neither thy death can be a revenge, nor thy overthrow a victory.'

'Thou dost well indeed,' said Zelmane, 'to impute thy case to the heavenly providence, which will have thy pride find itself, even in that whereof thou art most proud, punished by the weak sex which thou most contemnest.'

But then having sufficiently rested themselves, they renewed again their combat far more terribly than before; like nimble vaulters, who at the first and second leap do but stir and, as it were, awake the fiery and airy parts, which after in the other leaps they do with more excellency exercise. For in this pausing, each had brought to his thoughts the manner of the other's fighting, and the advantages which by that, and by the quality of their weapons, they might work themselves; and so again repeated the lesson they had said before more perfectly by the using of it. Anaxius oftener used blows, his huge force, as it were, more delighting therein, and the large protection of his shield animating him unto it: Pyrocles, of a more fine and deliver* strength, watching his time when to give fit thrusts, as, with the quick obeying of his body to his eye's quick commandment, he shunned any harm Anaxius could do to him: so would he soon have made an end of Anaxius, if he had not found him a man of wonderful and almost matchless excellency in matters of arms. Pyrocles used divers feignings to bring Anaxius on into some inconvenience; but Anaxius, keeping a sound manner of fighting, never offered but seeing fair cause, and then followed it with well governed violence. Thus spent they a great time striving to do, and with striving to do, wearying themselves more than with the very doing. Anaxius, finding Zelmane so near unto him that with little motion he might reach her, knitting all his strength together, at that time mainly foiled* at her face. But Zelmane strongly putting it by with his right-hand sword, coming in with her left foot and hand, would have given a sharp visitation to his right side, but that he was fain to leap away. Whereat ashamed, as having never done so much before in his life.[1]

\* \* \*

## A SUPPLEMENT OF THE SAID DEFECT BY SIR W. A.

The fire of rage then burning contempt out of his breast did burst forth in flames through his eyes and in smoke from his mouth, so that he was returning with a terrible madness (all the strength of his whole body transferred to the one hand for a singular service) which the resolute Zelmane did earnestly observe with a providently all-despising courage, whilst the ears of Anaxius were suddenly arrested by a sound, whereof they were only capable, which,

*deliver: nimble. foiled: thrust.

595

since in consort with his own humour, could only of him with authority have challenged a due attendance. Straight a martial noise (raised by the violence of invaders, and distractedness of others, dreadfully tumultuous) giving him intelligence what a bloody scene was acting without in the court of the castle (where he was expected as a special actor) though his eye, as harbinger of his blow, had already marked the room, where his bended arm threatened to lodge it, yet his feet did so suddenly ravish away the rest of his body that even his own thoughts, much more Zelmane's, were prevented by the suddenness of his flight – a flight, indeed, not from the fighting with one, but to the fighting with many, where he did look for an object worthy of the wrath of Anaxius. So that vanishing away as carried in a cloud of whirlwind, Zelmane either could not, or else would not reach him, as disdaining the base advantage of those dishonourable wounds which, though greatest shame to the flying receiver, can give no glory to the unresisted giver.

The impetuous storm that transported the spirit of Anaxius had quickly blown him down the stairs and up the door, his sword ushering his way, till his eyes were encountered with the beams of the lightning weapons of a small number, which rather seemed surprised within the castle than to have surprised the castle. Yet they had speedily purchased a great room for so small a company, challenging as their own all the bounds that their swords could compass: and in effect their enemies proved their fewness many, reckoning the Black Knight and his second (as cyphers are esteemed when valued by others, over which they are raised) not for the number which indeed they were, but for the number which they were worth. These three were quickly known by their wonted arms, but more by their wonted valour. The court had been a fitter list for two than a field for so many, where the narrowness of the place not giving place to sleight, there was no way but by plain force; so that the greatest cowards were as forward as the most courageous, fear making them bold, who saw no refuge but by fighting; which made the conflict exceeding cruel, either of the parties having more spurs than one to draw blood.

The Amphialians, besides their rage for being abused by an unexpected stratagem, and their desire to defend the place, being bound both by private interest and public vows, they had added further (to make up the accomplishment of a just wrath) the means of revenge (as they thought) on their master's murderer; looking no otherwise on the Black Knight than as on him who had buried all their hopes in the ruin of Amphialus, whereof to their further grief they had been idle witnesses. All this made them desperately endeavour that the eyes of Anaxius might be entertained with their victory before his ears could be burdened with their error: chiefly* at his coming, those of his own train kindled their courage at the torches of his eyes, prodigious comets of a deluge of blood.²

As for the pursued pursuers (like those who landing to make war in an island burn the ships which brought them thither, by the impossibility of their return to show the desperate necessity of their victory) they were assured they could neither advance nor retire but over the bellies of their enemies, yet were they not so desperate of their retreat as confident of their victory. The Black Knight, though all the giants* that fought against the gods had been there, he thought they could not hinder him from going where his heart was already, nor from prevailing where the prize was the delivery of his lady and friend, the double treasures of his soul, whereof any was valued above his life – yea, both were balanced with his honour; so that he did show not only the height of valour but a ravishing of his soul, and a transportation of magnanimity far from the level of ordinary aims, and even scarce within the prospect of more lofty thoughts. Yet neither love nor courage could blind his judgement in seeing his advantage; marching with his company ever next the wall,³ to prevent being compassed, though sometimes making brave sallies. Which Anaxius, at his first approach espying, upbraided his own troop as unworthy of his attendance, and all as traitors in receiving, or dastards in not expelling that (in his eyes) contemned crew; oftentimes urging them by their retiring to make way for him, and he alone would either beat them over the walls, or in the walls, for the truth is, they seemed all too small a sacrifice to appease his high indignation. It was superfluous labour for Alecto* to inflame

* *chiefly*: especially, *the giants*: who rebelled against Jupiter. *Alecto*: one of the Furies.

his soul with poisonous inspirations, for his soul might have furnished all the infernal furies with fury and yet have continued the most furious of all itself. Rage and disdain, burning his bosom, made him utter a roaring voice, as if his breath had been able to have blown away the world, which, for the sound that his sword made, could not distinctly be understood.

The first whom he encountered, lifting up his hand to strike, and withal opening his mouth as if intending some speech, his proposition was prevented by an active answer cutting him from the lips to the ears, so by opening his mouth restraining his speech. The Knight of the Sheep succeeding in his place, a vindictive heir, was exchanging blows with Anaxius with no disadvantage, when suddenly a dart (none knew to whose hand the honour of it was due) did wound him in the thigh, which he, doubtful to whom he stood debtor, did pay back to many an extraordinary interest, with the death of someone striving to defray every drop of his blood.

The Black Knight (black indeed to all his adversaries) when viewing the wonderful valour of Anaxius (with whom then rival in fame he entertained a terrible emulation) what bred terror in others bred in him contentment that his conquest (whereof he never doubted) might be endeared* by the difficulty, and his victory be honoured by so honourable an enemy, with whom, above all others, he laboured to meet, by the ruin of many making a room where they might fight.

But in the meantime the torrent of the violence of Anaxius was interrupted by a sudden tumult, seeming to proceed from an ambushment broken forth from the houses behind them. And no wonder though all thought so; the two swords of Zelmane, being riotous in their charges, were so covetous to extend their confines. She following, or rather (as a falcon in an earnest chase) flying down the stairs after him, did not overtake Anaxius but with her eyes till he was walled about with the armed multitude, and then (like a lioness lately enlarged, that had been long famished in prison) she ranged over all for her prey: but yet, like a cunning hound, that out of a whole herd of deer doth only single him out

* *endeared*: enhanced.

with whom she had entered first in hostility (a little drop of his blood having betrayed all the rest) she disdained to fight with any other, but would be resisted by none till she might unbend all her forces on Anaxius, whose sight as soon as her eyes had greedily swallowed, she burst forth:

'Base dastard, who hast abused the world with shadows of worth yet art void of all valour, having doubly forfeited the usurped title of honour in offering injurious violence to a woman and yet flying the just violence of a woman, to hide thyself (being protected by the shield of some trusted attender) where the sufficiency of others may conceal thy cowardice. But all this shall not defraud my wrath nor prevent thy punishment.'

Anaxius, more troubled with those words than if all the swords of the enemies had lighted upon him (who for the highest of all his wishes would have but wished her a man, yea an army of men) looked over his shoulder with an eye burning with disdain, as if one of his looks might have served to consume a woman, and at the same instant, uttering his rage another way, with a blow worthy of his arm he did cleave one before him through the helmet to the shoulders, making so, by being two headed, headless. But seeing Zelmane press near him, though he hoped for no honour from her, yet to prevent dishonour from her (shame kindling rage, and rage quenching reason) he commanded Armagines, his nephew, a youth of great valour, to take those foolish fellows prisoners who durst adventure within that castle without his leave, and to shut all the gates, that none of them might escape: and therewith whirling about and casting a sideward look on Zelmane, made an imperious sign with a threatening allurement (a disinviting inviting of her) to follow; which she performed with a countenance witnessing as great contentment as ever Venus did to meet with Mars; Mars and Venus at the same time having met within her mind, to make, though a less loving, yet a more martial meeting.[4]

The crowds of people in their way were quickly dispersed by the tempestuous breath of Anaxius, so that they had no hindrance, he being feared of all and she hated of none. Neither was their solitary retiring, in respect of their different seeming sex, suspiciously censured by any, the disdainfulness of their countenance bearing witness that they were led by hate to honour, and not by love to the contrary.

The place appointed by fortune to be famous by the famousness of this combat was a back court, which they found out at that time emptied of habitants; the stronger being gone to pursue others, and the weaker run to hide themselves; mediocrity being no more a virtue, where all was at height to make excellency eminent in extremity.

They two came here alone, for they would have no seconds, or rather were so far first as they could have no seconds, and every one of them, being confident in his own worth, could not mistrust another's. As if words had been too weak messengers of their wrath and swords only worthy to utter their minds, they began with that wherewith they hoped to end; none of them now could flatter himself so far against the proof of his own experienced knowledge as to contemn his fellow.

Anaxius at the first, rioting in rage and burning with a voluptuous appetite of blood, did abandon his hands to their accustomed prodigality which, contrary to the nature of that vice, was hurtful to the receiver and profitable for the spender. But Zelmane, well weighing with whom she had to deal, was more wary in her charges, and circumspectly managing the treasure of her strength, would not idly bestow it, but was liberal when occasion offered. It was hard to say whether the one was more frank or the other more thankful: the guerdon* never deferred, oft preventing* the gift, above the desire of the receiver, yet short of the giver's mind. Their thought, eye, hand and foot seemed chained to one motion, as all being tuned by violence to make up a harmony in horror. Never was courage better supported by skill and strength, nor skill and strength better accompanied by courage: the blows of every one of them seemed not only to strive with the other's, but even among themselves, for singularity;* the latter still (by being more observable) seeking to bury the remembrance of the former.

It seemed that those two were not retired from the battle, but that the battle was transferred where they were. The eye might

* guerdon: recompense. preventing: coming before. singularity: exceptional quality.

well have taken them to be two, but the ear would never have been persuaded that so mighty sounds could be sent but* from the weapons of a number. The environing windows with a sad solitariness seemed to bewail their want of eyes, which defrauded them the entertainment of that delectable terror and transporting sport.

Anaxius, more angry with himself than with his enemy that he should be so long in vanquishing where (when victorious) he would be but ashamed of the victory, all his active powers being highly bended both by choler and courage, he thus discharged his tongue:

'What spiteful god, jealous of my greatness or envying my glory, hath sent this devil in a woman's shape (as a cloud for Juno to Ixion)⁵ to mock me? But all this is one: though thou be a devil in a woman, or all the devils in one devil, I swear by this blow I will beat thee hence to the hells, to the eternal terror of all the dark region,' and with that lighted on Zelmane with such a huge force that all she could procure by the mediation of one of her swords was that what was intended wholly at her head, by the wrying* of her body did but wound her a little on the shoulder. This was so far from dismaying her that it did confirm (increase it could not) her resolution already at a height. Yet, though not more courage, she pretended* more fury, compassing him about to espy advantages; and oft giving him feigned alarms, as bragging to make a breach in his breast, advanced her right-hand sword, which Anaxius beat down and withal encroached to usurp a room in her right side: but Zelmane suddenly inclining to the left, gave him a flat blow with that hand's sword, which returned back clad with the spoils of that part of the body which it had forced.

Both thus being already allied by blood yet did strive for a more strict affinity, wounds, in regard of their frequency, being no more respected than blows were before. Though they met in divers colours, now both were clad in one livery as most suitable to their present estate, being servants to one master and rivals in preferment. Neither could showers of blood quench the winds of their wrath, which did blow it forth in great abundance till faintness would have fain persuaded both that they were mortal, and

* *sent but:* except. *wrying:* twisting. *pretended:* put forth.

though neither of them by another, yet both overcomable by death. Then despair came to reinforce the fight, joining with courage not as a companion, but as a servant; for courage never grew desperate, but despair grew courageous; both being resolved, if not conquering, none of them should survive the other's conquest, nor owe trophy but to death.

The greatest grief of the one was to die by a woman; and of the other, to die as a woman, both in respect of her apparel and (as she thought) action, being matched by one man who had o'er-matched multitudes of men. At last the great storms of blows being past, she rested one of her swords on the earth, either forced by faintness, or intending art, offering a thrust with the other, which Anaxius, perceiving, did speedily repel: and with that (gathering his distressed strength together, as ready to remove, but first bent to give a gallant farewell) ran forward with such a violent violence on Zelmane (nought being able to resist his unresistable force) that she presently interposing her reposed sword, though it ran him through the heart (or rather he his heart upon it) it could not hinder him from running her through the body, and both to the earth – a brave flash of a dying light, a mighty thunder of a quenched lightning! Thus did he overthrow his overthrower: not falling till none was able to stand before him, whilst though he were vanquished, none could vaunt of the victory. His breast fell above the hand with the sword, as if he would needs die embracing it, even after death adoring that idol of his life, and his dead weight striving with Zelmane's weak life; whilst she struggling to rise did break the sword, a part remaining under him, and the rest within her. Thus hard it was to force Anaxius, though he was dead, and impossible while he lived.

## CHAPTER 30

Zelmane, after her rising, did draw the other sword out of him, as bent to return, not interested in anything. She was stepping forward with a sword in every hand, and a part of one in her breast: a trophy of victory yet a badge of ruin; never better weaponed, never more unfit for fighting; when lo, all the followers of

Anaxius discomforted by his absence but more by the Black Knight's presence (Armagines having his death honoured by his hand) the rest were quickly discomfited, and, despairing to save the castle, sought to save themselves.

The Black Knight committed the following of their flight to others, as a dangerless action and therefore not worthy of him. Then fearing that elsewhere for another which he could no more find there for himself, he went by the direction of his eyes and the information of his ears to seek out the two retired champions, when suddenly he encountered his other self, marching like Pallas* from the giants' overthrow.

As soon as the eyes of Pyrocles – no, his soul, was ravished with the sight of Musidorus, it having infused a fresh vigour in his feeble members, and that physic (applied to his mind) triumphing over the infirmity of his body, he threw away his swords (only conquerable by kindness) and pulled out that which was in his body, that nothing might hinder him from embracing the image of his soul, which reflected his own thoughts. Their souls by a divine sympathy did first join, preventing* the elemental masses of the bodies. But, ah, whilst they were clasped in each other's arms (like two grafts grafted in one stock) the high tide of over-flowing affection restraining their tongues with astonishment as unable to express an unexpressible passion, Pyrocles, weakened with the loss of blood (the effects of hate) and in that weakness surcharged with kindness (the fruits of love) not able to abide the inter-choking of such extremities, the paleness of his face witnessed the parting of his spirits, so that not able to stand, Musidorus was forced to fall with him, or else would not stand after him. And at the suddenness of his unexpected adventure or vehemently re-spectable misadventure, like one who (unawares slipping from a great height) is choked betwixt the height and the lowness, ere he can consider either whence he fell or where he falls; being thrown from the top of contentment to be drowned in the depths of misery, he had his reasonable parts so hastily overwhelmed with confusion that he remained dead alive, as the other was living in death. At last, re-assembling his confounded senses from the rocks

* *Pallas*: who helped her father Jupiter in his war against the giants.
*preventing*: coming before.

of ruin, grief had gathered so much strength through weakness as to attempt an impossibility in manifesting itself:

'O what a monster of misery am I! Even when most fortunate, most unfortunate; who never had a lightning of comfort but that it was suddenly followed with a thunder of confusion. Twice was my felicity by land (that it might be washed for ever away) made a prey to the inexorable waves, whilst the relenting destinies pitying the rigour of their own decrees, to prevent their threatened effects, would have drowned me in (respecting the ocean of sorrow prepared to swallow me) that little drop of the sea. And, O, thrice happy I, if I had perished whilst I was altogether unhappy! Then, when a dejected shepherd offensive to the perfection of the world, I could hardly (being oppressed by contempt) make myself worthy to be disdained, disdain to be despised being a degree of grace. O would to God that I had died obscurely, whilst my life might still have lived famous with others, and my death have died with myself; whilst my not being known might have kept my dishonour unknown; even then when matched, matched by one, and in the presence of many fighting for one who was more dear to me than all the world. Ah me, most miserable in not being more miserable! Such a pestilentious influence poisoned the time of my nativity, that I have had a spark of happiness to clear me the way to destruction. I was carried high to be fit for a precipice, and that from that height I might behold how low the dungeons were wherein I was to fall. Even now I was so far from fear, as I was higher than hope, being in imagination master of all my wishes; yet at an instant, as if all that could be inflicted on myself were not sufficient to afflict me, being armed with resolution both to brave the terrors of death and to contemn the flatteries of life, I am tormented in another, whose sufferings could only make me tenderly sensible.'

And with that, sorrow (as it were sorry to be interrupted by utterance) did damn itself up to swell higher, feeding on the contemplation of itself within; where, when absolute tyrant of the breast, it might rather burst him than burst out.

Then he was lying down senselessly on his senseless friend, as in all estates striving to be still like him; when lo, he felt his breast beat, and thereafter saw his unclouded eyes weakly strive to shine again; thus first re-saluting the light, 'Oh where am I?'

Musidorus replied, 'With him who is hasting to die with you.'

'No,' said he, 'I have hasted to live with you.'

'Death or life,' said Musidorus, 'either of them must join us, but neither of them is able to part us.'

With that Pyrocles, weakly rising, entrusted his feet with their own burden, but Musidorus, jealous of the carriage of so precious a treasure, would needs aid them with his arm, his strength strengthening Pyrocles, and the weakness of Pyrocles weakening him.

Thus, whilst guided by one who was acquainted with the castle, they were seeking out a room where Pyrocles, reposing, might cause take a trial of the estate of his body, and repair the bloody breaches of the late battery (it being, though evil fortified, yet well defended) as they were walking along a gallery, they heard from a chamber neighbouring the side of it a dolorous sound, but so heavily delivered with a disorderly convoy, that, choked with sobs else drowned with tears, the pains of the bearer had so spoiled the birth that it could not be known; yet a secret sympathy, by an unexpressible working, did more wound the mind of Pyrocles than it was wounded by all the wounds of his body, he pitying the complaint, though not knowing from whom, nor for what. O, how the soul, apt for all impressions transcending reason, can comprehend unapprehensible things! This was the lamentation of the lamentable Philoclea.

The ladies after the departure of Zelmane, by the inundation in their ears of horrible sounds, were violently invited to come fearfully to a window overlooking the court, where they beheld the bloody effects of that whereof they were the innocent causes. At first the lilies of their cheeks overgrowing the roses, paleness had almost displaced beauty, were it not beauty was so powerful as to make paleness beautiful; yet their often-travelled memory instructed their judgement that misery, being at a height, could not but of force* either work the end of itself or a beginning of comfort, and they could expect no worse estate than that in which they were.

Pamela would fain have flattered herself to think that it was

*could not but of force: must of necessity.

Musidorus come to deliver her, but she had rather have still remained captive than to have drawn him to such a danger for her delivery; and having once apprehended that he was there, never a blow was given but that she was wounded with it, being ever sorry for the overthrown, never glad for the overthrower; either pity prevailing with the tenderness of her sex, or because she knew no danger could come by overcoming.

As for Philoclea, she who through the gentleness of her own nature would have smarted for any other who had been in danger, when she remembered the hazard of her treasure Zelmane (who, as she knew, did not use to be an idle spectator of so earnest a game) a multitude of thoughts, without art artificial,[1] did paint fear in her face and engrave grief in her bosom. Whilst they continued thus, Pamela, in vain striving to match majesty with affection, stood with a distracted stateliness and with a stately astonishment, where grief and fear in Philoclea made easily a consort in sorrow, with watery eyes (like the sun shining in a shower) weakly clearing a cloudy countenance; when suddenly they heard one cry, since the castle was won to set the ladies at liberty. But they who were well acquainted both with the frowns and smiles of fortune, as they had ever triumphed over the one, would not suffer themselves to be led captives by the other: neither could this accomplish their contentment, till they had the lords of that pleasant bondage which they did value more than unvaluable liberty; the constrained captivity of the body having nothing diminished the voluntary thraldom of the mind.

But ah, this smooth calm came only to make them the more sensible of the succeeding tempest, which the breath of one from below, roaring forth the death of Zelmane, did thunder up upon them. Pamela (like a rock amidst the sea, beaten both with the winds and with the waves, yet itself immovable) did receive this rigorous charge with a constant, though sad, countenance, and with fixed eyes witnessing the moving of her mind, yet neither uttering word nor tear, as disdaining to employ their weakness in so great a grief. Such might have been the gesture of Niobe hearing the news of her children's death,[2] ere she was metamorphosed into a stone; like one (majesty triumphing over misery) who would rather burst strongly within than be disburdened by bursting out in an abject manner.

But, ah me, the confounded Philoclea, who, being the weaker, had received the sharpest assault (an affectionate fury forcing from her an absolute passion, which a dutiful kindness through compassion only provoked in her sister) she, smothered with so monstrous a weight, did sink down under it to the earth.

This made Pamela forget her other grief without any comfort, transferring her affection from her friend to her more than friendly sister for whom she saw at that time her care might be more serviceable; wherewith she brought her to herself, and she herself to sorrow. At first the tongue and the eyes being too feeble instruments for so violent a passion, she used her hands, beating that breast which the most barbarous creature else in the world could not have done; offering those torn hairs as oblations to him after death, which had been the delights of his life; and deforming that face, the register of nature's wonders, confirmed by the admiration of men. Which when Pamela (of a patient become a physician) sought to hinder, she thus said:

'Alas, sister, you do not know what a treasure I have lost, even a treasure more worth than all the world was worthy to enjoy. Ah, pardon me thou, whom even death is not able to kill in my soul. Pardon me, who have ever concealed thy secret, now to discover mine own, for while my life lasts (short may it be, and long it shall not be) I will show to all the world that which, whilst thou livedst, I would have been ashamed to have shown to thyself, even thy perfection and mine affection. Neither do I regard how the conceits of others censure my carriage in this; for there is no eye now wherein I desire to appear precious, nor no opinion whereof I crave to make a purchase. Death may end my life but not my love, which, as it is infinite, must be immortal. I would gladly use means to dispatch this miserable life; but it were a shame for me if, after so great a disaster, sorrow only were not sufficient to kill me.'

And with that, beauty in the heaven of her face (two suns eclipsed) being wrapped up in paleness, she fell down grovelling on the ground.

## CHAPTER 31

Pyrocles, imagining what report might be made, and not doubting what effect it would work (bent to furnish physic for her mind ere he sought any for his own body) came in at the door, whom Pamela (her arms and her tongue rivals in kindness) embracing, said, 'Never more welcome, though ever welcome Zelmane; thou who ever art victorious, hast thou likewise brought thyself away a trophy from death?'

'Sweet ladies,' replied she, 'who would faint to fight for such divine creatures as you are? And who could have force to fight against you?'

Philoclea (who at first, either dull through excessive dolour, did not conceive her sister's words; or else suspecting, as she thought, her impossible desire to please her – all being doubtful to trust what they do extremely affect)* did misconceive her meaning. She was raising her eyes to examine her ears: but the most trusty of her senses* preventing both, by a palpable proof gave her an absolute assurance; so that ere she could think Zelmane was at all to be embraced, finding herself embraced by Zelmane, she was lifted up to a heaven of joy, as before she had been sunk down in a hell of grief; never absolutely her own, but either ravished or ruined. Spying the blood on Zelmane's garment, not knowing whether her own or her enemies', she grew pale; and then, looking on her sister, she blushed, suspecting that she suspected the cause of her paleness (conferring* it with her former plaints) to be more than a friendly kindness. But Zelmane, fearing what might be the effects of her fear, said that she expected a congratulation of her victory and not condoling of past danger, which was acquitted with the speechless answer of an affectionate look and a passionate pressing of her hand.

Then Pamela inquiring the perilous course of her short progress, she told how fortified with their fortune, trusting more to it than to her own valour, which, like their beauty, could not but prevail, she had first fatally overthrown the two brethren of Anaxius; and thereafter, fighting with himself, it was her chance (God streng-

* *affect*: desire. *the most trusty ... senses*: i.e. touch. *conferring*: considering it in conjunction with.

thening her weakness to punish his injustice) to kill him – she could not say overcome him: no, she was not ashamed to affirm that though he was killed, she thought him not overcome, seeing both he died with opinion and in action of victory, death preventing the knowledge of his last success. A rare happiness, his life and fortune having both but one bound.*

Both highly praising her valour and admiring her modesty, and glad of their own delivery whereof they thought her the author – thoughts striving to express themselves the more powerfully without words – they were acknowledging the same with a grateful countenance and kindly affecting looks, when Zelmane (not complementally hunting that which she fled, but like one who with a glass reflects the force of the sun somewhere else)[1] earnestly protested that she would be loth to usurp that which was due to another, especially in the owner's presence. And turning towards the Black Knight, who all the time stood aside as her attender (though armed, trembling for fear of one unarmed, who unarmed would not have been so afraid of an army in arms) she freely affirmed, 'There is the deliverer of us all, from whom we receive our liberty, to whom we owe ourselves, since it is that which makes us ourselves.'

Then the Black Knight, invited by the willing countenance of the princess, abasing his helmet, advanced more fearfully than to a battle to kiss her hand; when Zelmane courteously retired Philoclea a little distance from thence, as glad to confer with her as to give her friend occasion to confer with Pamela: who presently (whilst the roses of his lips made a flower of affection with the lilies of her hands) knowing her own Dorus, at the suddenness of the assault, the moving of her mind was betrayed by the changes of her countenance, the blood of her face ebbing and flowing according to the tide of affection: yet borrowing a mask from hate wherewith to hide love, she thus charged him, who already had yielded:

'How durst you thus presume to present yourself in my presence, being discharged it, when you deserved the uttermost that reason could devise, or fury execute? Hath my dejected estate emboldened you to exalt yourself against me?'

* bound: limit.

Then he, gathering courage from the extremity of despair, thus cleared his intention:

'True it is, lady of my life and shall be of my death, I was worthy then to have been banished from the world. But what a world of worlds? I was banished from your sight and (which is worst of all) deservedly. Neither come I now of contempt, but only to testify my obedience, which otherwise at this time might have been construed to a cowardice. Such a love as mine, wedded to virtue, can never be so adulterated by any accident – no, nor yet ravished by passion, as to bring forth a bastard disobedience, whereof my very conscience not being able to accuse my thoughts, I come to clear myself. But now, having performed all that was within the compass of my power, a part of my blood witnessing my affection, which I wish were confirmed by the rest; you may see, directress of my destiny, that no force can force me to anything, much less from your sight, save only your own will which is unto me a law, yea, an oracle. And now when you see I do it not for fear of others but only out of a reverence to you, if not for your satisfaction yet for my punishment, so to persecute him whom you hate I will go waste the remnant of my wretched days in some remote wilderness as not worthy to be seen of any, since odious in your sight: having, I hope, by many proofs prevailed thus much with your opinion, that after my death you will think there was some worth in me, though not worthy of your love.'

When he, full of humble affection, was retiring himself with a courtesy as low as his thoughts, she (thinking enough done to try him, yet without seeming to trust him, whilst, though guilty of grief, her countenance could accuse her of no care) as out of a fresh remembrance, said that she would not have Dametas to lose a servant nor Mopsa a suitor by her means; and if he would needs return towards the lodges, that he should first expect some employment homewards from her. Then he (as one who, fallen in the bottom of some deep water, coming to float above, in sight of land receiveth some comfort, though still in danger) began to reassemble his dispersed spirits again, looking more cheerfully. But ere his thoughts (every one of them overflowing another) could settle themselves in words, she, preventing the violence of so sudden a change, did call to her sister by accusing their indiscretion in holding these two so long, by talking with them, from looking to themselves. Which Philoclea allowed, trembling with an earnest fear to know in what estate Zelmane stood.

They two, injured by this courtesy, with an unwilling obedience accepted of it, more respecting the pleasure of others than their own necessity. Pamela, as only affecting Zelmane, offered her either all or a part of their chamber: and she, her tongue rebelling against her heart, refused what she desired, pretending a lothness to trouble them. Then the sisters offered to accompany them; but, after they had a while coloured true kindness with ordinary compliments, Zelmane prevailed against herself to go accompanied as she came: yet both looking as if they would have left their eyes behind them, as well as their hearts.

## CHAPTER 32

As soon as they were by themselves in a chamber, Zelmane disapparelling herself, the Black Knight, though better skilled in giving than in curing of wounds, yet lately experienced by passing the like danger, he would needs prove a surgeon: and after he had purchased things necessary, having considered his wounds, he found none (save the last that went through the body) dangerous, and it not deadly. Thereafter melting their minds in discourses, either of them had his own contentment doubled by hearing of the other's.

Then the Black Knight, taking leave for a while, locking the door behind him, went down to the court to try if any spark of the late fire remained as yet to quench. For after the opposite party (as if their arms were not sufficient to arm them unless their arms were armed with walls) ran to fortify themselves within houses, which had no strength save that which men were to afford them, he (who thought his own good fortune no better than a misfortune till he was assured that his friend had the like, without whom no happiness of his could be accomplished) recommending the remnant of the adversary's ruins to his two companions, had gone to learn if he were alike happy in all places: and they (fear freezing the courage, and dissolving the hearts of their scattered enemies) found quickly more throwing themselves weaponless at their feet than they could have leisure severally to raise, so that they were more weary, though more contented, with pardoning than they had been with punishing.

Some more crafty, or more fearful, cried out at the windows that they would render* upon security of pardon. But they, scorning to capitulate with fugitives, who would not have done it with them when fighters, and disdaining all that by the most large construction could be wrested to the sense of constraint, they would not equal them with those who were already humbled till they submitted in a more submissive manner, depending only on their free disposition. Which they (either trusting to the virtue of others, or mistrusting their own) having done, the Knight of the Sheep was constrained (his wound bleeding in great abundance which, being made by an empoisoned dart, had inflamed all his body) to retire. The other, having received the keys of the gate, committed the chief captives to keepers till the Black Knight's coming, who presently thereafter, exacting what conditions he pleased, did enlarge* them all. Then sentinels were set on the wall, and a company appointed to watch all night: when suddenly one came from their friend to desire them to come and take their last farewell of him: a request wonderfully grieving them, yet quickly granted; yea, performed ere answered.

Being met and all others retired, he with these words deeply wounded their souls:

'Dear friends, whom I may justly call so, though none of us as yet doth know another; I see I have acted my part, and the curtain must quickly be drawn. Death, the only period of all respects, doth dispense with a free speech. At a tilting in Iberia, where I was born, dedicated to the memory of the queen Andromana's marriage, a novice in arms, amongst others, I ran in a pastoral show against the Corinthian knights, whom the success had preferred in the opinion of the beholders: till the worthily admirable princes, Musidorus and Pyrocles, drawn forth by the young prince Palladius, brought back the reputation to our party, and there did such things as might have honoured Mars, if he had been in any of their places and made either of them worthy of his. Thereafter being drawn away from that country by an accident (the report whereof craves a longer time and a stronger breath than the

* *render*: surrender. *enlarge*: free.

heavens are like to afford me) their glory, tyrannizing over my rest, did kindle such flames in my bosom that, burning with a generous ardour, I did resolve leaving mine own country as too strict a bound for my thoughts, to try my fortune where I might either live famous or die unknown; vowing withal to travel till those princes were either the subject or witnesses of my valour.

'What passed in my way I pass over: perchance others may remember. At last, invited by fame, I came to this fatal country: it the band of my heart was, and now must be of my body: where first carried with curiosity, the fever of youth, I went to the Arcadian pastorals for my recreation but found the ruin of my rest. There, blinded with beholding and tormented with delight, my earnest eyes surfeited on the excellencies of the pattern of perfection, the quintessence of worth, even the most divinely divine Philoclea. Ah, too adventurous eyes! Neither could this content them, but they would needs offer up her picture on the altar of my heart, where by my thoughts their choice might be allowed, yea, and idolatrously advanced. For they, scorning the simple rudeness of the eyes, as easily defrauded of their too forwardly affected object, would securely entreasure it in a more precious place, by a piercing apprehension sinking it in the soul for ever. For a time, suffered as a stranger and a shepherd, known, as you know, by the name of Philisides, amongst the rest I had the means to pour forth my pliants before her, but never to her; and, though ore-thrown, not rendered, I had concluded never to have thrown the dice betwixt hope and despair, so betraying my estate to the tyranny of another's will. No: I was resolved she should never know her power in me till I had known her mind of me; so that, if she would not raise me, she should not have means to insult over me. Thus if I had not procured pity, I should not have exposed myself to disdain.

'In the haughtiness of my heart, thinking nothing impossible, I durst promise myself that, my deeds having purchased reputation, with words worthy of respect I might venture the process of my affection. In the meantime I joined joyfully with you in this late war now ended: though professing a general desire of glory, yet for a particular end, and happy end, since I end for her. But since whilst I lived I had not the means, as I wished, to content her, I crave not, by the knowledge of this, after death to discontent her.

It shall satisfy me that I die before my hopes; and she cannot grieve for the loss of that which she never knew to be hers.'

With this, the other* sliding apart to bear and bury his sorrow privately, the Black Knight, weeping, embraced him in his arms and told him what he was, saying he was glad that his vow was performed; he being a benefited witness, not the endangered subject of his valour. Then contentment, budding forth in his countenance, flourished in a smile, and having kissed his friends, desiring to live in their memory, wished them as contented lives as his was a death. He died as joyful as he left them sorrowful, who had known him a mirror of courage and courtesy, of learning and arms; so that it seemed that Mars had begotten him upon one of the Muses.[1]

Musidorus, exceedingly sorrowful for this irreparable loss, was yet more sorrowful when he remembered himself to be in danger of a greater; and recommending the direction of all below to the Knight of the Pole, he went himself up to visit his patient, whom he found, though lying, not resting; and though not sleeping, yet dreaming. As soon as he heard Musidorus, starting as one wakened out of a slumber, he looked on his face (grieved to see the impression of grief in it, he not knowing the cause) with an inquisitive amazement. But the other, preventing that threatened tempest, did blow away the clouds that were gathered in his countenance; telling him that he had no interest in the anguish which then did afflict him.

'What,' said Pyrocles, being passionately moved, 'can Musidorus have anything wherein I have no interest?'

'Aye,' said he, 'and for the present a greater wonder! My grief may breed you joy, I having lost a friend, and you a rival.' Then he began to discourse unto him what was passed. And beside that which was justly deserved, pity adorning praise and praise augmenting pity, a generous passion so conquered the unconquerable Pyrocles that he lamented him dead whom he had not known; no, nor would never have loved alive, and undoubtedly would have wished him no better success than he had. Yea, the very thing which before might have most discontented him did then most content him, having his judgement confirmed by the like in one of such worth.

* *the other*: the third knight, the Knight of the Pole.

After that, laid down in one bed together, friendship making them free and solitariness bold, whilst their minds began to be delivered all wherewith they had a long time travailed, a maid came to the door, sent by the two sisters, to visit Zelmane; who hearing two where she expected but one, and the one by the manner of his speech likely to be a man, did presently return, and reported to the ladies (who were lying together) that whereof her ears had given her sufficient assurance. At which news Pamela, burning within, sparkled forth these words to her sister:

'What wonder though strangers, ever wandering, wander from all things. Chiefly those of our sex, who being born to be bounded within houses, when they cannot be bounded within kingdoms, how can they be bounded by modesty? Yet, though I hate the deed, the respect of the doer, but more, of us* whose company she hath haunted (lest her reproach by the commentary of fame be too largely extended) binds me to conceal her shame that we blush not at it. But we must either free ourselves from her or she herself from this slander.'

'Oh,' but answered the ever (and now more than ever) mild Philoclea, 'we must not, sister, rashly condemn those whom we have oftentimes considerately approved, lest the change be in our judgement and not in them. No doubt, because of the indisposition of her body, it was necessary that she should have someone to accompany her. Perchance a woman mistaken; and if a man, who knows for what end? She, who being sound would acquaint herself with none, in this estate could not be acquainted with any.'

'It is an easy matter,' replied Pamela, 'for one who can deceive to dissemble. Neither is this a new acquaintance. You might have seen her use that knight who did come in with her rather kindly than courteously, a preceding friendship overpassing present respects; for where a great familiarity is, no ceremonial duty can be observed.'

Then Philoclea, having found her,* could hardly restrain the violence of a just laughter.

'As for that which you affirm last,' said she, 'I cannot deny it:

*but more, of us: the respect for ourselves. having found her: having recognized her real motive, jealousy.

no, I dare assure you – and assure yourself I will assure nothing without assurance – that knight is the man of the world whom Zelmane most dearly loves, and yet I know that neither would he offer nor she suffer her honour to be wronged as you imagine.'

This last wound was too deep for Pamela to speak after it: so that she (abandoning her heart to throw itself over the rock of unkindness, in danger to be drowned with her own tears) was thus prevented by Philoclea:

'Dear sister, and if any word can express more dearness more dear than that, your using me not only as a sister but as a friend in the highest degree of trust would make me ashamed to mistrust you, or that you should be beholden to any other than to me for my secret. So might my strangeness justify your unkindness, though you should discover and condemn that which I know you will conceal, perchance approve; and further being, by my imparting of it to you, made of the party, ere the report of others make you a judge, be bold, my tongue; for though my cheeks blush, yet they cover you. Be not ashamed, nay even glory to tell that Zelmane is the prince Pyrocles: he, whom you have heard so oft (yet ever to his honour) named; and, to define him unto you more particularly, the friend of Musidorus, over whom with him you are jealous; they lying now in one bed with no less love than I told you. Why he goes disguised with others, and why I am plain with you I need not tell; you may imagine. One God hath metamorphosed both, the one in a shepherd, the other in a woman; and we only can restore them to themselves, and themselves to the world, that they may grace it with the glory of their actions as they were wont to do.'

Then Philoclea, exchanging estates with her sister, words arrested by thoughts, she became sad and the other joyful; who (thinking herself well revenged of the past scorn, and having a sufficient pledge of her sister's secrecy) began to complain of their father's strict using of them by surmisings of his own minding to mar their fortunes, so that where he should rejoice at such an occasion, if coming to the knowledge thereof, he would not fail to disappoint it, perchance with the ruin of the princes; which would not only prove a particular loss for them, but (which she lamented more) a general loss for all the world; depriving it of those patterns of virtue, who in all their actions did but paint out the height of perfection, and encourage others to follow their footsteps in the way of worth. Therefore it behoved them to regard themselves, and seriously to consider a matter of so great importance. Then, both beginning to muse, night did cast the nets of sleep over their eyes, yet could not hinder their earnest thoughts from prosecuting the course of their own fancies; for what they were thinking when waking they still dreamed when sleeping.

## CHAPTER 33

But ere the morning star began to retire, as giving place to a greater light, whose coming it (as a forerunner) had only warned the world to attend, both awaked complaining of the night's length; and having with passionate discourses worn away darkness, as weary of them, they arose and hastily apparelled themselves though not in a curious yet in a comely manner. Then, with a pretended charity, they would needs go visit the diseased patient, being themselves impatient. A little before their coming, Musidorus being gone to give order for the burial of Philisides and (at the earnest desire of Pyrocles) of Anaxius, whose valour now had the full praise from which his own presumption had derogated much whilst he lived; as they approached to his chamber door they heard Pyrocles preparing his voice for the convoy of a sadly conceived and weakly delivered song, which they resolved not to interrupt, attending the letter which followed.

More dangerous darts than death, love throws, I spy,
Who by experience now know both their wounds:
Death pierc'd me all, yet could not make me die:
Love with a thought me in effect confounds.

The power of death, art sometimes may restrain,
Where love, I find, can never physic find:
Death only plagues the body but with pain,
Where love with pleasure doth torment the mind.

Death still to all alike none free doth leave;
Where partial love shafts but at some doth send:

Death with more mercy kills than love doth save:
Death's end breeds rest, love never rests to end.
  Death doth enlarge, where love imprisons still;
  Death forc'd by fates, love willingly doth kill.


As soon as this song was ended, Pamela opened the door, saluting him still (so to disguise her knowledge) by the name of Zelmane, and asked in what estate she was with herself, who returned this answer:

'How can I smart, having such angels to give me comfort? Or how can I feel pain in their presence, whose faces are heavens of pleasure?'

'Since,' said Pamela, 'being only unfortunate by falling in our company, the hazard of your life hath procured our liberty, so that accidentally, though far from our intention, we have been the causes of all your trouble, how can we think of your pain, but as of our own, or have any delight whilst you rest grieved?'

'Wonders of worth,' said Zelmane, 'I shall ever, whilst I live, reckon for my highest happiness my being honoured by your company; and as for my travails in this, they are by the success abundantly rewarded, since I could aspire to no higher good than I have compassed, having purchased you any contentment.'

Whilst that passionated Zelmane with an animated fervency did incorporate her hand with Philoclea's, whose speaking looks (however some time out of modesty obliquely moving) had a continual revolution about his face, the Black Knight's coming in drew Pamela's spirits from her thoughts to her eyes. A gentleman followed him, directed from Basilius; who after his duty done to the ladies, having shown them that their father and mother were in good health (invited by their inquiring attendance) told how the first, whom prodigal fame had breathed forth with news (hasted by himself, as who carried an acceptable message in hope of benefit or thanks) certified the king how the castle was won, and his daughters delivered by the Black Knight, who before had put a period to the victories of Amphialus. At this Pamela looking on Musidorus, blushed; and he (though by no gesture betraying his joy) rejoiced, not because he heard himself praised, but because she heard him praised; and that Anaxius in a single combat was killed by Zelmane, she not long over-living the victory.

The king hearing this (who of his gracious nature would rather save one friend than destroy all his enemies) as if the delivery of his daughters had been a matter of small moment and a gain too light to counterpoise so great a loss, did abandon his soul to the tyranny of sorrow even more than majesty in a prince or virtue in affliction, in the balances of reason, would have allowed of such weight. At this Zelmane's smile was accompanied with Philoclea's. But when he spake of Gynecia's griefs overgrowing the other, they grew pale, being afraid of the fountain from whence her tears did flow, lest it should drown them.

But whilst Gynecia (the messenger insisted) as run mad with anguish, inclosed in a chamber, would suffer none to come unto her, all wondered that her children being safe, a stranger's death or her husband's grief could weaken the known strength of her mind so much. The next messenger came, being the latter and thereby the better informed, who sugared the first news with the assurance of Zelmane's safety. Then the queen coming forth as after a great tempest, the sky of her countenance cleared, looking brighter than before. The king would have come himself here in person, but he was persuaded to send Philanax with a number of chosen men to receive the castle and ladies. Eftsoons* being curious to know who cured Zelmane, when it was told him that the knight who won the castle would trust none with that save himself, he was sorry that one of his worth should be put to such trouble, and would needs have an ordinary surgeon sought out to undertake the charge.

'In the meantime the queen came and brought out of a box a sovereign balm, which she hath sent by me to be applied to your wounds, fair Zelmane; not doubting but they will quickly become sound if her direction be observed, which is only that you rest and keep yourself quiet from company now and by the way, till she herself may use other remedies. And for this effect she entreats you, miracles of nature, her daughters, to forbear her company during this time, that your example (whose authority abused might embolden the indiscretion of inferiors) may be a law for

* *Eftsoons*: soon after.

others: and she assured me that she would by a secret spy learn how she were obeyed in this. Such a care hath she of this sweet lady's health.'

By the end of this commission well did Zelmane and Philoclea know at whom in particular those general injunctions did only aim. This enjoined abstinence did give Zelmane a surfeit in sorrow, who had rather have continued still infirm than to have recovered by so cruel a physic. And yet her misery was multiplied when she remembered the cause, whereof this (in respect of that which she did expect) was a slender issue, and but a little fury sent to afflict her out of that hell of Gynecia's breast into whose company she was shortly to enter. Now the Black Knight, purposing to depart before Philanax arrived, brought his companion, the Knight of the Pole, as a partner of his victory, to kiss the ladies' hands, extenuating his own part, and preferring his. Those who have true worth in themselves, can never envy it in another. Thereafter advising him privately to have their little company in a readiness, he went with an uncounterfeited reverence, humbling himself before the idol of his soul, to know her will: telling her, what he had done being only done for her, he would attend thanks from no other; neither would he be known till he might be known for hers. And she (her countenance rather lightening courtesy than affection) desired him to return to his old master, and he should be restored to the estate which by his fault he had before justly forfeited; wishing that he should carry himself more moderately thereafter, if he would not incur her indignation, and raze* all regard of him out of her memory.

Then Musidorus, as contented as one who had been brought from hell to heaven, with many vehement attestations to win trust with her, and imprecations against himself in case of perjury, wished (if ever his mind were so unhappy as to be surprised by any purpose tending in the least degree to grieve her) that he might never live till it took effect, but die ere it were discovered. And (like a wary gamester, who having once advantage is loth to adventure again) willing to seal up his ears with the acceptable sounds which they had received, he took leave, leaving his heart with her, and taking hers with him. Then went he towards Py-

* *raze:* blot out.

rocles, the joy of his heart shining through his face, and acquainted him with his unwilling absenting himself, referring all further conference till their meeting at the arbour. And having in a complimental\* manner craved, but not desired employment from Philoclea in any service after the funerals were performed, he marched with his troop away, the most part thinking that he went to meet Philanax: whilst Pamela from a window followed with her eyes, till clouds of dust did bury their object in the air.

## CHAPTER 34

Soon after their departure from the castle, about this time Philanax arrived, who, immediately after he had received the castle in the king's name, sought for the knight whose gift (though not given by him) he esteemed it to be. For he, being generously judicious, thought it more fit that princes should defray obligations by rewards (every man being inferior to him to whom he stands indebted) than to be behind with any by being beholden; and hearing that he was gone, by public inquiry for him and praises of him he witnessed to the world how highly his valour was valued. After he had saluted the princesses, he visited Zelmane and told her how careful his master was to have those wounds cured, which in his service had been procured, that thereafter he might otherwise express his gratefulness. But Zelmane affirmed that though that blood which was shed had been followed by all the rest of her body, with the king's former courtesies towards her, the deserving by the recompense was both preceded and exceeded. Then Philanax, loth to strive with deeds in words, desired her, if her health might serve, to provide for her removing with the rest tomorrow: otherwise, that should be done for her which she herself would direct.

Immediately after his departure Zelmane arose; and having apparelled herself, began to walk, not so much to try how she might comport with the intended journey as that she might pretend any means which might afford her the satisfaction of Philoclea's presence; where, violently carried by her thoughts, she came soon, but not so soon as she wished and was wished: where (Pamela

\* *complimental*: in elegant and ceremonious language.

apart entertaining her thoughts) she thus entered* with Philoclea:

'Dear love, o in what an ocean of troubles doth our estate continually float, yet hath never so much as attained the sight of any secure port. I see that this freedom will but bring us to a greater bondage: we are led from captivity, only to become captives. For where before those senseless walls were thought sufficient to guard us, we shall be watched now by one more jealous than Juno, with more eyes than ever Argus* had. I would willingly convey you where I might enjoy you, and you a kingdom: but this my infirmity first hindered, and the coming of Philanax hath altogether prevented. In the meantime, till for performing of that a longed for occasion come, I must arm myself against your father's folly and your mother's fury. The one's might easily be deluded, but the other's cannot be resisted but by a show of yielding, which I must cunningly counterfeit: and therefore trust no external show; for whoever have my countenance, you have my heart.'

Philoclea's words were, that she cared not where she went so it were with him, nor what she did so it were warranted by his directions; as bent rather to burn her breast than to let it lodge any thought which durst but doubt of the sufficiency of his intentions, since whatever circle they made, having always for their centre the excellency of his own worth. So parting, as if they had been to go to live in sundry kingdoms though going to live in one company, night invited them to repose.

The next morning being saluted by the trumpet's sounds, and all ready to remove, they were quickly transported over the lake; and as quickly, when landed, mounted by the provident care of Philanax to finish their journey. But ere they came two or three miles off the lodges, Basilius met them, who embraced his daughters: not that he would go first to them, but that he would be last with Zelmane, whom he had kissed with his eyes ere his lips were drawn from his daughters. And as soon as he had shown as much affection, encountering her, as his state before so many would permit, he said that notwithstanding her countenance was the treasure in the world whereof he was most covetous, yet it grieved

* *she thus entered*: broached the matter with. *Argus*: see Notes, II.14.6. (p. 856–7).

him that another should be so happy as to have procured her liberty rather than himself; and that it was his purpose, as a private adventurer, to have manifested his affection, fighting as a knight, not as a king, for her delivery.

Zelmane replying, that it had been against all reason that so great a prince, on whom the lives of so many did depend, should have been hazarded for the life of one whose fall could extend no further than to her own ruin:

'Your ruin?' said he, 'I wish that mine were first; for it could not but follow after. And do not think that the Black Knight or any other durst do more for you than I: yet such is the miserable estate of us kings that we cannot prove men, but are compelled to move in our own sphere.'

The journey's end cutting off their discourse, Gynecia was waiting on their lighting, and having first – duty tyrannizing over affection – carelessly kissed Pamela, disdainfully Philoclea, and vehemently Zelmane, thereafter inquiring of her wounds, thanks (though bestowing nothing defraying much) were courteously returned for the balm which was sent; she protesting that if no other thing could help, she would pull out her own heart, when Basilius interrupted them, coming to have lightened his heart by burdening his body* with his mistress' lighting.

Dametas came starting and leaping like a giddy kid to meet with Pamela; and as soon as she was lighted, for the first salutation, told her how much she was beholden to him, having shown his manhood and goodwill as much as the best fellow in those bounds could have done, swearing that he had ventured more for her than he would do for all the world again, and for his own life too:

'Aye,' quoth he, 'and when my man Dorus durst not be seen, who was thought a brave fellow, yet he feigned a business far from the noise of war, to seek sheep; but the truth is, to hide himself, whilst my deeds made all our army laugh for joy: so that during all that time of trouble, which I tremble yet to think upon, I never heard of him, till even now he sent me word by a shepherd whom he met on the way that he had found the ewes which had strayed, with great difficulty, and was driving them at leisure, for

* *burdening his body:* trying to lift her down from her horse.

fear they should miscarry. But when he comes, I promise I will make his cowardice be known for leaving me, when I would fain have left myself for fear.'

'O but,' said Pamela, 'you must not be offended, though every man be not so stout as you are. He may be an evil soldier, but yet a good shepherd: and I hope you keep him that he may keep sheep, not that he may kill men.'

'Now in good faith,' said he, 'I see you are not changed, for you were ever wise, and so do you continue still. I may well chide the fellow, but I will not beat him.'

Then all entering the lodge with Basilius, though the supper was ready, Gynecia would dress Zelmane's wounds first, and Basilius would see them dressed; so by his despised importunateness restraining the torrent of Gynecia's passions, which would but burst forth more furiously thereafter. This freeing Zelmane's ears at that time was but a relief to her, as they find who expel poison by counterpoison, she being as weary of him as afraid of the other.

Then sitting down to the supper, more curious of a surfeit to their eyes than for sustenance to the rest of the body; the eyes of Basilius were ever feeding on the face of Zelmane with a fearful earnestness, save sometimes when they were constrained to retire by the violence of his wife's looks, thinking that they with a jealous anger had upbraided his error, which she (otherwise busied) had never so much as observed. The one of her eyes was settled like a fixed star on Zelmane; the other (like a wandering comet threatening confusion where it shined) strayed betwixt Zelmane and her daughter Philoclea, watching and chastising with her look her stolen looks. Zelmane's languishing lights made the table envied, whilst her dejected looks did only bless it, as scorning to look on any since she might not look where she liked. Philoclea, chained by thoughts to Zelmane, did imitate her being pensive, because she was pensive: yet (like a cunning painter who, having fully fed his eyes with the affected object, turns back within himself that his imagination may engrave it the more exactly within his memory) she would sometimes with a thievishly adventurous look spy Zelmane's gesture, that she might the better counterfeit it in her countenance. As for Pamela, she kept her accustomed majesty, being absent where she was, and present where she was not. Then, the supper being ended, after some ambiguous speeches which might, for fear of being mistaken, be taken in two senses, or else were altogether estranged from the speaker's mind (speaking, as in a dream, not what they thought, but what they would be thought to think) everyone retired to the lodge where they had used afore to lie; Basilius having first invited them the next morning to see a pastoral represented by the ordinary shepherds, to congratulate their prosperous return.[1]

*From hence the history is again continued out of the author's own writings and conceits as followeth.*

## CHAPTER 35

After that Basilius (according to the oracle's promise) had received home his daughters, and settled himself again in his solitary course and accustomed company, there passed not many days ere the now fully recomforted Dorus, having waited a time of Zelmane's walking alone towards her little arbour, took leave of his master Dametas' husbandry to follow her. Near whereunto overtaking her, and sitting down together among the sweet flowers whereof that place was very plentiful, under the pleasant shade of a broad-leaved sycamore, they recounted one to another their strange pilgrimage of passions, omitting nothing which the openhearted friendship is wont to lay forth, where there is cause to communicate both joys and sorrows – for indeed there is no sweeter taste of friendship than the coupling of souls in this mutuality either of condoling or comforting; where the oppressed mind finds itself not altogether miserable, since it is sure of one which is feelingly sorry for his misery; and the joyful spends not his joy either alone or there where it may be envied, but may freely send it to such a well-grounded object, from whence he shall be sure to receive a sweet reflection of the same joy and (as in a clear mirror of sincere goodwill) see a lively picture of his own gladness.

But after much discourse on either part, Dorus (his heart scarce serving him to come to the point whereunto his then coming had been wholly directed, as loth in the kindest sort to discover to his friend his own unkindness) at length – one word emboldening another – made known to Zelmane how Pamela, upon his vehement oath to offer no force unto her till he had invested her in the duchy of Thessalia, had condescended to his stealing her away to the next seaport: that besides the strange humours she saw her father more and more falling into, and unreasonable restraint of her liberty (whereof she knew no cause but light grounded jealousies) added to the hate of that manner of life, and confidence she had in his virtue; the chiefest reason had won her to this was the late danger she stood in of losing him, the like whereof (not unlike to fall if this course were continued) she chose rather to die than again to undergo: that now they waited for nothing else but some fit time for their escape, by the absence of their three loathsome companions in whom folly engendered suspicion.

'And therefore now,' said Dorus, 'my dear cousin, to whom nature began my friendship, education confirmed it, and virtue hath made it eternal, here have I discovered the very foundation whereupon my life is built. Be you the judge betwixt me and my fortune. The violence of love is not unknown to you, and I know my case shall never want pity in your consideration. How all the joys of my heart do leave me in thinking I must for a time be absent from you! The eternal truth is witness unto me, I know I should not so sensibly feel the pangs of my last departure. But this enchantment of my restless desire hath such authority in myself above myself that I am become a slave unto it; I have no more freedom in mine own determinations. My thoughts are now all bent how to carry away my burdenous bliss. Yet, most beloved cousin, rather than you should think I do herein violate that holy band of true friendship wherein I unworthy am knit unto you, command me stay. Perchance the force of your commandment may work such impression into my heart that no reason of mine own can imprint into it. For the gods forbid the foul word of abandoning Pyrocles might ever be objected to the faithful Musidorus! But if you can spare my presence, whose presence no way serves you, and by the division of these two lodges is not oft with you: nay, if you can think my absence may, as it shall, stand you in stead, by bringing such an army hither as shall make Basilius, willing or unwilling, to know his own hap in granting you Philoclea, then I will cheerfully go about this my most desired enterprise, and shall think the better half of it already achieved, being begun in the fortunate hour of my friend's contentment.'

These words, as they were not knit together with such a constant course of flowing eloquence as Dorus was wont to use, so was his voice interrupted with sighs, and his countenance with interchanging colour dismayed; so much his own heart did find him faulty to unbend any way the continual use of their dear friendship. But Zelmane, who had all this while gladly hearkened to the other tidings of her friend's happy success, when this last determination of Dorus strake her attentive ears, she stayed a great while oppressed with a dead amazement. There came straight before her mind, made tender with woes, the images of her own fortune: her tedious longings; her causes to despair; the cumbersome folly of Basilius; the enraged jealousy of Gynecia; herself a prince without retinue; a man annoyed with the troubles of womankind, loathsomely loved, and dangerously loving: and now for the perfecting of all, her friend to be taken away by himself, to make the loss the greater by the unkindness. But within a while she resolutely passed over all inward objections, and preferring her friend's profit to her own desire, with a quiet but hearty look, she thus answered him:

'If I bare thee this love, virtuous Musidorus, for mine own sake, and that our friendship grew because I for my part might rejoice to enjoy such a friend, I should now so thoroughly feel mine own loss that I should call the heavens and earth to witness how cruelly ye rob me of my greatest comfort, measuring the breach of friendship by mine own passion. But because indeed I love thee for thyself, and in my judgement judge of thy worthiness to be loved, I am content to build my pleasure upon thy comfort; and then will I deem my hap in friendship great when I shall see thee, whom I love, happy. Let me be only sure thou lovest me still – the only price of true affection. Go therefore on, worthy Musidorus, with the guide of virtue and service of fortune. Let thy love be loved, thy desires prosperous, thy escape safe, and thy journey easy. Let everything yield this help to thy desert. For my part, absence shall not take thee from mine eyes, nor afflictions shall bar me from gladding in thy good, nor a possessed heart shall keep thee from the place it hath forever allotted unto thee.'

Dorus would fain have replied again, to have made a liberal confession that Zelmane had of her side the advantage of well performing friendship; but partly his own grief of parting from one he loved so dearly, partly the kind care in what state he should leave Zelmane, bred such a conflict in his mind that many times he wished he had either never attempted, or never revealed this secret enterprise. But Zelmane, who had now looked to the uttermost of it, and established her mind upon an assured determination:

'My only friend,' said she, 'since to so good towardness your courteous destinies have conducted you, let not a ceremonial* consideration of our mutual love be a bar unto it. I joy in your presence, but I joy more in your good. That friendship brings forth the fruits of enmity which prefers his own tenderness before his friend's damage. For my part, my greatest grief herein shall be I can be no further serviceable unto you.'

'O Zelmane,' said Dorus, with his eyes even covered with water, 'I did not think so soon to have displayed my determination unto you, but to have made my way first in your loving judgement. But alas, as your sweet disposition drew me so far, so doth it now strengthen me in it. To you, therefore, be the due commendation given, who can conquer me in love, and love in wisdom. As for me, then shall goodness turn to evil and ungratefulness be the token of a true heart, when Pyrocles shall not possess a principal seat in my soul, when the name of Pyrocles shall not be held of me in devout reverence.'

They would never have come to the cruel instant of parting nor to the ill-faring word of farewell, had not Zelmane seen afar off the old Basilius, who having performed a sacrifice to Apollo for his daughters', but principally for his mistress' happy return, had since been everywhere to seek her. And now being come within compass of discerning her, he began to frame the loveliest countenance he could, stroking up his legs, setting his beard in due order, and standing bolt upright.

'Alas,' said Zelmane, 'behold an evil fore-token of your sorrowful departure. Yonder see I one of my furies, which doth daily vex me. Farewell, farewell, my Musidorus. The gods make fortune

* *ceremonial*: ceremonious rather than sincere.

to wait on thy virtues, and make me wade through this lake of wretchedness.'

Dorus burst out into a flood of tears, wringing her fast by the hand.

'No, no,' said he, 'I go blindfold whither the course of my ill hap carries me; for now, too late, my heart gives me this our separating can never be prosperous. But if I live, attend me here shortly with an army.'

Thus both appalled with the grievous renting of their long combination (having first resolved with themselves that whatsoever fell unto them, they should never upon no occasion utter their names, for the conserving the honour of their royal parentage, but keep the names of Daiphantus and Palladius as before had been agreed between them) they took divers ways: Dorus to the lodge-ward, where his heavy eyes might be something refreshed; Zelmane towards Basilius, saying to herself with a scornful smiling, 'Yet hath not my friendly fortune deprived me of a pleasant companion.' But he having with much search come to her presence, doubt and desire bred a great quarrel in his mind; for his former experience had taught him to doubt, and true feeling of love made doubts dangerous.[1] But the working of his desire had ere long won the field, and therefore, with the most submissive manner his behaviour could yield;

'O goddess,' said he, 'towards whom I have the greatest feeling of religion, be not displeased at some show of devotion I have made to Apollo, since he (if he know anything) knows that my heart bears far more awful reverence to yourself than to his, or any other the like deity.'

'You will ever be deceived in me,' answered Zelmane; 'I will make myself no competitor with Apollo; neither can blasphemies to him be duties to me.'

With that Basilius took out of his bosom certain verses he had written, and kneeling down, presented them to her. They contained this:

> Phoebus, farewell; a sweeter saint I serve:
> The high conceits thy heav'nly wisdoms breed
> My thoughts forget: my thoughts which never swerve

From her in whom is sown their freedom's seed,
And in whose eyes my daily doom I read.

   Phoebus, farewell; a sweeter saint I serve:
Thou art far off, thy kingdom is above:
   She heav'n on earth with beauties doth preserve.
Thy beams I like, but her clear rays I love:
Thy force I fear, her force I still do prove.

   Phoebus, yield up thy title in my mind:
She doth possess: thy image is defac'd.
   But if thy rage some brave revenge will find
On her, who hath in me thy temple raz'd,
Employ thy might, that she my fires may taste;
     And how much more her worth surmounteth thee,
     Make her as much more base by loving me.

'This is my hymn to you,' said he, 'not left me by my ancestors, but begun in myself. The temple wherein it is daily sung is my soul; and the sacrifice I offer to you withal is all whatsoever I am.' Zelmane, who ever thought she found in his speeches the ill taste of a medicine and the operation of a poison, would have suffered a disdainful look to have been the only witness of her good acceptation, but that Basilius began afresh to lay before her many pitiful prayers, and in the end to conclude that he was fully of opinion it was only the unfortunateness of that place that hindered the prosperous course of his desires. And therefore, since the hateful influence which made him embrace this solitary life was now past over him (as he doubted not the judgement of Philanax would agree with his) and his late mishaps had taught him how perilous it was to commit a prince's state to a place so weakly guarded, he was now inclined to return to his palace in Mantinea; and there he hoped he should be better able to show how much he desired to make all he had hers – with many other such honey words which my pen grows almost weary to set down. This indeed nearly pierced Zelmane: for the good beginning she had there obtained of Philoclea made her desire to continue the same trade till unto the more perfecting of her desires; and to come to any public place she did deadly fear, lest her mask by many eyes might the sooner be discovered, and so her hopes stopped and the state of her joys endangered. Therefore a while she rested, musing at the daily changing labyrinth of her own fortune; but in herself determined it was her only best to keep him there, and with favours to make him love the place where the favours were received, as disgraces had made him apt to change the soil.

Therefore, casting a kind of corner look* upon him, 'It is truly said,' said she, 'that age cooleth the blood. How soon, good man, you are terrified before you receive any hurt! Do you not know that daintiness* is kindly* unto us, and that hard obtaining is the excuse of woman's granting? Yet speak I not as though you were like to obtain or I to grant, but because I would not have you imagine I am to be won by courtly vanities, or esteem a man the more because he hath handsome men to wait of him when he is afraid to live without them.'

You might have seen Basilius humbly swell, and, with a lowly look, stand upon his tiptoes, such diversity her words delivered unto him.

'O Hercules,' answered he, 'Basilius afraid! Or his blood cold that boils in such a furnace! Care I who is with me while I enjoy your presence, or is any place good or bad to me but as it pleaseth you to bless or curse it? O let me be but armed in your good grace, and I defy whatsoever there is or can be against me. No, no, your love is forcible, and my age is not without vigour.'

Zelmane thought it not good for his stomach to receive a surfeit of too much favour; and therefore thinking he had enough for the time to keep him from any sudden removing, with a certain gracious bowing down of her head towards him, she turned away, saying she would leave him at this time to see how temperately he could use so bountiful a measure of her kindness. Basilius, that thought every drop a flood that bred any refreshment, durst not further press her, but with an ancient modesty left her to the sweet repast of her own fancies.

*corner look: sly. daintiness: stand-offishness. kindly: natural.

## CHAPTER 36

Zelmane, as soon as he was departed, went towards Pamela's lodge in hope to have seen her friend Dorus, to have pleased herself with another painful farewell, and further to have taken some advice with him touching her own estate, whereof before sorrow had not suffered her to think. But being come even near the lodge, she saw the mouth of a cave, made, as it should seem, by nature in despite of* art, so fitly did the rich growing marble serve to beautify the vault of the first entry. Under foot the ground seemed mineral, yielding such a glistering show of gold in it as they say the river Tagus carries in his sandy bed. The cave framed out into many goodly spacious rooms, such as the self-liking* men have with long and learned delicacy found out the most easeful. There ran through it a little sweet river which had left the face of the earth to drown herself for a small way in this dark but pleasant mansion. The very first show of the place enticed the melancholy mind of Zelmane to yield herself over there to the flood of her own thoughts. And therefore, sitting down in the first entry of the cave's mouth, with a song she had lately made she gave a doleful way to her bitter affects.* She sung to this effect:

> Since that the stormy rage of passions dark
> (Of passions dark, made dark by beauty's light)
> With rebel force, hath clos'd in dungeon dark
> My mind, ere now led forth by reason's light:
>
> Since all the things which give mine eyes their light
> Do foster still the fruits of fancies dark,
> So that the windows of my inward light
> Do serve to make my inward powers dark:
>
> Since, as I say, both mind and senses dark
> Are hurt, not help'd, with piercing of the light,
> While that the light may show the horrors dark,
> But cannot make resolved darkness light:
>     I like this place where, at the least, the dark
>     May keep my thoughts from thought of wonted light.

*in despite of: in scorn of. self-liking: sybaritic. affects: passions.

Instead of an instrument, her song was accompanied with the wringing of her hands, the closing of her weary eyes, and even sometimes cut off with the swelling of her sighs, which did not suffer the voice to have his free and native passage. But, as she was a while musing upon her song, raising up her spirits which were something fallen into the weakness of lamentation, considering solitary complaints do no good to him whose help stands without himself,* she might afar off first hear a whispering sound which seemed to come from the inmost part of the cave, and being kept together with the close hollowness of the place, had, as in a trunk,* the more liberal access to her ears; and by and by she might perceive the same voice deliver itself into musical tunes, and with a base Lyra* give forth this song:

> Hark, plaintful ghosts, infernal furies, hark
> Unto my woes the hateful heavens do send,
> The heavens conspir'd to make my vital spark
> A wretched wreck, a glass of ruin's end.
>
> Seeing, alas, so mighty powers bend
> Their ireful shot against so weak a mark,
> Come cave, become my grave: come death, and lend
> Receipt to me within thy bosom dark.
>
> For what is life to daily dying mind,
> Where, drawing breath, I suck the air of woe;
> Where too much sight makes all the body blind,
> And highest thoughts downward most headlong throw?
> Thus then my form, and thus my state I find,
> Death wrapp'd in flesh, to living grave assign'd.

And pausing but a little, with moanful* melody it continued this octave:

> Like those sick folks, in whom strange humours flow,
> Can taste no sweets, the sour only please,
> So to my mind, while passions daily grow,

* *without himself*: in things outside his own control. *trunk*: tube. *Lyra*: lyre. *moanful*: lamenting.

Whose fiery chains upon his freedom seize,
  Joys strangers seem; I cannot bide their show,
  Nor brook aught else but well-acquainted woe.
  Bitter grief tastes me best, pain is my ease,
  Sick to the death, still loving my disease.

'O Venus,' said Zelmane, 'who is this so well acquainted with me that can make so lively a portraiture of my miseries? It is surely the spirit appointed to have care of me which doth now, in this dark place, bear part with the complaints of his unhappy charge. For if it be so that the heavens have at all times a measure of their wrathful harms, surely so many have come to my blissless lot that the rest of the world hath too small a portion to make with cause so wailful a lamentation. But,' said she, 'whatsoever thou be, I will seek thee out, for thy music well assures me we are at least-hand fellow prentices to one ungracious master.'

So rase she and went, guiding herself by the still plaining voice, till she saw upon a stone a little wax light set, and under it a piece of paper, with these verses very lately (as it should seem) written in it:

How is my sun, whose beams are shining bright,
Become the cause of my dark ugly night?
Or how do I, captiv'd in this dark plight,
Bewail the case, and in the cause delight?

My mangled mind huge horrors still do fright,
With sense possessed, and claim'd by reason's right:
Betwixt which two in me I have this fight,
Where who so wins, I put myself to flight.

Come, cloudy fears, close up my dazzled sight;
Sorrows, suck up the marrow of my might;
Due sighs, blow out all sparks of joyful light;
Tire on,* despair, upon my tired spright.
    An end, an end: my dull'd pen cannot write,
    Nor maz'd head think, nor falt'ring tongue recite.

        *Tire on: prey upon.

And hard underneath the sonnet were these words written:

> This cave is dark, but it had never light.
>> This wax doth waste itself, yet painless dies.
>>> These words are full of woes, yet feel they none.
>
> I darkened am, who once had clearest sight.
>> I waste my heart, which still new torment tries.
>>> I plain* with cause, my woes are all mine own.
>
>> No Cave, no wasting wax, no words of grief,
>>> Can hold, show, tell, my pains without relief.

She did not long stay to read the words, for not far off from the stone she might discern in a dark corner a lady lying with her face so prostrate upon the ground as she could neither know nor be known. But, as the general nature of man is desirous of knowledge, and sorrow especially glad to find fellows, she went as softly as she could convey her foot near unto her, where she heard these words come with vehement sobbings from her:

'O darkness,' said she, 'which dost lightsomely,* methinks, make me see the picture of my inward darkness, since I have chosen thee to be the secret witness of my sorrows, let them receive a safe receipt in thee; and esteem them not tedious, but, if it be possible, let the uttering them be some discharge to my overloaden breast. Alas, sorrow, now thou hast the full sack* of my conquered spirits, rest thyself awhile, and set not still new fire to thy own spoils! O accursed reason, how many eyes thou hast to see thy evils, and how dim, nay blind thou art in preventing them! Forlorn creature that I am, I would I might be freely wicked, since wickedness doth prevail; but the footsteps of my overtrodden virtue lie still as bitter accusations unto me. I am divided in myself: how can I stand? I am overthrown in myself: who shall raise me? Vice is but a nurse of new agonies, and the virtue I am divorced from makes the hateful comparison the more manifest. No, no, virtue, either I never had but a shadow of thee, or thou thyself art but a shadow. For how is my soul abandoned! How are all my powers laid waste! My desire is pained because it cannot hope, and if hope came, his best should be but mischief. O strange

* *plain:* lament. *lightsomely:* clearly. *sack:* conquest.

mixture of human minds: only so much good left as to make us languish in our own evils. Ye infernal furies (for it is too late for me to awake my dead virtue, or to place my comfort in the angry gods) ye infernal furies, I say, aid one that dedicates herself unto you: let my rage be satisfied, since the effect of it is fit for your service. Neither be afraid to make me too happy, since nothing can come to appease the smart of my guilty conscience. I desire but to assuage the sweltering of my hellish longing. Dejected Gynecia!'

Zelmane no sooner heard the name of Gynecia but that with a cold sweat all over her, as if she had been ready to tread upon a deadly stinging adder, she would have withdrawn herself; but her own passion made her yield more unquiet motions than she had done in coming, so that she was perceived and Gynecia suddenly risen up – for indeed it was Gynecia gotten into this cave (the same cave wherein Dametas had safely kept Pamela in the late uproar) to pass* her pangs with change of places. And as her mind ran still* upon Zelmane, her piercing lover's eye had soon found it was she. And seeing in her a countenance to fly away, she fell down at her feet, and catching fast hold of her:

'Alas,' said she, 'whither, or from whom dost thou fly away? The savagest beasts are won with service, and there is no flint but may be mollified. How is Gynecia so unworthy in thine eyes? Or whom cannot abundance of love make worthy? O think not that cruelty or ungratefulness can flow from a good mind! O weigh, alas, weigh with thyself the new effects of this mighty passion, that I, unfit for my state, uncomely for my sex, must become a suppliant at thy feet! By the happy woman that bare thee, by all the joys of thy heart and success of thy desire, I beseech thee turn thyself to some consideration of me, and rather show pity in now helping me than in too late repenting my death, which hourly threatens me.'

Zelmane, imputing it to one of her continual mishaps thus to have met with this lady, with a full weary countenance, 'Without doubt, Madam,' said she, 'where the desire is such as may be obtained, and the party well deserving as yourself, it must be a great excuse that may well colour a denial: but when the first motion carries with it a direct impossibility, then must the only answer be

* *pass*: escape. *still*: ever.

comfort without help, and sorrow to both parties; to you, not obtaining; to me, not able to grant.'

'O,' said Gynecia, 'how good leisure you have to frame these scornful answers. Is Gynecia thus to be despised? Am I so vile a worm in your sight? No, no, trust to it, hard-hearted tiger, I will not be the only actor of this tragedy! Since I must fall, I will press down some others with my ruins. Since I must burn, my spiteful neighbours shall feel of my fire. Dost thou not perceive that my diligent eyes have pierced through the cloudy mask of thy disguisement? Have I not told thee, O fool (if I were not much more fool!) that I know thou wouldst abuse us with thy outward show? Wilt thou still attend the rage of love in a woman's heart? The girl, thy well-chosen mistress, perchance shall defend thee when Basilius shall know how thou hast sotted his mind with falsehood, and falsely sought the dishonour of his house! Believe it, believe it, unkind creature, I will end my miseries with a notable example of revenge, and that accursed cradle* of mine shall feel the smart of my wound, thou of thy tyranny, and lastly (I confess) myself of mine own work.'

Zelmane, that had long before doubted herself to be discovered by her, and now plainly finding it, was (as the proverb saith) like them that hold the wolf by the ears, bitten while they hold, and slain if they loose. If she held her off in these wonted terms, she saw rage would make her love work the effects of hate: to grant unto her, her heart was so bound upon Philoclea, it had been worse than a thousand deaths. Yet found she it was necessary for her to come to a resolution, for Gynecia's sore could bide no leisure, and once discovered, besides the danger of Philoclea, her desires should be for ever utterly stopped. She remembered withal the words of Basilius, how apt he was to leave this life and return to his court, a great bar to her hopes. Lastly, she considered Dorus' enterprise might bring some strange alteration of this their well-liked fellowship. So that encompassed with these instant difficulties, she bent her spirits to think of a remedy which might at once both save her from them, and serve her to the accomplishment of her only pursuit. Lastly, she determined thus, that there was no way but to yield to the violence of their desires, since

* *that accursed cradle*: i.e. Philoclea.

striving did the more chafe them; and that following their own current, at length of itself it would bring her to the other side of her burning desires.

## CHAPTER 37

Now in the meanwhile, the divided Dorus, long divided between love and friendship, and now for his love divided from his friend, though indeed without prejudice of friendship's loyalty (which doth never bar the mind from his free satisfaction) yet still a cruel judge over himself, thought he was some ways faulty, and applied his mind how to amend it with a speedy and behoveful return. But then was his first study how to get away, whereto already he had Pamela's consent, confirmed and concluded under the name of Mopsa in her own presence – Dorus taking this way, that whatsoever he would have of Pamela he would ask her whether in such a case it were not best for Mopsa so to behave herself; in that sort making Mopsa's envy an instrument of that she did envy. So having passed over his first and most feared difficulty, he busied his spirits how to come to the harvest of his desires, whereof he had so fair a show. And thereunto (having gotten leave for some days of his master Dametas, who now accounted him as his son-in-law) he roamed round about the desert to find some unknown way that might bring him to the next seaport, as much as might be out of all course of other passengers. Which all very well succeeding him, and he having hired a barque for his life's traffic, and provided horses to carry her thither, returned homeward, now come to the last point of his care, how to go beyond the loathsome watchfulness of these three uncomely companions. And therein did wisely consider how they were to be taken with whom he had to deal; remembering that in the particularities of everybody's mind and fortune there are particular advantages by which they are to be held. The muddy mind of Dametas he found most easily stirred with covetousness: the cursed mischievous heart of Miso, most apt to be tickled with jealousy, as whose rotten brain could think well of nobody. But young mistress Mopsa, who could open her eyes upon nothing that did not all to be-wonder her, he thought curiosity the fittest bait for her.

And first for Dametas: Dorus having employed a whole day's work about a ten mile off from the lodge (quite contrary way to that he meant to take with Pamela) in digging and opening the ground under an ancient oak that stood there, in such sort as might longest hold Dametas' greedy hopes in some show of comfort, he came to his master with a countenance mixed betwixt cheerfulness and haste, and taking him by the right hand as if he had a great matter of secrecy to reveal unto him:

'Master,' said he, 'I did never think that the gods had appointed my mind, freely brought up, to have so longing a desire to serve you, but that they minded thereby to bring some extraordinary fruit to one so beloved of them as your honesty makes me think you are. This binds me even in conscience to disclose that which I persuade myself is allotted unto you, that your fortune may be of equal balance with your deserts.'

He said no further, because he would let Dametas play upon the bit a while; who not understanding what his words intended, yet well finding they carried no evil news, was so much the more desirous to know the matter as he had free scope to imagine what measure of good hap himself would. Therefore putting off his cap to him, which he never had done before, and assuring him he should have Mopsa though she had been all made of cloth of gold, he besought Dorus not to hold him long in hope, for that he found it a thing his heart was not able to bear.

'Master,' answered Dorus, 'you have so satisfied me with promising me the uttermost of my desired bliss, that if my duty bound me not, I were in it sufficiently rewarded. To you therefore shall my good hap be converted, and the fruit of my labour dedicated.'

Therewith he told him how under an ancient oak (the place he made him easily understand by sufficient marks he gave unto him) he had found, digging but a little depth, scatteringly lying a great number of rich medals; and that, piercing further into the ground, he had met with a great stone which, by the hollow sound it yielded, seemed to be the cover of some greater vault, and upon it a box of cypress with the name of the valiant Aristomenes[1] graven upon it; and that within the box he found certain verses, which signified that some depth again under that, all his treasures lay hidden, what time for the discord fell out in Arcadia he lived banished. Therewith he gave Dametas certain medals of gold he had long kept about him, and asked him (because it was a thing much to be kept secret and a matter one man in twenty hours might easily perform) whether he would have him go and seek the bottom of it, which he had refrained to do till he knew his mind – promising he would faithfully bring him what he found – or else that he himself would do it and be the first beholder of that comfortable spectacle.

No man need doubt which part Dametas would choose, whose fancy had already devoured all this great riches, and even now began to grudge at a partner, before he saw his own share. Therefore taking a strong jade, loaden with spades and mattocks, which he meant to bring back otherwise laden, he went in all speed thitherward, taking leave of nobody; only desiring Dorus he would look well to the princess Pamela, promising him mountains of his own labour, which nevertheless he little meant to perform – like a fool, not considering that no man is to be moved with part, that neglects the whole. Thus away went Dametas, having already made an image in his fancy what palaces he would build, how sumptuously he would fare, and among all other things, imagined what money to employ in making coffers to keep his money. His ten miles seemed twice so many leagues, and yet contrary to the nature of it, though it seemed long, it was not wearisome. Many times he cursed his horse's want of consideration that in so important a matter would make no greater speed: many times he wished himself the back of an ass to help to carry away the new sought riches (an unfortunate wisher, for if he had as well wished the head, it had been granted him).

At length being come to the tree which he hoped should bear so golden acorns, down went all his instruments, and forthwith to the renting up of the hurtless earth; where by and by he was caught with the lime* of a few promised medals, which was so perfect a pawn* unto him of his further expectation that he deemed a great number of hours well employed in groping further into it, which with logs and great stones was made as cumbersome as might be, till at length, with sweaty brows, he came to the great stone – a stone, God knows, full unlike to the cover of a

* *lime*: bird-lime. *pawn*: pledge.

monument; but yet there was the cypress box with 'Aristomenes' graven upon it, and these verses written in it:

> A banish'd man, long barr'd from his desire
> By inward lets,* of them his state possessed,
> Hid here his hopes, by which he might aspire
> To have his harms with wisdom's help redressed.
> Seek then and see what man esteemeth best:
> All is but this; this is our labour's hire:
> Of this we live, in this we find our rest;
> Who hold this fast no greater wealth require.
> Look further then, so shalt thou find at least
> A bait most fit for hungry minded guest.

He opened the box, and to his great comfort read them, and with fresh courage went about to lift up that stone.

But in the meantime, ere Dametas was half-a-mile gone to the treasure-ward, Dorus came to Miso, whom he found sitting in the chimney's end, babbling to herself, and showing in all her gestures that she was loathsomely weary of the world; not for any hope of a better life, but finding no one good, neither in mind nor body, whereout she might nourish a quiet thought, having long since hated each thing else, began now to hate herself. Before this sweet humoured dame Dorus set himself, and framed towards her such a smiling countenance as might seem to be mixed between a tickled mirth and a forced pity.

Miso, to whom cheerfulness in others was ever a sauce of envy in herself, took quickly mark of his behaviour, and with a look full of forworn* spite, 'Now the devil,' said she, 'take these villains that can never leave grinning because I am not so fair as mistress Mopsa! To see how this skipjack* looks at me!'

Dorus, that had the occasion he desired, 'Truly mistress,' answered he, 'my smiling is not at you but at them that are from you; and indeed I must needs a little accord my countenance with others' sport.' And therewithal took her in his arms, and rocking her to and fro, 'In faith, mistress,' said he, 'it is high time for you

---

*inward lets: opposition from within the state. forworn: long-held. skipjack: young puppy.

to bid us good night for ever, since others can possess your place in your own time.'

Miso, that was never void of malice enough to suspect the uttermost evil, to satisfy a further shrewdness took on a present mildness, and gently desired him to tell her what he meant; 'for,' said she, 'I am like enough to be knavishly dealt with by that churl my husband.'

Dorus fell off from the matter again, as if he had meant no such thing, till by much refusing her entreaty, and vehemently stirring up her desire to know, he had strengthened a credit in her to that he should say. And then with a formal* countenance, as if the conscience of the case had touched himself:

'Mistress,' said he, 'I am much perplexed in my own determination, for my thoughts do ever will me to do honestly; but my judgement fails me what is honest betwixt the general rule, that entrusted secrecies are holily to be deserved, and the particular exception, that the dishonest secrecies are to be revealed – especially there, where by revealing they may either be prevented, or at least amended. Yet in this balance your judgement weighs me down, because I have confidence in it that you will use what you know moderately, and rather take such faults as an advantage to your own good desert than by your bitter using it, be contented to be revenged on others with your own harms. So it is, mistress,' said he, 'that yesterday, driving my sheep up to the stately hill which lifts his head over the fair city of Mantinea, I happened upon the side of it, in a little falling of the ground which was a rampier against the sun's rage, to perceive a young maid, truly of the finest stamp of beauty; and that which made her beauty the more admirable, there was at all no art added to the helping of it: for her apparel was but such as shepherds' daughters are wont to wear; and as for her hair, it hung down at the free liberty of his goodly length, but that sometimes falling before the clear stars of her sight, she was forced to put it behind her ears, and so open again the treasures of her perfection which that for a while had in part hidden. In her lap there lay a shepherd, so wrapped up in that well-liked place that I could discern no piece of

* *formal*: solemn.

his face; but as mine eyes were attent* in that, her angel-like voice
strake mine ears with this song:

> My true love hath my heart, and I have his,
> By just exchange, one for the other giv'n.
> I hold his dear, and mine he cannot miss;
> There never was a better bargain driv'n.
>
> His heart in me keeps me and him in one;
> My heart in him his thoughts and senses guides:
> He loves my heart, for once it was his own;
> I cherish his, because in me it bides.
>
> His heart his wound received from my sight:
> My heart was wounded with his wounded heart;
> For as from me on him his hurt did light,
> So still me thought in me his hurt did smart:
> Both equal hurt, in this change sought our bliss:
> My true love hath my heart, and I have his.

'But, as if the shepherd that lay before her had been organs
which were only to be blown by her breath, she had no sooner
ended with the joining her sweet lips together, but that he re-
corded to her music this rural poesy:

> O words which fall like summer dew on me,
> O breath more sweet than is the growing bean:
> O tongue in which all honeyed liquors be,
> O voice that doth the thrush in shrillness stain,
> Do you say still, this is her promise due,
> That she is mine, as I to her am true.
>
> Gay hair, more gay than straw when harvest lies,
> Lips red and plum, as cherry's ruddy side,
> Eyes fair and great like fair great ox's eyes,
> O breast in which two white sheep swell in pride:
> Join you with me, to seal this promise due,
> That she be mine, as I to her am true.
>
> But thou white skin, as white as cruds* well pressed,

* *attent*: attentive to. *cruds*: curds.

643

So smooth as, sleekstone-like,* it smooths each part:
And thou, dear flesh, as soft as wool new dressed,
And yet as hard as brawn made hard by art:
First four but say, next four their saying seal,
But you must pay the gage of promis'd weal.[2]

'And with the conclusion of his song he embraced her about the knees. "O sweet Charita," said he, "when shall I enjoy the rest of my toiling thoughts? And when shall your blissful promise, now due, be verified with just performance?" With that I drew nearer to them and saw (for now he had lifted up his face to glass* himself in her fair eyes) that it was my master Dametas' – but here Miso interrupted his tale with railing at Dametas with all those exquisite terms which I was never good scold enough to imagine.

But Dorus, as if he had been much offended with her impatience, would proceed no further till she had vowed more stillness, 'For,' said he, 'if the first drum thus chafe you, what will you be when it comes to the blows?' Then he told her how, after many familiar entertainments betwixt them, Dametas (laying before her his great credit with the king, and withal giving her very fair presents, with promise of much more) had in the end concluded together to meet as that night at Mantinea in the Oudemian Street,[3] at Charita's uncle's house, about ten of the clock. After which bargain, Dametas had spied Dorus and, calling him to him, had with great bravery told him all his good hap, willing him in any case to return to the old witch Miso; ('for so indeed, mistress of liveliness and not of illwill, he termed you') and to make some honest excuse of his absence. ' "For," said he, kissing Charita, "if thou didst know what a life I lead with that drivel,* it would make thee even of pity receive me into thy only comfort." Now mistress,' said he, 'exercise your discretion, which if I were well assured of, I would wish you to go yourself to Mantinea, and (lying secret in some one of your gossips' houses till the time appointed come) so may you find them together, and using mercy, reform my master from his evil ways.'

There had nothing more enraged Miso than the praises Dorus gave to Charita's beauty, which made her jealousy swell the more

* *sleekstone*: smoothing-stone. *glass*: reflect. *drivel*: foul slut.

with the poison of envy. And that being increased with the presents she heard Dametas had given her (which all seemed torn out of her bowels) her hollow eyes yielded such wretched looks as one might well think Pluto at that time might have had her soul very good cheap. But when the fire of spite had fully caught hold of all her inward parts, then whosoever would have seen the picture of Alecto, or with what manner of countenance Medea killed her own children,[4] needed but take Miso for the full satisfaction of that point of his knowledge. She (that could before scarce go but supported by crutches) now flew about the house, borne up by the wings of anger: there was no one sort of mortal revenge that had ever come to her ears but presented itself now to her gentle mind. At length with few words – for her words were choked up with the rising of her revengeful heart – she ran down, and with her own hands saddled a mare of hers – a mare that seven year before had not been acquainted with the saddle – and so to Mantinea she went, casting* with herself how she might couple shame with the punishment of her accursed husband. But the person is not worthy in whose passion I should too long stand.

Therefore now must I tell you that mistress Mopsa (who was the last party Dorus was to practise his cunning withal) was at the parting of her parents attending upon the princess Pamela, whom because she found to be placed in her father's house, she knew it was for suspicion the king had of her. This made Mopsa with a right base nature (which joys to see any hard hap happen to them they deem happy) grow proud over her, and use great ostentation of her own diligence in prying curiously into each thing that Pamela did. Neither is there anything sooner overthrows a weak heart than opinion of authority, like too strong a liquor for so feeble a glass; which joined itself to the humour of envying Pamela's beauty so far, that oft she would say to herself, if she had been born a princess as well as Pamela, her perfections then should have been as well seen as Pamela's.

With this manner of woman and placed in these terms had Dorus to play his last part; which he would quickly have dispatched in tying her up in such a manner that she should little have hindered his enterprise, but that the virtuous Pamela (when

*casting: deliberating.

she saw him so minded) by countenance absolutely forbad it, resolutely determining she would not leave behind her any token of wrong, since the wrong done to herself was the best excuse of her escape. So that Dorus was compelled to take her in the manner he first thought of; and accordingly, Pamela sitting musing at the strange attempt she had condescended unto, and Mopsa hard by her looking in a glass with very partial eyes, Dorus put himself between them, and casting up his face to the top of the house, shrugging all over his body and stamping sometimes upon the ground, gave Mopsa occasion (who was as busy as a bee to know anything) to ask her lover Dorus what ailed him that made him use so strange a behaviour. He, as if his spirits had been ravished with some supernatural contemplation, stood still mute, sometimes rubbing his forehead, sometimes starting in himself, that he set Mopsa in such an itch of inquiry that she would have offered her maidenhead rather than be long kept from it.

Dorus not yet answering to the purpose, still keeping his amazement, 'O Hercules,' said he, 'resolve me in this doubt. A tree to grant one's wishes! Is this the cause of the king's solitary life? Which part shall I take? Happy in either; unhappy because I cannot know which were my best hap.'

These doubtful self-speeches made Mopsa yet in a further longing of knowing the matter; so that the pretty pig, laying her sweet burden about his neck, 'My Dorus,' said she, 'tell me these words or else I know not what will befall me. Honey Dorus, tell them me.'

Dorus having stretched her mind upon a right last:* 'Extremely loved Mopsa,' said he, 'the matters be so great as my heart fails me in the telling them; but since you hold the greatest seat in it, it is reason your desire should add life unto it.'

Therewith he told her a far fetched tale: how that many millions of years before, Jupiter, fallen out with Apollo,[5] had thrown him out of heaven, taking from him the privilege of a god; so that poor Apollo was fain to lead a very miserable life, unacquainted to work and never used to beg: that in this order, having in time learned to be Admetus' herdsman, he had (upon occasion of fetching a certain breed of beasts out of Arcadia) come to that

---

* *upon a right last*: like a shoe on its last, i.e. having got her interest to the full.

very desert where, wearied with travel, and resting himself in the boughs of a pleasant ash tree stood a little off from the lodge, he had with pitiful complaints gotten his father Jupiter's pardon, and so from that tree was received again to his golden sphere. But having that right nature of a god never to be ungrateful, to Admetus he had granted a double life: and because that tree was the chapel of his prosperous prayers, he had given it this quality, that whatsoever, of such estate and in such manner as he then was, sat down in that tree, they should obtain whatsoever they wished. This Basilius having understood by the oracle was the only cause which had made him try whether, framing himself to the state of an herdsman, he might have the privilege of wishing only granted to that degree; but that having often in vain attempted it, because indeed he was not such, he had now opened the secret to Dametas, making him swear he should wish according to his direction.

'But because,' said Dorus, 'Apollo was at that time with extreme grief muffled round about his face with a scarlet cloak Admetus had given him, and because they that must wish must be muffled in like sort and with like stuff, my master Dametas is gone I know not whither to provide him a scarlet cloak, and tomorrow doth appoint to return with it. My mistress, I cannot tell how, having gotten some inkling of it, is trudged to Mantinea to get herself a cloak before him, because she would have the first wish. My master, at his parting, of great trust* told me this secret, commanding me to see nobody should climb that tree. But now, my Mopsa,' said he, 'I have here the like cloak of mine own, and am not so very a fool, as though I keep his commandments in others, to bar myself. I rest only extremely perplexed, because having nothing in the world I wish for but the enjoying you and your favour, I think it a much pleasanter conquest to come to it by your own consent than to have it by such a charming force* as this is. Now therefore choose – since have you I will – in what sort I shall have you.'

But never child was so desirous of a gay puppet,* as Mopsa was to be in the tree, and therefore without squeamishness promising

* of great trust: in confidence. charming force: by force of magic charms. puppet: doll.

all he would, she conjured him by all her precious loves that she might have the first possession of the wishing tree, assuring him that for the enjoying her, he would never need to climb far. Dorus, to whom time was precious, made no great ceremonies with her; but helping her up to the top of the tree, from whence likewise she could ill come down without help, he muffled her round about the face so truly, that she herself could not undo it. And so he told her the manner was she should hold her mind in continual devotion to Apollo without making at all any noise, till at the furthest within twelve hours' space she should hear a voice call her by name three times; and that till the third time she must in no wise answer, 'and then you shall not need to doubt your coming down, for at that time,' said he, 'be sure to wish wisely; and in what shape soever he come unto you, speak boldly unto him, and your wish shall have as certain effect as I have a desire to enjoy your sweet loves.'

In this plight did he leave Mopsa, resolved in her heart to be the greatest lady of the world, and never after to feed of worse than frumenty.*

## CHAPTER 38

Thus Dorus, having delivered his hands of his three tormentors, took speedily the benefit of his device, and mounting the gracious Pamela upon a fair horse he had provided for her, he thrust himself forthwith into the wildest part of the desert, where he had left marks to guide him from place to place to the next seaport; disguising her very fitly with scarfs – although he rested assured he should meet that way with nobody till he came to his bark, into which he meant to enter by night. But Pamela, who, all this while transported with desire and troubled with fear, had never free scope of judgement to look with perfect consideration into her own enterprise, but even by the laws of love had bequeathed the care of herself upon him to whom she had given herself; now that the pang of desire with evident hope was quieted and most part of the fear passed, reason began to renew his shining in her heart and make her see herself in herself, and weigh with what wings she flew out of her native country and upon what ground she built so

* *frumenty*: a dish made of wheat boiled in milk with spices.

strong a determination. But love, fortified with her lover's presence, kept still his own in her heart; so that as they rid together, with her hand upon her faithful servant's shoulder, suddenly casting her bashful eyes to the ground and yet bending herself towards him (like the client that commits the cause of all his worth to a well-trusted advocate) from a mild spirit said unto him these sweetly delivered words:

'Prince Musidorus – for so my assured hope is I may justly call you, since with no other my heart would ever have yielded to go; and if so I do not rightly term you, all other words are as bootless as my deed miserable, and I as unfortunate as you wicked – my prince Musidorus, I say, now that the vehement shows of your faithful love towards me have brought my mind to answer it in so due a proportion that, contrary to all general rules of reason, I have laid in you my estate, my life, my honour: it is now your part to double your former care, and make me see your virtue no less in preserving than in obtaining, and your faith to be a faith as much in freedom as bondage. Tender now your own workmanship, and so govern your love towards me as I may still remain worthy to be loved. Your promise you remember, which here by the eternal givers of virtue I conjure you to observe. Let me be your own as I am, but by no unjust conquest. Let not our joys, which ought ever to last, be stained in our own consciences. Let no shadow of repentance steal into the sweet consideration of our mutual happiness. I have yielded to be your wife: stay then till the time that I may rightly be so: let no other defiled name burden my heart. What should I more say? If I have chosen well, all doubt is past, since your action only must determine whether I have done virtuously or shamefully in following you.'

Musidorus (that had more abundance of joy in his heart than Ulysses had what time with his own industry he stale the fatal Palladium,[1] imagined to be the only relic of Troy's safety) taking Pamela's hand, and many times kissing it, 'What I am,' said he, 'the gods I hope will shortly make your own eyes judges; and of my mind towards you, the meantime shall be my pledge unto you your contentment is dearer to me than mine own: and therefore doubt not of his mind, whose thoughts are so thralled unto you as you are to bend or slack them as it shall seem best unto you. You do wrong to yourself to make any doubt that a base estate could ever undertake so high an enterprise, or a spotted mind be able to behold your virtues. Thus much only I must confess I can never do: to make the world see you have chosen worthily, since all the world is not worthy of you.'

In such delightful discourses kept they on their journey, maintaining their hearts in that right harmony of affection which doth interchangeably deliver each to other the secret workings of their souls, till with the unused* travel the princess being weary, they lighted down in a fair thick wood which did entice them with the pleasantness of it to take their rest there. It was all of pine trees whose broad heads, meeting together, yielded a perfect shade to the ground, where their bodies gave a spacious and pleasant room to walk in. They were set in so perfect an order that every way the eye being full, yet no way was stopped. And even in the midst of them were there many sweet springs which did lose themselves upon the face of the earth. Here Musidorus drew out such provision of fruits and other cates* as he had brought for that day's repast, and laid it down upon the fair carpet of the green grass. But Pamela had much more pleasure to walk under those trees, making in their barks pretty knots which tied together the names of Musidorus and Pamela, sometimes intermixedly changing them, to Pamedorus and Musimela, with twenty other flowers of her travailing* fancies, which had bound themselves to a greater restraint than they could without much pain well endure. And to one tree (more beholding to her than the rest) she entrusted the treasure of her thoughts in these verses:

> Do not disdain, O straight up-raised pine,
> That wounding thee, my thoughts in thee I grave:
> Since that my thoughts, as straight as straightness thine,
> No smaller wound, alas, far deeper have:
>
> Deeper engraved, which salve nor time can save,
> Giv'n to my heart by more forewounded eyne:
> Thus cruel to myself, how canst thou crave
> My inward hurt should spare thy outward rine?*

* *unused*: unaccustomed. *cates*: delicacies. *travailing*: labouring. *rine*: rind, bark.

Yet still, fair tree, lift up thy stately line,
Live long, and long witness my chosen smart,
Which barr'd desires (barr'd by myself) impart;
   And in this growing-bark grow verses mine.
My heart my word, my word hath giv'n my heart:
The giver giv'n from gift shall never part.

Upon a root of the tree that the earth had left something barer
than the rest, she wrote this couplet:

        Sweet root, say thou, the root of my desire
        Was virtue clad in constant love's attire.

Musidorus, seeing her fancies drawn up to such pleasant contemplations, accompanied her in them, and made the trees as well
bear the badges of his passions, as this song engraved in them did
testify:

   You goodly pines, which still with brave ascent
In nature's pride your heads to heav'nward heave,
   Though you besides such graces earth hath lent,
Of some late grace a greater grace receive,

   By her who was (O blessed you) content
With her fair hand your tender barks to cleave,
   And so by you (O blessed you) hath sent
Such piercing words as no thoughts else conceive:

   Yet yield your grant: a baser hand may leave
His thoughts in you, where so sweet thoughts were spent;
   For how would you the mistress' thoughts bereave
Of waiting thoughts all to her service meant?

   Nay higher thoughts (though thralled thoughts) I call
My thoughts then hers, who first your rine did rent,
   Than hers, to whom my thoughts alonely* thrall
Rising from low, are to the highest bent;
   Where hers, whom worth makes highest over all
Coming from her, cannot but downward fall.

            * *alonely*: solely.

While Pamela, sitting her down under one of them, and making a posy of the fair undergrowing flowers, filled Musidorus' ears with the heavenly sound of her music which before he had never heard, so that it seemed unto him a new assault given to the castle of his heart, already conquered: which to signify, and withal reply to her sweet notes, he sang in a kind of still but ravishing tune a few verses. Her song was this, and his reply follows.

PAMELA: Like diverse flowers, whose divers beauties serve
   To deck the earth with his well-coloured weed,
     Though each of them his private form preserve,
   Yet joining forms one sight of beauty breed:

     Right so my thoughts, whereon my heart I feed;
   Right so my inward parts, and outward glass,
     Though each possess a diverse working kind,
   Yet all well knit to one fair end do pass:
     That he, to whom these sundry gifts I bind,
     All what I am, still one, his own, do find.

MUSIDORUS: All what you are, still one, his own to find,
   You that are born to be the world's eye,
     What were it else but to make each thing blind,
   And to the sun with waxen wings to fly?[2]

   No, no, such force with my small force to try
   Is not my skill, or reach of mortal mind.
     Call me but yours, my title is most high:
   Hold me most yours, then my long suit is sign'd.

   You none can claim but you yourself aright,
   For you do pass yourself, in virtue's might:
     So both are yours: I bound with gaged heart;
   You only yours, too far beyond desert.

In this virtuous wantonness, suffering their minds to descend to each tender enjoying their united thoughts, Pamela, having tasted of the fruits, and growing extreme sleepy (having been long kept from it with the perplexity of her dangerous attempt) laying her head in his lap, was invited by him to sleep with these softly uttered verses:

Lock up, fair lids, the treasure of my heart,
Preserve those beams, this age's only light:
   To her sweet sense, sweet sleep some ease impart,
Her sense too weak to bear her spirit's might.

And while, O sleep, thou closest up her sight,
(Her sight where love did forge her fairest dart)
   O harbour all her parts in easeful plight:
Let no strange dream make her fair body start.

But yet, O dream, if thou wilt not depart
In this rare subject from thy common right,
But wilt thyself in such a seat delight,
   Then take my shape, and play a lover's part:
Kiss her from me, and say unto her sprite,
Till her eyes shine, I live in darkest night.

The sweet Pamela was brought into a sweet sleep with this
song, which gave Musidorus opportunity at leisure to behold her
excellent beauties.[3] He thought her fair forehead was a field where
all his fancies fought, and every hair of her head seemed a strong
chain that tied him. Her fair lids then hiding her fairer eyes
seemed unto him sweet boxes of mother-of-pearl, rich in themselves, but containing in them far richer jewels. Her cheeks with
their colour most delicately mixed would have entertained his
eyes somewhile, but that the roses of her lips (whose separating
was wont to be accompanied with most wise speeches) now by
force drew his sight to mark how prettily they lay one over the
other, uniting their divided beauties; and through them the eye of
his fancy delivered to his memory the lying (as in ambush) under
her lips of those armed ranks, all armed in most pure white, and
keeping the most precise order of military discipline. And lest this
beauty might seem the picture of some excellent artificer, forth
there stale a soft breath, carrying good testimony of her inward
sweetness: and so stealing it came out, as it seemed loth to leave
his contentful mansion but that it hoped to be drawn in again to
that well-closed paradise – which did so tyrannize over Musidorus'
affects that he was compelled to put his face as low to hers as he
could, sucking the breath with such joy that he did determine in

himself there had been no life to a chameleon's,[4] if he might be suffered to enjoy that food.[5]

But long he was not suffered, being within a while interrupted by the coming of a company of clownish villains, armed with divers sorts of weapons, and for the rest, both in face and apparel so forwasted that they seemed to bear a great conformity with the savages: who (miserable in themselves, taught to increase their mischiefs in other bodies' harms) came with such cries that they both awaked Pamela and made Musidorus turn unto them full of a most violent rage, with the look of a she-tiger when her whelps are stolen away.

## CHAPTER 39

But Zelmane, whom I left in the cave hardly bestead* (having both great wits and stirring passions to deal with) makes me lend her my pen awhile to see with what dexterity she could put by her dangers. For having in one instant both to resist rage and go beyond wisdom (being to deal with a lady that had her wits awake in everything but in helping her own hurt) she saw now no other remedy in her case but to qualify her rage with hope, and to satisfy her wit with plainness. Yet lest too abrupt falling into it should yield too great advantage unto her, she thought good to come to it by degrees with this kind of insinuation:

'Your wise but very dark speeches, most excellent lady, are woven up in so intricate a manner as I know not how to proportion mine answer unto them, so are your prayers mixed with threats, and so is the show of your love hidden with the name of revenge, the natural effect of mortal hatred. You seem displeased with the opinion you have of my disguising, and yet if I be not disguised, you must needs be much more displeased. Hope then (the only succour of perplexed minds) being quite cut off, you desire my affection, and yet you yourself think my affection already bestowed. You pretend* cruelty before you have the subjection, and are jealous of keeping that which as yet you have not gotten. And that which is strangest in your jealousy is both the injustice of it (in being loth that should come to your daughter

* *hardly bestead*: hard-pressed. *pretend*: attempt.

which you deem good) and the vainness, since you two are in so diverse respects that there is no necessity one of you should fall to be a bar to the other. For neither (if I be such as you fancy) can I marry you, which must needs be the only end I can aspire to in her: neither need the marrying of her keep me from a grateful consideration how much you honour me in the love you vouchsafe to bear me.'

Gynecia, to whom the fearful agonies she still lived in made any small reprieval sweet, did quickly find her words falling to a better way of comfort; and therefore with a mind ready to show nothing could make it rebellious against Zelmane but too extreme tyranny, she thus said:

'Alas, too much beloved Zelmane, the thoughts are but outflowings of the mind, and the tongue is but a servant of the thoughts. Therefore marvel not that my words suffer contrarieties, since my mind doth hourly suffer in itself whole armies of mortal adversaries. But, alas, if I had the use of mine own reason, then should I not need, for want of it, to find myself in this desperate mischief: but because my reason is vanished, so have I likewise no power to correct my unreasonableness. Do you therefore accept the protection of my mind which hath no other resting place, and drive it not, by being unregarded, to put itself into unknown extremities. I desire but to have my affection answered, and to have a right reflection of my love in you. That granted, assure yourself mine own love will easily teach me to seek your contentment, and make me think my daughter a very mean price to keep still in mine eyes the food of my spirits. But take heed that contempt drive me not into despair, the most violent cause of that miserable effect.'

Zelmane (that already saw some fruit of her last determined fancy, so far as came to a mollifying of Gynecia's rage) seeing no other way to satisfy suspicion (which was held open with the continual pricks of love) resolved now with plainness to win trust, which trust she might after deceive with a greater subtilty. Therefore looking upon her with a more relenting grace than ever she had done before, pretending a great bashfulness before she could come to confess such a fault, she thus said unto her:

'Most worthy lady, I did never think till now that pity of

another could make me betray myself, nor that the sound of words could overthrow any wise body's determination. But your words, I think, have charmed me, and your grace bewitched me. Your compassion makes me open my heart to you and leave unharboured mine own thoughts. For proof of it, I will disclose my greatest secret, which well you might suspect but never know, and so have your wandering hope in a more painful wilderness, being neither way able to be lodged in a perfect resolution. I will, I say, unwrap my hidden estate, and after make you judge of it, perchance director. The truth is, I am a man: nay, I will say further to you, I am born a prince. And to make up your mind in a thorough understanding of me, since I came to this place, I may not deny I have had some sprinkling of I know not what good liking to my lady Philoclea. For how could I ever imagine the heavens would have rained down so much of your favour upon me, and of that side there was a show of possible hope, the most comfortable counsellor of love? The cause of this my changed attire was a journey two years ago I made among the Amazons, where, having sought to try my unfortunate valour, I met not one in all the country but was too hard for me, till in the end, in the presence of their queen Marpesia, I (hoping to prevail against her) challenged an old woman of fourscore years to fight on horseback to the uttermost with me: who, having overthrown me, for the saving of my life made me swear I should go like an unarmed Amazon till the coming of my beard did, with the discharge of my oath, deliver me of that bondage.'

Here Zelmane ended, not coming to a full conclusion because she would see what it wrought in Gynecia's mind, having in her speech sought to win a belief of her and (if it might be) by disgrace of herself to diminish Gynecia's affection. For the first it had much prevailed: but Gynecia, whose end of loving her was not her fighting, neither could her love (too deeply grounded) receive diminishment; and besides, she had seen herself sufficient proofs of Zelmane's admirable prowess. Therefore slightly* passing over that point of her feigned dishonour, but taking good hold of the confessing her manly sex, with the shamefast look of that suitor who, having already obtained much, is yet forced by want

* *slightly*: cunningly.

to demand more, put forth her sorrowful suit in these words:

'The gods,' said she, 'reward thee for thy virtuous pity of my overladen soul, who yet hath received some breath of comfort, by finding thy confession to maintain some possibility of my languishing hope. But alas, as they who seek to enrich themselves by mineral industry, the first labour is to find the mine, which to their cheerful comfort being found, if after any unlooked for stop or casual impediment keep them from getting the desired ore, they are so much the more grieved as the late conceived hope adds torment to their former want: so falls it out with me (happy or hapless woman, as it pleaseth you to ordain) who am now either to receive some guerdon of my most woeful labours or to return into a more wretched darkness, having had some glimmering of my blissful sun. O Zelmane, tread not upon a soul that lies under your foot. Let not the abasing of myself make me more base in your eyes, but judge of me according to that I am and have been, and let my errors be made excusable by the immortal name of love.'

With that, under a feigned rage tearing her clothes, she discovered some parts of her fair body, which if Zelmane's heart had not been so fully possessed as there was no place left for any new guest, no doubt it would have yielded to that gallant assault. But Zelmane, so much the more arming her determination as she saw such force threatened, yet still remembering she must wade betwixt constancy and courtesy, embracing Gynecia and once or twice kissing her:

'Dear lady,' said she, 'he were a great enemy to himself that would refuse such an offer in the purchase of which a man's life was blessedly bestowed. Nay, how can I ever yield due recompense for so excessive a favour? But having nothing to give you but myself, take that – I must confess, a small but a very free gift. What other affection soever I have had shall give place to as great perfection, working besides upon the bond of gratefulness. The gods forbid I should be so foolish as not to see, or so wicked as not to remember, how much my small deserts are over-balanced by your unspeakable goodness. Nay, happy may I well account my mishap among the Amazons, since that dishonour hath been so true a path to my greatest honour, and the changing of my out-

ward raiment hath clothed my mind in such inward contentation.* Take therefore, noble lady, as much comfort to your
heart as the full commandment of me can yield you. Wipe your
fair eyes and keep them for nobler services. And now I will presume thus much to say unto you, that you make of yourself for
my sake that my joys of my new obtained riches may be accomplished in you. But let us leave this place lest you be too long
missed, and henceforward quiet your mind from any further care,
for I will now, (to my too much joy), take the charge upon me
within few days to work your satisfaction and my felicity.'

Thus much she said, and withal led Gynecia out of the cave, for
well she saw the boiling mind of Gynecia did easily apprehend the
fitness of that lonely place. But indeed this direct promise of a
short space, joined with the cumbersome familiar* of womankind
(I mean modesty) stayed so Gynecia's mind that she took thus
much at that present for good payment, remaining with a painful
joy and a wearisome kind of comfort; not unlike to the condemned
prisoner, whose mind still running upon the violent arrival of his
cruel death, hears that his pardon is promised but not yet signed.
In this sort they both issued out of that obscure mansion, Gynecia
already half persuaded in herself (O weakness of human conceit)
that Zelmane's affection was turned towards her. For such, alas,
we are all: in such a mould are we cast, that with the too much
love we bear ourselves being first our own flatterers, we are easily
hooked with other's flattery, we are easily persuaded of other's
love.

But Zelmane, who had now to play her prize, seeing no way
things could long remain in that state and now finding her promise
had tied her trial to a small compass of time, began to throw her
thoughts into each corner of her invention how she might achieve
her life's enterprise. For well she knew deceit cannot otherwise be
maintained but by deceit: and how to deceive such heedful eyes,
and how to satisfy, and yet not satisfy such hopeful desires it was
no small skill. But both their thoughts were called from themselves with the sight of Basilius, who then lying down by his
daughter Philoclea upon the fair though natural bed of green

* contentation: satisfaction. familiar: inmate.

grass, seeing the sun what speed he made to leave our west to do his office in the other hemisphere, his inward muses made him in his best music sing this Madrigal:

> Why dost thou haste away
> O Titan fair, the giver of the day?
> Is it to carry news
> To western wights, what stars in east appear?
> Or dost thou think that here
> Is left a sun whose beams thy place may use?
> Yet stay and well peruse
> What be her gifts that make her equal thee;
> Bend all thy light to see
> In earthly clothes enclos'd a heavenly spark.
> Thy running course cannot such beauties mark.
> No, no, thy motions be
> Hastened from us with bar of shadow dark,
> Because that thou, the author of our sight,
> Disdain'st we see thee stain'd with other's light.

And having ended, 'Dear Philoclea,' said he, 'sing something that may divert my thoughts from the continual task of their ruinous harbour.'* She, obedient to him, and not unwilling to disburden her secret passion, made her sweet voice be heard in these words:

> O stealing time, the subject of delay,
> (Delay, the rack of unrefrain'd desire)
> What strange design hast thou my hopes to stay,
> My hopes which do but to mine own aspire?
>
> Mine own? O word on whose sweet sound doth prey
> My greedy soul, with gripe of inward fire:
> Thy title great I justly challenge may,
> Since in such phrase his faith he did attire.
>
> O time, become the chariot of my joys:
> As thou drawest on, so let my bliss draw near,
> Each moment lost, part of my hap destroys.

* *ruinous harbour*: painful place where they rest.

Thou art the father of occasion dear:
   Join with thy son to ease my long annoys;
In speedy help thank-worthy friends appear.


Philoclea brake off her song as soon as her mother with Zelmane came near unto them, rising up with a kindly bashfulness, being not ignorant of the spite her mother bare her, and stricken with the sight of that person whose love made all those troubles seem fair flowers of her dearest garland – nay, rather, all these troubles made the love increase. For as the arrival of enemies makes a town so fortify itself as ever after it remains stronger, so that a man may say enemies were no small cause to the town's strength; so to a mind once fixed in a well-pleased determination, who hopes by annoyance to overthrow it doth but teach it to knit together all his best grounds, and so perchance of a changeable purpose make an unchangeable resolution.

But no more did Philoclea see the wonted signs of Zelmane's affection towards her. She thought she saw another light in her eyes, with a bold and careless look upon her, (which was wont to be dazzled with her beauty) and the framing of her courtesies rather ceremonious* than affectionate: and that which worst liked her was that it proceeded with such quiet settledness as it rather threatened a full purpose* than any sudden passion. She found her behaviour bent altogether to her mother, and presumed in herself she discerned the well-acquainted face of his fancies now turned to another subject. She saw her mother's worthiness, and too well knew her affection. These, joining their diverse working powers together in her mind (but yet a prentice in the painful mystery of passions) brought Philoclea into a new traverse* of her thoughts, and made her keep her careful look the more attentive upon Zelmane's behaviour: who indeed (though with much pain, and condemning herself to commit a sacrilege against the sweet saint that lived in her inmost temple) yet strengthening herself in it (being the surest way to make Gynecia bite of her other baits) did so quite over-rule all wonted shows of love to Philoclea and convert them to Gynecia, that the part she played did work in

* *ceremonious*: formally polite. *threatened a full purpose*: gave promise of a resolved intention. *a new traverse*: a new tack.

both a full and lively persuasion. To Gynecia, such excessive comfort as the being preferred to a rival doth deliver to swelling desire. But to the delicate Philoclea, whose calm thoughts were unable to nourish any strong debate, it gave so stinging a hurt that, fainting under the force of her inward torment, she withdrew herself to the lodge and there, weary of supporting her own burden, cast herself upon her bed, suffering her sorrow to melt itself into abundance of tears. At length closing her eyes, as if each thing she saw was a picture of her mishap, and turning upon her heart-side which, with vehement panting, did summon her to consider her fortune, she thus bemoaned herself:

'Alas, Philoclea, is this the price of all thy pains? Is this the reward of thy given-away liberty? Hath too much yielding bred cruelty, or can too great acquaintance make me held for a stranger? Hath the choosing of a companion made me left alone; or doth granting desire cause the desire to be neglected? Alas, despised Philoclea, why didst thou not hold thy thoughts in their simple course, and content thyself with the love of thine own virtue, which would never have betrayed thee? Ah, silly* fool, didst thou look for truth in him that with his own mouth confessed his falsehood, for plain proceeding in him that still goes disguised? They say the falsest men will yet bear outward shows of a pure mind. But he that even outwardly bears the badge of treachery, what hells of wickedness must needs in the depth be contained? But, O, wicked mouth of mine, how darest thou thus blaspheme the ornament of the earth, the vessel of all virtue? O wretch that I am, that will anger the gods in dispraising their most excellent work! O no, no, there was no fault but in me, that could ever think so high eyes would look so low, or so great perfections would stain themselves with my unworthiness. Alas, why could I not see I was too weak a band to tie so heavenly a heart, I was not fit to limit the infinite course of his wonderful destinies? Was it ever like,* that upon only Philoclea his thoughts should rest? Ah, silly soul, that couldst please thyself with so impossible an imagination! An universal happiness is to flow from him. How was I so inveigled to hope I might be the mark of such a mind? He did thee no wrong, O Philoclea, he did thee no wrong. It was thy

* *silly:* ignorant. *like:* likely.

weakness to fancy the beams of the sun should give light to no eyes but thine!

'And yet, O Prince Pyrocles, for whom I may well begin to hate myself but can never leave to love thee, what triumph canst thou make of this conquest? What spoils wilt thou carry away of this my undeserved overthrow? Could thy force find out no fitter field than the feeble mind of a poor maid, who at the first sight did wish thee all happiness? Shall it be said the mirror of mankind hath been employed to destroy a hurtless gentlewoman? O Pyrocles, Pyrocles, let me yet call thee before the judgement of thine own virtue. Let me be accepted for a plaintiff in a cause which concerns my life. What need hadst thou to arm thy face with the enchanting mask of thy painted passions? What need hadst thou to fortify thy excellencies with so exquisite a cunning in making our own arts betray us? What needest thou descend so far from thy incomparable worthiness as to take on the habit of weak womankind? Was all this to win the undefended castle of a friend which, being won, thou wouldst after raze? Could so small a cause allure thee, or did not so unjust a cause stop thee? O me, what say I more? This is my case; my love hates me, virtue deals wickedly with me, and he does me wrong whose doings I can never account a wrong.'

With that, the sweet lady turning herself upon her weary bed, she haply* saw a lute, upon the belly of which Gynecia had written this song, what time Basilius imputed her jealous motions to proceed of the doubt she had of his untimely loves. Under which veil she (contented to cover her never ceasing anguish) had made the lute a monument of her mind; which Philoclea had never much marked, till now the fear of a competitor more stirred her than before the care of a mother.

The verses were these:

> My lute, within thyself thy tunes enclose;
> Thy mistress' song is now a sorrow's cry,
>     Her hand benumb'd with fortune's daily blows,
> Her mind amaz'd can neither's help apply.
>     Wear these my words as mourning weeds of woes;

* *haply:* by chance.

Black ink becomes the state wherein I die,
    And though my moans be not in music bound,
    Of written griefs yet be the silent ground.[1]

The world doth yield such ill-consorted* shows,
With circled course, which no wise stay can try,
    That childish stuff which knows not friends from foes,
    (Better despis'd) bewonder gazing eye.
    Thus noble gold down to the bottom goes,
When worthless cork aloft doth floating lie.
      Thus in thyself least strings are loudest found,
      And lowest stops do yield the highest sound.

Philoclea read them, and throwing down the lute, 'Is this the legacy you have bequeathed me, O kind mother of mine?' said she. 'Did you bestow the light upon me for this? Or did you bear me to be the author of my burial! A trim purchase you have made of your own shame: robbed your daughter to ruin yourself! The birds unreasonable yet use so much reason as to make nests for their tender young ones. My cruel mother turns me out of mine own harbour. Alas, plaint boots not,* for my case can receive no help; for who should give me help? Shall I fly to my parents? They are my murderers. Shall I go to him who, already being won and lost, must needs have killed all pity? Alas, I can bring no new intercessions: he knows already what I am is his. Shall I come home again to myself? O me, contemned wretch; I have given away myself.'

With that the poor soul beat her breast as if that had been guilty of her faults, neither thinking of revenge nor studying for remedy, but, sweeet creature, gave grief a free dominion, keeping her chamber a few days after, not needing to feign herself sick, feeling even in her soul the pangs of extreme pain. But little did Gynecia reck that, neither when she saw her go away from them, neither when she after found that sickness made her hide her fair face, so much had fancy prevailed against nature.

    * *ill-consorted*: inharmonious. *plaint boots not*: lamenting is of no avail.

## CHAPTER 40

But O you that have ever known how tender to every motion love
makes the lover's heart, how he measures all his joys upon her
contentment and doth with respectful eye hang all his behaviour
upon her eyes; judge, I pray you, now of Zelmane's troubled
thoughts when she saw Philoclea with an amazed kind of sorrow
carry away her sweet presence, and easily found (so happy a conjecture unhappy affection hath) that her demeanour was guilty of
that trespass. There was never foolish soft-hearted mother (that,
forced to beat her child, did weep first for his pains, and doing that
she was loth to do, did repent before she began) did find half that
motion in her weak mind as Zelmane did, now that she was forced
by reason to give an outward blow to her passions, and for the
lending of a small time, to seek the usury of all her desires.[1] The
unkindness she conceived Philoclea might conceive did wound her
soul: each tear she doubted she spent drowned all her comfort. Her
sickness was a death unto her. Often would she speak to the image
of Philoclea which lived and ruled in the highest of her inward
part, and use vehement oaths and protestations unto her that
nothing should ever falsify the free chosen vow she had made.
Often would she desire her that she would look well to Pyrocles'
heart, for as for her, she had no more interest in it to bestow it any
way: 'Alas,' would she say, 'only Philoclea, hast thou not so
much feeling of thine own force as to know no new conqueror can
prevail against thy conquests? Was ever any dazzled with the
moon that had used his eyes to the beams of the sun? Is he carried
away with a greedy desire of acorns that hath had his senses
ravished with a garden of most delightful fruits? O Philoclea, Philoclea, be thou but as merciful a princess to my mind as thou art a
true possessor, and I shall have as much cause of gladness as thou
hast no cause of misdoubting. O no, no, when a man's own heart is
the gage of his debt, when a man's own thoughts are willing
witnesses to his promise, lastly, when a man is the jailor over
himself, there is little doubt of breaking credit, and less doubt of
such an escape.'

In this combat of Zelmane's doubtful imaginations, in the end
reason, well-backed with the vehement desire to bring her matters

soon to the desired haven, did over-rule the boiling of her inward kindness, though, as I say, with such a manifest strife that both Basilius' and Gynecia's well-waiting eyes had marked her muses had laboured in deeper subject than ordinary: which she likewise perceiving they had perceived, awaking herself out of those thoughts, and principally caring how to satisfy Gynecia (whose judgement and passion she stood most in regard of) bowing her head to her attentive ears, 'Madam,' said she, 'with practice of my thoughts, I have found out a way by which your contentment shall draw on my happiness.'

Gynecia, delivering in her face as thankful a joyfulness as her heart could hold, said it was then time to retire themselves to their rest, for what with riding abroad the day before and late sitting up for eclogues, their bodies had dearly purchased that night's quiet.

So went they home to their lodge, Zelmane framing of both sides bountiful measures of loving countenances to either's joy and neither's jealousy: to the especial comfort of Basilius, whose weaker bowels were straight full with the least liquor of hope; so that still holding her by the hand and sometimes tickling it, he went by her with the most gay conceits that ever had entered his brains, growing now so hearted in his resolution that he little respected Gynecia's presence, but (with a lustier note than wonted) clearing his voice and cheering his spirits, looking still upon Zelmane (whom now the moon did beautify with her shining almost at the full) as if her eyes had been his song-book, he did the message of his mind in singing these verses:

> When two suns do appear,
> Some say it doth betoken wonders near,
> As prince's loss or change:
> Two gleaming suns of splendour like I see,
> And seeing feel in me
> Of prince's heart quite lost the ruin strange.
>
> But now each where doth range
> With ugly cloak the dark envious night,
> Who, full of guilty spite
> Such living beams should her black seat assail,
> Too weak for them, our weaker sight doth veil.

'No,' says fair moon, 'my light
Shall bar that wrong, and though it not prevail
Like to my brother's rays, yet those I send
Hurt not the face, which nothing can amend.'

And by that time being come to the lodge and visited the sweet Philoclea, with much less than natural care of the parents and much less than wonted kindness of Zelmane, each party, full fraught with diversely working fancies, made their pillows weak props of their over-loaden heads. Yet of all other were Zelmane's brains most turmoiled, troubled with love both active and passive, and lastly and especially, with care how to use her short limited time to the best purpose by some wise and happy diverting her two lovers' unwelcome desires. Zelmane, having had the night her only counsellor in the busy enterprise she was to undertake, and having all that time mused and yet not fully resolved how she might join prevailing with preventing, was offended with the day's bold entry into her chamber, as if he had now by custom grown an assured bringer of evil news: which she, taking a cittern to her, did lay to Aurora's charge, with these well sung verses:

Aurora,* now thou showest thy blushing light,
(Which oft to hope lays out a guileful bait,[2]
That trusts in time to find the way aright,
To ease those pains which on desire do wait)

Blush on for shame, that still with thee do light
On pensive souls (instead of restful bait)
Care upon care (instead of doing right)
To over pressed breasts, more grievous weight.

As oh! myself, whose woes are never light,
(Tied to the stake of doubt) strange passions bait,
While thy known course, observing nature's right,
Stirs me to think what dangers lie in wait:
For mischiefs great day after day doth show,
Make me still fear thy fair appearing show.

*Aurora: the dawn.

'Alas,' said she, 'am I not run into a strange gulf, that am fain for love to hurt her I love, and because I detest the others, to please them I detest? O only Philoclea, whose beauty is matched with nothing but with the unspeakable beauty of thy fairest mind, if thou didst see upon what a rack my tormented soul is set, little would you think I had any scope now to leap to any new change.'

With that with hasty hands she got herself up, turning her sight to everything, as if change of object might help her invention. So went she again to the cave, where forthwith it came into her head, that should be the fittest place to perform her exploit, of which she had now a kind of confused conceit, although she had not set down in her fancy the meeting with each particularity that might fall out. But as the painter doth at the first but show a rude proportion of the thing he imitates, which after with more curious hand he draws to the representing each lineament, so had her thoughts, beating about it continually, received into them a ground-plot of her device, although she had not in each part shaped it according to a full determination. But in this sort having early visited the morning's beauty in those pleasant deserts, she came to the king and queen, and told them that for the performance of certain country devotions (which only were to be exercised in solitariness) she did desire their leave she might for a few days lodge herself in the cave, the fresh sweetness of which did greatly delight her in that hot country; and that for that small space they would not otherwise trouble themselves in visiting her but at such times as she would come to wait upon them – which should be every day at certain hours: neither should it be long she would desire this privileged absence of them.

They (whose minds had already taken out that lesson, perfectly to yield a willing obedience to all her desires) with consenting countenance made her soon see her pleasure was a law unto them; both indeed inwardly glad of it: Basilius hoping that her dividing herself from them might yet give him some freer occasion of coming in secret unto her, whose favourable face had lately strengthened his fainting courage; but Gynecia of all other most joyous, holding herself assured that this was but a prologue to the play she had promised her.

Thus both flattering themselves with diversely grounded hopes, they rang a bell, which served to call certain poor women (which ever lay in cabins not far off to do the household services of both lodges, and never came to either but being called for) and commanded them to carry forthwith Zelmane's bed and furniture of her chamber into the pleasant cave, and to deck it up as finely as it was possible for them, that their soul's rest might rest her body to her best pleasing manner. That was with all diligence performed of them, and Zelmane already in possession of her new-chosen lodging where she, like one of Vesta's* nuns, entertained herself for a few days in all show of straitness;* yet once a day coming to do her duty to the king and queen, in whom the seldomness of the sight increased the more unquiet longing, though somewhat qualified as her countenance was decked* to either of them with more comfort than wonted – especially to Gynecia, who seeing her wholly neglecting her daughter Philoclea, had now promised herself a full possession of Zelmane's heart, still expecting the fruit of the happy and hoped for invention. But both she and Basilius kept such a continual watch about the precincts of the cave, that either of them was a bar to the other from having any secret communing with Zelmane.

While in the meantime the sweet Philoclea (forgotten of her father, despised of her mother, and in appearance left of Zelmane) had yielded up her soul to be a prey to sorrow and unkindness, not with raging conceit of revenge – as had passed through the stout and wise heart of her mother – but with a kindly meekness taking upon her the weight of her own woes, and suffering them to have so full a course as it did exceedingly weaken the estate of her body. As well for which cause, as for that she could not see Zelmane without expressing (more than she would) how far now her love was imprisoned in extremity of sorrow, she bound herself first to the limits of her own chamber, and after (grief breeding sickness) of her bed. But Zelmane, having now a full liberty to cast about every way how to bring her conceived attempt to a desired success, was oft so perplexed with the manifold difficulty of it, that sometimes she would resolve by force to take her away, though it were with the death of her parents; sometimes to go

* *Vesta*: patroness of the vestal virgins. *straitness*: austerity. *decked*: beautified.

away herself with Musidorus and bring both their forces, so to win her.

But lastly,* even the same day that Musidorus, by feeding the humour of his three loathsome guardians, had stolen away the princess Pamela (whether it were that love meant to match them every way, or that her friend's example had holpen her invention, or that indeed Zelmane forbare to practise her device till she found her friend had passed through his) – the same day, I say, she resolved on a way to rid out of the lodge her two cumbersome lovers, and in the night to carry away Philoclea – whereunto she was assured her own love, no less that her sister's, would easily win her consent; hoping that although their abrupt parting had not suffered her to demand of Musidorus which way he meant to direct his journey, yet either they should by some good fortune find him, or (if that course failed) yet they might well recover some town of the Helots near the frontiers of Arcadia, who, being newly again up in arms against the nobility, she knew would be as glad of her presence, as she of their protection.

Therefore having taken order for all things requisite for their going, and first put on a slight under-suit of man's apparel (which before for such purposes she had provided) she curiously trimmed herself to the beautifying of her beauties, that being now at her last trial she might come unto it in her bravest armour. And so putting on that kind of mild countenance which doth encourage the looker-on to hope for a gentle answer, according to her late-received manner, she left the pleasant darkness of her melancholy cave to go take her dinner of the King and Queen, and give unto them both a pleasant food of seeing the owner of their desires. But even as the Persians were anciently wont to leave no rising sun unsaluted, but as his fair beams appeared clearer unto them would they more heartily rejoice, laying upon them a great foretoken of their following fortunes; so was there no time that Zelmane encountered their eyes with her beloved presence, but that it bred a kind of burning devotion in them, yet so much the more gladding their greedy souls as her countenance were cleared with more favour unto them. Which now being determinately framed to the greatest descent of kindness, it took such hold of her unfortunate

* *lastly*: in the end.

lovers that (like children about a tender father from a long voyage
returned, with lovely childishness hang about him, and yet with
simple fear measure by his countenance how far he accepts their
boldness) so were these now thrown into so serviceable an
affection that the turning of Zelmane's eye was a strong stern*
enough to all their motions, wending no way but as the enchanting force of it guided them. But having made a light repast of the
pleasant fruits of that country, interlarding their food with such
manner of general discourses as lovers are wont to cover their
passions in when respect of a third person keeps them from plain
particulars, at the earnest entreaty of Basilius, Zelmane, first saluting the muses with a base viol hung hard by her, sent this
ambassade* in versified music to both her ill-requited lovers:

> Beauty hath force to catch the human sight;
> Sight doth bewitch the fancy evil awaked;
>    Fancy, we feel, includes all passion's might;
> Passion rebell'd oft reason's strength hath shaked.
>
> No wonder then, though sight my sight did taint,
> And though thereby my fancy was infected,
>    Though, yoked so, my mind with sickness faint,
> Had reason's weight for passion's ease rejected.
>
> But now the fit is past, and time hath giv'n
> Leisure to weigh what due desert requireth.
>    All thoughts so sprung are from their dwelling driv'n,
> And wisdom to his wonted seat aspireth,
>      Crying in me: 'Eye-hopes deceitful prove:
>      Things rightly priz'd, love is the band of love.'

And after her song with an affected modesty she threw down
her eye, as if the conscience of a secret grant her inward mind
made had suddenly cast a bashful veil over her. Which Basilius
finding, and thinking now was the time to urge his painful petition, beseeching his wife with more careful eye to accompany his
sickly daughter Philoclea, being rid for that time of her (who was
content to grant him any scope, that she might after have the like

* stern: director. ambassade: message.

freedom) with a gesture governed by the force of his passions, making his knees best supporters, he thus said unto her:

'If either,' said he, 'O lady of my life, my deadly pangs could bear delay or that this were the first time the same were manifested unto you, I would now but maintain still the remembrance of my misfortune without urging any further reward than time and pity might procure for me. But alas, since my martyrdom is no less painful than manifest, and that I no more feel the miserable danger than you know the assured truth thereof, why should my tongue deny his service to my heart? Why should I fear the breath of my words, who daily feel the flame of your works? Embrace in your sweet consideration, I beseech you, the misery of my case. Acknowledge yourself to be the cause, and think it is reason for you to redress the effects. Alas, let not certain imaginative rules, whose truth stands but upon opinion, keep so wise a mind from gratefulness and mercy, whose never-failing laws nature hath planted in us. I plainly lay my death unto you, the death of him that loves you, the death of him whose life you may save. Say your absolute determination, for hope itself is a pain while it is over-mastered with fear; and if you do resolve to be cruel, yet is the speediest condemnation, as in evils, most welcome.'

Zelmane, who had fully set to herself the train she would keep, yet knowing that who soonest means to yield doth well to make the bravest parley, keeping her countenance aloft:

'Noble prince,' said she, 'your words are too well couched to come out of a restless mind, and thanked be the Gods, your face threatens no danger of death. These are but those swelling speeches which give the uttermost name to every trifle, which all were worth nothing if they were not enamelled with the goodly outside of love. Truly love were very unlovely if it were half so deadly as you lovers (still living) term it. I think well it may have a certain childish vehemency which, for the time, to one desire will engage all the soul, so long as it lasteth. But with what impatience you yourself show, who confess the hope of it a pain, and think your own desire so unworthy as you would fain be rid of it, and so with over-much love sue hard for a hasty refusal.'

'A refusal!' cried out Basilius, amazed withal but pierced with the last. 'Now assure yourself whensoever you use that word definitively, it will be the undoubted doom of my approaching death. And then shall your own experience know in me how soon the spirits, dried up with anguish, leave the performance of their ministry whereupon our life dependeth. But alas, what a cruelty is this not only to torment but to think the torment slight! The terriblest tyrants would say by no man they killed, he died not, nor by no man they punished, that he escaped free; for of all other, there is least hope of mercy where there is no acknowledging of the pain, and with like cruelty are my words, breathed out from a flamy heart, accounted as messengers of a quiet mind. If I speak nothing, I choke myself and am in no way of relief; if simply, neglected; if confusedly, not understood. If by the bending together all my inward powers they bring forth any lively expressing of that they truly feel, that is a token (forsooth) the thoughts are at too much leisure. Thus is silence desperate, folly punished, and wit suspected – but indeed it is vain to say any more, for words can bind no belief. Lady, I say, determine of me. I must confess I cannot bear this battle in my mind, and therefore let me soon know what I may account of myself; for it is a hell of dolours when the mind, still in doubt for want of resolution, can make no resistance.'

'Indeed,' answered Zelmane, 'if I should grant to your request, I should show an example in myself that I esteem the holy band of chastity to be but an imaginative rule, as you termed it, and not the truest observance of nature, the most noble commandment that mankind can have over themselves, as indeed both learning teacheth and inward feeling assureth. But first shall Zelmane's grave become her marriage bed before my soul shall consent to his own shame, before I will leave a mark in myself of an unredeemable trespass. And yet must I confess that if ever my heart were stirred, it hath been with the manifest and manifold shows of the misery you live in for me. For in truth so it is, nature gives not to us, her degenerate children, any more general precept than one to help the other, one to feel a true compassion of the other's mishap. But yet if I were never so contented to speak with you (for further, never, O Basilius, look for at my hands) I know not how you can avoid your wife's jealous attendance but that her suspicion shall bring my honour into question.'

Basilius, whose small sails the least wind did fill, was forthwith as far gone into a large promising himself his desire as before he was stricken down with a threatened denial. And therefore bending his brows, as though he were not a man to take the matter as he had done, 'What,' said he, 'shall my wife become my mistress? Think you not that thus much time hath taught me to rule her? I will mew* the gentlewoman till she have cast all her feathers, if she rouse* herself against me.'

And with that he walked up and down, nodding his head as though they mistook him much that thought he was not his wife's master.

But Zelmane, now seeing it was time to conclude: 'Of your wisdom and manhood,' said she, 'I doubt not, but that sufficeth not me; for both they can hardly tame a malicious tongue and impossibly bar the freedom of thought, which be the things that must be only witnesses of honour or judges of dishonour. But that you may see I do not set light your affection, if tonight, after your wife be assuredly asleep – whereof by your love I conjure you to have a most precise care – you will steal handsomely to the cave unto me, there do I grant you as great proportion as you will take of free conference with me, ever remembering you seek no more, for so shall you but deceive yourself and for ever lose me.'

Basilius, that was old enough to know that women are not wont to appoint secret night meetings for the purchasing of land, holding himself already an undoubted possessor of his desires, kissing her hand, and lifting up his eyes to heaven as if the greatness of the benefit did go beyond all measure of thanks, said no more, lest stirring of more words might bring forth some, perhaps, contrary matter.

In which trance of joy Zelmane went from him, saying she would leave him to the remembrance of their appointment, and for her, she would go visit the Lady Philoclea. Into whose chamber being come, keeping still her late-taken-on gravity, and asking her how she did (rather in the way of dutiful honour than in any special affection) with extreme inward anguish to them both she turned from her, and taking the Queen Gynecia, led her into a bay window of the same chamber, determining in herself not to utter

* *mew*: cage. *rouse*: ruffle up her feathers.

to so excellent a wit as Gynecia had the uttermost point of her pretended device, but to keep the clause of it for the last instant, when the shortness of the time should not give her spirits leisure to look into all those doubts that easily enter to an open invention. But with smiling eyes and with a delivered-over grace, feigning as much love to her as she did counterfeit little love to Philoclea, she began with more credible than eloquent speech to tell her, that with much consideration of a matter so nearly importing her own fancy and Gynecia's honour, she had now concluded that the night following should be the fittest time for the joining together their several desires, what time sleep should perfectly do his office upon the king her husband, and that the one should come to the other into the cave – which place as it was the first receipt of their promised love, so it might have the first honour of the due performance: that the cause why those few days past she had not sought the like was lest the new change of her lodging might make the king more apt to mark any sudden event, which now the use of it would take out of his mind. 'And therefore now, most excellent lady,' said she, 'there resteth nothing but that quickly after supper you train up the king to visit his daughter Philoclea, and then feigning yourself not well at ease, by your going to bed draw him not long to be after you. In the meantime I will be gone home to my lodging, where I will attend you with no less devotion but, as I hope, with better fortune than Thisbe did the too-much-loving, and too-much-loved Pyramus.'

The blood that quickly came into Gynecia's fair face was the only answer she made, but that one might easily see contentment and consent were both to the full in her; which she did testify with the wringing Zelmane fast by the hand, closing her eyes, and letting her head fall, as if she would give her to know she was not ignorant of her fault, although she were transported with the violence of her evil.

## CHAPTER 41

But in this triple agreement did the day seem tedious of all sides, till his never erring course had given place to the night's succession. And the supper, by each hand hasted, was with no less speed ended when Gynecia, presenting heavy sleepiness in her countenance, brought up both Basilius and Zelmane to see Philoclea, still keeping her bed, and far more sick in mind than body, and more grieved than comforted with any such visitation. Thence Zelmane, wishing easeful rest to Philoclea, did seem to take that night's leave of this princely crew; when Gynecia, likewise seeming somewhat diseased, desired Basilius to stay a while with her daughter while she recommended her sickness to her bed's comfort – indeed desirous to determine again of the manner of her stealing away – to no less comfort to Basilius who the sooner she was asleep, the sooner hoped to come by his long-pursued prey. Thus both were bent to deceive each other and to take the advantage of either other's disadvantage.

But Gynecia having taken Zelmane into her bed-chamber to speak a little with her of their sweet determination, Zelmane upon a sudden, as though she had never thought of it before, 'Now the Gods forbid,' said she, 'so great a lady as you are should come to me, or that I should leave it to the hands of fortune if, by either the ill-governing of your passion or your husband's sudden waking, any danger might happen unto you! No, if there be any superiority in the points of true love, it shall be yours; if there be any danger (since myself am the author of this device) it is reason it should be mine. Therefore do you but leave with me the keys of the gate and upon yourself take my upper garment, that if any of Dametas' house see you, they may think you to be myself; and I will presently lie down in your place, so muffled for your supposed sickness as the king shall nothing know me. And then as soon as he is asleep will I (as it much better becomes me) wait upon you. But if the uttermost of mischiefs should happen, I can assure you the king's life shall sooner pay for it than your honour.'

And with the ending of her words she threw off her gown, not giving Gynecia any space to take the full image of this new change into her fancy: but seeing no ready objection against it in her heart, and knowing that there was no time then to stand long disputing (besides remembering the giver was to order the manner of his gift) yielded quickly to this conceit – indeed, not among the smallest causes, tickled thereunto by a certain wanton desire that her husband's deceit might be the more notable.

In this sort did Zelmane, nimbly disarraying herself, possess Gynecia's place, hiding her head in such a close manner as grievous and over-watched sickness is wont to invite to itself the solace of sleep. And of the other side the queen, putting on Zelmane's outmost apparel, went first into her closet, there quickly to beautify herself with the best and sweetest night-deckings. But there casting an hasty eye over her precious things, which ever since Zelmane's coming her head (otherwise occupied) had left unseen, she happened to see a bottle of gold, upon which down along were graved these verses:

> Let him drink this, whom long in arms to fold
> Thou dost desire, and with free power to hold.

She remembered the bottle, for it had been kept of long time by the kings of Cyprus as a thing of rare virtue, and given to her by her mother, when she being very young-married to her husband of much greater age, her mother (persuaded it was of property to force love with love effects) had made a precious present of it to this her beloved child – though it had been received rather by tradition to have such a quality than by any approved experiment. This Gynecia (according to the common disposition not only – though especially – of wives but of all other kinds of people not to esteem much one's own, but to think the labour lost employed about it) had never cared to give to her husband, but suffered his affection to run according to his own scope. But now that love of her particular choice had awakened her spirits, and perchance the very unlawfulness of it had a little blown the coal, among her other ornaments with glad mind she took most part of this liquor, putting it into a fair cup all set with diamonds: for what dares not love undertake, armed with the night and provoked with lust?

And thus down she went to the cave-ward, guided only by the moon's fair shining, suffering no other thought to have any familiarity with her brains but that which did present unto her a picture of her approaching contentment. She, that had long disdained this solitary life her husband had entered into, now wished it much more solitary, so she might only obtain the private presence of Zelmane. She, that before would not have gone so far, especially by night and to so dark a place, now took a pride in the same courage, and framed in her mind a pleasure out of the pain itself. Thus with thick-doubled paces she went to the cave, receiving to herself, for her first contentment, the only lying where Zelmane had done, whose pillow she kissed a thousand times for having borne the print of that beloved head. And so keeping with panting heart her travailing fancies so attentive, that the wind could stir nothing but that she stirred herself as if it had been the pace of the longed for Zelmane, she kept her side of the bed, defending only and cherishing the other side with her arms: till after a while waiting (counting with herself how many steps were betwixt the lodge and the cave, and oft accusing Zelmane of more curious stay than needed) she was visited with an unexpected guest.

For Basilius after his wife was departed to her feigned repose, as long as he remained with his daughter to give his wife time of unreadying herself, it was easily seen it was a very thorny abode he made there, and the discourses with which he entertained his daughter not unlike to those of earnest players when, in the midst of their game, trifling questions be put unto them: his eyes still looking about, and himself, still changing places, began to speak of a thing and brake it off before it were half done: to any speech Philoclea ministered unto him, with a sudden starting and casting up his head, he would make an answer far out of all grammar: a certain deep musing, and by and by out of it: uncertain motions, unstayed* graces. Having borne out the limit of a reasonable time with as much pain as it might be, he came darkling* into his chamber, forcing himself to tread as softly as he could. But the more curious* he was, the more he thought everything creaked under him; and his mind being out of the way with another thought, and his eyes not serving his turn in that dark place, each coffer or cupboard he met, one saluted his shins, another his elbows, sometimes ready in revenge to strike them again with his face. Till at length, fearing his wife were not fully asleep, he came, lifting up the clothes as gently as (I think) poor Pan did when, instead of Iole's bed, he came into the rough embracings of Hercules;[1] and laying himself down as tenderly as a new bride, rested a while with a very open ear to mark each breath of his supposed

* *unstayed:* restless. *darkling:* in the dark. *curious:* careful.

wife. And sometimes he himself would yield a long-fetched sigh, as though that had been a music to draw on another to sleep, till within a very little while, with the other party's well-counterfeit sleep (who was as willing to be rid of him as he was to be gone thence) assuring himself he left all safe there, in the same order stale out again; and putting on his night gown, with much groping and scrambling he gat himself out of the little house, and then did the moonlight serve to guide his feet.

Thus, with a great deal of pain did Basilius go to her whom he fled, and with much cunning left the person for whom he had employed all his cunning. But when Basilius was once gotten (as he thought) into a clear coast, what joy he then made, how each thing seemed vile in his sight in comparison of his fortune, how far already he deemed himself in the chief tower of his desires it were tedious to tell. Once* his heart could not choose but yield this song, as a fairing* of his contentment.

> Get hence, foul grief, the canker of the mind:
> Farewell, complaint, the miser's only pleasure:
>     Away, vain cares, by which few men do find
>             Their sought-for treasure.
>
> Ye helpless sighs, blow out your breath to nought;
> Tears, drown yourselves, for woe (your cause) is wasted;
>     Thought, think to end; too long the fruit of thought
>             My mind hath tasted.
>
> But thou, sure hope, tickle my leaping heart;
> Comfort, step thou in place of wonted sadness:
>     Fore-felt desire, begin to savour part
>             Of coming gladness.
>
> Let voice of sighs into clear music run;
> Eyes, let your tears with gazing now be mended;
>     Instead of thought, true pleasure be begun,
>             And never ended.

Thus imagining as then with himself, his joys so held him up that he never touched ground; and like a right old beaten soldier

*Once*: at once. *fairing*: token.

that knew well enough the greatest captains do never use long orations when it comes to the very point of execution, as soon as he was gotten into the cave and (to the joyful, though silent, expectation of Gynecia) come close to the bed, never recking* his promise to look for nothing but conference, he leaped into that side reserved for a more welcome guest, and laying his lovingest hold upon Gynecia: 'O Zelmane,' said he, 'embrace in your favour this humble servant of yours. Hold within me my heart which pants to leave his master to come unto you.'

In what case poor Gynecia was when she knew the voice and felt the body of her husband, fair ladies, it is better to know by imagination than experience. For straight was her mind assaulted, partly with the being deprived of her unquenched desire, but principally with the doubt that Zelmane had betrayed her to her husband, besides the renewed sting of jealousy what in the meantime might befall her daughter. But of the other side her love, with a fixed persuasion she had, taught her to seek all reason of hopes; and therein thought best, before discovering of herself, to mark the behaviour of her husband who (both in deeds and words still using her as taking her to be Zelmane) made Gynecia hope that this might be Basilius' own enterprise which Zelmane had not stayed,* lest she should discover* the matter which might be performed at another time. Which hope accompanied with Basilius' manner of dealing – he being at that time fuller of livelier fancies than many years before he had been – besides the remembrance of her daughter's sickness and late strange countenance betwixt her and Zelmane, all coming together into her mind (which was loth to condemn itself of an utter overthrow) made her frame herself not truly with a sugared joy, but with a determinate patience to let her husband think he had found a very gentle and supple-minded Zelmane; which he, good man, making full reckoning of, did melt in as much gladness as she was oppressed with divers ungrateful burdens.

*recking*: heeding. *stayed*: prevented. *discover*: reveal.

## CHAPTER 42

But Pyrocles (who had at this present no more to play the part of
Zelmane) having so naturally measured the manner of his breathing that Basilius made no doubt of his sound sleeping, and lain a
pretty while with a quiet unquietness to perform his intended
enterprise, as soon as (by the debate betwixt Basilius' shins and
the unregarding forms) he perceived that he had fully left the
lodge, after him went he with stealing steps (having his sword
under his arm, still doubting lest some mischance might turn Basilius back again) down to the gate of the lodge; which not content
to lock fast, he barred and fortified with as many devices as his wit
and haste would suffer him, that so he might have full time both
for making ready Philoclea and conveying her to her horse before
any might come in to find them missing. For further ends of those
ends, and what might ensue of this action, his love and courage
well-matched never looked after, holding for an assured ground,
that whosoever in great things will think to prevent all objections
must lie still and do nothing.

This determination thus weighed, the first part thus performed,
up to Philoclea's chamber door went Pyrocles, rapt from himself
with the excessive fore-feeling of his (as he assured himself)
near-coming contentment. Whatever pains he had taken, what
dangers he had run into, and especially those saucy pages of love,
doubts, griefs, languishing hopes and threatening despairs, came
all now to his mind in one rank to beautify his expected blissfulness, and to serve for a most fit sauce whose sourness might
give a kind of life to the delightful cheer his imagination fed upon.
All the great estate of his father, all his own glory, seemed unto
him but a trifling pomp whose good stands in other men's conceit,
in comparison of the true comfort he found in the depth of his
mind; and the knowledge of any misery that might ensue this
joyous adventure was recked of but as a slight purchase* of possessing the top of happiness – for so far were his thoughts passed
through all perils that already he conceived himself safely arrived
with his lady at the stately palace of Pella, among the exceeding
joys of his father and infinite congratulations of his friends, giving

* *purchase*: price.

order for the royal entertaining of Philoclea and for sumptuous shows and triumphs against their marriage. In the thought whereof as he found extremity of joy, so well found he that extremity is not without a certain joyful pain, by extending the heart beyond his wonted limits, and by so forcible a holding all the senses to one object that it confounds their mutual working, not without a charming kind of ravishing them from the free use of their own function.

Thus grieved only with too much gladness, being come to the door which should be the entry to his happiness, he was met with the latter end of a song which Philoclea (like a solitary nightingale* bewailing her guiltless punishment and helpless misfortune) had newly delivered over, meaning none should be judge of her passion but her own conscience. The song, having been accorded to a sweetly-played-on lute, contained these verses which she had lately with some art curiously written to enwrap her secret and resolute woes:

>    1     2      3     1     2      3
>   Virtue, beauty, and speech, did strike, wound, charm,
>
> 1     2   3      1     2     3
> My heart, eyes, ears, with wonder, love, delight:
>
>   1   2     3     1     2       3
>   First, second, last, did bind, enforce and arm,
>
>     1     2     3     1     2       3
> His works, shows, suits, with wit, grace and vows' might.
>
>      1     2     3   1   2      3
>   Thus honour, liking, trust, much, far, and deep,
>
> 1     2       3      1     2      3
> Held, pierc'd, possess'd, my judgement, sense and will,
>
>     1     2     3     1     2     3
>   Till wrong, contempt, deceit did grow, steal, creep,
>
> 1     2     3    1     2      3
> Bands, favour, faith, to break, defile and kill.
>
>     1     2     3   1    2      3
>   Then grief, unkindness, proof, took, kindled, taught,

*nightingale: see Notes, I.2.1. (p. 849).

 1               2   3   1    2      3
Well-grounded, noble, due, spite, rage, disdain:

  1  2  3            1     2     3
But ah, alas, (in vain) my mind, sight, thought,

    1      2      3   1   2    3
Doth him, his face, his words, leave, shun, refrain;

      1    2      3    1   2    3
For no thing, time, nor place, can loose, quench, ease,

    1     2      3    1   2    3
Mine own, embraced, sought, knot, fire, disease.

The force of love to those poor folk that feel it is many ways very strange, but no way stranger than that it doth so enchain the lover's judgement upon her that holds the reins of his mind, that whatsoever she doth is ever in his eyes best. And that best, being by the continual motion of our changing life turned by her to any other thing, that thing again becometh best; so that nature in each kind suffering but one superlative, the lover only admits no positive.\* If she sit still, that is best, for so is the conspiracy of her several graces held best together to make one perfect figure of beauty. If she walk, no doubt that is best, for, besides the making happy the more places by her steps, the very stirring adds a pleasing life to her native perfections. If she be silent, that without comparison is best, since by that means the untroubled eye most freely may devour the sweetness of his object. But if she speak, he will take it upon his death that is best, the quintessence of each word being distilled down into his affected soul.

Example of this was well to be seen in the given-over Pyrocles, who with panting breath and sometimes sighs (not such as sorrow restraining the inward parts doth make them glad to deliver, but such as the impatience of delay, with the unsurety of never so sure hope, is wont to breathe out) now being at the door; of the one side hearing her voice (which he thought, if the philosophers said true of the heavenly seven-sphered harmony,\* was by her not only represented but far surmounted) and of the other having his eyes over-filled with her beauty – for the king at his parting had

---

\* *positive*: absolute. *the seven-sphered harmony*: the 'music of the spheres'.

left the chamber open, and she at that time lay (as the heat of that country did well suffer) upon the top of her bed, having her beauties eclipsed with nothing but with a fair smock wrought all in flames of ash-colour silk and gold, lying so upon her right side that the left thigh down to the foot yielded his delightful proportion to the full view, which was seen by the help of a rich lamp which through the curtains a little drawn cast forth a light upon her, as the moon doth when it shines into a thin wood – Pyrocles, I say, was stopped with the violence of so many darts cast by Cupid all together upon him, that quite forgetting himself and thinking therein already he was in the best degree of felicity, he would have lost much of his time, and with too much love omitted the enterprise undertaken for his love, had not Philoclea's pitiful accusing of him forced him to bring his spirits again to a new bias. For she, laying her hand under her fair cheek, upon which there did privily trickle the sweet drops of her delightful, though sorrowful tears, made these words wait upon her moanful song:

'And hath that cruel Pyrocles,' said she, 'deserved thus much of me, that I should for his sake lift up my voice in my best tunes, and to him continually (with pouring out my plaint) make a disdained oblation? Shall my soul still do this honour to his unmerciful tyranny, by my lamenting his loss to show his worthiness and my weakness? He hears thee not, simple Philoclea; he hears thee not; and if he did, some hearts grow the harder the more they find their advantage. Alas, what a miserable constitution of mind have I! I disdain my fortune, and yet reverence him that disdains me. I accuse his ungratefulness, and have his virtue in admiration. O ye deaf heavens, I would either his injury could blot out mine affection, or my affection could forget his injury.'

With that, giving a pitiful but sweet screech, she took again the lute and began to sing this sonnet which might serve as an explaining to the other:

> The love which is imprinted in my soul
> With beauty's seal, and virtue fair disguis'd,
> With inward cries puts up a bitter roll
> Of huge complaints, that now it is despis'd.

Thus, thus the more I love, the wrong the more
Monstrous appears, long truth received late;
Wrong stirs remorsed Grief, grief's deadly sore
Unkindness breeds, unkindness fostereth hate.

But ah, the more I hate, the more I think
Whom I do hate; the more I think on him,
The more his matchless gifts do deeply sink
Into my breast, and loves renewed swim.
    What medicine then can such disease remove,
    Where love draws hate, and hate engendereth love?

But Pyrocles, that had heard his name accused and condemned
by the mouth which of all the world (and more than all the world)
he most loved, had then cause enough to call his mind to his
home, and with the most haste he could (for true love fears the
accident of an instant) to match the excusing of his fault with
declaration of his errand thither. And therefore, blown up and
down with as many contrary passions as Aeolus sent out winds
upon the Trojan relics guided upon the sea by the valiant
Aeneas,[1] he went into her chamber with such a pace as reverent
fear doth teach; where, kneeling down and having prepared a long
discourse for her, his eyes were so filled with her sight that (as if
they would have robbed all their fellows of their services) both his
heart fainted and his tongue failed in such sort that he could not
bring forth one word, but referred her understanding to his eyes'
language. But she in extremity amazed to see him there at so
undue a season, and ashamed that her beautiful body made so
naked a prospect, drawing in her delicate limbs into the weak
guard of the bed, and presenting in her face to him such a kind of
pitiful anger as might show this was only a fault therefore, because
she had a former grudge unto him, turning away her face from
him, she thus said unto him:

'O Zelmane or Pyrocles (for whether name I use it much skills
not, since by the one I was first deceived, and by the other now
betrayed) what strange motion is the guide of thy cruel mind
hither? Dost thou not think the day-torments thou hast given me
sufficient but that thou dost envy me the night's quiet? Wilt thou
give my sorrows no truce, but, by making me see before mine eyes

how much I have lost, offer me due cause of confirming my plaint? Or is thy heart so full of rancour that thou dost desire to feed thine eyes with the wretched spectacle of thine overthrown enemy, and so to satisfy the full measure of thy undeserved rage with the receiving into thy sight the unrelievable ruins of my desolate life? O Pyrocles, Pyrocles, for thine own virtue's sake, let miseries be no music unto thee, and be content to take to thyself some colour of excuse, that thou didst not know to what extremity thy inconstancy, or rather falsehood, hath brought me.'

Pyrocles, to whom every syllable she pronounced was a thunderbolt to his heart, equally distraught betwixt amazement and sorrow, abashed to see such a stop of his desires, grieved with her pain but tormented to find himself the author of it, with quaking lips and pale cheer:

'Alas, divine lady,' said he, 'your displeasure is so contrary to my desert and your words so far beyond all expectations, that I have least ability now I have most need to speak in the cause upon which my life dependeth. For my troth is so undoubtedly constant unto you, my heart is so assured a witness to itself of his unspotted faith, that having no one thing in me whereout any such sacrilege might arise, I have likewise nothing in so direct a thing to say for myself but sincere and vehement protestations. For in truth there may most words be spent where there is some probability to breed of both sides conjectural allegations. But so perfect a thing as my love is of you, as it suffers no question, so it seems to receive injury by addition of any words unto it. If my soul could have been polluted with treachery it would likewise have provided for itself due furniture of colourable answers; but as it stood upon the naked conscience of his untouched duty, so I must confess it is altogether unarmed against so unjust a violence as you lay upon me. Alas, let not the pains I have taken to serve you be now accounted injurious unto you. Let not the dangerous cunning I have used to please you be deemed a treason against you. Since I have deceived them whom you fear for your sake, do not you destroy me for their sake. What can I without you further do, or to what more forwardness can any counsel bring our desired happiness? I have provided whatsoever is needful for our going; I have rid them both out of the lodge so that there is none here to be hinderers or knowers of our departure but only the almighty powers, whom I invoke as triers of mine innocency and witnesses of my well-meaning. And if ever my thoughts did receive so much as a fainting in their affections, if they have not continually with more and more ardour from time to time pursued the possession of your sweetest favour, if ever in that possession they received either spot or falsehood, then let their most horrible plagues fall upon me; let mine eyes be deprived of the light, which did abase the heavenly beams that strake them; let my falsified tongue serve to no use but to bemoan mine own wretchedness; let my heart, empoisoned with detestable treason, be the seat of infernal sorrow; let my soul with the endless anguish of his conscience become his own tormentor.'

'O false mankind!' cried out the sweet Philoclea. 'How can an imposthumed[2] heart but yield forth evil matter by his mouth! Are oaths there to be believed where vows are broken? No no. Who doth wound the eternal justice of the gods cares little for abusing their names; and who, in doing wickedly, doth not fear due recompensing plagues, doth little fear that invoking of plagues will make them come ever a whit the sooner. But alas, what aileth this new conversion? Have you yet another sleight to play, or do you think to deceive me in Pyrocles' form as you have done in Zelmane's? Or rather, now you have betrayed me in both, is some third sex left you into which you can transform yourself to inveigle my simplicity? Enjoy, enjoy the conquest you have already won; and assure yourself you are come to the furthest point of your cunning. For my part, unkind Pyrocles, my only defence shall be belief of nothing; my comfort, my faithful innocency; and the punishment I desire of you shall be your own conscience.'

Philoclea's hard persevering in this unjust condemnation of him did so overthrow all the might of Pyrocles' mind (who saw that time would not serve to prove by deeds, and that the better words he used, the more they were suspected of deceitful cunning) that, void of all counsel and deprived of all comfort, finding best deserts punished and nearest hopes prevented, he did abandon the succour of himself, and suffered grief so to close his heart that (his breath failing him) with a dreadful shutting of his eyes, he fell down at her bedside, having had time to say no more but, 'Oh, whom dost thou kill, Philoclea?'

She, that little looked for such an extreme event* of her doings, starting out of her bed, like Venus rising from her mother the sea, not so much stricken down with amazement and grief of her fault as lifted up with the force of love and desire to help, she laid her fair body over his breast, and throwing no other water in his face but the stream of her tears, nor giving him other blows but the kissing of her well-formed mouth, her only cries were these lamentations:

'O unfortunate suspicion,' said she, 'the very mean to lose that we most suspect* to lose! O unkind kindness of mine, which returns an imagined wrong with an effectual* injury! O fool to make quarrel my supplication, or to use hate as the mediator of love! Childish Philoclea, hast thou thrown away the jewel wherein all thy pride consisted? Hast thou with too much haste over-run thyself?'

Then would she renew her kisses, and yet not finding the life return, redouble her plaints in this manner:

'O divine soul,' said she, 'whose virtue can possess no less than the highest place in heaven, if for mine eternal plague thou hast utterly left this most sweet mansion, before I follow thee with Thisbe's punishment* for my rash unwariness, hear this protestation of mine: that as the wrong I have done thee proceeded of a most sincere but unresistable affection, so led with this pitiful example, it shall end in the mortal* hate of myself and, if it may be, I will make my soul a tomb of thy memory.'[3]

At that word, with anguish of mind and weakness of body increased one by the other, and both augmented by this fearful accident, she had fallen down in a swoon but that Pyrocles, then first severing* his eyelids and quickly apprehending her danger (to him more than death), beyond all powers striving to recover the commandment of all his powers, stayed her from falling, and then lifting the sweet burden of her body in his arms, laid her again in her bed. So that she, but then the physician, was now become the patient, and he, to whom her weakness had been ser-

* *event*: outcome. *suspect*: fear. *effectual*: actual. *Thisbe's punishment*: suicide. *mortal*: resulting in death. *severing*: opening.

viceable, was now enforced to do service to her weakness: which performed by him, with that hearty care which the most careful love on the best loved subject in greatest extremity could employ, prevailed so far that ere long she was able (though in strength exceedingly dejected) to call home her wandering senses to yield attention to that her beloved Pyrocles had to deliver.

But he, lying down on the bed by her, holding her hand in his, with so kind an accusing her of unkindness as (in accusing her) he condemned himself, began from point to point to discover unto her all that had passed between his loathed lovers and him: how he had entertained, and by entertaining deceived both Basilius and Gynecia, and that with such a kind of deceit as either might see the cause in the other, but neither espy the effect in themselves: that all his favours to them had tended only to make them strangers to this his action; and all his strangeness to her, to the final obtaining of her long promised and now to be performed favour. Which device, seeing it had so well succeeded to the removing all other hindrances, that only her resolution remained for the taking their happy journey, he conjured her by all the love she had ever borne him she would make no longer delay to partake with him whatsoever honours the noble king of Macedon and all other Euarchus' dominions might yield him, especially since in this enterprise he had now waded so far as he could not possibly retire himself back without being overwhelmed with danger and dishonour. He needed not have used further arguments of persuasion; for that only conjuration had so forcibly bound all her spirits that (could her body have seconded her mind or her mind have strengthened her body) without respect of any worldy thing but only fear to be again unkind to Pyrocles, she had condescended to go with him. But raising herself a little in her bed, and finding her own inability in any sort to endure the air:

'My Pyrocles,' said she, with tearful eyes and a pitiful countenance such as well witnessed she had no will to deny anything she had power to perform, 'if you can convey me hence in such plight as you see me, I am most willing to make my extremest danger a testimony that I esteem no danger in regard of your virtuous satisfaction.'

But she fainted so fast that she was not able to utter the rest of her conceived speech; which also turned Pyrocles' thoughts from expecting further answer to the necessary care of reviving her in whose fainting himself was more than overthrown. And that having effected with all the sweet means his wits could devise, though his highest hopes were by this unexpected downfall sunk deeper than any degree of despair, yet lest the appearance of his inward grief might occasion her further discomfort, having racked* his face to a more comfortable semblance, he sought some show of reason to show she had no reason (either for him or for herself) so to be afflicted. Which in the sweet minded Philoclea (whose consideration was limited by his words, and whose conceit pierced no deeper than his outward countenance) wrought within a while such quietness of mind, and that quietness again such repose of body, that sleep (by his harbingers – weakness, weariness, and watchfulness) had quickly taken up his lodging in all her senses.

Then, indeed, had Pyrocles leisure to sit in judgement on himself and to hear his reason accuse his rashness; who, without forecast of doubt, without knowledge of his friend, without acquainting Philoclea with his purpose or being made acquainted with her present estate, had fallen headlong into that attempt, the success whereof he had long since set down to himself as the measure of all his other fortunes. But calling to mind how weakly they do that rather find fault with what cannot be amended than seek to amend wherein they have been faulty, he soon turned him from remembering what might have been done to considering what was now to be done, and when that consideration failed, what was now to be expected. Wherein having run over all the thoughts his reason (called to the strictest accounts) could bring before him, at length he lighted on this: that as long as Gynecia bewrayed* not the matter (which he thought she would not do, as well for her own honour and safety as for the hope she might still have of him, which is loth to die in a lover's heart) all the rest might turn to a pretty merriment, and inflame his lover Basilius again to cast about for the missed favour. And as naturally the heart stuffed up with woefulness is glad greedily to suck the thinnest air of comfort, so did he at the first embrace this conceit, as

* *racked*: painfully stretched. *bewrayed*: betrayed.

offering great hope, if not assurance of well-doing: till looking more nearly into it, and not able to answer the doubts and difficulties he saw therein more and more arising (the night being also far spent) his thoughts, even weary of their own burdens, fell to a straying kind of uncertainty; and his mind, standing only upon the nature of inward intelligences, left his body to give a sleeping respite to his vital spirits, which he, according to the quality of sorrow, received with greater greediness than ever in his life before. According to the nature of sorrow, I say, which is past care's remedy; for care, stirring the brains and making thin the spirits, breaketh rest; but those griefs wherein one is determined there is no preventing do breed a dull heaviness which easily clothes itself in sleep. So as laid down so near the beauty of the world, Philoclea, that their necks were subject each to other's chaste embracements, it seemed love had come thither to lay a plot in that picture of death, how gladly (if death came) their souls would go together.

## THE THIRD ECLOGUES[1]

Thyrsis, not with many painted words nor falsified promises had won the consent of his beloved Kala, but with a true and simple making her know he loved her, not forcing himself beyond his reach to buy her affection, but giving her such pretty presents as neither could weary him with the giving nor shame her for the taking. Thus, the first strawberries he could find were ever in a clean washed dish sent to Kala. Thus posies of the spring flowers were wrapped up in a little green silk and dedicated to Kala's breasts. Thus sometimes his sweetest cream, sometimes the best cakebread his mother made, were reserved for Kala's taste. Neither would he stick to kill a lamb when she would be content to come over the way unto him. But then, lo, how the house was swept, and rather no fire than any smoke left to trouble her. Then love songs were not dainty,* when she would hear them, and as much mannerly silence, when she would not. In going to church, great worship to Kala; so that all the parish said, never a maid they

* *dainty*: prudishly withheld.

knew so well waited on: and when dancing was about the may-
pole, nobody taken out but she, and he, after a leap or two to show
her his own activity, would frame all the rest of his dancing only
to grace her. As for her father's sheep, he had no less care of them
than his own, so that she might play her* as she would, warranted* with honest Thyrsis' carefulness. But if he spied Kala
favoured any one of the flock more than his fellows, then that was
cherished, shearing him so (when shorn he must be) as might most
become him; but while the wool was on, wrapping within it some
verses (wherein Thyrsis had a special gift) and making the innocent beast his unweeting* messenger. Thus constantly continuing, though he were none of the fairest, at length he won
Kala's heart, the honestest wench in all those quarters. And so
with consent of both parents (without which neither Thyrsis
would ask, nor Kala grant) their marrying day was appointed,
which because it fell out in this time, I think it shall not be im-
pertinent to remember a little our shepherds, while the other
greater persons are either sleeping or otherwise troubled.

Thyrsis' marriage-time once known, there needed no inviting of
the neighbours in that valley, for so well was Thyrsis beloved that
they were all ready to do him credit. Neither yet came they like
harpies to devour him; but one brought a fat pig, the other a
tender kid, the third a great goose: as for cheese, milk and butter
were the gossips'* presents. Thither came of strange shepherds
only the melancholy Philisides, for the virtuous Coriden had long
since left off all joyful solemnities. And as for Strephon and
Claius, they had lost their mistress, which put them into such
extreme sorrows as they could scarcely abide the light of the day,
much less the eyes of men. But of the Arcadian-born shepherds,
thither came good old Geron, young Histor – though unwilling –
and upright Dicus, merry Pas, and jolly Nico. As for Dametas,
they durst not presume (his pride was such) to invite him; and
Dorus they found might not be spared.

And there under a bower was made* of boughs (for Thyrsis'
house was not able to receive them) every one placed according to

* *play her*: enjoy herself. *warranted*: guaranteed. *unweeting*: un-
knowing. *gossip*: god-parent. *under a bower was made*: i.e. which was
made.

his age. The women – for such was the manner of the country – kept together to make good cheer among themselves, from which otherwise a certain painful modesty restrains them; and there might the sadder* matrons give good counsel to Kala who, poor soul, wept for fear of that she desired. But among the shepherds was all honest liberty – no fear of dangerous telltales who hunt greater preys, nor, indeed, minds in them to give telltales any occasion, but one questioning with another of the manuring his ground and governing his flock. The highest point they reached to was to talk of the holiness of marriage; to which purpose, as soon as their sober dinner was ended, Dicus instead of thanks sang this song with a clear voice and cheerful countenance:

> Let mother earth now deck herself in flowers,
> To see her offspring seek a good increase,
>     Where justest love doth vanquish Cupid's powers,
> And war of thoughts is swallowed up in peace;
>         Which never may decrease,
>         But like the turtles fair,
>         Live one in two, a well united pair:
>         Which that no chance may stain,
> O Hymen, long their coupled joys maintain.

> O Heav'n, awake, show forth thy stately face;
> Let not these slumbering clouds thy beauties hide,
>     But with thy cheerful presence help to grace
> The honest bridegroom and the bashful bride,
>         Whose loves may ever bide,
>         Like to the elm and vine,
>         With mutual embracements them to twine:
>         In which delightful pain,
> O Hymen, long their coupled joys maintain.

> Ye Muses all which chaste affects allow,
> And have to Thyrsis showed your secret skill,
>     To this chaste love your sacred favours bow,
> And so to him and her your gifts distil,

*sadder*: more sober.

That they all vice may kill,
    And like to lilies pure,
May please all eyes, and spotless may endure:
    Where that all bliss may reign,
O Hymen, long their coupled joys maintain.

Ye nymphs which in the waters empire have,
Since Thyrsis' music oft doth yield you praise,
    Grant to the thing which we for Thyrsis crave.
Let one time (but long first) close up their days,
    One grave their bodies seize,
    And like two rivers sweet,
    When they, though divers, do together meet,
One stream both streams contain:
O Hymen, long their coupled joys maintain.

Pan, father Pan, the God of silly sheep,
Whose care is cause that they in number grow,
    Have much more care of them that them do keep,
Since from these good the other's good doth flow;
    And make their issue show
    In number like the herd
Of younglings, which thyself with love hast rear'd,
    Or like the drops of rain.
O Hymen, long their coupled joys maintain.

Virtue, if not a God, yet God's chief part,
Be thou the knot of this their open vow,
    That still he be her head, she be his heart;
He lean to her, she unto him do bow,
    Each other still allow:
    Like oak and mistletoe,
    Her strength from him, his praise from her do grow;
    In which most lovely train,
O Hymen, long their coupled joys maintain.

But thou, foul Cupid, sire to lawless lust,
Be thou far hence with thy empoison'd dart,
    Which though of glitt'ring gold, shall here take rust,
Where simple love, which chasteness doth impart,

Avoids thy hurtful art,
Not needing charming skill,*
Such minds with sweet affections for to fill:
　Which being pure and plain,
O Hymen, long their coupled joys maintain.


All churlish words, shrewd answers, crabbed looks,
All privateness, self-seeking, inward spite,
　All waywardness, which nothing kindly brooks,
All strife for toys,* and claiming master's right,
　Be hence aye put to flight:
　All stirring husband's hate
　'Gainst neighbour's good for* womanish debate
　　Be fled as things most vain:
O Hymen, long their coupled joys maintain.


All peacock pride, and fruits of peacock's pride,
Longing to be with loss of substance gay,
　With recklessness what may thy house betide,
So that you may on higher slippers stay,
　For ever hence away:
　Yet let not sluttery,
　The sink of filth, be counted housewifery;
　　But keeping wholesome mean:
O Hymen, long their coupled joys maintain.


But above all, away vile jealousy,
The evil of eivls, just cause to be unjust:
　(How can he love, suspecting treachery?
How can she love where love cannot win trust?)
　Go snake, hide thee in dust,
　Ne dare once show thy face
　Where open hearts do hold so constant place,
　　That they thy sting restrain:
O Hymen, long their coupled joys maintain.


The earth is deck'd with flowers, the heav'ns display'd;

* *not needing charming skill:* skill with charms and love potions –
in contrast to Gynecia's bottle. *toys:* trifles. *for:* out of.

Muses grant gifts; nymphs, long and joined life;
   Pan, store of babes; virtue, their thoughts well staid:
Cupid's lust gone, and gone is bitter strife,
   Happy Man, happy Wife.
No pride shall them oppress,
Nor yet shall yield to loathsome sluttishness,
And jealousy is slain:
   For Hymen will their coupled joys maintain.

'Truly Dicus,' said Nico, 'although thou didst not grant me the prize the last day, when undoubtedly I wan it, yet must I needs say thou for thy part hast sung well and thriftily.'

Pas straight desired all the company they would bear witness that Nico had once in his life spoken wisely: 'For,' said he, 'I will tell it his Father, who will be a glad man when he hears such news.'

'Very true,' said Nico, 'but indeed so would not thine in like case, for he would look thou should'st live but one hour longer, that a discreet word wandered out of thy mouth.'

'And I pray thee,' said Pas, 'gentle Nico, tell me, what mischance it was that brought thee to taste so fine a meat?'

'Marry goodman blockhead,' said Nico, 'because he speaks against jealousy, the filthy traitor to true affection, and yet disguising itself in the raiment of love.'

'Sentences, sentences,'* cried Pas. 'Alas, how ripe-witted these young folks be nowadays! But well counselled shall that husband be, when his man comes to exhort him not to be jealous.'

'And so shall he,' answered Nico, 'for I have seen a fresh example, though it be not very fit to be known.'

'Come, come,' said Pas, 'be not so squeamish; I know thou longest more to tell it than we to hear it.'

But for all his words, Nico would not bestow his voice, till he was generally entreated of all the rest. And then with a merry marriage-look he sang this following discourse, for with a better grace he could sing than tell:

   A neighbour mine not long ago there was,
  (But nameless he, for blameless he shall be)

---

* *sentences*: sententious sayings without experience to support them.

That married had a trick* and bonny lass
As in a summer day a man might see;
   But he himself a foul unhandsome groom,
   And far unfit to hold so good a room.

Now whether moved with self-unworthiness,
Or with her beauty fit to make* a prey,
   Fell jealousy did so his brain oppress,
That if he absent were but half a day,
     He guessed the worst (you wot what is the worst)
     And in himself new doubting causes nursed.

While thus he feared the silly innocent,
Who yet was good, because she knew none ill,
   Unto his house a jolly shepherd went,
To whom our prince did bear a great good will,
     Because in wrestling, and in pastoral,
     He far did pass the rest of shepherds all.

And therefore he a courtier was be-named,
And as a courtier was with cheer received
   (For they have tongues to make a poor man blamed,
If he to them his duty misconceived)
     And for this courtier should well like his table,
     The good man bade his wife be serviceable.

And so she was, and all with good intent;
But few days past while she good manner used,
   But that her husband thought her service bent
To such an end as he might be abused;
     Yet like a coward fearing stranger's pride,
     He made the simple wench his wrath abide;

With chumpish* looks, hard words, and secret nips,
Grumbling at her when she his kindness sought,
   Asking her how she tasted courtier's lips,
He forced her think that which she never thought.
     In fine, he made her guess there was some sweet
     In that which he so fear'd that she should meet.

           * *trick:* trim. *make:* become. *chumpish:* boorish.

When once this entered was in woman's heart,
And that it had inflamed a new desire,
  There rested then to play a woman's part,
Fuel to seek and not to quench the fire,
    But (for his jealous eye she well did find)
    She studied cunning how the same to blind.

And thus she did. One day to him she came,
And (though against his will) on him she leaned,
  And out gan cry, 'Ah well away for shame,
If you help not, our wedlock will be stained.'
    The good man starting, asked what did her move.
    She sigh'd, and said the bad guest sought her love.

He, little looking that she should complain
Of that whereto he fear'd she was inclin'd,
  Bussing* her oft, and in his heart full fain,
He did demand what remedy to find,
    How they might get that guest from them to wend,
    And yet the prince (that lov'd him) not offend.

'Husband,' quoth she, 'go to him by and by,
And tell him you do find I do him love:
  And therefore pray him that of courtesy
He will absent himself, lest he should move
    A young girl's heart to that were shame for both,
    Whereto you know his honest heart were loth.

'Thus shall you show that him you do not doubt;
And as for me, sweet husband, I must bear.'
  Glad was the man when he had heard her out,
And did the same, although with mickle fear –
    For fear he did, lest he the young man might
    In choler put, with whom he would not fight.

The courtly shepherd much aghast at this,
Not seeing erst such token in the wife,
  Though full of scorn, would not his duty miss,
Knowing that evil becomes a household strife,

*Bussing*: kissing.

Did go his way, but sojourn'd near thereby,
That yet the ground hereof he might espy.

The wife thus having settled husband's brain,
Who would have sworn his spouse Diana was,
　Watched when she a further point might gain,
Which little time did fitly bring to pass,
　For to the court her man was called by name,
　Whither he needs must go for fear of blame.

Three days before that he must sure depart,
She written had (but in a hand disguised)
　A letter such which might from either part
Seem to proceed, so well it was devised.
　She seal'd it first, then she the sealing brake,
　And to her jealous husband did it take.

With weeping eyes (her eyes she taught to weep)
She told him that the courtier had it sent:
　'Alas,' quoth she, 'thus woman's shame doth creep.'
The good man read on both sides the content;
　It title had, 'Unto my only love':
　Subscription was, 'Yours most, if you will prove.'

The pistle* self such kind of words it had:
'My sweetest joy, the comfort of my sprite,
　So may thy flocks increase thy dear heart glad,
So may each thing even as thou wishest light,
　As thou wilt deign to read, and gently read
　This mourning ink in which my heart doth bleed.

'Long have I lov'd (alas, thou worthy art)
Long have I lov'd (alas, love craveth love)
　Long have I lov'd thyself. Alas my heart
Doth break, now tongue unto thy name doth move;
　And think not that thy answer answer is,
　But that it is my doom of bale or bliss.

'The jealous wretch must now to court be gone,
Ne can he fail, for prince hath for him sent.

* *pistle*: epistle.

Now is the time we may be here alone,
And give a long desire a sweet content.
   Thus shall you both reward a lover true,
   And eke revenge his wrong suspecting you.'

And this was all, and this the husband read
With chafe enough, till she him pacified,
   Desiring that no grief in him be bred,
Now that he had her words so truly tried,
   But that he would to him the letter show,
   That with his fault he might her goodness know.

That straight was done with many a boist'rous threat,
That to the king he would his sin declare;
   But now the courtier gan to smell the feat,
And with some words which showed little care,
   He stayed until the good man was departed,
   Then gave he him the blow which never smarted.

Thus may you see the jealous wretch was made
The pander of the thing he most did fear.
   Take heed, therefore, how you ensue that trade,
Lest the same marks of jealousy you bear.
   For sure, no jealousy can that prevent
   Whereto two parties once be full content.

'Behold,' said Pas, 'a whole dicker of wit.[2] He hath picked out such a tale with intention to keep a husband from jealousy, which were enough to make a sanctified husband jealous, to see subtleties so much in the feminine gender. But,' said he, 'I will strike Nico dead with the wise words that shall flow out of my gorge.' And without further entreaty thus sang:

Who doth desire that chaste his wife should be,
First be he true, for truth doth truth deserve:
   Then such be he as she his worth may see,
And one man still credit with her preserve.

Not toying kind,* nor causelessly unkind,
Not stirring thoughts, nor yet denying right,

     * *toying kind:* over-wanton.

Not spying faults, nor in plain errors blind,
Never hard hand, nor ever reins too light.

As far from want, as far from vain expense
(The one doth force, the latter doth entice):
Allow good company, but keep from thence
All filthy mouths that glory in their vice.
This done, thou hast no more, but leave the rest
To virtue, fortune, time and woman's breast.

'Well concluded,' said Nico. 'When he hath done all, he leaves the matter to his wife's discretion. Now whensoever thou marriest, let her discretion deck thy head with Actaeon's[3] ornament.'

Pas was so angry with his wish (being indeed towards marriage) that they might perchance have fallen to buffets, but that Dicus desired Philisides (who as a stranger sat among them, revolving in his mind all the tempests of evil fortunes he had passed) that he would do so much grace to the company as to sing one of his country songs. Philisides, knowing it no good manners to be squeamish of his cunning,* having put himself into their company, without further study began to utter that wherewith his thoughts were then, as always, most busied; and to show what a stranger he was to himself, spake of himself as of a third person, in this sort:

The lad Philisides
Lay by a river's side,
In flow'ry field a gladder eye to please:
His pipe was at his foot,
His lambs were him beside;
A widow turtle near on bared root
Sat wailing without boot.*
Each thing both sweet and sad
Did draw his boiling brain
To think, and think with pain
Of Mira's beams, eclips'd by absence bad;
And thus, with eyes made dim

* *cunning*: skill. *boot*: remedy.

With tears, he said, or sorrow said for him:
  'O earth, once answer give –
So may thy stately grace
  By north, or south still rich adorned live;
    So Mira long may be
On thy then blessed face
    Whose foot doth set a heav'n on cursed thee;
    I ask, now answer me:
  If th' author of thy bliss,
Phoebus, that shepherd high,
Do turn from thee his eye,
  Doth not thyself, when he long absent is,
Like rogue, all ragged go,
And pine away with daily wasting woe?

  'Tell me, you wanton brook –
So may your sliding race
  Shun loathed-loving banks with cunning crook;
    So in you ever new
Mira may look her face,
    And make you fair with shadow of her hue;
    So when to pay your due
  To mother sea you come,
She chide you not for stay,
Nor beat you for your play –
  Tell me, if your diverted springs become
Absented quite from you,
Are you not dried? Can you yourselves renew?

  'Tell me, you flowers fair,
Cowslip and columbine –
  So may you make this wholesome spring-time air
    With you embraced lie,
And lately thence untwine,
    But with dewdrops engender children high;
    So may you never die,
  But pull'd by Mira's hand,
Dress bosom hers, or head,
Or scatter on her bed –

Tell me, if husband spring-time leave your land,
When he from you is sent,
Wither not you, languish'd with discontent?

'Tell me, my silly pipe –
So may thee still betide*
  A cleanly cloth thy moistness for to wipe;
    So may the cherries red
Of Myra's lips divide
    Their sugared selves to kiss thy happy head;
    So may her ears be led,
  Her ears where music lives,
To hear and not despise
Thy liribliring* cries –
  Tell, if that breath, which thee thy sounding gives,
Be absent far from thee,
Absent alone canst thou then piping be?

'Tell me my lamb of gold –
So may'st thou long abide
  The day well fed, the night in faithful fold;
    So grow thy wool of note,
In time that richly dy'd
    It may be part of Mira's petticoat –
    Tell me, if wolves the throat
  Have caught of thy dear dam,
Or she from thee be stay'd,
Or thou from her be stray'd,
  Canst thou, poor lamb, become another's lamb?
Or rather till thou die,
Still for thy dam, with baa-waymenting* cry?

'Tell me, O turtle true –
So may no fortune breed
  To make thee nor thy better-loved rue;
    So may thy blessings swarm,

* *thee betide:* come to thee. *liribliring:* onomatopoeic coinage for sound of a pipe. *baa-waymenting:* bleating lament.

That Mira may thee feed
    With hand and mouth; with lap and breast keep warm –
    Tell me if greedy arm
  Do fondly take away
With traitor lime the one,
The other left alone;
    Tell me, poor wretch, parted from wretched prey,
Disdain not you the green?
Wailing till death, shun you not to be seen?

    'Earth, brook, flow'rs, pipe, lamb, dove,
Say all and I with them,
    "Absence is death or worse, to them that love."
    So I, unlucky lad,
Whom hills from her do hem,
    What fits me now but tears and sighings sad?
    O fortune too too bad,
  I rather would my sheep
Th'ad'st killed with a stroke,
Burnt cabin, lost my cloak,
    Than want one hour those eyes which my joys keep.
Oh, what doth wailing win?
Speech without end were better not begin.
    My song climb thou the wind,
Which Holland sweet now gently sendeth in,[4]
    That on his wings the level thou may'st find
To hit, but kissing hit
Her ears the weights of wit.
    If thou know not for whom thy master dies,
These marks shall make thee wise:
She is the herdess fair that shines in dark,
And gives her kids no food, but willow's bark.'*

    This said, at length he ended
His oft sigh-broken ditty,
    Then rase, but rase on legs with faintness bended,
    With skin in sorrow dyed,
With face the plot of pity,

  * *willows' bark*: the weeping willow, i.e. the food of sorrow.

With thoughts, which thoughts their own tormentors tried.
 He rase, and straight espied
  His ram, who to recover
 The ewe another loved,
 With him proud battle proved.
  He envied such a death in sight of lover,
 And always westward eyeing,
 More envied Phoebus for his western flying.

The whole company would gladly have taken this occasion of requesting Philisides in plainer sort to discover unto them his estate: which he willing to prevent (as knowing the relation thereof more fit for funerals than the time of a marriage) began to sing this song he had learned before he had ever subjected his thoughts to acknowledge no master but a mistress:

As I my little flock on Ister bank[5]
(A little flock; but well my pipe they couth)*
 Did piping lead, the sun already sank
Beyond our world, and e'er I got my booth,*
Each thing with mantle black the night did scothe;*
 Saving the glow-worm which would courteous be
 Of that small light oft watching shepherds see.

The welkin* had full niggardly enclosed
In coffer of dim clouds his silver groats,
Ycleped* stars; each thing to rest disposed;
The caves were full, the mountains void of goats;
The birds' eyes clos'd; closed their chirping notes.
 As for the nightingale, wood music's king,
 It August was, he deign'd not then to sing.

Amid my sheep, though I saw naught to fear,
Yet (for I nothing saw) I feared sore;
 Then found I which thing is a charge to bear,
As for my sheep I dreaded mickle more
Than ever for myself since I was bore.

* *couth:* recognized. *booth:* hut. *scothe:* scarf up (Robertson).
*welkin:* heavens. *Ycleped:* called.

I sat me down, for see to go ne could,
And sang unto my sheep lest stray they should.

The song I sang old Lanquet[6] had me taught;
Lanquet, the shepherd best swift Ister knew,
   For clerky rede,* and hating what is naught,
For faihtful heart, clean hands, and mouth as true:
With his sweet skill my skilless youth he drew
   To have a feeling taste of him that sits
   Beyond the heaven, far more beyond your wits.

He said the music best thilk power pleased
Was jump* concord between our wit and will,
   Where highest notes to godliness are raised,
And lowest sink not down to jot of ill:
With old true tales he wont mine ears to fill,
   How shepherds did of yore, how now they thrive,
   Spoiling their flock, or while 'twixt them they strive.

He liked me, but pitied lustful youth:
His good strong staff my slipp'ry years upbore:
   He still hop'd well because I loved truth;
Till forc'd to part, with heart and eyes e'en sore,
To worthy Coriden[7] he gave me o'er;
   But thus in oak's true shade recounted he,
   Which now in night's deep shade sheep heard of me.

Such manner time there was (what time I n'ot)*
When all this earth, this dam or mould of ours,
   Was only won'd* with such as beasts begot:
Unknown as then were they that builded towers:
The cattle wild, or tame, in nature's bowers
   Might freely roam, or rest, as seemed them:
   Man was not man their dwellings in to hem.

'The beasts had sure some beastly policy,
For nothing can endure where order n'is.
   For once the lion by the lamb did lie,
The fearful hind the leopard did kiss:

* *clerkly rede:* learned counsel. *jump:* exact. *n'ot:* know not. *won'd:*
inhabited.

Hurtless was tiger's paw, and serpent's hiss.
   This think I well, the beasts with courage clad
   Like senators a harmless empire had.


'At which whether the others did repine,
(For envy harb'reth most in feeblest hearts)
   Or that they all to changing did incline,
(As even in beasts their dams leave changing parts)
The multitude to Jove a suit imparts,
   With neighing, blaying,* braying, and barking,
   Roaring and howling for to have a king.


'A king, in language theirs they said they would
(For then their language was a perfect speech):
   The birds likewise with chirps, and pewing* could,
Cackling and chattering, that of Jove beseech.
Only the owl still warn'd them not to seech*
   So hastily that which they would repent;
   But saw they would, and he to deserts went.


'Jove wisely said (for wisdom wisely says)
'O beasts, take heed what you of me desire.
   Rulers will think all things made them to please,
And soon forget the swink* due to their hire:
But since you will, part of my heav'nly fire
   I will you lend; the rest yourselves must give,
   That it both seen and felt may with you live.'


'Full glad they were, and took the naked spright,
Which straight the earth yclothed in his clay:
   The lion, heart; the ounce* gave active might;
The horse, good shape; the sparrow, lust to play;
Nightingale, voice, enticing songs to say:
   Elephant gave a perfect memory;
   And parrot, ready tongue, that to apply.

---

* *blaying*: bleating. *pewing*: crying. *seech*: seek. *swink*: labour involved in their responsibility. *ounce*: leopard.

'The fox gave craft; the dog gave flattery:
Ass, patience; the mole, a working thought;
  Eagle, high look; wolf, secret cruelty;
Monkey, sweet breath; the cow, her fair eyes brought;
The ermine, whitest skin, spotted with nought;
  The sheep, mild seeming face; climbing, the bear.
  The stag did give the harm-eschewing fear.

'The hare, her sleights; the cat, his melancholy;
Ant, industry; and coney,* skill to build;
  Cranes, order; storks, to be appearing holy;
Chameleon, ease to change; duck, ease to yield:
Crocodile, tears, which might be falsely spill'd:
  Ape, great thing gave, though he did mowing* stand,
  The instrument of instruments, the hand.

'Each other beast likewise his present brings:
And (but they drad their prince they oft should want)
  They all consented were to give him wings:
And aye more awe towards him for to plant,
To their own work this privilege they grant,
  That from thenceforth to all eternity,
  No beast should freely speak, but only he.

'Thus man was made; thus man their lord became:
Who at the first, wanting, or hiding pride,
  He did to beasts' best use his cunning frame;
With water drink, herbs meat, and naked hide,
And fellow-like let his dominion slide;
  Not in his sayings saying "I", but "we";
  As if he meant his lordship common be.

'But when his seat so rooted he had found,
That they now skill'd not how from him to wend;
  Then gan in guiltless earth full many a wound,[8]
Iron to seek, which 'gainst itself should bend,
To tear the bowels, that god corn should send.
  But yet the common dam none did bemoan;
  Because (though hurt) they never heard her groan.

* *coney*: rabbit. *mowing*: 'mopping and mowing'.

'Then 'gan the factions in the beasts to breed;
Where helping weaker sort, the nobler beasts
 (As tigers, leopards, bears, and lions' seed)
Disdain'd with this, in deserts sought their rests;
Where famine ravin* taught their hungry chests,
  That craftily he forc'd them to do ill,
  Which being done, he afterwards would kill,

'For murders done, which never erst was seen,
By those great beasts. As for the weaker's good,
  He chose themselves his guarders for to been,
'Gainst those of might, of whom in fear they stood,
As horse, and dog, not great, but gentle blood:
  Blithe were the common cattle of the field,
  Tho' when they saw their foe'n of greatness kill'd.

'But they or spent, or made of slender might,
Then quickly did the meaner cattle find,
  The great beams gone,⁹ the house on shoulders light:
For by and by the horse fair bits did bind:
The dog was in a collar taught his kind.
  As for the gentle birds, like case might rue,
  When falcon they, and goss-hawk saw in mew.*

'Worst fell to smallest birds, and meanest herd,
Whom now his own, full like his own he used.
  Yet first but wool, or feathers off he tear'd;
And when they were well us'd to be abused,
For hungry throat their flesh with teeth he bruised:
  At length for glutton taste he did them kill:
  At last for sport their silly lives did spill.

'But yet, O man, rage not beyond thy need:
Deem it not glory to swell in tyranny.
  Thou art of blood, joy not to see things bleed:
Thou fearest death: think they are loth to die.
A plaint of guiltless hurt doth pierce the sky.
  And you poor beasts in patience bide your hell,
  Or know your strengths, and then you shall do well.'

    *ravin: preying on each other. mew: cage.

Thus did I sing and pipe eight sullen hours
To sheep, whom love, not knowledge, made to hear,
　　Now fancy's fits, now fortune's baleful stours:*
But then I homeward call'd my lambkins dear;
For to my dimmed eyes began to appear
　　The night grown old, her black head waxen grey,
　　Sure shepherd's sign, that morn should soon fetch day.

According to the nature of diverse ears, diverse judgements
straight followed; some praising his voice, others his words fit to
frame a pastoral style,[10] others the strangeness of the tale, and
scanning what he should mean by it. But old Geron (who had
borne him a grudge ever since in one of their eclogues he had
taken him up over-bitterly) took hold of this occasion to make his
revenge, and said he never saw thing worse proportioned than to
bring in a tale of he knew not what beasts at such a sport-meeting,
when rather some song of love or matter for joyful melody was to
be brought forth. 'But,' said he, 'this is the right conceit of young
men, who think then they speak wiseliest when they cannot
understand themselves.'

But little did the melancholic shepherd regard either his dis-
praises or the other's praises, who had set the foundation of his
honour there where he was most despised. And therefore he returning again to the train of his desolate pensiveness, Geron invited Histor to answer him in eclogue-wise; who indeed having
been long in love with the fair Kala, and now by Lalus overgone,
was grown into a detestation of marriage. But thus it was:

### GERON · HISTOR

GERON:　In faith, good Histor, long is your delay
　From holy marriage, sweet and surest mean
　　Our foolish lust in honest rules to stay.
　I pray thee do to Lalus' sample* lean:
　Thou seest how frisk and jolly now he is
　　That last day seem'd he could not chew a bean.
　Believe me man, there is no greater bliss
　　Than is the quiet joy of loving wife:

* *stours*: storms. *sample*: example.

Which whoso wants, half of himself doth miss.
    Friend without change, playfellow without strife,
Food without fulness, counsel without pride,
    Is this sweet doubling of our single life.

HISTOR: No doubt to whom so good chance did betide
    As for to find a pasture strawed* with gold,
    He were a fool if there he did not bide.
Who would not have a Phoenix if he could?
    The humming wasp, if it had not a sting,
Before all flies the wasp accept I would.
    But this bad world few golden fields doth bring:
Phoenix but one, of crows we millions have.
    The wasp seems gay but is a cumbrous thing.
If many Kala's our Arcadia gave,
    Lalus' example I would soon ensue,
And think I did myself from sorrow save.
    But of such wives we find a slender crew;
Shrewdness* so stirs, pride so puffs up the heart,
    They seldom ponder what to them is due.
With meagre looks, as if they still did smart,
    Puling and whimpering, or else scolding flat,
Make home more pain than following of the cart.
    Either dull silence, or eternal chat;
Still contrary to what her husband says;
    If he do praise the dog, she likes the cat.
Austere she is when he would honest plays,
    And gamesome then when he thinks on his sheep;
She bids him go, and yet from journey stays.
    She war doth ever with his kinsfolk keep,
And makes them fremd,* who friends by nature are,
    Envying shallow toys with malice deep.
And if forsooth there come some new found ware,
    The little coin his sweating brows have got
Must go for that, if for her lours he care:
    Or else, 'Nay faith, mine is the lucklest* lot

---

*strawed: strewn. *shrewdness:* shrewishness. *fremd:* unfriendly.
*lucklest:* most unlucky.

That ever fell to honest woman yet:
　　No wife but I hath such a man, God wot.'
Such is their speech who be of sober wit:
　　But who do let their tongues show well their rage,
Lord, what bye-words they speak, what spite they spit!
　　The house is made a very loathsome cage
Wherein the bird doth never sing, but cry
　　With such a will as nothing can assuage.
Dearly the servants do their wages buy,
　　Revil'd for each small fault, sometimes for none:
They better live that in a jail do lie.
　　Let other fouler sports away be blown,
For I seek not their shame, but still methinks
　　A better life it is to lie alone.


GERON: Who for each fickle fear from virtue shrinks
Shall in his life embrace no worthy thing:
　　No mortal man the cup of surety drinks.
The heav'ns do not good haps in handfuls bring,
　　But let us pick our good from out much bad,
That still our little world may know his king.
　　But certainly so long we may be glad
While that we do what nature doth require,
　　And for th' event* we never ought be sad.
Man oft is plagu'd with air, is burnt with fire,
　　In water drown'd, in earth his burial is;
And shall we not therefore their use desire?
　　Nature above all things requireth this,
That we our kind do labour to maintain:
　　Which drawn-out line doth hold all human bliss.
Thy father justly may of thee complain
　　If thou do not repay his deeds for thee
In granting unto him a grandsire's gain.
　　Thy Commonwealth may rightly grieved be,
Which must by this immortal be preserved,
　　If thus thou murder thy posterity.
His very being he hath not deserved

*th' event*: the future outcome.

Who for a self-conceit will that forbear
Whereby that being aye must be conserved.
  And God forbid women such cattle were
As you paint them: but well in you I find
  No man doth speak aright who speaks in fear.
Who only sees the ill is worse than blind.
  These fifty winters married have I been,
And yet find no such faults in womankind.
  I have a wife worthy to be a queen.
So well she can command, and yet obey:
  In ruling of a house so well she's seen.
And yet in all this time betwixt us tway,
  We bear our double yoke with such consent,
That never passed foul word, I dare well say.
  But these be your love-toys, which still are spent
In lawless games, and love not as you should,
  But with much study learn late to repent.
How well last day before our prince you could
  Blind Cupid's works with wonder testify!
Yet now the root of him abase you would.
  Go to, go to, and Cupid now apply
To that where thou thy Cupid may'st avow,
  And thou shalt find in women virtues lie.
Sweet supple minds which soon to wisdom bow
  Where they by wisdom's rule directed are,
And are not forc'd fond thraldom to allow.
  As we to get are fram'd, so they to spare:
We made for pain, our pains they made to cherish:
  We care abroad, and they of home have care.
O Histor, seek within thyself to flourish:
  Thy house by thee must live or else be gone:
And then who shall the name of Histor nourish?
  Riches of children pass a prince's throne;
Which touch the father's heart with secret joy,
  When without shame he saith, 'These be mine own.'
Marry, therefore, for marriage will destroy
  Those passions which to youthful head do climb,
Mothers and nurses of all vain annoy.

HISTOR: Perchance I will, but now methinks it time
    To go unto the bride, and use this day
    To speak with her while freely speak we may.

    He spake these words with such affection as a curious eye might easily have perceived he liked Thyrsis' fortune better than he loved his person. But then indeed did all arise and went to the women, where spending all the day and good part of the night in dancing, carolling and wassailing, lastly, they left Thyrsis where he long desired to be left, and with many unfeigned thanks returned every man to his home. But some of them, having to cross the way of the two lodges, might see a lady making doleful lamentations over a body which seemed dead unto them. But methinks Dametas cries unto me. If I come not the sooner to comfort him, he will leave off his golden work that hath already cost him so much labour and longing.

**THE END OF THE THIRD BOOK**

# The Fourth Book of the Countess
of Pembroke's Arcadia

## CHAPTER 1

The almighty wisdom (evermore delighting to show the world
that by unlikeliest means greatest matters may come to conclusion, that human reason may be the more humbled and more
willingly give place to divine providence) as at the first it brought
in Dametas to play a part in this royal pageant, so having continued him still an actor, now that all things were grown ripe for
an end, made his folly the instrument of revealing that which far
greater cunning had sought to conceal. For so it fell out that
Dametas, having spent the whole day in breaking up the cumbersome work of the pastor Dorus, and feeling in all his labour no
pain so much as that his hungry hopes received any stay, having
with the price of much sweat and weariness gotten up the huge
stone, which he thought should have such a golden lining, the
good man in the great bed that stone had made found nothing but
these two verses written upon a broad piece of vellum:

> Who hath his hire hath well his labour plac'd;
> Earth thou didst seek, and store of Earth thou hast.

What an inward discountenance* it was to master Dametas to
find his hope of wealth turned to poor verses (for which he never
cared much) nothing can describe but either the feeling in oneself
the state of such a mind Dametas had,[1] or at least the bethinking
what was Midas' fancy when, after the great pride he conceived to
be made judge between Gods, he was rewarded with the ornament
of an ass's ears.[2] Yet the deep apprehension he had received of
such riches could not so suddenly lose the colour that had so
thoroughly dyed his thick brain but that he turned and tossed the
poor bowels of the innocent earth, till the coming on of the night
and the tediousness of his fruitless labour made him content

* *discountenance*: abashment.

rather to exercise his discontentation at home than there. But forced he was (his horse being otherwise burdened with digging instruments) to return as he came most part of the way on foot, with such grudging lamentations as a nobler mind would (but more nobly) make for the loss of his mistress. For so far had he fed his foolish soul with the expectation of that which he reputed felicity, that he no less accounted himself miserable than if he had fallen from such an estate his fancy had embraced.

So then home again went Dametas, punished in conceit as in conceit* he had erred, till he found himself there from a fancied loss fallen to essential misery: for entering into his house three hours within night, instead of the lightsome countenance of Pamela (which gave such an inward decking to that lodge as proudest palaces might have cause to envy it) and of the grateful conversation of Dorus, whose witty behaviour made that loneliness to seem full of good company; instead of the loud scolding of Miso and the busy rumbling up and down of Mopsa (which, though they were so short as quite contrary to the others' praiseworthiness, yet were they far before them in filling of a house) he found nothing but a solitary darkness, which as naturally it breeds a kind of irksome ghastfulness, so it was to him a most present terror, remembering the charge he had left behind which he well knew imported no less than his life unto him. Therefore lighting a candle, there was no place a mouse could have dwelled in but that he with quaking diligence sought into. But when he saw he could see nothing of that he most cared for, then became he the right pattern of a wretch dejected with fear: for crying and howling, knocking his head to the wall, he began to make pitiful complaints where nobody could hear him, and, with too much dread he should not recover her, leave all consideration how to recover her. But at length looking like a she-goat when she casts her kid, for very sorrow he took in his own behalf, out of the lodge he went running as hard as he could, having now received the very form of hanging into his consideration.

Thus running as a man that would gladly have run from himself, it was his foolish fortune to espy, by the glimmering light the moon did then yield him, one standing aloft among the boughs of

* *conceit ... conceit*: self-conceit ... judgement.

a fair ash. He, that would have asked counsel at that time of a dog, cast up his face as if his tooth had been drawing, and with much bending his sight perceived it was mistress Mopsa, fitly seated there for her wit and dignity. There, I will not say with joy (for how could he taste of joy whose imagination was fallen from a palace to the gallows?) but yet with some refreshing of comfort, in hopes he should learn better tidings of her, he began to cry out: 'O Mopsa, my beloved chicken, here am I, thine own father Dametas, never in such a towardness of hanging if thou canst not help me.'

But never a word could his eloquence procure of Mopsa, who, indeed, was there attending for greater matters. This was yet a new burden to poor Dametas, who thought all the world was conspiring against him; and therefore with a silly choler he began another tune: 'Thou vile Mopsa,' said he, 'now the vengeance of my fatherly curse light overthwart* thee if thou do not straight answer me.'

But neither blessing nor cursing could prevail with Mopsa, who was now great with child with the expectation of her may-game hopes and did long to be delivered with the third time being named. Which by and by followed; for Dametas, rubbing his elbow, stamping and whining, seeing neither of these take place, began to throw stones at her and withal to conjure her by the name of hellish Mopsa. But when he had named her the third time, no chime can more suddenly follow the striking of a clock than she (verily thinking it was the god that used her father's voice, throwing her arms abroad and not considering she was muffled upon so high a tree) came fluttering down like a hooded hawk, like enough to have broken her neck but that the tree full of boughs tossed her from one bough to another, and lastly, well bruised, brought her to receive an unfriendly salutation of the earth. Dametas, as soon as she was down, came running to her, and finding her so close wrapt, pulled off the scarlet cloak – in good time for her, for with the soreness of the fall, if she had not had breath given her, she had delivered a foolish soul to Pluto.

But then Dametas began afresh to desire his daughter not to forget the pains he had taken for her in her childhood (which he

* *light overthwart*: fall upon.

was sure she could not remember) and to tell him where Pamela was.

'O good Apollo,' said Mopsa, 'if ever thou didst bear love to Phaeton's mother, let me have a king to my husband.'

'Alas, what speakest thou of Phaeton?' said Dametas. 'If by thy circumspect means I find not out Pamela, thy father will be hanged tomorrow.'

'It is no matter though he be hanged,' answered Mopsa. 'Do but thou make Dorus a king, and let him be my husband, good Apollo, for my courage doth much prick me toward him.'

'Ah Mopsa,' cried out Dametas, 'where is thy wit? Dost thou not know thy father? How hast thou forgotten thyself?'

'I do not ask wit of thee, mine own God,' said she, 'but I see thou wouldst have me remember my father, and indeed forget myself. No, no, a good husband!'

'Thou shalt have thy fill of husbands,' said Dametas, 'and do but answer me my question.'

'O I thank thee,' said Mopsa, 'with all my heart heartily, but let them be all kings.'

Dametas, seeing no other way prevail, fell down on his knees. 'Mopsa, Mopsa,' said he, 'do not thus cruelly torment me. I am already wretched enough. Alas, either help me or tell me thou canst not.'

She, that would not be behind Apollo in courtesy, kneeled down on the other side: 'I will never leave tormenting thee,' said Mopsa, 'until thou hast satisfied my longing, but I will proclaim thee a promise-breaker that even Jupiter shall hear it.'

'Now by the fostering thou hast received in this place, save my life,' said Dametas.

'Now by the fair ash,' answered Mopsa, 'where thou didst receive so great a good turn, grant post haste to my burning fancy.'

'O where is Pamela?' said Dametas. 'O, a lusty husband!' said Mopsa.

Dametas, that now verily assured himself his daughter was mad, began utterly to despair of his life; and therefore amazedly catching her in his arms to see whether he could bring her to herself, he might feel the weight of a great cudgel light upon his shoulders, and for the first greeting, he knew his wife Miso's voice by the calling him ribald villain, and asking him whether she could not serve his turn as well as Charita. For Miso, having according to Dorus' counsel gone to Mantinea and there harboured herself in an old acquaintance's house of hers, as soon as ten of the clock was stricken (where she had remained closely all that while, I think with such an amiable cheer as when jealous Juno sat cross-legged to hinder the child-birth of her husband's love)[3] with open mouth she went to the magistrate appointed over such matters, and there, with the most scolding invective her rage rather than eloquence could bring forth, she required his aid to take Dametas, who had left his duty to the king and his daughter, to commit adultery in the house of Charita's uncle in the Oudemian Street. But neither was the name of Charita remembered, nor any such street known. Yet such was the general mislike all men had of Dametas' unworthy advancement that every man was glad to make himself a minister of that which might redound to his shame; and therefore, with pans,[4] cries and laughters, there was no suspected place in all the city but was searched for under the title of Dametas; Miso ever foremost, encouraging them with all the shameful blazings* of his demeanour, increasing the sport of hunting her husband with her diligent barking; till at length, having done both him and herself as much infamous shame as such a tongue in such an action might perform, in the end not being able to find a thing that was not, to her mare again she went, having neither suspicion nor rage anything mitigated.

But (leaving behind her a sufficient comedy of her tragical fancies) away homeward she came, imputing the not finding her husband to any chance rather than to his innocency. For her heart being apt to receive and nourish a bitter thought, it had so swallowed up a determinate condemnation that in the very anatomy of her spirits one should have found nothing but devilish disdain and hateful jealousy. In this sort grunting out her mischievous spite, she came by the tree even as Dametas was making that ill-understood intercession to his foolish Mopsa. As soon as she heard her husband's voice, she verily thought she had her prey; and therefore stealing from her mare as softly as she could, she came creeping and halting behind him, even as he (thinking his daughter's

*blazings: proclaimings.

little wits had quite left her great noll*) began to take her in his arms, thinking perchance her feeling sense might call her mind parts unto her. But Miso, who saw nothing but through the choler of revengeful anger established upon the forejudgement of his trespass, undoubtedly resolving that Mopsa was Charita Dorus had told her of, mumping* out her hoarse chafe, she gave him the wooden salutation you heard of.

Dametas, that was not so sensible in anything as in blows, turned up his blubbered face like a great lout new whipped: 'Alas, thou woman,' said he, 'what hath thy poor husband deserved to have his own ill luck loaden with displeasure? Pamela is lost, Pamela is lost.'

Miso, still holding on the course of her former fancy, 'What tellest thou me, naughty varlet, of Pamela? Dost thou think that doth answer me for abusing the laws of marriage? Have I brought thee children, have I been a true wife unto thee, to be despised in mine old age?'

And ever among she would sauce her speeches with such bastinadoes that poor Dametas began now to think that either a general madding was fallen, or else that all this was but a vision. But as for visions, the smart of the cudgel put those out of his fancy; and therefore again turning to his wife, not knowing in the world what she meant, 'Miso,' said he, 'hereafter thou mayest examine me. Do but now tell me what is become of Pamela.'

'I will first examine this drab,' said she, and withal let fall her staff as hard as she could upon Mopsa, still taking her for Charita.

But Mopsa, that was already angry, thinking that she had hindered her from Apollo, leaped up and caught her by the throat, like to have strangled her but that Dametas from a condemned man was fain to become a judge and part this fray – such a picture of a rude discord, where each was out with the other two – and then getting the opportunity of their falling out to hold himself in surety* (who was indeed the veriest coward of the three) he renewed his earnest demand of them.

But it was a sport to see how the former conceits Dorus had printed in their imaginations kept still such dominion in them that Miso, though now she found and felt it was her daughter

* *noll*: noddle. *mumping*: mumbling. *chafe*: fury. *surety*: safety.

Mopsa, yet did Charita continually pass through her thoughts, which she uttered with such crabbed questions to Dametas that he (not possibly conceiving any part of her doubt) remained astonished, and the astonishment increased her doubt. And as for Mopsa, as first she did assuredly take him to be Apollo and thought her mother's coming did mar the bargain, so now much talking to and fro had delivered so much light into the misty mould of her capacity as to know him to be her father; yet remained there such footsteps of the foretaken opinion that she thought verily her father and mother were hasted thither to get the first wish. And therefore to whatsoever they asked of her she would never answer, but embracing the tree as if she feared it had been running away, 'Nay,' says she, 'I will have the first wish, for I was here first' – which they understood no more than Dametas did what Miso meant by Charita: till at length with much urging them, being indeed better able to persuade both than to meet hand to hand with either, he prevailed so much with them as to bring them into the lodge to see what loss their negligence had suffered.

Then indeed the near neighbourhood they bare to themselves made them leave other toys and look into what dangerous plight they were all fallen as soon as the king should know his daughter's escape. And as for the women, they began afresh to enter into their brawling whether* were in the fault. But Dametas, who did fear that among his other evils the thunderbolt of that storm would fall upon his shoulders, slipped away from them, but with so meagre a cheer as might much sooner engender laughter than pity.

'O true Arcadia,' would he say (tearing his hair and beard, and sometime for too much woe making unwieldy somersaults) 'how darest thou bear upon thee such a felonious traitor as I am? And you, false hearted trees, why would you make no noise to make her ungracious departure known? Ah Pamela, Pamela, how often when I brought thee in fine posies of all coloured flowers wouldst thou clap me on the cheek, and say thou wouldst be one day even with me? Was this thy meaning, to bring me to an even pair of gallows? Ah, ill-taught Dorus, that camest hither to learn good manners of me, did I ever teach thee to make thy master sweat out

*whether: as to which one.

721

his heart for nothing, and in the meantime to run away with thy mistress? O my dun cow, I did think some evil was towards me ever since the last day thou didst run away from me and held up thy tail so pitifully! Did I not see an eagle kill a cuckoo, which was a plain foretoken unto me Pamela should be my destruction? O wise Miso (if I durst say it to thy face) why didst thou suspect thy husband, that loveth a piece of cheese better than a woman? And thou, little Mopsa, that shalt inherit the shame of thy father's death, was it time for thee to climb trees, which should so shortly be my best burial? O that I could live without death, or die before I were aware! O heart, why hast thou no hands at commandment to dispatch thee? O hands, why want you a heart to kill this villain?'

In this sort did he inveigh against everything, sometimes thinking to run away while it was yet night; but he (that had included all the world* within his sheep-cote) thought that worse than any death. Sometime for dread of hanging he meant to hang himself, finding, as indeed it is, that fear is far more painful to cowardice than death to a true courage. But his fingers were nothing nimble in that action, and anything was let enough thereto, he being a true lover of himself without any rival.

But lastly, guided by a far greater constellation than his own, he remembered to search the other lodge, where it might be Pamela that night had retired herself. So thither with trembling hams he carried himself; but employing his double key (which the king for special credit had unworthily bestowed upon him) he found all the gates so barred that his key could not prevail, saving only one trap-door which went down into a vault by the cellar, which, as it was unknown of Pyrocles, so had he left it unregarded. But Dametas, that ever knew the buttery better than any other place, got in that way, and pacing softly to Philoclea's chamber (where he thought most likely to find Pamela) the door being left open, he entered in, and by the light of the lamp he might discern one on the bed by her[5] which he (although he took to be Pamela) yet thinking no surety enough in a matter touching his neck, he went hard to the bedside of these unfortunate lovers, who at that time, being not much before the break of day[6]

* *that included all the world*: who could conceive of nothing beyond.

(whether it were they were so divinely surprised, to bring this whole matter to the destined conclusion, or that the unresistable force of their sorrows had overthrown the wakeful use of their senses) were as then possessed with a mutual sleep, yet not forgetting with viny* embracements to give any eye a perfect model of affection. But Dametas, looking with the lamp in his hand (but neither with such a face nor mind upon these excellent creatures as Psyche did upon her unknown lover)[7] and giving every way freedom to his fearful eyes, did not only perceive it was Zelmane, and therefore much different from the lady he sought, but that this same Zelmane did more differ from the Zelmane he and others had ever taken her for, wherein the change of her apparel chiefly confirmed his opinion.

Satisfied with that, and not thinking it good to awake the sleeping lion, he went down again, taking with him Pyrocles' sword (wherewith upon his slight undersuit Pyrocles came only apparelled thither) being sure to leave no weapon in the chamber. And so making the door as fast as he could on the outside, hoping with the revealing of this (as he thought) greater fault, to make his own the less, or at least that this injury would so fill the king's head that he should not have leisure to chastise his negligence (like a fool, not considering that the more rage breeds the crueller punishment) he went first into the king's chamber, and not finding him there, he ran down crying with open mouth the king was betrayed, and that Zelmane did abuse his daughter. The noise he made (being a man of no few words) joined to the yelping sound of Miso and his unpleasant inheritrix,* brought together some number of the shepherds, to whom he – without any regard of reserving it for the king's knowledge – spattered out the bottom of his stomach, swearing by him he never knew that Zelmane (whom they had taken all that while to be a woman) was as arrant a man as himself was, whereof he had seen sufficient signs and tokens; and that he was as close as a butterfly with the lady Philoclea.

* *viny*: like the vine twisted round its support. *inheritrix*: i.e. Mopsa.

## CHAPTER 2

The poor men, jealous of their prince's honour, were ready with weapons to have entered the lodge, standing yet in some pause whether it were not best first to hear some news from the king himself, when by the sudden coming of other shepherds (which with astonished looks ran from one cry to the other) their griefs were surcharged with the evil tidings of the king's death. Turning therefore all their minds and eyes that way, they ran to the cave where they said he lay dead, the sun beginning now to send some promise of coming light, making haste, I think, to be spectator of the following tragedies. For Basilius, having past over the night more happy in contemplation than action, having had his spirits sublimed* with the sweet imagination of embracing the most desired Zelmane, doubting lest the cave's darkness might deceive him in the day's approach, thought it now season to return to his wedlock-bed, remembering the promise he had made Zelmane to observe due orders towards Gynecia. Therefore departing, but not departing without bequeathing by a will of words, sealed with many kisses, a full gift of all his love and life to his misconceived bedfellow, he went to the mouth of the cave, there to apparel himself; in which doing, the motion of his joy could not be bridled from uttering such like words:

'Blessed be thou, O night,' said he, 'that hast with thy sweet wings shrouded me in the vale of bliss. It is thou that art the first-gotten child of time; the day hath been but an usurper upon thy delightful inheritance. Thou invitest all living things to comfortable rest. Thou art the stop of strife, and the necessary truce of approaching battles.' And therewith he sung these verses to confirm his former praises:

> O night, the ease of care, the pledge of pleasure,
> Desire's best mean, harvest of hearts affected,
> The seat of peace, the throne which is erected
> Of human life to be the quiet measure,
>
> Be victor still of* Phoebus' golden treasure,

* *sublimed:* refined and raised. *victor still of:* over.

Who hath our sight with too much sight infected,
Whose light is cause we have our lives neglected,
   Turning all nature's course to self displeasure.

These stately stars in their now shining faces,
With sinless sleep, and silence (wisdom's mother)
   Witness his wrong, which by thy help is eased.
Thou art therefore of these our desert places
   The sure refuge; by thee and by no other
My soul is blest, sense joy'd, and fortune raised.

And yet further would his joys needs break forth. 'O Basilius,'
said he, 'the rest of thy time hath been but a dream unto thee: it is
now only thou beginnest to live, now only thou hast entered into
the way of blissfulness. Should fancy of marriage keep me from
this paradise, or opinion of I know not what promise bind me from
paying the right duties to nature and affection? O, who would
have thought there could have been such difference betwixt
women! Be jealous no more, O Gynecia, but yield to the pre-
eminence of more excellent gifts. Support thyself with such
marble pillars as she doth; deck thy breast with those alabaster
bowls that Zelmane doth: then accompanied with such a title,
perhaps thou mayest recover the possession of my otherwise inclined love. But alas, Gynecia, thou canst not show such evidence;
therefore thy plea is in vain.'

Gynecia heard all this he said, who had cast about her Zelmane's garment wherein she came thither, and had followed Basilius to the cave's entry, full of inward vexation betwixt the deadly
accusation of her own guiltiness and the spiteful doubt she had
Zelmane had abused her. But because (of the one side) finding the
king did think her to be Zelmane, she had liberty to imagine it
might rather be the king's own unbridled enterprise which had
barred Zelmane than Zelmane's cunning deceiving of her; and
that (of the other) if she should headily seek a violent revenge, her
own honour might be as much interested* as Zelmane endangered; she fell to this determination: first with fine handling of
the king to settle in him a perfect good opinion of her, and then, as

* *interested:* involved.

she should learn how things had passed, to take into herself new devised counsel. But this being her first action, having given un-looked for attendance to the king, she heard with what partiality he did prefer her to herself: she saw in him how much fancy doth not only darken reason but beguile sense: she found opinion mistress of the lover's judgement. Which serving as a good lesson to her good conceit, she went out to Basilius, setting herself in a grave behaviour and stately silence before him; until he (who, at the first thinking her by so much shadow as he could see to be Zelmane, was beginning his loving ceremonies) did now (being helped by the peeping light wherewith the morning did overcome the night's darkness) know her face and his error – which ac-knowledging in himself with starting back from her, she thus with a modest bitterness spake unto him:

'Alas, my Lord, well did your words decipher your mind, and well be those words confirmed with this gesture! Very loathsome must that woman be from whom a man hath cause to go back; and little better liked is that wife, before whom the husband prefers them he never knew! Alas, hath my faithful observing my part of duty made you think yourself ever a whit the more exempted? Hath that which should claim gratefulness been a cause of con-tempt? Is the being the mother of Pamela become an odious name unto you? If my life hitherto led have not avoided suspicion, if my violated truth to you be deserving of any punishment, I refuse not to be chastised with the most cruel torment of your displeasure; I refuse not misery purchased by mine own merit. Hard, I must needs say (although till now I never thought I should have had cause to say) is the destiny of womankind, the trial of whose virtue must stand upon the loving of them that employ all their industry not to be beloved! If Zelmane's young years had not had so much gravity hidden under a youthful face as your grey hairs have been but the vizor of unfitting youthfulness, your vicious mind had brought some fruits of repentance, and Gynecia might then have been with much more right so basely despised.'

Basilius (that was more ashamed to see himself so overtaken than Vulcan was when with much cunning he proved himself a cuckold)[1] began to make certain extravagant excuses: but the matter in itself hardly brooking any purgation (with the suddenness of the time which barred any good conjoined invention) made him sometimes allege one thing to which, by and by, he would bring in a contrary; one time with flat denial, another time with mitigating the fault (now brave, then humble) use such a stammering defensive that Gynecia (the violence of whose sore indeed ran another way) was content thus to fasten up the last stitch of her anger:

'Well, well, my Lord,' said she, 'it shall well become you so to govern yourself as you may be fit rather to direct me than to be judged of me, and rather to be a wise master of me than an unskilful pleader before me. Remember the wrong you have done is not only to me, but to your children whom you had of me; to your country, when they shall find they are commanded by him that cannot command his own undecent appetites; lastly, to yourself, since with these pains you do but build up a house of shame to dwell in. If from those movable goods of nature* (wherewith, in my first youth, my royal parents bestowed me upon you) bearing you children and increase of years have withdrawn me, consider, I pray you, that as you are the cause of the one, so in the other, time hath not left to work his never-failing effects in you. Truly, truly, Sir, very untimely are these fires in you. It is time for us both to let reason enjoy his due sovereignty. Let us not plant anew those weeds which by nature's course are content to fade.'

Basilius that would rather than his life the matter had been ended, the best rhetoric he had was flat demanding pardon of her, swearing it was the very force of Apollo's destiny* which had carried him thus from his own bias;* but that now, like as far travellers were taught to love their own country, he had such a lesson without book* of affection unto her as he would repay the debt of this error with the interest of a great deal more true honour than ever before he had done her.

'Neither am I to give pardon to you, my Lord,' said she, 'nor you to bear honour to me. I have taken this boldness, for the unfeigned love I owe unto you, to deliver my sorrow unto you much more for the care I have of your well-doing than for any other selffancy. For well I know that by your good estate my life is main-

---

* those movable goods of nature: beauty. Apollo's destiny: the destiny Apollo ordained. bias: natural course. without book: by heart.

tained; neither, if I would, can I separate myself from your fortune. For my part, therefore, I claim nothing but that which may be safest for yourself: my life, will, honour, and whatsoever else, shall be but a shadow of that body.'

How much Basilius' own shame had found him culpable and had already even in soul read his own condemnation, so much did this unexpected mildness of Gynecia captive his heart unto her, which otherwise perchance would have grown to a desperate carelessness. Therefore embracing her, and confessing that her virtue shined in his vice, he did even with a true resolved mind vow unto her that as long as he, unworthy of her, did live, she should be the furthest and only limit of his affection. He thanked the destinies that had wrought her honour out of his shame, and that had made his own striving to go amiss to be the best mean ever after to hold him in the right path.

Thus reconciled to Basilius' great contentation, who began something to mark himself in his own doings, his hard hap* guided his eye to the cup of gold wherein Gynecia had put the liquor meant for Zelmane, and having failed of that guest, was now carrying it home again. But he, whom perchance sorrow, perchance some long disaccustomed pains had made extremely thirsty, took it out of her hands, although she directly told him both of whom she had it, what the effect of it was, and the little proof she had seen thereof; hiding nothing from him but that she meant to minister it to another patient.

But the king, whose belly had no ears, and much drouth* kept from the desiring a taster,* finding it not unpleasant to his palate, drank it almost off, leaving very little to cover the cup's bottom. But within a while that from his stomach the drink had delivered to his principal veins his noisome vapours, first with a painful stretching and forced yawning, then with a dark yellowness dying his skin and a cold deadly sweat principally about his temples, his body, by natural course longing to deliver* his heavy burden to his earthly dam (wanting force in his knees, which utterly abandoned him) with heavy fall gave some proof whither the operation

* his hard hap: his evil fortune. drouth: thirst. desiring a taster: a taster to drink first to see if it were poisoned. longing to deliver: i.e. to fall down.

of that unknown potion tended. For, with pang-like groans and ghastly turning of his eyes, immediately all his limbs stiffened and his eyes fixed, he having had time to declare his case only in these words: 'O Gynecia, I die. Have care – ' Of what, or how much further he would have spoken, no man can tell.

For Gynecia, having well perceived the changing of his colour and those other evil signs, yet had not looked for such a sudden overthrow, but rather had bethought herself what was best for him. When she suddenly saw the matter come to that period, coming to him, and neither with any cries getting a word of him nor with any other possible means able to bring any living action from him, the height of all ugly sorrows did so horribly appear before her amazed mind that at first it did not only distract all power of speech from her but almost wit to consider, remaining as it were quick buried* in a grave of miseries. Her painful memory had straight filled her with the true shapes of all the fore-past mischiefs: her reason began to cry out against the filthy rebellion of sinful sense, and to tear itself with anguish for having made so weak a resistance: her conscience, a terrible witness of the inward wickedness, still nourishing this debateful fire: her complaint now not having an end to be directed unto, something to disburthen sorrow, but a necessary downfall of inward wretchedness. She saw the rigour of the laws was like to lay a shameful death upon her, which, being for that action undeserved, made it the more insupportable; and yet in depth of her soul most deserved, made it more miserable. At length, letting her tongue go as her dolorous thoughts guided it, she thus with lamenable demeanour spake:

'O bottomless pit of sorrow in which I cannot contain myself, having the firebrands of all furies within me; still falling, and yet by the infiniteness of it never fallen! Neither can I rid myself, being fettered with the everlasting consideration of it. For whither should I recommend the protection of my dishonoured fall? To the earh? It hath no life, and waits to be increased by the relics of my shamed carcass. To men, who are always cruel in their neighbours' faults, and make others' overthrow become the badge of their ill-masked virtue? To the heavens? O unspeakable torment of conscience which dare not look unto them! No sin can enter there. O,

*quick buried: buried alive.*

there is no receipt for polluted minds. Whither then wilt thou lead this captive of thine, O snaky despair? Alas, alas, was this the freeholding power that accursed poison hath granted unto me, that to be held the surer it should deprive life? Was this the folding in mine arms promised, that I should fold nothing but a dead body? O mother of mine, what a deathful suck have you given me? O Philoclea, Philoclea, well hath my mother revenged upon me my unmotherly hating of thee. O Zelmane, to whom yet (lest any misery should fail me) remain some sparks of my detestable love, if thou hast (as now, alas, now my mind assures me thou hast) deceived me, there is a fair stage prepared for thee, to see the tragical end of thy hated lover.'

With that word there flowed out two rivers of tears out of her fair eyes which before were dry, the remembrance of her other mischiefs being dried up in a furious fire of self detestation; love only, according to the temper of it, melting itself into those briny tokens of passion. Then turning her eyes again upon the body, she remembered a dream* she had had some nights before wherein, thinking herself called by Zelmane, passing a troublesome passage, she found a dead body which told her there should be her only rest. This no sooner caught hold of her remembrance, than that she, determining with herself it was a direct vision of her fore-appointed end, took a certain resolution to embrace death as soon as it should be offered unto her, and no way to seek the prolonging of her annoyed life. And therefore kissing the cold face of Basilius; 'And even so will I rest,' said she, 'and join this faulty soul of mine to thee, if so much the angry gods will grant me.'

## CHAPTER 3

As she was in this plight, the sun now climbing over the horizon, the first shepherds came by, who seeing the king in that case, and hearing the noise Dametas made of the Lady Philoclea, ran with the doleful tidings of Basilius' death unto him, who presently with all his company came to the cave's entry where the king's body lay: Dametas for his part more glad for the hope he had of

* See p. 376.

his private escape than sorry for the public loss his country received for a prince not to be misliked.* But in Gynecia nature prevailed above judgement, and the shame she conceived to be taken in that order overcame for that instant the former resolution; so that as soon as she saw the foremost of the pastoral troop, the wretched princess ran to have hid her face in the next woods, but with such a mind that she knew not almost herself what she could wish to be the ground of her safety. Dametas, that saw her run away in Zelmane's upper raiment and judging her to be so, thought certainly all the spirits in hell were come to play a tragedy in these woods, such strange change he saw every way – the king dead at the cave's mouth; the queen, as he thought, absent; Pamela fled away with Dorus; his wife and Mopsa in divers frenzies. But of all other things Zelmane conquered his capacity, suddenly from a woman grown to a man, and from a locked chamber gotten before him into the fields, which he gave the rest quickly to understand: for instead of doing anything as the exigent* required, he began to make circles and all those fantastical defences that he had ever heard were fortification against devils. But the other shepherds, who had both better wits and more faith, forthwith divided themselves, some of them running after Gynecia and esteeming her running away a great condemnation of her own guiltiness; others going to their prince to see what service was left for them, either in recovery of his life or honouring his death.

They that went after the queen had soon overtaken her, in whom now the first fears were stayed, and the resolution to die had repossessed his place in her mind. But when they saw it was the queen, to whom (besides the obedient duty they owed to her state) they had always carried a singular love for her courteous liberalities and other wise and virtuous parts which had filled all that people with affection and admiration, they were all suddenly stopped, beginning to ask pardon for their following her in that sort, and desiring her to be their good lady as she had ever been. But the queen (who now thirsted to be rid of herself, whom she hated above all things) with such an assured countenance as they

*not to be misliked: disliked by nobody. exigent: the demands of the moment.

have who already have dispensed with shame and digested the sorrows of death, she thus said unto them:

'Continue, continue, my friends: your doing is better than your excusing. The one argues assured faith; the other, want of assurance. If you loved your prince when he was able and willing to do you much good, which you could not then requite to him, do you now publish your gratefulness when it shall be seen to the world there are no hopes left to lead you unto it. Remember, remember you have lost Basilius, a prince to defend you, a father to care for you, a companion in your joys, a friend in your wants. And if you loved him, show you hate the author of his loss. It is I, faithful Arcadians, that have spoiled the country of their protector. I, none but I, was the minister of his unnatural end. Carry therefore my blood in your hands to testify your own innocency; neither spare for my title's sake, but consider it was he that so entitled me. And if you think of any benefits by my means, think with it that I was but the instrument and he the spring. What, stay ye, shepherds, whose great shepherd is gone? You need not fear a woman nor reverence your lord's murderer, nor have pity of her who hath not pity of herself.'

With this she presented her fair neck; to some by name, to others by signs, desiring them to do justice to the world, duty to their good king, honour to themselves, and favour to her. The poor men looked one upon the other, unused to be arbiters in princes' matters, and being now fallen into a great perplexity, betwixt a prince dead and a princess alive. But once* for them she might have gone whither she would, thinking it a sacrilege to touch her person; when she, finding she was not a sufficient orator to persuade her own death by their hands, 'Well,' said she, 'it is but so much more time of misery. For my part, I will not give my life so much pleasure from henceforward as to yield to his desire of his own choice of death. Since all the rest is taken away, yet let me excel in misery. Lead me therefore whither you will; only happy because I cannot be more wretched.'

But neither so much would the honest shepherds do, but rather with many tears bemoaned this increase of their former loss, till she was fain to lead them with a very strange spectacle – either

* *But once:* but certainly.

that a princess should be in the hands of shepherds, or a prisoner should direct her guardians, lastly, before either witness or accuser a lady condemn herself to death. But in such moanful march they went towards the other shepherds, who in the meantime had left nothing unassayed to revive the king; but all was bootless, and their sorrows increased the more they had suffered any hopes vainly to arise. Among other trials they made to know at least the cause of his end, having espied the unhappy cup, they gave the little liquor that was left to a dog of Dametas, in which within a short time it wrought the like effect; although Dametas did so much to recover him that for very love of his life he dashed out his brains.

But now altogether, and having Gynecia among them (who, to make herself the more odious, did continually record to their minds the excess of their loss) they yielded themselves over to all those forms of lamentation that doleful images do imprint in the honest but over-tender hearts, especially when they think the rebound of the evil falls to their own smart. Therefore after the ancient Greek manner, some of them remembering the nobility of his birth continued by being like his ancestors; others his shape, which though not excellent, yet favour and pity drew all things now to the highest point; others his peaceable government (the thing which most pleaseth men resolved to live of their own); others his liberality, which though it cannot light upon all men, yet all men naturally hoping it may be, they make it a most amiable virtue; some calling in question the greatness of his power, which increased the compassion to see the present change (having a doleful memory how he had tempered it with such familiar courtesy among them that they did more feel the fruits than see the pomps of his greatness): all with one consent giving him the sacred titles of good, just, merciful, the father of the people, the life of his country, they ran about his body, tearing their beards and garments; some sending their cries to heaven; other inventing particular howling music; many vowing to kill themselves at the day of his funerals; generally giving a true testimony that men are loving creatures when injuries put them not from their natural course, and how easy a thing it is for a prince by succession deeply to sink into the souls of his subjects – a more lively monument than Mausolus' tomb.[1]

But as with such hearty lamentation they dispersed among those woods their resounding shrieks, the sun, the perfectest mark of time, having now gotten up two hours' journey in his daily changing circle, their voice (helped with the only answering echo) came to the ears of the faithful and worthy gentleman Philanax, who at that time was coming to visit the king, accompanied with divers of the worthy Arcadian lords who with him had visited the places adjoining for the more assurance of Basilius' solitariness – a thing after the late mutiny he had usually done and, since the princesses' return, more diligently continued. Which having now likewise performed, thinking it as well his duty to see the king as of a good purpose (being so near) to receive his further direction, accompanied as above-said, he was this morning coming unto him when these unpleasant voices gave his mind an uncertain presage of his near-approaching sorrow. For by and by he saw the body of his dearly esteemed prince, and heard Gynecia's lamenting – not such as the turtle-like love is wont to make for the ever over-soon loss of her only loved mate, but with cursings of her life, detesting her own wickedness, seeming only therefore not to desire death because she would not show a love of anything.

The shepherds, especially Dametas, knowing him to be the second person in authority, gave forthwith relation unto him what they knew and had proved of this dolorous spectacle, besides the other accidents of his children. But he, principally touched with his master's loss, lighting from his horse with a heavy cheer, came and kneeled down by him, where, finding he could do no more than the shepherds had for his recovery, the constancy of his mind, surprised before he might call together his best rules, could not refrain such like words:

'Ah, dear master,' said he, 'what change it hath pleased the Almighty Justice to work in this place! How soon – not to your loss who have lived long to nature, and now live longer by your well deserved glory, but longest of all in the eternal mansion you now possess – but how soon, I say, to our ruin have you left the frail bark of your estate! O, that the words in most faithful duty delivered unto you when you first entered this solitary course might have wrought as much persuasion in you as they sprang from truth in me! Perchance your servant Philanax should not now have cause in your loss to bewail his own overthrow.' And therewith taking himself:* 'And indeed evil fitteth it me,' said he, 'to let go my heart to womanish complaints, since my prince being undoubtedly well, it rather shows love of myself which makes me bewail mine own loss. No, the true love must be proved in the honour of your memory, and that must be showed with seeking just revenge upon your unjust and unnatural enemies; and far more honourable it will be for your tomb to have the blood of your murderers sprinkled upon it than the tears of your friends. And if your soul look down upon this miserable earth, I doubt not it had much rather your death were accompanied with well-deserved punishment of the causers of it than with the heaping on it more sorrows with the end of them to whom you vouchsafed your affection. Let them lament that have woven the web of lamentation. Let their own deaths make them cry out for your death, that were the authors of it.'

Therewith carrying manful sorrow and vindicative* resolution in his face, he rose up, so looking on the poor guiltless princess, transported with an unjust justice, that his eyes were sufficient heralds for him to denounce a mortal hatred. She (whom furies of love, firebrands of her conscience, shame of the world, with the miserable loss of her husband towards whom now the disdain of herself bred more love, with the remembrance of her vision, where-with she – resolved assuredly the gods had appointed that shameful end to be her resting place – had set her mind to no other way but to death) used such like speeches to Philanax as she had before to the shepherds; willing him not to look upon her as a woman but a monster; not as a princess but a traitor to his prince; not as Basilius' wife but as Basilius' murderer. She told how the world required at his hands the just demonstration of his friendship: if he now forgot his prince, he should show he had never loved but his fortune, like those vermin that suck of the living blood and leave the body as soon as it is dead – poor princess, needlessly seeking to kindle him who did most deadly detest her; which he uttered in this bitter answer.

'Madam,' said he, 'you do well to hate yourself, for you cannot

* *taking himself*: pulling himself together. *vindicative*: vindictive.

hate a worse creature; and though we feel enough your hellish disposition, yet we need not doubt you are of counsel to yourself of much worse than we know. But now, fear not. You shall not long be cumbered with being guided by so evil a soul. Therefore prepare yourself that if it be possible you may deliver up your spirit so much purer as you more wash your wickedness with repentance.'

Then having presently given order for the bringing from Mantinea a great number of tents for the receipt of the principal Arcadians (the manner of that country being that where the prince died, there should be orders taken for the country's government, and in the place any murder was committed, the judgement should be given there, before the body was buried) both concurring in this matter, and already great part of the nobility being arrived, he delivered the princess to a gentleman of great trust. And as for Dametas, taking from him the keys of both the lodges, calling him the moth of his prince's estate and only spot* of his judgement, he caused him, with his wife and daughter, to be fettered up in as many chains and clogs* as they could bear, and every third hour to be cruelly whipped, till the determinate judgement should be given of all these matters. That done, having sent already at his coming to all the quarters of the country to seek Pamela, although with small hope of overtaking them, he himself went well accompanied to the lodge, where the two unfortunate lovers were attending a cruel conclusion of their long painful and late most painful affection.

## CHAPTER 4

Dametas' clownish eyes, having been the only discoverers of Pyrocles' stratagem, had no sooner taken a full view of them (which in some sights would rather have bred anything than an accusing mind) and locked the door upon these two young folks (now made prisoners for love as before they had been prisoners to love) but that immediately upon his going down (whether with noise Dametas made, or with the creeping in of the light, or rather that as extreme grief had procured his sleep, so extreme care had measured his sleep, giving his senses a very early salve to come to

* *spot*: blot. *clogs*: weights.

themselves) Pyrocles awaked: and being up, the first evil hand-sel* he had of the ill case wherein he was was the seeing himself deprived of his sword from which he had never separated himself in any occasion, and even that night, first by the king's bed and then there, had laid it (as he thought) safe; putting great part of the trust of his well-doing in his own courage so armed. For indeed the confidence in one's self is the chief nurse of magnanimity; which confidence notwithstanding doth not leave the care of ne-cessary furnitures for it: and therefore of all the Grecians Homer doth ever make Achilles the best armed. But that, as I say, was the first ill token. But by and by he perceived he was a prisoner before any arrest, for the door which he had left open was made so fast of the outside that for all the force he could employ unto it, he could not undo Dametas' doing.

Then went he to the windows to see if that way there were any escape for him and his dear lady. But as vain he found all his employment there, not having might to break out but only one bar, wherein notwithstanding he strained his sinews to the utter-most; and that he rather took out to use for other service than for any possibility he had to escape: for even then it was that Dametas, having gathered together the first coming shepherds, did blabber out what he had found in the lady Philoclea's chamber. Pyrocles markingly hearkened to all that Dametas said, whose voice and mind acquaintance had taught him sufficiently to know. But when he assuredly perceived that his being with the Lady Philoclea was fully discovered, and by the folly or malice, or rather malicious folly of Dametas, her honour therein touched in the highest degree; remembering withal the cruelty of the Arcadian laws, which without exception did condemn all to death who were found (as Dametas reported of them) in act of marriage with-out solemnity of marriage; assuring himself, besides the law, the king and the queen would use so much the more hate against their daughter as they had found themselves sotted* by him in the pursuit of their love; lastly, seeing they were not only in the way of death but fitly incaged for death, looking with a hearty grief upon the honour of love, the fellowless Philoclea (whose innocent soul now enjoying his own goodness did little know the danger of

* *handsel:* token. *soted:* made fools of.

his even fair, then sleeping, harbour)* his excellent wit, strengthened with virtue but guided by love, had soon described to himself a perfect vision of their present condition.

Wherein having presently cast a resolute reckoning of his own part of the misery, not only the chief but sole burden of his anguish consisted in the unworthy case which was like to fall upon the best deserving Philoclea. He saw the misfortune, not the mismeaning, of his work was like to bring that creature to end, in whom the world, as he thought, did begin to receive honour. He saw the weak judgement of man would condemn that as death-deserving vice in her which had in troth never broken the bonds of a true living virtue: and how often his eye turned to his attractive adamant*, so often did an unspeakable horror strike his noble heart to consider so unripe years, so faultless a beauty, the mansion of so pure goodness, should have her youth so untimely cut off, her natural perfections unnaturally consumed, her virtue rewarded with shame. Sometimes he would accuse himself of negligence, that had not more curiously looked to all the house-entries: and yet could he not imagine the way Dametas was gotten in; and to call back what might have been, to a man of wisdom and courage, carries but a vain shadow of discourse. Sometimes he could not choose but with a dissolution of his inward might lamentably consider with what face he might look upon his (till then) joy, Philoclea, when the next light waking should deliver unto her should perchance be the last of her hurtless life, and that the first time she should bend her excellent eyes upon him, she should see the accursed author of her dreadful end. And even this consideration, more than any other, did so set itself in his well-disposed mind that, dispersing his thoughts to all the ways that might be of her safety, finding a very small discourse in so narrow limits of time and place, at length in many difficulties he saw none bear any likelihood for her life but his death. For then he thought it would fall out that when they found his body dead (having no accuser but Dametas, as by his speech he found there was not) it might justly appear that either Philoclea in defending her honour, or else he himself in despairing of achieving, had left his carcass proof of his intent but witness of her clearness.

* *the sleeping harbour*: i.e. her body. *adamant*: magnet.

Having a small while stayed upon the greatness of his resolution and looked to the furthest of it: 'Be it so,' said the valiant Pyrocles. 'Never life for better cause nor to better end was bestowed; for if death be to follow this doing (which no death of mine could make me leave undone) who is to die so justly as myself? And if I must die, who can be so fit executioners as mine own hands, which, as they were accessories to the doing, so in killing me they shall suffer their own punishment?'

But then arose there a new impediment; for Dametas having carried away anything which he thought might hurt as tender a man as himself, he could find no fit instrument which might give him a final dispatch. At length, making the more haste lest his lady should awake, taking the iron bar, which (being sharper something at the one end than the other) he hoped (joined to his willing strength) might break off the slender thread of mortality, 'Truly,' said he, 'Fortune, thou hast well persevered mine enemy, that wilt grant me no fortune to be unfortunate, nor let me have an easy passage now I am to trouble thee no more. But,' said he, 'O bar, blessed in that thou hast done service to the chamber of the paragon of life, since thou couldst not help me to make a perfecter escape, yet serve my turn, I pray thee, that I may escape from myself.'

Therewithal yet once looking to fetch the last repast of his eyes, and new again transported with the pitiful case he left her in, kneeling down he thus prayed:

'O great maker and great ruler of this world,' said he, 'to thee do I sacrifice this blood of mine; and suffer, Lord, the errors of my youth to pass away therein, and let not the soul by thee made, and ever bending unto thee, be now rejected of thee. Neither be offended that I do abandon this body (to the government of which thou hadst placed me) without thy leave, since how can I know but that thy unsearchable mind is I should so do, since thou hast taken from me all means longer to abide in it? And since the difference stands but in a short time of dying, thou that hast framed my soul inclined to do good, how can I in this small space of mine benefit so much all the human kind, as in preserving thy perfectest workmanship, their chieftest honour? O Justice itself, howsoever thou determinest of me, let this excellent innocency not be oppressed! Let my life pay her loss. O Lord, give me some sign that I may die with this comfort.' And pausing a little, as if he had hoped for some token, and whensoever to the eternal darkness of the earth she doth follow me, let our spirits possess one place, and let them be more happy in that uniting.'

With that word, striking the bar upon his heart side with all the force he had, and falling withal upon to give it the througher passage, the bar in troth was too blunt to do the effect, although it pierced his skin and bruised his ribs very sore so that his breath was almost past him.

But the noise of his fall drave away sleep from the quiet senses of the dear Philoclea, whose sweet soul had an early salutation of a deadly spectacle unto her; with so much more astonishment as the falling asleep but a little before, she had retired herself from the uttermost point of woefulness,[1] and saw now again before her eyes the most cruel enterprise that human nature can undertake, without discerning any cause thereof. But the lively print of her affection had soon taught her not to stay long upon deliberation in so urgent a necessity. Therefore getting with speed her weak though well accorded limbs out of her sweetened bed (as when jewels are hastily pulled out of some rich coffer) she spared not the nakedness of her tender feet but, I think, borne as fast with desire as fear carried Daphne,* she came running to Pyrocles, and finding his spirits something troubled with the fall, she put by the bar that lay close to him, and straining him in her most beloved embracements:

'My comfort, my joy, my life,' said she, 'what haste have you to kill your Philoclea with the most cruel torment that ever lady suffered? Do you not yet persuade yourself that any hurt of yours is a death unto me, and that your death should be my hell? Alas, if any sudden mislike of me – for other cause I see none – have caused you to loathe yourself; if any fault or defect of mine hath bred this terriblest rage in you, rather let me suffer the bitterness of it, for so shall the deserver be punished, mankind preserved from such a ruin, and I for my part shall have that comfort, that I die by the noblest hand that ever drew sword.'

Pyrocles, grieved with his fortune that he had not in one instant

*Daphne:* in her flight from Apollo.

cut off all such deliberation, thinking his life only reserved to be bound to be the unhappy newsteller:

'Alas,' said he, 'my only star, why do you this wrong to God, yourself, and me, to speak of faults in you? No, no, most faultless, most perfect lady, it is your excellency that makes me hasten my desired end. It is the right I owe to the general nature that (though against private nature) makes me seek the preservation of all that she hath done in this age. Let me, let me die! There is no way to save your life, most worthy to be conserved, than that my death be your clearing.'

Then did he (with far more pain and backward lothness than the so near killing himself was, but yet driven with necessity to make her yield to that he thought was her safety) make her a short but pithy discourse what he had heard by Dametas' speeches, confirming the rest with a plain demonstration of their imprisonment. And then sought he new means of stopping his breath, but that by Philoclea's labour above her force he was stayed to hear her, in whom a man might perceive what a small difference in the working there is betwixt a simple voidness of evil and a judicial habit of virtue. For she, not with an unshaked magnanimity wherewith Pyrocles weighed and despised death, but with an innocent guiltlessness, not knowing why she should fear to deliver her unstained soul to God (helped with the true loving of Pyrocles, which made her think no life without him) did almost bring her mind to as quiet attending all accidents as the unmastered virtue of Pyrocles. Yet having with a pretty paleness (which did leave milken lines upon her rosy cheeks) paid a little duty to human fear, taking the prince by the hand and kissing the wound he had given himself:

'O the only life of my life and, if it fall out so, the comfort of my death,' said she, 'far, far from you be the doing me such wrong as to think I will receive my life as a purchase of your death; but well may you make my death so much more miserable as it shall anything be delayed after my only felicity. Do you think I can account of the moment of death like the unspeakable afflictions my soul should suffer so oft as I call Pyrocles to my mind, which should be as oft as I breathed? Should these eyes guide my steps, that had seen your murder? Should these hands feed me, that had not hindered such a mischief? Should this heart remain within me, at every pant to count the continual clock of my miseries? O no! If die we must, let us thank death he hath not divided so true a union! And truly, my Pyrocles, I have heard my father and other wise men say that the killing one's self is but a false colour of true courage, proceeding rather of fear of a further evil, either of torment or shame. For if it were a not respecting the harm, that would likewise make him not respect what might be done unto him; and hope being of all other the most contrary thing to fear, this being an utter banishment of hope, it seems to receive his ground in fear. Whatsoever (would they say) comes out of despair cannot bear the title of valour, which should be lifted up to such a height that, holding all things under itself, it should be able to maintain his greatness even in the midst of miseries. Lastly, they would say, God has appointed us captains of these our bodily forts which, without treason to that majesty, were never to be delivered over till they were re-demanded.'

Pyrocles (who had that for a law unto him not to leave Philoclea in anything unsatisfied) although he still remained in his former purpose and knew that time would grow short for it, yet hearing no noise (the shepherds being as then run to Basilius) with settled and humbled countenance as a man that should have spoken of a thing that did not concern himself, bearing even in his eyes sufficient shows that it was nothing but Philoclea's danger which did anything burden his heart, far stronger than fortune; having with vehement embracings of her got yet some fruit of his delayed end, he thus answered the wise innocency of Philoclea:

'Lady, most worthy not only of life but to be the very life of all things; the more notable demonstrations you make of the love so far beyond my desert with which it pleaseth you to overcome fortune in making me happy, the more am I, even in course of humanity (to leave that love's force which I neither can nor will leave) bound to seek requital's witness that I am not ungrateful: to do which, the infiniteness of your goodness being such as it cannot reach unto it, yet doing all I can, and paying my life (which is all I have) though it be far (without measure) short of your desert, yet shall I not die in debt to mine own duty. And truly, the more excellent arguments you made to keep me from this passage (imagined far more terrible than it is) the more plainly it makes me see what reason I have to prevent the loss not only Arcadia but all the face of the earth should receive, if such a tree – which even in his first spring doth not only bear most beautiful blossoms but most rare fruit – should be so untimely cut off.

'Therefore, O most truly beloved lady, to whom I desire for both our goods that these may be my last words, give me your consent even out of that wisdom which must needs see that (besides your unmatched betterness which perchance you will not see) it is fitter one die than both. And since you have sufficiently showed you love me, let me claim by that love you will be content rather to let me die contentedly than wretchedly, rather with a clear and joyful conscience than with desperate condemnation in myself that I, accursed villain, should be the mean of banishing from the sight of men the true example of virtue. And because there is nothing left me to be imagined which I so much desire as that the memory of Pyrocles may ever have an allowed place in your wise judgement, I am content to draw so much breath longer as, by answering the sweet objections you alleged, may bequeath (as I think) a right conceit unto you that this my doing is out of judgement, and not sprung of passion.

'Your father, you say, was wont to say that this like action doth more proceed of fear of further evil or shame than of a true courage. Truly first, they put a very guessing case, speaking of them who can never after come to tell with what mind they did it. And as for my part, I call the immortal truth to witness that no fear of torment can appal me, who know it is but diverse manners of apparelling death, and have long learned to set bodily pain but in the second form* of my being. And as for shame, how can I be ashamed of that for which my well meaning conscience will answer for me to God, and your unresistable beauty to the world? But to take that argument in his own force, and grant it done for avoiding of further pain or dishonour – for as for the name of fear, it is but an odious title of a passion given to that which true judgement performeth – grant, I say, it is to shun a worse case; and truly I do not see but that true fortitude, looking into all

* *second form*: the second rank.

human things with a persisting resolution, carried away neither with wonder of pleasing things nor astonishment of the unpleasant, doth not yet deprive itself of the discerning the difference of evil, but rather is the only virtue which, with an assured tranquillity, shuns the greater by the valiant entering into the less. Thus for his country's safety he will spend his life: for the saving of a limb he will not niggardly spare his goods: for the saving of all his body he will not spare the cutting off a limb – where indeed the weak-hearted man will rather die than see the face of a surgeon, who might with as good reason* say that the constant man abides the painful surgery for fear of a further evil, but he is content to wait for death itself. But neither is true; for neither hath the one any fear but a well-choosing judgement, nor the other hath any contentment but only fear; and not having a heart actively to perform a matter of pain, is forced passively to abide a greater damage. For to do requires a whole heart; to suffer falleth easiliest in the broken minds. And if in bodily torment thus, much more in shame, wherein (since valour is a virtue and virtue is ever limited) we must not run so infinitely as to think the valiant man is willingly to suffer anything, since the very suffering of some things is a certain proof of want of courage. And if anything unwillingly, among the chiefest may shame go; for if honour be to be held dear, his contrary is to be abhorred, and that not for fear but of a true election. For which is the less inconvenient, either the loss of some years more or less (for once* we know our lives be not immortal) or the submitting ourselves to each unworthy misery which the foolish world may lay upon us?

'As for their reason that fear is contrary to hope, neither do I defend fear nor much yield to the authority of hope, to either of which great inclining shows but a feeble reason which must be guided by his servants; and who builds not upon hope shall fear no earthquake of despair.

'Their last alleging of the heavenly powers, as it bears the greatest name so it is the only thing that at all bred any combat in my mind. And yet I do not see but that if God hath made us masters of anything, it is of our own lives out of which (without doing

* *who might with as good reason:* i.e. the weak-hearted man. for *once:* for certainly.

wrong to anybody) we are to issue at our own pleasure. And the same argument would as much prevail to say we should for no necessity lay away from us any of our joints, since they being made of him, without his warrant we should not depart from them; or if that may be, for a greater cause we may pass to a greater degree. And if we be lieutenants of God in this little castle, do you not think we must take warning of him to give over our charge when he leaves us unprovided of good means to tarry in it?'

'No, certainly do I not,' answered the sorrowful Philoclea, 'since it is not for us to appoint that mighty majesty what time he will help us: the uttermost instant is scope enough for him to revoke everything to one's own desire. And therefore to prejudicate his determination is but a doubt of goodness in him who is nothing but goodness. But when indeed he doth either by sickness or outward force lay death upon us, then are we to take knowledge that such is his pleasure, and to know that all is well that he doth. That we should be masters of ourselves we can show at all no title nor claim: since neither we made ourselves nor bought ourselves, we can stand upon no other right but his gift, which he must limit as it pleaseth him. Neither is there any proportion betwixt the loss of any other limb and that, since the one bends to the preserving all, the other to be destruction of all: the one takes not away the mind from the actions for which it is placed in the world; the other cuts off all possibility of his working.

'And truly, my most dear Pyrocles, I must needs protest unto you that I cannot think your defence even in rules of virtue sufficient. Sufficient and excellent it were if the question were of two outward things, wherein a man might by nature's freedom determine whether he would prefer shame to pain, present smaller torment to greater following, or no. But to this (besides the comparison of the matters' values) there is added of the one part a direct evil doing which maketh the balance of that side too much unequal; since a virtuous man without any respect (whether the grief be less or more) is never to do that which he cannot assure himself is allowable before the everliving rightfulness, but rather is to think honours or shames (which stand in other men's true or false judgements) pains or not pains (which yet never approach our souls) to be nothing in regard of an unspotted conscience. And these reasons do I remember I have heard good men bring in, that since it hath not his ground in an assured virtue, it proceeds rather of some other disguised passion.'

Pyrocles was not so much persuaded as delighted by her well-conceived and sweetly pronounced speeches: but when she had closed her pitiful discourse and (as it were) sealed up her delightful lips with the moistness of her tears which followed still one another like a precious rope of pearl; now thinking it high time:

'Be it as you say,' (said he) 'most virtuous beauty, in all the rest; but never can God himself persuade me that Pyrocles' life is not well lost for to preserve the most admirable Philoclea. Let that be, if it be possible, written on my tomb, and I will not envy Codrus' honour.'[2]

With that he would again have used the bar, meaning, if that failed, to leave his brains upon the wall; when Philoclea, now brought to that she most feared, kneeled down unto him, and embracing so his legs that without hurting her (which for nothing he would have done) he could not rid himself from her, she did, with all the conjuring words which the authority of love may lay, beseech him he would not now so cruelly abandon her, he would not leave her comfortless in that misery to which he had brought her: that then indeed she would even in her soul accuse him to have most foully betrayed her; that then she should have cause to curse the time that ever the name of Pyrocles came to her ears, which otherwise no death could make her do.

'Will you leave me,' said she, 'not only dishonoured, as supposed unchaste with you, but as a murderer of you? Will you give mine eyes such a picture of hell, before my near approaching death, as to see the murdered body of him I love more than all the lives nature can give?'

With that she sware by the highest cause of all devotions that if he did persevere in that cruel resolution, she would (though untruly) not only confess to her father that with her consent this act had been committed, but if that would not serve (after she had pulled out her own eyes made accursed by such a sight) she would give herself so terrible a death as she might think the pain of it would countervail the never-dying pain of her mind.

'Now therefore kill yourself to crown this virtuous action with
infamy. Kill yourself to make me (whom you say you love) as long
as I after live change my loving admiration of you to a detestable
abhorring your name. And so indeed you shall have the end you
shoot at, for instead of one death you shall give me a thousand,
and yet in the meantime deprive me of the help God may send me.'

Pyrocles, even over-weighed with her so wisely uttered
affection, finding her determination so fixed that his end should
but deprive them both of a present contentment and not avoid a
coming evil, as a man that ran not into it by a sudden qualm of
passion but by a true use of reason, preferring her life to his own,
now that wisdom did manifest unto him that way would not
prevail, he retired himself with as much tranquillity from it as
before he had gone unto it; like a man that had set the keeping or
leaving of the body as a thing without himself, and so had thereof
a freed and untroubled consideration. Therefore throwing away
the bar from him, and taking her up from the place where he
thought the consummating of all beauties very unworthily lay,
suffering all his senses to devour up their chiefest food, which he
assured himself they should shortly after for ever be deprived of:

'Well,' said he, 'most dear lady, whose contentment I prefer
before mine own, and judgement esteem more than mine own,
I yield unto your pleasure. The gods send you have not won your
own loss. For my part they are my witnesses that I think I do
more at your commandment in delaying my death than another
would in bestowing his life. But now,' said he, 'as thus far I have
yielded unto you, so grant me in recompense thus much again,
that I may find your love in granting as you have found your
authority in obtaining. My humble suit is you will say I came in
by force into your chamber – for so am I resolved now to affirm,
and that will be the best for us both – but in no case name my
name, that whatsoever come of me, my house be not dishonoured.'

## CHAPTER 5

Philoclea, fearing lest refusal would turn him back again to his
violent refuge, gave him a certain countenance that might show
she did yield to his request, the latter part whereof indeed she

meant for his sake to perform. Neither could they spend mor
words together; for Philanax, with twenty of the noblest per
sonages of Arcadia after him, were come into the lodge. Philanax
making the rest stay below for the reverence he bare to woman
hood, as stilly as he could came up to the door and opening it
drew the eyes of these two doleful lovers upon him; Philocle.
closing again for modesty sake within her bed the riches of he
beauties, but Pyrocles took hold of his bar, minding at least to di
before the excellent Philoclea should receive any outrage. But Phil
anax rested awhile upon himself, stricken with admiration at the
goodly shape of Pyrocles, whom before he had never seen; and
withal remembering, besides others, the notable act he had don
when with his courage and eloquence he had saved Basilius, per
chance the whole state, from utter ruin, he felt a kind of relenting
mind towards him. But when that same thought came waited on
with the remembrance of his master's death, which he by all pro
babilities thought he had been of council unto with the queen
compassion turned to hateful passion, and left in Philanax a
strange medley betwixt pity and revenge, betwixt liking and ab
horring.

'O lord,' said he to himself, 'what wonders doth nature in ou
time, to set wickedness so beautifully garnished! And that which
is strangest, out of one spring to make wonderful effects both o
virtue and vice to issue!'

Pyrocles, seeing him in such a muse, neither knowing the man
nor the cause of his coming but assuring himself it was for no
good, yet thought best to begin with him in this sort:

'Gentleman,' said he, 'what is the cause of your coming to my
lady Philoclea's chamber? Is it to defend her from such violence a
I might go about to offer unto her? If it be so, truly your coming i
vain, for her own virtue hath been a sufficient resistance: there
needs no strength to be added to so inviolate chastity. The excel
lency of her mind makes her body impregnable; which for my owr
part I had soon yielded to confess with going out of this place
(where I found but little comfort, being so disdainfully received
had I not been, I know not by whom, presently upon my coming
hither so locked into this chamber that I could never escape hence
where I was fettered in the most guilty shame that ever man was

seeing what a paradise of unspotted goodness my filthy thoughts sought to defile. If for that therefore you come, already, I assure you, your errand is performed. But if it be to bring me to any punishment whatsoever for having undertaken so unexcusable presumption, truly I bear such an accuser about me in mine own conscience that I willingly submit myself unto it. Only thus much let me demand of you, that you will be a witness unto the king what you hear me say, and oppose yourself that neither his sudden fury nor any other occasion may offer any hurt to this lady, in whom you see nature hath accomplished so much that I am fain to lay mine own faultiness as a foil of her purest excellency. I can say no more. But look upon her beauty; remember her blood; consider her years, and judge rightly of her virtues; and I doubt not a gentleman's mind will then be a sufficient instructor unto you in this, I may term it, miserable chance happened unto her by my unbridled audacity.'

Philanax was content to hear him out not for any favour he owed him, but to see whether he would reveal anything of the original cause and purpose of the king's death. But finding it so far from that that he named Basilius unto him as supposing him alive, thinking it rather cunning than ignorance:

'Young man,' said he, 'whom I have cause to hate before I have mean to know, you use but a point of skill by confessing the manifest smaller fault, to be believed hereafter in the denial of the greater. But for that matter, all passeth to one end, and hereafter we shall have leisure by torments to seek the truth, if the love of truth itself will not bring you unto it. As for my Lady Philoclea, if it so fall out as you say, it shall be the more fit for her years and comely for the great house she is come of that an ill-governed beauty hath not cancelled the rules of virtue. But howsoever it be, it is not for you to teach an Arcadian what reverent duty we owe to any of that progeny. But,' said he, 'come you with me without resistance, for the one cannot avail and the other may procure pity.'

'Pity!' said Pyrocles with a bitter smiling, disdained with so currish an answer, 'No, no, Arcadian, I can quickly have pity of myself, and I would think my life most miserable which should be a gift of thine. Only I demand this innocent lady's security, which until thou hast confirmed unto me by an oath, assure thyself the first that lays hands upon her shall leave his life for a testimony of his sacrilege.'

Philanax, with an inward scorn, thinking it most manifest they were both – he at least – of counsel with the king's death: 'Well,' said he, 'you speak much to me of the king. I do here swear unto you, by the love I have ever borne him, she shall have no worse (howsoever it fall out) than her own parents.'

'And upon that word of yours I yield,' said the poor Pyrocles, deceived by him that meant not to deceive him.

Then did Philanax deliver him into the hands of a nobleman in the company, everyone desirous to have him in his charge, so much did his goodly presence (wherein true valour shined) breed a delightful admiration in all the beholders. Philanax himself stayed with Philoclea to see whether of her he might learn some disclosing of this former conclusion. But she, sweet lady, whom first a kindly shamefastness had separated from Pyrocles (having been left in a more open view than her modesty would well bear) then the attending her father's coming, and studying how to behave herself towards him for both their safeties had called her spirits all within her; now that upon a sudden Pyrocles was delivered out of the chamber from her, at the first she was so surprised with the extreme stroke of the woeful sight that (like those that in their dreams are taken with some ugly vision, they would fain cry for help but have no force) so remained she awhile quite deprived not only of speech but almost of any other lively action. But when indeed Pyrocles was quite drawn from her eyes and that her vital strength began to return unto her, now not knowing what they did to Pyrocles but (according to the nature of love) fearing the worst, wringing her hands, and letting abundance of tears be the first part of her eloquence, bending her amber-crowned head over her bedside to the hard-hearted Philanax:

'O Philanax, Philanax,' said she, 'I know how much authority you have with my father: there is no man whose wisdom he so much esteems nor whose faith so much he reposeth upon. Remember how oft you have promised your service unto me, how oft you have given me occasion to believe that there was no lady in whose favour you more desired to remain; and if the remembrance be not unpleasant to your mind, or the rehearsal unfitting for my fortune, remember there was a time when I could deserve it. Now my chance is turned, let not your truth turn. I present myself unto you, the most humble and miserable suppliant living; neither shall my desire be great: I seek for no more life than I shall be found worthy of. If my blood may wash away the dishonour of Arcadia, spare it not, although through me it hath in deed never been dishonoured. My only suit is you will be a mean for me that, while I am suffered to enjoy this life, I may not be separated from him to whom the gods have joined me, and that you determine nothing of him more cruelly than you do of me. If you rightly judge of what hath passed, wherein the gods (that should have been of our marriage) are witnesses of our innocencies, then procure we may live together. But if my father will not so conceive of us, as the fault (if any were) was united, so let the punishment be united also.'

There was no man that ever loved either his prince or anything pertaining to him with a truer zeal than Philanax did. This made him, even to the depth of his heart, receive a most vehement grief to see his master made, as it were, more miserable after death. And for himself, calling to mind in what sort his life had been preserved by Philoclea what time taken by Amphialus he was like to suffer a cruel death, there was nothing could have kept him from falling to all tender pity but the perfect persuasion he had that all this was joined to the pack of his master's death, which the misconceived speech of marriage made him the more believe. Therefore first muttering to himself such like words: 'The violence the gentleman spake of is now turned to marriage: he alleged Mars, but she speaks of Venus. O unfortunate master! This hath been that fair devil Gynecia, sent away one of her daughters, prostituted the other, empoisoned thee to overthrow the diadem of Arcadia.' But at length thus unto herself he said:

'If your father, Madam, were now to speak unto, truly there should nobody be found a more ready advocate for you than myself; for I would suffer this fault, though very great, to be blotted out of my mind by your former-led life, your benefit towards myself, and being daughter to such a father. But since among yourselves you have taken him away in whom was the only power to have mercy, you must now be clothed in your own working, and look for none other than that which dead pitiless laws may allot unto you. For my part, I loved you for your virtue, but now where is that? I loved you in respect of a private benefit. What is that in comparison of the public loss? I loved you for your father. Unhappy folks, you have robbed the world of him.'

These words of her father were so little understood by the only well-understanding Philoclea that she desired him to tell her what he meant to speak in such dark sort unto her of her lord and father, whose displeasure was more dreadful unto her than her punishment: that she was free in her own conscience she had never deserved evil of him, no not in this last fact, wherein, if it pleased him to proceed with patience, he should find her choice had not been unfortunate.

He, that saw her words written in the plain table of her fair face, thought it impossible there should therein be contained deceit, and therefore so much the more abashed: 'Why,' said he, 'Madam, would you have me think you are not of conspiracy with the Princess Pamela's flight, and your father's death?'

With that word the sweet lady gave a pitiful cry, having straight in her face and breast abundance of witnesses that her heart was far from any such abominable consent. 'Ah, of all sides utterly ruined Philoclea,' said she, 'now indeed I may well suffer all conceit of hope to die in me. Dear father, where was I that might not do you my last service before soon after miserably following you!'

Philanax perceived the demonstration so lively and true in her that he easily acquitted her in his heart of that fact, and the more was moved to join with her in most hearty lamentation. But remembering him that the burden of the state and punishment of his master's murderers lay all upon him:

'Well,' said he, 'Madam, I can do nothing without all the states of Arcadia. What they will determine of you I know not. For my part, your speeches would much prevail with me but that I find not how to excuse your giving over your body to him that, for the last proof of his treason, lent his garments to disguise your miserable mother in the most vile fact she hath committed. Hard sure it will be to separate your causes, with whom you have so nearly joined yourself.'

'Neither do I desire it,' said the sweetly weeping Philoclea. 'Whatsoever you determine of him, do that likewise to me, for I know from the fountain of virtue nothing but virtue could ever proceed. Only as you find him faultless, let him find you favourable, and build not my dishonour upon surmises.'

Philanax, feeling his heart more and more mollifying unto her, renewed the image of his dead master in his fancy, and using that for the spurs of his revengeful choler, went suddenly without any more speech from the desolate lady, to whom now fortune seemed to threaten unripe death and undeserved shame among her least evils. But Philanax, leaving good guard upon the lodge, went himself to see the order of his other prisoners, whom even then as he issued he found increased by this unhoped means.

## CHAPTER 6

The noble Pamela, having delivered over the burden of her fearful cares to the natural ease of a well-refreshing sleep, reposed both mind and body upon the trusted support of her princely shepherd, when with the braying cries of a rascal company she was robbed of her quiet, so that at one instant she opened her eyes and the enraged Musidorus rose from her, enraged betwixt the doubt he had what these men would go about and the spite he conceived against their ill-pleasing presence. But the clowns, having with their hideous noise brought them both to their feet, had soon knowledge what guests they had found – for indeed these were the scummy remnant of those rebels whose naughty minds could not trust so much to the goodness of their prince as to lay their hangworthy necks upon the constancy of his promised pardon. Therefore when the rest (who as sheep had but followed their fellows) so sheepishly had submitted themselves, these only committed their safety to the thickest part of those desert woods; who as they were in the constitution of their minds little better than beasts, so were they apt to degenerate to a beastly kind of life, having now framed their gluttonish stomachs to have for food the wild benefits of nature, the uttermost end they had being but to draw out as much as they could the line of a tedious life.

In this sort vagabonding in those untrodden places, they were guided by the everlasting justice (using themselves to be punishers of their faults, and making their own actions the beginning of their chastisements) unhappily both for him and themselves to light on Musidorus; whom as soon as they saw turned towards them, they full well remembered it was he that, accompanied with Basilius, had come to the succour of Zelmane, and had left among some of them bloody tokens of his valour. As for Pamela, they had many times seen her. Thus first stirred up with a rustical revenge against him and then desire of spoil to help their miserable wants, but chiefly thinking it was the way to confirm their own pardon to bring the princess back unto her father (whom they were sure he would never have sent so far so slightly accompanied) they did, without any other denouncing of war, set all together upon the worthy Musidorus. Who (being beforehand as much inflamed against them) gave them so brave a welcome that the smart of some made the rest stand further off, crying and prating against him, but like bad curs rather barking than closing; he, in the meantime, placing his trembling lady to one of the pine trees, and so setting himself before her as might show the cause of his courage grew in himself, but the effect was only employed in her defence.

The villains, that now had a second proof how ill wards* they had for such a sword, turned all the course of their violence into throwing darts and stones – indeed the only way to overmaster the valour of Musidorus; who finding them some already touch, some fall so near his chiefest life, Pamela, that in the end some one or other might hap to do an unsuccourable mischief, setting all his hope in despair, ran out from his lady among them, who straight (like so many swine when a hardy mastiff sets upon them) dispersed themselves. But the first he overtook as he ran away, carrying his head as far before him as those manner of runnings are wont to do, with one blow, strake it so clean off that – it falling betwixt the hands, and the body falling upon it – it made a show as though the fellow had had great haste to gather up his head

*ill wards: little protection.

again. Another, the speed he made to run for the best game bare him full butt against a tree, so that tumbling back with a bruised face and a dreadful expectation, Musidorus was straight upon him, and parting with his sword one of his legs from him, left him to make a roaring lamentation that his mortar-treading was marred for ever. A third, finding his feet too slow as well as his hands too weak, suddenly turned back, beginning to open his lips for mercy. But before he had well entered a rudely compiled oration, Musidorus' blade was come between his jaws into his throat, and so the poor man rested there for ever with a very evil mouthful of an answer.

Musidorus in this furious chafe would have followed some other of these hateful wretches but that he heard his lady cry for help, whom three of this villainous crew had (whiles Musidorus followed their fellows) compassing about some trees, suddenly come upon and surprised, threatening to kill her if she cried, and meaning to convey her out of sight while the prince was making his bloodthirsty chase. But she that was resolved no worse thing could fall unto her than the being deprived of him on whom she had established all her comfort, with a pitiful cry fetched his eyes unto her, who then thinking so many weapons thrust into his eyes as with his eyes he saw bent against her, made all hearty speed to her succour. But one of them, wiser than his companions, set his dagger to her alabaster throat, swearing if he threw not away his sword, he would presently kill her. There was never poor scholar that, having instead of his book some playing toy about him, did more suddenly cast it from him at the child-feared presence of a cruel schoolmaster than the valiant Musidorus discharged himself of his only defence, when he saw it stood upon the instant point of his lady's life; and holding up his noble hands to so unworthy audience:

'O Arcadians, it is I that have done you the wrong. She is your princess,' said he; 'she never had will to hurt you, and you see she hath no power. Use your choler upon me that have better deserved it. Do not yourselves the wrong to do her any hurt, which in no time nor place will ever be forgiven you.'

They, that yet trusted not to his courtesy, bade him stand further off from his sword, which he obediently did – so far was love above all other thoughts in him. Then did they call together the rest of their fellows who, though they were few, yet according to their number possessed many places. And then began these savage senators to make a consultation what they should do: some wishing to spoil them of their jewels and let them go on their journey, for that if they carried them back, they were sure they should have least part of their prey: others, preferring their old homes to anything, desired to bring them to Basilius as pledges of their surety; and there wanted not which cried the safest way was to kill them both. To such an unworthy thraldom were these great and excellent personages brought. But the most part resisted to the killing of the princess, foreseeing their lives would never be safe after such a fact committed, and began to wish rather the spoil than death of Musidorus; when the villain that had his leg cut off came crawling towards them and, being helped to them by one of the company, began with a groaning voice and a disfigured face to demand the revenge of his blood, which (since he had spent with them in their defence) it were no reason he should be suffered by them to die discontented: the only contentment he required was that by their help with his own hands he might put his murderer to some cruel death – he would fain have cried more against Musidorus but that the much loss of blood, helped on with this vehemency, choked up the spirits of his life, leaving him to make betwixt his body and soul an ill-favoured partition.

But they, seeing their fellow in that sort die before their faces, did swell in new mortal rages, all resolved to kill him, but now only considering what manner of terrible death they should invent for him. Thus was a while the agreement of his slaying broken by the disagreement of the manner of it, and extremity of cruelty grew for a time to be the stop of cruelty. At length they were resolved every one to have a piece of him, and to become all as well hangmen as judges; when Pamela (tearing her hair and falling down among them, sometimes with all the sort of humble prayers, mixed with promises of great good turns, which they knew her state was able to perform; sometimes threatening them that if they killed him and not her, she would not only revenge it upon them but upon all their wives and children; bidding them consider that though they might think she was come away in her father's displeasure, yet they might be sure he would ever show himself a father; that the gods would never, if she lived, put her in so base estate but that she should have ability to plague such as they were; returning afresh to prayers and promises, and mixing the same again with threatenings) brought them (who were now grown colder in their fellow's cause, who was past aggravating the matter with his cries) to determine with themselves there was no way but either to kill them both or save them both. As for the killing, already they having answered themselves that that was a way to make them citizens of the woods for ever, they did in fine conclude they would return them back again to the king, which they did not doubt would be cause of a great reward besides their safety from their fore-deserved punishment.

Thus having, either by fortune or the force of these two lovers' inward working virtue, settled their cruel hearts to this gentler course, they took the two horses, and having set upon them their princely prisoners, they returned towards the lodge. The villains, having decked all their heads with laurel branches, as thinking they had done a notable act, singing and shouting, ran by them in hope to have brought them the same day again to the king. But the time was so far spent that they were forced to take up that night's lodging in the midst of the woods; where, while the clowns continued their watch about them, now that the night according to his dark nature did add a kind of desolation to the pensive hearts of these two afflicted lovers, Musidorus, taking the tender hand of Pamela and bedewing it with his tears, in this sort gave an issue to the swelling of his heart's grief:

'Most excellent lady,' said he, 'in what case think you am I with myself? How unmerciful judgements do I lay upon my soul now that I know not what god hath so reversed my well-meaning enterprise as, instead of doing you that honour which I hoped (and not without reason hoped) Thessalia should have yielded unto you, am now like to become a wretched instrument of your discomfort! Alas, how contrary an end have all the inclinations of my mind taken! My faith falls out a treason unto you, and the true honour I bear you is the field wherein your dishonour is like to be sown. But I invoke that universal and only wisdom (which, examining the depth of hearts, hath not his judgement fixed upon the event) to bear testimony with me that my desire, though in extremest vehemency, yet did not so overcharge my remembrance but that, as far as man's wit might be extended, I sought to prevent all things that might fall to your hurt. But now that all the evil fortunes of evil fortune have crossed my best framed intent, I am most miserable in that, that I cannot only not give you help but – which is worst of all – am barred from giving you counsel. For how should I open my mouth to counsel you in that wherein by my counsel you are most undeservedly fallen?'

The fair and wise Pamela, although full of cares of the unhappy turning of this matter yet seeing the grief of Musidorus only stirred for her, did so tread down all other motions with the true force of virtue that she thus answered him, having first kissed him (which before she had never done) either love so commanding her (which doubted how long they should enjoy one another) or of a lively spark of nobleness to descend in most favour to one when he is lowest in affliction.

'My dear and ever dear Musidorus,' said she, 'a great wrong do you to yourself, that will torment you thus with grief for the fault of fortune. Since a man is bound no further to himself than to do wisely, chance is only to trouble them that stand upon chance. But greater is the wrong (at least, if anything that comes from you may bear the name of wrong) you do unto me to think me either so childish as not to perceive your faithful faultlessness, or, perceiving it, so basely disposed as to let my heart be overthrown, standing upon itself in so unspotted a pureness. Hold for certain, most worthy Musidorus, it is yourself I love, which can no more be diminished by these showers of evil hap than flowers are marred with the timely rains of April. For how can I want comfort that have the true and living comfort of my unblemished virtue? And how can I want honour as long as Musidorus (in whom indeed honour is) doth honour me? Nothing bred from myself can discomfort me; and fools' opinions I will not reckon as dishonour.'

Musidorus looking up to the stars, 'O mind of minds,' said he, 'the living power of all things, which dost with all these eyes behold our ever-varying actions, accept into thy favourable ears this prayer of mine. If I may any longer hold out this dwelling on the earth which is called a life, grant me ability to deserve at this lady's hands the grace she hath showed unto me: grant me wisdom to know her wisdom, and goodness so to increase my love of her goodness that all mine own chosen desires be to myself but second to her determinations. Whatsoever I be, let it be to her service: let me herein be satisfied that for such infinite favours of virtue I have some way wrought her satisfaction. But if my last time approacheth and that I am no longer to be amongst mortal creatures, make yet my death serve her to some purpose, that hereafter she may not have cause to repent herself that she bestowed so excellent a mind upon Musidorus.'

Pamela could not choose but accord the conceit of their fortune to these passionate prayers, insomuch that her constant eyes yielded some tears, which wiping from her fair face with Musidorus' hand, speaking softly unto him, as if she had feared more anybody should be witness of her weakness than of anything else she had said, 'You see,' said she, 'my prince and only lord, what you work in me by your too much grieving for me. I pray you think I have no joy but in you, and if you fill that with sorrow, what do you leave for me? What is prepared for us we know not; but that with sorrow we cannot prevent it, we know. Now let us turn from these things, and think you how you will have me behave myself towards you in this matter.'

Musidorus finding the authority of her speech confirmed with direct necessity, the first care came to his mind was of his dear friend and cousin, Pyrocles, with whom long before he had concluded what names they should bear, if upon any occasion they were forced to give themselves out for great men and yet not make themselves fully known. Now fearing lest, if the princess should name him for Musidorus, the fame of their two being together would discover Pyrocles, holding her hand betwixt his hands a good while together:

'I did not think, most excellent princess,' said he, 'to have made any further request unto you, for having been already to you so unfortunate a suitor, I know not what modesty can bear any further demand. But the estate of one young man whom (next to you, far above myself) I love more than all the world; one worthy of all well-being for the notable constitution of his mind, and most unworthy to receive hurt by me whom he doth in all faith and constancy love

– the pity of him only goes beyond all resolution to the contrary.'

Then did he, to the princess' great admiration, tell her the whole story as far as he knew of it, and that when they made the grievous disjunction of their long company, they had concluded Musidorus should entitle himself Palladius, prince of Iberia, and Pyrocles should be Daiphantus of Lycia.

'Now,' said Musidorus, 'he keeping a woman's habit, is to use no other name than Zelmane. But I (that find it best, of the one side, for your honour it be known you went away with a prince and not with a shepherd; of the other side, accounting my death less evil than the betraying of that sweet friend of mine) will take this mean betwixt both; and using the name of Palladius, if the respect of a prince will stop your father's fury, that will serve as well as Musidorus, until Pyrocles' fortune being some way established, I may freely give good proof that the noble country of Thessalia is mine. And if that will not mitigate your father's opinion to mewards, nature, I hope, working in your excellencies, will make him deal well by you. For my part, the image of death is nothing fearful unto me, and this good I shall have reaped by it, that I shall leave my most esteemed friend in no danger to be disclosed by me. And besides, since I must confess I am not without a remorse of her case, my virtuous mother shall not know her son's violent death hid under the fame will go of Palladius. But as long as her years, now of good number, be counted among the living, she may joy herself with some possibility of my return.'

Pamela, promising him upon no occasion ever to name him, fell into extremity of weeping, as if her eyes had been content to spend all their seeing moistness now that there was speech of the loss of that which they held as their chiefest light. So that Musidorus was forced to repair her good counsels with sweet consolations, which continued betwixt them until it was about midnight that sleep, having stolen into their heavy senses and now absolutely commanding in their vital powers, left them delicately wound one in another's arms, quietly to wait for the coming of the morning. Which as soon as she appeared to play her part, laden (as you have heard) with so many well occasioned lamentations, their lobbish* guard (who all night had kept them-

* *lobbish*: clownish.

selves awake with prating how valiant deeds they had done when they ran away, and how fair a death their fellow had died who at his last gasp sued to be a hangman) awaked them and set them upon their horses, to whom the very shining force of excellent virtue, though in a very harsh subject, had wrought a kind of reverence in them. Musidorus as he rid among them (of whom they had no other hold but of Pamela) thinking it want of a well-squared* judgement to leave any means unassayed of saving their lives, to this purpose spake to his unseemly guardians, using a plain kind of phrase to make his speech the more credible:

'My masters,' said he, 'there is no man that is wise but hath, in whatsoever he doth, some purpose whereto he directs his doings, which so long he follows till he see that either that purpose is not worth the pains, or that another doing carries with it a better purpose. That you are wise in what you take in hand I have to my cost learned; that makes me desire you to tell me what is your end in carrying the princess and me back to her father.'

'Pardon,' said one. 'Reward,' cried another.

'Well,' said he, 'take both; although I know you are so wise to remember that hardly* they both will go together, being of so contrary a making. For the ground of pardon is an evil, neither any man pardons but remembers an evil done. The cause of reward is the opinion of some good act, and whoso rewardeth, that* holds the chief place of his fancy. Now one man of one company to have the same consideration both of good and evil, but that the conceit of pardoning (if it be pardoned) will take away the mind of rewarding, is very hard, if not impossible; for either even in justice will he punish the fault as well as reward the desert, or else in mercy balance the one by the other, so that the not chastising shall be a sufficient satisfying. Thus then you may see that in your own purpose rests great uncertainty.

'But I will grant that by this your deed you shall obtain your double purpose. Yet consider, I pray you, whether by another mean that may not better be obtained, and then I doubt not your wisdoms will teach you to take hold of the better. I am sure you know anybody were better have no need of a pardon than enjoy a

* *well-squared*: well-framed. *hardly*: with difficulty. *that*: i.e. that opinion.

pardon; for as it carries with it the surety of a preserved life, so bears it a continual note of a deserved death. This therefore (besides the danger you may run into, my Lady Pamela being the undoubted inheritrix of this state, if she shall hereafter seek to revenge your wrong done her) shall be continually cast in your teeth, as men dead by the law. The honester sort will disdain your company, and your children shall be the more basely reputed of, and you yourselves in every slight fault hereafter, as men once condemned, aptest to be overthrown.

'Now if you will (as I doubt not you will, for you are wise) turn your course and guard my Lady Pamela thitherward whither she was going first, you need not doubt to adventure your fortunes where she goes, and there shall you be assured (in a country as good and rich as this, of the same manners and language) to be so far from the conceit of a pardon as we both shall be forced to acknowledge we have received by your means whatsoever we hold dear in this life. And so for reward, judge you whether it be not more likely you shall there receive it where you have done no evil but singular and undeserved goodness, or here where this service of yours shall be diminished by your duty and blemished by your former fault. Yes: I protest and swear unto you, by the fair eyes of that lady, there shall no gentleman in all that country be preferred. You shall have riches, ease, pleasure, and that which is best to such worthy minds, you shall not be forced to cry mercy for a good fact. You only of all the Arcadians shall have the praise in continuing in your late valiant attempt, and not basely be brought under a halter for seeking the liberty of Arcadia.'

These words in their minds (who did nothing for any love of goodness, but only as their senses presented greater shows of profit) began to make them waver, and some to clap their hands and scratch their heads and swear it was the best way; others that would seem wiser than the rest, to capitulate* what tenements* they should have, what subsidies they should pay; others to talk of their wives, in doubt whether it were best to send for them or tò take new where they went; most, like fools, not readily thinking what was next to be done, but imagining what cheer they would make when they came there; one or two of the least discoursers

* *capitulate*: draw up conditions. *tenements*: holdings of property.

beginning to turn their faces towards the woods which they had left. But being now come within the plain near to the lodges, unhappily they espied a troop of horsemen. But then their false hearts had quickly, for the present fear, forsaken their last hopes; and therefore keeping on the way towards the lodge with songs and cries of joy, the horsemen, who were some of them Philanax had sent out to the search of Pamela, came galloping unto them, marvelling who they were that in such a general mourning durst sing joyful tunes and in so public a ruin wear the laurel tokens of victory; and that which seemed strangest, they might see two among them unarmed like prisoners, but riding like captains. But when they came nearer, they perceived the one was a lady, and the Lady Pamela. Then glad they had by hap found that which they so little hoped to meet withal, taking these clowns (who first resisted them for the desire they had to be the deliverers of the two excellent prisoners) learning that they were of those rebels which had made the dangerous uproar, as well under colour to punish that as this their last withstanding them, but indeed their principal cause being because they themselves would have the only praise of their own quest, they suffered not one of them to live. Marry,* three of the stubbornest of them they left their bodies hanging upon the trees, because their doing might carry the likelier form of judgement. Such an unlooked-for end did the life of justice work for the naughty-minded wretches, by subjects to be executed that would have executed princes, and to suffer that without law which by law they had deserved.

## CHAPTER 7

And thus these young folks, twice prisoners before any due arrest, delivered of their jailors but not of their jail, had rather change than respite of misery – these soldiers (that took them with very few words of entertainment) hasting to carry them to their lord Philanax: to whom they came even as he (going out of the Lady Philoclea's chamber) had overtaken Pyrocles whom before he had delivered to the custody of a nobleman of that country. When Pyrocles, led towards his prison, saw his friend Musidorus with

* *Marry:* a contemptuous exclamation.

the noble Lady Pamela in that inexpected sort returned, his grief (if any grief were in a mind which had placed everything according to his natural worth) was very much augmented; for besides some small hope he had if Musidorus had once been clear of Arcadia, by his dealing and authority to have brought his only gladsome desires to a good issue, the hard estate of his friend did no less – nay, rather more, vex him than his own. For so indeed it is ever found where valour and friendship are perfectly coupled in one heart; the reason being that the resolute man, having once digested in his judgement the worst extremity of his own case, and having either quite expelled or at least repelled all passion which ordinarily follows an overthrown fortune, not knowing his friend's mind so well as his own, nor with what patience he brooks his case (which is, as it were, the material cause of making a man happy or unhappy) doubts whether his friend accounts not himself more miserable, and so indeed be more lamentable. But as soon as Musidorus was brought by the soldiers near unto Philanax, Pyrocles, not knowing whether ever after he should be suffered to see his friend, and determining there could be no advantage by dissembling a not-knowing of him, leaped suddenly from their hands that held him, and passing with a strength strengthened with a true affection through them that encompassed Musidorus, he embraced him as fast as he could in his arms. And kissing his cheek,

'O, my Palladius,' said he, 'let not our virtue now abandon us. Let us prove our minds are no slaves to fortune, but in adversity can triumph over adversity.'

'Dear Daiphantus,' answered Musidorus, seeing by his apparel his being a man was revealed, 'I thank you for this best care of my best part. But fear not. I have kept too long company with you to want now a thorough determination of these things. I well know there is nothing evil but within us; the rest is either natural or accidental.'

Philanax, finding them of so near acquaintance, began presently to examine them apart; but such resolution he met within them that by no such means he could learn further than it pleased them to deliver; so that he thought best to put them both in one place, with espial of their words and behaviour, that way to sift out the more of these forepassed mischiefs; and for that purpose gave them both unto the nobleman who before had the custody of Pyrocles (by name Sympathus) leaving a trusty servant of his own to give diligent watch to what might pass betwixt them.

No man that hath ever passed through the school of affection needs doubt what a tormenting grief it was to the noble Pamela to have the company of him taken from her to whose virtuous company she had bound her life; but weighing with herself it was fit for her honour, till her doings were clearly manifested, that they should remain separate, kept down the rising tokens of grief, showing passion in nothing but her eyes, which accompanied Musidorus even unto the tent whither he and Pyrocles were led. Then, with a countenance more princely than she was wont, according to the wont of highest hearts (like the palm tree striving most upward when he is most burdened) she commanded Philanax to bring her to her father and mother that she might render them account of her doings.

Philanax, showing a sullen kind of reverence unto her, as a man that honoured her as his master's heir but much misliked her for her – in his conceit – dishonourable proceedings, told her what was past, rather to answer her than that he thought she was ignorant of it. But her good spirit did presently suffer a true compassionate affliction of those hard adventures which, with crossing her arms, looking a great while on the ground, with those eyes which let fall many tears, she well declared. But in the end, remembering how necessary it was for her not to lose herself in such an extremity, she strengthened her well-created heart and stoutly demanded Philanax what authority then they had to lay hands of her person, who being the undoubted heir, was then the lawful princess of that kingdom. Philanax answered, her grace knew the ancient laws of Arcadia bare she was to have no sway of government till she came to one and twenty years of age, or were married.

'And married I am,' replied the wise princess. 'Therefore I demand your due allegiance.'

'The gods forbid,' said Philanax, 'Arcadia should be a dowry of such marriages.' Besides, he told her, all the states of her country were evil satisfied touching her father's death, which likewise, according to the statutes of Arcadia, was even that day to be judged of, before the body were removed to receive his princely funerals. After that passed, she should have such obedience as by the laws was due unto her, desiring God she would show herself better in public government than she had done in private.

She would have spoken to the gentlemen and people gathered about her, but Philanax, fearing lest thereby some commotion might arise, or at least a hindrance of executing his master's murderers (which he longed after more than anything) hasted her up to the lodge where her sister was; and there, with a chosen company of soldiers to guard the place, left her with Philoclea, Pamela protesting they laid violent hands of her and that they entered into rebellious attempts against her. But high time it was for Philanax so to do, for already was all the whole multitude fallen into confused and dangerous divisions.

There was a notable example how great dissipations monarchal governments are subject unto. For now their prince and guide had left them, they had not experience to rule, and had not whom to obey. Public matters had ever been privately governed, so that they had no lively taste what was good for themselves, but everything was either vehemently desireful or extremely terrible. Neighbours' invasions, civil dissension, cruelty of the coming prince, and whatsoever in common sense carries a dreadful show, was in all men's heads, but in few how to prevent: hearkening on every rumour, suspecting everything, condemning them whom before they had honoured, making strange and impossible tales of the king's death: while they thought themselves in danger, wishing nothing but safety; as soon as persuasion of safety took them, desiring further benefits as amendment of forepassed faults (which faults, notwithstanding, none could tell either the grounds or effects of); all agreeing in the universal names of liking or misliking, but of what in especial points, infinitely disagreeing: altogether like a falling steeple, the parts whereof – as windows, stones, and pinnacles – were well, but the whole mass ruinous. And this was the general case of all, wherein notwithstanding, was an extreme medley of diversified thoughts – the great men looking to make themselves strong by factions; the gentlemen, some bending to them, some standing upon themselves, some desirous to overthrow those few which they thought were over them; the soldiers desirous of trouble as the nurse of spoil; and not much unlike to them, though in another way, were all the needy sort; the rich fearful, the wise careful.

This composition of conceits brought forth a dangerous tumult which yet would have been more dangerous, but that it had so many parts that nobody well knew against whom chiefly to oppose themselves. For some there were that cried to have the state altered and governed no more by a prince: marry, in the alteration, many would have the Lacedaemonian government of few chosen senators; others, the Athenian, where the people's voice held the chief authority. But these were rather the discoursing sort of men than the active, being a matter more in imagination than practice. But they that went nearest to the present case (as in a country that knew no government without a prince) were they that strove whom they should make, whereof a great number there were that would have the Princess Pamela presently to enjoy it; some, disdaining that she had (as it were) abandoned her own country, inclining more to Philoclea; and there wanted not of them which wished Gynecia were delivered and made regent till Pamela were worthily married. But great multitudes there were which, having been acquainted with the just government of Philanax, meant to establish him as lieutenant of the state, and these were the most popular sort who judged by the commodities* they felt.

But the principal men in honour and might, who had long before envied his greatness with Basilius, did much more spurn against any such preferment of him; for yet before, their envy had some kind of breathing out his rancour by laying his greatness as a fault to the prince's judgement, who showed in Dametas he might easily be deceived in men's value: but now if the prince's choice by so many mouths should be confirmed, what could they object to so rightly esteemed an excellency? They therefore were disposed sooner to yield to any thing than to his raising, and were content (for to cross Philanax) to stop those actions which otherwise they could not but think good. Philanax himself, as much hindered by those that did immoderately honour him (which brought both more envy and suspicion upon him) as by them that

* *commodities*: advantages.

did manifestly resist him, but standing only upon a constant desire of justice and a clear conscience, went forward stoutly in the action of his master's revenge which he thought himself particularly bound to. For the rest, as the ordering of the government, he accounted himself but as one, wherein notwithstanding he would employ all his loyal endeavour.

But among the noblemen, he that most openly set himself against him was named Timautus, a man of middle age but of extreme ambition, as one that had placed his uttermost good in greatness (thinking small difference by what means he came by it); of commendable wit, if he had not made it a servant to unbridled desires; cunning to creep into men's favours, which he prized only as they were serviceable unto him. He had been brought up in some soldiery, which he knew how to set out with more than deserved ostentation. Servile, though envious, to his betters, and no less tyrannically minded to them he had advantage of; counted revengeful, but indeed measuring both revenge and reward as the party might either help or hurt him; rather shameless than bold, and yet more bold in practices than in personal adventures. In sum, a man that could be as evil as he listed, and listed* as much as any advancement might thereby be gotten. As for virtue, he counted it but a school-name.*

He (even at the first assembling together) finding the great stroke Philanax carried among the people, thought it his readiest way of ambition to join with him: which though his pride did hardly brook, yet the other vice, carrying with it a more apparent object, prevailed over the weaker, so that with those liberal protestations of friendship which men that care not for their word are wont to bestow, he offered unto him the choice in marriage of either the sisters, so he would likewise help him to the other and make such a partition of the Arcadian estate: wishing him that since he loved his master because he was his master (which showed the love began in himself) he should rather (now occasion was presented) seek his own good substantially than affect the smoke of a glory by showing an untimely fidelity to him that could not reward it; and have all the fruit he should get in men's

* *listed:* liked. *a school-name:* a purely academic point.

opinions, which would be as divers as many, few agreeing to yield him due praise of his true heart.

But Philanax, who had limited his thoughts in that he esteemed good (to which he was neither carried by the vain tickling of uncertain fame, nor from which he would be transported by enjoying anything whereto the ignorant world gives the excellent name of goods) with great mislike of his offer, he made him so peremptory an answer – not without threatening if he found him foster any such fancy – that Timautus went with an inward spite from him whom before he had never loved; and measuring all men's marches by his own pace, rather thought it some further fetch* of Philanax (as that he would have all to himself alone) than was any way taken with the lovely beauty of his virtue, whose image he had so quite defaced in his own soul that he had left himself no eyes to behold it; but stayed waiting fit opportunity to execute his desires both for himself and against Philanax, when, by the bringing back of Pamela the people being divided into many motions (which both with murmuring noises, and putting themselves in several troops they well showed) he thought apt time was laid before him – the waters being (as the proverb saith) troubled and so the better for his fishing.

Therefore going among the chiefest lords whom he knew principally to repine at Philanax, and making a kind of convocation of them, he inveighed against his proceedings, drawing everything to the most malicious interpretation that malice itself could instruct him to do. He said, it was season for them to look to such a weed that else would over-grow them all. It was not now time to consult of the dead, but of the living, since such a sly wolf was entered among them that could make justice the cloak of tyranny, and love of his late master the destruction of his now-being children.

'Do you not see,' said he, 'how far his corruption hath stretched that he hath such a number of rascals' voices to declare him lieutenant, ready to make him prince but that he instructs them matters are not yet ripe for it? As for us, because we are too rich to be bought, he thinks us the fitter to be killed. Hath Arcadia bred no man but Philanax? Is she become a stepmother to all the rest

*fetch: trick.*

769

and hath given all her blessings to Philanax? Or if there be men amongst us, let us show we disdain to be servants to a servant! Let us make him know we are far worthier not to be slaves than he to be a master! Think you he hath made such haste in these matters to give them over to another man's hand? Think you he durst become the jailor of his princess but either* meaning to be her master or her murderer? And all this for the dear goodwill, forsooth, he bears to the king's memory, whose authority as he abused in his life, so he would now persevere to abuse his name after his death? O notable affection, for the love of the father to kill the wife and disinherit the children! O single-minded modesty, to aspire to no less than to the princely diadem! No, no, he hath veered all this while but to come the sooner to his affected end. But let us remember what we be: in quality his equals, in number far before him. Let us deliver the queen and our natural princesses, and leave them no longer under his authority whose proceedings would rather show that he himself had been the murderer of the king than a fit guardian of his posterity.'

These words pierced much into the minds already inclined that way, insomuch that most part of the nobility confirmed Timautus' speech and were ready to execute it, when Philanax came among them, and with a constant but reverent behaviour desired them they would not exercise private grudges in so common a necessity. He acknowledged himself a man, and a faulty man, to the clearing or satisfying of which he would at all times submit himself: since his end was to bring all things to an upright judgement, it should evil fit him to fly the judgement. 'But,' said he, 'my lords, let not Timautus' railing speech (who, whatsoever he finds evil in his own soul, can with ease lay it upon another) make me lose your good favour. Consider that all well-doing stands so in the middle betwixt his two contrary evils that it is a ready matter to cast a slanderous shade upon the most approved virtues. Who hath an evil tongue can call severity cruelty, and faithful diligence diligent ambition. But my end is not to excuse myself nor to accuse him: for both those, hereafter will be time enough. There is neither of us whose purging or punishing may so much import to Arcadia. Now I request you for your own honour's sake, and

*but either: without either.

770

require you by the duty you owe to this estate, that you do presently, according to the laws, take in hand the chastisement of our master's murderers and laying order for the government. By whomsoever it be done, so it be done, and justly done, I am satisfied. My labour hath been to frame things so as you might determine: now it is in you to determine. For my part, I call the heavens to witness the care of my heart stands to repay that wherein both I and most of you were tied to that prince, with whom all my love of worldly action is dead.'

As Philanax was speaking his last words there came one running to him with open mouth and fearful eyes, telling him that there were a great number of the people which were bent to take the young men out of Sympathus' hands and, as it should seem by their acclamations, were like enough to proclaim them princes.

'Nay,' said Philanax, speaking aloud and looking with a just anger upon the other noblemen, 'it is now season to hear Timautus' idle slanders while strangers become our lords, and Basilius' murderers sit in his throne! But whosoever is a true Arcadian let him follow me.'

With that he went toward the place he heard of, followed by those that had ever loved him, and some of the noblemen; some other remaining with Timautus who, in the meantime, was conspiring by strong hand to deliver Gynecia, of whom the weakest guard was had. But Philanax, where he went, found them all in an uproar, which thus was fallen out: the greatest multitude of people that were come to the death of Basilius were the Mantineans, as being the nearest city to the lodges. Among these, the chief man both in authority and love was Kalander – he that not long before had been host to the two princes; whom though he knew not so much as by name, yet besides the obligation he stood bound to them in for preserving the lives of his son and nephew, their noble behaviour had bred such love in his heart towards them as both with tears he parted from them when they left him under promise to return, and did keep their jewels and apparel as the relics of two demi-gods. Among others he had entered the prison and seen them, which forthwith so invested his soul both with sorrow and desire to help them (whom he tendered as his children) that calling his neighbours, the Mantineans, unto him, he told them all the praises of those two young men, swearing he thought the gods had provided for them better than they themselves could have imagined. He willed them to consider that when all was done, Basilius' children must enjoy the state: who since they had chosen, and chosen so as all the world could not mend their choice, why should they resist God's doing and their princesses' pleasure? This was the only way to purchase quietness without blood, where otherwise they should at one instant crown Pamela with a crown of gold and a dishonoured title, which whether ever she would forget, he thought it fit for them to weigh.

'Such,' said he, 'heroical greatness shines in their eyes, such an extraordinary majesty in all their actions, as surely either fortune by parentage or nature in creation hath made them princes. And yet a state already we have: we need but a man; who since he is presented unto you by the heavenly providence; embraced by our undoubted princess; worthy, for their youth, of compassion, for their beauty, of admiration, for their excellent virtue, to be monarchs of the world, shall we not be content with our own bliss? Shall we put out our eyes because another man cannot see? Or rather, like some men when too much good happens unto them, they think themselves in a dream and have not spirits to taste their own goods? No, no, my friends, believe me, I am so impartial that I know not their names, but so overcome with their virtue that I shall then think the destinies have ordained a perpetual flourishing to Arcadia when they shall allot such a governor unto it.'

This spoken by a man grave in years, great in authority, near allied to the prince, and known honest, prevailed so with all the Mantineans that with one voice they ran to deliver the two princes. But Philanax came in time to withstand them, both sides yet standing in arms, and rather wanting a beginning than minds to enter into a bloody conflict; which Philanax foreseeing, thought best to remove the prisoners secretly and (if need were) rather without form of justice to kill them than against justice (as he thought) to have them usurp the state. But there again arose a new trouble: for Sympathus, the nobleman that kept them, was so stricken in compassion with their excellent presence that, as he would not falsify his promise to Philanax to give them liberty, so yet would he not yield them to himself, fearing he would do them violence. Thus tumult upon tumult arising, the sun, I think, aweary to see their discords, had already gone down to his western lodging. But yet to know what the poor shepherds did, who were the first discriers of these matters, will not to some ears perchance be a tedious digression.

## THE FOURTH ECLOGUES

The shepherds, finding no place for them in these garboils,* to which their quiet hearts (whose highest ambition was in keeping themselves up in goodness) had at all no aptness, retired themselves from among the clamorous multitude; and as sorrow desires company, went up together to the western side of a hill, whose prospect extended it so far as they might well discern many of Arcadia's beauties. And there looking upon the sun's as-then-declining race,* the poor men sat pensive of their present miseries, as if they found a weariness of their woeful words: till at last good old Geron (who as he had longest tasted the benefits of Basilius' government, so seemed to have a special feeling of the present loss) wiping his eyes and long white beard, bedewed with great drops of tears, began in this sort to complain:

'Alas, poor sheep,' said he, 'which hitherto have enjoyed your fruitful pasture in such quietness as your wool, amongst other things, hath made this country famous, your best days are now passed. Now you must become the victual of an army, and perchance an army of foreign enemies. You are now not only to fear home-wolves but alien lions, now, I say, now that our right Basilius is deceased. Alas, sweet pastures, shall soldiers (that know not how to use you) possess you? Shall they that cannot speak Arcadian language be lords over your shepherds? For alas, with good cause may we look for any evil since Basilius, our only strength, is taken from us.'

To that all the other shepherds present uttered pitiful voices, especially the very born Arcadians; for as for the other, though

* *garboils*: disturbances. *race*: course.

humanity moved them to pity human cases – especially in a prince under whom they had found a refuge of their miseries, and justice equally* administered – yet could they not so naturally feel the lively touch of sorrow. Nevertheless, of that number one Agelastus (notably noted among them as well for his skill in poetry as for an austerely maintained sorrowfulness wherewith he seemed to despise the works of nature) framing an universal complaint in that universal mischief, uttered it in this sestine:[1]*

Since wailing is a bud of causeful sorrow,
Since sorrow is the follower of evil fortune,
Since no evil fortune equals public damage;
Now prince's loss hath made our damage public,
Sorrow, pay we to thee the rights of nature,
And inward grief seal up with outward wailing.

Why should we spare our voice from endless wailing,
Who justly make our hearts the seat of sorrow,
In such a case where it appears that nature
Doth add her force unto the sting of fortune;
Choosing alas, this our theatre public,
Where they would leave trophies of cruel damage?

Then since such powers conspired unto our damage
(Which may be known, but never helped with wailing)
Yet let us leave a monument in public
Of willing tears, torn hairs, and cries of sorrow,
For lost, lost is by blow of cruel fortune
Arcadia's gem, the noblest child of nature.

O nature doting, old; O blinded nature,
How hast thou torn thyself, sought thine own damage
In granting such a scope to filthy fortune,
By thy imp's* loss to fill the world with wailing!
Cast thy step-mother* eyes upon our sorrow:
Public our loss: so, see, thy shame is public.

*equally: fairly. sestine: sestina. imp: offspring. step-mother: unkind, unnatural.

O that we had, to make our woes more public,
Seas in our eyes, and brazen tongues by nature,
A yelling voice, and hearts compos'd of sorrow,
Breath made of flames, wits knowing naught but damage,
Our sports murdering ourselves, our musics wailing,
Our studies fixed upon the falls of fortune.

No, no, our mischief grows in this vile fortune,
That private pains cannot breathe out in public
The furious inward griefs with hellish wailing,
But forced are to burden feeble nature
With secret sense of our eternal damage,
And sorrow feed, feeding our souls with sorrow.

Since sorrow then concluded all our fortune,
With all our deaths show we this damage public:
His nature fears to die who lives still wailing.

It seemed that this complaint of Agelastus had awaked the spirits of the Arcadians, astonished before with exceedingness of sorrow; for he had scarcely ended when divers of them offered to follow his example in bewailing the general loss of that country which had been as well a nurse to strangers as a mother to Arcadians. Among the rest one, accounted good in that kind and made the better by the true feeling of sorrow, roared out a song of lamentation which, as well as might be, was gathered up in this form:[2]

Since that to death is gone the shepherd high,
Who most the silly shepherd's pipe did prize,
    Your doleful tunes sweet Muses now apply.
And you, O trees (if any life there lies
    In trees) now through your porous barks receive
The strange resound of these my causeful cries:
    And let my breath upon your branches cleave,
My breath distinguished into words of woe,
    That so I may signs of my sorrow leave.
But if among yourselves some one tree grow
    That aptest is to figure misery,

Let it embassage bear your griefs to show.
  The weeping myrrh I think will not deny
Her help to this, this justest cause of plaint.
  Your doleful tunes sweet Muses now apply.

And thou, poor earth, whom fortune doth attaint,*
  In nature's name to suffer such a harm
As for to lose thy gem, and such a saint,
  Upon thy face let coaly ravens swarm:
Let all the sea thy tears accounted be;
  Thy bowels with all-killing metals arm.
Let gold now rust, let diamonds waste in thee:
  Let pearls be wan with woe their dam doth bear:
Thyself henceforth the light do never see.
  And you, O flowers, which sometimes princes were,
Till these strange alterings you did hap to try,
  Of princes' loss yourselves for tokens rear:
Lily in mourning black thy whiteness dye:
  O Hyacinth, let Ai be on thee still.[3]
Your doleful tunes sweet Muses now apply.

O Echo, all these woods with roaring fill,
And do not only mark the accents last*
  But all, for all reach not my wailful will:
One Echo to another Echo cast
  Sound of my griefs, and let it never end,
Till that it hath all woods and waters passed.
  Nay, to the heav'ns your just complaining send,
And stay the stars' inconstant constant race,
  Till that they do unto our dolours bend:
And ask the reason of that special grace
  That they, which have no lives, should live so long,
And virtuous souls so soon should lose their place.
  Ask, if in great men good men do so throng,
That he for want of elbow-room must die;
  Or if that they be scant, if this be wrong.
Did Wisdom this our wretched time espy

---

* *attaint*: condemn. *accents last*: See Philisides' Echo song, p. 427.
*not*: OA and Ringler. '93 text, 'out'.

In one true chest to rob all virtue's treasure?
Your doleful tunes sweet Muses now apply.

And if that any counsel you to measure
　　You doleful tunes, to them still plaining* say,
'To well felt grief plaint is the only pleasure.'
　　O light of sun, which is entitled day,
O well thou dost that thou no longer bidest;
　　For mourning night her black weeds may display.
O Phoebus, with good cause thy face thou hidest,
　　Rather than have thy all-beholding eye
Fouled with this sight, while thou thy chariot guidest;
　　And well methings becomes this vaulty sky
A stately tomb to cover him deceased.
　　Your doleful tunes sweet Muses now apply.

O Philomela with thy breast oppressed
　　By shame and grief, help, help me to lament
Such cursed harms as cannot be redressed.
　　Or if thy mourning notes be fully spent,
Then give a quiet ear unto my plaining,
　　For I to teach the world complaint am bent.
You dimmy* clouds, which well employ your staining
　　This cheerful air with your obscured cheer,
Witness your woeful tears with daily raining.
　　And if, O sun, thou ever didst appear
In shape, which by man's eye might be perceived,
　　Virtue is dead, now set thy triumph here.
Now set thy triumph in this world, bereaved
　　Of what was good, where now no good doth lie:
And by thy pomp our loss will be conceived.
　　O notes of mine, yourselves together tie;
With too much grief methinks you are dissolved.
　　Your doleful tunes sweet Muses now apply.

Time ever old and young is still revolved
　　Within itself, and never tasteth end;
But mankind is for aye to nought resolved.

　　*plaining: uttering plaints. *dimmy:* dimmish.

The filthy snake her aged coat can mend,
And getting youth again, in youth doth flourish;
   But unto man age ever death doth send.
The very trees with grafting we can cherish,
   So that we can long time produce their time;
But man which helpeth them, helpless must perish
   Thus, thus the minds which over all do climb,
When they by years' experience get best graces,
   Must finish then by death's detested crime.
We last short while, and build long lasting places.
   Ah, let us all against foul nature cry:
We nature's works do help, she us defaces;
   For how can nature unto this reply,
That she her child, I say, her best child killeth?
   Your doleful tunes sweet Muses now apply.

Alas methinks my weakened voice but spilleth
   The vehement course of this just lamentation:
Methinks my sound no place with sorrow filleth.
   I know not I, but once in detestation*
I have myself, and all what life containeth,
   Since death on virtue's forth hath made invasion.
One word of woe another after traineth:*
   Ne do I care how rude be my invention,
So it be seen what sorrow in me reigneth.
   O elements, by whose (men say) contention
Our bodies be in living power maintained,
   Was this man's death the fruit of your dissension?
O physic's power, which (some say) hath restrained
Approach of death, alas, thou helpest meagrely,
   When once one is for Atropos* distrained.*
Great be physicians' brags, but aid is beggarly;
   When rooted moisture fails or groweth dry,
They leave off all, and say death comes too eagerly.
   They are but words therefore that men do buy

* *once in detestation*: once and for all. *traineth*: draweth. *Atropos*: the one of the three Fates whose task was to cut the thread of human life. *distrained*: seized.

Of any, since god Aesculapius[4] ceased.
  Your doleful tunes sweet Muses now apply.

Justice, justice is now, alas, oppressed:
  Bountifulness hath made his last conclusion:
Goodness for best attire in dust is dressed.
  Shepherds bewail your uttermost confusion;
And see by this picture to you presented,
  Death is our home, life is but a delusion.
For see, alas, who is from you absented.
  Absented? nay, I say, for ever banished
From such as were to die for him contented.
  Out of our sight in turn of hand is vanished
Shepherd of shepherds, whose well settled order
  Private with wealth, public with quiet garnished.
While he did live, far, far was all disorder,
  Example more prevailing than direction;
Far was home-strife, and far was foe from border,
  His life a law, his look a full correction.
As in his health we healthful were preserved,
  So in his sickness grew our sure infection,
His death our death. But ah, my muse hath swerved
  From such deep plaint as should such woes descry,
Which he of us for ever hath deserved.
  The style of heavy heart can never fly
So high as should make such a pain notorious:
  Cease Muse, therefore: thy dart, O death, apply,
And farewell prince, whom goodness hath made glorious.

Many were ready to have followed this course, but the day was
so wasted that only this rhyming sestine, delivered by one of great
account among them, could obtain favour to be heard:[5]

  Farewell, O sun, Arcadia's clearest light:
Farewell, O pearl, the poor man's plenteous treasure:
  Farewell, O golden staff, the weak man's might:
Farewell, O joy, the joyful's only pleasure:
  Wisdom, farewell, the skill-less man's direction:
  Farewell with thee, farewell all our affection.

For what place now is left for our affection,
Now that of purest lamp is quench'd the light,
   Which to our darkened minds was best direction,
     Now that the mine is lost of all our treasure,
     Now death hath swallowed up our worldly pleasure,
We orphans made, void of all public might?

   Orphans indeed, depriv'd of father's might:
     For he our father was in all affection,
In our well-doing placing all his pleasure,
   Still studying how to us to be a light.
As well he was in peace a safest treasure:
     In war his wit and word was our direction.

Whence, whence, alas, shall we seek our direction
     When that we fear our hateful neighbours' might,
   Who long have gap'd to get Arcadians' treasure?
Shall we now find a guide of such affection,
     Who for our sakes will think all travail light,
   And make his pain (to keep us safe) his pleasure?

No, no, for ever gone is all our pleasure;
     For ever wandering from all good direction;
   For ever blinded of our clearest sight:
For ever lamed of our surest might;
     For ever banish'd from well-plac'd affection;
For ever robb'd of all our royal treasure.

   Let tears for him therefore be all our treasure,
   And in our wailful naming him our pleasure:
   Let hating of ourselves be our affection,
And unto death bend still our thoughts' direction.
Let us against ourselves employ our might,
   And putting out our eyes seek we our light.

   Farewell our light, farewell our spoiled treasure:
   Farewell our might, farewell our daunted pleasure:
   Farewell direction, farewell all affection.

The night began to cast her dark canopy over them, and they

even weary with their woes bended homewards, hoping, by sleep forgetting themselves, to ease their present dolours; when they were met with a troop of twenty horse, the chief of which, asking them for the king and understanding the hard news, thereupon stayed among them expecting* the return of a messenger whom with speed he dispatched to Philanax.

*expecting: awaiting.

**THE END OF THE FOURTH BOOK**

# The Fifth Book of the Countess
of Pembroke's Arcadia

## CHAPTER 1

The dangerous division of men's minds, the ruinous renting of all estates, had now brought Arcadia to feel the pangs of uttermost peril – such convulsions never coming but that the life of that government draws near his necessary period – when to the honest and wise Philanax, equally distracted betwixt desire of his master's revenge and care of the state's establishment, there came (unlooked for) a Macedonian gentleman who in short but pithy manner delivered unto him that the renowned Euarchus, King of Macedon, purposing to have visited his old friend and confederate, the King Basilius, was now come within half a mile of the lodges; where having understood by certain shepherds the sudden death of their prince, had sent unto him (of whose authority and faith he had good knowledge) desiring him to advertise him in what security he might rest there for that night, where willingly he would (if safely he might) help to celebrate the funerals of his ancient companion and ally; adding he need not doubt, since he had brought but twenty in his company, he would be so unwise as to enter into any forcible attempt with so small force.

Philanax, having entertained the gentleman as well as in the midst of so many tumults he could, pausing awhile with himself, considering how it should not only be unjust and against the law of nations not well to receive a prince whom goodwill had brought among them, but (in respect of the greatness of his might) very dangerous to give him any cause of due offence; remembering withal the excellent trials of his equity, which made him more famous than his victories, he thought he might be the fittest instrument to redress the ruins they were in, since his goodness put him without suspicion, and his greatness beyond envy. Yet weighing with himself how hard many heads were to be bridled, and that in this monstrous confusion such mischief might be attempted of which late repentance should after be but a simple remedy, he judged best first to know how the people's minds would sway to this determination. Therefore desiring the gentleman to return to the King his master, and to beseech him (though with his pains) to stay for an hour or two where he was till he had set things in better order to receive him, he himself went first to the noblemen, then to Kalander and the principal Mantineans who were most opposite* unto him, desiring them that as the night had most blessedly stayed them from entering into civil blood, so they would be content in the night to assemble the people together to hear some news which he was to deliver unto them.

There is nothing more desirous of novelties than a man that fears his present fortune. Therefore they (whom mutual diffidence made doubtful of their utter destruction) were quickly persuaded to hear of any new matter which might alter, at least, if not help the nature of their fear – namely,* the chiefest men, who as they had most to lose so were most jealous of their own case, and were already grown as weary to be followers of Timautus' ambition as before they were enviers of Philanax's worthiness. As for Kalander and Sympathus, as in the one a virtuous friendship had made him seek to advance, in the other a natural commiseration had made him willing to protect, the excellent (though unfortunate) prisoners, so were they not against this convocation; for having nothing but just desires in them, they did not mistrust the justifying of them. Only Timautus laboured to have withdrawn them from this assembly, saying it was time to stop their ears from the ambitious charms of Philanax. Let them first deliver Gynecia and her daughters, which were fit persons to hear, and then they might begin to speak: that this was but Philanax's cunning to link broil upon broil, because he might avoid the answering of his trespasses, which as he had long intended, so had he prepared coloured speeches to disguise them. But as his words expressed rather a violence of rancour than any just ground of accusation, so pierced they no further than to some partial ears, the multitude yielding good attention to what Philanax would propose unto them; who (like a man whose best building was a well-framed

*opposite: opposed. namely: especially.

conscience) neither with plausible words nor fawning countenance, but even with the grave behaviour of a wise father whom nothing but love makes to chide, thus said unto them:

'I have,' said he, 'a great matter to deliver unto you, and thereout am I to make a greater demand of you: but truly, such hath this late proceeding been of yours that I know not what is not to be demanded of you. Methinks I may have reason to require of you (as men are wont among pirates) that the life of him that never hurt you may be safe. Methinks I am not without appearance of cause, as if you were Cyclops[1] or Cannibals, to desire that our prince's body, which hath thirty years maintained us in a flourishing peace, be not torn in pieces or devoured among you, but may be suffered to yield itself (which never was defiled with any of your bloods) to the natural rest of the earth. Methinks not as to Arcadians, renowned for your faith to prince and love of country, but as to sworn enemies of this sweet soil, I am to desire you that at least, if you will have strangers to your princes, yet you will not deliver the seigniory of this goodly kingdom to your noble king's murderers. Lastly, I have reason, as if I had to speak to madmen, to desire you to be good to yourselves; for before God, what either barbarous violence or unnatural folly hath not this day had his seat in your minds and left his footsteps in your actions? But in troth I love you too well to stand long displaying your faults. I would you yourselves did forget them so you did not fall again into them. For my part, I had much rather be an orator of your praises.

'But now (if you will suffer attentive judgement and not forejudging passion to be the weigher of my words) I will deliver unto you what a blessed mean the gods have sent unto you, if you list to embrace it. I think there is none among you so young, either in years or understanding, but hath heard the true fame of that just prince Euarchus, King of Macedon, a prince with whom our late master did ever hold most perfect alliance. He, even he, is this day come, having but twenty horse with him, within two miles of this place, hoping to have found the virtuous Basilius alive, but now willing to do honour to his death. Surely, surely the heavenly powers have in so full a time bestowed him on us to unite our divisions. For my part, therefore, I wish that, since among ourselves we cannot agree in so manifold partialities, we do put the ordering of all these things into his hands, as well touching the obsequies of the king, the punishment of his death, as the marriage and crowning of our princesses. He is both by experience and wisdom taught how to direct: his greatness such as no man can disdain to obey him: his equity such as no man need to fear him. Lastly, as he hath all these qualities to help, so hath he (though he would) no force to hurt. If therefore you so think good, since our laws bear that our prince's murder be chastised before his murdered body be buried, we may invite him to sit tomorrow in the judgement seat; which done, you may after proceed to the burial.'

When Philanax first named Euarchus' landing, there was a muttering murmur among the people, as though, in that evil ordered weakness of theirs, he had come to conquer their country. But when they understood he had so small a retinue, whispering one with another, and looking who should begin to confirm Philanax's proposition, at length Sympathus was the first that allowed it, then the rest of the noblemen; neither did Kalader strive, hoping so excellent a prince could not but deal graciously with two such young men: whose authority, joined to Philanax, all the popular sort followed. Timautus, still blinded with his own ambitious haste (not remembering factions are no longer to be trusted than the factious may be persuaded it is for their own good) would needs strive against the stream, exclaiming against Philanax that now he showed who it was that would betray his country to strangers. But well he found that who is too busy in the foundation of an house may pull the building about his ears. For the people (already tired with their own divisions, of which his clampring* had been a principal nurse, and, beginning now to espy a haven of rest, hated anything that should hinder them from it) asked one another whether this were not he whose evil tongue no man could escape, whether it were not Timautus that made the first mutinous oration to strengthen the troubles, whether Timautus, without their consent, had not gone about to deliver Gynecia. And thus inflaming one another against him, they threw him out of the assembly and after pursued him with stones and

* *clampring:* making false accusations.

staves, so that with loss of one of his eyes, sore wounded and beaten, he was fain to fly to Philanax's feet for succour of his life; giving a true lesson, that vice itself is forced to seek the sanctuary of virtue. For Philanax, who hated his evil but not his person, and knew that a just punishment might by the manner be unjustly done; remembering withal that although herein the people's rage might have hit rightly, yet if it were nourished in this, no man knew to what extremities it might extend itself; with earnest dealing and employing the uttermost of his authority he did protect the trembling Timautus. And then having taken a general oath that they should, in the nonage* of the princess or till these things were settled, yield full obedience to Euarchus so far as were not prejudicial to the laws, customs and liberties of Arcadia; and having taken a particular bond of Sympathus (under whom he had a servant of his own) that the prisoners should be kept close without conference with any man, he himself, honourably accompanied with a great number of torches, went to the King Euarchus, whose coming in this sort into Arcadia had thus fallen out.

CHAPTER 2

The woeful Prince Plangus receiving of Basilius no other succours, but only certain* to conduct him to Euarchus, made all possible speed towards Byzantium where he understood the king (having concluded all his wars with the winning of that town) had now for some good space made his abode. But being far gone on his way, he received certain intelligence that Euarchus was not only some days before returned into Macedon but since was gone with some haste to visit that coast of his country that lay towards Italy; the occasion given by the Latines, who (having already gotten into their hands, partly by conquest and partly by confederacy, the greatest part of Italy, and long gaped to devour Greece also) observing the present opportunity of Euarchus' absence and Basilius' solitariness (which two princes they knew to be in effect the whole strength of Greece) were even ready to lay an unjust gripe

* *nonage*: minority. *but only certain*: no other help except. See p. 406.

upon it, which after they might beautify with the noble name of conquest. Which purpose though they made not known by any solemn denouncing of war but contrariwise gave many tokens of continuing still their former amity, yet the staying of his subjects' ships trafficking as merchants into those parts, together with the daily preparation of shipping and other warlike provisions in ports most convenient for the transporting of soldiers, occasioned Euarchus (not unacquainted with such practices) first to suspect, then to discern, lastly to seek to prevent the intended mischief.

Yet thinking war never to be accepted until it be offered by the hand of necessity, he determined so long openly to hold them his friends as open hostility betrayed them not his enemies; not ceasing in the meantime by letters and messages to move the states of Greece, by uniting their strength, to make timely provision against this peril; by many reasons making them see that though in respect of place some of them might seem further removed from the first violence of the storm, yet being embarked in the same ship, the final wreck must needs be common to them all. And knowing the mighty force of example, with the weak effect of fair discourses not waited on with agreeable actions, what he persuaded them, himself performed, leaving in his own realm nothing either undone or unprovided which might be thought necessary for withstanding an invasion. His first care was to put his people in a readiness for war, and by his experienced soldiers to train the unskilful to martial exercises. For the better effecting whereof, as also for meeting with other inconveniences in such doubtful times incident to the most settled states, making of the divers regions of his whole kingdom so many divisions as he thought convenient, he appointed the charge of them to the greatest and of greatest trust he had about him, arming them with sufficient authority to levy forces within their several governments both for resisting the invading enemy, and punishing the disordered subject.

Having thus prepared the body and assured the heart of his country against any mischief that might attaint* it, he then took into his careful consideration the external parts, giving order both for the repairing and increasing his navy and for the fortifying of such places (especially on the sea coast) as either commodity* of

*attaint: infect. *commodity*: convenience.

landing, weakness of the country, or any other respect of advantage was likeliest to draw the enemy unto. But being none of them who think all things done for which they have once given direction, he followed everywhere his commandment with his presence, which witness of every man's slackness or diligence (chastising the one and encouraging the other) suffered not the fruit of any profitable counsel for want of timely taking to be lost.

And thus making one place succeed another in the progress of wisdom and virtue, he was now come to Aulon, a principal port of his realm, when the poor Plangus, extremely wearied with his long journey (desire of succouring Erona no more relieving than fear of not succouring her in time aggravating his travail) by a lamentable narration of his children's death called home his cares from encountering foreign enemies to suppress the insurrection of inward passions. The matter so heinous, the manner so villainous, the loss of such persons in so unripe years, in a time so dangerous to the whole state of Greece, how vehemently it moved to grief and compassion others (only not blind to the light of virtue nor deaf to the voice of their country) might perchance by a more cunning workman in lively colours be delivered. But the face of Euarchus' sorrow (to the one in nature, to both in affection a father, and judging the world so much the more unworthily deprived of those excellencies as himself was better judge of so excellent worthiness) can no otherwise be shadowed out by the skilfullest pencil than by covering it over with the veil of silence. And indeed that way himself took, with so patient a quietness receiving this pitiful relation that, all words of weakness suppressed, magnanimity seemed to triumph over misery. Only receiving of Plangus perfect instruction of all things concerning Plexirtus and Artaxia, with promise not only to aid him in delivering Erona, but also with vehement protestation never to return into Macedon till he had pursued the murderers to death, he dispatched with speed a ship for Byzantium, commanding the governor to provide all necessaries for the war against his own coming, which he purposed should be very shortly.

In this ship Plangus would needs go, impatient of stay for that in many days before he had understood nothing of his lady's estate. Soon after whose departure, news was brought to Euarchus that all the ships detained in Italy were returned. For the Latines (finding by Euarchus' proceedings their intent to be frustrate as before by his sudden return they doubted it was discovered, deeming it no wisdom to show the will, not having the ability to hurt) had not only in free and friendly manner dismissed them but for the time wholly omitted their enterprise, attending the opportunity of fitter occasion; by means whereof Euarchus, rid from the cumber of that war (likely otherwise to have stayed him longer) with so great a fleet as haste would suffer him to assemble, forthwith embarked for Byzantium. And now followed with fresh winds, he had in short time run a long course when on a night, encountered with an extreme tempest, his ships were so scattered that scarcely any two were left together.

As for the king's own ship, deprived of all company, sore bruised and weather-beaten, able no longer to brook the sea's churlish entertainment, a little before day it recovered* the shore. The first light made them see it was the unhappy coast of Laconia, for no other country could have shown the like evidence of unnatural war; which, having long endured between the nobility and the Helots, and once compounded* by Pyrocles under the name of Daiphantus, immediately upon his departure had broken out more violently than ever before. For the king, taking the opportunity of their captain's absence, refused to perform the conditions of peace as extorted from him by rebellious violence; whereupon they were again deeply entered into war, with so notable an hatred towards the very name of a king that Euarchus, though a stranger unto them, thought it not safe there to leave his person where neither his own force could be a defence, nor the sacred name of majesty a protection. Therefore calling to him an Arcadian (one that coming with Plangus had remained with Euarchus, desirous to see the wars) he demanded of him for the next place of surety where he might make his stay until he might hear somewhat of his fleet, or cause the ship to be repaired. The gentleman, glad to have this occasion of doing service to Euarchus and honour to Basilius (to whom he knew he should bring a most welcome guest) told him that if it pleased him to commit himself to Arcadia, a part whereof lay open to their view, he would under-

* *recovered*: reached. *once compounded*: formerly brought to peace.

take ere the next night were far spent to guide him safely to his master Basilius.

The present necessity much prevailed with Euarchus, yet more a certain virtuous desire to try whether by his authority he might withdraw Basilius from burying himself alive and to employ the rest of his old years in doing good, the only happy action of man's life. For besides the universal case of Greece, deprived by this means of a principal pillar, he weighed and pitied the pitiful state of the Arcadian people who were in worse case than if death had taken away their prince; for so yet their necessity would have placed someone to the helm. Now, a prince being and not doing like a prince, keeping and not exercising the place, they were in so much more evil case as they could not provide for their evil.

These rightly wise and virtuous considerations especially moved Euarchus to take his journey towards the desert, where arriving within night, and understanding to his great grief the news of the prince's death, he waited for his safe conduct from Philanax; in the meantime taking his rest under a tree, with no more affected pomps than as a man that knew (howsoever he was exalted) the beginning and end of his body was earth. But Philanax as soon as he was in sight of him, lighting from his horse, presented himself unto him in all those humble behaviours which not only the great reverence of the party but the conceit of one's own misery is wont to frame. Euarchus rase up unto him with so gracious a countenance as the goodness of his mind had long exercised him unto, careful so much more to descend in all courtesies as he saw him bear a low representation of his afflicted state. But to Philanax, as soon as by near looking on him he might perfectly behold him, the gravity of his countenance and years (not much unlike to his late deceased but ever beloved master) brought his form so lively into his memory and revived so all the thoughts of his wonted joys within him that, instead of speaking to Euarchus, he stood a while like a man gone a far journey from himself, calling as it were with his mind an account of his losses, imagining that this pain needed not if nature had not been violently stopped of her own course, and casting more loving than wise conceits what a world this would have been if this sudden accident had not interrupted it. And so far strayed he into this raving melancholy that his eyes, nimbler than his tongue, let fall a flood of tears, his voice being stopped with extremity of sobbing – so much had his friendship carried him to Basilius that he thought no age was timely for his death. But at length taking the occasion of* his own weeping, he thus did speak to Euarchus:

'Let not my tears, most worthily renowned prince, make my presence unpleasant or my speech unmarked of you; for the justice of the cause takes away the blame of any weakness in me, and the affinity that the same beareth to your greatness seems even lawfully to claim pity in you: a prince, of a prince's fall; a lover of justice, of a most unjust violence. And give me leave, excellent Euarchus, to say I am but the representer of all the late flourishing Arcadia, which now with mine eyes doth weep, with my tongue doth complain, with my knees doth lay itself at your feet which never have been unready to carry you to the virtuous protecting of innocents. Imagine, vouchsafe to imagine, most wise and good king, that here is before your eyes the pitiful spectacle of a most dolorously ending tragedy; wherein I do but play the part of all the new miserable province which, being spoiled of their guide, doth lie like a ship without a pilot, tumbling up and down in the uncertain waves, till it either run itself upon the rocks of self-division or be overthrown by the stormy wind of foreign force.

'Arcadia, finding herself in these desolate terms, doth speak (and I speak for her) to thee not vainly, puissant prince, that, since now she is not only robbed of the natural support of her lord but so suddenly robbed that she hath not breathing time to stand for her safety (so unfortunately, that it doth appal their minds, though they had leisure, and so mischievously, that it doth exceed both the suddenness and unfortunateness of it) thou wilt lend thine arm unto her and, as a man, take compassion of mankind; as a virtuous man, chastise most abominable vice; and as a prince, protect a people which all have with one voice called for thy goodness, thinking that as thou art only able, so thou art fully able, to redress their imminent ruins. They do, therefore, with as much confidence as necessity, fly unto you for succour; they lay themselves open to you – to you, I mean yourself such as you have ever

* *taking the occasion of*: using the occasion as the material of his speech.

been: that is to say, one that hath always had his determinations bounded with equity. They only reserve the right to Basilius' blood, the manner to the ancient prescribing of their laws. For the rest without exception they yield over unto you as to the elected protector of this kingdom, which name and office they beseech you (till you have laid a sufficient foundation of tranquillity) to take upon you.

'The particularity both of their statutes and demands you shall presently after understand. Now only I am to say unto you, that this country falls to be a fair field to prove whether the goodly tree of your virtue will live in all soils. Here, I say, will be seen whether either fear can make you short, or the lickerousness* of dominion make you beyond justice. And I can for conclusion say no more but this: you must think, upon my words and your answer depend not only the quiet but the lives of so many thousands which, for their ancient confederacy, in this their extreme necessity desire neither the expense of your treasure nor hazard of your subjects, but only the benefit of your wisdom, whose both glory and increase stands in the exercising of it.'

The sum of this request was utterly unlooked for of Euarchus, which made him the more diligent in marking his speech, and after his speech take the greater pause for a perfect resolution. For as (of the one side) he thought nature required nothing more of him than that he should be a help to them of like creation, and had his heart no whit commanded with fear, thinking his life well passed, having satisfied the tyranny of time with the course of many years, the expectation of the world with more than expected honour, lastly, the tribute due to his own mind with the daily offering of most virtuous actions; so (of the other) he weighed the just reproach that followed those who easily enter into other folk's business, with the opinion might* be conceived love of seigniory rather than of justice had made him embark himself thus into a matter nothing pertaining to him, especially in a time when earnest occasion of his own business so greatly required his presence. But in the end wisdom, being an essential and not an opinionate thing,[1] made him rather to bend to what was in itself good than what by evil minds might be judged not good; and therein did see

* *lickerousness*: lust for. *the opinion might*: which might.

that though that people did not belong unto him, yet doing good (which is not enclosed within any terms of people) did belong unto him, and if necessity forced him for some time to abide in Arcadia, the necessity of Arcadia might justly demand some fruit of abiding. To this, secret assurance of his own worthiness (which although it be never so well clothed in modesty, yet always lives in the worthiest minds) did much push him forward, saying unto himself the treasure of those inward gifts he had were bestowed by the heavens upon him to be beneficial and not idle. On which determination resting, and yet willing before he waded any further to examine well the depth of the other's proffer, he thus, with that well-appeased* gesture unpassionate nature bestoweth upon mankind, made answer to Philanax's most urgent petition:

'Although long experience hath made me know all men (and so princes, which be but men) to be subject to infinite casualties, the very constitution of our lives remaining in continual change, yet the affairs of this country, or at least my meeting so jumply* with them, makes me abashed with the strangeness of it. With much pain I am come hither to see my long approved friend, and now I find if I will see him, I must see him dead. After, for mine own security, I seek to be warranted mine own life; and there suddenly am I appointed to be a judge of other men's lives. Though a friend to him, yet am I a stranger to the country; and now of a stranger you would suddenly make a director. I might object to your desire my weakness, which age perhaps hath wrought in mind and body; and justly I may pretend the necessity of mine own affairs, to which, as I am by all true rules most nearly tied, so can they not long bear the delay of my absence. But though I would and could dispense with these difficulties, what assurance can I have of the people's will which, having so many circles of imaginations, can hardly be enclosed in one point? Who knows a people that knows not sudden opinion makes them hope, which hope if it be not answered, they fall in hate, choosing and refusing, erecting, and overthrowing according as the presentness of any fancy carries them! Even this their hasty drawing to me makes me think they will be as hastily withdrawn from me; for it is but one ground of inconstancy soon to take or soon to leave. It may be they have

* *well-appeased*: calm. *jumply*: exactly.

heard of Euarchus more than cause: their own eyes will be perhaps more curious* judges. Out of hearsay they may have builded many conceits which I cannot, perchance will not, perform. Then will undeserved repentance be a greater shame and injury unto me than their undeserved proffer is honour. And to conclude, I must be fully informed how the patient is minded before I can promise to undertake the cure.'

Philanax was not of the modern minds who make suitors magistrates, but did ever think the unwilling worthy man was fitter than the undeserving desirer. Therefore the more Euarchus drew back, the more he found in him that the cunningest pilot doth most dread the rocks, the more earnestly he pursued his public request unto him. He desired him not to make any weak excuses of his weakness, since so many examples had well proved his mind was strong to overpass the greatest troubles, and his body strong enough to obey his mind, and that so long as they were joined together, he knew Euarchus would think it no wearisome exercise to make them vessels of virtuous actions. The duty to his country he acknowledged; which as he had so settled as it was not to fear any sudden alteration, so, since it did want him,* as well it might endure a fruitful as an idle absence. As for the doubt he conceived of the people's constancy in this their election, he said it was such a doubt as all human actions are subject unto. Yet as much as in politic matters (which receive not geometrical* certainties) a man may assure himself, there was evident likelihood to be conceived of the continuance both in their unanimity and his worthiness, whereof the one was apt to be held and the other to hold, joined to the present necessity, the firmest band of mortal minds. In sum, he alleged so many reasons to Euarchus' mind, already inclined to enter into any virtuous action, that he yielded to take upon himself the judgement of the present cause, so as he might find indeed that such was the people's desire out of judgement and not faction.

Therefore mounting on their horses, they hasted to the lodges, where they found, though late in the night, the people wakefully watching for the issue of Philanax's embassage, no man thinking

* *curious*: careful. *since it did want him*: since it was already without him. *geometrical*: mathematical.

the matter would be well done without he had his voice in it, and each deeming his own eyes the best guardians of his throat in that unaccustomed tumult. But when they saw Philanax return, having on his right hand the King Euarchus on whom they had now placed the greatest burden of their fears, with joyful shouts and applauding acclamations they made him and the world quickly know that one man's sufficiency is more available than ten thousand's multitude – so evil balanced be the extremities of popular minds, and so much natural imperiousness there rests in a well-formed spirit. For, as if Euarchus had been born of the princely blood of Arcadia or that long and well-acquainted proof had engrafted him in their country, so flocked they about this stranger – most of them already from dejected fears rising to ambitious considerations who should catch the first hold of his favour; and then from those crying welcomes to babbling one with the other, some praising Philanax for his well-succeeding pains, others liking Euarchus' aspect, and as they judged his age by his face, so judging his wisdom by his age.

Euarchus passed through them like a man that did neither disdain a people nor yet was anything tickled with their flatteries, but always holding his own, a man might read a constant determination in his eyes. And in that sort dismounting among them, he forthwith demanded the convocation to be made; which accordingly was done with as much order and silence as it might appear Neptune had not more force to appease the rebellious wind than the admiration of an extraordinary virtue hath to temper a disordered multitude. He, being raised upon a place more high than the rest where he might be best understood, in this sort spake unto them:

'I understand,' said he, 'faithful Arcadians, by my Lord Philanax, that you have with one consent chosen me to be the judge of the late evils happened, orderer of the present disorders, and finally protector of this country till therein it be seen what the customs of Arcadia require.'

He could say no further, being stopped with a general cry that so it was, giving him all the honourable titles and happy wishes they could imagine. He beckoned unto them for silence, and then thus again proceeded:

'Well,' said he, 'how good choice you have made, the attending must be in you, the proof in me. But because it many times falls out we are much deceived in others, we being the first to deceive ourselves, I am to require you not to have an over-shooting expectation of me – the most cruel adversary of all honourable doings – nor promise yourselves wonders out of a sudden liking, but remember I am a man – that is to say, a creature whose reason is often darkened with error. Secondly, that you will lay your hearts void of foretaken opinions, else whatsoever I do or say will be measured by a wrong rule, like them that have the yellow jaundice, every thing seeming yellow unto them. Thirdly, whatsoever debates have risen among you may be utterly extinguished, knowing that even among the best men are diversities of opinions, which are no more in true reason to breed hatred than one that loves black should be angry with him that is clothed in white; for thoughts and conceits are the very apparel of the mind. Lastly, that you do not easily judge of your judge, but since you will have me to command, think it is your part to obey. And in reward of this, I will promise and protest unto you that to the uttermost of my skill, both in the general laws of nature, especially of Greece, and particular of Arcadia (wherein I must confess I am not unacquainted) I will not only see the past evils duly punished and your weal hereafter established, but for your defence in it, if need shall require, I will employ the forces and treasures of mine own country. In the meantime, this shall be the first order I will take, that no man, under pain of grievous punishment, name me by any other name but protector of Arcadia; for I will not leave any possible colour to any of my natural successors to make claim to this which by free election you have bestowed upon me. And so I vow unto you to depose myself of it as soon as the judgement is passed, the king buried, and his lawful successor appointed. For the first whereof – I mean the trying which be guilty of the king's death, and these other heinous trespasses – because your customs require such haste, I will no longer delay it than till tomorrow as soon as the sun shall give us fit opportunity. You may therefore retire yourselves to your rest, that you may be readier to be present at these so great important matters.'

## CHAPTER 3

With many allowing tokens was Euarchus' speech heard, who now by Philanax (that took the principal care of doing all due services unto him) was offered a lodging made ready for him – the rest of the people (as well as the small commodity of that place would suffer) yielding their weary heads to sleep. When lo, the night thoroughly spent in these mixed matters was for that time banished the face of the earth, and Euarchus, seeing the day begin to disclose his comfortable beauties, desiring nothing more than to join speed with justice, willed Philanax presently to make the judgement-place be put in order, and as soon as the people (who yet were not fully dispersed) might be brought together, to bring forth the prisoners and the king's body: which, the manner was, should in such cases be held in sight, though covered with black velvet, until they that were accused to be the murderers were quitted or condemned – whether the reason of the lay were to show the more grateful love to their prince, or by that spectacle the more to remember the judge of his duty. Philanax, who now thought in himself he approached to the just revenge he so much desired, went with all care and diligence to perform his charge.

But first it shall be well to know how the poor and princely prisoners passed this tedious night. There was never tyrant exercised his rage with more grievous torments upon any he most hated than afflicted Gynecia did crucify her own soul, after the guiltiness of her heart was surcharged with the suddenness of her husband's death; for although that effect came not from her mind, yet her mind being evil and the effect evil, she thought the justice of God had for the beginning of her pains coupled them together. This incessantly boiled in her breast, but most of all when, Philanax having closely imprisoned her, she was left more freely to suffer the fire brands of her own thoughts, especially when it grew dark, and had nothing left by her but a little lamp whose small light to a perplexed mind might rather yield fearful shadows than any assured sight. Then began the heaps of her miseries to weight down the platform of her judgement: then began despair to lay his ugly claws upon her: she began then to fear the heavenly powers she was wont to reverence, not like a child, but like an enemy. Neither kept she herself from blasphemous repining against her creation.

'O Gods,' would she cry out, 'why did you make me to destruction? If you love goodness, why did you not give me a good mind? Or if I cannot have it without your gift, why do you plague me? Is it in me to resist the mightiness of your power?'

Then would she imagine she saw strange sights and that she heard the cries of hellish ghosts. Then would she shriek out for succour, but no man coming unto her, she would fain have killed herself, but knew not how. At some times again, the very heaviness of her imaginations would close up her senses to a little sleep, but then did her dreams become her tormentors. One time it would seem unto her, Philanax was haling her by the hair of the head, and having put out her eyes, was ready to throw her into a burning furnace. Another time she would think she saw her husband making the complaint of his death to Pluto, and the magistrates of that infernal region contending in great debate to what eternal punishment they should allot her. But long her dreaming would not hold, but that it would fall upon Zelmane, to whom she would think she was crying for mercy, and that she did pass away by her in silence without any show of pitying her mischief.

Then waking out of a broken sleep and yet wishing she might ever have slept, new forms, but of the same miseries, would seize her mind. She feared death, and yet desired death. She had passed the uttermost of shame, and yet shame was one of her cruellest assaulters. She hated Pyrocles as the original of her mortal overthrow, and yet the love she had conceived to him had still a high authority of her passions.

'O Zelmane,' would she say (not knowing how near he himself was to as great a danger) 'now shalt thou glut thy eyes with the dishonoured death of thy enemy. Enemy? Alas, enemy, since so thou hast well showed thou wilt have me account thee. Couldst thou not as well have given me a determinate denial as to disguise thy first disguising with a double dissembling? Perchance if I had been utterly hopeless, the virtue was once in me might have called together his forces, and not have been led captive to this monstrous thraldom of punished wickedness.'

Then would her own knowing of good inflame anew the rage of despair, which becoming an unresisted lord in her breast, she had no other comfort but in death, which yet she had in horror when she thought of. But the wearisome detesting of herself made her long for the day's approach, at which time she determined to continue her former course in acknowledging anything which might hasten her end: wherein although she did not hope for the end of her torments, feeling already the beginning of hell-agonies, yet according to the nature of pain, the present being most intolerable, she desired to change that and put to adventure the ensuing. And thus rested the restless Gynecia.

No less sorrowful though less rageful were the minds of the Princess Pamela and the Lady Philoclea, whose only advantages were that they had not consented to so much evil and so were at greater peace with themselves, and that they were not left alone but might mutually bear part of each other's woes. For when Philanax, not regarding Pamela's princely protestations, had by force left her under guard with her sister, and that the two sisters were matched as well in the disgraces of fortune as they had been in the best beauties of nature, those things that till then bashfulness and mistrust had made them hold reserved one from the other, now fear (the underminer of all determinations) and necessity (the victorious rebel of all laws) forced them interchangeably to lay open – their passions then so swelling in them as they would have made auditors of stones rather than have swallowed up in silence the choking adventures were fallen unto them. Truly the hardest hearts which have at any time thought woman's tears to be a matter of slight compassion (imagining that fair weather will quickly after follow) would now have been mollified, and been compelled to confess that the fairer a diamond is, the more pity it is it should receive a blemish – although, no doubt, their faces did rather beautify sorrow than sorrow could darken that which even in darkness did shine.

But after they had (so long as their other afflictions would suffer them) with doleful ceremonies bemoaned their father's death, they sat down together apparelled as their misadventures had found them – Pamela in her journeying weeds now converted to another use, Philoclea only in her night-gown, which she thought should be the raiment of her funerals. But when the excellent creatures had, after much panting with their inward travail, gotten so much breathing power as to make a pitiful discourse one to the other what had befallen them, and that by the plain comparing the case they were in, they thoroughly found that their griefs were not more like in regard of themselves than like in respect of the subject (the two princes – as Pamela had learned of Musidorus – being so minded as they would ever make both their fortunes one) it did more unite and so strengthen their lamentation, seeing the one could not be miserable but that it must necessarily make the other miserable also. That, therefore, was the first matter their sweet mouths delivered, the declaring the passionate beginning, troublesome proceeding, and dangerous ending their never-ending loves had passed; and when at any time they entered into praises of the young princes, too long it would have exercised their tongues but that their memory forthwith warned them the more praiseworthy they were, the more at that time they were worthy of lamentation. Then again to crying and wringing of hands; and then anew, as unquiet grief sought each corner, to new discourses; from discourses to wishes; from wishes to prayers – especially the tender Philoclea, who as she was in years younger and had never lifted up her mind to any opinion of sovereignty, so was she the apter to yield to her misfortune; having no stronger debates in her mind than a man may say a most witty childhood is wont to nourish, as to imagine with herself why Philanax and the other noblemen should deal so cruelly by her that had never deserved evil of any of them; and how they could find in their hearts to imprison such a personage as she did figure Pyrocles, whom she thought all the world was bound to love as well as she did.

But Pamela, although endued with a virtuous mildness, yet the knowledge of herself and what was due unto her made her heart full of a stronger disdain against her adversity; so that she joined the vexation for her friend with the spite to see herself (as she thought) rebelliously detained, and mixed desirous thoughts to help with revengeful thoughts if she could not help. And as in pangs of death, the stronger heart feels the greater torment because it doth the more resist to his oppressor, so her mind, the nobler it was set and had already embraced the higher thoughts, so much more it did repine; and the more it repined, the more helpless wounds it gave unto itself. But when great part of the night was passed over the doleful music of these sweet ladies' complaints, and that leisure (though with some strife) had brought Pamela to know that an eagle when she is in a cage must not think to do like an eagle, remembering with themselves that it was likely the next day the lords would proceed against those they had imprisoned, they employed the rest of the night in writing unto them, with such earnestness as the matter required, but in such styles as the state of their thoughts was apt to fashion.

In the meantime, Pyrocles and Musidorus were recommended to so strong a guard as they might well see it was meant they should pay no less price than their lives for the getting out of that place: which they like men indeed, fortifying courage with the true rampire of patience, did so endure as they did rather appear governors of necessity than servants to fortune, the whole sum of their thoughts resting upon the safety of their ladies and their care one for the other, wherein (if at all) their hearts did seem to receive some softness. For sometimes Musidorus would feel such a motion to his friend and his unworthy case that he would fall into such kind of speeches:

'My Pyrocles,' would he say, 'how unhappy may I think Thessalia that hath been, as it were, the middle way to this evil estate of yours! For if you had not been there brought up, the sea should not have had this power thus to sever you from your dear father. I have therefore (if complaints do at any time become a man's heart) most cause to complain, since my country, which received the honour of Pyrocles' education, should be a step to his overthrow – if human chances can be counted an overthrow to him that stands upon virtue.'

'O excellent Musidorus,' answered Pyrocles, 'how do you teach me rather to fall out with myself and my fortune, since by you I have received all good, you only by me this affliction. To you and your virtuous mother I, in my tenderest years and father's greatest troubles, was sent for succour. There did I learn the sweet mysteries of philosophy. There had I your lively example to confirm that which I learned. There, lastly, had I your friendship, which no unhappiness can ever make me say but that hath made me happy. Now see how my destiny (the gods know, not my will) hath rewarded you. My father sends for you away out of your land, whence but for me you had not come. What after followed, you know. It was my love, not yours, which first stayed you here; and therefore if the heavens ever held a just proportion, it were I, and not you, that should feel the smart.'

'O blame not the heavens, sweet Pyrocles,' said Musidorus. 'As their course never alters, so is there nothing done by the unreachable ruler of them but hath an everlasting reason for it. And to say the truth of these things, we should deal ungratefully with nature if we should be forgetful receivers of her gifts, and so diligent auditors of the chances we like not. We have lived, and have lived to be good to ourselves and others. Our souls, which are put into the stirring earth of our bodies, have achieved the causes of their hither coming. They have known and honoured with knowledge the cause of their creation, and to many men (for in this time, place and fortune, it is lawful for us to speak gloriously) it hath been behoveful* that we should live. Since, then, eternity is not to be had in this conjunction,* what is to be lost by the seperaation but time? – which since it hath his end, when that is once come, all that is past is nothing, and by the protracting, nothing gotten but labour and care. Do not me, therefore, that wrong (who something in years, but much in all other deserts, am fitter to die than you) as to say you have brought me to any evil, since the love of you doth over-balance all bodily mischiefs, and those mischiefs be but mischiefs to the baser minds too much delighted with the kennel of this life. Neither will I any more yield to my passion of lamenting you, which, howsoever it might agree to my exceeding friendship, surely it would nothing to your exceeding virtue.'

'Add this to your noble speech, my dear cousin,' said Pyrocles, 'that if we complain of this our fortune, or seem to ourselves faulty in having one hurt the other, we show a repentance of the love we bear to these matchless creatures, or at least a doubt it should be over-dearly bought; which for my part (and so dare I answer for you) I call all the gods to witness I am so far from, that

* *behoveful*: beneficial, *this conjunction*: i.e. of our bodies and souls.

no shame, no torment, no death, would make me forgo the least part of the inward honour, essential pleasure and living life I have enjoyed in the presence of the faultless Philoclea.'

'Take the pre-eminence in all things but in true loving,' answered Musidorus, 'for the confession of that no death shall get of me.'

'Of that,' answered Pyrocles, soberly smiling, 'I perceive we shall have a debate in the other world, if at least there remain anything of remembrance in that place.'

'I do not think the contrary,' said Musidorus, 'although you know it is greatly held that with the death of body and senses (which are not only the beginning but dwelling and nourishing of passions, thoughts and imaginations) they failing, memory likewise fails which riseth only out of them, and then is there left nothing but the intellectual part or intelligence which (void of all moral virtues which stand in the mean of* perturbations) doth only live in the contemplative virtue and power of the omnipotent good, the soul of souls and universal life of this great work, and therefore is utterly void from the possibility of drawing to itself these sensible* considerations.'

'Certainly,' answered Pyrocles, 'I easily yield that we shall not know one another, and much less these past things, with a sensible or passionate knowledge; for the cause being taken away, the effect follows. Neither do I think we shall have such a memory as now we have, which is but a relic of the senses, or rather a print the senses have left of things past in our thoughts: but it shall be a vital power of that very intelligence which, as while it was here it held the chief seat of our life and was, as it were, the last resort to which of all our knowledges the highest appeal came, and so by that means was never ignorant of our actions (though many times rebelliously resisted, always with this prison darkened); so much more, being free of that prison, and returning to the life of all things where all infinite knowledge is, it cannot but be a right* intelligence (which is both his name and being)[1] of things both present and past, though void of imagining to itself anything; but (even grown like to his creator) hath all things with a spiritual

* *in the mean of:* under the conditions of. *sensible:* of the senses. *right:* true.

knowledge before it. The difference of which is as hard for us to conceive as it had been for us when we were in our mother's wombs to comprehend (if anybody would have told us) what kind of light we now in this life see, what kind of knowledge we now have: yet now we do not only feel our present being, but we conceive what we were before we were born, though remembrance make us not do it but knowledge, and though we are utterly without any remorse of any misery we might then suffer. Even such and much more odds shall there be at that second delivery of ours when, void of sensible memory or memorative* passion, we shall not see the colours but lives of all things that have been or can be, and shall (as I hope) know our friendship, though exempt from the earthly cares of friendship, having both united it and ourselves in that high and heavenly love of the unquenchable light.'

As he had ended his speech, Musidorus, looking with a heavenly joy upon him, sang this song unto him he had made before love turned his Muse to another subject:

> Since nature's works be good, and death doth serve
> As nature's work, why should we fear to die?
> Since fear is vain, but when it may preserve,
> Why should we fear that which we cannot fly?
>
> Fear is more pain than is the pain it fears,
> Disarming human minds of native might;
> While each conceit an ugly figure bears,
> Which were not evil, well view'd in reason's light.
>
> Our owly eyes,* which dimm'd with passions be,
> And scarce discern the dawn of coming day,
> Let them be clear'd, and now begin to see
> Our life is but a step in dusty way.
> Then let us hold the bliss of peaceful mind:
> Since this we feel, great loss we cannot find.

Thus did they, like quiet swans, sing their own obsequies, and virtuously enable* their minds against all extremities which they

---

* *memorative*: arising out of memory. *owly eyes*: used to darkness. *enable*: strengthen.

did think would fall upon them, especially resolving that the first care they would have should be by taking the fault upon themselves to clear the two ladies, of whose case, as of nothing else that had happened, they had not any knowledge – although their friendly host, the honest gentleman Kalander, seeking all means how to help them, had endeavoured to speak with them and to make them know who should be their judge. But the curious servant of Philanax forbade him the entry upon pain of death, for so it was agreed upon that no man should have any conference with them for fear of new tumults; insomuch that Kalander was constrained to retire himself, having yet obtained thus much, that he would deliver unto the two princes their apparel and jewels, which being left with him at Mantinea (wisely considering that their disguised weeds, which were all as then they had, would make them more odious in the sight of the judges) he had that night sent for and now brought unto them. They accepted their own with great thankfulness, knowing from whence it came, and attired themselves in it against the next day, which being indeed rich and princely, they accordingly determined to maintain the names of Palladius and Daiphantus as before it is mentioned.

## CHAPTER 4

Then gave they themselves to consider in what sort they might defend their causes, for they thought it no less vain to wish death than cowardly to fear it; till something before morning, a small slumber taking them, they were by and by after called up to come to the answer of no less than their lives imported.* But in this sort was the judgement ordered. As soon as the morning had taken a full possession of the element, Euarchus called unto him Philanax and willed him to draw out into the midst of the green, before the chief lodge, the throne of judgment seat in which Basilius was wont to sit and, according to their customs, was ever carried with the prince. For Euarchus did wisely consider the people to be naturally taken with exterior shows far more than with inward consideration of the material points, and therefore in this new entry into so entangled a matter, he would leave nothing which might

* *imported*: signified.

be either an armour or ornament unto him; and in these pompous ceremonies he well knew a secret of government much to consist. That was performed by the diligent Philanax, and therein Euarchus did set himself all clothed in black, with the principal men who could in that suddenness provide themselves of such mourning raiments; the whole people commanded to keep an orderly silence of each side, which was duly observed of them, partly for the desire they had to see a good conclusion of these matters, and partly stricken with admiration as well at the grave and princely presence of Eucharus as at the greatness of the cause which was then to come in question. As for Philanax, Euarchus would have done him the honour to sit by him, but he excused himself, desiring to be the accuser of the prisoners in his master's behalf; and therefore since he made himself a party, it was not convenient for him to sit in the judicial place.

Then was it awhile deliberated whether the two young ladies should be brought forth in open presence; but that was stopped by Philanax whose love and faith did descend from his master to his children, and only desired the smart should light upon the others whom he thought guilty of his death and dishonour, alleging for this that neither wisdom would they should be brought in presence of the people (which might hereupon grow to new uproars) nor justice required they should be drawn to any shame till somebody accused them. And as for Pamela, he protested the laws of Arcadia would not allow any judgement of her, although she herself were to determine nothing till age or marriage enabled her.

Then the king's body being laid upon a table, just before Euarchus and all covered over with black, the prisoners, namely, the queen and two young princes, were sent for to appear in the protector's name – which name was the cause they came not to knowledge how near a kinsman was to judge of them, but thought him to be some nobleman chosen by the country in this extremity. So extraordinary a course had the order of the heavens produced at this time that both nephew and son were not only prisoners, but unknown to their uncle and father, who of many years had not seen them. And Pyrocles was to plead for his life before that throne, in which throne lately before he had saved the king's life.

But first was Gynecia led forth in the same weeds that the day and night before she had worn, saving that instead of Zelmane's garment in which she was found, she had cast on a long cloak, which reached to the ground, of russet coarse cloth, with a poor felt hat which almost covered all her face, most part of her goodly hair (on which her hands had laid many a spiteful hold) so lying upon her shoulders as a man might well see had no artificial* carelessness; her eyes down on the ground of purpose not to look on Pyrocles' face, which she did not so much shun for the unkindness she conceived of her own overthrow as for the fear those motions in this short time of her life should be revived which she had with the passage of infinite sorrows mortified. Great was the compassion the people felt to see their princess' state and beauty so deformed by fortune and her own desert, whom they had ever found a lady most worthy of all honour.

But by and by the sight of the other two prisoners drew most of the eyes to that spectacle. Pyrocles came out led by Sympathus, clothed after the Greek manner in a long coat of white velvet reaching to the small of his leg, with great buttons of diamonds all along upon it. His neck without any collar, not so much as hidden with a ruff, did pass the whiteness of his garments, which was not much (in fashion) unlike to the crimson raiment our Knights of the Order* first put on. On his feet he had nothing but slippers which, after the ancient manner, were tied up with certain laces which were fastened under his knee, having wrapped about, with many pretty knots, his naked legs. His fair auburn hair (which he ware in great length and gave at that time a delightful show with being stirred up and down with the breath of a gentle wind) had nothing upon it but a white ribbon (in those days used for a diadem)* which, rolled once or twice about the uppermost part of his forehead, fell down upon his back, closed up at each end with the richest pearl were to be seen in the world. After him followed another nobleman guiding the noble Musidorus, who had upon him a long cloak, after the fashion of that which we call the Apostle's mantle,¹ made of purple satin – not that purple which we now have, and is but a counterfeit of the Getulian purple (which yet was far the meaner in price and estimation) but of the

---

* artificial: carefully arranged carelessness. Knights of the Order: of the Garter. diadem: badge of royalty.

right Tyrian purple[2] which was nearest to a colour betwixt our murrey* and scarlet. On his head, which was black and curled, he ware a Persian tiara, all set down with rows of so rich rubies as they were enough to speak for him that they had to judge of no mean personage.

In this sort, with erected countenances, did these unfortunate princes suffer themselves to be led, showing aright, by the comparison of them and Gynecia, how to divers persons compassion is diversely to be stirred. For as to Gynecia (a lady known of great estate and greatly esteemed) the more miserable representation was made of her sudden ruin, the more men's hearts were forced to bewail such an evident witness of weak humanity: so to these men (not regarded because unknown, but rather, besides the detestation of their fact, hated as strangers) the more they should have fallen down in an abject semblance, the more, instead of compassion, they should have gotten contempt; but therefore were to use, as I may term it, the more violence of magnanimity, and so to conquer the expectation of the lookers with an extraordinary virtue. And such effect indeed it wrought in the whole assembly, their eyes yet standing as it were in balance to whether of them they should most direct their sight. Musidorus was in stature so much higher than Pyrocles as commonly is gotten by one year's growth. His face, now beginning to have some tokens of a beard, was composed to a kind of manlike beauty. His colour was of a well-pleasing brownness, and the features of it such as they carried both delight and majesty; his countenance severe, and promising a mind much given to thinking. Pyrocles of a pure complexion, and of such a cheerful favour as might seem either a woman's face on a boy, or an excellent boy's face in a woman. His look gentle and bashful, which bred the more admiration, having showed such notable proofs of courage. Lastly, though both had both, if there were any odds, Musidorus was the more goodly and Pyrocles the more lovely.

But as soon as Musidorus saw himself so far forth led among the people that he knew to a great number of them his voice should be heard, misdoubting their intention to the Princess Pamela, of which he was more careful than of his own life, even as

* *murrey*: purple-red.

he went (though his leader sought to interrupt him) he thus with a loud voice spake unto them:

'And is it possible, O Arcadians,' said he, 'that you can forget the natural duty you owe to your Princess Pamela? Hath this soil been so little beholding to her noble ancestors? Hath so long a time rooted no surer love in your hearts to that line? Where is that faith to your prince's blood which hath not only preserved you from all dangers heretofore but hath spread your fame to all the nations in the world? Where is that justice the Arcadians were wont to flourish in, whose nature is to render to everyone his own? Will you now keep the right from your prince, who is the only giver of judgement, the key of justice, and life of your laws? Do you hope in a few years to set up such another race, which nothing but length of time can establish? Will you reward Basilius' children with ungratefulness, the very poison of manhood? Will you betray your long settled reputation with the foul name of traitors? Is this your mourning for your king's death, to increase his loss with his daughter's misery? Imagine your prince to look out of the heavens unto you: what do you think he could wish more at your hands than that you do well by his children? And what more honour, I pray you, can you do his obsequies than to satisfy his soul with a loving memory, as you do his body with an unfelt solemnity? What have you done with the Princess Pamela? Pamela, the just inheritrix of this country: Pamela, whom this earth may be happy that it shall be hereafter said she was born in Arcadia: Pamela, in herself your ornament; in her education, your foster child; and every way your only princess; what account can you render to yourselves of her? Truly I do not think that you all know what is become of her, so soon may a diamond be lost, so soon may the fairest light in the world be put out. But look, look unto it, O Arcadians. Be not so wilfully robbed of your greatest treasure. Make not yourselves ministers to private ambitions who do but use yourselves to put on your own yokes. Whatsoever you determine of us, who I must confess are but strangers, yet let not Basilius' daughters be strangers unto you. Lastly, howsoever you bar her from her public sovereignty (which if you do, little may we hope of equity where rebellion reigns) yet deny not that child's right unto her that she may come and do the last duties to her father's body. Deny not that happiness (if in such a case there be any happiness) to your late king, that his body may have his last touch of his dearest child.'

With such like broken manner of questions and speeches was Musidorus desirous, as much as in passing by them he could, to move the people to tender Pamela's fortune. But at length, by that they came to the judgement-place, both Sympathus and his guider had greatly satisfied him with the assurance they gave him this assembly of people had neither meaning nor power to do any hurt to the princess, whom they all acknowledged as their sovereign lady; but that the custom of Arcadia was such, till she had more years, the state of the country to be guided by a protector under whom he and his fellows were to receive their judgement. That eased Musidorus' heart of his most vehement care when he found his beloved lady to be out of danger. But Pyrocles, as soon as the queen of the one side, he and Musidorus of the other, were stayed before the face of their judge (having only for their bar³ the table on which the king's body lay) being nothing less vexed with the doubt of Philoclea than Musidorus was for Pamela, in this sort with a lowly behaviour and only then like a suppliant, he spake to the protector:

'Pardon me, most honoured judge,' said he, 'that uncommanded I begin my speech unto you, since both to you and me these words of mine shall be most necessary. To you, having the sacred exercise of justice in your hand, nothing appertains more properly than truth nakedly and freely set down. To me, being environed round about with many dangerous calamities, what can be more convenient than at least to be at peace with myself in having discharged my conscience in a most behoveful verity? Understand therefore, and truly understand, that the lady Philoclea (to whose unstained virtue it hath been my unspeakable misery that my name should become a blot) if she be accused, is most unjustly accused of any dishonourable fact which by my means she may be thought to have yielded unto. Whatsoever hath been done hath been my only attempt, which notwithstanding was never intended against her chastity. But whatsoever hath been informed was my fault. And I attest the heavens (to blaspheme which I am not now in fit tune) that so much as my coming into her chamber

811

was wholly unwitting unto her. This your wisdom may withal consider: if I would lie, I would lie for mine own behoof; I am not so old as to be weary of myself: but the very sting of my inward knowledge, joined with the consideration I must needs have what an infinite loss it should be to all those who love goodness in good folks if so pure a child of virtue should wrongfully be destroyed, compels me to use my tongue against myself, and receive the burden of what evil was upon mine own doing. Look therefore with pitiful eyes upon so fair beams, and that misfortune which by me hath fallen upon her, help to repair it with your public judgement, since whosoever deals cruelly with such a creature shows himself a hater of mankind and an envier of the world's bliss. And this petition I make, even in the name of justice, that before you proceed further against us, I may know how you conceive of her noble, though unfortunate action, and what judgement you will make of it.'

He had not spoken his last word when all the whole people, both of great and low estate, confirmed with an united murmur Pyrocles' demand, longing (for the love generally was borne Philoclea) to know what they might hope of her. Euarchus (though neither regarding a prisoner's passionate prayer nor bearing overplausible ears to a many-headed motion, yet well enough content to win their liking with things in themselves indifferent) was content first to seek as much as might be of Philoclea's behaviour in this matter: which being cleared by Pyrocles, and but weakly gainsaid by Philanax (who had framed both his own and Dametas' evidence most for her favour, and in truth could have gone no further than conjecture) yet finding by his wisdom that she was not altogether faultless, he pronounced she should all her life long be kept prisoner among certain women of religion like the Vestal nuns, so to repay the touched honour of her house with well observing a strict profession of chastity. Although this were a great prejudicating of Pyrocles' case, yet was he exceedingly joyous of it, being assured of his lady's life; and in the depth of his mind not sorry that what end soever he had, none should obtain the after enjoying that jewel whereon he had set his life's happiness.

After it was by public sentence delivered what should be done
with the sweet Philoclea – the laws of Arcadia bearing that what
was appointed by the magistrates in the nonage of the prince could
not afterwards be repealed – Euarchus, still using to himself no
other name but protector of Arcadia, commanded those that had
to say against the Queen Gynecia to proceed, because both her
estate required she should be first heard, and also for that she was
taken to be the principal in the greatest matter they were to judge
of. Philanax incontinently stepped forth, and showing in his
greedy eyes that he did thirst for her blood, began a well thought
on discourse of her (in his judgement) execrable wickedness. But
Gynecia, standing up before the judge, casting abroad her arms,
with her eyes hidden under the breadth of her unseemly hat,
laying open in all her gestures the despairful affliction to which
all the might of her reason was converted, with such like
words stopped Philanax as he was entering into his invective
oration:

'Stay, stay, Philanax,' said she, 'do not defile thy honest mouth
with those dishonourable speeches thou art about to utter against
a woman, now most wretched, lately thy mistress. Let either the
remembrance how great she was move thy heart to some reverence, or the seeing how low she is stir in thee some pity. It may be
truth doth make thee deal untruly, and love of justice frames
injustice in thee. Do not therefore (neither shalt thou need) tread
upon my desolate ruins. Thou shalt have that thou seekest, and
yet shalt not be oppressor of her who cannot choose but love thee
for thy singular faith to thy master. I do not speak this to procure
mercy or to prolong my life. No, no, I say unto you I will not live,
but I am only loth my death should be engrieved* with any
wrong thou shouldst do unto me. I have been too painful a judge
over myself to desire pardon in others' judgement. I have been too
cruel an executioner of my own soul to desire that execution of
justice should be stayed for me. Alas, they that know how sorrow
can rent the spirits, they that know what fiery hells are contained
in a self-condemning mind, need not fear that fear can keep such a
one from desiring to be separated from that which nothing but

* *engrieved*: made more grievous.

death can separate. I therefore say to thee, O just judge, that I, and only I, was the worker of Basilius' death. They were these hands that gave unto him that poisonous potion that hath brought death to him and loss to Arcadia. It was I, and none but I, that hastened his aged years to an unnatural end, and that have made all his people orphans of their royal father. I am the subject that have killed my prince. I am the wife that have murdered my husband. I am a degenerate woman, an undoer of this country, a shame of my children. What wouldst thou have said more, O Philanax! And all this I grant. There resteth then nothing else to say but that I desire you you will appoint quickly some to rid me of my life, rather than these hands which else are destined unto it, and that indeed it may be done with such speed as I may not long die in this life which I have in so great horror.'

With that she crossed her arms and sat down upon the ground, attending the judge's answer. But a great while it was before anybody could be heard speak, the whole people concurring in a lamentable cry, so much had Gynecia's words and behaviour stirred their hearts to a doleful compassion. Neither in truth could most of them in their judgements tell whether they should be more sorry for her fault or her misery, for the loss of her estate or loss of her virtue; but most were most moved with that which was under their eyes, the sense most subject to pity. But at length the reverent awe they stood in of Euarchus brought them to a silent waiting his determination: who, having well considered the abomination of the fact, attending more the manifest proof of so horrible a trespass (confessed by herself and proved by others) than anything relenting to those tragical phrases of hers (apter to stir a vulgar pity than his mind, which hated evil in what colours soever he found it) having considered a while with the principal men of the country and demanded their allowance, he definitively gave this sentence:

'That whereas, both in private and public respects, this woman had most heinously offended – in private (because marriage being the most holy conjunction that falls to mankind, out of which all families and so consequently all societies do proceed, which not only by community of goods but community of children is to knit the minds in a most perfect union; which whoso breaks, dissolves all humanity, no man living free from the danger of so near a neighbour) she had not only broken it, but broken it with death, and the most pretended* death that might be: in public respect (the prince's person being in all monarchal governments the very knot of the people's welfare and light of all their doings, to which they are not only in conscience but in necessity bound to be loyal) she had traitorously empoisoned him, neither regarding her country's profit, her own duty, nor the rigour of the laws – that therefore (as well for the due satisfaction to eternal justice and accomplishment of the Arcadian statutes as for the everlasting example to all wives and subjects) she should presently be conveyed to close prison, and there be kept with such food as might serve to sustain her alive until the day of her husband's burial, at which time she should be buried quick in the same tomb with him, that so his murder might be a murder to herself, and she forced to keep company with the body from which she had made so detestable a severance; and lastly, death might redress their disjoined conjunction of marriage.'

His judgement was received of the whole assembly as not with disliking so with great astonishment, the greatness of the matter and person, as it were, overpressing the might of their conceits. But when they did set it to the beam* with the monstrousness of her ugly misdeed, they could not but yield in their hearts there was no over-balancing. As for Gynecia (who had already settled her thoughts not only to look but long for this event, having, in this time of her vexation, found a sweetness in the rest she hoped by death) with a countenance witnessing she had beforehand so passed through all the degrees of sorrow that she had no new look to figure forth any more, rase up and offered forth her fair hands to be bound or led as they would, being indeed troubled with no part of this judgement but that her death was, as she thought, long delayed. They that were appointed for it conveyed her to the place she was in before, where the guard was relieved, and the number increased to keep her more sure for the time of her execution – none of them all that led her (though most of them were such whose hearts had been long hardened with the often exercising such officers) being able to bar tears from their eyes, and

* *pretended*: openly admitted. *set it to the beam*: weigh it against.

other manifest tokens of compassionate sorrow. So goodly a virtue is a resolute constancy that even in evil deservers it seems that party might have been notably well deserving.

Thus the excellent lady Gynecia, having passed five and thirty years of her age even to admiration of her beautiful mind and body, and having not, in her own knowledge ever spotted her soul with any wilful vice but her immoderate love of Zelmane, was brought first by the violence of that ill-answered passion, and then by the despairing conceit she took of the judgement of God in her husband's death and her own fortune, purposely to over-throw herself, and confirm by a wrong confession that abominable shame which, with her wisdom joined to the truth, perhaps she might have refelled.*

## CHAPTER 5

Then did Euarchus ask Philanax whether it were he that would charge the two young prisoners, or that some other should do it, and he sit according to his estate as an assistant in the judgement. Philanax told him, as before he had done, that he thought no man could lay manifest the naughtiness of those two young men with so much either truth or zeal as himself, and therefore he desired he might do his last service to his faithfully beloved master as to prosecute the traitorous causers of his death and dishonour; which being done, for his part he meant to give up all dealing in public affairs, since that man was gone who had made him love them.

Philanax thus being ready to speak, the two princes were commanded to tell their names, who answered, according to their agreements, that they were Daiphantus of Lycia and Palladius Prince of Iberia: which when they had said, they demanded to know by what authority they could judge of them, since they were not only foreigners, and so not born under their laws, but absolute princes, and therefore not to be touched by laws. But answer was presently made them that Arcadia laws were to have their force upon any were found in Arcadia, since strangers have scope to know the customs of a country before they put themselves in it; and when they once are entered, they must know that

* refelled: refuted.

what by many was made must not for one be broken – and so much less for a stranger, as he is to look for no privilege in that place to which in time of need his service is not to be expected. As for their being princes, whether they were so or no, the belief stood in their own words, which they had so diversely falsified as they did not deserve belief. But whatsoever they were, Arcadia was to acknowledge them but as private men, since they were neither by magistracy nor alliance to the princely blood to claim anything in that region. Therefore if they had offended (which now by the plaintiff and their defence was to be judged) against the laws of nations, by the laws of nations they were to be chastised; if against the peculiar ordinances of the province, those peculiar ordinances were to lay hold of them.

The princes stood a while upon that, demanding leisure to give perfect knowledge of their greatness; but when they were answered that in a case of a prince's death, the law of that country had ever been that immediate trial should be had, they were forced to yield, resolved that in those names they would as much as they could cover the shame of their royal parentage, and keep as long as might be (if evil were determined against them) the evil news from their careful kinsfolk; wherein the chief man they considered was Euarchus, whom the strange and secret working of justice had brought to be the judge over them. In such a shadow or rather pit of darkness the wormish mankind lives, that neither they know how to foresee nor what to fear, and are but like tennis balls, tossed by the racket of the higher powers. Thus both sides ready, it was determined (because their cases were separated) first Philanax should be heard against Pyrocles whom they termed Daiphantus, and that heard, the other's cause should follow, and so receive together such judgement as they should be found to have deserved.

But Philanax that was even short-breathed at the first with the extreme vehemency he had to speak against them, stroking once or twice his forehead, and wiping his eyes (which either wept, or he would at that time have them seem to weep) looking first upon Pyrocles as if he had proclaimed all hatefulness against him, humbly turning to Euarchus, who with quiet gravity showed great attention, he thus began his oration:

'That which all men who take upon them to accuse another are wont to desire, most worthy protector, to have many proofs of many faults in them they seek to have condemned, that is to me in this present action my greatest cumber and annoyance. For the number is so great and the quality so monstrous of the enormities this wretched young man hath committed, that neither I in myself can tell where to begin – my thoughts being confused with the horrible multitude of them – neither do I think your virtuous ears will be able to endure the report, but will rather imagine you hear some tragedy invented of the extremity of wickedness than a just recital of a wickedness indeed committed: for such is the disposition of the most sincere judgements that, as they can believe mean faults and such as man's nature may slide into, so when they pass to a certain degree – nay, when they pass all degrees of unspeakable naughtiness, then find they in themselves a hardness to give credit that human creatures can so from all humanity be transformed. But in myself the strength of my faith to my dead master will help the weakness of my memory: in you, your excellent love of justice will force you to vouchsafe attention.

'And as for the matter, it is so manifest; so pitiful evidences lie before your eyes of it, that I shall need to be but a brief recounter and no rhetorical enlarger of this most harmful mischief. I will therefore, in as few words as so huge a trespass can be contained, deliver unto you the sum of this miserable fact, leaving out a great number of particular tokens of his naughtiness, and only touching the essential points of this doleful case.

'This man – whom to begin withal I know not how to name, since being come into this country unaccompanied like a lost pilgrim, from a man grew a woman, from a woman a ravisher of women, thence a prisoner, and now a prince – but this Zelmane, this Daiphantus, this what you will (for any shape or title he can take upon him that hath no restraint of shame) having understood the solitary life my late master lived, and considering how open he had laid himself to any traitorous attempt, for the first mask of his falsehood disguised himself like a woman (which being the more simple and hurtless sex, might easier hide his subtle harmfulness) and presenting himself to my master, the most courteous prince that lived, was received of him with so great graciousness as might have bound not only any grateful mind but might have mollified any enemy's rancour. But this venomous serpent admitted thus into his bosom, as contagion will easily find a fit body for it, so had he quickly fallen into so near acquaintance with this naughty woman whom even now you have most justly condemned, that this was her right hand – she saw with no eyes but his nor seemed to have any life but in him, so glad she was to find one more cunning than herself in covering wickedness with a modest veil.

'What is to be thought passed betwixt two such virtuous creatures, whereof the one hath confessed murder and the other rape, I leave to your wise consideration; for my heart hastens to the miserable point of Basilius' murder, for the executing of which with more facility this young nymph of Diana's bringing up feigned certain rites she had to perform – so furious an impiety had carried him from all remembrance of goodness that he did not only not fear the gods (as the beholders and punishers of so ungodly a villainy) but did blasphemously use their sacred holy name as a minister unto it. And forsooth a cave hereby was chosen for the temple of his devotions, a cave of such darkness as did prognosticate he meant to please the infernal powers; for there this accursed caitiff, upon the altar of falsehood, sacrificed the life of the virtuous Basilius. By what means he trained him thither, alas, I know not, for if I might have known it, either my life had accompanied my master or this fellow's death had preserved him. But this may suffice, that in the mouth of this cave where this traitor had his lodging and chapel (when already master shepherd, his companion, had conveyed away the undoubted inheritrix of this country) was Gynecia found by the dead corpse of her husband newly empoisoned, apparelled in the garments of the young lady, and ready – no question – to have fled to some place according to their consort but that she was by certain honest shepherds arrested: while in the meantime (because there should be left no revenger of this bloody mischief) this noble Amazon was violently gotten into the chamber of the Lady Philoclea where, by the mingling as much as in him lay of her shame with his misdeed, he might enforce her to be the accessory to her father's death, and under the countenance of her and her sister (against whom they knew we would not rebel) seize as it were with one grip into their treacherous hands the regiment of this mighty province. But the almighty eye prevented him of the end of his mischief, by using a villain Dametas' hand to enclose him in there where, with as much fortification as in a house could be made, he thought himself in most security.

'Thus see you, most just judge, a short and simple story of the infamous misery fallen upon this country – indeed infamous, since by an effeminate man we should suffer a greater overthrow than our mightiest enemies have been ever able to lay upon us. And that all this, which I have said is most manifest, as well of the murdering of Basilius as the ravishing of Philoclea (for those two parts I establish of my accusation) who is of so incredulous a mind, or rather who will so stop his eyes from seeing a thing clearer than the light as not to hold for assured so palpable a matter? For to begin with his most cruel misdeed, is it to be imagined that Gynecia (a woman though wicked, yet witty) would have attempted and achieved an enterprise no less hazardous than horrible, without having some counsellor in the beginning, and some comforter in the performing? Had she (who showed her thoughts were so overruled with some strange desire as in despite of God, nature, and womanhood, to execute that in deeds which in words we cannot hear without trembling) had she, I say, no practice to lead her unto it? Or had she a practice without conspiracy? Or could she conspire without somebody to conspire with? And if one were, who so likely as this, to whom she communicated I am sure her mind, the world thinks her body? Neither let her words, taking the whole fault upon herself, be herein anything available; for to those persons who have vomited out of their souls all remnants of goodness there rests a certain pride in evil, and having else no shadow of glory left them, they glory to be constant in iniquity, and that, God knows, must be held out to the last gasp without revealing their accomplices, as thinking great courage is declared in being neither affeard of the heavens, nor ashamed of the world.

'But let Gynecia's action die with herself: what can all the earth answer for his coming hither? Why alone, if he be a prince? How so richly jewelled if he be not a prince? Why then a woman if now a man? Why now Daiphantus, if then Zelmane? Was all this play for nothing, or if it had an end, what end but the end of my dear master? Shall we doubt so many secret conferences with Gynecia, such feigned favour to the over-soon beguiled Basilius, a cave made a lodging, and the same lodging made a temple of his religion, lastly, such changes and traverses as a quiet poet could scarce fill a poem withal,[1] were directed to any less scope than to this monstrous murder? O snaky ambition, which can wind thyself in so many figures to slide thither thou desirest to come! O corrupted reason of mankind that can yield to deform thyself with so filthy desires! And, O, hopeless be those minds whom so unnatural desires do not with their own ugliness sufficiently terrify!

'But yet even of favour, let us grant him thus much more as to fancy that in these foretold things fortune might be a great actor perchance to an evil end, yet to a less evil end all these entangled devices were intended. But I beseech your ladyship, my Lady Daiphantus, tell me what excuse can you find for the changing your lodging with the queen that very instant she was to finish her execrable practice? How can you cloak the lending of your cloak unto her? Was all that by chance too? Had the stars sent such an influence unto you as you should be just weary of your lodging and garments when our prince was destined to the slaughter? What say you to this, O shameful and shameless creature, fit indeed to be the dishonour of both sexes? But alas, I spend too many words in so manifest and so miserable a matter. They must be four wild horses (which according to our laws are the executioners of men which murder our prince) which must decide this question with you.

'Yet see, so far had my zeal to my beloved prince transported me that I had almost forgotten my second part and his second abomination – I mean his violence offered to the Lady Philoclea wherewith, as if it had well become his womanhood, he came braving to the judgement-seat. Indeed our laws appoint not so cruel a death, although death too, for this fact as for the other. But whosoever well weighs it shall find it sprung out of the same fountain of mischievous naughtiness, the killing of the father, dishonouring the mother and ravishing the child. Alas, could not so many benefits received of my prince, the justice of nature, the right of hospitality, be a bridle to thy lust, if not to thy cruelty? Or if thou hadst – as surely thou hast – a heart recompensing goodness with hatred, could not his death (which is the last of revenges) satisfy thy malice, but thou must heap upon it the shame of his daughter? Were thy eyes so stony, thy breast to tigerish as the sweet and beautiful shows of Philoclea's virtue did not astonish thee? O woeful Arcadia, to whom the name of this mankind courtesan shall ever be remembered as a procurer of thy greatest loss!

'But too far I find my passion, yet honest passion, hath guided me: the case is every way too, too much unanswerable. It resteth in you, O excellent protector, to pronounce judgement; which if there be hope that such a young man may prove profitable to the world, who in the first exercise of his own determination far passed the arrantest stumpet in luxuriousness, the cunningest forger in falsehood, a player in disguising, a tiger in cruelty, a dragon in ungratefulness, let him be preserved like a jewel to do greater mischief. If his youth be not more defiled with treachery than the eldest man's age, let, I say, his youth be some cause of compassion. If he have not every way sought the overthrow of human society, if he have done anything like a prince, let his naming himself a prince breed a reverence of his base wickedness. If he have not broken all law of hospitality, and broken them in the most detestable degree that can be, let his being a guest be a sacred protection of his more than savage doings; or if his whorish beauty have not been as the high way of his wickedness, let the picture drawn upon so poisonous a wood be reserved to show how greatly colours can please us. But if it is, as it is – what should I say more? – a very spirit of hellish naughtiness; if his act be to be punished and his defiled person not to be pitied, then restore unto us our prince by duly punishing his murderers, for then we shall think him and his name to live when we shall see his killers to die. Restore to the excellent Philoclea her honour by taking out of the world her dishonour; and think that at this day, in this matter, are the eyes of the world upon you whether anything can sway your mind from a true administration of justice. Alas, though I have much more to say, I can say no more, for my tears and sighs interrupt my speech and force me to give myself over to my private sorrow.'

Thus when Philanax had uttered the uttermost of his malice, he made sorrow the cause of his conclusion. But while Philanax was in the course of his speech and did with such bitter reproaches defame the princely Pyrocles, it was well to be seen his heart was unused to bear such injuries, and his thoughts such as could arm themselves better against anything than shame. For sometimes blushing, his blood with divers motions coming and going, sometimes closing his eyes and laying his hand over them, sometimee giving such a look to Philanax as might show he assured himself he durst not so have spoken if they had been in indifferent place, with some impatiency he bare the length of his oration; which being ended, with as much modest humbleness to the judge as despiteful scorn to the accuser, with words to this purpose he defended his honour:

'My accuser's tale may well bear witness with me, most rightful judge, in how hard a case and environed with how many troubles I may esteem myself. For if he (who shows his tongue is not unacquainted with railing) was in an agony in the beginning of his speech with the multitude of matters he had to lay unto me, wherein, notwithstanding, the most evil could fall unto him was that he should not do so much evil as he would, how cumbered do you think may I acknowledge myself who, in things no less importing than my life, must be mine own advocate, without leisure to answer or foreknowledge what should be objected? In things, I say, promoted with so cunning a confusion, as having mingled truths with falsehoods, surmises with certainties, causes of no moment with matters capital, scolding with complaining, I can absolutely neither grant nor deny. Neither can I tell whether I come hither to be judged or before judgement to be punished, being compelled to bear such unworthy words far more grievous than any death unto me. But since the form of this government allows such tongue-liberty unto him, I will pick as well as I can out of his invective those few points which may seem of some purpose in the touching of me; hoping that as by your easy hearing of me you will show that though you hate evil, yet you wish men may prove themselves not evil, so in that he hath said, you will not weigh so much what he hath said as what he hath proved, remembering that truth is simple and naked, and that if he had guided himself under that banner, he needed not out of the way have sought so vile and false disgracings of me enough to make the untruest accusation believed. I will therefore, using truth as my best eloquence, repeat unto you as much as I know in this matter, and then, by the only clearness of the discourse, your wisdom, I know, will find the difference betwixt cavilling supposition and direct declaration.

'This Prince Palladius and I being inflamed with love (a passion far more easily reprehended than refrained) to the two peerless daughters of Basilius, and understanding how he had secluded himself from the world, that like princes there was no access unto him, we disguised ourselves in such forms as might soonest bring us to the revealing of our affections. The Prince Palladius had such event of his doings that, with Pamela's consent, he was to convey her out of the thraldom she lived in to receive the subjection of a greater people than her own, until her father's consent might be obtained. My fortune was more hard, for I bare no more love to the chaste Philoclea than Basilius (deceived in my sex) showed to me, insomuch that by his importunacy I could have no time to obtain the like favour of the pure Philoclea; till this policy I found: taking (under colour of some devotions) my lodging, to draw Basilius thither, with hope to enjoy me; which likewise I revealed to the queen, that she might keep my place and so make her husband see his error. While I in the meantime, being delivered of them both, and having locked so the doors as I hoped (if the immaculate Philoclea would condescend to go with me) there should be none to hinder our going, I was made prisoner there, I know not by what means, when (being repelled by her divine virtue) I would fainest have escaped. Here have you the thread to guide you in the labyrinth this man of his tongue had made so monstrous. Here see you the true discourse which he, mountebank-fashion,* doth make so wide a mouth over. Here may you conceive the reason why the queen had my garment, because in her going to the cave in the moon-shine night she might be taken for me, which he useth as the knot of all his wise assertions; so that as this double-minded fellow's accusation was double, double likewise my answer must perforce be, to the murder of Basilius and violence offered to the inviolate Philoclea.

* *mountebank-fashion*: like a showman.

'For the first, O heavenly gods, who would have thought any mouth could have been found so mercenary as to have opened so slight proofs of so horrible matters! His first argument is a question: who would imagine that Gynecia would accomplish such an act without some accessories, and if any, who but I? Truly I am so far from imagining anything, that till I saw these mourning tokens and heard Gynecia's confession, I never imagined the king was dead. And for my part, so vehemently and more like the manner of passionate than guilty folks I see the queen persecute herself, that I think condemnation may go too hastily over her, considering the unlikelihood, if not impossibility, her wisdom and virtue so long nourished should in one moment throw down itself to the uttermost end of wickedness. But whatsoever she hath done (which, as I say, I never believed) yet how unjustly should that aggravate my fault? – she found abroad, I within doors (for as for the wearing my garment, I have told you the cause) she seeking (as you say) to escape, I locking myself in a house – without perchance the conspiracy of one poor stranger might greatly enable her attempt, or the fortification of the lodge (as the trim man alleged) might make me hope to resist all Arcadia.

'And see how treacherously he seeks to draw from me my chiefest clearing, by preventing the credit of her words wherewith she had wholly taken the fault upon herself. An honest and impartial examiner! Her words may condemn her, but may not absolve me. Thus, void of all probable allegation, the craven crows upon my affliction, not leaving out any evil that ever he hath felt in his own soul to charge my youth withal. But who can look for a sweeter breath out of such a stomach or for honey from so filthy a spider! What should I say more? If in so inhuman a matter (which he himself confesseth) sincerest judgements are loathest to believe, and in the severest laws proofs clearer than the sun are required, his reasons are only the scum of a base malice, my answers most manifest, shining in their own truth. If there remain any doubt of it (because it stands betwixt his affirming and my denial) I offer, nay I desire, and humbly desire I may be granted the trial by combat, wherein let him be armed and me in my shirt, I doubt not justice will be my shield, and his heart will show itself as faint as it is false.

'Now come I to the second part of my offence, towards the young lady, which, howsoever you term it, so far forth as I have told you I confess and for her sake heartily lament. But if herein I offered force to her, love offered more force to me. Let her beauty be compared to my years and such effects will be found no miracles. But since it is thus as it is and that justice teacheth us not to love punishment but to fly to it for necessity, the salve of her honour (I mean as the world will take it, for else in truth it is most untouched) must be my marriage and not my death, since the one stops all mouths, the other becomes a doubtful fable. This matter requires no more words, and your experience (I hope) in these cases shall need no more; for myself, methinks I have showed already too much love of my life to bestow so many. But certainly it hath been love of truth which could not bear so unworthy falsehood, and love of justice that would brook no wrong to myself nor other, and makes me now, even in that respect, to desire you to be moved rather with pity at a just cause of tears than with the bloody tears this crocodile spends, who weeps to procure death and not to lament death. It will be no honour to Basilius' tomb to have guiltless blood sprinkled upon it, and much more may a judge over-weigh himself in cruelty than in clemency. It is hard, but it is excellent where it is found: a right knowledge when correction is necessary, when grace doth more avail. For my own respect, if I thought in wisdom I had deserved death, I would not desire life; for I know nature will condemn me to die though you do not, and longer I would not wish to draw this breath than I may keep myself unspotted of any horrible crime. Only I cannot, nor ever will deny the love of Philoclea, whose violence wrought violent effects in me.'

## CHAPTER 6

With that he finished his speech, casting up his eyes to the judge, and crossing his hands, which he held in their length before him, declaring a resolute patience in whatsoever should be done with him. Philanax, like a watchful adversary, curiously marked all that he said, saving that in the beginning he was interrupted by two letters which were brought him from the Princess Pamela and the Lady Philoclea; who having all that night considered and bewailed their estate, careful for their mother likewise (of whom they could never think so much evil) but considering with themselves that she assuredly should have so due trial by the laws as either she should not need their help or should be past their help, they looked to that which nearliest touched them, and each wrote in this sort for him in whom their lives' joy consisted:

The humble hearted Philoclea wrote much after this manner:

My Lords, what you will determine of me is to me uncertain; but what I have determined of myself I am most certain, which is no longer to enjoy my life than I may enjoy him for my husband whom the heavens for my highest glory have bestowed upon me. Those that judge him, let them execute me. Let my throat satisfy their hunger of murder. For alas, what hath he done that had not his original in me? Look upon him, I beseech you, with indifference,* and see whether in those eyes all virtue shines not. See whether that face could hide a murder. Take leisure to know him, and then yourselves will say it hath been too great an inhumanity to suspect such excellency. Are the gods, think you, deceived in their workmanship? Artificers will not use marble but to noble uses. Should those powers be so overshot as to frame so precious an image of their own but to honourable purposes? O speak with him, O hear him, O know him, and become not the putters-out of the world's light! Hope you to joy my father's soul with hurting him he loved above all the world? Shall a wrong suspicion make you forget the certain knowledge of those benefits this house hath received by him? Alas, alas, let not Arcadia for his loss be accursed of the whole earth and of all posterity. He is a great prince. I speak unto you that which I know, for I have seen most evident testimonies. Why should you hinder my advancement, who (if I have passed my childhood hurtless to any of you, if I have refused nobody to do what good I could, if I have often mitigated my father's anger) ever sought to maintain his favour towards you? – Nay, if I have held you all as fathers and brothers unto me, rob me not of more than my life comes unto. Tear not that which is inseparably joined to my soul. But if he rest misliked of you (which, O God, how can it be?) yet give him to me, let me have him. You know I pretend no right to your state, therefore is it but a private petition I make unto you. Or if you be hard-heartedly bent to appoint otherwise (which, oh, sooner let me die than know!) then, to end as I

*indifferency: impartiality.

began, let me by you be ordered to the same end, without,* for more cruelty, you mean to force Philoclea to use her own hands to kill one of your king's children.

Pamela's letter (which she meant to send to the general assembly of the Arcadian nobility, for so closely they were kept as they were utterly ignorant of the new taken orders) was thus framed:

In such a state, my Lords, you have placed me as I can neither write nor be silent. For how can I be silent, since you have left me nothing but my solitary words to testify my misery? And how should I write (for as for speech, I have none but my jailor that can hear me) who neither can resolve what to write, nor to whom to write? What to write is as hard for me to say as what I may not write, so little hope have I of any success, and so much hath no injury been left undone to me-wards. To whom to write where may I learn, since yet I wot not how to entitle you? Shall I call you my sovereigns? Set down your laws that I may do you homage. Shall I fall lower, and name you my fellows? Show me, I beseech you, the lord and master over us. But shall Basilius' heir name herself your princess? Alas, I am your prisoner. But whatsoever I be, or whatsoever you be, O, all you beholders of these doleful lines, this do I signify unto you, and signify it with a heart that shall ever remain in that opinion: the good or evil you do to the excellent prince was taken with me, and after by force from me, I will ever impute it as either way done to mine own person. He is a prince, and worthy to be my husband, and so is he my husband by me worthily chosen. Believe it, believe it, either you shall be traitors for murdering of me, or, if you let me live, the murderers of him shall smart as traitors. For what do you think I can think? Am I so childish as not to see wherein you touch him you condemn me? Can his shame be without my reproach? No, nor shall be, since nothing he hath done that I will not avow. Is this the comfort you bring me in my father's death, to make me fuller of shame than sorrow? Would you do this if it were not with full intention to prevent my power with slaughter? And so do, I pray you. It is high time for me to be weary of my life too long led, since you are weary of me before you have me. I say again, I say it infinitely unto you, I will not live without him, if it be not to revenge him. Either do justly in saving both, or wisely in killing both. If I be your princess, I command his preservation; if but a private person, then are we both to suffer. I take all

* *without:* unless.

truth to witness he hath done no fault but in going with me. Therefore, to conclude; in judging him you judge me. Neither conceive with
yourselves the matter you treat of is the life of a stranger (though
even in that name he deserved pity) nor of a shepherd (to which estate
love of me made such a prince descend) but determine most assuredly,
the life that is in question is of Pamela, Basilius' daughter.

Many blots had the tears of these sweet ladies made in their
letters, which many times they had altered, many times torn and
written anew, ever thinking something either wanted or were too
much, or would offend, or (which is worst) would breed denial.
But at last, the day warned them to dispatch, which they accordingly did, and calling one of their guard (for nobody else was
suffered to come near them) with great entreaty they requested
him that he would present them to the principal noblemen and
gentlemen together – for they had more confidence in the
numbers' favour than in any one, upon whom they would not lay
the lives they held so precious. But the fellow (trusty to Philanax,
who had placed him there) delivered them both to him what time
Pyrocles began to speak, which he suddenly opened, and seeing to
what they tended by the first words, was so far from publishing
them (whereby he feared in Euarchus' just mind either the princesses might be endangered or the prisoners preserved, of which
choice he knew not which to think the worst) that he would not
himself read them over, doubting his own heart might be
mollified, so bent upon revenge. Therefore utterly suppressing
them, he lent a spiteful ear to Pyrocles, and as soon as he had
ended, with a very willing heart desired Euarchus he might accept
the combat – although it would have framed but evil with him,
Pyrocles having never found any match near him besides Musidorus.

But Euarchus made answer, 'Since bodily strength is but a servant to the mind, it were very barbarous and preposterous that
force should be made judge over reason.'

Then would he also have replied in words unto him, but Euarchus, who knew what they could say was already said, taking their
arguments into his mind, commanded him to proceed against the
other prisoner and that then he would sentence them both together.

Philanax, nothing the milder for Pyrocles' purging himself, but rather (according to the nature of arguing, especially when it is bitter) so much the more vehement, entered thus into his speech against Musidorus, being so overgone with rage that he forgot in this oration his precise method of oratory.

'Behold, most noble protector, to what a state Arcadia is come, since such manner of men may challenge in combat the faithfullest of the nobility, and having merited the shamefullest of all deaths, dare name in marriage the princesses of this country. Certainly, my masters, I must say you were much out of taste if you had not rather enjoy such ladies than be hanged. But the one you have as much deserved as you have dishonoured the other.

'But now my speech must be directed to you, good master Dorus, who, with Pallas' help, perdy, are lately grown Palladius. Too much this sacred seat of justice grants unto such a fugitive bondslave, who, instead of these examinations, should be made confess with a whip that which a halter should punish. Are not you he, Sir, whose sheep-hook was prepared to be our sceptre, in whom lay the knot of all this tragedy? Or else, perchance, they that should gain little by it were dealers in the murder. You only, that had provided the fruits for yourself, knew nothing of it, knew nothing! Hath thy companion here infected thee with such impudency as even in the face of the world to deny that which all the world perceiveth? The other pleads ignorance, and you, I doubt not, will allege absence. But he was ignorant when he was hard by, and you had framed your absence just against the time the act should be committed – so fit a lieutenant he knew he had left of his wickedness, that for himself his safest mean was to convey away the lady of us all, who once out of the country, he knew we would come with olive branches of intercession unto her, and fall at his feet to beseech him to leave keeping of sheep and vouchsafe the tyrannizing over us – for to think they are princes, as they say, (although in our laws it behoves them nothing) I see at all no reason. These jewels certainly, with their disguising sleights, they have pilfered in their vagabonding race. And think you such princes should be so long without some followers after them? Truly if they be princes, it manifestly shows their virtues such as all their subjects are glad to be rid of them.

'But be they as they are, for we are to consider the matter and not the men. Basilius' murder hath been the cause of their coming; Basilius' murder they have most treacherously brought to pass; yet that, I doubt not, you will deny as well as your fellow. But how will you deny the stealing away the princess of this province, which is no less than treason? So notably hath the justice of the gods provided for the punishing of these malefactors, as if it were possible men would not believe the certain evidences of their principal mischief, yet have they discovered themselves sufficiently for their most just overthrow. I say therefore – to omit my chief matter of the king's death – this wolfish shepherd, this counterfeit prince hath traitorously, contrary to his allegiance (having made himself a servant and subject) attempted the depriving this country of our natural princess, and therefore by all right must receive the punishment of traitors. This matter is so assured as he himself will not deny it, being taken and brought back in the fact. This matter is so odious in nature, so shameful to the world, so contrary to all laws, so hurtful to us, so false in him, as if I should stand further in declaring or defacing it, I should either show great doubts in your wisdom or in your justice. Therefore I will transfer my care upon you, and attend (to my learning and comfort) the eternal example you will leave to all mankind of disguisers, falsifiers, adulterers, ravishers, murderers and traitors.'

Musidorus, while Philanax was speaking against his cousin and him, had looked round about him to see whether by any means he might come to have caught him in his arms and have killed him, so much had his disgracing words filled his breast with rage. But perceiving himself so guarded as he should rather show a passionate act than perform his revenge, his hand trembling with desire to strike, and all the veins in his face swelling, casting his eyes over the judgement seat:

'O gods,' said he, 'and have you spared my life to bear these injuries of such a drivel! Is this the justice of this place, to have such men as we are submitted not only to apparent falsehood but most shameful reviling? But mark, I pray you, the ungratefulness of the wretch, how utterly he hath forgotten the benefits both he and all this country hath received of us. For if ever men may remember their own noble deeds, it is then when their just defence and others' unjust unkindness doth require it. I omit our services

done to Basilius in the late war with Amphialus, importing no less
than his daughters' lives and his state's preservation. Were not we
the men that killed the wild beasts which otherwise had killed the
princesses if we had not succoured them? Consider, if it please
you, where had been Daiphantus' rape or my treason, if the sweet
beauties of the earth had then been devoured? Either think them
now dead, or remember they live by us: and yet full often this
telltale can acknowledge the loss they should have by their taking
away while maliciously he overpasseth* who were their pre-
servers. Neither let this be spoken of me as if I meant to balance
this evil with that good – for I must confess that saving of such
creatures was rewarded in the act itself – but only to manifest the
partial* jangling of this vile pickthank.*

'But if we be the traitors, where was your fidelity, O only
tongue-valiant gentleman, when not only the young princess, but
the king himself was defended from uttermost peril, partly by me,
but principally by this excellent young man's both wisdom and
valour? Were we, that made ourselves against hundreds of armed
men openly the shields of his life, like secretly to be his em-
poisoners? Did we then show his life to be dearer to us than our
own because we might after rob him of his life to die shamefully?
Truly, truly, master orator, whosoever hath hired you to be so
busy in their matters (who keep honester servants than yourself)
he should have bid you in so many railings bring some excuse for
yourself why in the greatest need of your prince, to whom you
pretend a miraculous goodwill, you were not then as forward to do
like a man yourself, or at least to accuse them that were slack in
that service. But commonly they use their feet for their defence
whose tongue is their weapon. Certainly a very simple subtlety it
had been in us to repose our lives in the daughters when we had
killed the father. But as this gentleman thinks to win the reputation of a copious talker by leaving nothing unsaid which a filthy
mind can imagine, so think I (or else all words are vain) that to
wise men's judgement our clearness in the King's death is
sufficiently notorious.

'But at length when the merchant hath set out his gilded bag-

*overpasseth: omits to mention. partial: biased. pickthank: syco-
phant.

gage, lastly he comes to some stuff of importance, and saith I conveyed away the princess of this country. And is she indeed your princess? I pray you then whom should I wait of else but her that was my mistress by my professed vow, and princess over me while I lived in this soil? Ask her why she went; ask not me why I served her. Since accounting me as a prince you have not to do with me, taking me as her servant, then take withal that I must obey her. But you will say I persuaded her to fly away. Certainly I will for no death deny it, knowing to what honour I should bring her from the thraldom by such fellows' counsel as you she was kept in. Shall persuasion to a prince grow treason to a prince? It might be error in me, but falsehood it could not be, since I made myself partaker of whatsoever I wished her unto. Who will ever counsel his king if his counsel be judged by the event,* and if it be not found wise, shall therefore be thought wicked?

'But if I be a traitor, I hope you will grant me a correlative to whom I shall be the traitor; for the princess against whom the treasons are considered, I am sure, will avow my faithfulness, without you will say that I am a traitor to her because I left the country, and a traitor to the country because I went with her. Here do I leave out my just excuses of love's force; which as thy narrow heart hath never had noble room enough in it to receive, so yet those manlike courages that by experience know how subject the virtuous minds are to love a most virtuous creature (witnessed to be such by the most excellent gifts of nature) will deem it a venial trespass to seek the satisfaction of honourable desires – honourable even in the curiousest points of honour, whereout there can no disgrace nor disparagement come unto her. Therefore, O judge (who I hope dost know what it is to be a judge: that your end is to preserve and not to destroy mankind; that laws are not made like lime-twigs or nets to catch everything that toucheth them, but rather like sea-marks to avoid* the shipwreck of ignorant passengers) since that our doing in the extremest interpretation is but a human error, and that of it you may make a profitable event (we being of such estate as their parents would not have misliked the affinity) you will not, I trust, at the persuasion of this brabbler* burn your house to make it clean, but like

* *event*: outcome. *avoid*: avert. *brabbler*: caviller.

a wise father turn even the fault of your children to any good that may come of it, since that is the fruit of wisdom and end of all judgements.'

## CHAPTER 7

While this matter was thus handling, a silent and, as it were, astonished attention possessed all the people; a kindly compassion moved the noble gentleman Sympathus. But as for Kalander, everything was spoken either by or for his own dear guests moved an effect in him – sometimes tears, sometimes hopeful looks, sometimes whispering persuasions in their ears that stood by him to seek the saving the two young princes. But the general multitude waited the judgement of Euarchus who, showing in his face no motions either at the one's or other's speech, letting pass the flowers of rhetoric and only marking whither their reasons tended; having made the question to be asked of Gynecia ( who continued to take the whole fault upon herself) and having caused Dametas and Miso and Mopsa (who by Philanax's order had been held in most cruel prison) to make a full declaration how much they knew of these passed matters, and then gathering as assured satisfaction to his own mind as in that case he could (not needing to take leisure for that whereof a long practice had bred a well-grounded habit in him) with a voice and gesture directed to the universal assembly, in this form pronounced sentence:

'This weighty matter, whereof presently we are to determine, doth at the first consideration yield two important doubts: the first, whether these men be to be judged; the second, how they are to be judged. The first doubt ariseth because they give themselves out for princes absolute, a sacred name, and to which any violence seems to be an impiety; for how can any laws, which are the bonds of all human society, be observed if the law-givers and law-rulers be not held in an untouched admiration? But hereto, although already they have been sufficiently answered, yet thus much again I will repeat unto you: that whatsoever they be or be not, here they be no princes, since betwixt prince and subject there is as necessary a relation as between father and son; and as there is no man a father but to his child, so is not a prince a prince but to his own subjects. Therefore is not this place to acknowledge in them any principality, without it should at the same time by a secret consent confess subjection.

'Yet hereto may be objected that the universal civility, the law of nations (all mankind being, as it were, co-inhabiters or world-citizens together) hath ever required public persons should be of all parties especially regarded, since not only in peace but in war, not only princes but heralds and trumpets are with great reason exempted from injuries. This point is true, but yet so true as they that will receive the benefit of a custom must not be the first to break it, for then can they not complain if they be not helped by that which they themselves hurt. If a prince do acts of hostility without denouncing war, if he break his oath of amity, or innumerable such other things contrary to the laws of arms, he must take heed how he fall into their hands whom he so wrongeth, for then is courtesy the best custom he can claim. Much more these men, who have not only left to do like* princes, but to be like princes, not only entered into Arcadia and so into the Arcadian orders, but into domestical services and so, by making themselves private, deprived themselves of respect due to their public calling. For no proportion it were of justice that a man might make himself no prince when he would do evil, and might anew create himself a prince when he would not suffer evil. Thus, therefore, by all laws of nature and nations, and especially by their own putting themselves out of the sanctuary of them, these young men cannot in justice avoid the judgement but, like private men, must have their doings either cleared, excused, or condemned.

'There resteth then the second point, how to judge well; and that must undoubtedly be done not by a free discourse of reason and skill of philosophy, but must be tied to the laws of Greece and municipal statutes of this kingdom. For although out of them these came, and to them must indeed refer their offspring, yet because philosophical discourses stand in the general consideration of things, they leave to every man a scope of his own interpretation, where the laws, applying themselves to the necessary use, fold us within assured bounds: which once broken, man's nature infinitely

* *not only left to do like*: ceased to behave like.

rangeth. Judged, therefore, they must be, and by your laws judged. Now the action offereth itself to due balance betwixt the accuser's twofold accusation and their answer accordingly applied; the questions being the one of a fact simply, the other of the quality of a fact. To the first they use direct denial; to the second, qualification and excuse. They deny the murder of the King; and against mighty presumptions bring forth some probable answers, which they do principally fortify with the Queen's acknowledging herself only culpable. Certainly as in equality of conjectures we are not to take hold of the worse, but rather to be glad we may find any hope that mankind is not grown monstrous (being, undoubtedly, less evil a guilty man should escape than a guiltless perish) so if in the rest they be spotless, then is this no further to be remembered. But if they have aggravated these suspicions with new evils, then are those suspicions so far to show themselves as to cause the other points to be thoroughly examined and with less favour weighed, since this no man can deny: they have been accidental, if not principal causes of the king's death.

'Now then we are to determine of the other matters which are laid to them, wherein they do not deny the fact, but deny, or at least diminish the fault. But first I may remember (though it were not first alleged by them) the services they had before done, truly honourable, and worthy of great reward, but not worthy to countervail* with a following wickedness. Reward is proper to well doing, punishment to evil doing, which must not be confounded, no more than good and evil are to be mingled. Therefore it hath been determined in all wisdoms that no man, because he hath done well before, should have his present evils spared, but rather so much the more punished as (having showed he knew how to be good) yet would against his knowledge be naught.

'The fact then is nakedly without passion or partiality to be viewed: wherein without all question they are equally culpable. For though he that terms himself Daiphantus were sooner disappointed of his purpose of conveying away the Lady Philoclea than he that persuaded the Princess Pamela to fly her country and accompanied her in it, yet seeing in causes of this nature the will by the rules of justice standeth for the deed, they are both alike to be

*countervail: counterbalance.

found guilty, and guilty of heinous ravishment. For though they ravished them not from themselves, yet they ravished them from him that owned them, which was their father – an act punished by all the Grecian laws by the loss of the head, as a most execrable theft. For if they must die who steal from us our goods, how much more they who steal from us that for which we gather our goods? And if our laws have it so in the private persons, much more forcible are they to be in princes' children, where one steals, as it were, the whole state and well-being of that people, being tied by the secret of a long use to be governed by none but the next of that blood. Neither let any man marvel our ancestors have been so severe in these cases, since, the example of the Phoenician Europa, but especially of the Grecian Helen, hath taught them what destroying fires have grown of such sparkles.[1] And although Helen was a wife and this but a child, that booteth not, since the principal cause of marrying wives is that we may have children of our own.

'But now let us see how these young men (truly for their persons worthy of pity, if they had rightly pitied themselves) do go about to mitigate the vehemency of their errors. Some of their excuses are common to both, some peculiar only to him that was the shepherd. Both remember the force of love and, as it were, the mending up of the matter by their marriage. If that unbridled desire which is entitled love might purge such a sickness as this, surely we should have many loving excuses of hateful mischief – nay, rather, no mischief should be committed that should not be veiled under the name of love. For as well he that steals might allege the love of money; he that murders, the love of revenge; he that rebels, the love of greatness, as the adulterer the love of a woman, since they do in all speeches affirm they love that which an ill-governed passion maketh them to follow. But love may have no such privilege. That sweet and heavenly uniting of the minds, which properly is called love, hath no other knot but virtue, and therefore if it be a right love, it can never slide into any action that is not virtuous.

'The other and indeed more effectual reason is that they may be married unto them, and so honourably redress the dishonour of them whom this matter seemeth most to touch. Surely if the question were what were convenient for the parties, and not what is just in the never changing justice, there might be much said in it. But herein we must consider that the laws look how to prevent by due examples that such things be not done, and not how to salve such things when they are done. For if the governors of justice shall take such a scope as to measure the foot of the law by a show of conveniency, and measure that conveniency not by the public society but by that which is fittest for them which offend, young men, strong men, and rich men shall ever find private conveniences how to palliate such committed disorders as to the public shall not only be inconvenient but pestilent. The marriage perchance might be fit for them, but very unfit were it to the state, to allow a pattern of such procurations of marriage. And thus much do they both allege.

'Further goes he that went with the princess Pamela, and requireth the benefit of a counsellor who hath place of free persuasion, and the reasonable excuse of a servant that did but wait of his mistress. Without all question, as counsellors have great cause to take heed how they advise anything directly opposite to the form of that present government – especially when they do it singly without public allowance – so yet is the case much more apparent, since neither she was an effectual princess (her father being then alive, and though he had been dead, she not come to the years of authority) nor he her servant in such manner to obey her, but by his own preferment first belonging to Dametas, and then to the king; and therefore if not by Arcadia laws, yet by household orders bound to have done nothing without his agreement. Thus therefore since the deeds accomplished by these two are both abominable and inexcusable, I do in the behalf of justice, and by the force of Arcadia laws, pronounce that Daiphantus shall be thrown out of a high tower to receive his death by his fall; Palladius shall be beheaded: the time, before the sun set; the place, in Mantinea; the executioner, Dametas: which office he shall execute all the days of his life for his beastly forgetting the careful duty he owed to his charge.'

## BOOK FIVE

## CHAPTER 8

This said, he turned himself to Philanax and two of the other noblemen, commanding them to see the judgement presently performed. Philanax, more greedy than any hunter of his prey, went straight to lay hold of the excellent prisoners, who, casting a farewell look one upon the other, represented in their faces as much unappalled constancy as the most excellent courage can deliver in outward graces. Yet if at all there were any show of change in them, it was that Pyrocles was something nearer to bashfulness and Musidorus to anger, both overruled by reason and resolution. But as with great number of armed men Philanax was descending unto them, and that Musidorus was beginning to say something in Pyrocles' behalf, behold Kalander, that with arms cast abroad and open mouth, came crying to Euarchus, holding a stranger in his hand that cried much more than he, desiring they might be heard speak before the prisoners were removed. Even the noble gentleman Sympathus aided them in it, and taking such as he could command, stopped Philanax, betwixt entreaty and force, from carrying away the princes until it were heard what new matters these men did bring.

So again mounting to the tribunal, they hearkened to the stranger's vehement speech or rather appassionate exclaiming. It was indeed Kalodulus, the faithful servant of Musidorus, to whom his master (when in despite of his best-grounded determinations he first became a slave to affection) had sent the shepherd Menalcas to be arrested; by the help of whose raiment in the meantime he advanced himself to that estate which he accounted most high, because it might be serviceable to that fancy which he had placed most high in his mind. For Menalcas, having faithfully performed his errand, was as faithfully imprisoned by Kalodulus; but as Kalodulus performed the first part of his duty in doing the commandment of his prince, so was he with abundance of sincere loyalty extremely perplexed, when he understood of Menalcas the strange disguising of his beloved master. For as the acts he and his cousin Pyrocles had done in Asia had filled all the ears of the Thessalians and Macedonians with no less joy than admiration, so was the fear of their loss no less grievous unto them, when by the

839

noise of report they understood of their lonely committing themselves to the sea, the issue of which they had no way learned. But now that by Menalcas he perceived where he was, guessing the like of Pyrocles, comparing the unusedness of this act with the unripeness of their age, seeing in general conjecture they could do it for nothing that might not fall out dangerous, he was somewhile troubled with himself what to do, betwixt doubt of their hurt and doubt of their displeasure. Often he was minded, as his safest and honestest way, to reveal it to the King Euarchus, that both his authority might prevent any damage to them, and under his wings he himself might remain safe; but considering a journey to Byzantium (where as yet he supposed Euarchus lay) would require more time than he was willing to remain doubtful of his prince's estate, he resolved at length to write the matter to Euarchus, and himself the while to go into Arcadia, uncertain what to do when he came thither, but determined to do his best service to his dear master, if by any good fortune he might find him.

And so it happened, that being even this day come to Mantinea, and as warely* and attentively as he could giving ear to all reports in hope to hear something of them he sought, he straight received a strange rumour of these things, but so uncertainly as popular reports carry so rare accidents. But this by all men he was willed, to seek out Kalander, a great gentleman of that country, who would soonest satisfy him of all these occurrents.* Thus instructed, he came (even about the midst of Euarchus' judgement) to the desert, where seeing great multitudes, and hearing unknown names of Palladius and Daiphantus, and not able to press to the place where Euarchus sat, he enquired for Kalander and was soon brought unto him, partly because he was generally known unto all men, and partly because he had withdrawn himself from the press when he perceived by Euarchus' words whither they tended, being not able to endure his guests' condemnation. He enquired forthwith of Kalander the cause of the assembly, and whether the fame were true of Euarchus' presence; who with many tears made a doleful recital unto him both of the Amazon and shepherd, setting forth their natural graces and lamenting their pitiful undoing. But his description made Kalodulus immediately know the

* *warely*: circumspectly. *occurrents*: occurrences.

shepherd was his duke, and so judging the other to be Pyrocles and speedily communicating it to Kalander who, he saw, did favour their case, they brake the press* with astonishing every man with their cries.

And being come to Euarchus, Kalodulus fell at his feet, telling him those he had judged were his own son and nephew, the one the comfort of Macedon, the other the only stay of Thessalia, with many such like words, but as from a man that assured himself in that matter he should need small speech: while Kalander made it known to all men what the prisoners were; to whom he cried they should salute their father and joy in the good hap the gods had sent them, who were no less glad than all the people amazed at the strange event of these matters. Even Philanax' own revengeful heart was mollified when he saw from divers parts of the world so near kinsmen should meet in such a necessity. And withal the fame of Pyrocles and Musidorus greatly drew him to a compassionate conceit, and had already unclothed his face of all show of malice.

But Euarchus staid a good while upon himself, like a valiant man that should receive a notable encounter, being vehemently stricken with the fatherly love of so excellent children, and studying with his best reason what his office required. At length with such a kind of gravity as was near to sorrow, he thus uttered his mind:

'I take witness of the immortal gods,' said he, 'O Arcadians, that what this day I have said hath been out of my assured persuasion what justice itself and your just laws require. Though strangers then to me, I had no desire to hurt them, but leaving aside all considerations of the persons, I weighed the matter which you committed into my hands with my most impartial and furthest reach of reason: and thereout have condemned them to lose their lives, contaminated with so many foul breaches of hospitality, civility, and virtue. Now, contrary to all expectations, I find them to be my only son and nephew, such upon whom you see what gifts nature hath bestowed; such who have so to the wonder of the world heretofore behaved themselves as might give just cause to the greatest hopes that in an excellent youth may be conceived:

* *brake the press*: broke through the crowd.

lastly, in few words, such in whom I placed all my mortal joys, and thought myself (now near my grave) to recover a new life.

'But alas, shall justice halt? Or shall she wink* in one's cause, which had lynx's eyes* in another's? Or rather shall all private respects give place to that holy name?* Be it so. Be it so. Let my grey hairs be laid in the dust with sorrow. Let the small remnant of my life be to me an inward and outward desolation, and to the world a gazing stock of wretched misery, but never, never let sacred righteousness fall. It is immortal, and immortally ought to be preserved. If rightly I have judged, then rightly I have judged mine own children, unless the name of a child should have force to change the never changing justice. No, no, Pyrocles, and Musidorus, I prefer you much before my life, but I prefer justice as far before you. While you did like yourselves, my body should willingly have been your shield, but I cannot keep you from the effects of your own doing: nay, I cannot in this case acknowledge you for mine; for never had I shepherd to my nephew, nor ever had woman to my son. Your vices have degraded you from being princes, and have disannulled your birthright. Therefore if there be anything left in you of princely virtue, show it in constant suffering that your unprincely dealing hath purchased unto you. For my part I must tell you, you have forced a father to rob himself of his children. Do you therefore, O Philanax, and you, my other lords of this country, see the judgement be rightly performed in time, place, and manner, as before appointed.'

With that, though he would have refrained them, a man might perceive the tears drop down his long white beard, which moved not only Kalodulus and Kalander to roaring lamentations, but all the assembly dolefully to record that pitiful spectacle. Philanax himself could not abstain from great shows of pitying sorrow and manifest withdrawing from performing the King's commandment. But Musidorus, having the hope of his safety and recovering of the Princess Pamela (which made him most desirous to live) so suddenly dashed; but especially moved for his dear Pyrocles, for whom he was ever resolved his last speech should be, and stirred up with rage of unkindness, he thus spake:

* *wink*: shut her eyes. *lynx's eyes*: noted for their keenness of sight. *that holy name*: justice.

'Enjoy thy bloody conquest, tyrannical Euarchus,' said he, 'for neither is convenient the title of a king to a murderer, nor the remembrance of kindred to a destroyer of his kindred. Go home and glory that it hath been in thy power shamefully to kill Musidorus. Let thy flattering orators dedicate crowns of laurel unto thee that the first of thy race thou hast overthrown a prince of Thessalia. But for me, I hope the Thessalians are not so degenerate from their ancestors but that they will revenge my injury and their loss upon thee. I hope my death is no more unjust to me than it shall be bitter to thee. Howsoever it be, my death shall triumph over thy cruelty. Neither as now would I live to make my life beholding unto thee. But if thy cruelty hath not so blinded thine eyes that thou canst not see thine own hurt; if thy heart be not so devilish as thou hast no power but to torment thyself, then look upon this young Pyrocles with a manlike eye, if not with a pitiful. Give not occasion to the whole earth to say: "See how the gods have made the tyrant tear his own bowels!" Examine the eyes and voices of all this people; and what all men see, be not blind in thine own case. Look, I say, look upon him, in whom the most curious searcher is able to find no fault but that he is thy son. Believe it, thy own subjects will detest thee for robbing them of such a prince, in whom they have right as well as thyself.'

Some more words to that purpose he would have spoken; but Pyrocles, who often had called to him, did now fully interrupt him, desiring him not to do him the wrong to give his father ill words before him, willing him to consider it was their own fault and not his injustice; and withal, to remember their resolution of well suffering all accidents, which this impatiency did seem to vary from: and then kneeling down with all humbleness, he took the speech in this order to Euarchus:

'If my daily prayers to the almighty gods had so far prevailed as to have granted me the end whereto I have directed my actions, I should rather have been now a comfort to your mind than an example of your justice; rather a preserver of your memory by my life than a monument of your judgement by my death. But since it hath pleased their unsearchable wisdoms to overthrow all the desires I had to serve you and make me become a shame unto you; since the last obedience I can show you is to die, vouchsafe yet, O

Father (if my fault have not made me altogether unworthy so to term you) vouchsafe, I say, to let the few and last words your son shall ever speak not be tedious unto you. And if the remembrance of my virtuous mother, who once was dear unto you, may bear any sway with you; if the name of Pyrocles have at any time been pleasant, let one request of mine, which shall not be for mine own life, be graciously accepted of you.

'What you owe to justice is performed in my death. A father to have executed his only son will leave a sufficient example for a greater crime than this. My blood will satisfy the highest point of equity: my blood will satisfy the hardest hearted in this country. O save the life of this prince. That is the only all I will with my last breath demand of you. With what face will you look upon your sister when, in reward of nourishing me in your greatest need, you take away – and in such sort take away – that which is more dear to her than all the world, and is the only comfort wherewith she nourisheth her old age? O give not such an occasion to the noble Thessalians for ever to curse the match that their prince did make with the Macedon blood. By my loss there follows no public loss, for you are to hold the seat, and to provide yourself perchance of a worthier successor. But how can you or all the earth recompense that damage that poor Thessalia shall sustain, who sending out (whom otherwise they would no more have spared than their own eyes) their prince to you, and you requesting to have him, by you he should thus dishonourably be extinguished? Set before you, I beseech you, the face of that miserable people, when no sooner shall the news come that you have met your nephew, but withal they shall hear that you have beheaded him. How many tears they shall spend, how many complaints they shall make, so many just execrations will light upon you.

'And take heed, O Father (for since my death answers my fault, while I live I will call upon that dear name) lest seeking too precise a course of justice, you be not thought most unjust in weakening your neighbours' mighty estate by taking away their only pillar. In me, in me this matter began: in me let it receive his ending. Assure yourself no man will doubt your severe observing the laws, when it shall be known Euarchus hath killed Pyrocles.

But the time of my ever farewell approacheth: if you do think my death sufficient for my fault, and do not desire to make my death more miserable than death, let these dying words of him that was once your son pierce your ears. Let Musidorus live, and Pyrocles shall live in him, and you shall not want a child.'

'A child,' cried out Musidorus, 'to him that kills Pyrocles?' With that again he fell to entreat for Pyrocles, and Pyrocles as fast for Musidorus, each employing his wit how to show himself most worthy to die; to such an admiration of all the beholders that most of them, examining the matter by their own passions, thought Euarchus (as often extraordinary excellencies, not being rightly conceived, do rather offend than please) an obstinate-hearted man, and such a one who being pitiless, his dominion must needs be insupportable. But Euarchus (that felt his own misery more than they and yet loved goodness more than himself) with such a sad assured behaviour as Cato killed himself withal,[1] when he had heard the uttermost of that their speech tended unto, he commanded again they should be carried away, rising up from the seat (which he would much rather have wished should have been his grave) and looking who would take the charge, whereto every one was exceeding backward.

But as this pitiful matter was entering into, those that were next the Duke's body might hear from under the velvet wherewith he was covered a great voice of groaning. Whereat every man astonished and their spirits (appalled with these former miseries) apt to take any strange conceit, when they might perfectly perceive the body stir, then some began to fear spirits, some to look for a miracle, most to imagine they knew not what. But Philanax and Kalander, whose eyes honest love (though to divers parties) held most attentive, leaped to the table and putting off the velvet cover, might plainly discern with as much wonder as gladness that the Duke lived. For so it was that the drink he had received was neither (as Gynecia first imagined) a love-potion nor (as it was after thought) a deadly poison, but a drink made by notable art and, as it was thought, not without natural magic, to procure for thirty hours such a deadly sleep as should oppress all show of life.

The cause of the making of this drink had first been that a princess of Cyprus, grandmother to Gynecia (being notably learned, and yet not able with all her learning to answer the objections of Cupid) did furiously love a young nobleman of her father's court; who fearing the king's rage, and not once daring either to attempt or accept so high a place, she made that sleeping drink, and found means by a trusty servant of hers (who of purpose invited him to his chamber) to procure him (that suspected no such thing) to receive it. Which done, he, no way able to resist, was secretly carried by him into a pleasant chamber in the midst of a garden she had of purpose provided for this enterprise; where that space of time, pleasing herself with seeing and cherishing of him, when the time came of the drink's end of working, and he more astonished than if he had fallen from the clouds, she bade him choose either then to marry her and to promise to fly away with her in a bark she had made ready, or else she would presently cry out, and show in what place he was, with oath he was come thither to ravish her. The nobleman in these straits, her beauty prevailed: he married her and escaped the realm with her; and after many strange adventures, were reconciled to the king her father, after whose death they reigned. But she, gratefully remembering the service that drink had done her, preserved in a bottle (made by singular art long to keep it without perishing) great quantity of it with the foretold inscription, which wrong interpreted by her daughter-in-law, the Queen of Cyprus, was given by her to Gynecia at the time of her marriage; and the drink, finding an old body of Basilius, had kept him some hours longer in the trance than it would have done a younger.

But a good while it was before good Basilius could come again to himself: in which time Euarchus (more glad than of the whole world's monarchy to be rid of his miserable magistracy, which even in justice he was now to surrender to the lawful prince of that country) came from the throne unto him, and there with much ado made him understand how these intricate matters had fallen out. Many garboils passed through his fancy before he could be persuaded Zelmane was other than a woman. At length remembering the oracle (which now indeed was accomplished not as before he had imagined) considering all had fallen out by the highest providence, and withal weighing in all these matters his own fault had been the greatest, the first thing he did was with all honourable pomp to send for Gynecia (who, poor lady, thought she was leading forth to her living burial) and, when she came, to recount before all the people the excellent virtue was in her, which she had not only maintained all her life most unspotted, but now was contented so miserably to die, to follow her husband. He told them how she had warned him to take heed of that drink; and so with all the exaltings of her that might be, he publicly desired her pardon for those errors he had committed. And so kissing her, left her to receive the most honourable fame of any princess throughout the world, all men thinking (saving only Pyrocles and Philoclea, who never bewrayed her) that she was the perfect mirror of all wifely love. Which though in that point undeserved, she did in the remnant of her life duly purchase, with observing all duty and faith to the example and glory of Greece. So uncertain are mortal judgements, the same person most infamous, and most famous, and neither justly.[2]

Then with princely entertainment to Euarchus, and many kind words to Pyrocles (whom still he dearly loved, though in a more virtuous kind) the marriage was concluded (to the inestimable joy of Euarchus, towards whom now Musidorus acknowledged his fault) betwixt these peerless princes and princesses: Philanax for his singular faith ever held dear of Basilius while he lived; and no less of Musidorus, who was to inherit that kingdom, and therein confirmed to him and his the second place of that province, with great increase of his living to maintain it: which like proportion he used to Kalodulus in Thessalia; highly honouring Kalander while he lived, and after his death continuing in the same measure to love and advance his son Clitophon. But as for Sympathus, Pyrocles (to whom his father in his own time gave the whole kingdom of Thrace) held him always about him, giving him in pure gift the great city of Abdera.

But the solemnities of these marriages, with the Arcadian pastorals, full of many comical adventures happening to those rural lovers; the strange stories of Artaxia and Plexirtus, Erona and Plangus, Helen and Amphialus, with the wonderful chances that befell them; the shepherdish loves of Menalcas with Kalodulus' daughter; the poor hopes of the poor Philisides in the pursuit of his affections; the strange continuance of Claius' and Strephon's desire; lastly, the son of Pyrocles, named Pyrophilus, and Melidora, the fair daughter of Pamela by Musidorus (who even at their birth entered into admirable fortunes) may awake some other spirit to exercise his pen in that wherewith mine is already dulled.

FINIS

# Notes

1. (p. 57) This dedication to the Countess of Pembroke was printed with the '90 Quarto and the subsequent Folios.

2. (p. 59) *To the Reader*: printed after the dedication in the '93 and subsequent Folios. H.S.: Hugh Sanford, secretary to the Earl of Pembroke and editor for the Countess.

3. (p. 59) *The disfigured face*: Sanford's sneer, mainly unjustified, at the inaccuracies of the '90 Quarto.

4. (p. 59) *Apelles*: the celebrated Greek painter who lived in the reign of Alexander the Great.

5. (p. 59) *roses*: a reference to *The Golden Ass of Apuleius*. Apuleius, turned into an ass, could only become a man again by eating roses.

6. (pp. 59–60) *lettuce ... lips*: proverbial: fodder for such asses.

## THE FIRST BOOK

1. 1. (p. 63) *places to call to memory*: the 'memory places' of the traditional art of memory. They consisted of visual scenes and images which the orator carried in his mind to help him recall his material.

2. 1. (p. 69) *nightingales ... wrong-caused sorrow*: Philomela, raped by Tereus, was turned into a nightingale and sings her sorrow all night through.

3. 1. (p. 74) Sidney fills Kalander's garden and house with traditional moral emblems expressing all the varied passions of love with which his story is to deal. *Aeneas*: founder of Rome and arch-hero of the Renaissance; the child of the virtuous love of Venus, in contrast to Cupid who sprang from her unregulated passions. *Actaeon*: turned into a stag and hunted by Diana's hounds for spying on the goddess as she bathed. He was a common Renaissance symbol of concupiscence. *Atalanta*: preserved her celibacy by outrunning all her suitors, until she was tempted by the golden apples of the Hesperides. *Helena*: of Troy. *Omphale*: for love of whom Hercules took on woman's attire. *Iole*: whose passion for Hercules led to his death by the shirt of Nessus.

3. 2. (p. 74) *bearing show of one being in deed*: appearing to be an actual person.

849

3. 3. (p. 74) *made by Philoclea*: presumably the image presented by Philoclea of which the painter makes the copy.

3. 4. (p. 77) The song about Mopsa endows her with the qualities most alien to the gods to whom they are attributed. Saturn was 'saturnine'; Pan, notoriously hairy; Juno, shrewish; Iris, the rainbow, always changing; Cupid, blind; Vulcan, limping. Momus was the scurrilous jester of the gods. *What length of verse*: the song is written in 'poulter's measure', a hackneyed metre associated with popular, semi-literate verse (Robertson).

4. 1. (p. 81) *to catch men's fancies*: I have followed the '90 text. '93, 'to each man's'.

4. 2. (p. 83) *such shepherds as Homer speaks of*: Homer in the *Iliad* commonly describes his rulers and heroes as 'shepherd of the people'.

4. 3. (p. 84) *their rural muse*: Sidney refers to the traditional modes of pastoral love songs, singing matches, allegorical satire – all of which are demonstrated in his Eclogues to the *Arcadia*.

4. 4. (p. 85) *Homer*: see the *Odyssey*, III, 70 where Nestor feasts Telemachus and his companions before asking their names and business.

4. 5. (p. 85) *Media*: the Medes, like the Persians, were noted for their luxurious and sybaritic style of living.

5. 1. (p. 89) *The evil step-mother*: Juno, the jealous wife of Jupiter who continually persecuted Hercules, Jupiter's son by Alcmena.

6. 1. (p. 96) *such kind of rhetoric*: plain language suitable to the speaker, without the embellishment of rhetorical figures.

8. 1. (p. 109) *that beauty is only confined to Arcadia*: the first hint that Pyrocles has already fallen in love with the picture of Philoclea, a point developed at the opening of Chapter 9.

9. 1. (p. 114) *Tarantula*: the venomous spider whose bite, it was believed, could only be cured by music.

10. 1. (p. 115) *children of summer*: Sidney may be referring to one of the many folk customs involving garlands and green liveries associated with May Day, the May King and Queen, Robin Hood, etc. A possible candidate is the ritual 'beating the bounds', where a garlanded procession, armed with staves and accompanied by boys, walked round the parish bounds, from time to time beating the boys in good-natured horse play. (See R. C. Chambers, *The Book of Days*.) Hence, perhaps, Sidney's reference to 'beating the guiltless earth'. There are 'green men' in contemporary dramatic entertainments, for example Nashe's *Summers Last Will and Testament*, 1600 where they have 'leaves and grass and straw and moss' sewn to their suits (ed. Wells, p. 137; Stratford-upon-Avon Library, I).

10. 2. (p. 115) *to beat the guiltless earth*: to flush the game when the hounds lost the scent.

10. 3. (p. 115) *Echo*: who pined away for love of Narcissus until she turned to stone, still retaining her voice.

12. 1. (p. 130) *resembling her he had once loved*: see p. 367.

12. 2. (p. 131) *The device*: an emblematic image, usually accompanied by a 'word', i.e. a motto indicating its meaning. Here Pyrocles, disguised as an Amazon, has for device, very appropriately, the picture of Hercules who, for love of Omphale, wore women's clothes and joined the women in spinning. Pyrocles' 'word' implies that he is no less a man for his disguise.

12. 3. (p. 131) *her other forces*: her beauty was beyond resistance.

12. 4. (p. 132) *insinuation ... division ... narration*: a metaphor based on the traditional scheme for an oration with its introduction, division into heads, and main statement.

12. 5. (p. 137) *painterly gloss*: a reference to Pyrocles' falling in love with Philoclea's picture.

13. 1. (p. 143) *taking myself with the manner*: 'mainour', a stolen thing found in a thief's possession when caught; hence 'caught redhanded'. Here Pyrocles catches himself red-handed in the crime of being amused at a time when he ought to be suffering the agonies of love.

13. 2. (p. 143) *Latona*: mother of Apollo and Diana by Jupiter. While seeking a place to bear her children she was refused water by some peasants whom Jupiter therefore turned into frogs.

13. 3. (p. 146) Pamela's 'word' for her device of a diamond in a mean setting resembles that of Pyrocles, p. 131.

13. 4. (p. 146) *Jupiter*: assumed the form of an eagle to carry off the boy Ganymede.

14. 1. (p. 148) *so sensibly ... Iris*: to see through the physical senses the demonstration of the heavenly rainbow.

14. 2. (p. 148) *common sense*: the faculty which collects sense data and lays them before the reason.

15. 1. (p. 152) *a seeled dove ... a kite*: both birds, although appearing free, are in fact prisoners and suffering. 'She' would seem to be Zelmane who uses them as emblems of her own state, prisoner to love.

15. 2. (p. 154) *one that both durst and knew*: the combination of daring with skill and knowledge which is Sidney's definition of true courage.

15. 3. (p. 154) *taken on than taken in*: put on outside like a suit of clothes rather than absorbed into one's nature.

16. 1. (p. 161) The real Zelmane was already dead by the time of the tournament. See p. 367.

17. 1.(p. 162) *lovely withal*: lovely in spite of his suntan, in Sidney's time associated with the peasantry and outdoor labour. True beauty is normally 'fair'.

17. 2. (p. 162) *Nature ... mean account*: Nature, unlike man, does not skimp on the workmanship in less important matters.

17. 3. (p. 164) *impresa ... 'Not so'*: An impresa was a device usually in the form of an image on the shield. The 'word' is 'not so' because his concealment, unlike that of the Sepia, is not out of a desire to escape.

17. 4. (p. 166) *star ... element of fire*: in the Ptolemaic cosmology, fire formed the highest layer of the material terrestrial elements, whereas the stars belonged to the higher celestial immaterial spheres.

18. 1. (p. 169) *Menalcas*: the shepherd whose clothes Musidorus had borrowed.

19. 1. (p. 176) *a hand in the margin of a book*: a common practice of Elizabethan printers to draw attention to gnomic sayings.

19. 2. (p. 176) *fiery*: the name 'Pyrocles' derives from the Greek word for fire.

19. 3. (p. 176) *Arethusa*: a nymph of Diana who, bathing in the river Alpheus, was pursued by the god of the river until Diana changed her into a fountain (Ovid, *Met.*, V, 572ff.). Miss Robertson points out that Sidney combines the description with that of Daphne pursued by Apollo (*Met.*, I, 530ff.).

19. 4. (p. 177) *contrary to his own kind*: lions were believed to lose their fierceness in the presence of royal blood.

19. 5. (p. 179) *Charon's ferry*: in which the souls of the dead were rowed over the river Styx to the infernal regions.

19. 6. (p. 180) *Gorgon*: the head of Medusa given by Perseus to Pallas who bore it ever after on her shield.

19. 7. (p. 180) *the Nemean lion*: the slaying of which was Hercules' first labour.

## THE FIRST ECLOGUES

1. (p. 183) The challenge to a singing match is in a tradition of pastoral song going back through Sannazaro and Montemayor to Vergil and Theocritus. Dorus follows the shifting stanza forms, verse patterns and varieties of rhyme set by Thyrsis, until the shepherd is forced to concede victory to his opponent's greater skill. The exercise allows Sidney to demonstrate his virtuosity in verse forms and to

illustrate the capacity for rhyme of the English language which he discusses in his *Apology for Poetry*.

2. (p. 184) *Hardly they herd*: 'the beasts singled out by good hunters find it hard to stay with the herd'.

3. (p. 184) *high ... attempt ... presumption*: Dorus refers continually to the love of the princess which inspires his verse; and both princes woo their ladies under cover of the pastoral veil.

4. (p. 184) *in translation*: a nymph who has been metamorphosed into Kala and improved by the change.

5. (p. 184) *inward assumption*: the gods have taken up their abode in her soul and keep it joined to her body so that their 'seat' will not perish.

6. (p. 185) *digression*: the gods forsake their own heaven to come to hers.

7. (p. 186) *prostrate lying*: Pamela's lying down when the bear appeared, p. 179.

8. (p. 187) The weeds, flowers, gins which Thyrsis offers are literal ones. In turning them into metaphors, Dorus hints here, as elsewhere, that he is not a real but a metaphorical shepherd. Sidney is playing with the convention of the poet as shepherd within the pastoral mode since Dorus invokes the Muse whereas Thyrsis invokes Pan the god of shepherds.

9. (p. 188) *the reputation*: Thyrsis admits that he is out-sung, but Dorus courteously returns the compliment since his ambition aims higher than to be a poet.

10. (p. 189) *elegiac verses*: one of Sidney's many experiments in classical metres.

11. (p. 189) *Heraclitus*: 'the mourner', so called on account of his pessimism. Desiring nothing, he was beyond the power of both Fortune and Nature.

12. (p. 190) *Thus not ending*: unlike the lute whose dead wood makes music, the human soul, though immortal, cannot go on singing Philoclea's praises after death.

13. (p. 191) In this long poem in hexameters, Dorus and Zelmane debate the advantages and disadvantages of their respective disguises, and the question of whose lot is the harder – Zelmane, who has access but cannot woo because disguised as a woman; Dorus who can speak as a man but is barred from wooing a princess by his lowly rank as a shepherd. They agree that Dorus is the better off.

14. (p. 195) A list of symbolic trees, in part traditional, in part of Sidney's own invention. Several of the manuscripts of the *Old Arcadia*, though not the '93 text, carry marginal notes explaining

the symbolism: Laurel: victory. Myrrh: lamentation. Olive: quietness. Myrtle: love. Willow: refusal. Cypress: death. Palms: happy marriage.

15. (p. 197) This long poem was not included in the *Old Arcadia* or '90 text but introduced by the countess into the '93 folio out of Sidney's stock of other poems. It has some relevance, however, to the dialogue between Strephon and Claius at the opening of the *Arcadia*.

16. (p. 197) *no height of style*: in terms of literary decorum, the pastoral was a 'low' genre, demanding a colloquial style.

17. (p. 198) *the ambitious lark*: a traditional method of catching larks by setting mirrors with nets around them.

18. (p. 199) May Day festivities were notorious for their pagan immorality and to get a 'green gown' was a normal euphemism for losing one's virginity. In this idyllic setting with the reference to 'chastest plays', it may, however, mean simply to get sweethearts.

19. (p. 199) *okerstay*: the mark he puts on with ochre to identify his sheep. It is a pillar standing unsupported, symbolic of his independence.

20. (p. 200) *bowls*: the nipples of her breasts are like the bias on a bowl.

21. (p. 203) *Barley-brake*: A country game involving three couples, one pair at each end and one pair in the middle (Hell). The object is for the couples at the opposite ends to change partners without being caught by the pair in the middle. For details, see Ringler, p. 495-6.

22. (p. 206) *Wilton*: the home of Sidney's sister, the Countess of Pembroke, where Sidney wrote the *Arcadia*.

23. (p. 208) *Creon's child*: Glauce, wife of Jason, whom Medea poisoned out of jealousy by means of a poisoned cloak.

## THE SECOND BOOK

2. 1. (p. 220) *laurel ... cypress*: emblematic of unfulfilled love. See the catalogue of trees, First Eclogues, p. 195 and note.

2. 2. (p. 221) *palm-trees*: were believed only to produce fruit when growing in pairs.

2. 3. (p. 225) *the balance*: Fortune alone weighs me and decides whether I am considered worthy or worthless.

2. 4. (p. 225) *hallidame*: Mopsa is making the common etymological error of confusing Hallidame – the Virgin – with halidom – God's kingdom.

2. 5. (p. 226) The same act carries different values when performed by different people.

2. 6. (p. 227) *for woes . . . long*: a neat way of telling Pamela that the events of his story did not in fact happen 'long since'.

3. 1. (p. 227) *matters for tragedies*: Musidorus is referring to his own birthplace and his own unhappy lot, of course, but Thessaly was the setting for many tragic happenings, from Deucalion's flood onwards. It includes mounts Olympus, Pelion, Ossa and Oeta; the last, the scene of Hercules' tragic death which Sidney may have had in mind. Seneca's *Hercules Oetaeus* was published in Thomas Newton's *Ten Tragedies* in 1581.

3. 2. (p. 230) *under that veil*: the pastoral was commonly defined as a mode of allegory which, under the veil of lowly shepherds, dealt with more important matters. Musidorus draws on this definition to hint that he himself is an allegorical, not a real, shepherd.

3. 3. (p. 232) *what kind of shepherd I was*: cf. p. 230. The song demonstrates that he is a shepherd in metaphor not reality.

4. 1. (p. 235) *method*: technical term in rhetoric denoting the reduction of ideas to simple order; see also p. 830.

5. 1. (p. 245) *drawing the curtain*: around the fourposter bed so that the candle-light in the room should not reveal her blushes.

5. 2. (p. 247) *run at the ring*: a jousting exercise, the object of which was to carry off on the point of the lance a metal ring suspended from a post.

5. 3. (p. 249) As a proof of his noble breeding, Musidorus demonstrates all the arts and skills which a cultivated nobleman of the Renaissance would be expected to be master of – riding, dancing, orating, acting, letter-writing, etc. For a full account of them see Castiglione's *Book of the Courtier*.

6. 1. (p. 257) *unhappy . . . grow*: Musidorus never misses an opportunity to plead his own case with Pamela, even in the middle of an analysis of the ideal king.

7. 1. (p. 258) This account of the princes' education follows the best Renaissance pattern, as laid down, for example in Sir Thomas Elyot's *Book named the Governor*.

7. 2. (p. 262) *wager . . . contention*: the winds and waves were having a wager as to which could sink the ship first.

10. 1. (p. 281) *places whence arguments*: the 'places' of logic, i.e. topics or positions out of which an argument could be developed. Plexirtus is drawn as a master of sophistry, able to move men by logic and rhetoric to beliefs and emotions which he himself does not share.

11. 1. (p. 285) A gap in the text at this point in '90 and all Folios. A British Museum copy of the 1598 folio has written in, in a con-

temporary hand: 'Sweete willow whose lovely bowes (boughs) gave shade'.

11. 2. (p. 287) *utterance ... invention*: two of the traditional divisions of rhetoric. Invention, concerned with the collection and selection of materials for the content of an oration. Utterance, the actual technique of delivery.

11. 3. (p. 287) In the *Old Arcadia* this poem is introduced at the end of Book III, as Pyrocles is about to consummate his love with Philoclea.

11. 4. (p. 290) *shadowing white*: using white to intensify the shadows and vice versa.

11. 5. (p. 290) *Atlas*: bore the heavens on his shoulders as her ankle supports the heavens of her calves.

11. 6. (p. 290) *Leda's swan*: the form in which Jupiter seduced her.

11. 7. (p. 290) A very far-fetched metaphor developed from 'doves'; covered with skin as a house was roofed over with lead: cf. 'upon the leads', p. 572.

12. 1. (p. 299) *Phaeton's dam*: Clymene who went mad with grief at her son's death. See Introduction, p. 43.

12. 2. (p. 299) *wittol*: a cuckold who accepts his role. In this case, Vulcan, god of fire, husband of Venus, cuckolded by Mars.

12. 3. (p. 300) *in moral rules*: 'Can I, who know the full extent of her sufferings, let my sorrow be cured by moral platitudes?'

12. 4. (p. 301) *condoling cause*: the man whose own good luck leaves him unafflicted with griefs will take on other men's miseries out of friendship.

14. 1. (p. 308) *cast daisies*: the 'dissembling daisy' was associated with fair promises by amorous bachelors. Hence 'to make improper proposals to'.

14. 2. (p. 308) *good old woman*: in the '90 and '93 texts Sidney has the dialect form 'wold' to suggest Miso's general uncouthness. A modern equivalent might be 'owd'.

14. 3. (p. 308) *fair Venus*: the '90 text has 'Fenus' on the first occasion that Miso uses the name, perhaps to suggest Miso's illiteracy. '93 changed to Venus. The reference to the priest which follows is Chaucerean in its double entendre.

14. 4. (p. 309) *glosses of deceits*: false images based on fictions. Sidney is adapting Plato's description of art as twice removed from the truth.

14. 5. (p. 309) *arrows two*: Cupid's two arrows caused love and hate respectively. *a third*: an allusion to horns and cuckoldry.

14. 6. (p. 309) *Argus, Io, Juno*: Juno turned Io into a cow because of

her husband Jupiter's love affair with her, and set the hundred-eyed Argus to keep watch, but Argus was killed by Mercury at Jupiter's command. Ringler points out that this version of Cupid's parentage is Sidney's own invention.

15. 1. (p. 317) *Proteus*: god of the sea who had the power to assume different forms.

16. 1. (p. 323) *Danae*: shut away by her father in a brazen tower, she was seduced by Jupiter who descended in the form of a shower of gold. A common theme in Renaissance painting.

16. 2. (p. 325) *Alecto*: one of the three Furies who lived in the underworld, where Proserpina, forcibly abducted there by Pluto, reigned as his queen for six months of the year, returning to earth each spring.

17. 1. (p. 329) *Pygmalion*: at whose prayer the statue he had carved, and with which he had fallen in love, came to life.

17. 2. (p. 331) *entertain ... parley*: keep him occupied in talk to prevent him from making love.

18. 1. (p. 332) *the giants*: one of the many references to the rebellion of the giants against Jupiter.

18. 2. (p. 338) For the original Dido, deserted by Aeneas, see Vergil, *Aeneid*, IV.

20. 1. (p. 347) *scutcheon ... supported*: a metaphor from heraldry. The scutcheon is a shield or device bearing the coat of arms. Supporters are mythological creatures depicted as holding up the shield. Here the display of her beauty to the eye is supported by the praises of her minions.

21. 1. (p. 353) '90, '93 have 'His Impresa was ...' followed by a break of one and a half lines.

21. 2. (p. 353) This is the first appearance of Philisides as the 'Knight of the Sheep' – the shepherd Knight – a role he continues to play on p. 543 and in Alexander's bridging passage. Ringler (p. 492) points out that Philisides has changed from being the lover of Mira as in the earlier eclogues and become identified with Astrophel, the lover of Stella, his 'Star'. Sidney's sonnet sequence, *Astrophel and Stella*, which made use of some autobiographical material, was written *c.* 1582, while Sidney was working on the revised *Arcadia*.

21. 3. (p. 354) Sidney drew on his own extensive experience of court jousting for his account of this tourney, especially perhaps the famous Devices at the Tilt-yard of 1581 where, as one of the Four Foster-Children of Desire, he helped to besiege the Fortress of Beauty. His friend, Fulke Greville, was another of the besiegers, and Sir Henry

Leigh (possibly Lelius) was among the defenders. A 'frozen knight' is mentioned among the combatants. The full account is contained in John Nichol, *Progresses and Public Processions of Queen Elizabeth*, Vol. II, which gives a valuable insight into the background of court chivalry of the period. See also Francis A. Yates, *Astraea* (Routledge, 1975), pp. 88–111: 'Elizabethan chivalry. The Romance of the Accession Day Tilts'. Sidney's romance is surprisingly close to the reality.

21. 4. (p. 355) See n. 3 above.

22. 1. (p. 358) For the description of Baccha, see Phalantus' tourney, pp. 158–9.

22. 2. (p. 360) *after some trial*: the princes, taking opposing sides, fought such impressive even though mock battles against each other that their followers felt totally dependent on them and took their advice.

24. 1. (p. 371) 'No prince could claim to be so high nor beggar to be so low as not to have heard of Arcadia.'

24. 2. (p. 372) *which abhorred all other knowledge*: 'which were too fearful to be disclosed to anyone else'.

24. 3. (p. 374) *children of Cadmus*: the soldiers who sprang up from the soil and slew each other when Cadmus sowed the dragon's teeth.

25. 1. (p. 378) *Arachne*: who challenged Pallas Athene to a trial of skill in weaving and was turned by the goddess into a spider.

25. 2. (p. 379) Sidney's adaptation of the popular tag, *tot homines, quot sententiae*.

25. 3. (p. 381) *Centaurs and Lapithes*: the drunken battle at the wedding of King Pirithous at which the Centaurs were destroyed. It was a common theme of Renaissance iconography.

26. 1. (p. 383) *laying out of commons*: apportioning more land for commons in opposition to the 'enclosures', increasing in the period.

27. 1. (p. 388) *Pelops*: Greek king after whom the southern Peninsula of Greece was named Peloponnese. *Minos*: King and Law-giver of Crete. It is appropriate that the villainous Clinias should quote these two heroes since both were involved in tragic circumstances. Pelops was father of the ill-fated line of Atreus and Thyestes; Minos, associated with the Minotaur.

27. 2. (p. 390) *Bacchus ... thunder*: Bacchus was the son of Jupiter, the 'Thunderer', by Semele who, desiring to see her divine lover in his full glory as a god, was consumed in his lightning. Bacchus, preserved by Jupiter, became among other things the god of wine.

28. 1. (p. 396) *Latona's son*: Latona, loved by Jupiter, was persecuted by the jealous Juno who set the serpent Python to follow her and

never allowed her to rest in one place to give birth to her child. She eventually reached Delos where she bore Diana and Apollo. Apollo slew Python.

29. 1. (p. 406) It is typical of Basilius' character that when asked for help by Plangus he sends him to Euarchus, the man of action, and contents himself with writing a poem on the situation.

## THE SECOND ECLOGUES

A collection of poems assembled from various other parts of the OA and the '90 versions, revealing the Countess's admiration for her brother's virtuosity, and Sidney's own passion for experiment in verse form.

1. (p. 408) *heavenly rules*: the concluding couplet, when Reason and Passion join hands in acclaiming the 'heavenly rules' which reconcile and transcend them both, could be the motto of the whole *Arcadia*.

2. (p. 410) *Largess, his hands* ...: 'love's hands are generosity, and never know how to be mean'.

3. (p. 410) *in her own infection*: 'in the love with which she has infected thee'.

4. (p. 411) *she spent herself*: 'Venus seems to have used up all her own riches in composing her'.

5. (p. 412) *The quiet mind ... diet me*: 'I would rather have a disquieted mind through loving her who does not love me, than possess the love of anyone else, however kind.'

6. (p. 413) This and the next eclogue originally belonged to the Fourth Eclogues of the OA, forming part of the lament at the death of Basilius, and their tone is over-tragic for their new situation. The double sestine consists of twelve stanzas which ring the changes twice over on the same six end-words, the final three-line envoy containing all six.

7. (p. 414) *deadly swannish music*: the mythical 'swan song' which swans were reputed to sing as they died.

8. (p. 415) *Dizain ... crown*: a poem of ten ten-line stanzas in which the first line of each new verse repeats the last line of the previous one; working round in a circle so that the last line of the poem repeats the first.

9. (p. 417) *Torpedo*: a favourite fish in Renaissance mythology which, according to Pliny, paralyses the angler who catches it.

10. (p. 417) *Basilisk*: also from Pliny: a mythological animal which kills with its look.

11. (p. 419) This eclogue from the First Eclogues of the OA, written

under Sidney's own pseudonym of Philisides, was omitted in the '90 text but restored by the Countess in '93.

12. (p. 419) *Or stop a breach*: 'Who can prevent the breaching of a wall who never saw a cannon?'

13. (p. 423) Also from the First Eclogues of the OA, omitted in '90.

14. (p. 424) 'Brag when there is no danger, but be obsequious to anyone aboard.'

15. (p. 424) *I con thee thank*: 'You say, "Thank you".'

16. (p. 426) In the '90 text the Echo eclogue is given to a 'young melancholy shepheard, Lamon'. In '93, the Countess restored it to Philisides as in OA, following her consistent policy of reviving her brother's memory. Sidney's own intention, as revealed in '90, seems to have been to play down Philisides.

17. (p. 429) After 'hard'. OA and '90 have the line:
    'Hard to be got, but got, constant to be held very steels. Eels.'
The Countess may have omitted this line as indecorous in a romance involving heroic women.

18. (p. 430) *Europa*: carried off by Jupiter in the guise of a bull. *Adonis*: killed by the boar. *Venus' net*: with which her husband Vulcan caught her in the middle of her love affair with Mars. *the sleepy kiss*: Endymion, beloved by the Moon who visited him each night in his sleep on Mount Latmos.

19. (p. 433) Zelmane's song of love's war is balanced by Dorus' of the solitary life in the woods, the two reflecting the roles of Amazon and shepherd respectively. The last verse of Dorus' song, however, widens the definition of solitariness to include Pamela.

## THE THIRD BOOK

1. 1. (p. 439) *And to revenge*: those who turn towards revenge would be revenged in a way appropriate to the crime, outdoing it if possible.

1. 2. (p. 440) *Cimmerian*: the Cimmerians, mentioned by Homer as a nation living on the edge of the earth in darkness and mist.

2. 1. (p. 441) *greedy Phoebus*: they were sunburned, cf. p. 162.

2. 2. (p. 446) 'People's guesses at what I wanted produced more results then than my expressed desires now.'

5. 1. (p. 461) *the seeled dove*: cf. p. 152. Used by the falconer presumably to train hawks for the 'mounty' (p. 236).

8. 1. (p. 471) *chases*: technical term from the old game of tennis applied to the second bounce of the ball after the player has failed to return it.

8. 2. (p. 473) *authority ... knowledge*: without any followers or impresa to indicate who he was.

8. 3. (p. 474) *Ceres' servants*: threshers. Ceres was goddess of harvest.

9. 1. (p. 475) This poem in praise of Mira, the 'admired one', was sung by Philisides in the Fourth Eclogues of the OA, but '90, following its usual pattern, omitted Philisides and gave it to Amphialus as a sequence of dramatic relief clumsily inserted after the battle scene in Chapter 8. '93 left this unchanged. The poem is Sidney's adaptation of the judgement of Paris (Ringler, p. 418); but its theme, the decay of belief in the planetary deities, is common to the period, perhaps related to the changing conceptions of astronomy and the challenge to the Ptolemaic system. Giordano Bruno's *Spaccio della bestia Trionfante*, 'The expulsion of the Triumphant Beast', written in England and dedicated to Sidney a little later (1585), makes the same point about the decline of the old gods.

9. 2. (p. 476) *the never moving ground*: the earth was the fixed centre around which the celestial spheres revolved in the Ptolemaic cosmology.

9. 3. (p. 477) Sidney uses Horace's well-known tag about the labouring mountain bringing forth *ridiculus mus*.

9. 4. (p. 479) Saturn, the original lord of the gods, was deposed by his son Jupiter.

9. 5. (p. 479) *better wit than lot*: it is more fitting for us that a reasoned judgement rather than mere chance should decide our fates.

9. 6. (p. 479) *Paris' doom*: the judgement of Paris, when Venus was awarded the prize for beauty.

9. 7. (p. 480) All texts have a brief gap at this point.

10. 1. (p. 485) *they become laws to themselves*: i.e. men ('90 text). '93, 'laws themselves'.

10. 2. (p. 486) *Cranes ... Pygmies*: whose traditional enmity is mentioned by Homer, *Iliad*, III, 5ff. ; Ovid, *Met.*, VI, 90, etc.

10. 3. (p. 489) *on which opinion*: the opinion that all is by chance.

10. 4. (p. 489) Pamela is referring to the crystalline sphere which, in the Ptolemaic system, enclosed the sublunar levels of creation. The lighter elements, air and fire, rose to the top; the heavier, water and earth, fell to the centre.

10. 5. (p. 489) The words 'Fortune ... these' and 'eternity ... inconstancy' were included in '90 but not in '93. As they are clearly Sidney's attempt to clarify the argument, I include them.

11. 1. (p. 493) *melancholy ... choler*: the slow cold and hot fiery humours, leading respectively to defence and attack.

11. 2. (p. 496) The pale colours of autumn fields after harvest.

11. 3. (p. 497) An appropriate 'word' for the 'hateless' combat which is proposed.

12. 1. (p. 504) *two palm trees*: the emblem of married love, see Notes, First Eclogues, 14 (p. 853) and II. 2.2. (p. 854).

13. 1. (p. 512) To complete the parody of the heroic mode, Sidney makes Dametas include a parody hexameter in his device.

14. 1. (p. 518) *amplify*: a technical term from rhetoric: the use of all the figures and techniques to build up a total effect. The metaphor is continued in 'declamations', 'methodized'.

15. 1. (p. 521) *Thraso*: the archetypal bragging soldier, taken from Terence's play, *The Eunuch*.

15. 2. (p. 522) *brick-wall*: corruption of 'bricole', the rebound of the ball from the side wall in real tennis. Here, the music is metaphorically rebounding off Anaxius towards Philoclea.

15. 3. (p. 523) *unpossessed minds*: minds not yet attending but called to attention by the sound of the horns.

17. 1. (p. 533) *Antiope*: Queen of the Amazons carried off by Theseus, to whom she bore Hippolytus. In some versions of the myth she is identified with Hippolyte; cf. Shakespeare's A *Midsummer Night's Dream*.

17. 2. (p. 533) *Iole*: whose father was killed by Hercules for breaking his promise to give him Iole for wife. It was on account of Hercules' love for Iole that Dejanira sent him the shirt of Nessus by which he was poisoned.

18. 1. (p. 537) See Vergil, *Aeneid*, VIII, 372; 'more courteous', because Venus got her way by inflaming Vulcan with desire for her.

18. 2. (p. 543) *The knight of the sheep* – Philisides, the shepherd knight. See Notes, II. 21.2. (p. 857).

18. 3. (p. 543) The Knight of the Pole is never explicitly identified but would seem to be Kalander's son, Clitophon, whose love of Musidorus made him always follow the hero.

19. 1. (p. 549) *instead of stopped words*: when her speech became too broken to continue.

20. 1. (p. 551) *Diana's temple*: at Ephesus, one of the seven wonders of the world, burnt down on the night that Alexander the Great was born.

22. 1. (p. 560) *haled her wit to her courage*: while she forced her intelligence to subject itself to the demands of her courage, she destroyed its proper function.

26. 1. (p. 579) *consort*: The '90 text has at the end of Chapter 25 a funeral song which, in the OA and '93 onwards, forms part of the Fourth Eclogues. Hence the musical reference in 'consort'.

26. 2. (p. 581) *his reverence*: the reverence in which they held him caused them to withhold their pleading.

27. 1. (p. 585) *which ought always to be one*: which should also be in accord with that harmony, i.e. it is not yet the right time to assume that death is inevitable.

27. 2. (p. 586) *in dark wonted speeches*: the difficult riddles in terms of which oracles usually express their meaning.

28. 1. (p. 589) *if heroical courage ... amazed*: if her courage had not been of the truly heroical kind which is governed by reason, she would have fallen into frenzy.

28. 2. (p. 589) *his hairy forehead*: cf. 'catching occasion by the forelock'.

28. 3. (p. 590) *an angry goddess against ravishers*: because she herself was ravished by Pluto.

28. 4. (p. 593) *Pallas*: goddess not only of wisdom but also of the conduct of war.

29. 1. (p. 595) The revised *Arcadia* ends at this point. '93 inserts:

How this combat ended, how the ladies by the coming of the discovered forces were delivered and restored to Basilius; and how Dorus again returned to his old master Dametas, is altogether unknown. What afterward chanced, out of the author's own writings and conceits hath been supplied, as followeth:

It then continues as at 625.

The Folio of 1621 inserts instead:

Thus far the worthy Author had revised or inlarged that first written Arcadia of his, which only passed from hand to hand, and was never printed: having a purpose like wise to have new ordered, augmented, and concluded the rest, had he not been prevented by untimely death. So that all which followeth here of this work, remained as it was done and sent away in several loose sheets (being never after reviewed, nor so much as seen altogether by himself) without any certain disposition or perfect order. Yet for that it was his, howsoever deprived of the just grace it should have had, was held too good to be lost; and therefore with much labour were the best coherencies that could be gathered out of those scattered papers made, and after-wards printed as now it is, only by her Noble care to whose dear hand they were first committed, and for whose delight and entertainment only undertaken.

What conclusion it should have had or how far the work have been extended (had it had his last hand thereunto) was only known to his own spirit, where only those admirable Images were (and no where else) to be cast.

And here we are likewise utterly deprived of the relation how this combat ended, and how the ladies by discovery of the approaching forces were delivered and restored to Basilius: how Dorus returned to his old master Dametas: all which unfortunate maim we must be content to suffer with the rest.

Alexander's section is headed 'A supplement of the said defect'.

29. 2. (p. 597) *prodigious comets*: like comets and prodigies foretelling tragedies.

29. 3. (p. 597) *ever next the wall*: keeping close to the wall so that they could not be surrounded.

29. 4. (p. 599) *Mars and Venus*: god of war and goddess of love. Meeting within her mind, the warlike instincts of Pyrocles are fuelled by the amorous ones.

29. 5. (p. 601) *Ixion*: who attempted to seduce Juno, but Jupiter sent a cloud in her likeness, upon which Ixion begot centaurs.

30. 1. (p. 606) *without art artificial*: her thoughts, though spontaneous and natural, yet like an artist painted and engraved.

30. 2. (p. 606) *Niobe*: 'all tears', whose pride in her children was punished by Apollo and Diana who slew them all. Grief turned her to stone.

31. 1. (p. 609) *not complementally*: not putting on a show of modesty in order to elicit praise for herself, but drawing attention to the merits of another person.

32. 1. (p. 614) Sir William Alexander uses the death of the Knight of the Sheep to pay a moving tribute to Sidney, both as a soldier and a poet. See the reference at the conclusion of his bridging passage, Notes, III. 34.1. below. It is a nice touch to make Sidney in love with his own Philoclea.

34. 1. (p. 625) Alexander's bridging passage concludes with the following envoy:

If this little Essay have not that perfection which is required for supplying the want of that place for which it was intended, yet shall it serve for shadow to give a lustre to the rest. I have only herein conformed myself to that which preceded my beginning, & was known to be that admirable Author's own, but do differ in some things from that which follows, specially in the death of Philisides, making choice of a course whereby I might best manifest what affection I bear to the memory of him, whom I took to be alluded unto by that name, & whom I only by this imperfect parcel (designing more) had a mind to honour.

S.W.A.

35. 1. (p. 629) *dangerous*: in the medieval sense of frightening, off-putting.

37. 1. (p. 639) *Aristomenes*: an earlier hero of Arcadian history whom Sidney seems to have invented.

37. 2. (p. 644) *first four*: words, breath, tongue, voice. *next four*: hair, lips, eyes, breast. *But you*: skin, flesh.

The two songs which Musidorus invents are comically unsuitable, especially the second which he attributes to Dametas, knowing that Miso's jealousy will blind her to its inappropriateness.

37. 3. (p. 644) *Oudemian*: 'without inhabitants' (Ringler).

37. 4. (p. 645) *Medea*: killed her children to gain revenge on Jason their father, who had deserted her.

37. 5. (p. 646) Apollo was banished by Jupiter for killing the Cyclops, and lived for nine years as a shepherd serving Admetus, King of Thessaly. For this reason the god had special regard for shepherds. Musidorus invents variations on a well-known myth for Mopsa's benefit.

38. 1. (p. 649) *Palladium*: the image of Pallas Athena worshipped by the Trojans. The safety of Troy depended on its presence, and when Ulysses stole it, the city fell.

38. 2. (p. 652) *waxen wings*: reference to Icarus who made himself wings which he attached with wax. Flying too near the sun, the wax melted and he fell into the ocean and was drowned. He was a common Renaissance image of ambition.

38. 3. (p. 653) This part by part description of Pamela's beauties is a rhetorical 'icon' traditionally associated with love scenes. cf. the long poem, p. 287 and Notes, II. 11.3. (p. 856). Originally given to Pyrocles at the parallel situation in his story.

38. 4. (p. 654) *no life to a chameleon*: no life to be compared with that of a chameleon which was believed to live on air (cf. *Hamlet*, 'I eat the air, promise crammed').

38. 5. (p. 654) At this point, as part of the process of cleaning up the *Old Arcadia*, the following passage was omitted in '93 and subsequent Folios:

But each of these having in his heart a several working, all joined together did so draw his will into the nature of their confederacy that now his promise began to have but a fainting force, and each thought that rose against those desires was received but as a stranger to his counsel, well experiencing in himself that no vow is so strong as the avoiding of occasions. So that rising softly from her, overmastered with the fury of delight, having all his senses partial against himself and enclined to his well-beloved adversary, he was bent to take the vantage of the weakness of the watch, and see whether at that season he could win the bulwark before timely help might come. And now he began to make his approaches, when to the just punishment of his broken promise, and most unfortuned bar of his long pursued and achieved desires, there came by a dozen clownish villains armed with divers sorts of weapons.

39. 1. (p. 663) *ground*: a pun. The lute itself is the ground on which the poem is written; but 'ground' is also a musical term, the basic melody around which a descant is composed.

40. 1. (p. 664) *for the lending*: lending a little time to Gynecia in the hope of gaining, as interest, the fulfilment of his desires towards Philoclea.

40. 2. (p. 666) The poem is built round a three-fold pun on 'bait' – 'guileful bait', to trap; 'restful bait', an inn or place of relaxation; 'passions bait', baited by passions as at a bear-baiting.

41. 1. (p. 677) *Pan, Iole*. Ovid, *Fasti*, II, 303ff., where the story is told of Faunus and Omphale instead of Pan and Iole. Faunus got into the wrong bed because Hercules was dressed in woman's clothes; Sidney has confused the two mistresses of Hercules.

42. 1. (p. 684) *Aeolus*: god of the winds who did his best to wreck Aeneas and his companions on their voyage home after the fall of Troy.

42. 2. (p. 686) *imposthumed*: corrupted and festering: a brutal metaphor and pun to describe what Philoclea believes to be an unforgivable act.

42. 3. (p. 687) From this point the OA proceeds as follows:

But as she was rising, perchance to have begun some such enterprize, Pyrocles, severing his eye lids and having for his first object her beloved beauty (which wrought in him not unlike to those who, lying abroad, are so moved by the morning sun to pay the tribute of their sight to his fairness) he was almost in as much danger of having his spirits again overpressed with this too excessive joy; but that she (finding him alive and forgetting natural bashfulness) for the late fear of his loss, with her dear embracements added strength to his life. So that coming again to the use of his feet, and lifting the sweet burden of Philoclea in his arms, he laid her on her bed again, having so free scope of his serviceable sight that there came into his mind a song the shepheard Philisides had in his hearing sung of the beauties of his unkind mistress, which in Pyrocles' judgement was fully accomplished in Philoclea. The song was this:

Here follows the long poetic icon, in '93 given to Pyrocles at the scene of bathing in the river Ladon, pp. 287–91. The OA then goes on:

But do not think, fair ladies, his thoughts had such leisure as to run over so long a ditty: the only general fancy of it came into his mind fixed upon the sense of the sweet subject. Where, using the benefit of the time, and fortifying himself with the confessing her late fault to make her now the sooner yield to penance, turning the past griefs and unkindness to the excess of all kind joys (as passion is apt to slide into all contrary) beginning now to envy Argus' thousand eyes and Briareus' hundred hands, fighting against a weak resistance which did strive to be overcome; he gives me occasion to leave him in so happy a plight, lest my pen might seem to grudge at the due bliss of these poor lovers, whose loyalty had but small respite of their fiery agonies. And now Lalus' pipe doth come to my hearing, which invites me to his marriage that in this season was celebrated between him and his handsome Kala, whom long he had loved: which I hope (fair ladies) your ears be not so full of great matters that you will disdain to hear.

## THE THIRD ECLOGUES

1. (p. 690) These are unchanged from OA except for the addition of 'The lad Philisides' from Sidney's earlier 'Mira' poems. As in the First Eclogues, the shepherd Lalus of OA is renamed Thyrsis in '93, but the editor failed to make the change in the song between Geron and Histor on p. 709. The Third Eclogues are mainly concerned with marriage, and have ironic relevance to the main story – even more in the OA where Pyrocles and Philoclea have just consummated their love illegally.

2. (p. 699) *dicker*: ten; half a score being a normal unit of exchange. Here Pas accuses Nico of having offered a measure of wit big enough to arouse mistrust rather than trust in marriage.

3. (p. 700) *Actaeon's ornament*: cuckold's horns. Notes, I. 3.1. (p. 849).

4. (p. 703) *Holland*. The wind blowing from Holland, suggesting a

location for the poem in East Anglia; which may be why, as Ringler suggests, Sidney did not include it in his Greek *Arcadia*.

5. (p. 704) This poem, containing much autobiographical material, was sung by Philisides in the OA but assigned to an anonymous shepherd as part of the first Eclogues in '90 and restored to its original position and singer in '93. Its subject is the social hierarchy and for this reason it may have been set on the Danube (Ister) to camouflage its topicality. It is written in unusually colloquial dialect and archaic language, perhaps, to conform to the normal pattern of pastoral allegory veiling more serious matters under homely tales.

6. (p. 705) *Lanquet*: Hubert Lanquet, protestant statesman and Sidney's friend; the poet was with him in Vienna in 1573–4.

7. (p. 705) *Coriden* ('90, '93): in OA, Coredens; occasionally changed to the conventional pastoral Coridon in '93. Possibly a pseudonym for Sidney's friend, Edward Wotton, six years older and in Vienna with him.

8. (p. 707) *The guiltless earth*: conventional description of what happened after the Fall and the loss of the Golden Age, cf. *Paradise Lost*, I, lines 684–93.

9. (p. 708) *The great beams gone*: through his fable Sidney makes a plea for the retention of a strong aristocracy as a defence against unlimited monarchy.

10. (p. 709) *a pastoral style*: the very deliberate colloquialism of this poem is part of the decorum of 'a lowly shepherd's tale'. Geron shows his ignorance of pastoral convention in censuring it.

## THE FOURTH BOOK

1. 1. (p. 715) *but either*: 'there is no way of understanding how Dametas felt except either by undergoing a similar experience or ...'

1. 2. (p. 715) Midas was given ass's ears for judging Pan to be a better musician than Apollo.

1. 3. (p. 719) *jealous Juno*: she delayed Alcmena's giving birth to Hercules in this way.

1. 4. (p. 719) *pans*: the OA version. ' '93 has 'panic'. Miss Robertson retains 'pans', suggesting that Sidney refers to the beating of metal vessels to make a noise and flush out the game, and that the hunt for Dametas is a sort of 'skimmity ride'. The '93 'panic' would therefore be the 'learned and pedantic emendation of Hugh Sanford' (p. 467). For a similar transformation, cf. Chaucer's noisy chase after the fox in 'The Nun's Priest's Tale', and Dryden's version, 'with panic horror of pursuing dogs'.

1. 5. (p. 722) *one on the bed by her*: OA has 'one abed with her'.
1. 6. (p. 722) *break of day*: OA continues:

Who at that time, being not much before the break of day (whether it were they were so by foreappointment surprised to bring their fault to open punishment; or that the too high degree of their joys had overthrown the wakeful use of their senses; or that their soul, lifted up with extremity of love after mutual satisfaction, had left their bodies dearly joined to unite themselves together so much more freely as they were freer of that earthly prison; or whatsoever other cause might be imagined of it) but so it was that they were as then possessed with a mutual sleep.

1. 7. (p. 723) *Psyche*: who insisted on discovering the identity of her divine lover, Cupid.
2. 1. (p. 726) Vulcan made a net in which his wife, Venus, was caught with Mars and exposed in public to the gods.
3. 1. (p. 733) *Mausolus' tomb*: the mausoleum, tomb of King Mausolus and one of the seven wonders of the world.
4. 1. (p. 740) the *uttermost point of woefulness*: in OA 'the uttermost point of contentment'.
4. 2. (p. 746) *Codrus*: the last King of Athens who, causing himself to be killed in battle to fulfil a prophecy that the side should win whose king was killed, was honoured by a decree ordaining that he should have no successors and that the city should henceforth be ruled by Archons.


## THE FOURTH ECLOGUES

1. (p. 774) This song was introduced in the OA at the point where the shepherds first discover Basilius' body.
2. (p. 775) The song forming part of the Fourth Eclogues in OA, was transferred in '90 to the end of Book III, Chapter 25, when Helen takes away Amphialus' body, see Notes, III. 26. 1. (p. 862). '93 restored it to its original place.
3. (p. 776) *Ai*: Ovid, *Met.*, X 170–215. Hyacinthus was accidentally slain by Apollo, and from his blood sprang the flower whose leaves bear the markings of the exclamation of woe, Ai.
4. (p. 779) *Aesculapius*: Son of Apollo, killed by Jupiter for restoring men to life. He became the god of medicine.
5. (p. 779) From the Fourth Eclogue of OA, omitted in '90.

## THE FIFTH BOOK

**1. 1.** (p. 785) *Cyclops*: the race of one-eyed giants, one of whom devoured Ulysses' followers.

**2, 1.** (p. 793) *essential ... opinionate*: an absolute, not a thing depending on fluctuating opinion. Sidney is referring to the famous Platonic distinction of the divided line, between the absolute and the relative.

**3. 1.** (p. 804) *intelligence (which is both his name and being)*: from *inter* and *legere*, to bring together; in this case, things both present and past, i.e. to know all things simultaneously.

**4. 1.** (p. 808) *apostle's mantle*: the kind of mantle which the Apostles were often depicted as wearing.

**4. 2.** (p. 809) *Getulian ... Tyrian*: Miss Robertson (p. 481) quotes the distinction between Getulian purple from the Libyan coast, and the true Tyrian purple from the murex shell.

**4. 3.** (p. 811) *their bar*: cf. the oracle, p. 395 'who at thy bier as at a bar shall plead'.

**5. 1.** (p. 821) *a quiet poet*: presumably 'could scarcely get into a single poem'.

**7. 1.** (p. 837) The 'destroying fires' apply especially to the burning of Troy as a result of Helen's rape by Paris. Europa was carried off by Jupiter, and the quest of her brother Cadmus to find her led to the sowing of the dragon's teeth and the mutual slaughter of the armed men who sprang up from them.

**8. 1.** (p. 845) *Cato*: the Roman hero who committed suicide after reading Plato on the immortality of the soul, rather than submit to Caesar and see Rome cease to be a republic.

**8. 2.** (p. 847) A typically caustic remark even as the story comes to its romantic and happy ending.

## MORE ABOUT PENGUINS
## AND PELICANS

*Penguinews*, which appears every month, contains details of all the new books issued by Penguins as they are published. From time to time it is supplemented by *Penguins in Print*, which is our complete list of almost 5,000 titles.

A specimen copy of *Penguinews* will be sent to you free on request. Please write to Dept EP, Penguin Books Ltd, Harmondsworth, Middlesex, for your copy.

*In the U.S.A.:* For a complete list of books available from Penguins in the United States write to Dept CS, Penguin Books, 625 Madison Avenue, New York, New York 10022.

*In Canada:* For a complete list of books available from Penguins in Canada write to Penguin Books Canada Ltd, 2801 John Street, Markham, Ontario L3R 1B4.

# PENGUIN ENGLISH POETS

EDMUND SPENSER

## THE FAERIE QUEENE

*Edited by Thomas P. Roche Jr and C. Patrick O'Donnell Jr*

*The Faerie Queene*, Spenser's masterpiece, is among the most influential poems in the English language. It was the first epic in English and established the possibilities of heroic poetry in the English tradition. Although Milton called Spenser a better teacher than Scotus or Aquinas, the rhythmical music and rhetorical control of *The Faerie Queene* have, no less than its learning, delighted poets for four centuries. Eighteenth-century poets imitated Spenser with abandon and Wordsworth, Keats and Tennyson were deeply influenced by the sensuousness of the poem.

Spenser's intention was to rival or surpass the epic romances of the Italian poets Ariosto and Tasso through the 'darke conceit' of his poem, which brilliantly unites the medieval romance and renaissance epic. Spenser is the culmination of an ancient tradition begun by Virgil, yet the tone and atmosphere of *The Faerie Queene* are distinctively his own. C. S. Lewis remarked of the poem: 'I never meet a man who says he used to like *The Faerie Queene*.'

# THE PENGUIN ENGLISH LIBRARY

### BEN JONSON

## THREE COMEDIES

#### VOLPONE / THE ALCHEMIST
#### BARTHOLOMEW FAIR

*Edited by Michael Jamieson*

As Shakespeare's nearest rival on the English stage, Ben Jonson both gained and suffered. Productions of recent years have, as it were, rediscovered him as a comic dramatist of genius and a master of language. This volume contains his best-known comedies.

*Volpone*, which is perhaps his greatest, and *The Alchemist* are both *tours de force* of brilliant knavery, unflagging in wit and comic invention. *Bartholomew Fair*, an earthier work, portrays Jonson's fellow Londoners in festive mood – bawdy, energetic, and never at a loss for words.

### JOHN MILTON

## SELECTED PROSE

*Edited by C. A. Patrides*

In prose which is at once magnificent and impressively varied John Milton entered passionately and eloquently into the religious, personal and political controversies of a divided age. The 'three species of liberty' to which he was committed – ecclesiastical, domestic and civil – are represented in this edition, which includes five of his treatises in full: *Of Education, Areopagitica, The Tenure of Kings and Magistrates, A Treatise of Civil Power* and *The Readie and Easie Way to Establish a Free Commonwealth*. In addition there are abridged texts of his famous arguments concerning reformation and divorce.

This volume also contains two early biographies, by John Aubrey and Edward Phillips, Milton's nephew, while the editor's explanatory introduction and extended bibliography will be of the greatest use to students.

# THE PENGUIN ENGLISH LIBRARY

## THREE
## JACOBEAN TRAGEDIES

*Edited by Gāmini Salgādo*

Renaissance humanism had reached a crisis by the early seventeenth century. It was followed by a period of mental unrest, a sense of moral corruption and ambiguity which provoked the Jacobean dramatists to embittered satire and images of tragic retribution.

John Webster (*c.* 1570–1625) in *The White Devil* paints a sinister and merciless world ruled by all the refinements of cunning and intrigue, whilst in *The Revenger's Tragedy*, one of the most powerful of the Jacobean tragedies, Cyril Tourneur (c. 1570–1626) displays in a macabre ballet the emotional conflicts and vices typical of the age. *The Changeling* is perhaps the supreme achievement of Thomas Middleton (1580–1627) – a masterpiece of brooding intensity.

### JOHN WEBSTER

## THREE PLAYS

*Edited by David Gunby*

In calling Webster the 'Tussaud Laureate' Bernard Shaw spoke for all the critics who have complained of the atmosphere of charnel-house and torture-chamber in his plays. Certainly he can be morbid, macabre and melodramatic and exploits to the full the theatrical possibilities of cruelty and violent death. But critics have too often identified Webster's views with those of his characters and neglected his superb poetry and excellent craftsmanship. Though he was writing at a time of social confusion and pessimism, it is possible to see his own universe as an essentially moral one and his vision as deeply religious.

On the evidence of the three plays in this volume, surely, Webster can be regarded as a great poet and second only to Shakespeare as an English tragedian.

# THE PENGUIN ENGLISH LIBRARY

## TUDOR INTERLUDES

### Edited by Peter Happé

*Tudor Interludes* draws on ten plays, either complete or in extract, which have been chosen to represent the loosely defined dramatic form known as the 'Interlude'. Interludes preceded the full flowering of the Elizabethan theatre and are thought to have been designed for banquets or other forms of entertainment. Both popular and aristocratic specimens have survived, and each style is represented here. The plays include *Fulgens and Lucres, Youth, The Play of the Wether, Wit and Science, Respublica, Apius and Virginia* and *Like Will to Like*. The interludes have been only slightly modernized and are printed with extensive glossaries.

# THE PENGUIN ENGLISH LIBRARY

SIR THOMAS MALORY

## LE MORTE D'ARTHUR

IN TWO VOLUMES

*With an Introduction by John Lawlor*

Writing in the uncertain times of the Wars of the Roses Sir Thomas Malory looked wistfully back to the days of a great king, to a dead age of chivalry, and to a national disaster wreaked by treachery. The various parts of this most famous of medieval legends – the love of Launcelot and Guenever, the quest for the Holy Grail, the fellowship of the Round Table, the treason of Mordred – are handled by him as separate episodes: yet they are given a unity by the magic of his prose style.

In the edition of 1485, which this volume follows, it can now be seen what part Caxton played as Malory's first editor. Eight tales of earthly chivalry were welded by him into one book, to compose a story which gains strength, pace, and pathos as it moves towards the inevitable tragedy of Arthur's death.